CHEAT AND CHARMER

Random House / New York

CHEAT
and
CHARMER

A Novel

ELIZABETH FRANK

Copyright © 2004 by Elizabeth Frank

All rights reserved under International and Pan-American Copyright Conventions. Published in the United States by Random House, an imprint of The Random House Publishing Group, a division of Random House, Inc., New York, and simultaneously in Canada by Random House of Canada Limited, Toronto.

RANDOM HOUSE and colophon are registered trademarks of Random House, Inc.

ISBN 0-7394-5209-6

Printed in the United States of America

For Annie and Valentin

I to my perils
   Of cheat and charmer
   Came clad in armour
   By stars benign.
Hope lies to mortals
   And most believe her,
   But man's deceiver
   Was never mine.

The thoughts of others
   Were light and fleeting,
   Of lovers' meeting
   Or luck or fame.
Mine were of trouble,
   And mine were steady,
   So I was ready
   When trouble came.

—A. E. HOUSMAN

PART

One

[1951]

The band launched into an old swing tune and the other couples fell away, clearing the floor for Jake and Dinah Lasker, who were dancing with tremendous rhythm and style. Tall and broad-shouldered, his thinning hair black and wavy, Jake led smoothly, his timing practiced and understated as he released his wife in an outward spin and then snapped her back toward him in an inward spiral. Under her flaring green satin dress, Dinah's legs and ankles were what any dance director would have considered professionally great—long and well proportioned, with slender, graceful ankles. She wasn't otherwise especially beautiful, at least not by the impossible standards of the motion picture industry, but she was a comely woman, with regular features and warm, guileless eyes. She wore her brown hair in a pageboy, with a side wave swept up and locked into place with a simple gold barrette. Had she been two inches taller, she could easily have had a career as a model; good clothes looked wonderful on her, and she danced with the same naturalness and trust in her body with which she walked and gestured.

After a wave of applause, Irv Engel, the tuxedoed president and head of production at Marathon Pictures, returned the baton to its rightful owner and beckoned the Laskers to join him. Engel was strikingly tall and thin, round-shouldered, with transparent eyeglass frames and, at the moment, a big horsy smile that seemed inconsistent with his furrow-browed demeanor at the studio. "God, it's fun watching you two dance," he remarked, as he clamped his long arms around both Dinah's and Jake's shoulders and steered them from one table to the next, each with a pink damask tablecloth and napkins, heavy silver, and gardenias afloat in a crystal bowl from whose center rose a small flickering candle. It was early summer and, like most Southern California evenings at this time of year, fragrant with ocean air, pine trees, and night-blooming jasmine.

It seemed to Dinah that Irv was unusually attentive tonight, flattering her in front of all the guests, oohing and aahing about her great legs, and going on and on about her as a paragon of Hollywood wifeliness. Nevertheless she hung back, keeping her eyes on Jake, wanting the night's glory to be completely his. She took in the sound of voices low in conversation, the gusts of sudden, often profane laughter, and the familiar scents—perfume and coffee and cigarette smoke, brandy and cigars. Finally, seeing an opportunity, she slipped away from Irv and her husband and headed toward a round table otherwise deserted except for a lone woman who was staring out in unfathomable melancholy at the turquoise depths of the swimming pool.

As Dinah swept the folds of her dress to one side, let her satin high heels drop to the terra-cotta tiles, and put her stocking feet up on the empty chair beside her, the woman, a small blonde, glanced at her with interest. "My, my, Dinah, you and Jake certainly look good on the dance floor."

"Thanks, Anya," Dinah gasped. "But I forgot I was wearing high heels. I damn near k-k-k-killed myself."

"The two of you have such style together. It's a pleasure to watch."

"We're having such a good time tonight, Anya. It's a wonderful p-p-p— Jesus, I can dance but I can't say this word!" She screwed up her eyes with effort and tried again. "P-p-p-party. There. I got it out."

Dinah withdrew a Camel from a pack inside the beaded cigarette case in her black satin clutch, pausing for a moment, as if she had seen something unexpected inside the bag. Dinah was always conscious of her stutter around Anya Engel, and always uncomfortable, no doubt because Anya herself had a most peculiar problem. Although she had well-formed, delicate features, her mouth was twisted to the side of her face, and looked like a porthole, through which words were issued with a muffled precision— the result, Dinah had heard, of a sudden stroke after childbirth from which Anya had all but completely recovered, except for this single affliction. Dinah had learned early in life never to avoid mentioning her stutter. Consequently, her patience with people who kept silent about their so-called defects, imperfections, or handicaps had its limits, and in all the years Dinah had known her, Anya Engel had never once mentioned hers. Dinah would have liked her better if she had, but from the beginning she had regarded the wife of her husband's boss as an East Coast snob who considered *her* an uneducated shiksa, a nobody from nowhere whose great legs were an enviable but nevertheless suspicious sign of her lumpen origins. Anya Engel had always let it be known that she was a Radcliffe graduate and an *artist,* aloof from and superior to the movie business. During the many evenings the Laskers had been guests at the Engels' Pacific Palisades hacienda, Anya had often disappeared after dinner without explanation, and on weekends at their Palm Springs "compound," as Irv called it, Irv talked movies and politics with Jake, Dinah knitted sweaters, and Anya stood at an easel set well apart from the conversation, painting landscapes of the mountains and the desert and correcting Jake's pronunciation when he complimented her on her "fauve" palette.

Dinah was perfectly clear about one thing. This was not the night for a heart-to-heart about the trials of having flaws in a town that worshiped physical perfection. Tonight belonged to Jake. The Engels were giving this party to honor the thirty-nine-year-old producer-writer-director, the huge success of his recent picture, *Cousin Jonnycake,* and the three-picture deal that Jake had signed earlier in the week. And so Dinah had to make conversation with Anya, never an easy thing to do.

"Do you and Irv like to dance?"

"Well, we never had much of a chance. He was always the bandleader, so I danced with the other fellows. And he hated that." She smiled, and Dinah thought, She's telling me how much her husband loves her. "It's how we became engaged," Anya continued. " 'Just so they know you're taken,' he used to say."

"Cute," said Dinah. "Very c-c-c-cute." She glanced at the large square diamond next to Anya's wedding band. Imagine being able to afford a rock like that during the Depression, she said to herself—not for the first time, either.

"Tell me, Dinah, what do you hear from Veevi these days?"

"She's fine," she said, surprised. She had not been thinking about her sister.

"Beautiful girl. Really," Anya went on, "the most beautiful creature I ever saw."

"It's true," Dinah readily agreed. "When people see her for the first time, it's as if they've been thrown from a horse. Knocks the breath right out of them."

"It must have been hard for you."

Dinah looked straight at Anya with her large brown eyes. "Hard? How so?" She knew perfectly well what Anya meant. This is why I can't stand her, she said to herself. She does it every time; she reminds me of the old days, the awful nothing days.

"Well, if I had a sister who was the most beautiful girl in the world . . ."

"Oh, I think I've managed pretty well," Dinah said, lighting a cigarette, her voice brittle.

"Of course, I don't know about you," Anya said carefully, "but it was certainly hard for me. Coming out here right after we were married and finding everyone in Irv's family positively smitten with her. I remember Lionel and Edy sent a car for us and we drove up to the house, and they were all there to meet us, and there was Irv's poor brother Talcott, standing there with his arm around a girl dressed in a dirndl. She had the most stunning face I've ever seen. Don't think I didn't see Irv's jaw drop. He moped around the house, took long drives by himself, could barely look at me. Imagine, me a new bride, and I come out here, and suddenly he's got this enormous crush on Veevi."

"Well, he wasn't the only one," Dinah said. "Every writer in Hollywood was cr-cr-cr-cr-crazy about her."

"But I said to him," Anya continued, " 'Look here, if you don't snap out of it I'm going right back home to New York, and I mean tonight.' " She laughed. "That did it."

"I guess it worked," Dinah said. "But she did have that effect on people."

"She certainly did." Anya reached across the table and patted Dinah's hand. "I remember so well what you were like all those years ago. It wasn't easy for you, dear, and I'm so glad to see you . . . finally getting . . . well, you know, what you deserve," she said, the words coming thickly but distinctly through the moist porthole.

"Thank you, Anya," Dinah said, withdrawing her hand. She understood now. Anya was reminding her, on this night of Jake's triumph, of the days when Dinah wasn't Mrs. Jake Lasker but just Veevi Milligan's older, not-quite-beautiful sister, a poor, unmarried secretary working for an oil company. What business was it of Anya's to keep watch over her life and bring up that miserable past? What are you, she wanted to say, my fucking biographer? She wanted to strike back, say something coarse and cruel—*How do you manage to go down on Irv with that thing?* But of course she said nothing of the kind.

"Is Veevi still married to Michael Albrecht?"

"*St-St-St-Still?* Yes, of course."

"That must be some marriage—the most beautiful girl in the world and the most talented man of our time. I've read all his novels. He won't let Irv option any of them. Imagine," Anya sneered, "someone brave enough to turn his back on this town! Does he love her very much? Is she divinely happy?"

"Divinely," Dinah said, and grasped at once that Anya was not divinely happy, whatever else she may have been. "She's divinely, magnificently, sp-sp-spectacularly happy, in Paris, away from Hollywood." Yes, she told herself, that's what it is. Anya wants Europe, and she's stuck here in L.A. She smiled. "Excuse me, dear," she said, standing up and sliding her feet into her heels. "I'm off to the powder room."

Anya Engel's dark eyes, vivid and alive in her tortured little face, became dreamy. "How I'd love to live in Paris." She sat back in her chair and looked out over the swimming pool. "She'd be a fool ever to come back here."

"Oh, but I don't think she ever will. She hates this t-t-t-town even more than you do," said Dinah, leaving Anya sitting by herself, with something inconsolable in her expression.

Inside the house, a Negro maid wearing a black uniform and a starched white organdy apron and cap led Dinah to the powder suite, where she stretched out on a chaise longue after asking for aspirin and water. Her head throbbed, and she dug her knuckles into her temples. Her breathing was rapid, and the light hurt her eyes. She had a horrible taste in her mouth.

After the maid returned, and again disappeared, Dinah lay back, waiting for the aspirin to start working. Suddenly she sat up, opened her black clutch, and withdrew a folded piece of pink paper. She read what was written on it, and quickly put it back in her bag.

Earlier that day, Dinah had been sitting in the breakfast room watching the bulldozer scoop gigantic mouthfuls of earth out of what, until only a few days before, had been a formal English garden with a brick retaining wall and a stone lion's head that gushed a stream of water into a small oval pool. A crew had invaded and ravaged the clipped box hedges and the beds of flowers—snapdragons, asters, pansies, chrysanthemums—that Dinah had lovingly tended since she and Jake had moved into the house the year before. Her dismay growing, she watched as the orange and lemon trees were ripped out by the roots and promptly thrown into the incinerator. In their place rose heaps of black dirt beside a big rectangular hole that grew bigger and deeper every day. Dinah didn't like to swim. When she was twelve, her father, who had promised to teach her how to swim, tossed her off a pier into the too-deep waters of Lake Arrowhead. Somehow she had managed not to drown, but she had feared the water ever since. Once it became clear that *Cousin Jonnycake* was going to be a hit, however, Jake had insisted on putting in a pool. He'd been sent to camp every summer on Lake Michigan and, later, had been a member of the swim team at the University of Chicago. Though the war in Korea had made it much more expensive to buy concrete and tiles, he was going to have his pool.

Most of the year, it was light and sunny in the breakfast room, but in June the morning fog almost never burned off until lunchtime, and a gray glare hovered outside the window. It depressed her, reminding her of the Pittsburgh of her earliest memories—humid summer days, damp winter twilights, chapped, frozen upper lips, she and her sister keeping each other awake all night with whooping cough, their chests smeared with foul-smelling mustard plasters. This descent into the past—the only thing that threatened her contented daily routine—was halted when the doors separating the breakfast room from the kitchen swung open and Gussie Crittenden, the Laskers' Negro housekeeper, chanting "Coming through," flew in to set down the day's mail on the black-and-white marble lazy Susan, and flew out again, too busy to hear Dinah's thank-you.

The mail wasn't particularly interesting—the trades, a large manila envelope from the business manager with checks to sign, a ballot for Jake from the Screenwriters Guild. For her father there were two items—an envelope from his Masonic Lodge and a blue tissue-paper-thin airmail letter from Veevi. Dinah would keep both of them in a kitchen drawer, along with the rest of his accumulated mail, until the next time his Airstream pulled into the driveway, and there was no telling when that would be. God only knew what wilderness he'd taken off to—Death Valley, maybe, or Yosemite, or redwood country. He would disappear for months on end, send a post-card with two lines, and then show up without warning, in a worn denim shirt, dusty hiking boots, suspenders, and an old canvas hat. The next morning he would come into the kitchen all dressed up in the same dark blue woolen pin-striped suit he had worn on the train to California in January 1922, take his mail out to the garden, and commence the solemn ritual of reading the letters his younger daughter, Veevi, had written him from Paris.

Dinah was planning to pick up Peter and Lorna from school that after-noon and take them into Beverly Hills to shop for camp clothes, but as she wrote out her list in shorthand, she paused from time to time to stare at the tight buds on the camellia bushes outside. During a brief respite from the din of the bulldozer, she heard the front doorbell and shouted to Gussie to please get it. "If it's the Fuller Brush man again," she said, "tell him to forget it. I've told him three times already I've finished p-p-p-painting the rooms upstairs."

Gussie rushed through the breakfast room toward the front door and returned in a moment. "Mrs. Lasker," she said uneasily, "there's a man at the door says he got to see you personally. He done refused to tell me his name and I don't know what he wants. I best be coming with you to the door."

"Thanks, Gus," Dinah said, reluctantly getting up. "It's just one of those p-p-p-pain-in-the-ass real estate guys. I'll get rid of him." At least once or twice a week people came to the door to ask if she had plans to put the house on the market. Again because of the war, construction materials were nowhere to be found, people weren't building, and good houses were at a premium.

When she opened the front door the man she saw was a stranger. He was wearing a light gray hat, his white shirtsleeves were rolled up, and he was holding his jacket over his shoulder. He quickly scanned her face with impassive eyes, one of them squinting to avoid the smoke that curled up from the cigarette that he removed from the thin line of his lips. "Are you Dinah Milligan Lasker?"

"Yes, I am," she said, and in that instant he shoved an envelope at her. "You are hereby served." Tossing his still-burning cigarette into one of the rosebushes behind the box hedge, he turned aside and walked quickly along the redbrick path to the driveway. She stood there, paralyzed and blinking, as he drove off in a black sedan. The whole encounter had taken less than a minute.

※

How on earth, she wondered now, as the aspirin eased her headache, had she managed to dance with Irv and Jake or down even one glass of champagne? More astonishing still was how she, who was almost constitutionally unable to keep a secret from Jake, hadn't said a word to him when he came home from the studio late that afternoon, elated, expansive, joking with the guys on the pool crew, playing a brief game of catch with Peter, then thumping upstairs and locking the bedroom door, grabbing her by the crotch and steering her to his bed, where he insisted on some highly athletic pre-party efforts at starting the first of the three new babies (one per picture) he'd promised her in light of his newly secure situation at Marathon. After their lovemaking, while she raised her legs and rested them against the bedroom wall, he had fallen into a deep sleep with the bedspread pulled high over his head. When she woke him up to get ready for the evening, he asked her to keep him company. So after her shower, dressed in a light blue bathrobe, she went through his dressing corridor and the extra bedroom he used as an office to his bathroom, announcing her presence with " 'Here I am, all freshly b-b-b-bathed and scented,' " in imitation of Jessica Tandy's soft southern accent, and perched herself on the closed toilet seat. She sipped Scotch on the rocks and smoked a cigarette while he regaled her with the dirty lyrics he had written to "It Could Happen to You," which he crooned in a Yiddish accent. She watched him shave and breathed in the scent of Yardley's gooey green brilliantine, which he slicked on over his thinning hair, and broke up when he grabbed the Oscar from the shelf he'd had installed for it and kissed it on the mouth. Later, when she came downstairs, hair, clothes, and makeup in place, she found him sitting at the kitchen table with Gussie and the kids, stealing bites from their Gussie Fried Chicken and Gussie Sugar Rice and telling them about plans for his next movie—the locations he would use, the visits to the set he would arrange for them, the movie stars they were going to meet.

She had said nothing during the long drive out Sunset to the Palisades, nothing throughout the long glittering evening, the smiles, the hugs, the jokes, the congratulations, the dinner, and the dancing. Her head was still throbbing, but it was time to go back to the party. Standing before the mirror and applying bright red arcs of lipstick to her full mouth, she looked hard at herself and adjusted her expression until it became the smooth empty plate of a party face, then she pressed a handkerchief between her lips, blotting the fresh lipstick, snapped her clutch, and went back to the Engels' patio. Anya had disappeared from the table and, it seemed, from the party itself. Dinah wasn't surprised; Anya hardly ever lasted out a whole evening.

⁂

The party was still going on at one. Enchanted by the spring air, the guests danced on and on, and told stories and forgot that the maid was asleep in the den, her aching feet propped up on the ottoman, and the TV long since gone to snow, while the children threw off blankets, and the neighborhood cats prowled through the ivy, searching for mice and momentarily stopping the cricket song.

Eventually, however, the band stopped playing. The musicians packed up their instruments, and Dinah and Jake, after the requisite farewells, were sprung into the night. The parking valet, a blond kid with a crew cut, brought them their dark green Cadillac and, stifling a yawn, held the door open for Dinah as Jake slipped him a buck. Moments later, the Laskers were wending their way down the serpentine streets of Pacific Palisades and soon came to a gentle stop at Capri and Sunset, where the traffic light glowed red. Showing no fatigue and whistling contentedly and vaguely off-key, Jake reached over to stroke the back of Dinah's neck. "Lovely evening, darling, wasn't it?"

"Mmm," she murmured. Her hands clutched her purse.

"That was a helluva speech he made. Actually, I was kind of embarrassed. If I believed everything he said I'd be the biggest schmuck in America."

She opened the purse but took out only a cigarette. "I think he meant it."

"Honestly?"

"Yeah, honestly."

Just after dinner, looking, with his bow tie and slightly rounded shoulders, exactly like a college president, Engel had gone over to the microphone and tapped it with the bandleader's baton. "Ladies and gentlemen, friends and members of the Marathon family and this great industry of

ours," he began. "Tonight we celebrate, just among ourselves, without re-
porters, photographers, and sculptured ice swans, the achievements of a
man who has made Marathon Pictures synonymous with quality entertainment. In picture after picture, Jake Lasker has touched the hearts of real
people. My friends, Jake Lasker knows how to make America laugh. Jake
Lasker keeps alive the one thing without which no democracy can survive.
I am speaking of *irreverence*: the ridiculing of authority, the poke in the ribs
at pretension and folly, scoundrels and fools—and the rest of my relatives.
But seriously, friends, in America today humor and democracy go hand in
hand. If we forget that, then we forget ourselves, and that's when the wind-
bags, the fanatics, and the pious frauds take over. I won't name names. We
all know who they are. They're dangerous. Very dangerous. Well, let *Cousin
Jonnycake* tell 'em a thing or two. What else was this country built on but
the native shrewdness of country bumpkins like Cousin Jonnycake, or the
guts and persistence of greenhorns like my father? Like millions of others,
Lionel Engel landed in this country at the age of sixteen with two bucks in
his pocket and not a single word of English. And where did he end up?
With a major studio, his own table at Hillcrest, and a corned beef sandwich
created in his name!

"So just think about it, friends: where would we be without the little
guy, the guy who outsmarts the city slickers? That's what makes *Cousin
Jonnycake* the American classic it is. You could send that picture all over
the world and say to millions of people, 'Now, *that's* America.'

"So—" He picked up a glass of champagne from a tray held at shoulder
height by a Negro butler in livery and white gloves. "Here's to you, Jake
Lasker—to you and your wonderful wife, Dinah, and your wonderful
kids—and your example to all of us that Hollywood's a place where wholesome family life goes hand in hand with first-class family entertainment.
And here's to many more wonderful years and classic pictures we know
you're gonna make right on the back lot of Marathon, because I'm gonna
hold you to every last word of your deal! You belong here, and we're for you
one thousand percent."

"You mean that's my cut of the gross?" Jake piped up. "I can live with
that!"

Now, recalling the laughter and applause, Dinah gnawed the inside of
her cheek and sighed.

"Tired, sweetheart?" he asked.

She sighed again.

"Are you okay, darling?" He took his eyes off the road and scrutinized her face. "You looked a little pale tonight. You don't think you're preggers, do you?"

They were at the stop where the UCLA campus torqued away from Sunset. To the left he could see the ghostly white of the statue of the Virgin Mary on the front lawn of Marymount School. Aware of the tightness of his belt, he was looking forward to getting home, taking off his clothes, and putting on the pajama top and boxer shorts that constituted his sleepwear. He also had very tightly fitting teeth, with no spaces in between, and as he waited for the light to change, not pressing Dinah to answer his query, he slid his thumbnail between two molars and tried to dislodge a piece of food.

"I'm not pr-pr-pr-preggers, Jake."

"Oh, too bad, darling."

"But something did happen today."

"Oh?" he said distractedly.

She opened her purse and took out the pink document. "A guy in a gray hat came to the front door today and served me." She rustled the piece of paper. "It's a subpoena."

"The Committee?"

"Yeah."

He glanced over at her. "And?"

"They want me to testify in Washington, in three weeks."

The light changed. Dinah put the document back in her purse and snapped it shut. Jake pressed down on the accelerator. "Well," he said, "as your mother used to say, 'Oh-shit-oh-dear.' You waited all day and all night to the end of the party to tell me, didn't you, honey?"

He reached over and stroked her neck and shoulder.

She felt tears welling up, but she didn't want to cry.

"Listen," she said. "I'll just go and do it. I don't care. I don't want anything to happen to you or the kids."

"Wait, honey. We've got to talk about it. You can't just decide like that. You'd have to live with it for the rest of your life."

"So?"

"You don't mean that, honey."

"Sure I do. It's s-s-s-simple, Jake. If I don't . . ."

"Sweetheart. Calm down. We'll talk about it at home."

With his right hand still planted on the nape of her neck, he steered with his left hand, his elbow jutting out the window, weaving almost drunkenly from lane to lane, as if he were the only driver on the road.

"We are not going to lose everything we've worked for just because I spent a f-f-f-few years trying to get a secondhand college education."

"Shh. When we get home we'll sit down and have some hot chocolate and discuss this like two rational people."

"I don't care about being rational, and there's nothing to discuss!" She wanted the whole matter settled right then, at that instant. The thought of waiting, thinking it over, having discussions, weighing pros and cons, filled her with dread. "I'll do it, and then we'll go on just like before. I won't let them ruin our life. Or your career," she said.

"What makes you think this has anything to do with me? There's nothing on that subpoena that says anything about me, is there?"

"Oh, Jake, come on. *I* don't matter to them. Any idiot can f-f-f-figure that out. If *I* refuse to testify, *you'll* be up shit creek. They'll blacklist you. We'll have to sell the house and move. Though God only knows where. To Mexico, maybe, like the Allens and the Salanders and the Gorkys."

"So? What's so terrible about that? I can write anywhere."

"Where would you get work? We'd starve, have chronic turista, and live like holy fucking martyrs for the rest of our lives. Angry forever and grateful to friends for sending us secondhand cashmere sweaters, like the ones Evelyn Morocco and I sent Pat Gorky in Cuernavaca last week."

"Well, Mexico's out. It's gotta be someplace with a delicatessen."

He yawned, a loud, luxurious, full-bodied yawn, the yawn of a tired child who has had a long, good day and expects to have another one tomorrow, and the day after that, and the day after that—forever. The yawn was real, but in every other way he was performing. He had no intention of letting her know it, but the subpoena was a shock. He hadn't been expecting it, but he had decided, in the instant following Dinah's announcement, exactly what he would have to do.

"Honey, relax. I'll go in and see Irv first thing tomorrow morning."

"And what do you think he's going to say? You know damn well he's completely knuckled to the Committee. That's why that speech was pure horseshit."

"I thought you said he meant it."

"The part about you, yes. The rest—forget it, Ch-Ch-Ch-"

"Charlie," he said, completing her sentence.

"Look, darling," he said, moving his hand to her thigh. "We'll face this just like we do everything else: together. We're one person, you and I. One body. If you're in trouble I'm in trouble. Whatever happens to you happens to me."

"So you always say," she said, giving in to a leaden fatigue. She put the cigarette out, slid over, and rested her head against his shoulder.

At home, she left him behind in the kitchen while she made her way to the den, where she found Gussie sleeping in her uniform, her cheek against her fist, her long legs in their lace-up shoes stretched out on the ottoman. On the television, slender phantoms hunched and crouched as they careened around the track in *Roller Derby,* Gussie's favorite late-night program. Dinah gently touched her shoulder. "We're home, Gus."

"All right, Mrs. Lasker," Gussie said, waking instantly. "Let's go up then."

An artful arrangement of blue irises rose from a crystal vase at the center of the Early American table next to the love seat. Gussie leaned over and began to gather up the cut stems.

"Leave them, Gus. They can wait till morning. The fl-fl-flowers look great. You always do such wonderful things with them. Ready?"

They went upstairs together, and then parted at the landing, Gussie going to her room above the garage and Dinah to the master bedroom, where, as she had expected, she found Lorna, who was almost four, asleep in Jake's bed.

"Mommy," the child murmured as Dinah gathered her up in her arms. Jake stood on the landing, holding a tray with two cups of hot chocolate. "Want me to take her?" he asked, holding out the tray. She shook her head. "Maybe next year. She's still small enough for me to do it."

"Do you think by the time she gets to college she'll be sleeping all night in her own bed?" Dinah smiled. Jake had made this crack before, usually when he was the one carrying the warm bundle of sleeping child back to her own bed.

Dinah pulled the covers up over Lorna, sweeping her heavy blond hair away from her face. That hair came from her side, the Milligan side; her father had been blond as a child. Already it was beginning to darken to a honey-colored brown. Lorna stirred and opened her eyes. "Pretty dresses," she mumbled. For a moment, it looked as if she were trying to decide whether to wake up and talk, as she loved to do, about the dresses at the parties her mother went to, but she closed her eyes, content, it seemed, with her mother's presence. Dinah waited, listening to her daughter's even breathing, and then bent over and kissed her on a spot between lip and chin.

She walked softly through the children's bathroom to Peter's room, where she found him curled up tightly under the covers, his hair—black like Jake's, straight like hers—framing his oval face. That afternoon, he'd said that he didn't want to go to day camp this summer. He wanted to start clarinet lessons instead. She'd had to tell him, for the third time, "The clarinet teacher says you should wait until you're seven. That way all your front teeth will be in, and you'll be ready to start." He had lost just one of the two front upper teeth; the other one was loose, though not very, and the bottom ones were still tightly in place. But the month before he'd been walking with her in Beverly Hills past a music shop where they'd paused to look at the instruments in the window. He'd let go of her hand and pointed to a set of separate pieces lying within the red velvet compartments of a hard black case. "What is that one?" he'd asked. "A clarinet," she'd said. "I want to play it," he'd announced. And to her surprise he'd said it again every day since then, so that she'd found a teacher and discussed the best time to start lessons. Meanwhile she'd taken out her Benny Goodman 78s and played them for him. "Yes," he'd said thoughtfully, "I want to play the clarinet."

Along the corridor between Lorna's and Peter's rooms there was another room, small and empty, but freshly painted in a pale green. Dinah had marked it out as the baby's room the previous fall, when she and Jake had first looked at the house, into which they had moved three months later. Lorna would be four in a few weeks, and Peter seven in September; she herself was almost thirty-nine, and if they were going to have a third child the time to start was now. She went into the room and looked out the window at the backyard lights illuminating the big gaping hole where the pool was being built. Suddenly she imagined them—she and Jake, the two kids, and probably Jake's mother—in a cramped stucco apartment in the Valley, stuffy and hot in 105-degree weather, Jake working in a butcher shop, as he'd done in college, she typing in an office somewhere. No third child, no clarinet lessons, no fencing lessons, no future for the kids, certainly no college, Jake's mother beaming at her nervously and asking the children for kisses.

She felt Jake glide into the room and put his hands on her shoulders.

"Bet I know what you're thinking," he said. He had already changed into his slippers and bathrobe.

"I can't do it," she said.

"Of course not."

"We'll have to sell the house."

"Okay, we'll have to sell the house. So what?"

He squeezed her shoulders.

"They'll throw me in jail."

"So, we'll visit you."

"No b-b-b-baby," she said.

"Wait a minute. Don't I get conjugal visits?" He put his arm around her. "Come on, let's have the hot chocolate."

Back in their own room, she disappeared into her dressing suite to change into her pajamas. When she returned, the hot chocolate was cold, so they got into her bed, though they usually started out in his, and he stayed with her there throughout what little was left of the brief, uneasy night.

At eleven-thirty the next morning, Jake Lasker watched carefully as Irv Engel pulled the pipe away from his girlish mouth, and stretched out a long arm over stacks of scripts in colored binders to retrieve a gold lighter on the far end of the Art Deco desk. Jake let his eyes wander as Engel theatrically pondered, and duly noted again what he had duly noted many times before: the beige silk walls and the signed photos of Irv shaking hands with Franklin Roosevelt, Harry Truman, Winston Churchill, and other dignitaries; of Anya Engel handing an unwieldy bouquet of bird-of-paradise blooms to Eleanor Roosevelt; laminated citations from the guilds; and framed color posters of Marathon's biggest hits—among them the old thirties blockbuster *Away in a Manger* (the *true* story of the journey of the wise men—with one of them played by Bill Robinson, considered a daring casting choice at the time), Stu Krieger's thriller *Fat Chance,* with Art Squires, and, most recently, Jake's own *Cousin Jonnycake.*

Another poster caught his eye. He and Dinah had the same one at home, carefully wrapped up in the attic. A beautiful young woman, Genevieve Milligan, stares in fascination and horror at a series of cards she holds in her hand. The face of the jack of clubs is that of Robert Montgomery, and he is wearing a gray Confederate uniform; the second—the queen of spades—has the face of Alice Brady, made up as an old woman, and she is dressed in a ball gown and has a tiara in her elaborately coiffed eighteenth-century wig, eyes glittering with demented malice; another, a joker, is none other than Emil Jannings. In the background an open window reveals a city at night, in flames—Richmond, Virginia. Across the top, in big letters, stand the names of the four stars and the title: QUEEN OF

SPADES. Below: **Produced by Willie Weil. Written by Dorshka Albrecht and Stefan Ventura. Directed by Stefan Ventura.**

On the office walls there also hung a small Klee, a drawing by Picasso, a Schwitters collage, and several portraits by Anya Engel of the two Engel boys with green noses, orange cheeks, blue chins, and purple hair.

"Frankly, I'm as puzzled as you are," said the studio head, after lighting his pipe. "Why Dinah, of all people? Don't tell me *she* was in the Party."

"Actually, she was."

Engel puffed and considered. "But why do they care about that? Was she important? Was she a big shot?"

"Hardly."

"Then it doesn't make any sense. Unless, of course, it's you they're after. *You* as a possible target I can understand. For you the Party would have been impossible to avoid."

"What makes you think that?"

"Believe me, Jake, I know you better than you think I do. You're one of those guys who joined the Party because you could only make it with shiksas, and you were looking for college-educated Communist blondes because they were easy and didn't make trouble the next morning." He grinned wickedly.

"Ordinarily, Irv, I'd say you know me *very* well," said Jake with an obliging laugh. He pushed back his glasses. "But you're only half right. I never joined the Party. I went to some meetings, the usual shindigs for Spain, the Anti-Nazi League, that sort of thing. I even spent a few evenings out here at workers' school. After writing jokes all day for George Joy's Crystaldent show, you can imagine how much fun it was to be instructed in the theory of surplus value by people of insufficient talent. I knew a lot of people in the Party, but somehow or other I just couldn't take that step. I'm not much of a joiner."

"Unless it's your country club," said Engel. "And the guilds."

"You know," Jake said with a perfunctory laugh, "I remember one time, at the University of Chicago, waking up in the apartment I was sharing with some guys and going into the bathroom and finding some fellow I'd never seen before sitting up completely dressed in the bathtub reading a newspaper. I was a little embarrassed, so I said, 'What's the weather going to be today?' And he said, 'I don't know. I never read the capitalist press.' But joining? That I never did. Dinah—that's a different story. Because of Veevi and Ventura."

Engel's eyes lit up. Very few people had the right to call Genevieve Milligan Ventura Albrecht by her nickname, and among those who did even fewer knew its genesis in the deep past, when Dinah, a stuttering child of three, unable to master the recalcitrant syllables of her baby sister's name, Genevieve, had taken the third, and easiest, and turned it into two.

"By God, that was some world," Engel said. "Tell me, Jake, I've always wanted to ask you this: when did she find out about about—?"

"Ventura? Right after the war, in Paris, when she and Mike had found each other again and he got his OSS pals to make inquiries."

"So what's the story? What really happened?"

"Maybe somebody sold him out, maybe it was just bad luck. I don't know, and I don't think anybody does for sure. He was involved with a group of foreign Communists, mostly Jews—Poles, Romanians, Bulgarians like himself, young guys, sometimes just teenagers. Their families were poor immigrants who'd come to France years before, and the Nazis had rounded them up and shipped them off to the camps. So these boys were desperadoes, they had nothing to lose, really, and they wanted to kill Nazis. Stefan was the same age as their fathers, had contacts in the French Party, and because he'd been a director he knew how to get people to do things— you remember him, don't you? I only saw him once, before I knew Veevi and Dinah, but I'll never forget that big calm man, with his intelligent, kind of amused-looking face. He was a lovely guy, a true mensch. Anyway, he was put in charge of these boys, told them their assignments, found them hiding places, helped them make bombs. He was a kind of Resistance scoutmaster, if that isn't too grotesque a way of putting it, and carried out their actions with them. Through Willie Weil—"

"I know Willie," said Engel.

"Ventura'd become a French citizen before he came out here, so he had a French passport, but he had an accent and a foreign-sounding last name, and—I don't have to tell you—the other kind of passport, the one you get at your bris. So he was in real danger. They all were, really, and that includes Veevi. She was in on it from the beginning. I mean, she did fantastic things—carrying pipe bombs in her purse and handing them to one of the boys on the street, who would light the fuses and toss them into garbage cans just as Nazi officers were passing by on their evening constitutionals. Stefan and his boys did a lot of damage in Paris, and when it got too hot there and they went into the country they did railroad sabotage, blew up bridges—things like that. Heroic stuff—the real thing. Stefan had a feeling the Gestapo was closing in, and according to Veevi he wasn't so sure about the Party higher-ups. But he had friends from the old days—from after Berlin but before Hollywood—and he made sure they got Veevi a phony French passport that made her the American widow of a French aristocrat, and she and her daughter moved back and forth between a château belonging to a countess who was also a Communist and a farmhouse belonging to friends of hers. She sweated out the war there, terrified that someone would remember her from her American movies. But they got Stefan."

"Who? The Gestapo?"

"Who else? Of course the Gestapo."

"And?"

"First they beat him up, then they tortured him, then they decided they hadn't had enough fun, so they brought out another guy who'd been arrested with him, cut off their balls, tied their legs together, and told them to race each other in the snow. Then they shot them."

The words tore through the comfortable office, with its elegant appointments, like a savage smell, and Engel, always unshockable, never at a loss, swallowed, teared up, squeezed his eyes shut, and motioned with his hands for Jake to stop. "Please," he said hoarsely. "I'm sorry I asked."

Jake thought, Always a line. Even now there has to be a ready-made line. He felt overwhelming—but brief—contempt for the man and the industry to which they both belonged. Jake watched as Irv tapped the bowl of his pipe upside down on a crystal ashtray, and shifted his tall, lean body in his chair as if he could not get comfortable. "I'm afraid my father never did realize what he had in this man. He was a great artist. His fate"—Oh God, thought Jake, here it comes, another Engel-logue—"and his"—he searched for the word—"*contribution* should be acknowledged and commemorated in some, ah, appropriate way one day by this studio, while at the same time our"—he dug his pipe into a Dunhill pouch, packing it with the tips of his delicate fingers. "Our—um, not—um—help me out here, Jake—"

"Culpability?"

"No. Our, uh"—he scratched his head, which was, Jake noted enviously, as full of hair as a toupeed evangelist's—"*difficulties* in giving him the wide berth his talent, I mean, uh, genius, required, did, regretfully, play a role in his, uh, decision to return to Europe on the eve of war." He glanced around, and Jake saw that he wasn't finished. "But that decision was his own, and I have to believe he made it with open eyes. Let's face it, Jake," he said almost in a whisper, as if there were somebody listening under the table. "Who in their right mind went *back* to Europe in 1939? The man had to be suicidal."

But you did nothing to stop him, Jake thought. You were in love with Veevi, and sore at her for marrying Ventura; you could have gone to your father and argued with him to keep Ventura on, but you didn't do a goddamn thing. You let them both go.

"There was nothing left for him here, Irv."

"You know, in this business if you're patient enough something always turns up."

Not true, Jake said again to himself. It's what everybody out here is terrified of: if you're finished, you're finished for good.

"So," Jake said, "if Dinah refuses to testify and I'm blacklisted, there's nothing to worry about? I'll just sell shoes till I get a phone call from you?"

"Okay, okay," said Engel, rearranging paperweights and pens. "Let's get serious. Let's talk about you and Dinah. She was in the Party and you weren't, and they've got her number now and you want to know what to do. Is that the situation?"

"That's the situation. Now," said Jake, slapping his thighs with both hands, "you've got to understand my wife. She's—she's *frighteningly* loyal. She'd do anything for me. If I ask her to testify, she'll testify. She's willing to do it. If she could have done it last night at your party she would have. But I don't want her to go through it if she doesn't absolutely have to."

"Well, what about you, Jake? Can you live with Dinah's testifying for you?"

Jake bit his lip, hesitating. "I don't know, Irv. That's a tough one."

They both knew it meant he could but wasn't going to say so.

"So what are you asking, dear boy? You want I should be the heavy?" Engel said, in imitation of his immigrant father.

"Tell me the truth. What'll happen if she refuses."

"What'll happen to *her* or to *you*?"

"Me."

Engel looked at his watch. "Tell you what. I have to get tough with a certain director, a friend of yours and mine, though I can't tell you his name, but I know you know who I mean. I'm supposed to be on his set in five minutes to yell at him about going over-budget—something I rarely have to worry about with you, which is another reason you're a very valuable commodity." He picked up the phone. "Carlotta, set up a call for me with the legal department at exactly one-thirty. And at exactly two o'clock get me Van Zandvoort Aldrich. On his private phone."

"*The* V. Z. Aldrich?" Jake asked. "Of the Hudson-Hyde Trust?"

"The one and only. I'm expecting him out here at the end of the week. He comes to inspect the premises about twice a year," added Engel, putting the phone back. "Most often when his wife's in Paris for the spring collections."

V. Z. Aldrich was the head of the New York bank behind Marathon. "We met him at your house, Irv, remember? He tried to get me to arrange a date for him with Fiona Henley. I told him she'd gone back to England when we finished shooting. What else could I say? That she's a dyke and is serviced by her maid?"

"Very diplomatic of you."

"He told me how much he loved *Cousin Jonnycake,*" Jake continued. " 'Young man,' he said, 'it took real chutzpah to make that picture.' " Jake pronounced the word with the *ch* sound in *cheese,* or *chump.*

"And he also asked you, if I'm not mistaken, whether you'd signed the loyalty oath, and you fudged and said you were planning to, and by God the next day after that dinner in you trotted, and out came your pen, and to a chorus of angels you signed that goddamn loyalty oath and God did not smite you with leprosy. You woke up the next morning and you were still the same talented, successful guy you were the day before. Look, I understand what you're going through—you love your wife, you're edgy, you don't want to put her through this. Take the day off, play golf, have fun, then meet me back here at five o'clock. I'll have some answers for you."

Jake sighed, slapped his thighs again, and got up to leave. "Five," he said. "I'll be here."

※

Back in his own office, Jake had his secretary, Gladys, put a call through to Dinah and described to her in detail the meeting with Irv and the plan to see him again later that day. "I'll call you the minute it's over."

"Gee," she said, "it's gonna be a *long* afternoon for you."

"Yeah, and my legs are restless as hell. I'm torn between trying to work on the script and just going over to Finlandia to sweat out the tension. Maybe I'll drop in and see my mother."

"So *go*," she said. "*Go*."

He summoned Gladys and gave her the scenes he had been working on that morning, with instructions to insert them in the light blue third-draft binder.

"Oh, this'll be fun," she said, taking the yellow legal pages, which were covered in Jake's spider-web-thin scrawl.

"You still like it?"

Gladys was a small dark young woman who smoked Kools and chewed Juicy Fruit gum while she typed, and her Brooklyn-accented voice was always raspy and precise, with whistle-sharp sibilants. "So far I love it, I swear," she said. "Would I lie to you?"

"Maybe you're a bit too close to it."

"Naw. I read it out loud to my brother and sister-in-law last Sunday, when I finished typing those pages I took home, and they howled. Really howled. That sequence where the guy is hiding under the table listening to the spies talking about the bomb plans, scratching one guy's knee and tapping the other guy's, trying to keep it all in sync." She looked up at him and, seeing him search for something in the top drawer of his desk, reached into her blouse pocket and threw him a stick of gum, which he caught with one hand, unwrapped immediately, and popped into his mouth. He liked their little wordless understandings and always felt comfortable around her.

"You like that part?" he asked her, chewing noisily as he went to the closet for his jacket and his baseball cap.

"It's terrific." Her small, eager face, resplendent with loyalty, followed his every movement. "Has George seen it yet?"

"I was going to show it to him this week, but I think I'll wait a little till we have more pages."

"He's committed before on a lot less than this."

"Yeah, but you know, I just wanna wait awhile. Between you and me, maybe he's not the only guy who could do it. How many George Joy pictures have I made, after all?"

"Five," said Gladys, counting them on her fingers while she silently reviewed the titles. "Five pictures since 1944. I know, 'cause I've typed the scripts for every last one of them."

And, he thought, what the hell are you going to do if Dinah refuses to testify and you're out of a job? He couldn't imagine working without Gladys. And what about Gussie? What would happen to Gussie?

"Well, maybe there's . . ." His voice trailed off.

She looked at him, understanding that there was something he wasn't saying but that she couldn't ask him about. Yet, not wanting to appear to have secrets from her, he felt he had to confide to her at least something she could be trusted with. "I'd like to see just once what would happen if I worked with somebody else. Do you think I could shoot this picture with Wynn Tooling?"

"The English comedian? That is one sensational idea, Jake. I mean, sensational."

"You think so?"

"I think so."

He wanted so much to tell her about the subpoena.

"Jake," she said, "if you shoot it in England, could you take me with you? I've never been to Europe."

"Semper fi, kiddo. If the Brits'll let me, that is. They've got complicated labor laws. But I'd pull every string I could." And he meant it, too.

"You know," she said matter-of-factly, putting a new page into the type-writer. "I'd like to see the world one day."

"I know you would, Gladys."

He looked at her and felt how much he liked her, and wished, some-how, that he could do more for her. Then, as he started toward the door, he paused and asked her to call his mother and tell her he would be stopping by sometime in the afternoon.

He drove along Santa Monica, not Sunset. He wasn't going to Finlandia, and hadn't intended to go there in the first place. Stopping in a parking lot in West Hollywood, he entered a phone booth, where he took a blue address book from his jacket pocket and dialed, slouching against the glass windows. A minute or two later, he got back into the sea-green 1950 Cadillac and pulled into Santa Monica again, then made a right on Harper, which rose steeply toward Sunset. He parked just above Fountain, to be safe; his mother rarely walked to that end of the block.

It never failed to amuse him that the girl happened to live in the same building as his mother. It was just the sort of farcical circumstance he adored, and he wished he could use it in a picture someday. Will the time ever come, he often wondered, when American movies can show this sort of thing? Luckily, the two women lived on different floors—his mother on the fourth, the girl on the seventh—and, again luckily, in different parts of the building, which was a very large white stucco Spanish Colonial. Bonnie's place fronted west, on Harper, while his mother's looked out to the east and the north, toward the San Bernardino Mountains, over layers of scalloped terra-cotta roofs.

It winded Jake a little to climb the stairs, but he knew that his mother, with her arthritic knee, never used them, relying solely on the elevator. Nor was he likely, this way, to run into the elderly couple who lived across the hall from her and whose son was a well-known television director.

There really was very little danger, he reminded himself. Still, he always got the jitters when he came to see Bonnie. In a way, he knew, it was part of the fun. He had met her at Joe Brogan's, the bar across the street from the wrought-iron gate at the entrance to Marathon. Cutting *Cousin Jonny-cake,* planning to stay late into the night, he had taken a late-afternoon break for a beer and pretzels and the baseball scores. As soon as he walked in, he saw Johnny O'Rourke and Sammy Hart, the songwriting team, both of them real swingers, talking to a couple of Marathon starlets, a blonde and a brunette. The fellows called him over, and at one point, when the brunette had gone to the ladies' room, he asked Johnny what she was like. "Oh nice, nice," said the affable lyricist. "A sweet, easygoing kid. Here, I'll give you her number."

Always well provided for himself, O'Rourke was generous with his friends, often passing along current or ex-girlfriends. In these arrangements, everyone understood everyone else: the men wanted discretion and no fuss, and the girls—every single one of them—a break.

When the brunette, whose name was Bonita—"My friends call me Bonnie"—returned to the table, Jake talked with her for a while and then, after calling his cutter, drove her home. That's when he discovered that she lived in the Ensenada House, the same building as his mother. At the door, she invited him in for a drink. Minutes later he and Bonnie were in bed and having a very nice time. When he called her again, it was a weekend, the middle of a Saturday afternoon, and he was banking on his mother's having gone to his sister's in the Valley. With Dinah, he had used his most reliable alibi—that he had to go to Finlandia for a steambath and a massage—anything to relieve his tension over the final cut.

He'd been having girls on the side for some time now, but there hadn't been anyone he'd seen more than once or twice. At first he'd used the three-bedroom apartment in the Hollywood Hills that George Joy rented for meetings with his writers. They all had keys, and there was a tacit understanding that you were supposed to call five or ten minutes ahead to make sure the coast was clear. But Jake found this arrangement distasteful. It lacked class, and he disliked the feeling that at any moment George himself or one of the boys, most of whom were married, might unexpectedly show up with a broad, despite the rule about phoning ahead. So he'd been limiting himself to girls who lived alone in their own apartments. But there hadn't been many of these, either—two or three at most, which wasn't anything compared to some of the other guys. And then, as he had repeatedly explained to his analyst, Sandy Litvak, he didn't know what to do about the guilt, the lousy feeling that would creep up on him from time to time—mostly when, in the throes of screenplay insomnia, he would wake Dinah up and ask her to rub his back. She was a deep sleeper, but she never re-fused him, and then he would feel pretty low. Of course, a lot of the time he felt no guilt at all, and thought often of a line he'd heard from an old vaudevillian he'd worked for years before: "How do I know I love my wife? 'Cause I'm so comfortable cheating on her." He simply put Dinah and family in one compartment and girls in another—the same with his work, his golf game, his kids, his mother, Las Vegas, donations to Israel, and so on. And for some time now Bonnie had been tucked away right there in the drawer marked Convenient, for her place was on the way to and from the studio, and she had thus become, over the past eighteen months, a fixture in his life.

Calling her up, seeing if she was free, he had repeatedly told Litvak dur-ing the weeks when he was finishing up five expensive years of analysis—which had come to a successful end last July, in time for the analyst's August vacation—always made him feel as if he were seventeen years old and back in Chicago, trying to score with girls on Seventy-first Street and South Shore Drive. He liked the gamble of it, the footloose feeling. Most of all, he liked that kind of sex. "What kind?" Litvak had always pressed him. "Oh, you know goddamn well what kind, Sandy," Jake had said. "We've been over this before."

"Yes," said Litvak. "So I will tell you once again: the kind where there's absolutely no chance whatsoever that you've just been fucking Mommy."

"Oh, Sandy, forget the old whore-madonna thing just once, for Christ's sake. All I mean is I like and need that easy, uncomplicated kind where you don't have to romance them and spend an hour and a half working on them. Tell me something, Sandy, why does it take my wife such a long time to hit a home run?"

"Could it be," said Litvak, with the little giggle that Jake found so en-dearing, "that she senses your impatience?"

"I'm not impatient," said Jake. "In my opinion, and according to some very satisfied ladies I've known, I'm a very generous, considerate guy in the sack. But Christ, I'm exhausted." It was so different with Bonnie. She seemed to have a nice time, at least she told him so, and it didn't take all day. After visiting her, he said, he always felt healthy, renewed, and hygienic—and very deserving, too, especially when he considered, as he often did on the drive home, how hard he worked to provide for his family. And another good thing, he told Litvak, was that spending an hour or two with Bonnie always made him eager to get home to Dinah and the kids. "I mean, this is something that you, as my analyst, ought to write me a prescription for. She's probably done me more good than you and vitamins and a weekly golf game all rolled together!"

There was something else he couldn't kid himself about, he told Litvak. If he ever had to go without other women, he would die. As far as Jake Lasker was concerned, faithful husbands were fools. Women were one of the great pleasures, and any man who denied himself that particular cup of bliss was missing out on life. He couldn't think of even one friend who was faithful to his wife. Of course, some guys handled these things like complete amateurs and risked real trouble at home. But Jake made sure he wasn't one of them. To his way of thinking, either you did things with a touch of class or you were a schmuck.

"I bet you do it, too," he said to Litvak. "With a psychiatric nurse, maybe? I can imagine the possibilities."

"Oh?" said the analyst. "Tell me, did your father have other women?"

"Of course he did. You know that already. In fact, everything we're talking about we've talked about before. A million times."

"Yes?" said Litvak. "So you tell me what it means."

"It means that I see you as my father and if it's okay for you, then it's okay for me."

"Exactly."

"But, Sandy," Jake said, laughing, "the problem is, you treat all the comedy writers in Hollywood, and one of them—I won't say who—happened to see you not so long ago with a broad at a restaurant in Malibu."

Silence.

"Necking," Jake added. Expecting the doctor's giggle, he heard, again, only silence. "Well?" said Jake.

"And how does that make you feel?" said Litvak.

"How does that make me feel? It makes me feel, one, that you're human, two, that there's nothing wrong with me that isn't wrong with you, and three, why the hell do I keep coming here when I could spend my dough on putting in a pool? I'm sick of pretending I've got something to work out when we both know I'm never going to change and that I'm the same charming, lovable, incredibly talented, and incorrigibly infantile guy I was when I started coming here five years and ten thousand bucks ago. I could put two kids through college on what I've paid you and they would know more about anything than I've ever learned about myself on this couch. That's how it makes me feel."

"Yes?" said Litvak. "Anything else?"

"Yeah," said Jake. "I'm just curious about something. Was it a lady analyst?"

He sat at Bonnie's kitchen table talking about his script, but he wished he could tell her about the subpoena, because she listened so well. He really couldn't, though. She had girlfriends on the lot who were banging guys who couldn't be trusted with this information. Nevertheless, since he had finished his analysis and stopped seeing Sandy Litvak four times a week, he missed having someone to talk to, and realized just now how much he wanted not just a girl on the side but a confidante, someone to whom he could tell everything.

Still, Bonnie was just so nice to be around. She was from New Mexico—she said she was half Indian and half Irish, and she had great cheekbones and a quietness about her that calmed him. She never initiated anything and she never held back. She came over now and put a glass of ice-cold root beer on the table, and he grabbed her by the waist and stuck his head right between her breasts. The silk of her kimono was cool against his hands.

"Oh," she said mildly, "you wanna lay down for a while."

She always used this phrase, and it always crossed his mind that Dinah would have winced at her grammar.

She picked up his glass and walked ahead of him into the bedroom. Her matter-of-factness aroused him powerfully. *Immediate gratification,* he said to himself, echoing Sandy Litvak's phrase. *The powerful pleasure of immediate gratification.* He stretched out with his arms behind his head and she began to fiddle with him, unzipping him, sticking her hand inside the boxer shorts ironed to a crisp yesterday by Miss Fanny in the laundry room at home and freeing what Jake himself noticed was an uncommonly splendid erection, stopping to unbutton his shirt, unbuckle his belt. She pulled the shorts down to his ankles, and then whisked them completely off, pausing to unlace his shoes and pull them off, too, along with his socks, leaving him only his T-shirt. Yet, when she lay down beside him and sought his erection, she discovered that it had drooped, and nothing she did, with hand or mouth, seemed able to revive its former architectural magnificence. "Hey, what's the matter?" she said, glancing up at him with gentle concern.

"Gee, honey," he murmured drowsily, "I don't know. I seem to be awfully tired all of a sudden. Didn't sleep much last night."

"Why's that?"

"Just the usual. The script," he murmured.

"Well, take a nap. I'll be next door learning some lines." She began to sit up.

"Don't go," he said, pulling her back down. She nestled in beside him on the left side. "Right side, honey," he said, and she simply climbed over him, so that he caught a whiff of the Maja soap she showered with. Jake was deaf in his left ear, from a case of childhood mumps, and some gymnastic ingenuity was required from the women in his life.

"You got a job?" he asked lazily.

"Sure do. Lady-in-waiting in *Ferdinand and Isabella*."

"Good for you. Did I have anything to do with it?"

"Hey you, don't you remember? You sent me over to Jimmy McRoberts and he liked me."

"Oh geez, honey, yes," he said sleepily. "That's great. I'm sorry I forgot. You know I've got so much on my mind." He could hardly keep his eyes open.

"Oh, go to sleep," she said with a laugh, getting up and going back into the living room. "I'm just gonna get the script."

He slept the sleep he could never get at home—the sleep of pure escape from his screenplay, from the day's writing, from his kids, wife, house, and mortgage. From insurance premiums, college savings, guild dues, agent's percentages, business manager's percentages, club fees, private school bus fees, summer camp fees, dentist and doctor bills, car repairs, maid's, laundress's, gardener's, and pool man's salaries. His mother's monthly rent and support checks. The checks he sent to help his sister. From the relentless, ever-present worry over whether he was any good and how long his luck would hold out. And today, above everything else, from the subpoena, coming, as it had, at the worst possible time, just when he had reached the top of his game.

With Bonnie there was no talk about the house and the cars. No discussions about whom to invite to a party or whom they owed. No arguments about his habit of leaving Dinah to play golf on Sundays just when his sister was coming over with their mother. Bonnie had skin like silk. She was nice to him and didn't ask for anything. She was good in the sack. It was that simple.

When he woke up half an hour later, she was lying naked beside him, sideways with her rear end resting against his thighs. It was as easy as breathing to slide into her tight wet heat. She made no sound, and moved up against him; whatever was happening to her seemed to be taking place at a great distance, so lost was he in his own pleasure, which soon tore up his spine like a lit fuse.

A little less than an hour later, having slept some more, showered, and dressed, he kissed her lightly at the door. As always, she didn't ask him whether or when he would call again. "Thanks, honey," he said. "That was great."

She smiled and smoothed back her hair.

"You okay for dough?"

"Yeah, fine," she said, noticing his hand going to his pocket.

"Well, go have some fun. Go down to the beach and have dinner some-where with a friend," he said, putting a fifty-dollar bill in her hand, which softly closed around it. He was grateful to her, he felt wonderful, and for just that instant he loved her very much.

Nevertheless, as he started down the red-and-green-carpeted stairs, she ceased to exist for him, and she would wait in a limbo of nonbeing, like a reel of film in a metal can, until the next time he thought of her. What worried him now was how to hold on to a life where he could have her and other girls like her. If Dinah refused to testify, if he had to leave Holly-wood, if he no longer had serious dough and a big name, girls like Bonnie wouldn't waste two minutes on him.

❧

Downstairs at his mother's, in an identically laid-out apartment, he stuffed a handful of stale peppermints and calcified green and orange gumdrops into his mouth. His mother kept cut-crystal jars next to every slipcovered piece of furniture, and you couldn't move without catching your eye on rainbow-colored candies or foil-wrapped Hershey's Kisses. Rose Lasker came in from the kitchen, carrying a small tray with a large piece of pound cake and a steaming cup of fresh coffee, with cream and sugar. She limped a little from the arthritis in her knee. "I said 'No thanks, Ma,'" he yelled at her, accepting the plate nonetheless and digging in. "Are you trying to kill me? One of these days I'm gonna have a heart attack and it'll be because of you." Within seconds he had devoured the cake. His mother, joyously watching him eat, asked him if he wanted another piece. "Just bring the rest of it," he answered in self-disgust. "The whole goddamn thing."

He wanted to tell her about the subpoena, too, but he couldn't risk it. She would drive him crazy with her what's-going-to-happen-to-me? worry and fear. So he listened to her latest reports about Chicagoans she kept in touch with, those who were still there as well as those who were now living in Los Angeles, uprooted and transplanted by their grown-up, guilt-ridden, successful children. As she reeled off her usual mix of gossip and chit-chat, along with her favorite subjects—strokes, heart attacks, prostate, uterine, and bladder troubles, gout, cancer, deafness, blindness, diabetes, Parkinson's, senility, operations, and good and bad deaths—he was plunged into deep gloom. If Dinah testified . . . If he couldn't find work . . . If they lost the house . . . If he couldn't afford his mother's rent . . . Then, oh dear God, she'd have to move in with them. Every hypothetical spelled loss and suffocation, and seemed to stop his digestion cold. And each time his mother got up and went into the kitchen to get him some other high-calorie, artery-clogging treat, he could hear the familiar, sickening swish of her nylon stockings rubbing together between her fat thighs. It was the one sound in the universe he could not stand.

When Jake showed up again at Irv Engel's office just before five, Carlotta Moran, his secretary, resigned herself to being at the office for at least another half hour. Mr. Engel had told her to hold all calls. There was going to be a social at her church tonight, and she wanted to go home and fix herself up for it. She had every intention of finding another husband, this time one with money, and there was a widower with nice manners she had her eye on.

After she led Mr. Lasker into Mr. Engel's office, she strained to listen to the conversation on the other side of the door but could catch only indecipherable murmurs and, from time to time, shouting, by two different voices: Mr. Engel's shrill and shrieking, and Mr. Lasker's deep, gravelly, and explosive.

At five-forty, Mr. Lasker came out, murmured good night, and, with a preoccupied look on his face and his lips tightly pressed together, quickly left. After a moment, she heard a buzz: "Get me V.Z.A. again, honey. The Greenwich number. After that you can go on home."

"Yes, Mr. Engel," she said. "Sure you don't need me to stay?" She took care to sound just as bright and cooperative as she had been all day, as she was every day. She had worked for Mr. Engel's father and was close to sixty. One tiny expression of weariness or resentment and she would be gone, she knew. The secretarial pool at Marathon swelled every day with younger, prettier women who would do *anything* to work for a top executive in the business.

❧

"Jake, I don't have to tell you," Engel began. "I believe in you, and there's nothing I wouldn't do at this studio or in this town for you."

Just say it, Jake thought. Just get it over with.

"I also know I don't have to tell you how much I abhor the investigations and the terrible things they've done to this industry." Engel shook his head. "It's Salem all over again, each side vilifying and reviling the other, each bringing out the worst instincts in the other—cowardice, sneakiness, knavery—"

Where would he be without the thesaurus? thought Jake.

"And you know where I stand, Jake. You know I was one of the first, the very first, to speak out in public against the Committee. You know I was on that plane to Washington with you and all those other good people. You saw my statement in the *New York Times* and the *Los Angeles Times,* and the ones I put in the trades, too. You know how hard I have fought to keep certain people we both admire from losing their jobs."

"Yes, Irv," Jake said. "Believe me, I do know and everyone in the industry knows you've done all you can, but the fact remains that those guys are out on their asses. So tell me, right now, Irv. I've got to know right now, because I'm right in mid-screenplay and I've got two kids to send to college, in addition to a monthly nut the size of a football: what's gonna happen if Dinah refuses to testify?"

"You'll never work in Hollywood again."

Jake sat perfectly still, his hands clasped together in his lap. He had known that this was what Irv was going to say. But hearing it, as opposed to expecting to hear it, was an altogether different thing.

"That long, huh?" he said finally.

"Not here at Marathon, not at Metro, not at Paramount, Universal, Warner Brothers, Columbia, RKO—forget it. You won't be able to get through the front gate. Not even as an extra."

"What about the three-picture deal I just signed? What about 'Jake Lasker knows how to make America laugh' and all the other sweet nothings you said last night?"

"That was last night. Today's today," Engel said without expression. "This is what I called V.Z.A. and the legal department about. The contract is out. Without Dinah's testimony, you'll become a known subversive."

"*Me?* A 'known subversive'? How do you figure that?"

"Being married to a known subversive makes you a known subversive."

"Guilt by association?"

"Exactly. You'd be in violation of the loyalty oath, so there'd be no obligation on our side."

"But I *signed* that fucking loyalty oath!" Jake shouted. "That goddamn idiotic unconstitutional loyalty oath that I never wanted to sign in the first place."

"That was before they subpoenaed your wife. Who knew they'd go after her?" Engel shrugged.

"Is that what those loyalty oaths are for? Fucking escape clauses for you guys? It's obscene, Irv," Jake shouted again.

"Don't you shout at me, Jake Lasker," said Engel, his own voice rising. "I'm as much a victim of this as you are. I *writhe* with shame thinking about what I've had to do. But my job is to keep this studio running and the bankers in New York happy, a contradiction in the best of times, so that when this madness is over we'll still have a Marathon studio where guys like you can keep on making pictures like *Cousin Jonnycake*. If I'm out, God knows who they'll stick in here to run the place."

"I hear you've worked out deals for people."

Engel pounded on his desk. "Like who? Name me one single person! There are no deals with the Committee." His voice had become an impassioned falsetto. "You don't know the hours I've spent on the phone, at this desk, screaming at the top of my lungs at the boys in New York. All they ever say is 'Protect our investment.'"

"What about protecting me? Aren't I an investment? You need dough from New York, but you need talent from here!"

"Look, Jake. You know we're the only studio in Hollywood history that's ever given a damn about writers. My father believed in writers and I believe in writers, and we treat 'em just as good as movie stars here. But do you think V. Z. Aldrich and the blue-blooded board of the Hudson-Hyde Trust give a good goddamn about writers? As far as these genteel gentiles are concerned, writers are what Harry Cohn called them: 'schmucks with type-writers.' In the same class with nannies and broads—almost as useful and much more expendable. I have to fight these guys every time I pay a writer what he's worth. They're schmucks with airplanes—big private airplanes—who come out here when their wives are planning charity balls and tell me which broads to send up to the hotel. Before I get paid, they get laid. And that, on top of our profits, is how we finance great American popular art like yours. Believe me, Jake, V.Z.A.'s got friends in Washington and he wants to keep 'em. What a *macher* he is with the Republican Party I don't have to tell you. I've begged him to let me keep one writer after another. Frank Ford, Eric Riswold, Burt Allen, Archie Collier, Dan Salander, Joel Kanin—top guys, the best in the business. He axed every single one. Not to mention actors, actresses, producers, directors. My orders are very strict: 'Get rid of the stink of pink or we get rid of you.' Deals? Forget it."

But Engel, as Jake well knew, was lying. He'd been allowed to keep Lance Drake, a huge Marathon star whose last two pictures had grossed more than ten million dollars worldwide. Nobody had had to work very hard to convince Van Zandvoort Aldrich about the importance of keeping Marathon's cash cow. Aldrich had called Dick Nixon in Washington and promised a big contribution to the young man's next campaign if he could persuade his colleagues on the Committee to let the Drake matter drop; then he'd called Engel and dictated a letter in which Drake would say how sorry he was to have been duped in his young and innocent days into giv-ing money to the Hollywood Anti-Nazi League. In exchange for the letter, Engel and Drake got no publicity and a dropped subpoena.

But Lance Drake was a major movie star, not a screenwriter.

"You do realize what kind of position this puts Dinah in, don't you? She hates the idea of informing, but she doesn't want me to lose my job. Can't you say something to Aldrich? What kind of a threat could she be? She's just a *housewife,* for Christ's sake."

Engel slumped back in his chair. "No can do, my boy."

"Jesus Christ, Irv, how can I let my wife go to jail for a year? We've got two little kids at home. Have you thought of that?"

"Did I say anything about Dinah's going to jail? Listen, Jake—" he said, leaning forward. "If I thought Dinah should take the First or the Fifth, by God I'd tell you. Believe it or not, I've advised some of my own people to do it—even though I knew I'd have to fire them, and told them so. *I have never demanded that someone who works for me double-cross his own conscience—*"

Where had he heard *that* line before? Jake wondered. Later on he remembered reading it in Engel's open letter in the trades, during the hearings on the Ten.

"Jake," Engel continued, "you've got to look at it this way. Dinah's not the one with the *talent* in this case. *You* are. For Christ's sake, why should *we* be deprived of *you*—a very hot creative talent, right in your prime—just because you happen to be married to a woman—a *wonderful* woman, Dinah is one of my *favorite* people in the whole world, an absolute *paragon* of what a Hollywood wife should be, an attractive, no-bullshit dame utterly devoted to you and your two beautiful children—*but,* let's say it now, out loud, a woman who was, if we have to face it, at one time, like a lot of other very young people of goodwill who didn't know any better, a member of the Communist Party?"

He pulled on an earlobe and cocked his head before adding: "Unless, um, she's still got some kind of attachment to it?"

"Hell no. She left years ago."

"How many years ago is 'years ago'?"

"During the war—before we were married. I kinda told her she'd have to get out if we were ever to have any kind of a future together."

"Well, then, what's the *problem*? Get her to testify, Jake. Tell her it's for you. For us. For the Marathon family."

"What about naming people?"

"What about it?"

"Can't she just name herself?"

Engel sighed deeply and, clasping his hands together, looked at Jake as if he were a teacher who had kept a slow pupil after school to explain a simple math problem. "That, Jake, is where the Committee has the world by the balls. You can't just show up and talk about yourself. That's the whole point. You're there to name names. If you don't, you're through. But"—he shrugged—"names, schnames. *They've already got all the names they want.* They've had 'em from the beginning. They don't care about names. What they want is humiliation, degradation, and demoralization. They want to crush the Left and the New Deal and the Democratic Party, or what's left of it," he said. "And they know the best way to do that is to turn people against each other, so the martyrs hate the stool pigeons and the stool pigeons hate the martyrs. There's no Left left in a situation like that."

"I don't know, Irv. I can't force her to do it."

"Sure you can," said Engel, fixing his eyes on Jake. "If I know one thing about Dinah, it's that she loves you. She loves you more than you've got any right to be loved. She loves you more than she should."

"What's that supposed to mean?" Jake said.

"I know it because that's how Anya feels about me. She hates it out here. Every day is torture for her. She wants to live in New York, she wants to live in Paris, she wants art galleries and museums. I say, 'What can I do, baby? I gotta stay here and mind the store.' And she sticks it out because she's crazy about me, the way Dinah's crazy about you. I can feel it, I can see it. She looks at you the way Anya looks at me. She'll do anything you ask. Actually, you don't even have to ask her. She'll do it anyway. Let's not forget I know something about your wife."

"You do?" said Jake. "And what's that?"

"I knew her before you did, before you ever came out here."

"What're you saying, Irv?"

"Oh, it's not that. I never had anything going with her. I was one of those perfect idiots in love with Veevi. But I saw what life was like for her when nobody knew she was alive. She was waiting for something; you could see it in her eyes. You're not only the best thing that ever happened to her, Jake, you're the *only* thing that ever happened to her."

"My wife," said Jake with dignity, "had and still has more class than any woman I've ever known, including her sister. Don't ever talk to me that way about her again."

He stood up to go.

"Jake, listen," said Engel. "I'm sorry. I spoke out of line. Don't blow it, Jakie. Don't fuck things up. I want you here, at this studio. You know what I'm saying?"

He stood up, smiled a broad, warm, utterly seductive smile, and went over to Jake and put his arm around him.

"I don't know, Irv. You got any relatives in the shoe business? I used to sell shoes in college. Shoes, meat, bicycles. Maybe I could be a bicycle salesman."

"It's not gonna come to that," Engel said quietly. "Listen to me. Be extra-special nice to her. Be, you know, romantic. Lay off the broads for a while—"

"What do you mean?" said Jake, surprised.

"Come on," said Engel. "You don't have to pretend with me. That Bonnie Alvarez is a nice girl. Needs a different last name, though. Maybe we'll change it to Austen and see if she gets somewhere."

Jake laughed. "Don't tell me you've got plans for her yourself?"

"Who, me? Nah. I'll tell you something, my boy," said Engel, squeezing Jake's shoulder. "I know this is going to sound very square, but I don't play around. I'm faithful to Anya. I mean, I *make a point* of it. Maybe I didn't so much when I was younger, but"—he shook his head sagely—"I don't think I'm missing anything. Luckily for me, she never found out. You know, one false step and there's your whole family. And then, oh my God, *alimony.* Christ, forget it, it ain't worth it."

Jake nodded automatically but offered nothing in reply. Engel added, "Let me say it again, Jake. Dinah loves you. She's gonna do it and never look back. She's gonna do it for *you.* So don't be careless, 'cause you're gonna owe her."

"Got it."

"Good boy."

There was one last pure Engelism, as Jake later reported it to Dinah. Just as they reached the office door, he said, Engel gave his shoulder an especially tight squeeze. "Just promise me one thing, Jake," he said. "When this all blows over, and the country wakes up and realizes what it's done to itself, I'm gonna write a script with you and you're gonna direct it, and together we're gonna tell the *truth* about this period—and we'll do it with *humor.*"

"Let's do that, Irv," Jake said, disengaging himself from Engel's embrace. "Let's definitely do that."

4

*S*he stops and checks her watch: 2 P.M. exactly. A thousand years ago she had won silver cups in dance contests in the ballroom on the same floor, the mezzanine of the Hollywood-Griffith Hotel. Once a château-esque blue extravagance, it is now faded to gray, deep in the smoggy bowels of an already decrepit and tatterdemalion Hollywood Boulevard. She pauses in front of the conference room and by design she's alone, without counsel, and not in Washington, as she had feared. A deal has been worked out. Jake found a lawyer who has arranged a closed "executive" session right here at home in L.A., and fixed it so that she would show up alone and thus demonstrate greater good faith and co-operation on her part than if she had come with a lawyer at her side. Nevertheless, she breathes fast, and her intestines rumble; she trembles and sweats. Calm down, she orders herself. The lawyer, who has had lots of experience representing "friendly witnesses," has told her it's going to be easy and fast.

She knocks at a door. Ever the director, Jake had gone through her closet the night before, taking a dress from the rack and saying, "This'll do very nicely. I want you to look very Pasadena Garden Club." It's a cream silk printed with a pattern of small horseshoes and jockeys astride horses. She is wearing smart brown-and-white open-toed heels and cream-colored gloves, and she stands straight and tall. She is pulled together: a little powder, red lipstick, and mascara, hair and nails perfect, the gold barrette locked into its usual place.

The door opens and she faces a thin man with limp hair. The way he holds his head back at a stiff angle and doesn't quite look her in the eye reminds her of a heron. "Mrs. Lasker?" he asks in a surprisingly quiet voice.

"Yes."

"I'm Horace Marlow. Please come in." He gestures toward a large table piled high with manila folders. At the far end of the table she sees a fat man with puffy jowls and a crew cut. Marlow introduces her to him, but she recognizes him from the newspapers and loathes him on sight: the Honorable Curtis P. Kingman, Republican congressman from Orange County. In a corner of the room, by the open windows and the maroon velvet drapes, a stenographer with glasses and bright red lips sits at a card table with a steno machine.

"Are you ready to be sworn in, Mrs. Lasker?" Marlow inquires.

"I am."

"Please raise your hand."

As he recites the oath, she tries to identify his accent. It sounds midwestern to her ears; there's a slight twang. An Okie? she wonders. Why would an Okie be on *their* side? Hasn't he read *The Grapes of Wrath*?

The swearing-in completed, Marlow motions for her to sit down. Then he moves to the opposite side of the table and begins to look through a file. Clearing his throat twice, three times, he makes another strange birdlike movement with his head, jutting it forward and then back again, where it stays, slightly tilted, so that when he looks at her she gets only a sidelong view of his face. He asks her to recite her full name and address and then to confirm that she is appearing under subpoena. She obliges, and he continues.

"Where were you born, Mrs. Lasker?"

"In Pittsburgh, Pennsylvania."

"Could you elaborate, please?"

"I was born at the Homeopathic Hospital in Pittsburgh, Pennsylvania. My family lived in Beaver Falls and my father was a steel salesman. We moved to California in January 1922, when I was nine."

"Would you give us a brief résumé of your educational background?"

"Public schools in Pittsburgh and Philadelphia, then Selma Avenue School in Hollywood, then Hollywood High School, from which I graduated"—she stutters on this one—"in June 1930. I was supposed to begin UCLA in the fall of 1930, but the Depression had hit and I went to work."

His face registers nothing when she stutters, although Burt Unwin, her lawyer, has cited it in his negotiations as the major reason for the executive session. If you put her on the stand in Washington, in full public view, he'd warned Marlow and Kingman, she'll be tongue-tied and the hearing will take a very long time. Maybe Mrs. Lasker would be unable to speak at all.

She glances coldly at Kingman, noting his lumpish face.

"Were you a dancer in motion pictures under the name of Dinah Milligan?"

"Yes, briefly. But it wasn't 'under' that name. It *is* my name, or was, before I married." She catches herself too late. Unwin has instructed her: Don't tell them more than they ask for.

"Can you give us some background concerning your career?"

"I became a dancer in pictures while I was still in high school in order to help support my family. May I smoke?"

"By all means." She lights a cigarette, and Marlow reaches over and pushes an ashtray toward her. It's full of cigarette butts, and she wonders how many people they've already seen that day.

"Please continue."

"Dancing wasn't steady enough, so after graduation I got a job as a secretary at the Sprague P-P-P-Paper Company. I was there for five years and then I got another job, at Claggett Oil, where I was executive secretary."

"Continue, please."

"Actually, between those jobs I worked for L. J. Saber for one week. He was the founder of Marathon Pictures, and he fired me when he heard me stuttering on the phone. Later, after Claggett Oil, I became a secretary for Mr. Reginald Pertwee at American Artists Corporation," she continues. "It was and still is a well-known entertainment agency in Beverly Hills. Eventually I became a writer on the NBC radio show *Hey There, Patsy Kimball!*"

"Are you now or have you ever been a member of the Communist Party?" The voice isn't Marlow's but Kingman's, and it's gruff and phlegmy. He's bored and wants to get the session over with. She hates the way he pronounces the word—*Comm*-unn-ist.

"Yes, sir. That is, I am not now a member of the Communist Party, but I was at one time."

"Can you tell us when you joined the Communist Party?" asks Marlow.

"I joined sometime late in 1937 or '38."

"Do you recall who recruited you to the Communist Party?"

"No one 'recruited' me. As I remember it, I went to a party somewhere. Some of the other guests were raising money for ambulances in Spain or refugees fleeing from Hitler, I don't remember which. Maybe it was both.

There was some interesting conversation, and I was invited to another one, and eventually I just started going to more gatherings. One day I joined."

"Do you remember who invited you to this party?"

It had been Renna Schlossberg—Renna Goldman back then. They were getting bored with going ice-skating in Westwood every weekend. Renna knew about this meeting and they'd gone together. Dinah replies, "Just some fellow I had a date with. I don't remember his name—I never went out with him again."

"You are certain you don't remember his name?" Kingman barks from his end of the table.

Unwin had said: *Unless you knew for a fact that someone really was a member, don't name them.*

"Oh yes, I'm certain. I have a t-t-terrible memory for names."

She looks squarely at Kingman as she speaks. She fears him, and despises him, gross feature by gross feature. For some reason she doesn't despise Marlow; he intrigues her. He looks as if he could have been one of those unsmiling Party guys or union organizers from the aircraft industry or dock workers in San Pedro: envoys from the world of real "toilers" (the word everyone used to make fun of from the badly translated Soviet pamphlets they used to have to do "reports" on), men who from time to time showed up at meetings, and had romantic, iron faces and hard eyes and were absolutely sure of themselves. Except that, with his oddly angled body, Marlow doesn't look that tough. He seems tense.

"Where was this meeting held?" Marlow asks.

"Honestly, I don't mean to be so vague, but I just don't remember."

She is about to light another cigarette but interrupts herself. It's time to give them something. "Somewhere in West Los Angeles, maybe, near UCLA, near Veteran. I'm not sure."

"But you did go back there and you subsequently joined the Communist Party?" Marlow asks.

"Yes, I did."

"Were you assigned to any particular unit?"

"I was asked to do clerical work. Typing, mostly. Stuffing envelopes. I think all of it had to do with Sp-Sp-Spain—meetings for Spain and fund-raisers for Spain."

"Where did you do this typing?"

"It would depend. Sometimes one person's house, sometimes another's.

On Saturday mornings. I can't say I showed up very reliably. I worked hard during the week and was often very tired on weekends."

"Did you attend specific meetings for any regular period of time?"

"Not regularly. I'd say I went on and off."

"Do you recall where these meetings were held?"

"Well, that's difficult for me to answer. It was a long t-t-t-time ago."

"Mrs. Lasker," Marlow says, his voice a degree louder. "Do you recall where *some* of those meetings were held?"

"I remember driving somewhere in Westwood, between Olympic and P-P-P-Pico. A house—someone's house; I don't remember whose. I did some secretarial work there, I remember."

"Do you recall who was present at these meetings?"

"No, I don't."

"You can't remember the name of a *single person* who was present at these meetings?"

"They were not people I was familiar with. I was still a secretary. I wasn't in radio yet—I didn't begin working for AAC until 1941. I was shy and didn't mingle easily. I felt uneducated. I tried to l-l-l-listen to what was being said, but I didn't start conversations. With my speech, you understand, I was not very f-f-f-forthcoming."

"Surely, Mrs. Lasker," growls the Honorable Curtis P. Kingman, "you can remember the names of some of the people at these meetings. Mr. Marlow and I have all afternoon to help you refresh your memory."

She does not sigh, she does not glare, she does not take on the stony, intransigent expression of a person who has decided to become difficult. Indeed, she sits back in her chair and lights a cigarette and tries to give the impression that she is a lady whose current life has no connection whatsoever to the life about which she is being interrogated and that searching her memory is a far greater ordeal than she had anticipated. "Well," she says finally, "I went to meetings at the homes of the screenwriters Norman M-M-M—You have to bear with me, gentlemen, because I could never say this fellow's name. Norman—" She shuts her eyes to concentrate, takes a deep breath, and exhales "Metzger. Norman Metzger. And Anatole K-K-Klein. They were the ones who gave me secretarial work." Her stutter is genuine; these names have always been impossible for her to say, although she has had them ready for several days and has practiced saying them.

Kingman looks at Marlow and blinks impassively. There is no new thrill here for them. She hasn't named anyone new. Metzger and Klein have long since served their jail terms. One of them has moved to England; the other lives in Mexico. Nothing she says about them now can harm them, or so she wants to believe.

"Mr. Metzger and Mr. Klein are known to this committee," Marlow says. "Is there anyone else you remember?"

"I'd just have to rack my brains, Mr. Marlow. I really do have such a t-t-t-terrible time with names."

"Would you please tell us, Mrs. Lasker," says Marlow, lighting a cigarette, "your reasons for joining the Communist Party."

Unwin has coached her: *Be sincere, don't be vague; make a speech if you have to.*

"The Depression was still going on," she begins. "My family was hit quite hard. My father was already in his sixties and couldn't find a job. No one could. B-B-B-Boys I had graduated with who were supposed to go to college couldn't find jobs anywhere. We were young and we saw that there were"—the next word was impossible for her, so she sounded it out syllable by syllable—"e-c-c-c-co-nom-ic reasons for this, and we wanted to find out about them and do something about them, too. I couldn't afford college. The Party was the only place where I could talk to people about books and ideas and what was going on in the world. People in the offices where I worked didn't read much. It was so bewildering, really, to have everything we took for granted just sort of crash all of a sudden. It was awful to see the hardships. In the Party I learned why this had happened, and why it didn't have to happen again."

She pauses, and takes in Marlow's face. It is expressionless; he has heard some variation of this speech a thousand times. But she has warmed to her topic and, much to her surprise, wants to keep talking. "And then more than anything else there was fascism—Franco and Hitler and Mussolini. The Communist Party seemed to be the only group that realized how dangerous they were or knew what to do about them. The Party seemed to care about people—ordinary people who had it tough. They raised money for floods and disasters. And they were the only people who wanted to help the Negroes and do something to end segregation. My G-G-G-God," she bursts out, "nobody else was doing anything! I loved Roosevelt, but even his ideas seemed to us too little too late."

She has never spoken like this before, never made statements, discussed her life, or shared her convictions with strangers, much less hostile ones, never seen herself as a part of the times or of history. She speaks with a growing wonder that she has, indeed, lived through a distinct period, and she is surprised at the ease with which she talks about it. But she stops herself. She has said too much. What, she asks herself, am I even doing here?

"Tell us, Mrs. Lasker," Marlow begins brightly. "Did you ever attend Communist Party meetings at the home of the actress Genevieve Milligan Ventura Albrecht?"

Startled, Dinah looks up at him. "My s-s-s-sister?"

"Then it is true, Mrs. Lasker, that you have a sister named Genevieve Milligan, an actress who was married to the late film director Stefan Ventura and who now resides in Paris with her present husband, the writer Michael Albrecht?"

"Yes. That is true," she says dully. Oh God, she thinks, I should have known. The men questioning her and the woman with the red talons poised above the steno machine all go still. A stagnant orange haze hangs outside the window, and the smoke from her cigarette scrapes her lungs like glass dust.

"Did you go to meetings of the Communist Party at the home of your sister, Mrs. Lasker?" Marlow persists.

"It's difficult to know exactly how to answer your question, Mr. Marlow," she says finally. "I assume you are aware that my brother-in-law, Stefan Ventura, worked for the French Resistance. He was captured by the Nazis, tortured, mutilated, and murdered by them. My sister and Mr. Ventura left for France early in 1939. Later on, my sister and her child were hidden by friends in the French countryside, where they spent the rest of the war." She speaks slowly, carefully, measuring every word, stuttering hardly at all. "I rarely went to my sister's house when she and Mr. Ventura lived here, and when I did go there it was only for social events."

Kingman breaks in, adjusting his gray-suited bulk in his chair and unclenching his hands. "Surely you are aware, Mrs. Lasker, that other cooperative witnesses have identified your sister and Stefan Ventura as members of the Communist Party? Here's what one witness said: 'They had the most distinguished Stalinist salon on the West Coast.'"

He pronounces it *sal*-lawn.

"Well, this is the first I've ever heard of it. I am busy morning till night raising a family, and I have no time to follow who's been saying what about whom. My sister has not lived in this country for many years, and she and I have always led s-s-s-separate lives."

"Nevertheless, you would know your sister's political sympathies," Marlow says in his tight monotone.

"Not n-n-n-necessarily."

"That certainly seems at odds with the facts, Mrs. Lasker," says Marlow, pinching the skin on his neck. "According to our records, you resided at your sister's home in the Malibu Colony from 1936 until 1938. Others have said you were well acquainted with the many European Communists and agitators who stayed at her home."

" 'Communists and agitators'? Excuse me, Mr. Marlow, but your inf-f-f-formation is incorrect. I spent brief stretches of time at my sister's and every once in a while I stayed overnight in one of the guest rooms, but I had my own apartment and that's where I lived. You could hardly call the people who stayed at my sister's or visited her home 'agitators.' Who was or wasn't a Communist I just don't know, and frankly I don't care. If some of them *were* Communists, I'm sure they had their reasons. My God, don't you remember those times? People were running for their lives. My sister's guests were often famous and distinguished p-p-people, or so I was told, but when I met them they had usually just arrived, and they were in very rough shape. They had just been through hell, and they looked it, too. The Nazis had taken their money and property, and they were impoverished, and terrified, and had barely gotten out alive. I remember a woman, a famous singer from Berlin, who had seen her fiancé shot in the street before her eyes. There was another man whose mother died in Lisbon before they could get on the boat. Every single one of them was d-d-desperately worried about people who'd been left behind and whom they couldn't get out and who were in fact killed later on in the gas chambers. You do remember the gas chambers, gentlemen, don't you?"

"Was a Mrs. Dorshka Albrecht a frequent guest of your sister's?" Marlow asks, ignoring her taunt.

"She wasn't a guest. Mrs. Albrecht collaborated with Stefan Ventura on the screenplays for his movies, and she actually lived at the house. She had worked with him in the early twenties, in Berlin, and when he left for Paris in the early thirties, he arranged for her to go, too. She was a selfless, tireless friend to everyone who needed her. She sponsored one refugee after another. Many times she gave her last cent to get people out."

"Was Mrs. Albrecht a member of the Communist Party?"

"I don't know. I never saw her at any meetings."

"Mrs. Albrecht has been identified to us as a well-known Communist," says Kingman.

"Then why are you asking me?" she snaps. "Look, gentlemen, I lived a separate life from my sister's. Even when I spent weekends at her house I lived a separate life. I was not yet in show business. Now, l-l-l-l-let me tell you something: people who are *in* show business take very little notice of people who are *not* in show business. Even the very nicest, kindest people in show business, people who worry about the poor and the hungry and the oppressed and the exploited, don't really want to know you if you're not in show business. To spend even an instant talking to someone outside the business is a big waste of their time. In fact, they're c-c-c-completely un-interested in you and automatically bored to death with you if you're not in it. I was not yet in it in the late thirties. What I was, gentlemen, was a genuine proletarian—a wage earner without prop-p-p-perty . . . sorry, I had an old Ford—a secretary in an oil company. I was invisible, as far as they were concerned. I spent my days taking dictation and typing letters for Mr. Winston Grundy at Claggett Oil in downtown L.A., and when the brilliant American screenwriters and movie stars and the famous European ge-niuses who came to my sister's house met me their eyes gl-gl-gl-glazed over. But I didn't care. I went there because I had just been divorced and I was lonely, and my sister's guests were interesting, damn interesting, every last one of them. I had never known anyone like them, and so it was sort of my way of finding out what was going on in the world. And my sister needed me to help out—to shop for groceries, help with the cooking and cleaning up. On weekends she had at least twenty people for every meal, and she didn't believe in having servants."

"Isn't that a Communist belief?" growls Kingman.

"You'd have to ask her," she says. "All I can tell you is that I made more whipped cream with an eggbeater on any given Saturday than either of you will ever eat in a l-l-l-lifetime, and I served Mrs. Albrecht's schnitzel and Sacher torte, and passed around the coffee and made sure the refugees had everything they needed. When I was around them, I felt terribly shy and uneducated. I would be told that this person or that was a famous writer or a famous composer, but I didn't know who the hell they were. I hadn't gone to college, I didn't understand German, I'd never heard of the books they'd written or the music they'd composed. I didn't know what their politics were; hell, I didn't know that politics was something you had. So when I visited my sister I just kept quiet and listened to all these people, and helped out when I was asked to, and who knew who was or wasn't a Communist?"

"How is that possible?" Kingman snarls. "You are avoiding the question!"

"Mr. Kingman, I can't say that I knew absolutely for sure who was or wasn't a Communist." She pauses, then adds, "You know, some people were what we used to call fellow travelers. I am sure, sir, that you remember the phrase."

"So you say there were fellow travelers at your sister's and this Ventura fellow's?"

"I think, Mr. Kingman, that you ought to speak more respectfully of a man who gave his life f-f-f-fighting against Hitler."

Before Kingman can answer, Marlow takes over. "Mrs. Lasker," he says quietly. "What did people talk about at your sister's?"

"The Spanish Civil War was the big thing at the time. And Hitler, of course, and the trials in Moscow, and, later on, the Pact." She takes a deep breath. "You know, gentlemen, my sister didn't have to join organizations. People flocked to her and Stefan."

"What was Stefan Ventura's background?" Kingman asks suspiciously. "Was he Spanish?"

"He was a Bulgarian Jew, from an old Italian-Jewish family that had come to that part of the world centuries ago, after some pope or other decided it was time to kick out the Jews. They got absorbed into the Bulgarian Sephardic world."

She senses that neither Kingman nor Marlow has the slightest idea of what she's talking about.

"Are you sure he wasn't a Spanish Communist?" Kingman says, raising his eyebrows.

"I am quite sure he wasn't, sir. He did study moviemaking in Moscow as a young man and then he went to Berlin, where he made a number of very good pictures."

"When was he in Moscow, Mrs. Lasker?" asks Marlow with sudden interest.

"During the Revolution." She lets this sink in.

"But even though others have unhesitatingly identified Ventura and your sister as Communists, you can't say one way or another whether they were members of the Communist Party?"

"That's correct, Mr. Marlow."

"Is it true, Mrs. Lasker," Marlow goes on, "that your husband, Jacob Lasker, known professionally as Jake Lasker, was not then or at any other time a member of the Communist Party?"

"That is true. He believed a person could be anti-fascist and anti-Nazi without being a Communist."

"Well, that's very interesting," Kingman interrupts. "But, Mrs. Lasker, be that as it may, can you give us the names of some of the people you saw at Communist Party meetings?"

Here it is, she thinks. At least they're off Veevi for now.

"Well, let's see," she says, and takes a deep breath. "I've already mentioned—you know, the men whose n-n-n-names I find so hard to say. Perhaps you could refresh my memory a little, since you already seem to know who it is you want me to name."

"Mrs. Lasker!" Kingman booms. His face is flushed. Even his eyelids look inflamed. "You are trying the patience of this committee! Mr. Ornstein led us to expect you were willing to give us your full cooperation. We can only know that you are sincere in your desire to help us get to the bottom of this terrible scourge of anti-Americanism if you willingly tell us the names of those people whom you saw at Communist Party meetings and at your sister and Mr. Ventura's home, and at the homes of other known Communists as well."

"Do not shout at me, sir. I said I would c-c-c-cooperate and I am trying to do so now."

"Let me ask you again whom you remember from the time of your membership in the Communist Party," Marlow says, plucking at his neck.

She sighs. "All right, gentlemen, I shall give you some names. Gilbert Moore—he was a screenwriter and a novelist. A Harvard graduate. He was a member of the Party around the time I joined. He was known as a kind of a th-th-th—this is an awfully hard word for me to say so please be patient—a th-th-th-th-theoretician. Later on he left the industry, and I have no idea what happened to him."

"Did you know a woman named Renna Goldman, now Mrs. Joseph Schlossberg?" Marlow asks.

"Yes, I did."

"Did you see her at meetings?"

"Sometimes."

"She claims she recruited you into the Communist Party."

So she's the one, Dinah thinks.

"I believe I already told you that nobody recruited me. Renna told me about various meetings, but, as I told you, I went to my first meeting with some fellow I knew."

"And she claims that you and your sister were very close, that you knew all about your sister's membership in the Party, and that you frequently consorted with known Communists and were fully aware of who was a member of the Party and who wasn't."

"Mr. Marlow, I don't see why you need me to answer questions about myself, since Mrs. Schlossberg seems to have given you all the answers you want."

"Mrs. Lasker!" Kingman barks again. "Unless you are willing to be specific, we will have to conclude that you are unwilling to cooperate with us."

She looks at him in silence.

"Unless concerned people like yourself help us root out this terrible conspiracy of Communism," Marlow adds, his tone reasonable, "our lives and the lives of our children won't be worth living."

"Oh, come on," she says. "You don't expect people to t-t-take that seriously, do you? Frankly, gentlemen, I don't happen to think there *is* or ever *was* a Communist conspiracy in this country. You guys are just wasting everyone's time and taxes with all this hys-s-s-steria. And you're r-r-r-ruining people's lives. Now, you and I know that I'm not here because I want to be. I was subpoenaed, and I came. I should be picking up my kids at school, gentlemen." She reaches for her purse, pushes her chair away from the table, and begins to stand up. "Anyway, I've told you all I know, and there just isn't any more."

Jake's career and her children's future—her reasons for agreeing to testify—dissolve in the stark wrongness of the occasion—the relentlessness of her interrogators, the poisonous absurdity of their words, the stale air in this suffocating room.

"*Sit down!* Mrs. Lasker!" Kingman booms. "You have not been excused. Moreover, you will be cited immediately for contempt of Congress unless you answer one question—namely, whether your sister was or was not a member of the Communist Party. Now, I'm puzzled and I think Mr. Marlow here is puzzled, too. Why would you tell the Committee that you're willing to cooperate with us and then come down here and just lead us down the garden path? I can't understand why you would waste your time and ours, unless this is some kind of Communist trick you have up your sleeve. I can tell you one thing with great certainty: my colleagues in the House of Representatives will not look kindly on a person whom they believe to be toying with and mocking the good faith of the American people and this duly constituted congressional committee. Finally, I think you'd agree that it would be an even greater pity if your husband, Jake Lasker, who isn't now and never has been a member of the Communist Party, were to find himself deprived of professional opportunities and professional standing because of his contaminating association with an uncooperative witness and known subversive, who may for all we know still be an active member of the Communist Party."

Dinah can only stare at him.

"Now, Mrs. Lasker," Kingman rasps, "was your sister, known at that time as Genevieve Milligan Ventura, a member of the Communist Party?"

Her eyes brightening with hate, Dinah takes out a cigarette and lights it, holding it between her thumb and forefinger, as her father, or a truck driver, would, with the ash end pointing backward, and she leans forward and, under the table, defiantly spreads her knees. Half-moons of clammy sweat soak through her dress, and underneath her nylon slip her girdle binds and pinches her flesh. "Mr. Kingman, I want to make sure I understand you. You are saying that if I don't give you my sister's name you will bl-bl-blacklist my husband?"

"As a loyal American citizen, I remind you that *there is no blacklist*," declares Kingman.

"Then what the hell do you call the threat you just made? What you just said is that unless I give you my sister's name, my husband will never work in Hollywood again."

"I did not say that."

"You certainly implied it. You made a threat."

"Put it on the record that the witness refuses to cooperate with this committee," Kingman shouts over her to the stenographer, and bangs his fist on the table. "And note that I hereby cite Mrs. Lasker for contempt of Congress."

"Mr. Kingman, are we on the record?"

"Yes, Mrs. Lasker," he shouts.

"Good. Because I want to make sure that the stenographer is recording that you are trying to hound and int-t-t-imidate me."

"Miss Mulrooney is taking down every word we say, Mrs. Lasker," Kingman says, white spittle gathering at the corners of his mouth. "And I wish to add that you are refusing to cooperate with this committee and that I shall momentarily issue the citation for contempt."

"Miss Mulr-r-r-ooney," Dinah calls out, although the woman remains motionless at the sound of her name, "just make sure you get this: that this committee has threatened my husband with blacklisting if I don't name my sister."

"Mrs. Lasker," Marlow coolly resumes, as though he hasn't heard a word of this last exchange. "I have a copy here of a list of those who paid membership dues to the Communist Party on September 4, 1938. Your name is on the list, and so is the name of Genevieve Ventura. Can you remember now whether or not your sister was a member of the Communist Party?" he asks.

The noose tightens. The trapdoor breaks beneath her. "At that t-t-t-time," Dinah answers, "she was."

"Do you know when she joined the Communist Party?"

"Truthfully, I do not know for sure."

"And were the late Mr. Ventura and Mrs. Albrecht members as well?"

"Are their names on your list?"

"Not on this list, Mrs. Lasker. But"—he coughs—"their names are on another list I happen to have right here, from March 1937, of contributors to a fund for an ambulance corps in Spain. The money was collected after a speech given by a Frenchman who came to California, a well-known Communist agitator and author André Malrowks."

"Malraux," she corrects him.

"Thank you. Mr. Malraux spoke at a party meeting at your sister's home in the Malibu Colony. Mr. and Mrs. Ventura and Mrs. Albrecht each wrote a check for one hundred and fifty dollars. Do you know whether or not Mr. Ventura and Mrs. Albrecht were members of the Communist Party?"

"You're barking up the wrong tree, sir. I wasn't there that day, and I can't tell you about things I didn't see."

"I doubt that, Mrs. Lasker," says Kingman.

"This may surprise you, sir, but I don't care what you think."

"Did Mr. Ventura have friends in Mexico City?" asks Marlow.

"Yes."

"Elaborate, please."

"He and my sister eloped to Mexico City, and it was there that they were married. They stayed with friends."

"Do you know who they were?"

"I don't remember their names." She hesitates. "You know, Mr. Marlow, there was a lot going on at the time that I didn't understand."

"Can you explain please?"

"Don't you listen, Mr. Marlow? I just said there were things I didn't understand about those days. How can I elaborate when I don't know, didn't know, hadn't figured it out, and still haven't?"

That's it, she tells herself. Not another word.

He looks at her as if deciding whether to pursue this line of questioning. She can hear Kingman's raspy breathing. Marlow takes his glasses off and pinches the bridge of his nose. She sees the red mark they have left before he puts them back on. Both men stare at her, as if they have forgotten what they wanted to ask her.

Finally, Marlow resumes his questions. "Did you ever meet an Andor Somogyi?"

"Somogyi? It rings a bell, but I can't quite place it."

"Mrs. Lasker, who arranged for Mr. Ventura and your sister to return to France?"

"Actually, come to think of it, it may have been that guy you just mentioned—Andor Somogyi. He was a big man, if I remember, with a very thick accent and a big jaw. He came up once, I think, from Mexico City for a few days."

"Was he a member of the Communist Party?"

"I don't know. I saw him once, gave him a cup of coffee, and never saw him again."

"He was a Stalinist agent, Mrs. Lasker, and he arranged for your sister and her husband to go to France, where they were well looked after by other loyal Stalinists," Marlow says dispassionately, "until one of them betrayed Stefan Ventura and sold him out to the Nazis."

How have they gotten hold of this information? she wonders. Who told them?

"Tell us, Mrs. Lasker," Marlow continues. "What makes you think it was Andor Somogyi who arranged for Mr. and Mrs. Ventura to go to Europe?"

"Because when I told them I thought it was crazy to go, my sister said, 'Don't worry, Somogyi's taking care of everything. Someone's going to meet us in Marseilles.' Why she thought that would have k-k-k-kept me from worrying, I haven't the faintest idea," she adds. "I was worried sick about her from the day they left until the war was over."

"Were you and your husband members of the Committee for the First Amendment?" Marlow asks.

This non sequitur startles her. "Why, yes."

"In other words, you and your husband flew to Washington with other prominent members of the motion picture industry to express opposition to these congressional hearings?"

"Yes."

"Mrs. Lasker?" Marlow says gently. "When did you leave the Communist Party?"

"I stopped going to meetings just before I married Jake Lasker. He insisted that I stop, and, frankly, I had come to dislike the way they were run."

"Please elaborate for us, Mrs. Lasker. I know you're tired." How considerate he's become now that I've ratted on Veevi and Dorshka and Stefan, she thinks.

"I disc-c-c-covered that there always seemed to be a small group of people who would decide beforehand what the larger group was supposed to do or vote on."

"Who were these people?"

"Well, M-M-M-Metzger and K-K-K-Klein, for sure. And Guy Bergman. Those men were always telling us what the line was to be at any particular moment, no matter how illogical. One day we're isolationists and pacifists and war is an imperialist plot; the next we're in it with Uncle Joe, all-for-one and one-for-all. Once there was a new stand about something, you couldn't qu-qu-qu-question or oppose it. People who did were accused of disloyalty, reaction, counter-this and counter-that. I found the rigidity of thinking intolerable," she says simply, delivering lines that were, for her, true enough but which her lawyer has coached her to say. "About the Soviet Union, for instance. I was much more concerned about what was wrong with America than with what was right about Russia," she says pointedly. "I mean, tell me, gentlemen, what's the difference between you g-g-g-guys and Stalin, if I may ask?"

Marlow smiles, a frozen, mirthless smile. She looks over at Kingman. He is wiping his nose with a clotted white handkerchief, and for a moment she fights the urge to gag.

"When did you completely sever your relationship to or your membership in the Communist Party?" he asks her, putting the foul handkerchief in his pocket.

"In January, right after I was married. I was actually packing up my apartment when some fellow stopped by and asked me if I had stopped coming. I told him I had decided to quit and he agreed it was my right to do so. That was it. I wasn't important enough for them to make a fuss over."

"Did he threaten you with reprisals of any kind?" Kingman says.

"No. You're up to your ears in clichés, you know," she says. "Nobody recr-cr-cr-cruited me, and nobody ever threatened me about anything— ever. Unlike you."

Marlow thumbs through some papers; he scans a document and glances up at her. "Did you make contributions to the Sleepy Lagoon Defense Fund?"

"Yes, I did. I have the checks here if you want to see them. Mr. Ornstein suggested I bring them."

"That won't be necessary. Thank you very much, Mrs. Lasker," Marlow says. "You are free to go."

She stares at them. Is that it?

"Mrs. Lasker," Marlow says politely when she doesn't move. "I do apologize, but we have another witness waiting outside."

"Yes," she says, "I heard you the first time."

Out in the hallway, her knees wobble. She feels rubbery and light-headed, as if she has forgotten how to walk. Her heart races, and she leans against the wall, and then something catches her attention. Up ahead, near the tall cigarette receptacles next to the elevator, she sees two men in dark suits. One of them is going bald and carries a briefcase. She figures him for a lawyer. She recognizes the other just as he recognizes her. Oh shit, she swears to herself. Art Squires, formerly Aaron Skebelsky, who had come out to Hollywood from the Group Theatre and Broadway and never looked back, not after all those Warner Brothers pictures in which he played gangsters and boxers and sexy doomed tough guys from the streets. He is pale and looks nervous, smoking a cigarette with the same hard, fast drags he'd used for the death row scenes in *Fat Chance,* which had won him an Academy Award for best actor the year before. He's giving her a certain look, though, as if seeing her means he can turn back into somebody he would much rather be than the poor scared son of a bitch she knows he knows she's seeing. "Dinah honey," he murmurs. "Of all people . . ."

She feels a sudden sexual heat—she can't help it. Years ago, during one of those awful periods before they were married, when Jake, after telling her he loved her, would consequently stop calling, she had gone to a Party meeting and Art Squires was there. And after Guy Bergman got up and explained that the night's discussion topic would be "from each according to his ability, to each according to his need," Squires had quipped, "I don't know if it's a good way to run a country, but it sure sounds like a great idea for an orgy." She had laughed out loud when nobody else had. Afterward he had taken her to a club, and while they were dancing he'd said, "I bet you'd be an animal in bed." She went home with him that night. And now, from time to time, standing at a stoplight or tying the kids' shoelaces, she'd remember that night—which had been, indeed, memorable.

He bends over to kiss her. "Oh, Dinah sweetie, not you, too?"

She turns aside, so that the kiss lands on her jawline, and looks unsmilingly into his anxious face. "Don't go in there, Artie. Just turn around and get in the elevator and go home. Right now."

"That bad, huh?" He shrugs and throws an arm around her shoulders. "Come on," he whispers, and again she feels that heat. "Didja name me?"

The elevator doors open and she slips out from under him and gives him a bitter smile. "No, not you, Artie. Not you."

5

*H*oney, pull yourself together."

"I just need a few minutes." Her voice quavered and her legs sagged, and she sat down on the hard phone-booth seat and leaned against the wall.

"Are you there? Dinah?"

"Yeah, I'm here. Jesus Christ, Jake."

"It's over. Finished. Come home."

"You sound impatient."

"Honey, please. I'm concerned about you. Do you want me to come and get you?"

"No. I have the car. What would we do with the other one?"

Suddenly they were talking car talk, L.A. two-car talk, and it was an ordinary day once again, except that she felt as if all the blood had drained out of her.

"I can drive you back there tomorrow on my way to the studio."

"Forget it. I'll drive home."

"Good. I'll just call Irv and fill him in, and then I'm on my way. I'll take Melrose. You take Sunset. You might even get home before me."

Moments later, as Dinah stood waiting for the valet to drive her old Pontiac station wagon up to the hotel entrance, an uninvited image of Kingman's clotted handkerchief flashed across her mind and she gagged. Her sweat-stained dress was cold and clammy against her skin, and there was a foul taste in her mouth. It was about three-thirty, and the sky was a poisonous gray-orange haze. The decaying boulevard seemed like a bad imitation of the place that had once enchanted her. As a nine-year-old girl, newly arrived in Los Angeles, she had roller-skated past Grauman's Egyptian every day to watch it being built. She'd stared at Charlie Chaplin and Mary Pickford through the windows of Armstrong-Schroeder's, hoping they would notice her and make her a child star.

She tipped the valet and, pulling out to the edge of the road, squeezed her way into the caravan of automobiles filing westward into the malignant afternoon sun. Reaching Sunset Strip, she found the traffic heavy and slow, and though she knew where she was going, it seemed to her that she was no longer in a familiar place. She despised everything she saw—the hideous billboards, the endless interior design shops with fancy white wrought-iron garden furniture placed out on the sidewalk, the view south into the city's sprawling anonymous flatlands, where, because of what she'd done today, she reminded herself, she and Jake would never have to live.

She pressed hard on the accelerator, hugged the long curves out of Beverly Hills, and soon turned right off Sunset onto Delfern, where suddenly all was silence and calm. There were no sidewalks, and not a single moving car, only an occasional gardener's truck parked by the curb. Late-afternoon sprinklers whipped iridescent sprays of water over flower beds and lawns. The sweet smell of freshly cut grass hung in the air. Pampered wives, back from lunch and shopping, took dreamless naps in bedrooms hung with heavy silk drapes. Children gathered in front of the TV set, their fingers pruny from swimming. It was the hour when the maid, working without hurry, set the table with the good silver and the laundress checked her watch. Another hour and she would shut down the presser and begin the slow walk to the bus stop and the long ride home with her friends to the Crenshaw, where her employers have never been.

Shame shot through Dinah like a hot dye in her veins, and she clutched the wheel at the sight of every imperturbable mansion. She passed the house, as she did every day, where Bugsy Siegel had been murdered and thought, Somebody caught him off guard, too, and she remembered the newspaper photo of him wearing a dark suit, slumped against a sofa, blood pouring out of what had been his eye.

Turning into her own driveway, she saw the green Caddy in the garage. Thank God he's home, she thought, and began to shake with dread and relief. She hadn't wanted to come home and not find him there. The two trucks parked in front of the house meant the pool guys were still at work.

They had been set to pour the cement into the huge excavated hole in the backyard today, and by now it had probably been done. Jake was probably in the backyard watching and exulting.

She turned off the ignition and rested her head on the steering wheel, preparing herself for the next wave of shame. But it didn't come, and, gathering her purse and keys, she got out of the car. In another moment she was opening the screen door and stepping into the laundry porch, where she was met by the blissful aromas of freshly washed and ironed clothes and the roast slowly cooking in the oven.

6

*J*ake had imagined and even blocked the scene, and he therefore knew exactly what to do. He had raced home, taking the shortcut he had discovered in the forested hills behind Sunset, sensing that if she got home before he did she would simply fall apart. Kibitzing with the pool crew, he watched for her arrival, and the moment he saw her silhouette in the breakfast room he broke away and came into the house. Wordlessly, he steered her upstairs and into their room, locking the door. He drew her over to his bed, not hers, and pulled her down beside him and held her, kissing her gently all over her face—something he ordinarily never did. He lifted her chin and looked into her eyes, and she saw his drawn and worried expression, his cheeks dark and rough with five o'clock shadow. Then he held her again. Was now the right time? No, not yet. He would wait till later. Though limp beside him, she tried to turn her face away. "Ugh," she said. "My breath must be awful." He took her face in both his hands. "That doesn't matter. There isn't anything about you I don't adore."

Without letting go of her, he turned slightly and lay back. Her head rested on his shoulder, her face in his neck. "Did I ever tell my wife I love her?" he said. This had become a special line between them after they had heard it addressed to Rose Lasker by Jake's father, Eli Lasker, as he lay dying in an oxygen tent in Cedars of Lebanon Hospital, in November 1946, after a thirty-five-year marriage in which he had shown his wife almost no affection whatsoever.

"I went to see Irv," Jake began. "I told him it was over. He said he was 'pleased and sad.' Pleased because of your courage, he said, and sad that you'd had to do it at all. 'Marathon Pictures is forever in Dinah's debt,' he said. I'm supposed to tell you that. And he sent his love. Don't be surprised if a million roses arrive sometime in the next twenty-four hours. And don't be surprised if they don't."

"A m-m-m-million roses? He's out of his mind. Tell him I want fifteen full-length s-s-s-sable coats, a lifetime charge account at Bergdorf's, and my name over the studio gate," she said, her voice cracking from fatigue. She liked his attentions but wasn't fooled for a minute; she knew they were rehearsed. "Did you tell him about the Veevi part?"

"Uh-huh."

"And?"

"All he said was 'It's a rotten business.' "

"I wish you hadn't told him. It'll get around."

"Of course it'll get around—the Committee will let it out! Everyone will know—everyone from Hollywood to New York to London to Paris. Don't let it get to you," he said lightly. "Your job is done, we're safe and sound, and you don't have to explain yourself to anyone ever again."

He wanted her to unburden herself so that he could pick up the muddy handfuls of doubt and remorse and squeeze them into firm, smooth equivocations. Since by her silence she wasn't allowing him to do that, he decided to try anyway. "You have to remember they have all the names they want. It's a degradation ritual, nothing more. And if it's hurting Veevi you're worried about, forget it. Nothing whatsoever is ever going to hurt Genevieve Milligan Ventura Albrecht, and you know that better than anyone." He slowly drew his arm out from under her shoulders, where it had gone to sleep. "She's blissfully married to one of the most important American writers of our time, and since he happens to loathe America and everything about it, *and* since they *both* hate Hollywood and have no intention of ever coming back, nothing you said today will have the slightest effect on him or her, now or in the foreseeable future."

"What about the unforeseeable f-f-f-future?"

"That's not going to happen. But if for some strange reason they do go after her, it won't be because of you. You can't be the first person who ever named her. They already *knew* her name, because they *asked* you about her. You simply confirmed information they already had. Someone else gave them her name."

"But, Jake, you don't get it. I *named* her."

"So what? You've got to be absolutely clear about this or you'll drive yourself crazy over it, and that means trouble for us. You and me."

She seemed not to hear what he said. "I don't know. I have a b-b-b-bad feeling about it. I feel guilty as all hell."

"I'm telling you, darling, your sister's never coming back here again, and it has nothing to do with HUAC. Mike's not gonna let her out of his sight for a second. Didn't you tell me he has to have her in the room when he's writing? She sits there reading or knitting afghans, for Christ's sake, while he hunts and punches at the typewriter. Mommy stays while baby plays 'the lonely writer facing the naked page' and all that horseshit."

She sat bolt upright. She was still wearing her silk dress, and it was wrinkled and disheveled. Her expression frightened him: she was staring past him, reminding him of the mental patients whose photographs he often saw in *U.S. Camera*. It was a look of abstraction and inwardness, as if she were listening to a voice that only she could hear. She turned away, lit a cigarette, and looked out the window. "Jake? What would we have done if I had walked out of there today, like I almost did? Like I should have."

Bingo. Now he could finally get to work on her. "Well, for one thing, I wouldn't have had to finish this goddamn screenplay."

She laughed, not wanting to, and he saw that he had her back. She had lost that crazy pensive look of a moment ago. "Listen," he went on, "we would have done whatever we had to, darling, whatever would have been necessary. I sold newspaper advertising in college, and shoes, and I worked in a butcher shop. I pulled a rickshaw at the World's Fair. I could do any of those things again. If it weren't for my bursitis, I'd make a hell of a caddy over at the club."

He drew her back down beside him, enfolding her again in his arms. "But the point is, sweetheart, you didn't walk out. You stuck it out, and Christ knows you must have hated every minute of it. I understand that, darling, and I know the only reason you did it is because of me and the kids. So be very clear about this: I would have loved you just as much and just as forever as I love you now if you had walked out of there. And I would have admired you and been amazed at your courage. As I am now. And we would have made it somehow. I'm a reasonably healthy man in the prime of life, and I would have done what I've always done—namely, provide for you and the kids. We would have made it. But because you went through that ring of fire today, we *do* have a choice. And if you think you can't stand the thought of living in this town and in this industry another minute, I'll quit. I'll walk away. We'll move to Europe. Or Mexico. Or—"

"Jake, you're so full of sh-sh-sh-shit," she said.

He laughed, and then fell silent, waiting for a sign that would tell him whether he was succeeding. Tears wouldn't have surprised him, but she didn't cry. Was it over yet, or was she going to put on a hair shirt for the rest of her life? He had to cauterize her misgivings and doubts—and *right now*—or they would infect everything.

He reached over, stroking her arm lightly. "Maybe we are being a little selfish about this, but we have kids to raise—and we're not escaping to Europe and pretending we're too good for this town. So you went in there and named names. So what? You didn't do it because you wanted to, honey. You did what you had to do, hating it, as any decent person would, but now it's over, and I can make pictures and give you and the kids everything you need. We're not going to pretend you didn't testify, but we're not going to hang a scarlet *T* around your neck, either. You had a chance to fuck it all up, everything we have together, the kids' futures, my work, and all in the name of a bunch of abstractions you don't believe in anymore, but you didn't. So don't fuck it up with endless guilt, darling, please."

"Hush, Jake," she said. "Stop the filibuster. I can't l-l-l-listen anymore."

Soon it would be time for dinner. Gussie would probably send up one of the kids to knock on their door. She was relaxed, finally. Her breathing slowed and she slipped into a half sleep. Jake had stopped talking, but only for a moment, and as he felt her drifting off he whispered: "Don't you imagine for one second that I'm telling you I love you because of what you did for me today. I've always loved you. I'm not so good at all that romantic stuff—I know I could do a lot better in that department. But the girl I love is the girl who had it in her to go and face those guys. I know that girl, and I've loved her ever since I met her."

She raised her head and, opening one eye, gave him a skeptical look. "Oh yeah? If that's so, why'd I have to tell you 'marry me or we're through'? Huh? Just answer that one, b-b-b-buster."

"I plead the Fifth." He watched her for a moment, congratulating himself for his tact in not attempting to make love to her. Later would be better; he had to give her time.

⁂

After dinner with the children, they went for a long drive along the Pacific Coast Highway. Jake parked the car at the beach, and they took off their shoes and walked together, arms around each other's waists. "Remember when," Jake said, "we tried to camp out here and we had the two sleeping bags and"—she took over—"you were so c-c-c-cold you put on three sweaters and your overcoat and a knit cap and gloves and got inside your sleeping bag and then said to me, 'Let's do it'?" "And all those nights we danced to Fats Waller," he said, "and we'd do it on the floor and on the sofa and then again in the shower and after that at four in the morning and one more time at six and then you had to go home and get ready for work?"

The memories continued—memories of lovemaking in sleeping cars on the way to New York, hotels in Coronado and Acapulco, raftered lodges on salmon-fishing trips in Oregon. The secret fear they each harbored—that perhaps they'd been married too long and the passion had died—melted away as the memories kindled the sharpest desire they had felt in years.

And so, while the great cornball ocean served up a succession of crashing waves, they sank to their knees, and tumbled backward, trying to ignore the cold air and colder sand. They hugged and writhed and kissed, Dinah hiking up her dress while Jake tugged at her girdle and garters. Dinah reached out and groped for Jake's fly, tugging and tugging. The zipper yielded, then stuck. In a lustful lunge, she tightened her grip on the metal pull and yanked hard. "Honoré de Balzac! Honoré de Balzac!" Jake cried out in alarm, and Dinah dissolved in a fusillade of wanton laughter.

"Oh, honey, your thing's not c-c-c-caught, is it? Jesus, did I hurt you? Come on," she whispered, pulling down her dress. "Let's get the hell out of here and go home to our own bed."

"Yours or mine?"

"I don't care. As long as it doesn't have sand in it!"

*O*n the way downstairs the next morning, she felt moist and squishy between her legs, and as she moved she could smell, underneath her light bathrobe, the pungent scent of Jake's semen now resident many hours within her. This was something women never discussed, she thought, the way the lingering semen, the fermenting smell of it, was proof that you belonged to your husband. It made you feel like a watered plant: you would live a few more days. She would wait until evening to shower, wanting to spend the day knowing it was there, washing away its traces only before bed, so that Jake might not meet with the smell and find offensively female that which, after all, had come from himself. Maybe last night they'd hit the jackpot. Maybe six weeks from now she would feel little spasms low in her belly, followed by barely perceptible flutters and fugitive cramps, always for her the signs of the nesting egg settling in for its nine-month sleep. She longed for the heavy tiredness and tender breasts, the headaches and nausea, which she had borne twice before and was eager to bear again.

On the table in the breakfast room, she found a note: "Darling, see front page Met. section, p. 4. I adore you. J."

She poured herself a cup of coffee, drew the paper closer, and read:

"RED" INQUIRY TESTIMONY REVEALED
Westwood Housewife Tells of
Break with CP Unit

Testimony of a Westwood housewife at an executive hearing of the House Un-American Activities Committee appears in an official transcript of the proceedings released to the press yesterday evening.

Mrs. Dinah Milligan Lasker, 39, wife of producer-writer-director Jake Lasker, and a former motion picture dancer and radio writer, testified in closed session that she had been a member of the Communist Party between 1938 and 1944—leaving it because she found the party's "rigidity of thinking intolerable."

Mrs. Lasker gave her testimony at the Hollywood-Griffith Hotel on May 28 to Congressman Curtis P. Kingman and Committee Investigator Horace Marlow.

The article continued with excerpts from her testimony. Seeing her words in print surprised Dinah. She didn't remember what exactly she had said, only the bad air, the sweat growing cold in her silk dress, Marlow picking at his neck, Kingman's revolting handkerchief.

"Mrs. Lasker named as fellow Communists the screenwriters Norman Metzger, Anatole Klein, and Guy Bergman," the article said, "as well as the well-known actors' agent Renna Schlossberg. She referred to the possible Communist Party membership of former screenwriter Dorshka Albrecht and the late European director Stefan Ventura. However, she unequivocally affirmed that her sister, the actress Genevieve Milligan, was a member of the Communist Party in Los Angeles from 1936 until the departure for Europe of Miss Milligan and her then husband, Mr. Ventura, in early 1939. Miss Milligan, who has retired from the screen, currently lives in France and is married to the American writer Michael Albrecht. Said Congressman Kingman, 'Mrs. Lasker's willingness to testify about her past association with the Communist Party is an encouraging sign of loyalty and patriotism. We hope other former Communists will come forward and cooperate with us as fully as she has, and help us root out this blight on our American way of life.' "

Dinah grabbed the newspaper, her coffee cup and Camels, and raced up the back stairs to Jake's office. There was something she had to do at once, and she had no time to lose.

She locked the door and sat down at Jake's mahogany desk, with its worn, tooled-leather trim. A gray steel typing table was at a right angle to the desk, and held a big black Royal typewriter, the keys marked with gold letters. Feeling suddenly hesitant and frightened, Dinah forced herself to go on. Opening a drawer, she saw a single sheet of paper with the typed heading "Random Notes." She picked it up and read. It contained lines, some heard, some made up, that Jake had collected, thinking they might be useful someday in his work. There were names in front of some of the lines. After the name "Pop"—her father—her husband had written: "If you see a Jew or a Negro coming down the street, cross over to the other side, or you'll lose ten percent." Having heard her father say that repeatedly during her childhood, she was sixteen when she finally said to him, "Ten percent of *what*, Pop?"

"Who made me a judge?" Jake had typed out. "You're askin' me, and I'm the judge." That was Gussie's, from one of their conversations about baseball.

There were others:

"Far be it from me to ever take a walk with you on an upset stomach again."

"HE: (referring to a child): Is he the sort of child that's interested in Mother Goose?
SHE: No. He's the kind that's more interested in goosing Mother."

"HOLLYWOOD TYPE: If you're not going to be home this afternoon, I can bring Rita Hayworth over to swim in your pool."

"PRODUCER: I want a story with some fresh clichés."

"OLD COMEDIAN IN NEW YORK AT THE STAGE DELICATESSEN: What's the most humiliating thing that can happen to a man? You wake up with a hard-on, bump into a wall, and break your nose."

Somewhere in a file cabinet there were dozens of these. At night, when he couldn't sleep, Jake came in here and typed until all hours of the morning. Gussie was always finding little slips of paper with lines scribbled on them when she turned his pockets out before doing the laundry. She kept them in envelopes and would give them to him when he passed through the kitchen, saying "Here, Mr. Lasker, I got some more of them state secrets for you."

Dinah hurriedly stuck the sheet back in the drawer, feeling a little guilty for trespassing. Jake didn't mind it when she used his office, but she shouldn't be going through his things. Remembering that he kept the typing paper in the bottom drawer, she retrieved two sheets and fitted them together against the platen before rolling them through.

At first, she wrote easily. Her typing was still fast and accurate. Then she stopped. A fit of yawning overtook her, and she felt heavy-limbed and dull. She lit a cigarette and, chewing at the edge of her red manicured thumbnail, stared out at the fog. More stupefying yawns overcame her, but she forced herself to type as fast as she could. Her fingers flew—the old speed, developed over eleven years of office work, returned, and the typewriter rang with one little zing after another as she filled up the page.

She stopped, glanced over what she had written, and pulled the paper out, tearing it and dropping the pieces in the wastebasket. Then she inserted fresh paper and began typing again.

"*It was you they wanted me to name,*" she wrote. The fresh ribbon made the letters clear and black, and the underlining nearly cut through the good bond paper, making her think back vividly to Maggie Reilly, the bitch supervisor at Sprague Paper, who used to run her hand along the back of each typed sheet and make the girls retype any pages on which her fingertips could detect the minuscule nubs of dotted *i*'s. Dinah remembered, too, in a flood of conjured-up odors and textures, the paper cuffs she used to put on to prevent carbon-paper stains, the Ediphone earphones that would muss her permanent, the rat droppings that would fall down into the ladies' room sinks from nests in the dust and oil that accumulated from the printing presses on the floor above.

Hurriedly, she wrote:

> *They kept trying to get me to say you'd been a Communist.*
> *I realize this will be hard to believe, but I really tried to get out of saying anything. I tried to have the worst case of amnesia anyone had ever seen. Finally, I decided to walk out. But they stopped me and then said Jake would never work in Hollywood again if I didn't name you.*
>
> *Look, I'm not going to make excuses. I did it, Vee. I named you. They asked about Stefan and Dorshka, and I said I didn't know, which is the truth. I don't think they were listening very hard or even cared what I said. One thing I'm sure of—whatever I said, they already seemed to know. I keep telling myself I should have named the Nine-*

teen and the Ten and everybody else who's already been named—they can't be hurt twice, after all—but of course that wouldn't have made any difference. The fun for them was in not letting Jake off the hook until I had named you.

It was stupid of me to think this couldn't happen, Vee. Jake and I had always just assumed that I wasn't important enough for them to bother with. I guess we just took it for granted that we were safe and that they would leave us alone. It certainly does seem as if they're scraping the bottom of the barrel, having run out of big names to hound.

I can't tell you how sorry I am. I don't give a good goddamn what anybody in or out of Hollywood thinks of me, but the whole point of deciding to testify in the first place was to protect my family. And you are my family. I keep telling myself you're safe in Europe and don't want to live here, and of course I also realize that I'm not the first person in the world to name you, but I'm still worried that this whole lousy business might have very unpleasant consequences for you—and Mike, too. You must, both of you—and I can't say this strongly enough—you must let us know if anything happens. We will do whatever we can to help.

I don't know what else to say except that if things are well with you, then they are well with me.

xxxxxxx D.

Moments later, still wearing her bathrobe, she flew out the back door and raced barefoot down the driveway to the mailbox, which she flung open. She tossed her letter into it as if the force of her motion could make it fly halfway across the globe and land that instant in Paris.

Later, as she dressed for the day, a sudden impulse came over her and she returned to Jake's office. She rolled another two sheets into the typewriter, and wrote:

I'm not sorry for what I did. You've always had everything—love, beauty, the world's adoration—and you always will. Nothing can hurt

you. There was no choice. I never would and never will—ever—
choose you over Jake. If you think for an instant I would have spared
you and damned Jake and me to the dreary petit-bourgeois hell we all
came from, you're crazy. You can write or not write; I don't care.

Whatever you do, stay where you are. Be happy, beautiful, cherished, sought after, and adored. And hate me if you like. But just stay
the hell away. Be and do all those things where you are, in your own
world, not mine. If you think I don't know what you thought and said
about me all those years when you were with Stefan, you're dead
wrong. I know how you used to laugh at my clothes and pity me because of my job and condescend to me about my education, though you
didn't even graduate from high school, and I did. I went to work, goddamnit, to support you and Mom and Pop when you hadn't been discovered yet. You snickered to your fancy friends, all those guys you
screwed once, about my stuttering mispronunciation of all those European writers you knew and flirted with day in and day out while
Stefan was at the studio or working in the upstairs office with Dorshka.

There you were, with all Stalinist Hollywood at your feet, waving
your scented handkerchiefs at every novelist and screenwriter who
kissed your feet. It wasn't enough, though, was it? You couldn't stand
for anyone else to have anything, Veevi—especially me. Whatever there
was to have in the world, you were going to have it, not me.

You never introduced me to anyone. It was Stefan and Dorshka who
were kind to me, not you. I was your chief maid and bottlewasher.

So just stay in Paris and be the revered widow of the great martyred
hero whom you never loved, not even for one minute. Be muse to the
Greatest Writer of Our Time. I'll stay out of your life, and you just stay
the hell out of mine.

She lit a cigarette and inhaled deeply. The words on the page, in their neat
blocks, looked back at her: *Do you recognize us?* they seemed to say. *You
should. You just wrote us down yourself. You can't take us back. What are you
going to do with us? We're yours, all right. You can't pretend we're not.* She
thought immediately of movies in which a character leans into a fireplace

and drops a letter into a blaze or lights a corner of a page and watches it slowly go up in flames, and, yanking the letter out of the typewriter, she went into the bathroom, lifted the toilet seat, flicked her gold lighter, and lit the edge of the paper. Then she kneeled over the toilet and watched it crumble into the hissing water.

Returning to Jake's desk, she gathered up the newspaper and was just beginning to fold it when she saw another item she'd missed: HUAC CITES ACTOR ART SQUIRES FOR CONTEMPT. Artie had refused to name names and was going to jail for ten months. Of course, she knew, he would never work in Hollywood again. She took the paper downstairs and out to the incinerator, and set it on fire, too. It burned quickly, and she slammed the iron door of the incinerator to keep the searing smoke and ashes from blowing into her face.

*A*s she looked for a parking space later that afternoon, Dinah wondered how Dorshka Albrecht had ended up living on a street lined with fraternity houses. This woman—who had once been a star of the great stages of Vienna, Prague, and Berlin; who had married the renowned Austrian poet Joachim Albrecht and, after his death, written screenplays for Murnau, Lang, Pabst, Lubitsch, and Ventura; who had taken into her bed heaven knows how many eager and grateful artists, actors, composers, and playwrights—today, this woman walked alone to Westwood Village and back. Dressed in loose slacks and a man's shirt, a pair of blue sneakers on her feet, she carried her groceries past gangly college boys who had no idea who she was or the world she had come from.

With determined steps, Dinah walked up the sun-dappled path to the front door of Dorshka's apartment. The doorbell chimed two notes, high and low, when she pressed the button. In her mind she had a vivid picture of her friend and expected her to look and sound just the same, even though it had been years since she had last seen her, she recalled guiltily— the summer of '46, when, after their marriage, Veevi and Mike had flown from Paris to Los Angeles for a brief trip. Dorshka was too proud to call, Dinah supposed, and though Dinah had always been fond of Dorshka and had seen her often during the war, when both of them were grim and desperate about Veevi, Stefan, and Mike, she hadn't tried as hard as she might have to stay in touch. Jake's success, Dinah suspected, would have been hard on Dorshka, and she would not have wanted anyone to know it.

Subpoenaed early in the investigations, she had refused to testify and had lost her U.S. passport and been blacklisted. So of course she couldn't find work as a screenwriter—work that, in any case, had been scarce enough since the end of the war. After the Venturas left, she had written movies exclusively for the great Austrian beauty Lily Keller, and she might have gone on writing them forever, except that after the war Keller surprised everyone by going into seclusion on Vancouver Island. Since Dorshka was associated only with Lily, projects stopped coming her way, and she had to live on her savings, which lasted only a few years, given that she had spent thousands of dollars getting people out of Europe. She stopped going to parties, where she might have made new contacts or revived old ones: she would have been pitied or, worse, flattered into irrelevance by her association with a vanished past that had been the present as recently as five years before—an interval in Hollywood tantamount to prehistoric aeons. Through Veevi's letters, Dinah knew that Mike regularly sent his mother checks, which she reluctantly accepted. Dorshka also coached young Hollywood "hopefuls" in diction, dialogue, and dialect "for the stage and screen"—something for which she had long been famous. That is, she had been known in the thirties for interrupting young Americans and correcting what she considered to be their offensively nasal pronunciation.

Now, as Dinah heard the lengthening syllables of "Coming!"—an extended high note balanced by an equally extended low one, as if she were echoing the doorbell chime—she couldn't help remembering how she and Veevi would laugh at the way Dorshka had corrected their diction. "Now say, 'Faaaaather,' " she had gravely instructed them. Only, because of Dorshka's heavy Polish accent, it came out as "Faaaaah-zer." She had also taken it upon herself to instruct them in what she called "the arts of the courtesan." They were to put cold cream every day in their vaginas (*"faginas"*), never let their husbands see them completely naked, and always, even during sex, leave a little something on. Never, ever were they to refuse their husbands or balk at doing anything out of the ordinary, no matter how complicated or fanciful the position.

When the front door opened, Dinah saw that Dorshka was indeed unchanged—still tall and erect, still broad-shouldered, still big-breasted. The short, curly hair, once red, was perhaps a little snowier than Dinah remembered, but the extraordinary skin was still smooth and taut, and as free of wrinkles as a freshly ironed satin pillowcase. The cheeks were still high and pink, the large blue eyes intelligent and clear. Dinah had always loved Dorshka's looks, which were striking and dramatic, though not, perhaps, what you would call beautiful. Her wide face and round nose were offset by a thin mouth whose characteristically sardonic smile, had it been less warm, would have resembled a permanent sneer. It was this smile more than anything that marked Dorshka, for Dinah, as a European. No American Dinah had ever seen had a smile like that. It blended infinite tolerance with infinite skepticism, ready warmth with minimal expectation.

The older woman threw her arms around Dinah and led her into the cool apartment, where she had lived now for many years. Shortly after his own arrival in Hollywood in 1934, Stefan Ventura, her former lover and dearest friend, had arranged for her to leave Paris with her teenage son, Mike, and come to Los Angeles as an employee of Lionel Engel's Marathon Pictures. She had always managed to create a certain ambience around her. In her room at Veevi's, and now here in the apartment, there were plants in terra-cotta pots, a record player and stacks of records, opened letters strewn over the top of a desk, where there also lay a paper knife in the shape of a miniature scimitar. Books were everywhere, evidence of a rich but largely interior and now solitary existence.

"I've prepared a little treat," Dorshka said, disappearing briefly into the kitchen and returning with a pot of hot coffee and two huge slices of cake. "You look tired, my dear. It takes such hard work to breathe here. So many automobiles making all of this terrible smog. When I came here in the thirties, already there were too many cars, but now they choke the life out of the place. And the public transportation! For a bus you wait on the corner an hour and a half. And if you walk anywhere the police stop you and think you are some kind of crazy."

Dinah gratefully took the coffee and tasted the cake—a Sacher torte, the kind Dorshka used to make in the old days, so that there would always be something to fill the stomachs of the refugees, who had always just arrived from Lisbon or Marseilles and whom Dinah so often discovered on the Venturas' chintz sofas as they slept the dead sleep of the truly exhausted. Dressed in their rumpled yet dignified traveling clothes, their worn shoes arranged neatly on the antique braided Early American rug, they woke shy and disoriented day and night to the pounding of the surf and the smell of baking chocolate, which wafted through the house with a welcoming and familiar scent. After Stefan and Veevi left for France, and Dorshka moved to this apartment in Westwood, she kept on finding beds, apartments, and jobs for the recent arrivals, and, above all, giving them money.

"You know," Dinah said as they settled in the living room, "you sound just the way you used to. Everything was—wait, let me see if I can r-r-r-remember the word—everything was '*schrecklich.*' "

"Oh God, yes, we complained all the time about everything. Nothing was good enough for us refugees! We must have seemed an ungrateful lot to you."

"No, not that. Just int-t-t-timidating. I remember Veevi saying, 'So-and-so's the most important novelist or composer of the twentieth century,' but I didn't know who the hell anyone was, and I didn't want people to know how ignorant I was. I just felt sorry for them, especially when they first arrived. They always looked so b-b-b-bedraggled. It was hard to see how great they were when I'd find them sleeping on the sofas in their stocking f-f-f-feet. I couldn't understand a word they said, either, though I knew they were cultured and educated, and even when you or Stefan explained what they were talking about, I still didn't understand any of it. And then it always seemed like they couldn't bear anything about us and were always finding fault with everything. God, they made me nervous!"

"Well, it drove me crazy, too. My God, how they complained! Though, as you know, things here at that time weren't only *schrecklich.* Thomas Mann used to tell me how much he loved the scent of orange blossoms. It was still paradise then. Even Brecht, when he came, had to admit it to me every once in a while." She paused. "Once in a very long while." And they laughed together about this, because over the years Dinah had managed to catch up, to a certain extent.

She would happily have chatted on in this vein with Dorshka if it weren't for the mounting constriction in her chest, which threatened to squeeze the life out of her. She clenched her hands into fists that she held in her lap.

"D-D-D-D-Dorshka . . ."

"Ach, you struggle still with the *stottern*?"

"Struggle? I don't know if it's a struggle, Dorshka. I don't fight it anymore. It's just always there."

"I could cure it, you know."

"Oh, Dorshka dear, thank you, but no one would know me without it—least of all m-m-m-myself. But there's something I need to t-t-t-tell you."

"Yes, darling?"

She knows, thought Dinah. It's in her mouth, in that smile. But Dinah went ahead in a rush, so that Dorshka couldn't get a word in edgewise. She told Dorshka what she had done, and at the end she said, "I wanted to tell you myself, because no matter how you hear about it, I'm still the one who should be telling you. And because I wanted to ask you what you think it might mean for Veevi and Mike. I wrote to them this morning. And I'm concerned, of course, very concerned, about you and them. J-J-Jake and I want to help if you need it."

There was silence. She didn't think that Dorshka would ask her to leave, but her hands were cold and clammy and her chest still tight.

"Tell me, Dinah," Dorshka said, sternly but not unkindly. "Why did you do this thing you must now live with for the rest of your life?"

Dinah let out a long breath and searched for words. When she spoke, however, it was matter-of-factly. "It didn't seem right that Jake should be punished because of me."

"But does it seem right to you that you have become an *informer?*"

She waited for the grand resonance of Dorshka's stage projection to fade; surely even the walls of the fraternity houses down the block had registered the vibrations. "I don't like the word 'informer,' " she said. "But I can live with it. I don't like what I did. It's wrong, and I know it. I didn't do it thinking there was anything *right* about it. And I didn't believe I could justify it, if only I could see it from a certain angle—that's Jake's way of thinking, not mine. I don't like hurting people. But I don't feel loyalty to the Party. I was glad to get out when I did. Of course I don't like the Committee, either. Can't st-st-st-stand either of them. I didn't do it to choose one b-b-big idea over the other—American horsesh-sh-sh-shit over Communist horseshit."

"Why did you do it, then?"

"It's v-v-v-very simple—to save Jake's career. Irv said I'd have to testify or Jake would never work in Hollywood again."

"Yes. I know all about that. He said the same thing to me when, like a fool, I went to talk to him."

"I haven't come here to ask you to forgive me," Dinah said. "I came to offer help, if and when you need it."

"Dinah darling, don't be silly. What kind of help can you give me? For four years already I'm on their damn blacklist. What more can they do to me? Look, sweetheart, I would love to get the hell out of this lousy country and move to Switzerland, but I can't. And do you know why? Because they took my passport. They can't deport me because, no doubt much to their regret, I am now an American citizen. Can you imagine a more idiotic situation?"

"It's the beatenest thing," Dinah said, lapsing into one of her father's Arkansas expressions.

"So, it's for love you have done this terrible thing, yes?"

"What other reason could I possibly have?"

Dorshka searched her face. "And the rest of the world—?"

"There is no 'rest of the world' for me, Dorshka. When did the rest of the world ever give a good goddamn about me? You remember what things were like for me at Veevi and Stefan's. Just the other night Anya Engel was telling me, in that sickly sweet way of hers, how f-f-f-fucking glad she is that I managed to land a guy like Jake. Well, thanks a lot. All those geniuses from Europe, the br-br-br-brilliant Party people, the fellow travelers, all those writers from New York—oh, they wanted to sleep with me, all right. I had great legs and I looked good in a bathing suit. But they thought I was the maid!"

"Yes, it's true," Dorshka said, nodding. At once Dinah felt enormous relief. She wasn't making it up; it had all actually been the way she remembered it. "All those people—what snobs they were!" The way Dorshka pronounced it, the word sounded like *snops*. "Frightful snobs."

"Do you remember Clement Wallach, the Czech playwright?"

"Of course I remember him. He was married to my old friend Henrietta Sternberg. They moved to New York after the war, and he died a couple of years ago, but she and I still write to each other. What about him?"

"God, how my heart went out to him. Straight off a freighter from Mexico to San Pedro. Had a monocle, remember? And a long cigarette holder. And Henrietta had bad headaches, migraines or something, and she would ask me to bring her c-c-c-cold compresses. They had been through so much, and I felt so sorry for them, and then one day out in my car, when I was showing him the difference between the brakes and the clutch and she was dozing in the backseat, he stuck his hand up my skirt, the old c-c-c-coot."

Dinah looked brightly at Dorshka. "As I told the committee boys downtown yesterday, it is one thing to be a pr-pr-pr-pr-proletarian *in* the industry and another thing to be a proletarian *out* of the industry. I was a proletarian non grata. And, oh boy, did all that change when I became a radio writer. Suddenly I was a hot ticket. When Clement Wallach heard about the show, he said, 'Why don't we take a nice little drive and I can help you develop your conception of the character.' "

"I knew nothing of this!" Dorshka said, laughing.

"It was even worse when it got around that I was seeing Jake. Oh boy, the Party wanted him so badly they were dr-dr-drooling. Why didn't I bring him around? Maybe I could get him to write some jokes for the folksingers they were bringing to a h-h-h-hootenanny."

"A what?"

"A hootenanny. Don't you remember? You know, where you sing the Internationale and folk songs. 'There once was a union maid' and all that sort of thing. I remember this one very well. We were going to collect bandages and blankets and winter underwear for partisan groups in Yugoslavia. But Jake *hates* folk music, and he isn't too crazy about labor songs, either. 'It's not the politics, it's just that they're all so goddamn square,' he'd say. He said I'd have to leave the Party or we were through. And then I gave him my own ultimatum and—well, I won't go into all that. But I'd lost interest in the P-P-P-Party anyway. It just didn't matter anymore to me one way or the other."

"That's because you had found what you were looking for. I remember the first time you brought him over here. How happy you were!"

Dinah could hear something ironic and not altogether kind in Dorshka's words, and she looked at her uncertainly. "And still am, Dorshka."

"But tell me something, darling. Didn't Jake try to stop you?"

"Maybe a little, in a halfhearted way. But I could see right through him. He was desperate for me to do it. He can't live without working, and I can't live if he can't live."

"Dinah, we're not talking about life and death here. Just money."

"I know, Dorshka. It must seem incomprehensible to you. You've saved so many people from death. I mean horrible death—Auschwitz death, shooting and starving death. This isn't even remotely on that scale. No one was holding a gun to my head. I get it, I really do. It's a terrible thing to inform on people because you don't want your husband to lose his job. It's not even as if his life were in danger."

"So at least about this you do not kid yourself."

"I don't expect you to understand—I'm not noble, like you. I just can't stand the thought of doing anything to hurt my husband and kids."

"Aren't you worried about what your children will think?"

"They can think what they like, when the t-t-t-time comes. The one thing they'll know is that I did it because I loved their father."

"I think, you know, that this attitude is something which you find maybe only in America."

Dinah looked puzzled. "What attitude?" She found her mind alert, sharpened, as if, having undergone that interrogation yesterday, she was ready for more questions. And yet she didn't understand what Dorshka was saying.

"This not giving a damn about what the others think because love justifies all."

Dinah shrugged. "I don't know, Dorshka, if it's American or not. Does it matter? I don't care about people I don't love. The problem, though, is that in addition to Jake I also love you and my s-s-s-s-sister." She said this simply and directly; she was not asking Dorshka for anything.

"Not the way you love Jake."

"Ah, Dorshka, come on. I don't want anything b-b-b-bad to happen to you or Veevi because of me."

"But you named us. We are expendable."

Dinah's eyes wandered along the walls and lit momentarily on a still life by Vlaminck of some lemons and a pitcher. Dorshka had brought it over with her so long ago. "No, you're not. Not to me."

"But you sacrificed us."

"Jake is my husband, the father of my children."

"You also believe in all this dreary American nonsense about falling in love forever and worshiping your husband."

Startled, and menaced by this remark, Dinah drew back. "It's not nonsense, Dorshka. It's what I've always wanted. And now I have what I want and I want what I have, and I'm going to protect it no m-m-m-matter what."

"Really, my dear," Dorshka said without harshness.

Dinah noticed how long Dorshka's legs looked in her men's slacks—

long, sturdy, energetic legs. "But you're the one who used to say, 'Love is a gift you must always accept freely, without doubt and questions.' " She said this dramatically, with head held high in the air and hand over the heart, in affectionate imitation.

"I wasn't talking about *marriage*," Dorshka said drily.

Dinah looked bewildered. "You mean, *affairs?*"

Dorshka shrugged.

"Oh Jesus, Dorshka, I'm a real dope about that kind of thing."

"No doubt you are. Tell me, have you had a romance since you married Jake?"

"A *romance?* Of course not!"

"Well, that's too bad for you," Dorshka teased. "You and every other chaste wife in this Calvinist country will end up looking like boiled cabbages. You must live, Dinah, while you have the chance!"

"Dorshka, don't waste your breath. I'm a simple American housewife in love with her husband. I wasn't going to go to jail—that would have hurt my kids. I'd rather accept the dishonor than hurt them and Jake."

"NO!" Dorshka brought her fist down on the armchair. "Don't you see? You say you don't want to hurt your children. But you already have, by doing what you did! You will say to your children: I was an *informer.* I named names because I didn't want you to suffer. Do you honestly think they will be grateful? That they will thank you? No. Even if *you* don't feel any guilt, or think you don't, *they* will, because they will know, without any doubt, that for them you broke the most fundamental moral law to—"

"The most f-f-f-fundamental m-m-m-moral *what?* The moral *law?* That must be something you talk about in college when you read a lot of philosophers. I don't think that way. I don't go around asking myself if I obeyed the fundamental moral law today. I ask myself if I bought enough milk and eggs, and did I p-p-p-pick up Jake's golf shoes and should I order some more redwood rounds for the front path. M-M-Moral law? That sounds like something from a *Saturday Review,* something I have to look up."

Without answering, Dorshka got up and went to her desk and handed Dinah a newspaper clipping. "I saw it this morning," she said. "So I knew you had done this before I had any idea I would be seeing you today. And I tell you something, Dinah darling. When I saw this, my heart, well, it just sank. What you have brought upon yourself, of this you have no idea."

Dinah felt intensely aware of her friend's self-possession, her love affairs, her loneliness, her difficulties both surmounted and endured. Her old breasts drooped under the short-sleeved man's shirt, having become comfortably obsolete. She had been born to a large life, but here she was, confined and straitened, without an ounce of self-pity.

"Didn't you ever do something you didn't want to do but had to do, or thought you had to do?" Dinah asked.

"Yes, of course," she said. "But it was just, you know, private stupidity."

"It's nice of you to want to save my soul," Dinah said. "But you know, you're used to thinking about things in a European way. Complicated and s-s-s-sophisticated. I don't know how to do that. I'm not an intellectual, Dorshka. I go by my guts and I don't have the head for abstract ideas. I just came here today to say that I hope I haven't hurt you, but that if I have and if you need anything . . ." She glanced at her watch. "I've got to get home before the kids get back from school—"

"Ach, Dinah, you American women let your children run your lives. But please, stay a little longer." She folded up the newspaper clipping and stuck it in her shirt pocket, from which she also took out a letter. It was a light-blue tissue-paper-thin aerogram. Dinah recognized it immediately. Withdrawing her glasses from her breast pocket, Dorshka began to read aloud in her thickly accented, full second-balcony voice:

Mike is working hard on revisions but wants to get out of Paris, so we've taken a house in St-Jean-de-Luz for the summer. It should be rather jolly. Hunt and Felicity are coming, too. Hunt has finally convinced Mike to let him make a movie out of The Confession, *so they're going to work on the screenplay in the mornings and fish in the afternoons or go to bullfights—ghastly but beautiful. Life has offered to pay him a small fortune to do a photo essay on Gastaing, the ever-astonishing Basque sculptor who is a friend of ours, with Béla (known as Bill) Nemeth, also a character, always dashing all over the world to take pictures of wars. You'd like him—a shock-of-hair-over-the-eye, live-today-for-tomorrow etc. etc. sort of guy. Women are crazy about him, and Mike adores him. So he's coming, too, and bringing his girlfriend, Rue Melville. She's Canadian, divorced, has lived in Paris since the war, has endless private income and thick champagne-blond braids she ties around her head—why I don't know, because it makes her look too* mädchen-*like for my taste—gets to spend about two*

weeks with Bill three times a year, and keeps a very close watch on him
when she does. We three girls will do the shopping and cooking, which
will mean daily hilarity at the market, since Felicity and Rue love to
make fun of my French—still terrible despite thirteen years here.
Three witches to stir the pot for the daily bouillabaisse will also be fun,
though I guess I can tell you now I've been forbidden to eat shellfish be-
cause I'm pregnant—

"Pregnant?" said Dinah, interrupting her. "I thought Mike didn't want
children."

"Shh. Just listen." Dorshka read on:

As you know, Mike is not the family type, but this was an accident, and
he says he's glad. Maybe by the time the baby arrives (in the middle of
winter, poor thing!), we'll find some way to convince the U.S. govern-
ment that you're hardly a security risk and bring you over here for good.
We both wish you could come and live with us and Claire and the
baby. We do miss you terribly.

Dorshka put the letter down on the coffee table and snorted. "Thanks
to those bastards at HUAC, my devoted son has enjoyed complete immu-
nity over the past four years from the slightest threat of a visit from me. All
this about missing me and wanting me to live there with them is complete
nonsense. If they miss me so much, what's to stop them from coming here,
after all?"

"Well, for one thing they hate it here. They're card-carrying expatriates
and have taken an oath to despise everything 'made in the U.S.A.' "

"Ha! Do you know what they want? They want to be left alone. What
couple as wrapped up in each other as they are could stand to have anyone
else around—least of all a mother-in-law? Oh, they have their friends, but
their friends are all alike—romantic, living for love and experience."

"As you did?"

"Yes, as I did. And I'm damn glad of it too, now that *that's* all finished."
She smiled triumphantly at Dinah.

"She's pregnant," Dinah murmured. She felt suddenly tired and, glancing again at her watch, decided that she really must go. Yet she made no
move to get up and instead sank back in her chair.

Dorshka mistook this for concern. "You know, my dear," she said gently,

"I think for now you don't have to worry about them. They are fine. And since you make this bargain with the Devil—you name names and in exchange your perfect happiness continues undisturbed—you should now enjoy life to the fullest. That, you owe yourself. To tell you the truth"—and her eyes filled with tears that sparkled and brimmed but did not spill over—"I envy you. You girls are still in the middle of your lives. You are so much in love with your husbands. So you owe it to someone like me to live fully, and live well, so that I can see once again before I die what life should be like."

The tears fell, then, and Dorshka withdrew a handkerchief from her pocket and in silence wiped her eyes.

At that moment, Dinah knew without a doubt that she had finally seen what it was about Dorshka that had made her a legend for audiences in Berlin and Prague.

She leaned forward across the coffee table and took the older woman's hands in her own. "I l-l-love you dearly, D-D-D-Dorshka. You were kind to me today, and you didn't have to be."

"I love you too, my dear. Only . . ."

They let go of each other's grasp and got up at the same time.

". . . you must be prepared if they decide—"

"Never to speak to me again?" Dinah said sharply.

"Yes."

"But will you speak to me?"

"Haven't I done so today?"

At the door, Dorshka sighed and Dinah's heart sank. She's wonderful, Dinah thought, but she can never leave anything unsaid. Everything has to come out somehow. It was Dorshka's great strength, she would have admitted at once, but it could also be trying. "You know," Dorshka began. And Dinah moved imperceptibly closer to the door, even though she knew she would not be able to leave without one more dose of moral instruction. "It's a pity, really, because always I have liked Jake. He's a charming boy. And he has so much talent."

"Do you think so? I thought you didn't like his pictures."

"Oh, but I do."

"But . . . ?"

Dinah could have been out the door in an instant, but she stayed rooted, waiting for the needle, reminding herself that Dorshka, who had been able to get so many people out in time, had not managed to save her own family. Her mother, her two sisters, her three brothers, and their families had all been murdered in Auschwitz. And then she had lost Stefan, learning of his death through her son, Mike, who had tracked down Ventura's surviving comrades in M.O.I. and listened to their stories. Out of this, Mike's second novel, *The Confession,* had been written. It was about a German-born and German-speaking naturalized American soldier's attempt to track down the Gestapo officers who had tortured and killed his father, a Resistance fighter in France. Dinah had interpreted the book to mean that Mike believed that Stefan Ventura was his father—though no one, not even Dorshka, knew it for sure.

"They win," said Dorshka. "These terrible HUACkers win when they turn people who should stand together against each other. They split them into good guys and bad guys. I myself wouldn't testify, but I won't stop talking to you—because I don't want them to win. I don't want to let them cut us off from each other. But at the same time, since I, too, must listen to my guts, I suppose that I wouldn't so much like to talk to Jake. He has influence over you, and he could have told you not to do it."

Dinah nodded, her lips pressed tightly together. There was nothing she could say. She kissed Dorshka again and then stepped soundlessly out into the hazy afternoon and began walking toward her car.

She waited until she had reached the stoplight at Veteran and Sunset to light a cigarette and release her own tears. *Pregnant.* Veevi was pregnant again. And Dinah, with her two children, felt that she herself would never again conceive. The old envy, the oldest feeling she had ever known, turned the warm Los Angeles afternoon into a dreary Pittsburgh landscape—heavy, deadening, and gray. For the second time in two days, she felt desolate and bereft.

It was Veevi and Mike's love that assaulted her now. That passionate mutual adoring love, as Veevi described it in her letters, in which they were the entire world to each other. It wasn't, Dinah acknowledged sickeningly, what Jake had ever felt for her or ever would feel. She had eagerly accepted him last night, and responded to him with every muscle and nerve, and believed with all her heart in his passion, as if, finally, he had given her the truest, deepest part of himself. Yet something about it was wrong, and false. It wasn't the Jake she knew. He just wasn't that considerate, that slow and patient, that generous, by nature or by habit. It had been a performance. He'd been *thanking* her. She hadn't wanted to see it then, but she couldn't avoid seeing it now. Oh, he loved her, all right, in his own way, but it wasn't the wild, consuming adoration Mike felt for Veevi. It never would be that, either. And with this realization the thought snaked through her and began twisting itself around her: Mike would never have let Veevi testify for him. Never. Never. *Never.*

*I*t was a late summer evening some weeks later. Although Dinah had just devoured three morsels of rumaki, the euphoria created by the combined tastes of chicken liver, water chestnuts, and bacon had lasted for only a moment, not nearly long enough to assuage either her hunger pangs or the edgy feeling that had been plaguing her all day. Not simply all day—for the whole of the past week. "Aren't we going to Mort Berman's next Thursday?" Jake had asked. He had been heavily in screenplay, and it would be their first big party since she had testified. This one wasn't to be missed. It was a hundred-dollar-a-plate luau for the Democratic Party, with the guest of honor Adlai Stevenson, governor of Illinois, due to arrive later that evening. Rumor had it that he might run for president next year.

Searching the patio for familiar faces, Dinah moved toward a cluster of people who had gathered around Mel Gordon. She was just in time to hear him deliver the punch line, in a Yiddish accent: "Doctor, I too miscalculated. I only *thought* I had to fart."

She was fond of Mel and his wife, Annie, and liked everyone else in the group, too—Marv and Ruthie Weiskopf, Dolly and Phil Levinson, Irwin and Bea Katzenbach, Hy and Esther Rosen—and now her laughter mingled happily with theirs. Though Mort, an entrenched Hollywood bachelor, usually went around with a faster, sportier crowd than the Laskers, he had invited some of the couples from their set as well, and Dinah relaxed, feeling safe with them. She looked for Jake and caught him in profile, head tilted slightly forward, drink in his right hand, the other cupping his deaf left ear. He was listening to Joe Schlossberg, who had called the day Jake's Marathon deal was announced in the trades and offered to represent him, saying he could get Jake ten times what Reggie Pertwee or anybody else in Hollywood could promise.

"I'm famished," Dinah murmured to Ruthie Weiskopf.

"Me, too, but I don't see a crumb of food. Do you?"

Her own stomach growling, Dinah scanned the crowded patio for the waiter with the hors d'oeuvres tray, only to encounter Sid Plotkin's lascivious stare. *I want you,* he mouthed at her. She shot him a broad smile and mouthed back: *Sor-ry.* Sid was the kind of person you'd expect to see at a Mort Berman party—any kind of Mort Berman party, whether it was for the Democrats or for the guys who spent the day at the track (after they'd written that day's quota of jokes for George Joy—some of them had worked for him since the Stone Age). Sid was and would always be a George Joy writer: divorced, a Santa Anita habitué, often found in Palm Springs and Vegas, never with the same girl twice.

From the moment in 1941 when Jake had first taken her to NBC to watch a Crystaldent broadcast and introduced her to Joy's stable of writers, Sid had faithfully made a pass at Dinah every time they'd met. It had been going on for so long now that it was simply a reflexive gag—not funny, not unfunny either, although Dinah never doubted that Sid's lust was real and that a response from her would have meant real trouble. She found him what she called "seriously unattractive," unlike Art Squires, she thought, blushing uneasily, as she remembered their encounter the day she gave her testimony to the Committee. Sid Plotkin was no Art Squires, though. He was trim and compact in a self-regarding, tennis-playing, neither-short-nor-tall sort of way, but had a repellent, fishlike face, with round eyes that were too close together. Jake called him, in private, the Human Salmon. "Watch out for him. He's just another horny Jewish comedy writer lusting for shiksa legs," Jake had testily warned her years ago when she reported Plotkin's pass-making to him.

Undeterred, Sid held up his hands in mock prayer. Dinah shook her head again, and he let his fall limply to the side in a parody of disappointment. All right, she told herself, enough of that. Turning toward the buffet table, she noticed that it was piled with food at last. "Look, Ruthie," she said, grabbing Ruthie Weiskopf's elbow.

"Let's go," said Ruthie, a warm, freckled woman whose husband had written and produced a hit television comedy series about a private secretary.

The two women were headed toward the cold roast beef when a woman with upswept hair and a perfectly round, rouged face, resembling a pink pom-pom, suddenly loomed ahead and stopped them cold. "Now, you come right over here with me," she commanded, dragging Dinah away from Ruthie. "Talk to me, Dinah," she said. "Joe and I read it in the paper. Aren't you relieved it's *over*?"

On the way to the party Jake had warned her: "For Christ's sake, if you see her, just be nice. Don't get huffy or noble. We don't know for a fact that she's the one who nailed you. And don't forget, whatever you do, it's an elemental fact of the motion picture industry that among professional agents there are a handful whose names carry more prestige than all the rest put together, and Joe and Renna Schlossberg are the two halves of one of those names."

"I know that," she had said. "And if you think I went through the whole goddamn business of t-t-t-testifying only to blow up at the person who I'm ninety-nine and forty-four one-hundredths percent sure named me, you must think I'm a real h-h-h-horse's ass."

"Yes, I'm glad it's over," she said to Renna Schlossberg, who, as she squeezed Dinah's hand, made a sound somewhere between a yelp and a squeal. "Though, frankly, I think I would rather have had a tooth pulled. Without novocaine."

"Really? They were very nice to me."

Well, you sure as hell were nice to them, she didn't say.

Dinah smiled. Where had Renna picked up that god-awful squeal?

"But that Kingman. God. A real American type, don't you think? Now, Marlow—he's interesting. He's got that—that kind of redneck purity about him. You know what I mean? Skinny. Craggy. *Very* Carradine."

"Got him in mind for *The Grapes of HUAC*?"

Another yelp. Then, softly, "Do you hate me, Dinah?"

Bingo. "For naming me? N-N-N-Not a chance, Renna. It's over, that's all. I don't want to think about it."

Renna tugged at the hem of her black sheath, trying to cover her plump knees. "Well, anyway," she went on, searching Dinah's face, "Joe showed me the article and I wanted to call, but I wasn't sure you'd want to talk."

"Well, what's there to s-s-s-say? We both did it, and now it's done."

"You know, honey, I'm not a bit sorry," Renna said. "Those days are a joke. When I think of myself as a *Communist"*—she uttered the word with another squeal—"it's like trying to remember a time when I was a *virgin*. I mean, was it ever *possible*? It's so absurd, really. The thought of it *today*. I mean, anybody with a brain in their head got out. I left, you left, everybody who wasn't a schmuck got out. We outgrew it. When they subpoenaed me, I said to Joe, 'Joe, it's just like they want to get me for having been a Girl Scout. For a minute and a half of my life.' "

Dinah reached into her black clutch for a cigarette. "How's the baby?"

The pom-pom face sobered. "Funny you should ask. Do you want to know the real reason I testified? I'll tell you. The adoption agency wouldn't let us have the baby unless I did."

"But who told them? How did they even know?"

"The agency checks your background. They go to the FBI, and these days they go way back, too. If they come up with something hot, they tell the Committee. That's how come they can ask all those questions. 'Did you or did you not picket Warner Brothers every Saturday morning during the labor strike of 19-blah-blah-blah?' I had to clear myself before they'd let me have Debby. Christ, Dinah, what's more important—giving a baby a home or sparing certain people you and I both know from being identified as deluded schmucks? And tell me something. Why did the Party have to be so damn secretive? None of this would have happened if from the beginning everyone had just said, 'Yeah, we're Communists. So what?' "

"Of course," Dinah said. "But how's the baby?" She was staring at Renna's jewelry: a large square-cut diamond ring, a diamond bracelet, diamond-and-ruby earrings. She remembered when Renna was a reader at Paramount and, like her, owned exactly two dresses plus one ice-skating outfit and a bathing suit. She was the one friend Dinah had made at Veevi and Stefan's all-day-all-night Saturdays. And it was Renna who'd started taking Dinah to meetings in town, during the week, when it was too far to drive to the ones over in Malibu.

"Dinah, I shit you not: she's sensational, the love of my life." Renna's pink cheeks glowed. "I wasn't going to live without a child."

"No, no, of course not. I'm very happy for you. But just tell me, Renna, why *did* you name me?"

The doll-like face, flushing under the two rosettes of rouge, seemed to give off a pink steam. The Kewpie mouth went still, then the lips pursed. Dinah heard a sharp intake of breath. "I told you—because we couldn't adopt Debby unless I did, and I wasn't going to lose my chance at getting a kid."

"No, I don't mean why did you testify. I asked why *me*? Why did you name *me*?"

"Because, I swear on my client list," said Renna, squeezing Dinah's forearm, "I never thought they'd bother you. I thought they might go after some of the big names I named, though they'd grabbed most of them already. But never you. I mean, what are you today? You're just a *housewife*." She threw her head back and laughed. "You're not in the industry anymore. You haven't written a word since you married Jake. And, well . . ." she said with a gulp, "I thought you'd understand. And maybe I'm not the only one who named you. Have you thought of that?"

"Renna dear, I'm just curious. I'm not ang-g-g-g . . ."

"Tell me something," Renna broke in, her voice quavering. "How many paragons of virtue do you know? This is show business, for heaven's sake. Show me one person in this town who hasn't gotten into bed with someone they hate because they wanted a deal. I mean, really, fuck 'em all. And fuck you, too."

Dinah took her arm. "Come on, darlin', it's over. Let's eat!" But Renna squeezed Dinah's hand again and gazed into her face, and Dinah couldn't look away. The pom-pom cheeks and Betty Boop mouth begged absolution.

"Okay, Renna," Dinah said. "I forgive you. Okay? F-F-Forgive me, too."

"I'm so sorry, Dinah. I guess if it hadn't been for me—"

"Oh, Renna," Dinah said, putting her arms around her old friend. "Forget it, honey. If it hadn't been for you, I wouldn't have met Jake. I wouldn't have had my kids. I wouldn't have had *anything*."

Renna took a rumpled handkerchief from her bag and daintily wiped her eyes. "I still remember the day Jake called me at the studio and said, 'Do you know any nice girls? I want to meet a nice girl.' And I said, 'I know this girl who ice-skates with me. She has brown eyes and brown hair and she's five-five and the nicest person I know.' " Then she batted her eyes and gave a brief squealing laugh, and Dinah felt with a stab of nostalgia Renna's old warmth toward her.

"Now, listen," Renna said. "Do me a favor and tell Jake I think he should kick that limey faggot Reggie Pertwee right in the ass and let Joe and me make the two of you really rich. Like you deserve to be. Like we all deserve to be!"

A peck on Dinah's cheek, a tug at the hem of her dress, plump knees in motion, and Renna was off to zero in on a new target, Kermit Strauss. A flushed and fluffy homing pigeon, she stage-whispered his name before making her way toward the New York playwright, who had a smash on Broadway, and whose ears stuck out at a ninety-degree angle.

Deserted as abruptly as she'd been kidnapped, Dinah steadied herself by looking for Jake, whom she soon discovered talking to a tall, slim girl in a white dress, her dark hair pulled back very tight from her "gamine" face, as the magazines would have said. Dinah studied her for a moment. This must be Charm School Posture Number 35: the girl was holding a drink in her right hand, resting her elbow on her left, and listening with worshipful attention to something Jake was saying. Dinah had seen the girl in a picture recently, and liked her, but couldn't remember the name of either the picture or the girl. Light-headed from hunger, Scotch, and cigarettes, she started toward the buffet table. Leslie something? Brill? Or was it a French name? Bridou? Britain? A real show-biz name, made up, too euphonious. She hoped she wouldn't have to be introduced to her. *How do you do, Miss Br-Br-Br—?* The stuttering would throw the girl into a panic. *Hello, dear,* Dinah sometimes said to these girls, of whom she had met countless specimens at countless parties. But it made her feel matronly. She was far from ready to take that tone.

This young beauty made her think of Veevi, the fairest of them all, and plunged her back into the dread in which she now lived, day after day. Her sister hadn't written back.

She saw Sid Plotkin, balancing a plate piled high with shrimp and pineapple chunks, looking for someone to latch on to, and she realized that if she didn't join Jake and the girl, Sid was likely to sidle right up to her. So she struggled to remember the girl's name—not that it mattered. There were thousands of these girls in Hollywood, and they all had pretty names she couldn't remember. But she had to remember this girl's name to keep back the cold wave of terror that threatened to engulf her each time she thought of her sister. And she thought of Veevi many times a day, and all night; she was never not thinking about Veevi. Yet right now she had to find out the girl's name or nothing would ever be right again. She stamped out her cigarette on the terra-cotta deck and scanned the crowd for Nelly Steiner. Nelly, she figured, would know that girl's name. Nelly always knew who was who in the current crop of starlets. She found Nelly perched on the diving board, next to a woman Dinah recognized, by her perfectly turned-under pageboy, as Evelyn Morocco, the wife of Mel Gordon's partner, Izzie Morocco.

So she started for Nelly, feeling that everything would soon be fine again. When she was within a few feet of the diving board, Dinah noticed Nelly suddenly raise a hand and cut it through the air. She's been here since 1939, Dinah thought affectionately, and she's still so *German*. She's still got that rigid, almost military way of waving hello. Still, Dinah rejoiced in the sight of the one friend in Hollywood whom she genuinely loved. She was about to call out, *I see you, I see you, I'm on my way over.* But there was no need; she was there. "Does anyone know the name of that girl who finds my husband so f-f-f-fascinating?" she sang out. "Leslie something or other?"

"Well, you oughtta know!" hissed Evelyn Morocco. "You're the one who knows everybody's name around here!" She glared at Dinah before stalking off on her dyed-to-match open-toed black satin high heels.

Dinah recoiled, but Nelly pulled her down beside her on the diving board. "Are you blind? I tried to warn you! My God, didn't you see me holding up my hand?"

"I thought you were just waving hello."

"Waving hello? You dummy! I was telling you to stay away!"

Dinah looked around to see if anyone was watching. Evelyn had disappeared—probably, Dinah thought, to reapply lipstick and fix her hair, which she had mussed with the violence of her movements.

"So Evelyn Morocco's s-s-s-sore at me."

"Very."

Dinah looked at Nelly, whom, despite their friendship, she had not called in the six or seven weeks since her testimony. "And you? Are you sore at me, too?"

"What do you think?"

"Well, you're talking to me. Oh, God!" Dinah felt a wave of panic overtake her. "Where's Izzie? Where's Jake?"

"Don't bother about them right now. Look, you're shaking!"

And she was. She barely managed to take a cigarette out of her purse and light it. "What did she say to you?"

"Oh, come on, Dinah, you don't really want to hear it, do you?"

"Of course I want to hear it." Dinah slid her shoes off and, moving down slightly on the diving board, dangled her feet over the shimmering water. She felt weak-kneed and out of breath.

"She said if she'd known you were going to be here tonight she wouldn't have come," said Nelly in her distinct, slightly lisping accent. "And that Mort obviously didn't know you had testified, because if he had, he wouldn't have invited you. She said she's going to write a letter to the big Democrats here requesting that you and Renna and anybody else who testified be removed from lists of volunteers and donors and I don't know what else."

Dinah let out a loud volley of laughter. "That's rich. Izzie's agent is Renna Schlossberg! And Izzie and Jake have worked together, and they might work together again! Is she really going to make Izzie break with all these people, and give up her two yearly trips to Bergdorf's? Miss 'My-hair-needs-New York,' as she's famous for s-s-s-saying."

" 'I don't expect integrity from people like Renna, but from Dinah Lasker it's a different story.' Those were Evelyn's exact words," said Nelly.

" 'Integrity'? Since when has that word even been in Evelyn Morocco's v-v-v-vocabulary?"

On the diving board next to Dinah was a glass somebody had abandoned. The ice had dissolved into a warm puddle of Scotch. Dinah picked it up and finished it off, and, swinging her legs over to the firm ground, planted her feet squarely on the concrete, facing Nelly. She looked, despite her black cocktail dress, like an old Appalachian farmer in overalls. "So I'm Miss Lost Int-t-tegrity of 1951," she said. "That's a good one. Do you want to know the last conversation I had with Evelyn M-M-M-Morocco?" she said to Nelly. "I was p-p-p-p-picking my kids up at school, and she was there, waiting for hers. So I got out of the car to stretch my legs and say hello, and she looked at whatever it was I was wearing—a shirt and pants from J-J-Jax or something—and she said, 'Now, that's the way you should dress all the time.' " Dinah snorted. "She's the kind of dame that if your purse and shoes don't match, you're in big tr-tr-tr-trouble."

She leaned down and extinguished her cigarette in the pool, then flicked it into the azalea bushes nearby. "Yikes! I better find J-J-Jake. God only knows what she might say to him."

Dinah felt Nelly's hand on her wrist, restraining her. "He's a big boy, Dinah," she said. "Let him take care of himself. Now, sit down. I'm going to get us some food."

Dinah didn't hear her; she was falling into a reverie. One Sunday afternoon a few summers ago, she and Jake had taken the kids swimming up at the Steiners' house, in Stone Canyon. The usual crowd was there—the

Weiskopfs, the Breitners, the Katzenbachs, the Gordons, and the Moroccos. They all had the same standing invitation for every Sunday, and the backyard of the Steiners' Bel-Air colonial, which looked out from a mountaintop of thyme, yucca, and wild mustard across the descending foothills to the Pacific, rang with the sounds of children splashing and shouting, as the adults talked and told stories and laughed. Except for Marv Weiskopf, who had a hit TV show, the husbands were all high-priced screenwriters. Mel and Izzie had been a writing team since the late thirties. They'd started out in radio, then moved into movies, and both occasionally worked with other guys they had known from the George Joy Crystaldent show. All the wives had been in the industry, too. Dinah, of course, had been a radio writer, briefly. And Bea Katzenbach, the only wife who still worked, wrote with her husband, Irwin. Even though they had all known one another for years, Evelyn had always rubbed Dinah the wrong way. Some of it, Dinah was willing to admit, was outright envy. Evelyn came from a rich family in New York, had gone to Fieldston and Bennington (the year it opened), and flew back to New York every spring and fall to buy expensive clothes. On weekends in Palm Springs with the Engels, she would whisper with Anya about art and ballet and become silent whenever Dinah tried to join in, as if there were nothing the three of them could possibly have in common. She and Anya took private art lessons in a studio built onto her garage, where the teacher instructed them in painting semiabstract murals of mythological figures doing peculiar ritualistic things in inexplicable postures.

   That afternoon at the Steiners', Dinah remembered, Evelyn had been trying to get everyone to sign a petition on behalf of the teacher, Hernando Nuñez—a Mexican artist who had known Rivera, Siqueiros, and Orozco— who was being deported for being a Communist. When she asked Phil Breitner, Dinah remembered, he barely looked up from his *New York Times* crossword puzzle, shook his head, and said he never signed anything, since he might wake up the next morning feeling just the opposite of what he'd felt the day before. Jake apologized, but said he wouldn't sign because he'd recently signed a loyalty oath at Marathon and vowed to himself he'd never sign anything again. Neither Irwin nor Bea Katzenbach signed, saying they agreed with Phil and Jake. Mel Gordon was about to sign, but Annie, his wife, said, "If you sign that thing with the situation the way it is today, I will personally escort you to the psychiatric ward at L.A. County General." Dinah, however, had signed. Jake scowled, but he didn't stop her. Evelyn, who had never done anything more radical than vote for Roosevelt and

Wallace, stuck the petition back inside her pool bag, saying she was very disappointed in all of them, except for Dinah. After all, the hearings were basically over in Hollywood, so why was everyone so afraid? The fact was, her teacher wouldn't be on the verge of being thrown out of the country if somebody hadn't named him, and as far as she was concerned it was the finks who named names who ought to be thrown out.

At this, Nelly Steiner looked up from her embroidery. "You really must be fantastically innocent to think it's all over," she said, with her slight lisp. "These things are never over when people think they are. You have to be careful." To which Evelyn, in her hundred-dollar bathing suit from Bergdorf's, replied, "It's a question of principle. A fink is a fink is a fink."

"Uhhhhnnnnnnnh. Uhhhhnnnnnnnnnh." Those two long, high-pitched wailing moans, full of East Broadway and Henry Street and Saturday mornings in *cheder,* came out of the mouth of a wiry brown body lying in glistening splendor as the sun beat down upon his outstretched limbs. His bald head shone like an oiled brown egg, while a blob of white cream on the end of his nose offset his high cheekbones. "Sign, schmign, it doesn't make a bit of difference. If you ask me, the real shits are the studio heads and the bankers in New York who won't stand up to the Committee. The whole thing is so terrible I want to cry." Thus spoke Manny Steiner, who believed only in baseball, working at home, and getting paid on time.

As their kids got in and out of the pool and asked for towels and snacks, the grown-ups discussed people they knew who had testified and those who had refused, their own little group somehow forming an island relatively untouched by the investigations. Dinah was in fact the only one who had actually belonged to the Party, but none of the others knew about it. Even Nelly didn't know. It was during a lull in the conversation that Evelyn Morocco chose to say something. "I think you're all scared of nothing, and I'm very disappointed in you." Dinah had wanted to say, *Who the hell are you to be disappointed in anyone?* Evelyn had never joined the Party—at least not out in Los Angeles, or Dinah would have known about it. She and her trust fund had arrived in Hollywood early in 1942. It had taken her about four months to land Izzie Morocco, whom Jake had gone to high school with back in Chicago and who, like Jake, had had it drilled into him by his parents that "it's just as easy to marry a rich girl as a poor girl," advice Jake had resolutely ignored—just as he had ignored parental orders to marry a rich *Jewish* girl. When Jake started taking Dinah to parties, Evelyn made it perfectly clear that she was an interloper.

Now, two plates in hand, Nelly was carefully making her way back to Dinah and the diving board when she saw Dinah stride across the patio, her fists clenched and a look of terrible purpose on her face.

It was the bangs Dinah kept her eyes on—the perfect black bangs and the perfect black pageboy and the perfect black satin dinner suit, the whole outfit forming a stark silhouette against the balmy summer twilight. Evelyn Morocco was absorbed, as she often was, in a whispery tête-à-tête with a woman Dinah didn't know, when Dinah came up sideways to her and tapped her on the shoulder.

Looking up, Evelyn scarcely had time to blanch. "Now, l-l-l-listen to me, you horse's ass," Dinah said, pointing her finger in Evelyn's face. "You and I have known each other for a long time and we're not exactly cr-cr-cr-crazy about each other, but if you're going to judge me, then do it for the right reasons, for Ch-Ch-Christ's sake. Don't pretend you've got some high f-f-f-fucking moral standard that's better than anyone else's. What you don't like about me is that I'm an uneducated long-l-l-l-legged shiksa who can dance better than you and say 'shit' in front of men and get away with it. And before I came along, you had Izzy and Phil and Manny and Jake all to yourself, like some kind of a qu-qu-queen bee. Sure, I was in the P-P-P-Party, and I don't recall ever seeing you anywhere near it. So don't you d-d-d-dare judge me for trying to live with something you never even had the guts to do in the first place."

It was over before people realized a scene had taken place. Evelyn burst into tears and ran into the Berman house; Nelly walked over and took Dinah's elbow. Dinah gently shook her off. She felt exhilarated but faint. "It's okay. I feel fine," she said. "But I'm gonna pass out if I don't eat something."

"Did you absolutely have to talk back to her?" Jake said as they were driving home later that night. Dinah glanced away from the winding road ahead, as Jake, in his usual relaxed way, changed lanes without signaling. He was trying hard to sound evenhanded and unruffled.

"Yeah, I did."

"Well, next time, maybe we should take out an ad in the trades."

"Oh, for Christ's sake, Jake. She's a c-c-c-cunt and a phony and I wasn't going to let her get away with it."

She waited for him to say something, but he only hummed a tuneless melody, then whistled for a while.

"You're off-key, Jake."

He stopped whistling and looked over at her. She had her face turned to the right window, away from him. "Why're you so sore?" he said.

"Because you're not backing me up."

"I thought you would have realized that this kind of thing is going to happen again and again," he said. "You're going to have to get used to it. A lot of people are going to cut you, and say things to you that you won't like. I thought you said you were prepared for it and didn't give a good goddamn what anybody thought."

"I am. I can take whatever people say. Only just not from that f-f-f-fucking Evelyn Morocco."

"But what if I want to work with Izzy again? This could make it awkward."

"Okay, I'm sorry," she said bitterly. "It won't happen again." Tears filled her eyes, and she opened the window and looked out at the night. Jake started whistling again, and soon made a sharp right onto their street.

*S*eptember came, bringing fierce dry heat. Temperatures of a hundred or higher penetrated the brick walls of the Tudor house, baking its usually cool interior. Every window was open, inviting sluggish cross-drafts to collide. Peter and and Lorna slept restlessly on sheets spread out over the living-room sofas, while Gussie took a fan to her room above the garage and had to move the sports pages and her *Daily Word* prayer booklets off the night table away from the gusts of cooling air. Making love late in the night, Jake and Dinah soaked the sheets with sweat. Afterward, Jake fell at once into a damp sleep, while Dinah, having slid a pillow underneath her buttocks and elevated her legs against the wall, lay quietly listening to the whooshing sounds of cars on Sunset as the tickling wetness on her skin slowly evaporated in the dark.

It had worked twice before and it should work again, she told herself— although it had been months now that they'd been trying, without success.

Then the heat broke, and the days were clear and balmy, the nights dripping with the scent of jasmine. Mothers and kids came over after school to swim in the new pool, and on Sundays Jake's entire family—his mother and sister and her husband and kids—showed up and stayed all afternoon and for dinner. People they used to invite only for evening parties now came over with their kids. Time and again the diving board gave off its peculiar dull plunk, like a sound in a cartoon, followed by the crash of kids cannonballing into the water.

Los Angeles was, once again, paradise, and Dinah felt renewed and re-vived. Her whole body seemed inhabited again by the nine-year-old girl she had been that day in January 1922 when she had stepped down onto the platform of Union Station, taken a deep breath of delicious air, and en-

tered into an entirely new existence. It had been a perfect morning. To the
east rose mountains with the sharpest outlines, their snowcaps dazzling in
the blue radiance of the sky. It was so warm that Dinah and Veevi had immediately torn off their hats and coats and run madly around, waving their
arms, frolicking, wanting to take off their stockings and kick off their
shoes. Dinah had never felt so happy, ever, and was suddenly sharply aware
of that, aware that she had been unhappy before, terribly unhappy, but
hadn't even known it. It was from this moment that she had begun to
watch herself living her life.

The good weather made her think of Veevi. "Still no word," she sometimes said to Jake, usually in the evening as he was loosening his belt and
trying to decide whether to hit golf balls in their bedroom with his putting
machine or go downstairs into his darkroom to develop a roll of film or
search the icebox for kosher pickles or take a late swim or, when he had run
out of escapes, reluctantly go back to his office at the other end of his
dressing corridor and keep working on the umpteenth draft of the new picture. "What does it matter?" he said. "You've got to stop this, Dinah, and
put it behind you."

One day a blue aerogram with French stamps and Veevi's return address arrived from Paris. It was addressed to Ed Milligan and had been postmarked
some ten days earlier. So that meant, Dinah reflected, as she placed it in
the special envelope in which she saved her father's Social Security checks
and announcements from his Shriner and Masonic lodges, that Veevi and
Mike had no doubt returned to Paris from St-Jean-de-Luz and had seen
her letter but were refusing to answer it. She was dying to know what was
in the letter, but she had no idea when her father would next show up. He
was probably still somewhere up in the Sierras, having sent a postcard in
the middle of the summer from Yosemite: "I was here in 1905, before I met
your mother. Pop." She called the trailer park in Alhambra that he considered home and asked Mrs. Snyder, the proprietress, if she knew where he
was. "Dunno, dearie, but I wouldn't worry if I was you," she said. "He'll be
by one of these days, when it starts gettin' cold up in the mountains."

In frustration, she went to her bedroom and shook all of Veevi's letters
out of the envelope she kept them in. The place names jumped out at her:
Beaulieu, Villefranche, Cap Ferrat, Pamplona, St-Jean-de-Luz, Biarritz,

Klosters, not to mention London, Paris, and Rome. The letters were full of stories about other people—Mike and Veevi's friends, who were always between pictures or novels or safaris or wars. The friends who were novelists were always contemptuously turning their novels into screenplays; the screenwriters were always piously doing their "real" work, writing novels. The journalist and photographer friends went only to the most dangerous places from which they returned with prize-winning articles and pictures. Veevi casually referred to pilots and jockeys, English lords, Texas heiresses, and assorted Americans doing business in Paris. Not a few of these people had had a "good" war, and Veevi often said things like "Mike knew him in the OSS." She and Mike enjoyed life: mornings were for writing, afternoons for sport, evenings for the nomadic pursuit of pleasure. Reading the names and places—bars and clubs and bistros—Dinah felt a reluctant envy, as if she were supposed to want what Veevi had. But, gathering up the letters and stuffing them back into the manila envelope, she knew she wouldn't be able to endure that life. Didn't the Albrechts and their friends ever stay home for dinner? Didn't they ever eat with their kids? She and Jake knew people here in Hollywood who were out every night and whose kids ate only with the help, but it was something she and Jake had decided not to do. They went out, they entertained, but not every night. They ate with their kids. And Dinah loved the hours she had to herself to garden and read.

She stared at the envelope, not sure what she had been looking for, but certain that she hadn't found it.

The days grew cooler; it was time for jackets and sweaters. Dinah took to sitting in the den, brooding, in the late afternoons, knitting and smoking while the kids watched TV before dinner. Occasionally she took a sip of Scotch on the rocks and watched the rain disappear into the rising mists of the heated pool. There was no sign of a letter from Veevi.

She threw herself into physical activity. On clear days, dressed in blue jeans and one of Jake's old shirts, she worked in the garden in the front of the house, clipping the box hedges, deadheading the roses, helping Joe, the old Irish gardener, whose bald head and baseball cap always reminded her of her father, pour fertilizer from heavy bags onto the soil and spray against aphids. She replanted flowers in the small patch of dirt left uncovered by the pool crew in the backyard. On Sunday evenings, she and Jake stood side by side barbecuing hot dogs and hamburgers for the hordes of people who still brought their kids over to swim, even though it turned dark earlier and the kids came out of the heated water and into the chilly air with blue lips and shivering limbs.

She spent two long mornings a week working with Nelly Steiner at the Democratic Party office in Beverly Hills, typing and stuffing envelopes and wetting down stamps with a sponge. In the afternoons, she picked up Lorna and Peter from school, took Lorna to her ballet lesson and Peter for an ice cream cone at Wil Wright's. Then the three of them went on errands to the hardware store or the grocery store, and then home, where Gussie was waiting to help carry the bags into the house.

She finished a sweater for Lorna and started one for Jake, and never once stopped thinking about Veevi's silence. She forgot about Evelyn Morocco and remained perfectly cool when Tildy Mizener cut her dead at Chasen's; she was unperturbed when, at about six one evening in November, at the stoplight in front of the Indian fountain at the junction of Wilshire and Santa Monica, she glanced at the car next to hers and saw Jill Bergman, Guy Bergman's wife, staring at her with eyes like blue knives and mouthing the word *fink*. She mentioned it casually that night to Jake, who didn't even look up from the *Herald Examiner*'s sports page.

Nevertheless, the letter that did not come gnawed deeper and deeper toward some dark center of dread that seemed to open up and gape at her just when she was cutting carnations and marigolds for Thanksgiving and trimming the Christmas tree with Jake and Gussie and the kids. Her father showed up just in time for Christmas. She waited anxiously when he disappeared into his trailer, parked in the Laskers' driveway, to read his mail. But there was no sign on his face, later that evening, that Veevi had said anything especially disturbing. "She's having another baby, I hear," Dinah said to him, knowing he would have been too embarrassed to volunteer this piece of information. "Guess so," he said, adding nothing more. He was kind this year, bringing presents for the children and sitting down at the piano to play and sing his old-time songs. She decided not to ask any more questions, but she kept wondering if there was some way she could get into the trailer without getting caught. She suggested that he take a walk with the kids, but he never left the house. He liked to spend the day in the kitchen with Gussie, listening to the radio and reading the papers. The kitchen windows looked out directly on the driveway and the trailer, so it was impossible for her to slip in there unseen. Then she had an idea: she would send Gussie and Pop out with the kids to look at Christmas decorations in the neighborhood. They would be gone for several hours if they covered Beverly Hills, Holmby Hills, Bel-Air, and Westwood. What did it matter that she and Jake had already done this with the kids on Christmas Eve? But the day after Christmas she came into the kitchen and found him sitting at the Formica table with Gussie and Lorna reading the letter again. She saw that it was already mightily creased, having been folded and refolded many times. As she poured herself a cup of coffee, she noted how he folded it up yet again and put it back in the breast pocket of his suit jacket. She would never have found it in the trailer, she realized.

And so she gave up. What, after all, was she hoping to hear? Veevi's silence said it all, she reminded herself. Then, coming home late one Saturday morning in early April, after picking up paper plates and cups for a birthday party later that day for Jake's sister Elsinore's son, she saw a white envelope in the breakfast room. It wasn't the familiar thin aerogram, but the stamps on it were French. As she picked it up her heart beat wildly. So, this is it, she said to herself, and quickly called Jake at the studio. "Can't it wait till I come home?" he asked brusquely, annoyed at the interruption. She was about to tell him to go to hell and hang up, but before she could stutter the words out his tone changed. "Okay, shoot," he said. She began to read the densely typed pages.

March 30, 1952

Jake and Dinah,

A week or so after Dinah's letter arrived, Veevi was subpoenaed by the Committee, which acted through the embassy here. We retained, at considerable expense, an American lawyer we know here. He went over various impossibilities, but in the end Veevi had to appear before an epicene little toady from the FBI who had no doubt been shipped over in some metal cage for the sole purpose of interrogating her. Among other things, he told her that although many other "friendly" witnesses had named her, it was the testimony of her sister, Mrs. Jake Lasker, that had linked her most conclusively to the Party. Now, would she please confirm that the aforementioned sister had been a member of the aforementioned Communist Party? No, she replied, she wouldn't.

Well, how about some other names? Again no—no names, no nothing. Sorry, fellas, I'm not going to play. The epicene little toady got very mad, and instructed the gentleman from the embassy's legal depart- ment to issue a contempt citation and confiscate her passport, which they did on the spot. So from here on in she can't travel in or out of France, except to return to the U.S.A., which she can't leave again once she's there. This is a great pity, really, since six weeks ago she gave birth to a daughter, Coco, whom she would like to bring to L.A. to meet her grandparents—in particular your father, whose every letter has but one cry, "When are you coming home?" This is now entirely out of the question, of course, and, given his age, it is extremely doubtful that he and Veevi will ever lay eyes on each other again.

So, my dear in-laws, since you have chosen to do the unthinkable, I guess I'll just have to say the unsayable: the two of you are beneath contempt. You are rat finks, squealers, canaries, stoolies—indeed, you beggar my thesaurus. But do you recognize yourselves in these un- pleasant derogations? Of course not! Why? Because you're so "nice," and "nice" people don't deliberately or willingly do the wrong thing. Of course, we know how very sorry you are. Please, just drop your little tergiversations, your abject expressions of worry, your wretched pleas to help or do something to make the guilt go away.

Now I'll tell you about Veevi. She had a rough delivery—a Cae- sarean here at the American hospital—is very weak, and continues to be stunned by your perfidy. For Christ's sake, hasn't she been through enough? Isn't hiding from the Nazi butchers for four years and risking her life in the Resistance and finding out what happened to Stefan enough for one lifetime?

You've betrayed her past, her history. Worst of all, you've betrayed Stefan and everything he died for. Does the word betrayal shock you? Of course it doesn't, because you live in a world where it means noth- ing. It is in fact soullessness that is the absolute condition of your wearisome, self-important little lives. Is naming names and giving those gray-suited Torquemadas what they want any different from what you already do—daily, hourly, by the minute? Does a friend's picture stink? You tell him you love it. Your lousy little formulaic sentimental comedies are all about giving people what they want and taking every- thing you can get.

Not for you the iron clamp of principle, the dark night of a blind fu-

ture. Veevi chose to follow Stefan—my father—into that dark night when everyone was running in the other direction. She knew they could die. This is courage you will never have, Jake—not you, who allowed your wife to abase herself for you, and not you either, Dinah, who could have saved us all, and especially yourself, had you walked out on those bastards, which, for one brief instant you apparently almost did. Well, my dear lady, almost ain't good enough.

Perhaps, Jake, if you had ever seen explode before your eyes into a million crimson, never-to-be-reconstituted bits the strong, vital flesh of a nineteen-year-old Tennessee boy who had in boot camp sweetly asked you to teach his big, awkward hands how to tie his wonderful-unto-tears bad-taste tie because he wanted to go out that night and get drunk and find a French girl against the coming of the brutal dawn, when he would be sent into battle, you would know what losses you could bear, what lines you wouldn't cross.

But the only lines you know are the ones you write—the one-liners, the tedious jokes. The world spins its webs of evil and you remain a clown among clowns, punching out a laugh a minute from your script of a hundred and twenty pages, no more and no less. If you bring it in under budget, your conscience is clean, you can sleep at night, and God loves you.

Know, both of you, beyond all possibility of doubt, that you have spoken your last to Veevi. You will never see her again. As you grow fatter and fatter feeding off the carrion of your murdered ethics, may your self-forgiveness torture you until the chickenshit in which you're sunk up to your necks forms a loathsome crust upon the skin of your life and reveals you to the world as the moral lepers that you are. You have denied history, you have denied truth, you have denied decency, you have denied your flesh and blood. You have denied everything except the tenderness with which you cherish your infinitely beloved selves.

Mike

There was a silence on Jake's end.

"Well?" she said.

"I'm going to the commissary. I hear the corned beef is pretty good today. What're you gonna do?"

"J-J-J-AKE!!!"

"Darling, listen to me. Take this overwritten, sanctimonious crap and flush it down the toilet. If you allow that strutting, logorrheic gasbag to cause you one instant of doubt or discomfort, I will come home and personally horsewhip you."

But Dinah wasn't listening. Clutching the phone tightly, she felt the full force of the irreversible hit her, like saltwater rushing into her mouth, while her sister seemed suddenly to have been sucked away by a vicious riptide of bitter black foam.

"Honey? Honey?" Jake's anxious voice came over the telephone. "Are you there?"

There was no answer.

"Pull yourself together. He's a nasty, preening, arrogant son of a bitch pissing words all over us. It's nothing, it doesn't mean anything. It's just writing, just a morning's writing to him. Look, honey," he pleaded with her, "forget it, please. I love you. We're a unit, a team, and whatever happens to you happens to me. Everything's fine, darling. I'm going to take care of you forever. Get it?"

She was supposed to say "Got it," and he was supposed to say "Good," but the words wouldn't come.

"Dinah?"

Still there was no answer.

"Look, I'll come home right away."

This helped her collect herself. She didn't want to see him, not now. "No," she said woodenly. "I'll be all right. Elsinore's having that birthday p-p-party this afternoon for Jerry. Ten three-year-olds, and"—she laughed a hard laugh—"a hired clown. I told her I'd get the cake, and I've gotta go and pick it up."

"Good," he said. "That's just what you need right now. Your regular routine."

As she drove to the bakery on Sunset Strip, she found herself drifting into the past. She saw herself and Veevi roller-skating home from school, going for chocolate sodas on Hollywood Boulevard, waiting for a glimpse of Charlie Chaplin, Mary Pickford, and Douglas Fairbanks as their big car drove up to Musso & Frank's. How many times had Dinah skated back and forth in front of the restaurant, hoping they would see her and "discover"

her! But when Chaplin put his face to the window one day, a rose between his teeth, miming a swooning lover, and beckoning with his index finger, it was Veevi, not Dinah, to whom his passionate gestures were addressed. Parking the car and stepping out onto the pavement, Dinah remembered how her sister had smiled mysteriously at Chaplin, and felt again in her wrist the violence with which she had yanked her sister's hand away from the window, not letting go, while Veevi stumbled after her, trying to catch up.

PART

Two

1

"Why are you doing this?" Jake bellowed as he padded across the floor wearing nothing but his bedroom slippers. "If you ask me, darling, it's an exercise in absolute futility and gratuitous decency that will be totally lost on your sister and that pompous, pharisaical lout to whom she happens to be married."

Jake and Dinah were up early. They had celebrated New Year's Eve the night before at the Steiners' but were having their own open house later in the afternoon, and there was much to be done. Dinah, seated at Jake's desk, was still in her bathrobe and, on top of her usual morning befuddlement, looked tired and unrefreshed. Her sleep had been interrupted again and again by the hot, dry Santa Anas, which rattled the windowpanes and made the tree branches scrape against the roof like ghosts clawing to get in.

"You can think what you l-l-l-like," she said, shrinking from the alarming energy with which he barreled into the bathroom and turned on the shower full blast. "Anyway, I didn't ask you," she murmured out of his hearing.

He began to sing almost immediately, belting out "I saw yours last night and got that ooooold feeling. . . ." She knew what he was trying to do but too set on her purpose to laugh, she turned to the black Royal and dug in.

January 1, 1953

Dear Veevi,

Pop died suddenly on December 23rd. Mrs. Snyder called to say he'd had a heart attack and was taken to L.A. County General. But when Jake and I got there it was too late. He'd died in the ambulance. We had him cremated, and put his ashes under the same rosebush where we put Mom's, in the same little green cemetery in Westwood. I suppose he would have liked it better if we'd tossed them into the falls at Yosemite or scattered them under a redwood, but it just seemed simpler this way.

I went out to the trailer the day after Christmas and found his will in a strongbox. It's very brief, and Jake's secretary, Gladys, is sending a mimeo. What little he had, he left to you and the girls.

She wrote and then erased "and nothing to my 'Jew-kids,' as he called them." The erasure was visible and messy, so she yanked the paper out of the typewriter, crumpled it, and threw it into the wastebasket. Then she stuck another two sheets of paper into the typewriter, reached into the wastebasket, smoothed out the first sheet, copied over the parts she had already written minus the part about the "Jew-kids," re-crumpled the first draft, threw it again into the wastebasket, and continued:

I've told Mrs. Snyder to put the trailer on the market. When it's sold, I'll send you the money minus her commission. He had no bank accounts, but in the strongbox, along with the will, there was about twelve thousand in cash. Gladys is wiring that to you as well.

When I was cleaning out the trailer, I found your letters to him, and Gladys is returning these to you along with photographs you've sent, postcards, Claire's drawings, photos of Coco, etc.

Did I ever tell you about the time Jake and I and our friends the Steiners drove down to Palm Springs to spend a weekend with the Engels? This must have been three or four years ago. Just as we reached the edge of town, Manny Steiner turned to me and said, "Hey, Dinah, isn't that your old man?" We backed up to take a look, and sure enough, there was the silver Airstream parked just off the highway and

Pop sitting in a foldout easy chair under the trailer awning reading the paper and listening to the baseball game on a homemade transistor radio, just as happy as pie. We hadn't seen him in months, and my eyes almost fell out of my head, but it was Pop, all right, with his pipe, railroad engineer's cap, suspenders, sneakers and all. Somehow or other he'd figured out how to hook up the trailer to the public utilities, and he had electricity and hot water—everything he needed. We stopped and said hello, and the next morning he came to the Engels' for breakfast and went riding with us, which of course he knew how to do better than anyone else.

Irv kept staring at him, as if he'd walked out of a ghost town, and when I told him Pop had been on the Oklahoma Land Run in 1889, at the age of sixteen, and earned a Mississippi riverboat pilot's license in 1891, he damn near fainted and kept saying, "My God, he's the genuine article! Where have you been keeping him all these years?" It's the only time I ever saw Irv Engel turn shy in front of anybody. Well, finally, Pop got off his horse to join me for a smoke. "Mr. Milligan, would you like to be in pictures?" asked Irv, still on horseback. "Thanks but no thanks, Engel," said Pop. "It's a damn fool business if you ask me." And then, as Irv pulled away, Pop added, supposedly to me but still in Irv's hearing, "Too many goddamn Jews." Irv did a double take. I thought he would fall right off his horse. So right then and there I bawled hell out of Pop, but he was just as cool as could be. "Don't go beatin' your gums. I don't give a good goddamn what he thinks," he said. "His white-slaver Jew father took my Genevieve away from me." Jake kept winking at Irv as if to remind him what an "American type" Pop was and not to take him seriously, but I shooed them away and got him out of there fast. The next day when I drove over to see him, he was gone—had taken off, as he used to say, "without so much as kiss my ass or have an apple."

You were the only person he ever loved.

D.

Dinah pulled the letter out of the typewriter and laid it down flat and carefully reread it. Never having given much thought before to censoring what she wrote her sister, she was aware now of having left out a good deal. At the hospital, she had removed her father's Masonic ring, with its little round diamond at the junction of the two compass legs interlaced with the square. He'd left her nothing, but she remembered how he'd posed for pictures in mock grandeur, his Shriners' fez perched on his head, his thumbs in his lapel, and she simply took the ring, whether she was supposed to have it or not.

Nor did she mention that among his belongings she had found wrapped Christmas presents with little tags inscribed in her father's elegant, old-fashioned hand: "To Genevieve, With All My Love, Pop," "To Claire, With Love from Papa Milligan," " To Coco, With Love from Grandpa," "To Mike, Cheers, from Ed." These, too, she would give to Jake so that Gladys could send them to Paris. Dinah made no mention of a letter, lying on her father's unmade bed, which she had nearly memorized:

November 15, 1952

Dearest Pop,

It's awful to have to tell you this, but we aren't coming after all. It's not that we don't want to. It's that we can't. A few weeks ago, the American Embassy here ordered us to come in for a "special talk." When we showed up, we were told that if we went back to America my passport would be taken away and I wouldn't be able to go back to France. The only way to get it would be for me to snitch on people we had known years ago who are accused of being Communists, of all things. It's hard to imagine anything so silly. Really, it's all such a frightful bore. You and I always feel the same way about everything, and I know you'd find it as ridiculous as I do. But I do feel dreadful about having to disappoint you. There may be a solution, though. Mike and Claire and I want you to think about coming here, and not just for a visit. Move here, Pop. Come live with us permanently—in Paris, and wherever else we go. Mike wants me to tell you that everything you love is here—mountains, fishing, horses and, of course, us.

Think it over, Pop. I miss you so much. Wire me about dates and Mike will send you a ticket and arrange to have you taken to the airport. You will have to get a passport. Ask Dinah to go with you, and bring your birth certificate. I imagine you're not too keen on flying,

*though if you give it a try I dare say you'd rather like it. I'm dying to
take you all around Paris and show you the sights. Claire wants to take
you to the zoo.*

xxxxx V.

*P.S. If you want more details about this political nonsense, ask Dinah
when you go there for Christmas. She can tell you why the government
has all these crazy ideas about me. Of course, I know you can't stand
being at her house. V.*

Everything about the letter bewildered and confused her. She stared at
the date, feeling stupid, until she figured out that this wasn't the letter her
father had received at Christmas last year. That one she found inside a polished wooden box, lined with green satin quilting, that he kept next to his
bed; that letter, much to her puzzlement, said nothing about a visit, nothing about Dinah's testimony, and nothing about Veevi's own subpoena in
Paris—nothing, in fact, except that her pregnancy was going well and that
she missed him as usual. After staring again at the date of the more recent
letter and realizing that Veevi was reporting her hearing in Paris as if it had
happened only a few weeks ago, and not more than a year before, a thin fil-
ament of white-hot anger raced through her. What the hell is this? she said
to herself. Some kind of monkey business? She went over the dates again
and again. Mike said in *his* letter that Veevi had been subpoenaed very
soon after Dinah testified. But hadn't that been almost a year and a half
ago?

She remembered very clearly that Mike's letter to her and Jake had
come last spring, the day of that birthday party for Elsinore's kid, which
had been a nightmare: screaming kids tracking water into the house, ice
cream dripping all over the pool deck, Elsinore running Gussie ragged, the
goddamn hired clown asking her if he could leave his head shots with her
to show Jake, she running into the den to take a hit of Scotch from time to
time just to get through the afternoon. So she wondered, if Veevi's passport
had been taken away that long ago, how could she have promised to come
for this Christmas? It didn't make sense. It didn't add up—it was a complete riddle. And that invitation to their father to come to Paris—
completely insincere. What was she going to do, take him out to bistros
every night with the gang? Veevi, Dinah was quite sure, had issued it know-

ing perfectly well he would never take her up on it. He had lived nearly eighty years without once flying. Sometime in '47, Veevi had written her to encourage him to come, and Dinah, sitting companionably out in the garden with her father while Lorna napped in her baby carriage, had said, "You oughtta fly to Paris, Pop," to which he had sensibly replied, "If God wanted me to fly, he'd have stuck a feather up my ass."

But it was now, recently, that Veevi had written about the passport, and done so, it seemed to Dinah, with a peculiar malice and arch innuendo that seemed at odds with the direct tone she usually took with their father. It was as if she had written it expecting him to read it out loud to Dinah, thereby forcing her to explain herself to the old man. And this in itself was strange and mean, because Dinah and Veevi had never done that sort of thing. They had never once quarreled—at least not openly—for as long as she could remember, and they had never involved their parents in their lives. There had been what Dinah called "moments"—brief and unacknowledged flickers of anger, envy, and resentment that quickly dampened. But having heard stories from friends about great roaring battles between them and their sisters, Dinah knew that she and Veevi were different, and perhaps a bit odd in this respect. They had never screamed or shouted, never gone for months without speaking to each other, never called each other names. Even though Dinah had come to the conclusion that this was strange and not quite *normal*, she was glad of it, because the idea of openly fighting with Veevi filled her with horror.

Dinah took the letter and put it in her purse, and then, thinking better of it, returned it to the pile that would be sent back to Veevi. She'd decided not to say anything to Jake about it. He would see another reason in it for her not to write Veevi about their father's death, and Dinah was determined to write—to be almost spitefully decent under the circumstances. Just what those circumstances were, she hadn't a clue, but it also seemed wrong to feel such anger at her sister. There had to be an explanation. Surely Veevi wouldn't play their father for a fool or deliberately lie to him and deceive him.

That afternoon, as Dinah sat with Mrs. Snyder in her stuffy office, going over arrangements for selling the trailer and occasionally glancing out the window to see lights flashing on small Christmas trees crammed inside the trailers in the trailer park, she learned that her father had arrived back from the mountains late in the night. At about noon the next day, he'd come to Mrs. Snyder's office and picked up the package of mail that Dinah had sent after she'd received a postcard from Dutch Flat with a black-and-white picture of an old run-down saloon and the message "It's colder than a witch's tit here. Home for Christmas. Forward mail to Mrs. Snyder. Yours, Pop." Then, Mrs. Snyder said, maybe fifteen or twenty minutes later, she happened to look out the window and saw him stagger out of the trailer, clutching his chest, and collapse on the ground. Naturally, she'd called the ambulance right away, and Dinah just afterward.

At the funeral home, where she had seen him laid out in blue pajamas, his hard face not tranquil but stilled, Dinah kept trying to figure out what her father had been doing when the pain hit him. Now she knew, and the image of him clutching his chest displaced forever and with terrible clarity what had always been her favorite way of conjuring him up: sitting back in his rocking chair, right leg crossed over left knee, puffing on a pipe, reading the paper.

She had wanted him home for Christmas. Her children loved him but were afraid of him. He was gruff with them, often rebuking Lorna for carrying around a naked doll. But he sat with her once for an entire afternoon when she was home from school with a cold, and read a book he had brought her about a little dragon named Horace who lived in London, at the bottom of the Thames. He set up a canvas tent for Peter in the backyard, before the pool was built, and stayed out there overnight with him, making a campfire and cooking bacon and eggs in an iron skillet. And Lorna and Peter stayed in the trailer with him from time to time, and were fascinated by the sight of his tobacco-stained false teeth sitting overnight in a glass of water. It was true, she acknowledged, that he disliked the largeness and luxury of her house. More often than not, when the family was watching *Toast of the Town* with Jake's mother, Rose, who always came over on Sundays and spent the night, Pop would get up suddenly, look at her and say, "So long, Sadie," to her (she nodding and smiling, never letting on that she'd heard the anti-Semitic insult), and go into the kitchen to have a smoke with Gussie, who served him whatever he wanted and with whom he felt comfortable and superior. They would both leave the house at the same time—he to his trailer, she to her apartment above the garage, and Gussie told Dinah that he always waited until she had climbed up the wooden stairway, turned the key in the lock, and said to him, "It's all right, Mr. Milligan. You go on in to bed."

The last time Dinah had seen him, in May, he'd simply shown up one day, parked the Airstream in the driveway, breezed into the house, stayed for dinner, demonstrated to Peter how to spit brown tobacco juice in a straight line right into the bamboo bushes near the pool, played the piano, sung his old songs, danced a sailor's hornpipe, and taken off the next morning for the Sierras. He'd seemed happy enough to be in her house. Still, he must have said something to Veevi in a letter about not being able to stand it, and once again she felt the old hurt, as old as her memory, as old as her life.

That he had never loved her she was certain. He had wanted a son for his firstborn, and long ago, for the first three years of her life, not disguising his disappointment, he had called her Papa's Baby Boy. Then one day her aunt and uncle had swooped her up and put her in the backseat of their pink Winton and taken her away to their big house in Wilkinsburg. There everything was brown velvet, and her aunt would put her in a hot bath and scrub her neck with Old Dutch Cleanser and talk to a medium named Black Hawk, who she said was always leaving messages in chalk for her on a blackboard in the sewing room. The day they'd taken her home to Beaver Falls she'd run up the stairs and found her mother sitting up in bed wearing a white lace cap and holding a very small wriggling animal that kept rooting at her breast. "What's that?" Dinah had asked. "That's your baby sister," her father said. "Her name is Genevieve. Isn't she a beauty?" Dinah didn't think so.

Her father had had a Model T. On Saturdays they would wash the car together and inspect the parts and repair whatever needed fixing. She was proud of being able to say the big grown-up words—car words like *crankshaft* and *universal joint*. One Saturday, while her mother nursed the new baby on the front porch and she and her father were inspecting the engine, she began to say, "Did you check the carburetor, Daddy?" but something strange happened; the word *carburetor* got stuck. It fired and fired again, and she felt the sound "c-c-c-c-c" jamming her throat, but it wouldn't, couldn't, didn't, come out. The same thing happened again and again that day, and she remembered the way her father looked at her without saying anything, running his eyes over her with an expression of horrified curiosity. From that time on, every waking hour became a struggle against the dark foot in her throat that crushed her words as they fought their way up toward the open air.

Why don't you go into analysis and get yourself straightened out about all this? Jake had said to her more than once. You need to unearth your memories, get into your unconscious. I don't have any unearthed memories, she'd tell Jake. Perhaps it would be better if I did.

When she finished making arrangements with Mrs. Snyder, she returned to the trailer. Stretching out on her father's bed, she held his pillow to her face and sobbed into it, smelling his lonely old smell. It had been three days since the trailer last received an infusion of acrid pipe smoke, and Mrs. Snyder had decided to air out the place for prospective buyers. A hot dry Santa Ana was blowing through the open windows, ruthlessly taking away every last trace of her father.

The spareness of the trailer made her think of Pop's life. He had been a handsome man, tall and slender, with well-defined Scotch-Irish features. He had strong, deft hands, and could build anything, fix anything, charm the poison out of a snake, and tell stories like no one except Jake. But his life had been a series of failures, one after another, always following success, which he couldn't stand. He had sold steel, and was good at it, but every time he got promoted he'd go out and get drunk, wreck the company car, disappear for two weeks, and come home stinking and sorry. A thirty-second-degree Mason, and a Shriner, he'd had to accept Shriner charity after going on a binge and wrecking the car in the summer of 1930, just after Dinah graduated from high school. Having fractured three vertebrae near his neck, he came home from the Shriner rest home completely broke and unable to work, and she'd put aside her plans to start UCLA in the fall, and had gotten a secretarial job instead. He'd given up after that and allowed her to support the family, but she remembered his bitterness, and his permanent contempt for himself, which pursued him everywhere: on his camping trips to the Sierras, on his prospecting trips to the Mojave, on his pilgrimages to the redwoods, under whose shade he would have somebody take his picture, which he would send her to show the kids, with the caption, "Grandpa and the redwoods: guess who's older?"

Later, in the kitchen, she noticed a small tin percolator on the two-burner stove. It was heavy with old cold coffee. A white tin cup, chipped at the rim, sat in the sink, an inch or so of coffee thickening into a sludge at the bottom. "Cough-on-the-puddypot"—put on the coffeepot—he used to say to her mother in the mornings, after they'd moved from Beaver Falls to

Pittsburgh and from Pittsburgh to Philadelphia, a new start coming every two years in the wake of the triple tsunami: promotion, binge, and lost job. Once more he was hopeful, once more he would tap-dance down the stairs, revving up to go out and be the best goddamn steel salesman the Mossberger Knife and Forge Company had ever seen.

·⚜·

After rereading her letter to Veevi a second, third, and fourth time, during which Jake emerged from the bathroom in fresh shorts and T-shirt, shaking his head at her, Dinah searched for an envelope in his desk, pushing aside the clutter: notebooks, business cards, photos, a box of the Wrigley's Doublemint he went through by the pack, sharpened pencils, Scotch tape, scissors, paper clips, boxes of brass studs for the three-hole binders in different colors he used for his scripts, each color signifying a different stage of revision. Among the business cards were innumerable scraps of paper with names, addresses, phone numbers, and availability dates for cameramen, makeup men, stuntmen, doubles, costume people, production designers, actors, actresses, cutters, composers, arrangers, assistant directors—all of them wanting a job. Except when he was writing, she reflected, Jake came into contact with hundreds of people—many of whom she knew nothing about and would never even meet—while her days included long stretches of time alone. Dinah was glad not to have to be around people. She found her own company sufficient and her own thoughts absorbing, and she rarely had lunch with other wives. Nevertheless, seeing these slips of paper, she was reminded of her high school days, when she'd needed a job and had danced in pictures. She had been proud of herself and her high school newspaper had run articles about her, with photographs. But even then, what she had longed for was to be loved, married, and safe, free of the fear of losing her job and not being able to support herself and her parents. After marrying Jake, she had never, ever, wanted to go back to those days, and she never missed working. Yet all these people he came into contact with sometimes made her feel something akin to an envy of her former self—as if she had once been another person, someone she admired who had survived an ordeal, even if it was just the everyday ordeal of having to put food on the table. Sometimes she was haunted by the thought that there was something not quite right in her being free of that struggle.

She found the kind of envelope she was looking for, a plain white one, not the kind that had MRS. JAKE LASKER and their address printed on the back flap. She folded the letter, stuffed it into the envelope, and thought, I might as well be throwing this off the Santa Monica pier. There's not a chance in hell I'm ever going to hear from her again. But she put a stamp on it.

Jake, now dressed, told her he was going to take the kids and pick up his mother and bring her over for the day. "By the way, did Groucho call to say he's coming?" he asked.

"Groucho's coming."

"Good. My mother will have an orgasm—one of the two or three of her life. And, honey, for Christ's sake, this time make sure you don't give him a drink in a green-bottomed glass," Jake said. "I ran into him at Hillcrest the other day, and I thought I'd never hear the end of it. 'I like to see my Scotch when I'm drinking it,' he said."

"I better warn Peter," Dinah said. "Groucho scares him to death."

Jake scowled.

"Don't start now," she said. "Don't be hard on Pete about this. Groucho's awful with little kids. Don't you remember how he snapped at Peter the last t-t-t-time he was here?"

"Two minutes after Groucho arrives, we'll send my mother upstairs to watch TV in our room with Pete, and that will take care of that," Jake said, as if he'd just discovered fire.

"Fine," said Dinah, not really listening to him. There was something she had to do today, and as soon as Jake was out the door she reached for the phone and called Dorshka.

et us find something out of the wind
if that's possible," Dorshka suggested. It was now a little after one o'clock
and very gusty at the open-air tables of the Brentwood Mart. Dorshka was
tying a faded scarf of blue silk under her chin.

Dinah recognized it, and she remembered admiring this touch of high
style in a woman who was otherwise indifferent to fashion. Expensive silk
scarves were the one luxury Dorshka had permitted herself during the days
when she was pouring almost every cent of her high screenwriting fees into
getting refugees out of Europe. She would cover her head with one of these
silk scarves—bright red or emerald green—whenever she drove her red
Buick convertible with the top down. It was exhilarating to see her dashing
around in that car, wisps of red hair escaping from under the scarf. Sometimes she was alone; sometimes with Michael, who sat in the front seat
with his arms crossed, shrinking a little from his mother's flamboyance and
the humiliation of not being old enough to drive; and sometimes with her
lover, Bernhard, who sat back in the sunshine with his eyes closed, blissfully happy.

The two old friends settled at a table sheltered by a big canvas umbrella. "That's more like it," Dorshka said, taking a deep breath. "These
winds—they are relentless, like a big stampede of cattle. Very American!"
Then she gestured discreetly at a woman sitting nearby, a movie star who
was reading the newspaper and, with the tip of the nail on her pinkie,
scratching a tiny itch just inside her right nostril.

"Ah," Dorshka whispered, "today she thinks herself invisible, like the
rest of us civilians. Celebrating the arrival of the New Year with a delicious

hour or two of complete anonymity. Enjoying with all her heart the privileges of the nobody, because so few people are out today."

Dinah loved the expression on Dorshka's face—her mouth taut with a sardonic downturn. "Oh, Dorshka, you must have been s-s-s-something onstage," she said. "Like a great gilded g-g-goblet of vitality and intelligence."

Dorshka smiled at the compliment.

"The critics always compared me to wild beasts. Wild *female* beasts. My Medea was a lioness. My Lady Macbeth a tigress. My Phèdre a—good heavens, now, what *was* my Phèdre?" Dorshka laughed. "But you know, in all these roles it was Ventura's direction that brought it out in me. 'Be strong in grief. Be strong in madness. Be strong in hatred. Even in *weakness* be strong. Don't be a little weak. Be a lot weak!' "

She sighed. "It's been so many years now, and still . . . every day I think of him. My best friend."

"Why didn't you two get married?"

"But, darling, I was already married! Didn't you know that? To Albrecht. And then, when he died, already Stefan and I were working together, and when you spend all day every day working with a man, well—even with lovers it just turns into something else. And it doesn't matter a bit."

Abashed, Dinah struggled to find something to say. The simple mention of Stefan's name opened a valve in her memory and at once something warm, but also troubling, surged through her. "What I liked best about Stefan," she observed shyly, "was that he took the time to explain to me what people were saying—you know, when everyone was speaking German. I was so l-l-l-lost—I didn't understand anything—and he was patient and kind."

"Yes," said Dorshka. "I remember how you two would sometimes laugh when he translated something. Always it was the complaints! He thought they were so funny."

"He was nice to me even though I wasn't, you know, important. He was nice to my mother and father, too."

"I'm sorry about your father, dear," Dorshka said, putting her hand over Dinah's. "He was a real American character."

"I suppose he was. But to me he was just a lonely, embittered old coot who adored my sister and couldn't get along with anybody else."

"You loved him very much."

"I did. He didn't love me."

"No," said Dorshka, not contradicting her. "He didn't. I could tell. I think he liked you, though."

"Yes, but for a child that isn't enough. But no matter. You can't spend your whole life wishing somebody l-l-l-loved you who didn't. Tell me something, dear," Dinah said, plunging ahead. "Did Veevi write anything about coming here for Christmas?—I mean, this Christmas, the one we had last week?"

"No, I don't think so." Dorshka looked puzzled. "Why?"

"Pop seemed to think she was coming, with everyone—Mike, Claire, the baby." She told Dorshka about finding the presents, and the letter, in her father's trailer. "Why would she say they were coming when her passport had been taken away? And why now? Why would she come if it meant she wouldn't be able to leave again?"

"Certainly it's odd, but I don't know anything about it, my dear," Dorshka said, glancing a little to the side. Dinah wondered if she was telling the truth.

"Do me a favor and don't say anything to them about it now. I clearly wasn't supp-p-p-posed to be in on it." She hesitated. "Have they said anything to you about—?"

"Your little talk with the boys?"

Dinah nodded.

"Well, I know they know. I know that Mike wrote to you a year ago. But I haven't seen you, dear, since you came to see me." She smiled at Dinah, who was too absorbed to register embarrassment.

"I suppose," she blurted, "he was so disappointed by Veevi's not coming that his heart just broke. Because of me. He d-d-d-died because of what I did. He must have felt he'd never see her again."

"Oh, Dinah, who knows about all this?" Dorshka scrutinized Dinah's face. "The main thing is, you must be absolutely clear about what you have done and what you haven't done—or else you will torture yourself and everybody else who knows you, and that will not be good for any of us."

Dinah stared down into her coffee cup. Dorshka was offering comfort, but she was also lecturing. Dinah wanted her friend's reassurance, but right now she also felt a keen resentment against Dorshka and her European wisdom, aged and cooled in the cellars of experience, mellowed by education, books, acting, theater, music, and love affairs, none of which Dinah possessed in any comparable degree. How on earth did one get to be like that? How did one get free of the muddle, the sheer incomprehensibility, of everything? Sitting across the plain wooden table from her friend, with the wind blowing hard against the overhead umbrella, Dinah yearned to know what Dorshka knew—she craved Dorshka's ability to make the distinctions and discriminations that she found it impossible to make—but at the same time she hated it when Dorshka treated her as if she knew nothing.

"You see, darling, sometimes our actions have consequences—"

"Dorshka, please! I'm not twelve. I know what I did and why. I can l-l-l-live with myself."

"And that's why you called me on this nice New Year's Day, right?" Dorshka countered. "Of myself or Veevi I am not speaking, Dinah, but of you. By doing this thing, it is yourself you have hurt the most, no?"

"You've said that to me before. It's not true, and I don't want to hear it again."

"Dinah, the trouble with you is that you don't want to hear anything—not from me or anyone else. Like most Americans, you think that you don't have to pay attention to what the world says about you. But you are wrong, Dinah, very wrong. There is no self without the world of other people. Thinking you have done this for love and that therefore it doesn't matter what people think is foolish and naïve. So maybe you hurt your sister and maybe not, or maybe you hurt your father and maybe not. What I am telling you is that the person you injure the most is you—not because of what will happen but because of what already has."

"Look, Dorshka, I know one thing: I haven't done anything to myself that I wasn't prepared to do. I did what I did to keep what I have—because what I have is what I want, and I never had anything before. But I don't like the feeling that maybe—maybe I killed my father."

Dorshka shook her head. "Dinah, come now, you cannot say that this is what you did. It is too easy! Much harder is not to know. And you never will know. *Never!* And anyway, would you have done it if in advance you had known this would happen?"

"You mean, would I have done it if someone had said to me, 'If you t-t-t-testify, you will start something that will end with the death of your father'?"

"Yes. That is exactly what I mean."

"Well, no. I mean, of course not."

"You would have gone to jail? Moved to Mexico?"

Dinah heaved a big sigh. "I don't know. Honestly. What you say to yourself is, Go ahead and get it over with. The sooner you do it, the sooner you'll have your life back like it was before. You don't really think about anything else."

"And you thought this way?"

"Dorshka, I did it to keep my husband from being hurt; I didn't think about whether I'd be hurting anyone else."

"And your friends?"

"What 'fr-fr-fr-friends'?" Dinah exploded. "That's what all these martyrs say: 'Don't rat on your friends.' What f-f-f-fucking fr-fr-fr-friends did I have in the Party? I haven't seen those people in years. They were Veevi's friends, not mine!"

"You know, Dinah, I am afraid that it was Jake who made you do it. If so, he's a *Schwein.*"

"You've said that before, Dorshka, and dammit, it's not true. Nobody made me do it—not Jake, not anybody. I *chose* to do it. And it's not that I *did* it that's driving me nuts, only what's happened *because* I did it."

"Ach, now you talk sophistry. This is disingenuous."

"I'm talking *what*? Save it for a Double-Crostic, Dorshka. Don't talk to me about big concepts and morality and all that jazz, because my eyes'll gl-gl-gl-glaze over. I testified so that my husband could keep working, and I did it because I love him—end of story. I can live with that part of it. I can live without hearing from my sister, or even seeing her again, if that's what she wants. But having Pop die—that, I didn't expect."

"Didn't it ever cross your mind that they would ask you about Veevi?"

"No. I didn't think *I* mattered. It never occurred to me they'd come after me. I'm just a housewife, I'm not a radio writer anymore, I don't have a college education, and I spend my time gardening and schlepping kids and groceries in my station wagon. Was I dumb to think they would never come after me? God yes. Dumb doesn't begin to say it. And I just wish, you know, I just wish Veevi would get in touch. I worry about her. Do you think she's okay?"

"Dinah, dear," Dorshka said with finality. "Look here. There's no mystery—no surprise. She learned that one's passport is not a piece of personal property. And for this, as you know, she and Mike have cut you. This business with your father . . . Well, who knows what that was about? But you and Veevi are out of each other's lives for now. Do you wish absolution? To be forgiven automatically?"

Dinah pondered. "No, it isn't absolution I came for," she said, suddenly aware that there was an entirely different conversation she wanted to have with Dorshka. There were questions she wanted to ask, questions that were years old. But they were like things stored away so long ago in the attic that to come upon them was to experience bafflement, a kind of amnesia even.

She looked over at Dorshka. The grand old woman had loosened her scarf and her broad face seemed to drink in the January light and the rushing winds. Dinah asked her if she had been disappointed by the election.

"I had no hopes, so I am not disappointed," Dorshka replied. "American politics used to fascinate me. I used to think, Well, maybe here there is real democracy. Now it is nothing but a bore. Tell me, even if Stevenson had won the last election, what would he have done for this brutal and hypocritical country? Would he have helped the Negroes? No one here is ever going to help the Negroes. Would he have stopped the McCarthys over here and defended the 'premature anti-fascists'? Is it a surprise that they elect Eisenhower? The war is over seven years and who wins? A blue-eyed general with a German name! And how happy they will be to live under this authority, this military guy! What did all of you expect?" A worldly shrug. "I am sick to death of America. The stupid McCarran Act. The steel strike. And this horrible Korean War. I tell you, I am with all of it fed up—up to here." She made a cutting motion across her throat and smiled wearily—and a bit theatrically, Dinah thought, conceding, however, that she had earned the right to be wearily theatrical.

"I want to talk to you about something else, Dorshka," Dinah said.

"Yes, my dear? What?"

"Well, the old days."

"And what about them?"

"Why did Stefan and Veevi go to Europe? I never understood that."

"He was finished here—you knew that."

"But it was suicide to leave then."

Dorshka shrugged. "He thought it was suicide to stay."

There were other questions Dinah wanted to ask, but Dorshka's blue eyes reflected a certain wariness.

"But didn't you think there would be trouble? Wasn't it like walking into the jaws of, I don't know, d-d-d-death or something?"

"Well, yes. I worried, like everyone else. But Stefan had good friends over there."

Dinah felt certain that Dorshka knew something that Dinah wasn't supposed to know. Enough for now. She glanced at her watch.

"I see you've got to get cracking," Dorshka observed. "It's too windy here anyway." And she retied the blue scarf around her luminous head.

"Some people are stopping by this afternoon," Dinah said. "Would you like to come over?"

Of course Dorshka understood that the open house had been planned well in advance and that Dinah hadn't thought to invite her earlier. "No thanks, my dear. I shall curl up with a good book today. But come whenever you like. I'm glad you still want to see your old Dorshka."

"No, Dorshka, it's the other way around—I'm glad you still want to see *me*."

Dinah felt her hand blanketed by Dorshka's own. "This has not exactly been for you a bed of roses and wine," said the old woman.

Dinah laughed kindly. "Oh, Dorshka—"

"What—did I say it wrong? Come, tell me how it is supposed to go?"

"A bed of r-r-r-roses. And it's 'days of wine and roses'—meaning happy, romantic days, days when you're in love and life is sweet and all that sort of thing."

"Oh God, what can I say? I'm an imbecile!"

They had a good laugh together as they returned, arm in arm, to Dinah's car.

Dinah didn't have much time before she had to get home. Probably Jake's sister Elsinore and her husband and kids were already there, and then after four o'clock there would be a stream of people coming by for drinks and a buffet. In the den, the guys would shout at the top of their lungs over the Rose Bowl. Dinah would distribute gifts to the kids from under the Christmas tree. Later, Jake would run a couple of movies he'd brought from the studio. The only open grocery store was down on Pico, and she needed to pick up extra tonic and ginger ale. Nevertheless, she found herself instead driving straight up to Rabbit Hill, where she sometimes brought the children to fly kites. A plateau high above the UCLA football field, it was now covered in a fresh rippling green in celebration of what passed for winter in Los Angeles.

Dinah parked at the summit and gazed out over the redbrick Romanesque Revival buildings of the university. She remembered when this was still open country—home to rattlesnakes, coyotes, and jackrabbits. In those days the area was covered with patches of lavender, wild mustard, and yucca, a word that had delighted her as a child, though she had found it then, and still found it, impossibly difficult to say. When she had first arrived in California and spent time roller-skating by herself up and down the streets of Hollywood, she used to stop now and then and ask the neighbors who stood there with hoses in hand spraying their flowers to identify the things that grew in their yards. They soon learned the name of the curious child. "Why, that's bougainvillea, Dinah," "That's pittosporum," "That's wisteria," "That's a cherimoya," they explained, and she saw how they tried not to flinch when they heard her struggling to say the words. Learned them, however, she had. She mastered the names of things growing in yards and gardens and mountains and canyons, and at night, after her sister had fallen asleep beside her, a tight curled crescent of lightly breathing child, Dinah would repeat them over and over to herself, without stuttering, in a low chant, remembering their scents and colors, and the way her fingers felt when she touched them: *jacaranda, eucalyptus, oleander, yucca, manzanita, cypress, ceanothus, purple sage.*

Now, as she sat smoking in the car, the windows rolled down, she said their names again. The words had spelled enchantment in those days, when she had practiced ballet, tap, and adagio on the sidewalk, knowing that one day she was going to be a famous movie star.

How long had that lasted, that brief eternity after the Milligans arrived in California, when she'd been happy day after day with a joy that coursed through her lithe and agile body? Two years, she remembered, exactly two years—1922 to 1924—and then her father had gone on his first California binge and come back without a job and they'd moved to a two-room apartment with peeling wallpaper in Boyle Heights, where Alice, their mother, had had to wash the lice out of their hair with kerosene. But like all Pop's binges, this one passed, and soon they moved to a little stucco house in Hollywood, with wisteria hanging down over the porch and a big juniper tree in the front yard. Ed Milligan had found a job selling steel again, Alice's diamond engagement ring was redeemed from the pawnshop, and, since her feet were one size bigger, Dinah got a new pair of roller skates. So you could be happy, she concluded, for a while. It never lasted—something would always wreck it. But then it could come back, and you sucked on it for as long as you could, as if it were an Eskimo Pie melting in the sun after school. If you could roller-skate up and down Hollywood Boulevard by yourself, and get a chocolate soda because Pop was working and Mom gave you a nickel, and you didn't have to look after your sister every minute of the day; if you could stop and talk to the three-thousand-year-old Egyptian guy who wore a turban and made pottery on a wheel in the courtyard of Grauman's Egyptian, and listen to him tell stories about building pyramids and playing with King Tut, then that was happiness—and you could enjoy it and not worry about how long it would last.

But could she do that now? Dinah wondered as she sat tensely in the car, the smoke from her cigarette slowly curling out the window. So far so good: more than a year and a half had passed since she'd testified, and things were fine. It had rocked her, but she'd regained her equilibrium. Jake was working, the kids were growing, life was fine. There were people coming to the house today. So she'd lost her sister. That wasn't a tragedy, was it?

Oh, come on, she said to herself. Forget it, forget it.

Yet she hunched behind the wheel, taking long drags on her cigarette, her heart pounding. The beautiful day oppressed her, even angered her. She remembered her father coming downstairs after their first six months in California and going out to the porch to pick up the newspaper and growling, "Another goddamn beautiful day." That pure air outside seemed false, like an aging actress who had made herself up to have the color and eyes of an ingenue. Something inside her felt ready to burst with exasperation. Since her father's death, everything had become muddled and complicated. Even after talking to Dorshka, she didn't understand anything except that her father had died and that it was somehow her fault.

She had been remembering things from the past, thinking about them for months now, but she couldn't bring herself to probe and resurrect those old days with Dorshka. It seemed that they mattered somehow, that they held clues, but she didn't know to what. All she knew was that because of them, her fate had changed—that is, because of them she had emerged from some kind of invertebrate life and had found that she could pull herself out of the lower-middle-class muck and drag herself up, slowly and agonizingly, onto the beachhead of a larger world, which held out other possibilities—a picked-up education and love—consuming love.

She glanced again at her watch and felt that she really had to get going, but instead she reclined against the seat. There were no other cars here this afternoon, but Rabbit Hill was a well-known spot for necking. Kids drove up at night in their souped-up Fords and Chevys; sometimes, when she brought the children here to fly their kites, she saw used condoms in the dirt. She remembered her own years of high school groping, and then, later, the contorted postures of backseat sex. After she started going with Jake, it seemed that it had all happened to another person, although at parties she sometimes told the story of the Saturday night she had been necking with a boy in the living room of her parents' West Hollywood bungalow, when her father woke up and decided to have a smoke. Noiselessly gliding up to the sofa in his bare feet and dressed in a long nightshirt, he sat down in the dark, right on top of Dinah and her date. "All hell broke loose," she would say. "Pop screamed, I screamed, and the boy screamed. Then he ran out of the house and I never saw him again."

Except that it hadn't happened *quite* that way. The boy, like so many of the fellows Dinah went out with, happened to catch sight of Veevi the next time he came over, and that was the end of Dinah's romance. In fact that boy, Lester Wooten, finding himself only one among a crowd of Veevi's adorers, had made himself her valet, and would show up late on Saturday afternoons to iron her dress before she went out with someone else. For this constant display of devotion, Lester waited for his reward. And what was that? Nothing more than a look, a swift, patronizing glance that he took as assurance, even for the briefest instant, that he was the court favorite. He would never know that as he loped up the little brick path to their house, Veevi, all of fourteen and besieged with suitors, would murmur to Dinah and Alice from behind the screen door, "Oh God, here comes that drip Lester Wooten again."

After that calamity, whenever Dinah and Veevi both had dates on a Saturday night, Dinah made sure the boy arrived at the house after Veevi left and always refused to invite him in later. She allowed no kissing at the front door, but agreed to drive somewhere to neck before her date took her home, and in this way discovered Rabbit Hill, though it hadn't yet had a name.

Those first stirrings of pleasure, but also of strange waves of a nausea-like shame, had been shattering. And the surprise of it: so *this* was what Pop's warnings and Mom's evasions were all about! Dinah took to physical love as if it were a suddenly discovered and hitherto unsuspected talent. The swells of shame became weaker than the trances of pleasure that overcame her during long sessions of kissing and groping. She remained "good," however, through the end of high school and for several years afterward, mindful of Pop's thoroughly unoriginal and oft-repeated warning that "familiarity breeds contempt." That this was true, she and Veevi knew from what they called their parents' "sex fights," during which the girls would make faces at each other and cover their ears with their pillows as they overheard, late in the night, "Please, Alice, please," from their parents' bedroom and their mother's muffled explosions of anger. The next morning they would see the red rubber douche bag and its revolting syringe hanging over the towel rack in the bathroom, and again they would make faces, because they sensed it had something to do with those fights during the night. Occasionally, they asked their mother to explain the facts of life to them. Her lemon-mouthed circumlocutions cracked them up; they would get into bed later and repeat what she had said until they doubled up with laughter, tears running down their cheeks. But for Dinah, everything about sex seemed nevertheless alien and scary. From whispered hints at school, she heard that the first time would hurt, and she became afraid. Then one night she sat on the toilet seat as Veevi, then thirteen, took a bubble bath and laughingly described, amid a sea of pink foam, how she had recently lost her virginity to a much older boy. Had it hurt? Dinah wanted to know. Yes, but not for long, Veevi had answered, and lifted her manicured foot to turn on the hot water again. The pain went away. Actually, doing it was sort of fun, she said, especially if you could be on top; it was like riding a horse (the new boyfriend had just given her one, at his family's Topanga ranch). It wasn't true, either, what their father had said, that boys didn't respect you if you did it with them; the boyfriend was crazy about her and would do anything for her now that she had "gone all the way" with him. Dinah remained unpersuaded. The mechanics, as Veevi described them, seemed horrible, and she decided then and there that this was something she could easily postpone until some sublime great love would make it inevitable, painless, and glorious.

Later, Dinah necked and petted on Rabbit Hill with Dexter Cleary, the boy she won dance contests with. They did all but "it" in the backseat and the front seat of his Chevy, with her on her back, on her side, and on his lap, and when the interior of the car became steamy and she rolled down the window to drink in the wine of the California night, she marveled at the pleasure she was feeling and wondered what the things she *wasn't* doing were like. But she wasn't in love with Dexter, and in the end she found it easy to say no. She was going to high school and dancing in pictures and contests and planning to go to UCLA in the fall. On summer nights when it stayed light until late, she could look out the front window while necking with a boy—and there were several after Dexter—and see the university, and imagine the boys she would meet in college—intelligent, ambitious, good-looking fellows, good dancers, who would tell her she was pretty, like her for having a sense of humor, and take her any day over her sister.

Then just as she graduated the Depression hit, her father got drunk, cracked up the car, and crushed his third, fourth, and fifth vertebrae. While he was convalescing as a charity case at the Shriner home, she said good-bye to her dream of UCLA and got a job; thank God she had taken typing at Hollywood High. Two years later, in the fall of 1932, driving west on Wilshire in the blinding sun after a dreary day's work at Sprague Paper, she pulled into a gas station and was startled when a tall young man with wiry blond hair poked his head through the window. "Hey, Dinah Milligan! I've been wondering what happened to you!"

Everett Gilfillen told her he had admired her in high school but had never had the courage to ask her out. How 'bout now? When he picked her up in his Ford to take her to the movies, he told her she looked pretty, and, much to her astonishment, later in the evening over ice cream sodas he said that he liked her stutter. It was cute, he told her boldly, taking her hand across the table with a grown-up assurance that gave her flutters in the groin. When he finally met Veevi, he took no interest in her. Her sister called Everett "dull," and Dinah wondered if there was something wrong with him for being so immune to Veevi's dazzle. She said so to her mother, who put her plump arms around Dinah and said, "Sweetie pie, haven't I always told you your time would come?"

Everett was the first man Dinah slept with, and because of that she married him—after a number of pregnancy scares, and muscles made stiff and sore from vehicular fornication on Rabbit Hill. Sitting now in her station wagon on New Year's Day, 1953, she recalled Everett's hot breath, his urgent hands sliding past her garters, his helpless, in-the-way, boiling-over erections, her long open legs colliding at peculiar angles with the steering wheel and dashboard, the way he would put his arm around her afterward, when they were sitting up again, knowing they would have to leave soon. The very first time they did it—and it *had* hurt—he had apologized. He told her he loved her, and every time after that he told her he loved her, and she liked hearing him say it. Her parents told her he was a fine boy and a good catch. After they were married at the Christian Science church in

Hollywood—Dinah in a white dress and veil Mom had made for her—she and Everett moved into their own apartment in West Hollywood, established a routine in bed, and planned the life they would have if the Depression ever ended. For their wedding present, his father had given him a job in the family restaurant, but Everett wanted a business of his own.

But I knew then, she said to herself now, lighting a new cigarette, checking her watch but desperate to stay with her memories, feeling like a thief who has broken into a home and come upon a treasure just as the owners are pulling into the driveway, I knew then that I'd married him just to get away from home—from Pop sitting every day in a rocking chair on the porch, his old slippers on his feet and his neck in a brace, snapping at Mom, who snapped right back at him. Her mother had married her father in 1911, when she was eighteen and he was thirty-eight, and on the second day of their honeymoon, in Norfolk, Virginia, he'd told her to stay in the hotel while he went to see a man who owed him money. At about four in the morning, he'd come back drunk and stumbling, his money belt stolen—he didn't believe in banks, which he said were controlled by the Jews—and his two front teeth knocked out. Dinah was born nine months later.

Shortly after Dinah married Everett, Veevi started dancing in pictures, at Marathon. Things happened fast once Talcott Engel set eyes on her. The elder son of Marathon's founder, Lionel Engel, Tal started bringing Veevi to his parents' beach house and Veevi invited Dinah. Once—only once—Everett had come with her, but he brooded all afternoon, because he'd left his parents to take care of the restaurant, and he was worried that something would go wrong. He had nothing to say to anyone he met. Dinah felt guilty. She'd felt sorry for him as he drove home stiffly upright to keep his sunburned back from rubbing up against the car upholstery, that is, until he said, "You better watch it—they're all Roosevelt lovers. They'll sell the country out to the reds and the other Jewish elements. Did you see all those Jews jabbering at each other today? They sure do stick together. Just you wait and see. Father Coughlin has a lot to say about them, yes sirree, and if you spent Sunday afternoons with me instead of with that chichi crowd you'd figure it out for yourself, like I have."

"Everett," she said. "Your thinking about J-J-J-Jews is icky. Keep it to yourself, okay?" They drove the rest of the way home in silence, and she smoked and looked out the window and thought, I've got to live with him for the rest of my life.

Soon enough, Dinah stopped listening to Everett. She was much more interested in thinking about the things people talked about at the Engels'. She would situate herself on the margins of the lively group of men and women—writers and actors—who gathered around Veevi. Stretched out on a pool chaise with her shining brown hair done up in braids and a straw hat shading her face, her only makeup bright red lipstick and mascara, she reigned as an icon of perfection. Her every gesture was graceful; Veevi was incapable of an awkward or a clumsy movement. No one questioned her right to sovereignty—least of all herself. Veevi's self-assurance, Dinah marveled, was absolute. Wherever she was, there was laughter, her own a gay chortling gasp, often laced with mockery.

For a while, Dinah didn't understand the new words she was hearing at the Engels'. She didn't know what people meant when they referred to the "Comintern" and the "popular front" and "workers' committees" and "five-year plans." But she caught on fairly quickly. People talked, it seemed to her, both seriously and ironically at the same moment. "Hey, all you toilers on the Marathon lot," said Clifford Boatwright, Jr., one afternoon. "Just a reminder: tomorrow night, my house, come one come all. Mrs. Parker and Mr. Stewart are coming to talk to us about forming an anti-Nazi league." Boatwright was from the East Coast, the only son of a journalist famous for his squibs and jibes at American provincialism, and he'd grown up knowing all the famous writers of the teens and twenties. He wasn't handsome—at least, according to Veevi—but he had taut skin drawn over a face with a high forehead and high cheekbones, and his expression was simultaneously vigilant and mischievous. Dinah thought something was going on between him and Veevi. "I can't help it if he's crazy about me," Veevi said with a shrug when Dinah asked her about it. Boatwright wasn't Jewish, but he was the one who explained to Veevi, who then explained to Dinah, that they were "shiksas." He also translated *schmuck, schlemiel, meshuga,* and other Yiddish terms for them, and did so with such pleasure, such appreciation of nuances, that it was as if he were introducing them to fine wines.

By this time Veevi had become a movie star. The fan magazines said simply that she'd been "discovered on the Marathon lot," but the real story was different. Dinah had taught her all the dance steps she would need to get a job, and she became a dancer in the chorus of an ice-skating movie at Marathon. One afternoon, Tal Engel spotted her taking a break in the midday sun with the other dancers outside the freezing soundstage. She knew who he was and complained about working conditions—the long hours, the treacherous condition of the ice rink. She was beautiful and fearless, and he was smitten. He did nothing about her complaints, but had her tested instead and put under contract. While Dinah spent her days typing and her evenings doing the laundry, Veevi starred in "costume dramas," in which she played one ingenue after another, usually a princess or a countess endangered by medieval upstarts or French assassins. Audiences loved her, but she complained to Dinah that she felt silly when she acted and hated being on display. Money and fame came easily, however, as well as a house of her own in Beverly Hills. Sometimes during the week, in the evenings, Dinah dropped in to borrow books from the "library," as it was called. On her lunch hour, over a ham-and-cheese sandwich and a Coke in a nearby coffee shop, or on a bench in Echo Park, Dinah would manage to read a few pages. When she started in on *The Communist Manifesto,* she hid it inside a Mary Roberts Rinehart novel—Everett would have had a fit. She used the same novel to hide *The ABC of Communism.* When she started reading *Capital,* she put it inside the dust jacket for *The Grapes of Wrath. Capital* was very slow going, and she had no one to talk to about it. She certainly couldn't ask Tal Engel to explain it. He was obsessed with Veevi, eager to lift her out of her background, hungry to have her all to himself; obviously he wasn't interested in talking to Dinah, and he already resented the time she spent with Veevi, who, Dinah could see, wasn't in love with him. At the Engels', people were nice enough to her— she was asked to join volleyball games and to dance when music was piped out to the pool deck—but a couple of years went by and nobody paid any real attention to her.

Dinah took a deep breath and closed her eyes. The Santa Anas were still blowing hard, slanting the blades of fresh grass on the hill. She would be late to her own open house, late to greet her guests, late to get them drinks, to laugh and joke, and find them a place by the fireplace in the den. She remembered now just how shy and insignificant she had felt during those early years. The way those people talked! She was sure they had all been to college. They were so quick, and they always had so much to say! Whatever they talked about, they looked at from a thousand different angles: fascism and Spain and Roosevelt and strikes and Stalin and Clifford Odets and the

New Deal and the Group Theatre and Hitler and *The New Yorker* and a million other interesting things that were new to Dinah.

Sometimes she found herself stretched out on a towel among the crowd gathered around Norma Levine. Small-boned, with elegantly coiffed strawberry-blond hair, she never went into the pool but wore expensive bathing suits and used a cigarette holder. She had written stories for *The New Yorker* before she gave in to the lure of a two-thousand-dollar-a-week salary in Hollywood. Dinah loved listening to her, because she often caught Dinah's eye when she spoke, as if she were seeking confirmation from her, and because she was always telling stories or anecdotes or remembering bits and pieces of things—as if the world consisted of nothing but stories.

Dinah suddenly remembered how startled she had been upon hearing Norma say, "All I know is the girl walking in front of me turned to the other girl and said, 'And what did I get out of it? Nothing but pleasure!'" It was the way people laughed when they heard lines like that that Dinah had wondered about. How did they know *when* to laugh, and *what* was funny? For every utterance, there always seemed to be a web of unspoken mutual understandings. Dinah also noticed Veevi watching Norma, watching and listening, as if Veevi were deciding how best to handle this rival, who was seductive not because she was beautiful—which she wasn't—but because she was interesting and intelligent and fun. And so Dinah studied Norma, too: the ease with which she told stories, the way she nodded her head sagely while listening to others, the impression she gave that sitting around and talking was the most interesting and absorbing thing in the world. Once Norma told a story about an actor from the Group Theatre—Art Squires, whom Dinah would later get to know but who, in the summer of 1935, had only just come to L.A. under contract to Warner Brothers. "So get this," Norma said, squinting against the sun, so that her entire face now seemed centered by her full red mouth, "Phoebe, his wife, goes out and buys *a hundred and thirty-six* pairs of shoes." She enunciates the syllables very slowly and pauses before adding, "And when he calls his mother-in-law to tell her they've just bought a forty-room mansion with an oak-paneled living room and a screening room for fifty and a wine cellar for hundreds of bottles of vintage-this and vintage-that, her first comment is, 'Is there swimming on the premises?'" which Levine—at some point Dinah began thinking of her by her last name—delivered the line in a perfect Yiddish accent. Dinah saw Veevi taking in Levine's success, and saw how, the following Sunday, as Levine emerged from the dressing room and started walking toward them in the sun, Veevi said sotto voce, "Oh, here comes Twinkle-Tits." Someone laughed, then somebody else, and then, when Levine arrived, Veevi said to her, "Great bathing suit, Norma. Looks terrific on you. Where'd you get it?"

But Dinah also realized that it didn't make all that much difference whether or not Veevi spoke. She was so lovely to look at that all she had to do was exist. Nothing else was required of her. Clifford Boatwright stood up in front of her one day and said, in front of everyone, "If eyes were made for seeing, / Then Beauty is its own excuse for being," and bowed, with one hand on his belly and the other behind his back, like a cowlicked boy of ten who has just finished reciting at a school assembly.

No one got more pleasure out of the sheer fact of Veevi's existing than Lionel J. Engel, who talked incessantly of the day when he would give her and Tal an "extravanganza-type" wedding by the ocean, with all Hollywood present, although so far the young couple hadn't set a date. L.J. liked having Veevi by his side when eminent drop-ins dropped in on Sundays. Since she, however, much preferred the company of the young writers from New York, she always managed to get from one side of the pool to the other— from the shady side with the red-and-white-striped umbrellas, where L.J. and his producer pals sat and went for "dips" in the pool, to the dazzling sunny side, where the younger set slathered themselves in suntan lotion, and, when they reached the broiling point, threw the Spanish Loyalists to the wind and hurled themselves into the water in an ecstasy of aquatic self-immolation. L.J. was always sending a maid or a butler over to summon her while she was in the midst of the political discussions. Later on, she would ask Dinah to fill her in on who had said what—which, naturally, helped Dinah in her poolside education.

Among the Sunday drop-ins were the sons and daughters of other Hollywood pioneers—they'd gone to the same birthday parties and Ivy League colleges as the Engel boys. Some of them were younger men who were fond of L.J.; they appreciated him—he wasn't quite the cliché they accused their own fathers of being.

Dinah had learned that *The Haberdasher,* the novel that Talcott Engel had published at the age of twenty-two, was closely modeled on something that had happened in real life, when L.J. had visited him at Princeton. Invited to dinner at his son's mostly non-Jewish fraternity, the old man had sensed both his son's tremulous fear of being embarrassed by him and the other boys' anti-Semitic truculence. When one scion of a Connecticut insurance dynasty turned to him at table and said, "Tell me, Mr. Engel, have you ever read Voltaire?" L.J. answered, with a faint smile and a deliberately thickened accent, "You mean Vol-taire Vin-chell?" This incident was captured word for word in Tal's novel. His narrator said, "By this inspired gesture of preemptive and ironic self-deprecation, Dad redeemed himself so completely in my eyes that I quit college and asked him for a job in the mailroom at the studio," which is where his rise to the top begins. As for Tal, he had finished Princeton, but he hadn't started in the mailroom: he started almost at the top, as the head of the story department. From there, his father wanted him to become head of production—though everybody else knew that what Tal really wanted was to quit the business and move with Veevi to Vermont to write novels. He was simply waiting for his younger brother, Irving, to finish college.

One Sunday morning in the early summer of 1936, Dinah was standing in the kitchen in the tiny, hot West Hollywood apartment where she and Everett lived, her bathing suit rolled up in a towel. As usual, she asked if he wanted to go out to the Engels' that day. "Not on your life," he said. "And I don't see how you can stand going out there week after week with all those pushy Jewboys who think they own the world. Hell, they don't *think* they own the world. They *do* own the world. Roosevelt's in the hands of the Jew bankers. And can't you see that those Engel boys and their friends are all just a bunch of Jew Communists puttin' one over on the old man? Everybody there's always talkin' about how great it is in Russia and how Russia's damn near heaven on earth. Well, if you ask me, they oughtta be put up against a wall and shot, the whole pack of 'em."

"Everett," she said quietly, "how is it possible for the Jews to own Roosevelt on the one hand and be C-C-C-Communists on the other? Isn't that a c-c-c-contradiction?"

"Don't you contradiction me, Dinah. Father Coughlin says the Jews'll do anything to keep in power. They fake being Communists so they can keep on being capitalists. They've got it all figured out—they have since the beginning of time. They're all in it together, with the banks. Come on, it's as clear as one and one makes two."

She didn't feel like arguing with him—he no longer interested her. All she knew was that she lived for those Sundays at the beach. Last Sunday he had needled and wheedled her into staying in town. They had spent the afternoon working at the restaurant, and then his mother had given them tickets to go hear Aimee Semple McPherson at the Angelus Temple. When the great evangelist accidentally spilled a few drops from a glass of water on an electric microphone and knocked herself out, Dinah let out a rapid-machine-gun burst of laughter. Everett was so furious that he shut her up by digging his fingers deep into her shoulder, bruising her. For the third week in a row, they didn't have sex, and Everett turned up the volume on Father Coughlin, whom he listened to by himself while Dinah ironed clothes in the kitchen.

So this Sunday she went out to the Engels' alone, and in the late afternoon, sitting with Veevi's friends on the warm pool deck, her towel draped around her shoulders just like everyone else, and ignoring her stutter, she told a story—the one about McPherson. To her delight, everyone laughed. Norma Levine took off her dark glasses and smiled at her, as if Dinah were there for the first time.

And then, though it was not on the subject, or any other subject, Dinah ventured another story—about the time when she and Veevi were little girls and their father invited his boss over for tea. When the man arrived, they could all see that he had a very large nose—a huge nose, an enormous nose. She and Veevi kept staring at it, and their mother kept giving them looks, trying to get them to stop. Then her mother poured the tea. And as she handed the cup to the gentleman, she said, "Would you like cream and sugar in your nose?"

Again, laughter—loud chesty laughter. Then a rather hefty man she couldn't remember ever seeing before asked her to tell him the story again, and the Aimee Semple McPherson story as well. They went off by themselves to sit at the edge of the pool so they could dangle their legs in the water, and she repeated the stories. This time he laughed till tears streamed down his cheeks. His English wasn't bad, just slow and deliberate, and he had a thick accent that she couldn't identify. Shyly, she asked him where he was from, and he replied that he had been born in a town called Razgrad. Did she know where that was? Hadn't a clue, she said. It's in Bulgaria, he answered, and she confessed that she didn't know where that was, either. "Is it in Europe?" she asked, and then added, "I must seem like an idiot to you. But I sure as hell don't know where it is." He described the complicated geography of the Balkans and then told her that as a young man he had gone first to Moscow and then Berlin to work in the movies. His name was Stefan Ventura, he said, and he had arrived in America only a week ago. He was a director and was going to make movies. He had been promised a free hand by L. J. Engel, who had arranged his passage from France.

"Why does your name sound Sp-Sp-Spanish?" she asked him.

He explained to her that he was a Sephardic Jew, and that his ancestors had come to Bulgaria hundreds of years ago after being expelled from Italy, where they had gone after being expelled from Spain. "Many Jews here in America, they speak Yiddish, but my family, we speak Ladino. Have you ever heard it?"

He sang a little snatch of something in Ladino, in a gloriously deep voice, and she recognized the word *Hermosa* and smiled. Dinah adored him instantly. Two minutes after he introduced himself, she would have died for him. Already in his forties, he was the first European at the Engels' with whom Dinah had ever had a conversation, the first one she had actually ever met. He was a large man with a hunkering yet gentle and uncertain gait, as if he felt his body to be powerful but not necessarily graceful. If he did not shave twice a day, his face looked as if it were smudged with charcoal. In his fingers he always held a lit cigarette. Although he had been in Los Angeles for only a short time, the California sun had already turned his face brown.

Dinah found his large blue eyes arresting. He had a way of screwing them up, partly as a barrier against the rising smoke of his cigarette, but partly to concentrate, it seemed. It was a look that contained its own opposites—mocking appraisal and at the same time complete bewilderment. When he laughed again at her story, it was with a slow thunderous motion welling upward from a cavern deep within his chest. "I can see this moment very well," he said. "The lady is full of excitement and then suddenly she is knocked out—isn't that what you say? Knocked out like a boxer, lying cold on the stage in her long white robe. It is delicious. Come," he said, gesturing for her to get up. "I will get us something to drink, and you will tell me more about this fruit compote of a city."

Dinah felt him looking at her movements and her body with interest, and the blood rushed to her cheeks. Her insides convulsed with a faint sexual nausea—simultaneous shame and desire—and she sensed that he could observe that, too. He asked her about herself. She told him about being born in Pittsburgh and moving to Philadelphia and then coming out to California with her family in 1922. She told him about the miserable summer heat and bitter cold of the East, and that when she got off the train she thought she had landed in paradise. "It's different now, there are more people, but it is still p-p-paradise for me," she said.

He kept asking questions, and soon she was telling him about her father and his father before him—how her grandfather had fought in the Civil War, but on the wrong side, for the South, because the girl he loved in Little Rock, Arkansas, wouldn't marry him unless he volunteered for the Confederacy. Then he'd ended up at Andersonville. Did he know what Andersonville was? She explained that it was this terrible kind of camp, in Georgia, where men from the Union had starved and died like flies, but her grandfather had been a guard there, and then, after the war, when he'd gone back for a visit to his home town of Bellaire, Ohio, they'd almost lynched him, and had the rope and the tree all ready, when suddenly somebody cried out, "Say, that's Ed Milligan. Don't string him up! He got us blankets and medicine and extra food!"

Suddenly Ventura thrust out a large hand and gripped her forearm. "Your grandfather fight in the Civil War? Yes? For the South? Is this the story you tell me just now?"

She nodded.

"Oh, my God—I must tell you, this is a wonderful chance. Please, do something for me. Please read a story I give you. Here."

The next thing she knew, he pulled a small book out of his jacket pocket. "You know Pushkin?"

She shook her head, embarrassed.

"No matter. Read this translation, please, and tell me: can I from this make a movie about the American Civil War? Read it, please, quick. It take maybe one hour. Then please to telephone me." He took a fountain pen from his pocket and wrote a number inside the book, under his name, and when she looked at the letters and numbers she found them enchanting. They were different from any letters and numbers she had ever seen— taller, with slanting lines and loops and flourishes. The seven had a horizontal line through it, and the one looked almost like a seven. So this was Europe, she thought—this flowing, elegant way of writing letters and numbers.

"Okay," she said simply. "I'll read it at work."

"Work? You make a movie now? You have a good role?"

"No." She smiled. "I'm not an actress. I'm not in the m-m-m-movies at all—at least not anymore."

"You not in the movies? How can this be? You are so beautiful I think you must be an actress."

No one had ever spoken to her this way, and she tried not to show him how it made her feel. She explained that she used to dance in pictures but that she had gone to work after high school at a paper company and now had a new job as a secretary for a big oil company. Then, sensing that he would understand immediately, she tried out words she had been hearing at the Engels' but had never used before. "I'm a real proletarian. L-L-L-Lumpen as all hell. I don't think there's anyone here who makes less than a thousand a week. I take home eighty d-d-d-dollars a month. I'm lucky to have a job at all. But you're right. At one time I wanted to be an actress. But, as you can see, I stutter."

"You what? I don't know this word."

"I can't say certain words." Of course, now that she was describing the problem she wasn't stuttering. So she imitated herself stuttering.

"Ah, I see," he said. "But it's charming, this—what do you call it?—'stutter.' If you are not an actress, is not because you stutter."

"How can someone be an actress if she stutters? What if Hamlet said, 'To b-b-b-be or not to b-b-b-be'?"

"It would be very interesting, I think. We see he truly hesitates!"

So far, she hadn't identified herself as Veevi's sister or said anything about being married. Instead, she kept saying to herself, My God, at last someone out here has noticed me, and look who it is. A famous director. A big, strong, handsome guy. A smart guy—an interesting, warm guy. Every artery, every vein in her body swelled with love.

"Please, can you help me? Please to find someone to teach me to drive?"

"You want to learn how to drive?"

"They send a car and chauffeur. The chauffeur tell me he want to act in the movies." Another big laugh thundered from Ventura's chest. "When I learn to drive, I will tell the chauffeur, 'You sit in the back and I drive you.'"

Dinah said she would teach him.

"Wonderful. We go now."

"Now?"

"Yes, now! Why not?"

She felt others' eyes upon her as she and Ventura, his hand lightly touching her elbow, made their way from the crowded poolside toward the stone path to the highway. For once she was the object of attention, and she enjoyed it. It seemed as if her life had been transformed in an instant. Everett came to mind for a moment, and then all thoughts of him vanished.

In the car, she explained the different gears and instructed him to watch her shift from one to the other as she steered the 1930 Ford along the Pacific Coast Highway all the way to Zuma Beach. There she found a stretch of gravel that had been laid down as a parking lot. It was late in the day and only a few cars remained, and there was plenty of room for him to practice. They changed places, and she told him where to put his feet and hands, leaning toward him but not deliberately touching him. He made the usual errors, and laughed at them, but he wasn't embarrassed, and, unlike her husband and her father, showed no particular interest in proving himself competent with a machine. It didn't seem important to him to learn how to handle a car—just a necessary skill he had to acquire. She had never known a man who was indifferent to engines, and found it astonishing. At one point, he bumped into a parked car and she looked around, worried that its owner would come rushing up from the beach, kicking sand clouds behind him, but nothing happened. She told Ventura how to shift into reverse, and he lurched the car backward. "I stop now," he said. "Otherwise I kill us both. Come, let us to walk a little."

By this time the sun had dipped below the horizon and the air was getting cooler. People were packing up picnic baskets, shaking sand out of towels, ordering kids to pick up their pails and shovels and carry beach balls to the car. Ventura took off his shoes and socks, and Dinah took off hers. After tucking them into the sand, they began to walk north. The sight of his white feet gave her a heart-squeeze of pity and embarrassment—they seemed so tender and European, not like the rough brown extremities of the California boys she knew.

Ventura took her elbow. "I am going to make great American movies," he said in his resonant bass. "I take old stories from Europe and make them American. The old man, Engel—they call him L.J.," he said, laughing, "was born in Odessa. Is not so far from Razgrad, and I am Jew and he is Jew, and he say to me, 'We are landsmen, almost.' I hope he still think so after I make a movie."

Dinah told him that someone (it was Veevi) had recently gotten her a job as L.J.'s secretary. The first day, she noticed how overstuffed his filing cabinets were, so she offered to go through them and throw out the old, unnecessary files. Fine, he said, but make copies of them first. Then, a few days later, he heard her talking on the phone, realized she had a stutter, and fired her. He had no idea that she came to his beach house on Sundays. And it made no difference that she was Veevi's sister. She had quit her job at the paper company, there were no other secretarial jobs at the studio, and she had panicked. She had to have a job, she told Ventura. Her father hadn't worked in years; her mother made a few dollars altering people's clothes, but mostly she just looked after her father. At the unemployment office they'd told her that there was an opening at Claggett Oil, where she had been working for the past several months. "I don't know why I'm t-t-t-telling you all this," she said finally.

"Because," he said, stopping, turning her around, and putting his big hands on her shoulders, "you are a very nice girl."

For a moment she thought he was going to give her a grandfatherly pinch on the cheek, but then he embraced her and kissed her, holding her so tightly she felt the breath squeezed out of her. The stubble from his afternoon shadow was so rough it scraped against her chin. Nothing in her life had prepared her for such an embrace, such a kiss, but she didn't resist.

This is *it*: I am going to love him for the rest of my life, she thought. He let go of her, and they walked some more, grazing each other's arms and shoulders. It was dusk, and the beach was deserted. As they walked large waves broke, rushing and foaming up toward their ankles. "Look," she said. "The tide is coming in." He took her hand and for a while they stood facing the ocean, watching the waves. He let go of her hand and took her arm. "We go back now?" They turned around and headed back, their feet lightly splashing in the cold water that kept returning and swirling upward to the edges of the packed wet sand. Then he stopped and took her in his arms and kissed her again. "Will you come to my house tonight?" he said, his voice deep and tender.

She turned her face away and put her head on his shoulder. "I c-c-can't. I'm married," she said. And she explained that her husband was a bigot who thought everyone at the Engels' was a Jew and a Communist. But she had to go home to him.

"Why you marry such an imbecile?"

"I don't know," she answered. She almost said, "I didn't know any Jews at the time!"

He crushed her to him. "You are a nice, sweet girl. Not a movie girl. You smell like California. This anti-Semite imbecile husband—does he tell you that?"

"No." The sound came out muffled as she pressed her face to his chest.

Awkwardly, they slid down to the sand and he lowered himself onto her. From his throat came deep murmurs. He called her "Bebcho" again and again, and she loved the way the word sounded, like a bubble of thick honey. Kissing her, he scraped his face along her cheek, her neck. Her chin stung with the scraping, and she didn't care.

Still, when he finally plunged inside her and seemed to devour her, she felt that it was not her he wanted but something else—release from loneliness, perhaps, and from uncertainty and worries he hadn't even begun to mention.

Afterward, as they drove back in silence toward Santa Monica, she kept her eyes on the road and chewed the inside of her cheek. He reached over to squeeze her hand, and her thigh, but his touch seemed kind, not passionate, and she knew at once that she had made a mistake.

When they walked back into the Engels' house, everyone had already eaten. They were having coffee in the living room, which had enough chintz-covered sofas to accommodate at least thirty people. Thus, there was an audience for Ventura, who, accepting a cognac, explained to Lionel and Edy Engel and their guests that he had just had his first driving lesson. With various physical gestures, he began to caricature himself. Realizing that his story was also meant to protect her, Dinah slipped away to the powder room, where, almost immediately, Veevi barged in.

"Great whisker burn," she said, her eyes glittering. "You can only see it about a mile away."

Dinah was putting on fresh lipstick and observed her sister's face behind her in the mirror. "I don't know what you're talking about. I got t-t-t-too much sun."

"Oh, come on. That's a whisker burn. Besides, the sun went down a long time ago."

"Okay, so it's a wh-wh-wh-whisker burn. So what?"

"Well, don't get any ideas. He's supposedly a great lecher. He's bedded every great European actress in the world, including Dietrich. God only knows what kind of pain in the ass he'll be with *me* once we start shooting the picture. You did it with him, didn't you?"

"You can't be serious," Dinah said, using one of Veevi's pet phrases. "Why would I do something d-d-d-dumb like that?"

"You've got that look. I know you, Ina," Veevi said, using Dinah's nickname.

Dinah looked at herself in the mirror. She did have that look. "You're doing a picture with him?" she said.

"That's what they tell me," Veevi said, and shrugged. "Some Russian thing he wants to do American. The thing is, I haven't actually met him yet. How on earth could you even neck with him, Dinah? He's so old. And hairy. It would be like necking with a gorilla." She made a face.

"Listen, Vee. I've got to get home to Everett."

"When are you going to wise up and leave that creep?" Veevi said.

Not answering, Dinah told her sister to thank the Engels for her and was out of the house in seconds.

In the car, she found Ventura's book and put it in the bag with her beach things. Then, in a storm of blind will, she drove back to town. What had happened with him that afternoon felt like a jagged wooden splinter in her heart, and it had to be brutally yanked out at once. By the time she pulled into the garage, everything she had felt and done that afternoon had been utterly erased, along with her hopes for a great love and an existence somehow larger than the one she had now.

Everett was lying in bed in his pajamas listening to the radio, and she told him that the day had been boring and that she wasn't going out to the Engels' again.

"It's about time you came to your senses," he said. But when he wanted to make love, she said she had gotten scraped by sand while bodysurfing and was just too sore all over to do anything. He looked at her chin and went to get some iodine, which burned as he applied it on a raw patch of skin. The next night, however, she couldn't find an excuse.

She stopped phoning her sister, and when Veevi called to ask about her, Dinah said she was tired from work. On Sundays, she helped out at the restaurant, thrusting her hands into mounds of raw hamburger meat and listening to the conversations between Everett and his father. They used the same words her father did: *Jewboy, kike, nigger, wop, chink.* They said things like "The world is going to hell in a handbasket" and "That Adolf Hitler has some good ideas. They ought to pay more attention to him over here." On Saturdays she went to the library, trying to remember the names of writers whose names she had heard at the Engels'. In this way she found Hemingway and Saroyan, Steinbeck and Sinclair Lewis. But she was careful to cover them in the jackets from the Christian Science books Everett's mother liked to lend her. For Christmas that year, she gave Dinah Anne Morrow Lindbergh's *North to the Orient,* the jacket of which was soon used for camouflage while the book itself remained unread. Out at the Engels', Dinah had heard that Lindbergh was a big pal of Hitler's.

And then four months later her mother called to announce that Veevi and Ventura had eloped to Mexico City and that they had just wired to say they were coming home. The next time Dinah saw her sister and the director, it was on a Sunday at the beach house in Malibu the suddenly famous couple had just bought, where they were having a reception. Dinah went with her mother and father. Everett, always indifferent to Veevi, had insisted on going to work at the restaurant.

Dinah's breath came in shallow gasps, and she was afraid her knees would buckle. Her hands were damp, and her heart was racing. A large crowd had gathered in the broad sun-filled living room, all its windows open to the ocean air, and Dinah recognized many faces. Tal Engel's brother, Irv, was sitting on a sofa between two women. On his right was Norma Levine; to his left sat a small blonde with shy, intelligent eyes. He was holding hands with her, but seemed preoccupied. She was appraising the house and scrutinizing faces as if she were trying to decide whom she ought to be afraid of, whom she should try to meet, and whom she could safely ignore. A college girl from the East, thought Dinah, noticing the girl's very correct beige outfit and cloche. At the sight of the diamond on the girl's left hand, Dinah's heart sank. They're all getting married, she thought.

She looked around for Tal Engel, but he was nowhere in sight, though she saw L.J. and Edy holding glasses of champagne and talking with various people who, at least up till now, had been regulars at their house on weekends. How, Dinah wondered, had Veevi broken things off with Tal, and when? How soon after Dinah's own little episode with Ventura had he met Veevi and fallen in love with her? That same night, after she had gone home, when he had finished regaling the crowd with the story of his driving lesson? Perhaps even before she turned off the Pacific Coast Highway onto Sunset!

But what was she doing here? She ought to be with her husband, living the life she had chosen—the life, she reminded herself, of the ignorant, bigoted, small-minded petit-bourgeois drudge. If only she could find a way to get out of it, she thought, sipping her champagne, which gave her, instantly, a headache. There had to be some way out. But it wasn't going to happen here, in her newly married and famous sister's beachfront living room with the Early American antiques and big braided rugs.

Hoping to postpone the moment when she would have to face the happy couple and offer her congratulations, she made her way out to the veranda. It was a terrible mistake to have come, but she was stuck, because of her parents. They were sitting in silence side by side on a sofa, eating large slices of wedding cake. She felt sorry for them. No one was interested in them, and they had long ago ceased to be interested in each other.

She felt like going for a walk along the water, but there was the problem of her stockings. She couldn't very well take them off here. She stood hesitating near the wooden steps leading down to the sand when she felt a large, heavy hand clamp down on her shoulder and pivot her around.

"Ah, it *is* you! *Tseluvki, tseluvki,* kisses, kisses," said a deep voice that could only be Ventura's. He caught her in a tight hug and kissed her on both cheeks. "I see you and I think, Ah, I find you again!" he said. "And where is the imbecile husband?"

She shook her head.

"He not come this time, too? No?" He grabbed her hand. "It's . . ."

"Dinah," she said.

"Dinah! Yes, Dinah! Such an American name! Come, Dinah, and meet my beautiful young wife. You will be great friends, I know."

He had forgotten her name. Do not cry, she commanded herself. You are now Sarah Bernhardt. Hold yourself erect. Do not falter!

He took her by the elbow and steered her over to her sister, who was stunning in a simple red crepe dress. Veevi leaned forward to be kissed, hardly a gesture Dinah was used to. But she kissed her sister and embraced her. The muscles in her face were sagging and twitching with the need to cry, but she forced herself to smile.

"Veevi," said Dinah to Ventura, "is my sister. Congr-gr-gr-gratulations to you both."

If he was surprised, he didn't show it. "Then you are my sister, too. And you still teach me to drive?"

"If you l-l-l-like," Dinah said a little stiffly.

"Darling," said Veevi, taking Ventura's arm. "I told you I had a sister. Dinah's the best driver I know. You can feel completely safe with her." She glanced up at him with a look Dinah would have called adoring, except that she didn't for a moment believe that Veevi adored him, any more than she had adored, or even loved, Tal Engel. Then Veevi caught Dinah's eye, and in her look Dinah saw her sister saying, "You didn't honestly think you had a chance, did you?" It was a look that demanded acknowledgment of a fait accompli, not so much a triumph but merely the simple fact of what was Veevi's due, and therefore in the cosmic order of things. Veevi was going to take whatever life gave her. Her look said, "I'm out of it now, out of that lower-middle-class hell that you, with your hopeless lack of style and your awful stutter and your loser husband, are doomed to stay in for the rest of your life. You want to be there? Fine. But me? I'm out of it, forever."

"I know you'll both be very happy," Dinah said, capitulating at once, looking back and forth from her sister's eyes to Ventura's face, which revealed nothing—not so much as a flicker of memory to acknowledge what had happened between them.

"I hope you come and see us often," said Ventura. "Our house is your house."

"Oh," she said, "I have a job, and I help my husband at the restaurant on w-w-w-weekends, and it's an awfully long ride from Hollywood out to Malibu. But th-th-th-thanks." She didn't understand why he seemed to like her so much, yet his kind eyes lingered on her face, and she felt that he genuinely wanted to be friends. It was more than she could stand for the moment. "Well, I'm going to find M-M-M-Mom and Pop and see if they're ready to go home. Mom's probably trying to wash all the dishes, and Pop's wishing he were somewhere in the Sierras. Have you met him yet?" she said pointedly to Ventura.

"For only a moment. I don't think he likes me," Ventura said, grinning.

"You have to remember that my sister is the love of his life. That and the fact that he's a real, one-hundred-percent red-blooded American b-b-b-bigot. Very d-d-d-democratic—hates everyone equally. If you keep those things in mind, you and he will do just fine. Oh," she added. "I almost forgot. Stefan, I have your Pushkin. May I keep it? You won't mind, will you? I gather the picture's already been made!"

He laughed. "Would you like to see it?"

"Of course," she said.

"Ah, then you come to a preview. Right, darling?" he said to Veevi. "When we know where, we tell you and you come."

"Of course," said Veevi. "But I'm warning you: Dinah has a sharp tongue and strong opinions."

For a moment Dinah felt embraced by both of them, and she began to feel that she might enjoy coming again. Then she wandered off and went back out to the veranda, where she stared at the ocean—immense, blue, free of people. *I thought you said doing it with him would be like doing it with a gorilla,* pounded through her head. *I thought you said he was a lecher.* He must have taken one look at Veevi and just about died, she thought.

Still, she couldn't deny that she wanted to know him better. He wanted to be friends? Fine. They would be like brother and sister. She would make him laugh. Perhaps next time he would even remember her name.

It took her almost two more years, but one Saturday morning she got up at five and on the table in the breakfast nook she placed a note she had typed at the office: *Dear Everett, It's over. Good-bye, Dinah.* Taking the suitcase she had packed and hidden away the night before, she went noiselessly out to her car and drove into the fading dark toward Malibu. Veevi had met her one day after work in the park across from the Beverly Hills Hotel and given her a key, so she was able to let herself in. She knew which guest bedroom to go to, and she had already left some of her things there.

The next day she slept late, and didn't wake until after noon. When she came downstairs, she met Veevi and Stefan, who were grinning up at her. "Look outside," Veevi said, laughing and holding out a cup of hot coffee. When Dinah went outside, she saw that Everett had evidently found a truck and, in a rage, filled it with things Dinah had left behind and driven it all the way out to Malibu and dumped their belongings on the ground. She could see where the broken plates and old clothes and the lamp he had tossed into the pale green ice plant were bobbing in the wind, and for a few seconds she realized that she had hurt him terribly and thought she was going to cry. Then she and Veevi and Stefan had a good laugh together, and she knew at once that one part of her life was over. "I have left the p-p-p-petit b-b-b-b—oh shit, you know what I mean," she added, smiling happily. "I am now an official cadre in the vanguard of the div-v-v-vorciat."

Stefan came up to her and touched her elbow.

"Come have breakfast, comrade," Veevi said.

For the moment Dinah felt at home. She didn't move in permanently, however. To drive all the way from Malibu to her job in downtown Los Angeles took too long and used up too much gas. So she took her small savings and rented a small apartment—an "in-law" attached to a house—in Laurel Canyon. It was the first apartment she had ever had to herself. Nevertheless, Veevi assured her that the room in Malibu was permanently hers, and Dinah began spending weekends there, driving back either very late Sunday evening or very early Monday morning. Ventura and Veevi's first movie together, *Queen of Spades,* set in antebellum Richmond, had come out the year before and done well, though not spectacularly, and they had just finished another movie, a Western whose box-office prospects were uncertain. Stefan wanted to do something serious, another Western, but in the vein of the pictures he had made in the twenties and early thirties in Berlin and Paris, but with an American flavor. He'd convinced L. J. Engel—with Irv's support, now that Tal had left Hollywood and moved to Vermont to write novels—to let him come up with a screenplay based on the story of Oedipus. But, as he now explained to Dinah, just that week he'd had a series of big meetings, big discussions, and big arguments about the story—with L.J. and Irv and then with Irv alone, who had to explain why his father was insisting that every mention of the mother-son incest theme had to go or the picture wouldn't be made. Yes on the father-son murder story, no on the blinding. Of course there had to be a girl's part for Veevi and the Oedipus character has to end up with her. So Jocasta was Johanna—gorgeous, young, "and not some old bag with sagging tits," Irv had told Stefan. Ed, the town sheriff, is in love with her. Fine on Ed as a mysterious gunslinger who wandered into town years earlier and got rid of all the local bad guys, became sheriff, but still wants to solve the mystery of why all the cattle are dying. And okay, okay—maybe for just a little while there can be this horrible question of Johanna and Ed being brother and sister, but it's got to be a big mistake. Fine, let the Indians be the ones who straighten it all out, but nix on the hermaphrodite business, just make him a nice normal blind Indian, no half-man, half-woman freak—and Dorshka will have to work out the details. Let there be a lot of Indian hocus-pocus for the oracles—that's fine, but no mother-son hanky-panky (or, as L.J. pronounced it, "henky-penky"). This is America—no dirty stuff. Mainly, make the ending happy. Johanna and Ed have to end up together even if Ed decides he can't show his face to the world for a while—let him go off and be a rancher with her at his side. Fine, there's plenty of ways for a person to get lost in the Wild West.

Stefan wanted to keep as much Sophocles as he could, wanted to have Ed discover that Johanna was his sister after he marries her, but L.J.'s response was to repeat "Over my dead body" until he was hoarse.

Stefan now looked at Dinah across the breakfast table. "Do you think that Americans will like this story?"

"I dunno, Stefan," she said. She had never read the Sophocles, never even heard of it. "It sounds kind of d-d-depressing. Things are still awfully tough here. Maybe people just want to be entertained."

She saw that Veevi was watching her with a bright, inquisitive expression, as if testing her, and she could feel that she had somehow failed.

"Is good for people to forget their troubles and feel maybe something for the other guy's troubles, no?" he said. "But maybe this is not so for Americans?"

"I don't think people want to feel any worse than they already d-d-d-do," Dinah said. "But what do I know? I've never even heard of S-S-S-Sophocles. Is this where the Oedipus complex comes from?"

Stefan didn't answer her, and Dinah saw for the first time how troubled and anxious he had become.

All the same, the house was always swarming with people. On Saturdays and Sundays nearly everyone Dinah used to see at the Engels' was now at the Venturas'. Dinah had been getting to know a few of the same people at Party meetings in Westwood on weekday evenings, when she attended workers' classes and fulfilled her assignment. She had to type endless letters from screenwriters and Party big shots like Anatole Klein, Norman Metzger, and Guy Bergman on the subject of fund-raising for the Loyalists in Spain. Like everyone else, she was in a fever about Spain and glad to feel useful, and through the workers' classes she was beginning to see her whole life in a different way. She viewed her father now as a proletarian who nursed petit-bourgeois dreams and was doomed to failure. Through the theory of surplus value she saw how Claggett Oil sucked the blood out of everyone who worked there, including herself. Booms and depressions she now understood as the cogs and wheels of a carefully manipulated system guaranteed to grind down the human beings who oiled and turned it. Why didn't I ever realize this before? she often said to herself. It's so simple. It's so obvious. The situation of Negroes could be seen as class warfare between petit bourgeois elements, like Everett and his family, and the dark-skinned landless proletariat they hated and feared. Even Roosevelt, whom she loved, wasn't going to change things that much, and neither was the New Deal. She had become a believer. She feared the fascists, and hated Hitler, Franco, and Mussolini. Everyone said that Stalin was great and Trotsky terrible, and she supposed this must be true, but all she really wanted was to fall in love, get married, and have children.

Some months before she left Everett, she drove out to Malibu for a weekend and found, in the kitchen, a striking woman with short flyaway red hair, broad football player's shoulders, a great shelf of a bosom, and a forthright expression. "I am Dorshka Albrecht. Who are you?" the woman said, extending her hand.

Later that day, as they took a walk on the beach, Veevi explained to Dinah that years ago, when he had directed her in the theater in Berlin, Stefan had had a passionate affair with Dorshka, and this had eventually become a friendship and they had subsequently collaborated on screenplays. Dorshka had followed him to Paris after he left Berlin in '33, and now he'd finally persuaded L.J. to bring her over from Paris to work with him. So here she was just off the boat and already under contract to Marathon. As Dinah and Veevi returned from their walk, they paused to watch Stefan wrestling at the water's edge with a boy—a beautiful boy, about fourteen or fifteen, slender and muscular—who grabbed Stefan tightly around the waist and lifted him up. Staggering momentarily under the weight of the older, heavier man, who was laughing out loud, the boy dug his legs into the shifting sand and seemed to be on the verge of collapsing backward in a heap when he turned sharply and in an instant flipped the older man on his back. Stefan laughed again. Picking himself up and shaking the sand from his hair, he rushed the boy and repeated the boy's movements—so that this time it was the boy who landed on his back in the sand. They were smiling, growling, shouting, and laughing together in German. "Who's that handsome k-k-k-kid?" Dinah asked Veevi, who explained that it was Michael Albrecht, Dorshka's son by the Austrian poet Joachim Albrecht, who had died some years ago, but to whom she had been married for many years. Stefan had known him forever, and had become a father to Michael. "Stefan's so happy now," Veevi said. "He adores Michael, and they're always wrestling and talking about sports together. Michael wants to learn American football, and," she added, "how to drive." Dinah, who found herself envying Veevi for having yet another new person in her life—a handsome stepson, someone she could talk about in an indulgent and parental tone—immediately offered to give the boy driving lessons. "He'll love it," Veevi said. "But he's so beautiful to look at, make sure you keep your eyes on the road."

Veevi seemed relieved to have Dorshka living in her home. "She's very domestic," Veevi said. "She wants to do all the cooking, which is great for me, since all I want to do is read." Dorshka in fact immediately took over the management of the household, bought a big convertible, and put everyone who met her at ease. She was kind and warm to Dinah, who loved her. In a matter of weeks, Dorshka was able to get her lover, the playwright Bernhard Mendelsohn, out of Germany. A short taciturn man with a great sprouting head of salt-and-pepper hair, he seemed pleasantly bewildered to have ended up in Southern California and became, like Dorshka and Michael, a permanent member of the Malibu household.

But the Venturas' was also the gathering place for the American-born set—in their twenties and thirties, always diving headlong into the biggest waves as capitalism breathed its last. They adored Veevi, and they respected Stefan so much that they didn't quite know what to say to him when he talked about sustained close-ups, his good friends Fritz Lang and F. W. Murnau, and the films of his beloved countryman Zlatan Dudov. And they were in awe of the refugees and exiles who also reclined on the veranda, usually fully clothed, with just their shoes and socks off, speaking German, Hungarian, Russian, and Polish to one another. From time to time one of the Americans spoke Yiddish with a refugee, but the refugees were startled, even nonplussed, by the Americans' exuberant warmth and familiarity. They walked with slow, heavy steps along the beach, stopped to gather shells, and seemed older, to Dinah, by a full generation—older, careworn, and tired. A number of them were angry, too, and hostile. Dinah remembered now, as the sun-warmed wheel of her Pontiac station wagon became hot to the touch, how Dorshka had laughed in exasperation when Cliff Boatwright had cracked (in an accent) about a dachshund belonging to a newly arrived and decidedly imperious refugee couple, "In Germany, I was a Great Dane."

Dinah lies on her stomach on a towel. The sun beats down on her back as she listens to Cliff Boatwright describe his meetings with a Russian writer during a recent trip to Moscow.

"Spoilsport. Loser. Malcontent," breaks in Anatole Klein with a contemptuous snort. In his bathing trunks he has long hairy legs and arms, a simian jaw, and hungry black eyes. "What's his name, anyway? Believe me, he knows you're from Hollywood. A counterrevolutionary saboteur. Wants you to hide him in his suitcase and bring him over here for the moola."

"I think it was Yuri Kaminetsky. Does that sound right?"

"Screenwriter. Stinks," says Klein.

"A no-talent hack. A lousy petit-bourgeois wrecker and opportunist if you ask me," chimes in Guy Bergman, who is bald and has a mustache and speaks in a deep voice tinged with contempt. Veevi barely turns her head.

Curious how they always make fun of those words until they get mad, and then they use them against one another, Dinah thinks.

"Didn't seem that way to me," says Boatwright, who, with three good screenwriting credits to his name, has also recently published a novel. "Seemed to me he was scared shitless." Dinah has seen him impish and mischievous with Veevi, and so overcome with adoration for her that it has sometimes seemed as if his taut face would dissolve in tenderness like melted wax, but now he fixes Bergman and Klein with a cold stare. Dinah notes the way Veevi is looking at him, waiting for him to unlock his eyes from his adversaries and find hers so that she can single him out for a private understanding that, when they detect it, will unnerve the other two men.

"He's played out. Has nothing left to say. End of story," says Bergman.

"Speaking of stories, gentlemen," says Boatwright, glancing rapidly from Bergman and Klein to Veevi and back. "I got your letter the other day."

"Not here, Boatie," says Klein. "This isn't the place . . ."

"Why isn't it the place? Why can't I talk about it now?"

"Not now, Clifford," says Bergman.

"Oh for Christ's sake," Veevi says, shading her eyes with her hand. "Stop acting like commissars. Just say whatever you have to say and then go play volleyball or something."

"Who the hell are you guys anyway to say anything to me about my book?" says Boatwright. "I'm not going to sit around and wait for a goddamn summons from you guys. You got a problem with what I've written, go write a review."

"Not so fast, Boatie. We've got some questions about class-angling in your book," says Bergman. He's a stocky fellow, Dinah notices, and from where she's lying she can see the toes of his sandy right foot jiggling in the shadow of the umbrella.

"What kind of questions?"

"Well, you say you've read the letter. We've invited you to come and talk about it."

" 'Invited'? I wouldn't call that an invitation. That's a summons! A subpoena! I don't recognize your right to issue it. I'm not answerable to you—not when it comes to my work. You heard the lady. If you have questions, ask me now. Right here."

"We've told you when and we've told you where. Show up and we'll ask. Stay away and face the consequences."

" 'Face the consequences'? What're you gonna do? Excommunicate me? Hold an auto-da-fé in the Hollywood Bowl? What is it you think you can do to me?"

"It's a question of discipline, Boatwright. Party discipline," says Klein.

"Sorry, fellas. Ask me now or forget it. I'm busy. I'm in screenplay. I don't have time for a goddamn inquisition."

"Remember this," says Klein. " 'Social weapon.' "

"Good God," says Veevi, with a sardonic laugh. "The two of you sound like street-corner bullies." She looks at Klein and Bergman in imperious disbelief, while she and Boatwright exchange glances that Dinah characterizes to herself as adoring. The two commissars seem to collapse, visibly, like punctured beach balls. Their ribs sink in, their bellies roll over the tops of their swimming trunks. Boatwright gets up and walks away; Veevi lies back, closes her eyes, and extends her legs, which are not as long as Dinah's but are just as shapely. Dinah is sure now that something is going on between Veevi and Boatwright, but she doesn't want to think about it. Instead, she heads toward the kitchen to see if she can help out with the care and feeding of the new crop of refugees from Europe.

Working in Everett's parents' restaurant had given Dinah kitchen skills and good serving technique, and she often found herself traveling back and forth between living room and kitchen, carrying trays piled with thick sandwiches of salami and cheese on pumpernickel and rye, followed by slices of cake as big as bricks and slathered with whipped cream, which people devoured from the fine old English china Tal Engel had given Veevi. They drank tea and coffee and smoked cigarettes and talked. When they ate fruit, they took their time, wielding a small knife in the most artful way, cutting apples and pears into lovely slices rather than sinking their jaws into them as the Americans did. A ripe pear or a plate of apricots and nuts and a glass of wine after dinner was a perfect dessert for Stefan, Dinah saw, much to her surprise, for she had never dreamed of combining fruit and wine.

Hearing German spoken confounded her. If ever a language seemed to bark rejection at a stutterer, it was German. Yet she gradually began to have the strange feeling that she could understand what was being said, even though she didn't get individual words. She could sense when someone was complaining or arguing or gossiping or telling a story. And sometimes one of them would look away, and then she knew that things more terrible than she had ever seen or imagined were being remembered. Sitting on the veranda once with Stefan and a handsome, recently arrived, shabbily dressed middle-aged couple, she heard the story (which Stefan translated for her) of how they had gotten out of Austria by hiding in an industrial-size coffee urn in the supply car of a passenger train bound for Strasbourg. The clothes they were wearing now were the clothes they had worn then; they had no others. That night they would sleep in the so-called maid's room— it was for overflow guests; Veevi and Stefan didn't have a maid—and soon, with Dorshka's help, would find an apartment and work, perhaps at UCLA, where the man, a scientist, hoped to get something in the chemistry department. There was also a young woman, athletic and pretty, who spoke very correct English and had a slight lisp. She came to the screen door one afternoon and asked Dinah if there was a place to rinse her feet, since she had just come out of the ocean—"So refreshing!" she said—but she didn't want to trek sand into the house. "Oh, come in, come in, there's s-s-s-sand all over the place," Dinah said, liking her at once. Later, the young woman came into the kitchen and volunteered to help. In this way Dinah learned that Nelly Rosenzweig had been an art student in Berlin and then moved to London with her mother, a widow who had sunk deeper and deeper into depression, and finally hanged herself from the chandelier in the room of the boardinghouse where they'd lived in Golders Green. On what was left of the money from her mother's jewelry, Nelly had sailed to New York and then taken the train to Los Angeles, where she had just landed a job as an assistant in the art department at Marathon. Years later, Dinah would meet Nelly again, at Groucho Marx's, with her husband, Manny Steiner, and they became fast friends.

At night, exhausted from the studio, Dorshka would sit down at the typewriter to write letters and fill out forms for the refugees. Dinah would bring her coffee to help her stay awake. "They're going to kill all the Jews," she would say matter-of-factly. "How am I going to get everyone out?" Sometimes she held her head in her hands and cried. "We need our friends," she said again and again to Veevi and Stefan, and it took Dinah a long time to figure out that she didn't mean friends in a general sense but rather special people in the Party—and not just in America, either, but everywhere—especially in Mexico and France.

After months of listening to and watching the refugees, however, Dinah began to see that not everything they talked about had to do with the situation in Europe. Some of the loudest conversations that took place in the comfortable living room, with its chintz-covered sofas and braided rugs, had nothing to do with Hitler and the Nazis and desperate attempts to survive, or even about movie studios and the absurdities of Los Angeles life. Some of them were intrigues and quarrels as old as the Holy Roman Empire (about which Stefan had given Dinah a brief and useful history). A conductor with a lurching gait and an eye patch quarreled one Sunday afternoon with a tall, unsmiling composer until the conductor, in a rage, picked up a large pewter plate, spilling its load of fruit on the floor, and brought it down on the head of the composer—or would have, except that the composer calmly ducked, as if he were used to assaults from his enraged compatriot, who wouldn't stop shrieking at him until Dorshka rushed in and, with a torrent of Yiddish, dragged him back to the kitchen for a bawling out that could be heard all the way to Santa Barbara.

Once in a while, one of the refugees spoke to Dinah directly. A handsome blond actor who had been in two of Stefan's Berlin movies showed up one Sunday with an old man dressed in a frayed double-breasted brown suit. The old man said nothing, but Dinah noticed that when he tried to eat his piece of Sacher torte his hand trembled so fiercely that crumbs fell all over the rug. The actor took a linen napkin and tried to pick up the crumbs, embarrassed but uncertain what to do. Dinah went and sat down between them and, putting her hand on the old man's, with its transparent blue-veined skin and age spots, steadied it as he lifted the fork to his mouth. He smiled, abashed, grateful. She could see that he was enjoying the cake, that he wanted to eat it. "My mother and father wait for weeks for the Portuguese visas," the handsome actor said, startling her with his English. *"Aber es gab so schrecklich wenig zu essen,"* he continued in German to Stefan. *"Meine Eltern waren alt und schwach—kurz gesagt, meine Mutter starb."* "His parents were old and weak," Stefan translated for her as she put the old man's hand down and simply lifted the cake-loaded fork to his mouth, which he now opened and shut like a baby bird. "And his mother died." *"Aber mein Vater—es ist ein Wunder, dass er es Ueberlebt hat. Ich gehe jeden Tag mit ihm in Santa Monica spazieren, und dann schaut er mich immer an und fragt: 'Sag mir, lebe ich? Bin ich noch am Leben?'"* "He says," Stefan explained to her, "that every day he takes his father for a walk in Santa Monica. And the father looks at him and says, 'Tell me, am I alive? Am I still alive?'"

While his father sat back and dozed, engulfed by the comfortable sofa, the handsome actor, whom Stefan had introduced to Dinah as Heinz Kirschner (after the war he would have a very successful Hollywood career playing Nazi officers), took her aside and asked her if she would like to change jobs. She looked into his square-jawed, blue-eyed, apparently Aryan face, so like those of the Nazis in the newsreels, and wondered how the Nazis could always be so sure about who was or wasn't Jewish, while he explained to her that he needed a companion-housekeeper for his father while he was on the set of the movie he'd soon be starting at MGM. To put him into a home for old people would kill him, the actor said, and Dinah said, "Of course you couldn't p-p-p-possibly do that." But she, too, had to be away all day at her job, she explained. He pleaded with her: she looked after everyone so well here. Dinah smiled and said, "Oh, no, I don't work here; I'm Veevi Ventura's s-s-s-sister." He blushed and apologized profusely, took her hand and kissed it, and for the rest of the afternoon Dinah sleepwalked—once again—in a febrile dream of instant romance, until everyone left and Veevi invited her to keep her company while she took a bath. Then Dinah asked Veevi about the handsome actor. "Forget it," Veevi said, reaching toward the faucet to replenish the supply of hot water. "He's a fairy. Couldn't you tell?"

"Hell no!" Dinah said, not caring if she appeared naïve to her sister. "Damn it, Vee, there isn't anybody for me."

Unlike their mother, who always managed to say something deliciously banal and comforting to Dinah when she complained that there weren't any men out there, Veevi said nothing.

But there was another man who interested her, a great modern song-writer, apparently: Frank—real name Ferenc—Herzog. He wore round steel-rimmed glasses and had a head of thick light brown curly hair flecked with gray, and what Norma Levine referred to as "a large corporation." He came often on Sundays, and he always showed up with his dog, Boris, a German shepherd, whom she overheard him describe as a "dedicated Bol-shevik and crotch-sniffer." Dinah and Frank Herzog shared a silent laugh once when Boris went into a state of olfactory ecstasy as he attempted to burrow into the nether regions of a certain statuesque and overdressed Vi-ennese lady, famous for having married a rather long roster of celebrated men—the last an architect with whom she had migrated across the seas to Beverly Hills, a necessity she was said to have bitterly and loudly blamed on his being Jewish. Herzog asked Dinah to take a walk on the beach with him. The dog had no interest in molesting her, particularly since she kept throwing her sandal into the swirls of foamy water, from which he de-lighted to retrieve it for her. She was, furthermore, extremely wary of tak-ing long walks on the beach with interesting European men just off the boat, and kept a wide space between the songwriter and herself. He asked her who she was and what she did, and where he could buy ink, composi-tion paper, and phonograph records. When they got back, Veevi was still holding court on the patio and Dinah observed her sister looking at her with curiosity, but when Veevi asked her if she wanted to come upstairs and talk while they changed into slacks and shirts for dinner, Dinah said she had promised to help Dorshka in the kitchen. She knew now to avoid Veevi's comments on men whose attention she had won.

That night Frank Herzog sat at the piano and sang some of his songs—in German, of course—but he kept seeking out Dinah's eyes, and before the evening was over he invited her to dinner the following Wednesday. He apologized for asking her to drive all the way out to his little house in Santa Monica, and explained that he did not yet know Los Angeles, or even how to drive well enough to come for her himself—and in any case, he wanted to show her what he was working on.

The night of their date, feeling sophisticated and shrewd, determined not to repeat what had happened with Ventura, Dinah headed out to Santa Monica, wearing her one glamorous dress (a black silk studio hand-me-down from Veevi). She had spent extra money on gas and was worried about exceeding her weekly budget, but she soon pushed that to the back of her mind. Herzog took a great interest in her, asking all about her work.

"It's not v-v-v-very interesting," she said. "I type all day, take dictation, and hate my supervisor." Herzog had cooked a goulash with red cabbage and buttered noodles, and she expressed admiration and almost, but not quite, cleaned her plate, remembering her father's admonition to "walk away from the table a little bit hungry." After dinner—she surprised herself by not offering to clear the dishes—he played songs from the score he was working on. The story was from some old American novel nobody had ever heard of, about a man who practices mesmerism and casts spells on beautiful young women. It's got horror in it, and fantasy, he explained excitedly, and he was having such fun writing the songs. They had motifs from American folk music, which he had been studying and had fallen in love with. Would she like him to play some for her? Could she recognize the American songs? He played, and she sang along softly with the tunes, indeed recognizing all of them, and then she offered to sing two songs her father used to sing to her and her sister when they were little and that she'd never heard anywhere else.

"Yes, please do," he said. "I would like very much to hear these songs."

" 'I went way out to Kansas,' " she began simply, and unself-consciously, " 'where they told me I would find / Money growin' round like apples on a tree / But it was just like Dinah told me / There was nothin' of the kind / And the weather was so cold / I like to froze.' "

Herzog's eyes lit up. Dinah didn't have a strong voice, but she was a natural alto and could carry a tune. As she moved into the refrain, Herzog accompanied her, sight-reading, as it were, from her face and the tune:

I'm gwyin' back,
I'm gwyin' back,
To my Dinah and my little baby Ben,
To the little whitewashed cabin
With the grapevine o'er the door,
And the old moss-covered chimney at the end.

Then she sang another, which was fast and funny. When she finished, he was looking at her with joy in his face.

"Will you write down these songs? Such wonderful songs!"

"Sure," she said, and he ran into his study and came back with paper and pencils.

As she wrote down the words, he asked if she had been named for the Dinah in the song.

"Yes," she said. "It's a sad song, though, isn't it? I got the name from the sad song, and my sister, Genevieve, got the fancy French name from God knows where. I l-l-l-like my name, though," she added, printing the lyrics in small capitals so that he could read them clearly. "That song's nice, isn't it?"

"Yes, I, too, love this song. I steal it from you completely!" he added, and they shared a laugh. He was, like Stefan, older than she, well into his forties. She liked him, liked his cozy house, with the piano that took up nearly the entire living room and the big German shepherd snoozing and sighing on the rug.

Later, he brought in coffee and they sat at either end of the sofa, talking. He told her about the Nazis' forbidding performances of his music, shutting down the theater where he'd had many successes, calling his work decadent, Communist, Jewish. At ten o'clock, though she wanted to keep on talking—or, rather, listening—she glanced at her watch. The drive back was long, she told him, and she had better go. At this he reached across the sofa for one of her hands, which he took in both of his and kissed. She had secretly laughed at all the hand-kissing that went on at the Venturas', thinking it a silly custom, and was surprised by the tenderness in the gesture and the sexual way it stirred her. Then he spoke: "I must be here for three months. I am alone, and I do not like all this Hollywood"—he waved his hand—"nonsense. Ventura is an old friend of mine and I am very fond of the fellow, but, forgive me for saying so, he is a bit of a fool. Your sister has beauty and charm, but she does not truly care for him—anyone can see that, and Dorshka fusses around him like a grandmother, and nobody sees that they will eat him alive here. You are different. I see something in you right away. You are not part of the movies, and I like that very much. Excuse me, I mean to say, I like *you* very much. I would like for you to come and live with me here, in this house. You could give away—"

"Give up?"

"Give up your job. You say you would like to read more—why not come and live with me and read all day? There is one circumstance and I will not hide it from you. I am married. My wife is an actress and a singer, a great one, and she is in New York now, working in a show I have written just for her. It is doing very well. When I leave here, I will go back to her and we will work together on another show for her. Then I will come back here, as long as I have luck getting work in this crazy place. My wife and I, we have what you call an understanding, because so much time we are separated. Certain questions we don't ask each other. No doubt, of passing the time when we are not together, she has her own ways. I will never leave her and she will never leave me. Making troubles she will not do for me, and I also don't make troubles. And I would take good care of you and I would not hurt your pride."

Herzog let go of her hand. Dinah looked at him with her candid brown eyes and wondered why she had the rottenest luck with men of anyone she knew. She turned and leaned over her knees and clasped her arms together, and looked sideways at him. "Your arrangement sounds very nice. I'd love to quit my job and live with you. It sounds like a wonderful life. But after a while you'll go back to New York, to your wife, and then I'll be stuck in this house with nothing to do. I want to fall in love with someone, Mr. Herzog, and get m-m-m-married. I want to have kids. I don't want to be a mistress, even of a very nice and interesting guy like you. So I'm going to go home now."

But he leaned forward and took her hand and began to pull her toward him. If she kissed him, she would never go home, and with a force of will that surprised her, she pulled away.

"Dinah darling, you have nothing to fear. I think you are a fine girl, a splendid girl. I would take care of you. And you wouldn't be lonely when I'm not here. I know good, interesting people here. They would make sure you weren't too much alone. And always, I would come back."

"Thank you, Frank," she said, pointedly using his first name now. "You're being awfully nice about this. But I'm not all that s-s-s-sophisticated about some things, and I don't sleep with married men. I want kids."

He leaned forward, took her face in his hands, and kissed her. "You are a good American girl."

Stefan had said the same thing to her. Who did they think she was, she wondered, Rebecca of Sunnybrook Farm, for Christ's sake?

"For you, something is either wrong or right, *ja*? But you know you refuse yourself—and me—something good for us both. You are—what do they call it?—a puritan!"

Dinah wanted badly to stay. He had warm eyes, and she loved it that he had seen something in her that interested him. "Well, I dunno. Maybe I am," she said, standing up. "But I don't think it's that. I just want the usual things—you know, a nice guy and some kids. Thanks for dinner and for playing your songs. And for inviting me to l-l-l-live with you."

She put on her little black hat, also a hand-me-down from Veevi and the Marathon wardrobe department, and pulled her car keys out of her purse as he walked her out to her car. The night air was cool and sweet, and she imagined what it would have been like to live in that house and fall asleep with him every night to the sound of the ocean. But then, she reminded herself, he would go back to New York and she'd be all by herself. The ocean can sound angry and restless if you're alone in a dark house.

"Will you at least come and have dinner with me again?" he asked her, opening the door of her old Ford.

She turned and threw her arms around him, kissing him on the mouth, holding him to her, and then quickly broke away, and got into the car.

"Oh, Frank," she said, smiling, feeling as if she were in a movie. "We'd just end up like we are right now, with you inviting me to dinner again and me waiting for the engine to t-t-t-turn over."

Then in the spring of 1938, after a Party meeting, Dinah got to talking with Owen Darrow, a screenwriter who was considered by the members of the Potemkin Club, as the unit was called, the most brilliant explainer of Marxist theory among them. He besieged her with phone calls, insisting that she have dinner with him every night, and she capitulated easily, fascinated by the clear and ready speech with which he answered questions. Fluency— articulate, unobstructed utterance—hypnotized her. She was spellbound at the meeting when he said that Litvinov, Radek, Rykov, Yagoda, and Bukharin were all Trotskyist wreckers and saboteurs who were actively aiding fascism and Hitler. "Look at the evidence," he said. "Is anybody here really going to stand up and say that hundreds of pages of testimony and innumerable eyewitness reports are all fabricated, all lies? Make no mistake about it: people who defame the Moscow trials are dedicated enemies of American progressivism. They ought to be damn grateful to the Soviet government and its great leader, Stalin, for exposing these traitors before they can do more harm than they already have."

Owen Darrow had a grim, humorless poise and everyone listened to him with what seemed to Dinah a mixture of reverence and gratitude for having figured out all the positions in advance. When they spoke at meetings, Norman Metzger, Guy Bergman, and Anatole Klein always turned to him for confirmation. It was as if he knew just what they were going to ask him and had the answers at his fingertips, and she marveled at the sheer coherence of their exchanges. Dinah had never experienced anything like that, and she wondered if it was like what went on in college.

Darrow was a hefty guy, with transparent green eyes and closely cropped sandy-brown hair. He was handsome, but he wasn't a good athlete and didn't like volleyball or bodysurfing out at Veevi's. He lived in town, not far from Laurel Canyon, picked Dinah up for meetings, and took her out on dates. He said right away that he was in love with her and was sure she was the one. "Let's give it some time, and then it's home to meet Mother and plan the wedding," he said.

When they visited her sister's, and were visibly a couple, Veevi beamed at Dinah and said, "Well, you've got an interesting fish on the line." He was patient with Dinah, in the beginning. She admired his ready opinions, and when he told her what to think she accepted it—after all, he was much smarter than she was. Of all the Communists they knew, he seemed to her the most genuine. When they went out for seafood and beer in Long Beach with union guys he knew, longshoremen in the Party, he loosened up and was right at home with them, so much that when it came time to go back to Los Angeles she had to do the driving.

But after a few months Owen revealed another side of himself. By then, she was practically living at his apartment, on South Doheny. Gradually, she noticed that he drank beer from morning till night, and liked to play with himself while listening to the sexual vocalizations of a couple whose amorous encounters took place in the building across the way. Dinah would wake up in the middle of the night, hearing what sounded like the yelps of a chained puppy, and see him lurking near the window, holding a pair of binoculars with his left hand and sawing the air with a furious vibration of his right. His own efforts with her a few hours earlier had been aborted, seemingly owing to the effects of beer. He often told her that he loved her, but he said it with a look of contrition, as if he were forever making up for some sin he had committed.

At meetings, he continued to perform with his usual stern brilliance, and was treated respectfully by the Party people out at her sister's. Then he handed in the script he was working on and no one liked it and his contract wasn't renewed. When he wasn't railing against the imperialist saboteurs, exploiters, social parasites, lynchers, and union busters, he bitterly denounced every person in the industry more successful than himself—including Stefan, whom he called a sellout. The things that were strange about him got stranger, and she found that she could no longer explain them away by telling herself he was "creative." For instance, when he wasn't too drunk to make love, he demanded that she be just as vocal and uninhibited as the invisible female half of the couple across the way. This was extremely difficult for her: once, when trying to make the same yelping-puppy sounds as her neighbor, she burst into laughter, and Owen didn't find it amusing at all. Yet whenever she put her arm around him or reached up to kiss him, he told her he couldn't stand it and that he hated it when women were affectionate with him. Why? she wanted to know. Because he didn't *deserve* it, he said, because he wanted her to be more *critical* of him.

Every so often after dinner, he would take down a worn edition of Boswell's *Life of Johnson,* open it to a few dog-eared pages, read a passage or two out loud, and cry. Disconcerted at first, she tried to comfort him, but he seemed to enjoy these sessions of weeping and always chose the same passages. One was about Johnson's standing out in the rain in some English town whose name she couldn't remember. Even before Owen reached the end of the passage, his voice would quaver and the tears would roll down his cheeks. Sometimes he read a passage about Johnson's vowing that his cat Hodge would not be shot, and this one dissolved him. He sobbed piteously. Dinah didn't know what to say to him at these times, and just waited them out. She'd sit on the sofa, one leg tucked under her, and watch her cigarette ash grow longer.

As spring turned to summer, he began to find fault with her. She wasn't womanly enough, he said. She didn't cook enough, or sew. She countered that she was exhausted from typing all day, sewed when she had to but found it boring, and had never been all that interested in food. When she came for dinner he cooked, she pointed out, so he never gave her much of a chance to see what she could do. Then he said he didn't think she was a real Communist at heart but was in the Party only because she felt sorry for people like her father. Well, what's wrong with that? she wanted to know. Weren't there lots of people like that in the Party, who felt terrible about what was happening to their families? If you join for personal reasons, you leave for personal reasons, he told her with a sternness that used to impress her but now struck her as tedious.

He received phone calls from people in other cities. At least once a week, there were evening visits from Metzger, Klein, Bergman, and others. Dinah was told to stay in the bedroom, but she knew that they were strategizing for the upcoming meeting and trying to figure out how the votes would go. Owen had explained to her that this was "democratic centralism" and the best possible way to get across to people the great decisions Comrade Stalin was making for the world, for which he needed the support of the rank and file. This seemed peculiar to Dinah, but she told herself that she was too dumb and uneducated to come up with a good reason to oppose this way of doing things. Besides, Owen always had an answer for everything.

One night she woke up and saw him standing at the open window, completely absorbed in the orchestrations next door (this time there were not only shrill yelps but frequent arpeggios, and a few outright howls), and ministering to his member. As she lay under the sheets observing him, Dinah suddenly saw a small bat fly into the room and begin to knock itself against the ceiling. The sight of Owen running naked in black socks around the moonlit bedroom trying to protect his dwindling erection with one hand and swat the bat with a broom in the other was too much for her: she was besieged by violent waves of laughter. Having succeeded in harrying the bat out the window, he turned to her and said, in an aggrieved voice, "I don't see what's so damned funny."

"Once," she said, beginning to laugh again so hard that she could barely speak, "Veevi and I were going to bed and a big m-m-m-moth flew into our room. We were scared of it and screamed for our father. He came in, wearing"—she said, her whole body shaking—"a long white nightgown and a nightcap. And while he was looking all around, trying to find the moth, it landed on his"—her eyes filled with tears, and she coughed—"*b-b-b-big t-t-t-toe*. The two of us burst out laughing. He looked at us as if we were completely crazy and said, 'This is no time for jollification.'"

Owen stood there, stark naked, not laughing. This made everything worse: seeing Owen's desolate face and shriveling penis, she simply rolled over on her side, her behind inadvertently exposed, and laughed again into the pillow on her side of his bed.

That night he went to sleep with his back to her. At about 4 A.M. she got up, got dressed, and, as she had done with Everett, left a note, which she placed on the kitchen counter: *Even when the revolution comes, we still won't laugh at the same things. Good-bye. D.* She stopped going to the Potemkin Club meetings, and heard, some months later, that Owen's agent hadn't been able to interest anyone in his new screenplay and that he'd gone back to New York.

She went on to have casual affairs. Sex in itself became interesting, and she developed skills. She took men home to her apartment in Laurel Canyon, and gave herself easily to them, but there was no one she especially cared for. Some of the men had nothing to do with the movies or the Party. A few she picked up at the ice rink in Westwood, where she went skating with her Party friend Renna Goldman. But they were often broke or had dead-end jobs, and, worst of all, didn't read books. One day she said to Renna, "I don't care if I am a Communist. From now on, no more low-wage earners."

Renna approved, and they agreed that this would require a new kind of "party" discipline. No more men from the skating rink or, in Dinah's case, from work. No one without a college education. No one who didn't read. No one without a sense of humor—this was the great problem with the fellows she met at Party meetings. No one outside the movie industry and no one who wasn't being paid, and paid well, for his writing.

So Dinah started going back to Veevi's, often with Renna in tow. At the Venturas' there were always people who fascinated her, amused her, intimidated her. Veevi and Stefan let their house be used for all sorts of causes—Communist Party fund-raisers and art auctions for Spain, farmworker-strike fund-raisers, union fund-raisers, anti-segregation fund-raisers, Democratic Party fund-raisers. Famous European writers came and gave speeches about the Loyalists and the Nazis and the looming threat of war. There was a constant stream of new visitors.

One night a tall young man with a round open face, black curly hair, and glasses he continually pushed back along his nose wandered into the kitchen, picked up a fork, and began eating leftovers of Dorshka's pot roast right off the used plates. "My God," he exclaimed with his mouth full, "I haven't eaten food like this since I left Chicago! Jesus, this is delicious." Dinah was trying to think of something to say when he added, "Say, where's the legendary beauty Veevi Ventura? Point her out to me, will ya?"

Dinah motioned for him to look out the kitchen window at the patio, which was lit up with bright lights and jammed with people. "She's over there," she said with a nod. "The one with the braids. Surrounded by her usual crowd of ad-d-d-doring admirers." Still eating leftovers, he looked out and watched Veevi for a while. "That is without doubt the single most sensational-looking woman I have ever seen in my *ganze leben*," he said.

"Your what?"

"My entire life. I'm Jake Lasker, by the way. Who're you?"

"I'm Mrs. Ventura's sister. Why don't you go out there and introduce yourself? There's always room for one more sh-sh-sheep in the fl-fl-flock." He gave her a funny look, which she returned. His seemed to say, "You mean you don't think I'm charming?" And hers answered, "No, not in the least." Then she untied the gingham apron she was wearing, hung it on the back of a chair, left the kitchen, and forgot him.

That night Stefan introduced the famous French writer André Malraux, who had come to Los Angeles to talk about the desperate need for medical supplies in Spain. After Stefan finished his introduction, Malraux warmly clasped his hands and startled Dinah by kissing him on both cheeks. Malraux had a dark, movie-star romantic look. He was wearing a rumpled suit, and Dinah thought him handsome in an exceedingly intelligent and troubled way. Then she silently scolded herself for finding so many European men attractive. By this time, she shouldn't be so impressionable—a word she had picked up from Norma Levine. After his speech he was surrounded by people she had never seen before, people who had traveled all the way up the coast from Mexico who seemed to know Stefan as well. Dinah was sitting in a corner of the sofa, studying the group around Malraux, when she took a sip of coffee and immediately felt like throwing up. Rushing upstairs to the bathroom, she vomited, and realized that she wasn't late, as she had imagined, but probably pregnant by one of the men she'd been sleeping with. Veevi had put her in touch with a gynecologist and she had a diaphragm now, and used it, but supposed uneasily that she must have taken it out too soon one morning, wanting to put the night before and the man she had brought home with her behind her once and for all.

Through the Beverly Hills gynecologist, Veevi found her an abortionist who had an office between Pico and Olympic, just west of La Cienega; Veevi said he took care of all the Marathon actresses who managed to get knocked up. He had dirty fingernails, smoked a cigar, and never took off his hat. The night before, her mother came over, asked no questions, slept in her bed with her as the sound of eucalyptus trees rustled outside, and held her until it was time to leave. For the rest of her life Dinah would remember that night and her mother's dry, warm hand holding hers, and how it had felt to try to sleep nestled against her mother's firm plumpness, her body prematurely worn and thickened from the years of housework and worry. Alice waited for Dinah outside in the car. Afterward, she took Dinah home, made her tea and buttered toast, and pulled up a chair to the edge of the bed, where she kept watch while Dinah slept. Dinah called in sick for two days but dared not take a third.

There wasn't anyone out there, she complained to her sister. She was going to die an old maid.

"Well, if you keep turning down people like Frank Herzog you will," said Veevi. "How could you be so dumb? You passed that up. Frank Herzog! The greatest songwriter of the twentieth century, for Christ's sake. You don't just walk away from someone like that! Do you know the people you could have met through him?"

Dinah always answered that she didn't want to be a married man's mistress.

"You wouldn't have ended up with him, you dope," Veevi said. "You would have *started* with him and then, at the right time, met someone else in his league and made your move."

"You mean I should have used him?" Dinah said.

"Well, why not? He would've been using you. That's how it works. Haven't you figured that out?"

"No," Dinah answered. "I haven't. By God I *am* d-d-d-dumb. That sort of thing never even occurred to me."

The only relief from the feeling that her life was going nowhere was helping out with the exiles. There, at least, she thought, she was useful. Saturday and Sunday mornings she gave driving lessons, and chauffeured people around to do their errands. They condescended to her but were nonetheless kind, and were clearly grateful to her. She asked Stefan what their lives had been like, and he told her to read Proust, which she did in the park on her lunch hour and before turning off the light at night. She began to liken weekends at the Venturas' to the world of the Guermantes, where she could imagine herself invisibly blending in. She watched and listened, all by herself, and felt she was learning things—indefinable things, things that were somehow important to know. She felt less shy about talking to the exiles. She was bringing coffee to a famous novelist with dark lines and puffy bags under his eyes and a little patch of a mustache when she heard him using the words *"Rosenbusche"* and *"Orangen und Oleander und Akazien."* Then he said to the woman seated behind him, *"In der Nacht ist der Duft schwer and suess. Das ist der Jasmin, der in der Nacht blueht,"* and Dinah caught his eye and said, "Night-blooming jasmine?" amazing even herself. He nodded, with a sharp bob of the head, and gave her a thin, formal smile.

Her interest in meeting new men, however, waned. Looking for someone seemed pointless—there wasn't anyone, she kept telling herself. Renna was just beginning to go out with the man she would later marry, and she invited Dinah to go to the movies with them, but the more lovey-dovey the two of them got, the more uncomfortable she became. More refugees arrived, bringing horrible stories, but Dinah felt, nevertheless, through her pity and concern, that those things were happening a long way from her own life. The Party people always seemed to know what to say, and the articles she read in the *New Masses* and *Daily Worker* were all for Spain but opposed a war with Germany, and she didn't know what to think. The Moscow trials confused her. Without Owen to direct her thinking, she couldn't make sense of the reasons anymore.

Then, one night late in the year—and as she sat now in her big Pontiac station wagon at the top of Rabbit Hill some fourteen years later her limbs stiffened and she gnawed the inside of her cheek with the memory—she went downstairs from her room in Veevi's house, restless, unable to sleep, wondering what to do about her life, wakeful because she knew she had to get up early in the morning and go back to her job, which she loathed. I'll just go down to the water's edge for a while and smell the ocean air, she thought. That'll make me drowsy.

She was careful to open and close the screen door quietly, not wanting to make any noise. The house was full of people—mostly couples, sharing beds, and it made her miserable to think of them when she was so alone. Veevi and Stefan's bedroom was just upstairs. Dorshka and her lover, Bernhard, had the maid's apartment at the back of the house, and there was a newly arrived couple from Hungary in the second guest bedroom next to her own. Tomorrow night she would come back after work and drive them to an apartment in Santa Monica that Dorshka had rented for them. Her son, Mike, as everyone now called him, also had a room upstairs. He also had to get up early for school. He drove there in the old Chevy his mother had bought him to keep him from running away and joining the Abraham Lincoln Brigade—which he had threatened to do many times. Mike cherished that car, Dinah thought fondly, with all his teenage heart.

Near the water's edge, however, in the darkness, she froze. The sounds were unmistakable. A young male voice cried, "Darling!" There was a woman's laugh, then, "Shh," and more laughter. Then the first voice, in lightly accented English: "You told me yourself he snores like a moose!" Dinah felt her stomach turn. Her heart pounded and she gasped for breath, horrified at what she was hearing and at the thought that she herself might be heard. Slithering backward, like an amphibious creature returning to the sea, wishing she were unconscious, numb, unable to see or hear, she began to feel a cold damp grittiness—wet sand—seeping into her nightgown, which quickly grew sloshy and heavy. She shivered as she felt the wind on her skin. Her vision sharpened, and she could make out the pale muscular back of Michael Albrecht as he leaned over a body that she knew was her sister's, whose wide-open, ocean-wet kneecaps threw off a pale luster.

Dinah made out the two glistening bodies moving together in the night. Moreover, she realized that for them it wasn't the first time: they were too intent, too slow, too purposeful. They know what they're doing, she said to herself. They've got a routine already.

She stuck her sandy fingers in her ears, as if she were at a movie listening to the cries of men being shot or killed, but she was becoming so cold she needed to cross her arms under her head and somehow try to curl up within herself. At last she heard what was unmistakably the end. Fine, she thought, they'll go in now. But then she saw the red glow of burning cigarettes in the darkness, and heard low laughter.

"For me it's not so bad. I can sleep as late as I want," Veevi was saying. "But *you*, you poor thing, have to get up and go to *school* tomorrow morning."

"Yeah," Mike said. "First period's chemistry and second period's geometry. Through those I will sleep. Then I have English. *The Red Badge of Courage*. For that one I wake up."

Dinah was relieved to hear them getting up, but then she heard "Shh! Get down! The cigarettes! Put them out!" from Michael, and she froze again: without doubt, she had been discovered. But there was only more quiet laughter and, looking up, she saw what they were seeing: Dorshka and her lover Bernhard, bundled up in lumpy terry-cloth bathrobes, standing at the kitchen sink, eating big slabs of cake with their fingers, sharing milk from the bottle. "Hey, darling, look! It's Mutti and Bernhard. They've been doing what we've been doing and now they are having a little snack!"

"How dear," Veevi said drily. "How very dear."

"He's the best lover she's ever had. Imagine that, the old guy."

"Who told you that?"

"She did."

"Dorshka told you? She talks about that sort of thing with you? My mother always made a terrible face if we asked her about it. My father warned us about white slavers, but he would have shot himself rather than talk to us about sex."

"Your father would rather shoot anything, period. By the way, you know, don't you, that Stefan is probably my father?"

"I'd forgotten that," she said gaily. "Then we're committing incest and not just adultery?"

"Two for the price of one, as you Americans say."

There was a silence. Then Dinah heard sighs, whispers, murmurs. Oh, Jesus Christ, they're at it again. Please don't, she silently pleaded with them. But they only became quiet again. She could hear the waves, and feel them reaching up to her feet.

The kitchen went dark and time passed and Veevi and Michael had another cigarette. Finally, they rose from the sand and walked slowly back to the house, but not together: Veevi, who from the rustling sound Dinah heard must have put her short, filmy, expensive handmade silk nightgown back on, went first, and Michael followed a good five minutes later.

Once they had disappeared into the house, Dinah made her way back along the path. Her body was stiff and sore and wobbly from lying in the cold sand. There was sand in her teeth and in her ears. The lower half of her nightgown was soaked. Her eyes burned from wind and salt. Hearing them make love had aroused her, against her will, and she felt disgusted with herself and ashamed. She was beside herself thinking of Stefan— heartsick for him, revolted, appalled, furious.

It must have been only a few weeks later that Western Union couriers started showing up at Malibu at all hours, bringing cables from Mexico and France. Veevi told Dinah that no matter how early she woke in the morning, Stefan had already been up for hours. There was talk of his moving to another studio, of their moving to New York—or to Mexico. At one point Stefan and Veevi actually drove down to Mexico City, where, they said vaguely, they saw some old friends of his, the ones who had driven north that time to hear Malraux. Dinah suspected they were Party friends, but when she asked Veevi who they were, Veevi just shrugged and said, "Oh, I don't know, people from Stefan's UFA days—you know, movie people from Berlin. I can't keep track of them all." When they came back, Veevi got Dorshka to start teaching her French. They sat out on the veranda and Dorshka drilled her and corrected her pronunciation. Unlike Stefan, Dorshka was still working, on assignment for Marathon. She felt awful about it since things had gone bad there for Stefan, she told Dinah, but what could she do? She needed money to get people out.

Then Veevi called Dinah at home one night in Laurel Canyon. An old and respected French production company had offered to back Stefan in anything he wanted to do and he had said yes. They were taking the train to New York in two days; could Dinah take a couple of sick days and help her pack things for storage and then drive them to Union Station?

"How can you go to Europe right n-n-n-now?" Dinah exclaimed. "Are you out of your minds? Everybody's trying to get out!"

"Don't worry," Veevi said mysteriously. "Stefan has friends over there who need him and they'll look after us."

At the station, Dinah and Dorshka kept looking at each other. It was January 1939, and they understood that they might never see Veevi and Stefan again. Veevi wrote from New York that Michael had come down from the boarding school in Connecticut to which he had just been sent to see them at their hotel, and that Stefan had taken him out in a bitter wind for a long walk through Central Park, but she didn't say what they had talked about. "Don't worry about us," she wrote on the hotel stationery. "Hollywood is finished with Stefan, and Stefan is finished with Hollywood. And thank God for that. Of course I will miss you and Dorshka, but as far as I'm concerned I'm putting America behind me for good. For the first time in my life I'm going to a place where I belong. I owe everything to Stefan, and if he wishes to go into the lion's den, I'll go with him."

I don't get it, Dinah kept saying to herself as she read and reread the letter at work. Had she hallucinated that scene on the beach? "I didn't want anyone to know this before we left, because it would have caused too much fuss, but I'm pregnant," Veevi had added. With whose child? Dinah wondered.

In March, Veevi wrote from Paris to say that she and Stefan were fine. They were living in a friend's apartment until they found a place of their own. Dinah had her own news to report: their mother was divorcing Pop and planning to marry her high school sweetheart, Lloyd Muir. Mom had run into him one day last year on the Marathon lot when she was visiting Veevi. A widower with grown children, he had been living in Los Angeles for years and played first violin in the studio orchestra. Pop was devastated, she told Veevi, and she was giving him as much as she could from her savings to help him buy a trailer; if she and Stefan had any money at all, perhaps they could wire some to him. Veevi wrote that they needed all they had for themselves.

In July, Veevi gave birth to a daughter, Claire. All along Dinah had been wondering if going to France with Stefan had been, for Veevi, a kind of alibi. Mike, of course, was still in high school, and who knows if Veevi and Stefan had been having sex during his last awful weeks at Marathon. But it had nothing to do with her, Dinah told herself, so she let the questions fade along with the memory of that terrible night on the beach. Meanwhile, she found herself alone for the first time in her life, her family scattered hither and yon. Alice and Lloyd moved into the Venturas' house, keeping watch over it until it was sold. Dorshka moved to an apartment on Landfair, in Westwood. Ed Milligan, unable, Dinah knew, to find pleasure or comfort in her company and grieving far more over Veevi than his wife, took off for the Sierras. Then came the Pact, and Poland.

Only Dinah's life stood still.

She sat up now, with a start. Shadows were falling on Rabbit Hill, and in a sudden panic she checked her watch and saw that it was close to four. She should have been home long ago. Jake would be furious if she wasn't there to greet their guests. What was the point of dredging up those old days, anyway? she asked herself as she tore down the road toward Sunset, a cloud of dust rising behind the car. It was only self-indulgence to wallow in unanswerable questions. Would things have been any different for her if she'd never joined the Party? Would it have been better for her if she'd gone back to men like Everett, whose idea of a great time was a DeMolay dance or a state picnic every year? Not on your life, buster, she murmured to herself, turning left onto Westwood Boulevard. Then she remembered one sad phone call at the beginning of the war. Tal Engel had called to ask if she'd had any news of her sister. They got to talking—by that time, she was working in radio—and Tal invited her out to dinner. But he didn't show up or even call to apologize. A few days later, Renna told Dinah he had died the night before of pneumonia. L.J. was retiring, and Irv was taking over as head of Marathon Pictures.

Things might have been different, but so what? In a few minutes she would load up the car with extra bottles of ginger ale and tonic and then rush home to her husband and kids and guests. She had what she wanted, and wanted what she had. She'd tell Groucho the story about Mom and the guy with the big nose. He'd like it, she was sure. When Groucho loved a story, he didn't laugh; his mouth, with the broad mustache, twitched very faintly and he had a concentrated look, as if he were focusing on a delicious taste. "It's too funny to laugh," he would say. That story and ten minutes of watching her dance the Charleston—she always did that for him whenever he came over—and he was a happy man.

$\mathcal{L}$ooking up from his yellow legal pad, Jake sighed and swiveled his chair, landing, like a chip on a roulette wheel, in front of his office window. He hated writing at the studio, and could take little pleasure in the scene he had just mapped out, knowing that until he worked out a finish for the story, there was no satisfaction in what he had already done. He was restless, too, feeling that he ought to be more patient with Dinah. Despite her avowals to the contrary, she seemed to have put her life in limbo as she waited to hear from Veevi. The HUAC episode was lingering in their lives, like a bad smell. There had to be something he could do to get her to put the whole thing behind her. He didn't approve of her writing to Veevi or visiting Dorshka or involving herself in anybody's life but his and the children's. I don't give a fuck about Veevi, he had told her, and I wish to hell you didn't, either. Another thing that bothered him was that she went to sleep right away in her own bed, not coming into his, not giving him back rubs, and seemed uninterested in sex. She still wanted another baby, but these past few weeks, what with Pop Milligan dying and all the worrying over Veevi, she hadn't shown the slightest interest; yet here he was thinking that he really ought to stay away from girls—in other words, make a real sacrifice of his comfort and pleasure and put his energies into making Dinah pregnant. He'd seen Bonnie last week, and promised himself it was for the last time. So rejection from his own wife was the last thing he needed.

Every day he woke up full of fight and promise, and every night he went to bed beaten and desolate. Sandy Litvak, his analyst, had often told him that he had an infantile personality, which was why, he said, "you have such a need for gratification. Happiness is beyond us; all any of us can obtain, realistically, is gratification, though you seem to need it constantly in both oral and genital forms." But now Jake was trying, he said in imaginary conversations with Litvak, to be a grown-up. He was trying to diet and to stay away from broads, and to withstand the overwhelming anxiety of finding a finish for his story. The pressure was almost unbearable, and yet he had decided to give up Bonnie. I'm trying to be a mensch, he reminded himself. The result was that he felt irritable and edgy.

That mood was now broken by a welcome sight: young Hunt Crandell walking toward the writers' building, Irv beside him, his long arm draped around Hunt's athletic shoulders in imprisoning affection.

"Hey, boychik!" shouted Jake, sticking his head out the window. "What's a nice goyishe kid like you doing in a place like this?"

"Just lucky, I guess," came the instant reply, which all three men recognized as the punch line to any one of a dozen jokes about girls found in compromising positions. "I was just on my way up to see you." A man in his early thirties, with clean-cut classic American features, grinned up at Jake from under the window.

"So get your Parisian ass right up here this minute!" Jake shouted back at Hunt.

"Okay—but ship the lad right back to me after lunch," Irv instructed, pointing to his watch.

"Over and out," said Jake, and pulled his head in. Quickly, he rearranged the papers on his desk. He had a real talent for sitting at people's desks and reading their correspondence upside down, and he assumed others did it too, so whenever he knew he had a visitor coming he scooped up all his papers and stuffed them into a drawer.

Hunt had also met Dinah in the old days, at the Engels' beach house. They used to play volleyball and horse around together, like brother and sister. Later, Hunt became close friends with Mike Albrecht. Stefan had given him a job as a gofer on the disastrous Oedipus movie, and had brought him into the cutting room to learn the trade. After the war, the army had put him to work shooting and cutting documentary footage for the Nuremberg trials, and on a visit to Paris he had looked up his fellow OSS buddy Michael Albrecht, who said to him, "You'll never guess who I'm marrying tomorrow," which was how Hunt ended up serving as best man at Mike and Veevi's wedding.

By that time he'd already been married for three years to Felicity Moore, an exuberant, leggy beauty who came from an old lumber family in

Tacoma. She was a bright and savvy ex-deb with leftist yearnings and a trust fund, and when she took off for New York at the age of nineteen it was with a clear understanding that destiny would provide her with a lifetime's worth of interesting, clever, talented people. Knowing herself equal to the company she wished to keep, she was hardly surprised when writers fell for her, wrote stories about her, and couldn't keep up with her on the tennis court. She dressed well and drank well, had perfect manners, enormous tact, and an infinite capacity for fun. She wasn't a prude and she disliked making judgments, but when she did she was forthright and didn't back down.

Felicity's blue eyes were large and bright and she had a way of opening them wide when she told a story. Her laughter was high-pitched and explosive, and she was sharp—she understood nuances and got everything right away. She was well-read, not Jewish, and hated anti-Semitism. Dinah loved her, and Jake did, too, though of course he had kept his desire to sleep with her to himself, having become fascinated by her lithe and athletic body while he and Hunt were cutting Jake's *Utopia, Incorporated* in 1947.

It was after Mike wrote Jake from Paris about Hunt that Jake gave him a job—his first as a cutter on a full-length feature. Afterward, he and Felicity began dividing their time between L.A. and Paris, where Mike had met the legendary producer Willie Weil and persuaded him to let Hunt direct the movie version of Mike's short story "Heart's Blood," which Mike refused to let anyone in Hollywood make. It was about a married American woman in Paris who has a love affair with a young French jockey, a veteran of the Resistance. He is killed in a big race. She later learns that her husband, a major American importer of German cars, had paid her lover to fix the race, and she finds a way to take revenge on him. A small-budget (and French-subsidized) art-house success in the States and a moneymaker in Europe, the picture secured Hunt the interest of the Hollywood majors, especially Marathon, where his early friendship with Irv Engel had done him no harm at all. He was in L.A. with Willie Weil, he told Jake, to make a deal for a picture he wanted to direct in Africa.

That same night, after Jake and Hunt had met at the lot, they caught up over dinner at Chasen's with Dinah and Felicity. Felicity told a story about Mike, though it was really a story about Ben Knight, the novelist whom both Mike and Hunt shared as a best friend. Mike had gone skiing in Switzerland with Knight's eight-year-old son, Stevie, and Stevie's Swiss ski instructor, Kristl, a pretty young woman from the village, who probably had a crush on Mike. Always one to push himself, and everyone else, further than they could go, Mike insisted on leaving the trails and skiing in faraway untouched deep snow. He got separated from Kristl and Stevie, and there was an avalanche. Mike heard cries and raced to locate them, but by the time he spotted Stevie, covered to his cap in snow and clinging to a tree trunk, the girl had been swept away. Not knowing whether to search for the girl or take the terrified boy back to the village, he decided to stay and look for the girl and send the boy back on his own. Stevie was a good skier, and he found his way back to the village and went for his father, who called out the rescue teams to help look for Kristl.

After hours of searching, they found her, but she was dead, her body crushed, one arm sticking out of the snow. That night, Ben Knight knocked on Mike's door at the lodge. "Look," he said. "This was a local girl and she's dead. The first thing you're gonna want to do is slip out of here, any way you can. But since you can't leave tonight, tomorrow morning I'm meeting you downstairs at eight and we're going to walk together from one end of town to the other. Life will go on as usual. What happened was an act of God—very regrettable, but nothing to hide from." And that was what they did, Felicity continued—they walked up and down the main street, greeting all the local people, saying good morning in Swiss-German. "Well, I can tell you one thing," Felicity concluded. "Odile was none too happy about that. Wouldn't even look at him over the fondue pot—not for a whole evening."

"Who's Odile?" Dinah asked.

"Fe-li-ci-ty," said Hunt.

"Oh shit," Felicity said, her eyes opening wide. "Have I stepped in it? Oh dear. Why don't you tell them, darling," she said to Hunt.

"No, baby—*you* tell them. You're the one who had to open your big mouth."

"You don't know?" Felicity said weakly to Jake and Dinah.

"Know what?"

Looking up so suddenly that he spilled vanilla ice cream on his shirt, or would have, except that the super-athlete Hunt quickly stuck out his spoon and caught it in mid-drip, Jake said, "Haven't a clue."

"Is Veevi all right, Felicity?" asked Dinah.

"No, she isn't," Felicity answered.

"Jesus Christ, will one of you just t-t-t-tell me what's going on?" pleaded Dinah, taking out a cigarette.

"Darlings," said Felicity, "it just couldn't be worse."

Jake saw the color drain out of Dinah's face. He leaned forward and cupped his deaf left ear.

"At the end of the summer—not *last* summer, but the summer *before* last, Mike told Veevi that he'd fallen in love with a French girl—Odile Boisvert. She's an actress, not bad for her age, which is immensely young— twenty-one, if that. And so bloody beautiful you could cry. Not Veevi's kind of beauty either, but cool, blond, elegant—very high-couture. She used to be a model, I think. Mike moved into the girl's flat, and they spend a lot of time skiing in Klosters. So, for Genevieve that in itself has been tough enough. But there's more."

Dinah felt as if she had turned into a block of stone.

"Well, she was *pregnant* and was having a very hard time. The baby was in a peculiar position and she had to spend a lot of time in bed until the birth in late winter. Mike kept telling Genevieve that he loved her even if he was no longer *in* love with her, and said he'd be there for the birth. But he was working on a new novel and he was very sadistic—just awful. Some- how he let Veevi know that he had to have Odile with him—you know, just like he used to tell Genevieve how much he needed her to be there with him while he heroically, or maybe it's existentially, faced the blank page and all that sort of thing."

"This has been going on for over a year?" Dinah asked.

Felicity sighed. "What makes me so mad is how damn noble Genevieve is being about the whole thing. 'It's not his fault,' she keeps saying. 'You can't choose the person you're going to fall in love with—it's not up to you.' She's convinced herself that if she just hangs on long enough he'll come back. That it's all a big reaction to the baby, which was an accident. Mike wanted her to get an abortion, but it was too late, or she didn't tell him until it was too late. He's fond enough of Claire, but he panicked, she says—thought that with another child they were going to have a regular family life, and if there's one thing Mike Albrecht isn't cut out for it's family life and everything that goes with it."

"I don't know . . ." said Hunt. "You're making it sound too tragic, sweetie. She meets us at Fouquet's, on her own, and nobody lets her pay. She doesn't look like a martyr to me."

"Well, we figured something fishy's been going on," said Jake, stabbing his fork into Dinah's banana shortcake. "By the way, we've also got something to tell you."

"We know," Felicity said. "Veevi told us." She hesitated before adding, "If you don't want to talk about it, you don't have to."

"Of course we want to talk about it!" Jake said, and then went on to tell the whole story of Dinah's testimony. When he finished, Dinah mentioned the letter she'd received from Mike.

"What a sanctimonious schmuck," said Jake, taking a spoon and mushing up the remaining streaks of whipped cream, hot fudge sauce, and bananas from Dinah's plate. "I can't stand guys like that."

"Haven't you ever been in love?" said Felicity.

"Not that way," Jake answered.

"Gee, thanks a lot, b-b-b-buster," said Dinah, looking across the table and grabbing the spoon away from him.

"Ah, honey, you know what I mean," said Jake. "I'm talking about Mike's way. That all-consuming fuck-what-people-think kind of thing."

"No, dear," said Dinah, patting him on the wrist. "That certainly ain't you." Then she looked at Felicity. "Has she said anything to you about wanting to come home?"

"Oh, Dinah, it's hard to say. You ought to know by now that your sister isn't a creature of intentions. Impulses, maybe. Instincts, perhaps. She's blind, frightened. A couple of times she said something about leaving, that she couldn't stand seeing Mike with Odile, but she just hangs on."

"Why?" said Dinah. "It must be hell for her there."

"She's been insanely in love with Michael ever since they found each other in Paris, right after the war," said Felicity.

It was long before that, Dinah almost said.

"She's desperate," Felicity continued. "By day she lies in bed crying. At night she goes to Fouquet's and pretends that nothing's wrong. All she thinks about is how to get Mike back. But it's hopeless, Dinah. He's *gone*. He told her he's gone. I think he's a perfect cad, myself."

"Now look, Felicity," Hunt said to her, "enough of that. Mike is my closest friend, and I won't have you passing judgment on him. He's suffering just as much as she is."

"Nonsense, darling," said Felicity. "He can't be. He's in love. Nobody just ran out on him. I don't care if he's God's best friend, he's a son of a bitch."

"Does Dorshka know?" Dinah said.

"Yes. Genevieve says that she and Mike have written her separate letters."

"Recently?"

"No. A while ago. Around Christmas, I think, or just before."

Jake caught Dinah's eye: "I told you so," his look said. Dinah had come home after her lunch with Dorshka, and told Jake how "genuine" Dorshka was, and he had said, "There's something full-of-shit about her."

The check came, and Jake grabbed it. Then the four of them strolled out into the balmy winter evening. Dinah ached to go home, crawl under the covers, and brood about Veevi's situation. As it turned out, the Crandells wanted to make it an early evening, so the two couples got into the Laskers' Cadillac and headed toward Sunset and the Beverly Hills Hotel, where the Crandells were staying.

Hunt sat in front with Jake, while Dinah and Felicity sat in the back and listened to the two men talk. Was it true, Jake asked, that Willie Weil seemed willing to relieve writers and directors of every responsibility except that of actually coming up with a story and making a picture? Was he a son of a bitch? Did Hunt think Jake and Weil could get along? Dinah was astonished to hear Jake confess that he was getting restless at Marathon and that he'd been wondering if he and Dinah ought to move to Europe.

Felicity turned to Dinah. "True?" she said. "That would be great for us."

"Who knows? Jake doesn't know what he wants," Dinah whispered to her. "Or, rather, he wants everything." She hesitated, then added, "It's exhausting."

Before dropping the Crandells at the hotel, Jake made a date with Hunt to play golf on Sunday. Dinah and Felicity agreed to have lunch the following week. On Saturday, however, Felicity phoned. She had to fly back to Paris right away. The French nanny had called to say that both kids had come down with chicken pox and that she had never had it and was going to quit and leave them with the cook if Madame Crandell did not return "toot sweet," as Felicity pronounced it. "Please tell Veevi I'll do anything for her!" Dinah cried. "Tell her I'll come over and I'll pack her up and get her and Claire and the baby over here. I'll deal with the embassy or the consulate or whatever the hell we've got over there—whatever she wants. Tell her she can hate me or not—it doesn't matter. She's my sister, my family, and I'll take care of everything if she'll let me."

Felicity promised to give Veevi the message but told Dinah not to get her hopes up. "I don't think it's a question of politics, darling. Just heart-break."

Later that night, Jake patted a space beside him on the bed. As Dinah obediently got in next to him, she told him to ask Gladys to make a plane reservation for her. "I'm going to Paris to get Veevi."

"Oh no you aren't," he said.

"Oh yes I am. I've got to make sure she's all right."

"That's exactly what you don't have to do, Dinah. You haven't heard from her—she's effectively said 'fuck you' to both of us. As far as I'm concerned, she's on her own. Let's turn off the lights and make a baby. Don't make Veevi the baby. If you do, it'll never end."

"Okay, Jake, okay. But I'll come to England with you and I'll go see her."

Jake was superstitious about his projects and rarely discussed them with friends until principal photography had started. What he hadn't shared with Hunt Crandell was that it looked as if his new picture would soon be set. He had a commitment from Wynn Tooling, the English movie star, and was revising the script, putting in business geared specifically to Tooling's genius for physical comedy. All the second-unit material—exteriors, the car chase—would be shot in and around London. He didn't want the respon-sibility of having Dinah with him during the days. And he had high hopes for extracurricular fun at night. Most of all, he didn't want Dinah to get tangled up in Veevi's life.

"Wait a little while, honey, and let's see how things shape up," he coun-seled her. "They usually take care of themselves."

"She's in trouble, Jake. And alone."

"Veevi has more friends than anyone we know. And don't forget—she stopped speaking to you. What makes you so sure she'll want to see you?"

He turned on the radio and started listening to the baseball game, and Dinah turned out the lights and got into her own bed. The smooth, ironed sheets enveloped her, but she felt small and cold.

*J*ake pulled the sheet of engraved stationery out of the hotel typewriter on which he had been contentedly hunting and punching, set it down on the night table beside the bed, and stepped out onto the balcony overlooking Hyde Park. He sucked on his Monte Cristo, gazing momentarily at its emerald green sunspots and feeling the prickles of sweat break out on his scalp as the rich, spicy smoke invaded his senses. He had been feeling wonderful ever since arriving in London. He was happy with everything: the red double-decker buses slowly lumbering up Park Lane, the towering green trees retreating into dusky shadow in the park, the exteriors and the chase he had been shooting for the past two weeks. One day, he told himself, he was going to shoot a scene from just this angle. The POV shot would be right from this balcony. The heavies would be chasing the hero up Park Lane, in and out of buses, and he'd work in the park and the trees and the vista up to Marble Arch and put in the tobacco-stained old fellow from the news kiosk on the corner—the one who'd made him laugh out loud the other day: "Me muvver started me on the tit. De-licious. An' it's only Guinness what gives me the same de-loit."

Sighing with an unquenchable desire for more—for more of *every-thing*—he chewed the cigar and gazed out over the park, savoring the sounds of a big city—like the Chicago he had known as a kid. Los Angeles was nowheresville compared to London. He had craved the roar of ceaseless activity, the smell of wet raincoats, the stink of buses. He wanted to get the kids out of L.A. and into a place with museums and theaters—not to mention gambling clubs for himself. He would start with a town house, in one of the big squares. Then good "public" schools for the kids, a country house, and flats in Paris and New York. He wanted to be free of studios and to go wherever he liked. He wanted to make pictures cheaply and live out in the world, not in L.A., which was nothing but a company town. Come to think of it, why stop at Paris and New York? He wanted a place in Cap Ferrat or Biarritz, and another in Klosters. And what about Italy? He'd love a little place in Italy. He puffed and yearned and puffed and yearned, relishing what he had and what he didn't have and what he wanted and what he was free to want, and all of it made him wild to work and convinced him that he could make it all happen.

Finally, he glanced at his watch and went inside. Unbelting his bathrobe, he lay down on the wide bed in his T-shirt and shorts and, by the light of a yellow silk lamp with fringe and gilded tassels that he knew Dinah would find hilarious, reached for the letter he had just finished writing. *Honey,* it began,

> *Today we finished another marvelous week of exteriors out at Marlow (incredibly lovely, near an equally lovely spot on the Thames called, believe it or not, Maidenhead—I forgot to ask whose). We're about two-thirds done on the chase, the trick car has—knock on wood—been behaving well, and the English weather, which is, as you know, the dreariest in the world, has favored us with fairly constant sunshine and no rain. I love working here and I love being here. The crew call me "Guv," and as long as they get their tea breaks exactly on schedule (which they call "shed-ule"), they couldn't be sweeter or more helpful. Wynn Tooling is a darling—a consummate professional, always ready, genuinely nice. Thinking I might be lonely, he and his wife, Diana, invited me out to their house last Sunday afternoon. She's the daughter of Constance Fletcher—remember her? Since "retiring from the stage," she has established herself in regal comfort not a mile from the Toolings in Henley, which happens to be right next to Maidenhead. I had the Rolls—finally a car long enough for me to stretch out my legs in—and the chauffeur from Elstree (very nice for a little Jewish kid from Hyde Park—Hyde Park, Chicago that is), and I invited Felicity along. She's in town for a few days' shopping at Harrods before they leave for Kenya. Except for missing you terribly, and both of us wanting to show you a thousand things, we had a great afternoon, ending up at a neighbor of the Toolings' Wynn would only identify as Lady Peel. Well, Felicity was nervous and so was I. Being here is one thing.*

Meeting the quality another. Felicity kept giving me strained looks, and I began to wonder whether men are supposed to curtsy.

Expecting a shelf-bosomed dowager with pearls and a lorgnette, I was dumbfounded when the diminutive creature announced to us by the butler turned out to be none other than Bea Lillie, very elegant, thoroughly crocked, and utterly adorable in her big house on the Thames. And she most certainly is Lady Peel, by virtue of her marriage to a descendant of the fellow who came up with that capital invention the London police, or "bobbies."

Tea was served, but nobody drank it. Instead, there were rivers of gin. Then Wynn said, "Darling, do be a love and show Jake the Queen and the Crapper." Whereupon Bea Lillie suddenly became, right before our eyes, none other than Queen Victoria on the occasion of Her Majesty's introduction to the first modern water closet at Buckingham Palace. On her head she placed a little white lace handkerchief. Then she folded her arms tightly across her chest and somehow managed to both puff out her cheeks and pinch in her mouth, and bang, there she was, the aged queen herself, approaching and inspecting, with high royal skepticism, the first royal loo. She raised her imaginary but voluminous skirts and gently and suspiciously lowered her royal behind onto the royal can. The look on her face as she passed what can only be called royal water, the human bliss of it—checked by monarchical noblesse, as if it would be a betrayal of her subjects to enjoy the moment too voluptuously—made me ache for a camera. Moments later she stands, suspiciously inspects the bowl, tentatively reaches out, and then, in a wild burst of royal courage, as if she were taking upon herself the fate of the empire, pulls, or rather yanks, the chain—suddenly starting at the noise and jumping back, then leaning forward and peering downward with amazement as the royal effluvia are hydraulically propelled through the labyrinthine pipes of the palace plumbing out into London's sewers, whence they make their democratic way to the ever-flowing Thames. Christ, honey, I wish you'd been there. You know Felicity's laugh. Well, you could hear it all the way to Windsor Palace.

Anyway, the point is that it's only over here that we can meet people like that. I would love to write something for Bea Lillie, and I think I have a knack for English stage comedy. It isn't so far from Vaudeville shtick, and can be very broad and very, very funny. And think how close London is to the rest of Europe! I could make pictures in a dozen dif-

ferent places over here. I'm finally going to Paris first thing tomorrow morning, taking the seven o'clock plane from Heathrow with Felicity and staying at the Raphael. According to her, it's much classier and quieter than the George V. Now, about your letter. Don't worry, I haven't forgotten it, and if I can somehow find a way to see Veevi, and if she'll condescend to talk to me, I'll give it to her. I promise, though as you know, I still think you're making a big mistake. By the way, Felicity seems much less worried about her than she was in L.A., though she thinks V.'s apparent equanimity is based on her tenacious but totally mistaken assumption that if she just waits it out long enough Mike will come back—something Felicity says ain't gonna happen. I'm telling you all this very reluctantly, because I know it will only make that albatross of an already overdeveloped sense of guilt toward your sister hang more heavily around your pretty little neck. Please, darling, I'm begging you, don't drive yourself crazy over this. I will honestly try to deliver your letter by hand as you've asked, but I'm not going to force myself on her. As I wrote you the other night, she never called me back when I called her two weeks ago and there's only so much I can do or, frankly, am willing to do.

God, I love this town, and I know you would, too. I can't tell you how being over here makes me want to get the hell out of Hollywood for good, and move here, the sooner the better. I wake up here and think, Why on earth would anybody want to live in L.A.? Why be chained to that goddamn industry? I've never felt so at home anywhere as I do here. Think of it, honey: the Dorch is just around the corner from where Disraeli lived. In America I'm a Jew; over here I'm a Yank who knows how to make the English laugh. It's romantic and silly of me, I suppose, but I love walking here and feeling surrounded by history. If I could just show it to you, I know you'd understand. As usual, whenever I'm away from you I feel only half alive. I wish you were here right now so we could go beddy-bye and then spend the day looking for a smashy house for the four (or more) of us. And about that "more": anything to report?

So let's start talking this over as soon as I get home. Let's sell the house. If Gussie's willing to come, let's bring her with us. I want the kids to go to good English schools and get a real education. I want to live in a town where people talk about something besides the movies. I want to walk in the parks. I want to start over and write plays, and I've *got some novels up my sleeve. Just being away makes me realize that every day I'm in L.A. I walk around with a slight depression. Over here it's gone and I feel like a new man.*

Darling, I love you and miss your sweet brown eyes and your great long legs. I miss your laugh and your stutter. Just promise me, honey, that wherever we live, whatever we do, we're doing it as one person, one body, forever.

Kiss the kids for me, and don't forget our nightly date: when it's ten o'clock here it's two there, and, baby, I've been thinking of you at exactly that time and hope you've been thinking of me. When the picture is done let's go someplace great together, just you and me, and get back to work on supplying the world with another little Lasker.

All my love,

When he finished rereading the letter, he found his gold ballpoint pen and signed his initial—*J.* He could just imagine Dinah reading it in her bathrobe at the breakfast table, and felt a little teary. If he did say so himself, he wrote a damn good love letter, and his chest expanded with the pleasure and reassurance he knew she would feel upon reading it. He wasn't so good at hugging and kissing, didn't like to hold hands or put his arm around her, but he knew how to lay down the words.

He glanced at his watch: time to shave and shower for the evening. He hastily folded the letter and put it in an envelope and began to whistle "I'm gonna sit right down and write myself a letter." But the tune trailed off; he felt overcome by the desire to take a little nap. He called the hotel operator and instructed her to ring him in exactly twenty minutes. Then he lay down on the large bed and drew the bedspread up to the hollow just under his nose. Luxuriously, he abandoned himself to thoughts of Felicity's legs. Long and tanned, crossed, and sheathed in nylon stockings in the backseat of the Rolls earlier in the week, when she had driven out with him to watch him shoot, those legs had held out delightful promise. As he grew hard he thought, I really ought to just take this nap, and besides, what if she says yes? Then I've gone and shot it all and can't get it up later. But then he thought sternly yet comfortingly, Nonsense, this is pure nonsense. Since when haven't I been able to do it at least twice in one night? Reaching for himself, he added, Besides, there's nothing that relaxes me better or faster and does a better job of putting me to sleep.

An hour later, thoroughly refreshed, he stood before the mirror in full uniform: dark blue suit, light blue shirt, and tie, all from Dick Carroll; over his left arm a tan Burberry raincoat. He was hungry, happy, and counting on almost certain success with Felicity. The campaign had been going reasonably well. He had restrained himself earlier in the week. She had gone back to Shepperton with him to watch the dailies, and then they'd had a late dinner together at a bistro in Beauchamp Place. Exhausted, he had fallen asleep in the Rolls on the way back to the Connaught, where she was staying. Embarrassed when she gently jostled him to say good night, he had taken her up in the lift and kissed her at the door. She invited him in for a nightcap, and when they sat down at opposite ends of the sofa, she let her shoes drop to the floor and stretched her legs out across his lap. While they talked, he lightly stroked her feet and ankles. They necked. But by then it was past midnight and he had to be up at six for the next day's shooting, so he left, with things unspoken between them. Last night, he had once again taken her out to dinner in Mayfair, and as they walked arm in arm afterward around Grosvenor Square he said, "Look, I think you're sensational. You love Hunt and I love Dinah and we both know the code of the hills. I won't be a pain in the ass and neither will you. So come back to my room with me. On Saturday, we'll fly to Paris together just as we planned."

"You're very dear," she said, looking at him with her intelligent blue eyes. "Can I think about it?"

"Of course. There's always tomorrow night, too."

Vaguely embarrassed by the Rolls-Royce slowly trailing him and Felicity, he dismissed the chauffeur for the night. He hadn't felt this good in a long time. It was like the early days in Chicago, after college and before he had come out to Hollywood. He had hated his job selling advertising for the *Jewish Daily Messenger,* and lived for the nights, when he would work on his novel, *Beef* (which now lay untouched in an envelope in his attic). He was disgusted with his false starts and his constant failure to get down on paper what he had it in him to say, but he was desperate to grab on to the possibilities of life. At about ten every night, he'd go out for a walk, ravenous for success and money and women. And he had loved, in those days, left-wing Jewish girls, college girls, but sometimes also working girls— Polish and Catholic girls, with whom he could have unromantic companionable sex, who didn't expect him to say "I love you" and would have laughed at him if he had.

"Of course you can think about it, baby," he said to Felicity softly. "But

I really am crazy about you. We're friends. Real friends. That doesn't change one way or the other. And it's about the friendliest thing two people can do."

The line had come to him some weeks ago and he had jotted it down in the little memo book he kept in his jacket pocket, thinking it would make a good opening line in a song for the Broadway musical that was slowly simmering in his mind—a musical about his grandfather's saloon, in Chicago, in the 1890s. This song would be the first line to be sung by the young medical student to the even younger Polish waitress who lived with his family and worked for them and whom he wished to sweet-talk into bed.

On Felicity's instructions, he arrived at Fouquet's ahead of the Crandells and ordered a Scotch on the rocks at the bar. Although he was apprehensive about seeing Veevi and running into Mike Albrecht, he couldn't help being exhilarated. He was in Paris, and he could concentrate on his impressions without diluting them by having to share them with Dinah. He hardly had a chance to take in the place before Veevi came in, flanked by Hunt and Felicity, those two golden sentries, who issued convincing cries of surprise and joy at finding him there. He moved fast, not giving Veevi a chance to rebuff him, and leaned forward to kiss her on both cheeks, as Felicity had taught him. Veevi automatically raised her face to his, as if finding him there was the most natural thing in the world.

So she wasn't going to cut him, he thought. Doubtless she had other, more pressing things weighing on her than Dinah's testifying, so he could put his mind to rest about that. Clearly, she wasn't going to make a scene, and, anyway, from everything he knew about her, that wasn't her style.

To Jake, who often told Dinah what to wear and enjoyed supervising the wardrobes of actresses in his pictures, Veevi's simple attire suggested a woman who wished to keep herself up and was determined to look subdued, chic, and, it seemed to him, very French. Whereas Felicity had clothed her lithe and athletic body in a sporty little navy blue sheath (the feeling of her tanned legs clamped against his lower back was still fresh in his memory from last night at the Connaught, where she'd told him that she'd considered his proposition and agreed that their friendship required nothing less), Veevi was in a black silk shirtwaist, a string of small pearls around her neck and a pearl in each earlobe. This arrangement set off her face, still stunning, with its clear and regular features. She wore red lipstick on her wide mouth, mascara on her eyelashes; her thick brown shoulder-length hair was brushed back in a wave and to the side. When she looked at him, her face registered no sadness or heartbreak or surprise or annoyance. It seemed to say, "Oh, it's you. Hmm."

He felt himself floating through waves of people and then anchored at a table near the bar with his sister-in-law and the Crandells. A hand on his thigh caressed him; Felicity offered a stream of amusing prattle. What a terrific dame, he thought, knows just what to do. She told the Lady Peel story, and Veevi laughed, and then there was talk about the London stage, and comparisons with plays currently running in Paris, and Felicity pointed out an English actress who was standing at the bar with her third husband, Lord Hindlip. Then Hunt asked Jake about his picture and the English crews, exercising the tact—cultivated over the years—that well-bred moviemakers used with one another: they confined themselves to questions likely to receive cheerful answers and carefully avoided those sparked by rumor and malice.

Hunt and Jake agreed that going back to Hollywood was a depressing thought after shooting a picture in England, and Jake said he'd fallen in love with London and wanted to move there but was tied for the time being to Marathon; he made a face as if he had indigestion. Felicity and Veevi perked up their ears to the whispers and murmurs around them that meant serious gossip, and Hunt kept talking about all the problems he would have to face on the picture he was going to be shooting in Kenya. Somehow, tonight, Jake decided, he would try to give Dinah's letter to Veevi. He would find a way to manage it; after all, he was in excellent company, and felt blissful and affectionate toward the whole world. Hunt was a decent fellow, charming and expert at putting everyone at ease. Did he have any idea, Jake wondered, of what had gone on between himself and Felicity? She had said, last night, of her husband, "He's my best friend. We don't ask each other questions we shouldn't." Now, why couldn't he and Dinah have an arrangement like that?

It surprised him that he felt so good. Life didn't get better than this—this blaze of good Scotch and attractive people, all of them in the prime of life, all of them singled out by destiny, it seemed, for lives of infinite pleasure. People stopped by their table, and in the space of about twenty minutes he met a bullfighter and his girlfriend, two writers for the Luce magazines, the bureau chief for the *International Herald-Tribune,* an American working for the Paris branch of a big New York law firm, an English director and his wife, a prince from Saudi Arabia with a beautiful French model on his arm, an English colonel and his debutante daughter, an American jockey, and an Italian count who manufactured racing cars and was accompanied by his blond wife, who was a fashion designer, and taller than he. Some recognized Jake's name, or pretended to, and asked about mutual friends in Hollywood—usually big-name stars who weren't in the Laskers' set, but none of it made any difference. He was accepted and that was that, and by people he had been nervous about meeting, expecting them to be standoffish, a little patronizing even, since he was only a comedy writer, and the corner of social Hollywood he and Dinah belonged to was hardly the most glamorous of the many worlds at that moment in glorious collision right before his eyes.

A couple joined them at the table. Jake recognized the man at once from dust jacket photos. He was the novelist Ben Knight, and he was with his pretty wife, Sylvia, who nodded curtly, did not extend her hand, and gave Jake a guarded smile that made him suspect that she knew all about Dinah's testimony and had opinions about it. But Knight took Jake's hand with both of his in an athlete's crushing grip and inquired how his movie was going, and Jake just about levitated as he felt himself invisibly replaced inside his own skin by another version of himself—someone he had long desired to become but never quite dared to believe in.

To have Knight speak to him in this way—as a social if not an artistic equal—was the first stamp in a new passport. Jake, who read other people's books very slowly and very competitively, had read Knight's World War II novel, *The Innocent and the Beautiful,* and had been knocked out by it, thinking it better by far than Norman Mailer, Irwin Shaw, James Jones, and Mike Albrecht. But these days he found himself with less time and patience to read and hadn't kept up with Knight's career, except for an occasional story in *The New Yorker*. He was aware, of course, that it was Knight who spoke for this particular crowd, especially the American expatriates, and that their lives, including this little scene right now at the bar in Fouquet's, were his meat.

Much later in the evening, after dinner at a bistro whose name he couldn't remember, Jake found himself at a club. He had no idea where he was, but you had to go down a flight of steps to get in, and a more intimate group had migrated there from the restaurant and now huddled together at a few small tables. It was then, remembering his errand, that Jake took a sip of cognac and asked Felicity to dance to a slow tune. The band—a sax, a bass, and a piano player—were American Negroes and wore dark glasses.

"Careful," she said under her breath as they reached the floor. "Not too close."

"Ne worry-ez pas," he replied, having been instructed over dinner in the art of forming French negatives. He steadied her against his large chest and belly to maintain the pressure of his body against hers but held her hand and her back at a stiffly correct distance. "So what's the story with Veevi? She looks fine to me. And not particularly interested in me one way or the other. You'd hardly know I'm her brother-in-law."

"She's like that with everyone. Rather cagey, really. Unless you bring things up, she won't say a word. Has she asked you about Dinah and the kids?"

He withheld his answer, pressed her closer, and whispered, "Look, I know what I said about my same-city rule, but how about slipping away sometime tomorrow and coming over to my room?"

He had told her that he never took a woman to bed when she was in the same city as her husband.

"In two words: *im-possible*. By the way, who's Hunt dancing with?"

"Veevi. They're about four feet from your shoulder."

"In that case I'll bet you anything—Jake Lasker, get that hard thing of yours away from me right now; we've had our fun—the great Albrecht and the ever lovely Odile Boisvert have just shown up and Hunt is helping Veevi over the first of her nightly Stations of the Cross. He's really such a gent, that husband of mine."

Jake separated his body very slightly from Felicity's and searched the room. "Yup, I see them. They're at our table, with the Knights."

"Are you prepared for that?"

"*Mais oui, mademoiselle.*"

"*Madame,* dearie." Whispering into his ear, so that it looked almost as if they were dancing cheek to cheek, Felicity said, "I wish Veevi didn't do this to herself. It happens almost every night. She has this uncanny instinct about showing up wherever they show up."

Felicity disengaged one long bare tennis-firm forearm and waved. Mike Albrecht casually saluted Felicity and Jake but, like Veevi earlier in the evening, made no gesture of special recognition. "That's the HUAC cold shoulder," said Jake. "No outright incivility, but no warmth, either."

"Well, what did you expect?"

"I expect nothing, but I'm interested in everything," he replied, taking advantage of the crowded dance floor to push up against her.

"Well, essentially, he's stuck. We're sitting with the Knights, and he came here thinking he'd see Ben, which is what he does every night. They adore each other, these fellows—have to see each other every day or they get a headache. So you come with the dinner, so to speak."

Jake took a good look at the young woman with Mike—very young, with short blond hair and a magnificent face. So the unthinkable had happened: Mike had found a girl with a face that trumped Veevi's. The girl returned Jake's look blankly and briefly, hardly lifting her eyes from Mike for a second.

"Come on," Felicity said. "Let's go back."

Mike stood up and kissed Felicity, and nodded curtly to Jake but didn't offer his hand. Before he could sit down, Hunt and Veevi had swept up to the table: more hugs, more kisses, and Hunt, acting as if he hadn't seen the very attenuated exchange between Mike and Jake, blurted out, "You know, Mike, Jake did a swell job of looking after Felicity in London. Jake, tell him the Lady Peel story," and suddenly the story was being told yet again, with Felicity and Hunt laughing as if they were hearing it for the first time.

Mike smiled, because it would have been unsporting not to, and then Knight vacuumed everyone up into his aura as he began holding forth. To Jake, it seemed as if he were an old lion in a den of cubs, even though Ben and Jake were the same age and Hunt and Mike were only six or seven years younger. Knight had published a book two months ago and reviews were still coming in. "Say, anybody see that *Times* review? That guy oughtta be shot." And again Jake was taken prisoner by Knight's raspy voice. He lit into Greg Schuyler, the director who was the thinly disguised subject of Knight's most recent novel—the protagonist goes to Latin America to make a movie but gets caught up in a revolution and is eventually responsible for the slaughter of hundreds of peasants. How could that reviewer in the *New York Times* say the book had too much Conrad in it. "You guys know Greg. Tell me, did I have to go to Conrad to write that book? And who is this guy Chesterton Keith, anyway? Some fucking English professor? What does he know about anything? Says I'm losing touch with America. Listen to this!" He pulled a carefully folded piece of paper out of his jacket pocket. " 'At the end of the war,' " he began, " 'Knight was the brightest talent in a constellation of major new American voices that were out to give definitive expression to the war and its aftermath.' Obviously that means you too, Mike, you know that," Knight interrupted with a nod in Mike's direction. " 'But it's becoming all too apparent that Knight's prodigious output of a novel every two years is putting a fatal strain on his powers of invention. The slickness of his prose, the convenient twists of his plots, and the obvious and heavy-handed use of Conrad betoken the wholesale commercialization and cheapening of his once formidable gift. He needs to come home, to sink himself once again in American life and put his finger on its pulse, if he is to recover the muscular freshness of the stories that bedazzled us in the thirties. Native sons need native soil.' "

Knight grinned and put the clipping back in his pocket.

"Balls," said Hunt. He lifted his glass. "Complete and utter balls."

"Or bollocks," Felicity said. "As the British put it."

"A Provincial Professor of Crappy Criticism," said Veevi in a burst of alliteration. "The High Chair of Bad Writing."

Knight beamed at Veevi, basking in her loyalty.

"And besides," said Sylvia Knight, in a remark her husband paid no attention to, "all the other reviews have been raves."

"But it's always that one lousy review that keeps you up at night," Jake volunteered.

"You bet your ass," Knight said, looking at him with sudden recognition and respect.

Jake was fascinated and astonished. It would never have occurred to him that Knight would be bothered by a bad review. He himself would take to his bed for a day and contemplate suicide. But Ben Knight? "Hey, Hunt! You know Greg Schuyler. Tell him," Knight said, nodding at Jake. "How much of that book did I have to make up, huh?"

"You're fucking lucky Greg didn't sue you," said Hunt, laughing.

"Ah, he knows I love him," said Knight, clasping his Scotch with his hand and moving it in toward his chest like a little girl holding a kitten to her breast.

"He knows it," said Mike. "He loves you, too."

"Where the hell is he, anyway?" said Knight.

"In the Camargues. Buying horses," said Mike. "Listen, Ben, I'll write that *Times* eunuch a letter."

Ah, one of your letters, Jake thought. We know about your letters.

Knight waved his forefinger back and forth like a windshield wiper. "Forget it. Never write a reviewer. Ever. Conrad," he said again. "Can you believe it?" he asked Jake point-blank. Jake hadn't read the book, but Dinah had. She'd liked it. Jake shook his head. "No. It's beyond belief."

"See," Knight said to his pals. "He can't believe it, either. Those New York literary eunuchs over there, with their reviews. Clifton-fucking-Fadiman types." But then he grinned, and Jake, who had feared that Knight might be on the verge of getting sloppily drunk, saw that he was, at least for the moment, in fine form. Jake was glad; he didn't want to be disappointed in Knight. He wanted to believe in the big talent, as if it were all packed between Knight's football player's shoulders. He liked the tender way Knight looked at his friends. He liked feeling spellbound, and he liked both Knight's visible appetites and his unapologetic reverence for them. He remembered reading in one of his *New Yorker* stories about a man whose wife asks him as he's getting into bed whether he's brushed his teeth. No, the man says, I haven't. Aren't you going to? she says. No, he answers. I like going to sleep with the taste of food and wine in my mouth.

For now, Jake calculated, Knight was in one piece. But stacking up the man's passions and lusts against the prodigious hard work that he had to do to support the apartment in Paris and the chalet in Klosters, Jake wondered how long he could take it. Would the body outlast the talent? Could the talent survive the body? One novel had already been made into a movie. There would have to be more movies, no matter what Knight said about staying out of Hollywood—if only to meet his liquor bills. Jake observed the tender eyes and the close-cropped curly hair, the robust features, sensed the ready virility and insatiable hungers, noticed the broken capillaries in Knight's broad cheeks, and read there a palimpsest of booze, broads, gallantry, competition, physical joy, and professional exertion, all of it gathered into Knight's luminous defiance of time and inevitable decay.

But just as he found himself admiring the man, swept up in his atmosphere, almost dissolving with boozy camaraderie, Jake suddenly felt cautious and aloof. No, he told himself, I love this scene, but let one or two nights be enough. Knight is the real thing, all right, but Knight needs this all the time. He's got to have subalterns and vassals, he's got to be Arthur at the Round Table. And Mike Albrecht, who had also been hailed as the greatest of the postwar writers, was one of the courtiers. He looked like Ben Knight's son. Anyone could see, Jake reflected, that Albrecht was

Lancelot to Knight's King Arthur. Knight loved his friends but needed them to live his life *with* him and their own lives *for* him. But aren't I like that, too? he argued back at himself. Don't I do the same thing? Writers are cannibals, aren't they?

Yet as he drank more and relaxed more and felt tired and comfortable, none of his warnings to himself seemed to matter. Felicity's hand, which had gripped tennis racquets and other men's cocks with guiltless gusto, slid down his thigh under the table where he, his wife's sister, her estranged husband, the husband's new girl, and the Crandells were intimately gathered around Ben Knight. Everyone seemed to be ignoring the many private complications behind this public conviviality, although Knight, Jake thought, had to be taking everything in. One day soon, Jake reflected, he'd take a copy of *The New Yorker* into the john with him and find this scene in one of Knight's well-wrought stories. Knight would get the scents, the flavors, the small gestures, the glances; he'd make the story hinge on one one-line comment—so gentle, so ironic—that made everything irreversible. But Jake? What would he make of it? he wondered. He hadn't a clue how to handle material like this. Where was the comedy? He couldn't see it— not yet, at least. These were people who laughed at others but not at themselves. They were too romantic and attractive. When things went wrong for them, as they had for Veevi, what did they do? Was his talent—inexorably comic—up to finding a story in their lives?

Still, pitting himself against Knight, imagining some future novel he vaguely felt he'd have to write, Jake consciously took in the details. *Notice everything you can,* he ordered himself. Notice the way Mike and Veevi sit here at the same table. She looks him in the eye; he looks away. Everything in her dares him to repudiate what's gone on between them. But it doesn't matter to him; the past is over. So when he looks back, it's with impersonal kindness, without love, and it kills her, that loveless look, because she once had it all with him, they had once been consumed with each other. Now each is determined only to be civil. But notice how Veevi plants her elbows on the table, no doubt to make Mike's girl see how comfortable she is, how thoroughly she belongs. "I had him first; I'll get him back," those elbows, like a shield with crossed swords, seem to say.

Mike likes the rivalry between the two women. He looks at Veevi but puts his arm around Odile, who turns her face to him and makes a kissy face right there for Veevi to see. Undaunted, Veevi excludes the girl whenever she laughs or talks, and Mike looks back and forth between the two and then at Veevi, pained. These people are fucking savages, Jake tells himself. But Knight's noticing it, too, he sees, and relishes every minute.

Over dinner with Felicity at Les Ambassadeurs earlier in the week, Jake had heard the story and imagined the scene: Veevi, lying in bed at the American Hospital, having just had a tough delivery. In comes Mike, overcoat on his arm, hair tousled. A nurse comes in and gives the baby to Veevi, who looks at Mike and says, "She's you, top to toe—absolutely you." He doesn't sit down, but stands by the bed. "I'm sorry, baby," he says. He kisses her on the forehead. She looks up at him, smiles. He looks at the baby. "I'll send you something." She waits for him to say something more, but he doesn't. "You'd better go." He shakes his head. It's not his fault. It's just the way things happen.

It was a scene for a Knight story. The Mike character would be gruffly tender, would look at her as if summoning up remembrance of bedtimes past. She would be beautiful, the brown hair gleaming on the shoulders. She would claim him by asking for nothing, not just letting him go but pushing him away. And the story would be good. It would be tight, the Paris details understated, perfect. Or Mike would put it in a first-person novel and pity the man more than the woman. The man would be just about to leave for a war, or be in a war. Yes, it would make a good story. Only, Jake didn't believe any of it. You don't leave your wife when she's pregnant and then make yourself the victim. You don't fall in love and say you were struck by lightning. So you fool around, you have dames on the side. But you don't get serious! You don't live as if the word *alimony* doesn't exist. And what about Veevi? he wondered. Her pink cheeks were flushed, eyes shining; she was fingering her pearls, putting on the brave-and-noble act. What kind of a woman was she, really? Spends four years hiding out in the countryside, risking her neck for the Free French, loses Stefan to an unspeakable death, but it's losing Mike she takes the hardest. Losing him was the worst thing that had happened to her. He could see it in her face. She was still beautiful, but anyone could see that she was not as beautiful as Odile Boisvert, who had almost twenty years' advantage over her. Veevi was bright and chatty, and she was knocking herself out, Jake saw, to conceal the torture of sitting at the same table with Mike and the girl. It was a heroic and foolish spectacle, and Jake pitied her terribly and thought Mike Albrecht was a swine. Gets on his high moral horse in that letter, then cuts out on a pregnant wife. Jake would die before he treated Dinah that way.

What kind of a prick cuts out on a pregnant wife? Oh, he understood wanting to do it. And how. There wasn't anything natural about sleeping with the same woman for the rest of your life. But to screw up everything at home because the fucking was good with someone younger? Hadn't Mike figured out by now that fucking the same person year in and year out *always* gets boring? What had Manny Steiner once said? "Fucking your own wife is like striking out the pitcher."

He wondered whether he was getting drunk. The place was jammed now. People were dancing, and he had to cup his deaf ear to make out what was being said around him. Something about hydrogen bombs, bomb shelters, the movie *From Here to Eternity,* had he seen *The Crucible* in New York? It was hard to talk. He fell silent.

"Catch this one," Felicity whispered in his ear, and nodded toward a tall, dark, hunkering fellow who stealthily approached Ben Knight and slapped his hands squarely down on the novelist's shoulders.

Knight jumped to his feet and clasped the man in a tight embrace, and the two kissed repeatedly on both cheeks, which made Jake shift uncomfortably in his seat. If he moved to Europe, would he have to start kissing his friends? *"Mon vieux!"* cried Knight—the words unfamiliar to Jake, who nevertheless understood them to be a cry of affection. Voices filled the air in unison: "Nemeth! Nemeth! Nemeth! My God, it's Nemeth!"

Jake's eyes sought an explanation from Felicity, who whispered, "Bill, born Bela, Nemeth."

Jake nodded in recognition.

"Just back from Indochina, I think," Felicity continued, "or wherever the forces of light are pitted against the forces of darkness—or something like that. Girls adore him. He goes to war zones just to escape their maenad cries."

Jake saw tears in Hunt's eyes. "Jesus Christ, where the hell have you been?" he cried, also kissing and hugging the man, who continually tossed his head back in an attempt to get a very black shock of hair out of the way of an eye almost closed shut against the plume of smoke that rose from the cigarette dangling between his full lips. Jake knew who he was: Nemeth, the greatest war photographer of the age, renowned for getting himself into the same terrifying and dangerous situations as the men whose photos he took.

Jake immediately envied everything about the guy—the hair, the rumpled jacket, the dark eyes that said he'd been everywhere, seen everything, and fucked every woman he'd ever wanted. Of course women found him irresistible. Jake himself did; everyone did. The women at the table, already beautiful, already lovely for Knight, brightened even more in Nemeth's presence. Jake reached for the little leather notebook he kept in his jacket pocket, placed it surreptitiously on his right knee, noted the date, the place, and Nemeth's name, followed by the words "Use this someday: sees himself the way dames do. Knows why they want him. Excited by their desire for him."

As he wrote, Felicity's right hand squeezed his left thigh. "Get up," she whispered.

Then he saw why he had to stand up: to greet the woman standing next to the handsome Hungarian photographer. She was in her early thirties, a clear-faced and decidedly American beauty, with champagne-colored hair pulled back and held by a black velvet bow. Sylvia Knight led the woman by the hand and stopped near Jake, who hurriedly stuck his notebook into his trouser pocket. Sylvia introduced her as Rue Melville. Later, he learned that she had grown up on a cattle ranch in Montana, married into an old New York family, and upon her divorce received a very nice settlement that allowed her to keep a house in New York and a flat in Paris. Thus she was always available to fly to Paris at a moment's notice to join Bill Nemeth for the two and four days at a time he spent between months-long assignments for *Life* magazine, which regularly shipped him and his cameras off to whatever wars were being waged around the world—and of course there were always several to choose from.

Jake wondered whether Felicity had ever banged the guy. He hoped she hadn't, but conceded for a disheartening moment that she probably had. After all, he said to himself, who wouldn't?

He felt someone poking him in the shoulder. Before he could turn around, Felicity was almost shouting at him. "Jake! *Faites attention*. It's your sister-in-law." Jake, turning to the left, encountered Veevi's faintly mocking eyes.

"Care to dance?"

"I thought you'd never ask," he answered.

He understood at once that this particular display was for Mike's benefit.

Once they moved onto the crowded dance floor, he felt a sensation as he held his wife's sister's body close to his own that he would only have described as eerie. He had never danced with Veevi before, but they moved together smoothly, and that in itself made him feel uneasy, because it re-minded him so much of Dinah. There was no doubt about it: the Milligan girls were born dancers. He led well, as always, and she followed easily. She was shorter than Dinah, by two or three inches, and light of foot. In a sense, she was Dinah without the leggy energy he liked so much. There was a scent, too, that reminded him of his wife in its warm, creaturely cleanliness, though the perfume was different from anything Dinah wore—headier, stronger, inescapable. Do people in families smell the same? he wondered.

He thought he should make his move. But how should he begin? There was something about Veevi that put him off—he couldn't say what. But he had made a promise to Dinah.

"You look good," he said. "Everything okay with you?"

"Everything's swell. You like Paris?"

"Love it," he said, "though the language drives me crazy. Tell me some-thing. If a word in French ends with an *e* and a *t,* you don't pronounce the *t*. Right? So why does everyone here call that place we met at tonight Fouquet's?" (He sounded out the *t*.)

She laughed. "Haven't the foggiest."

"You're not fluent?"

"Nope. *Je ne parle pas français,*" she said with an exaggerated American accent. "I have a bad ear, they say."

"Really? After all these years?"

"Well, I can manage with a little grocery French."

"As in, 'May I squeeze that melon?' as my mother used to say?"

"Haven't a clue how to say that! God, it's nerve-racking, because you don't just go to one store here. It's a daily pilgrimage, really. This is a one-store-for-each-thing sort of country. You go off in the morning with your lit-tle string bag and you stop at the bakery for bread and then you go to the butcher shop for meat and then there's the vegetable guy and the fruit man. But they know me and I point to things and they say the word, and I nod, and everyone's happy. You should see Felicity, though. She could hold philosophical conversations with them if she had to. So could Sylvia Knight. Not me." Veevi said all of this with a light laugh so that it seemed amusing, but then Jake realized that she was still seeing herself as part of a set of three inseparable couples—the Knights, the Crandells, and the Al-brechts.

They danced in silence until the music stopped. As he took her lightly by the elbow and began to lead her off the floor, he paused and put his hand inside his jacket and pulled out an envelope. "I almost forgot to give this to you."

"It can wait till tomorrow," she said, pushing his hand and the envelope away. "If you have any time—want me to show you around?"

He brightened immediately. "Wonderful! I'd love it! I was just going to walk around on my own. You know, whistling 'An American in Paris' to my-self."

"Off-key, natch."

"Can we go to the Louvre?" He heard the word *loove* come out of his mouth. I must sound like a talking elephant, he said to himself.

"Why not?" she said. "But only if you can say it with that *rh* at the end. Otherwise they don't let you in."

Relieved that he would now have a chance to give Veevi Dinah's letter, he was anxious to get back to the table and Ben Knight, who interested him at the moment far more than his sister-in-law. So he steered her back. "Oh, Villie Vile," he heard Felicity saying. "You dear old thing, what brings you to the metropolis?" She was embracing a short, stocky, barrel-chested man. The legendary producer looked as if he could have been Ben Knight's father: both of them had the same tough, handsome streetwise face as Jake's uncles in Chicago, with high cheekbones and elegant Semitic noses.

The impeccably tailored Willie Weil kissed Felicity and then, as Jake and Veevi neared him, reached for Veevi's hand and brought it to his lips, pulling her to him in a courtly embrace that made Jake uneasy, packed as it was with sexual bravado, the kind that he himself, he liked to think, had as well, though in rather more self-mocking, and occasionally self-doubting, supply.

"Meet my brother-in-law, Jake Lasker," said Veevi.

Jake and Willie Weil shook hands. My God, he's got Uncle Max's hand-shake too, Jake thought: knuckle-crushing. He felt himself being scruti-nized by a pair of inquisitive blue eyes. "So you're the talented Jake Lasker," said Weil. "I've enjoyed your pictures. Tell me, how do you like working with my friend Wynn Tooling? Do you know he adores you? Do you like your suite at the Dorch? Because if you don't, you know, just let me know and I'll call the queen and arrange another."

Once again tonight, Jake felt himself drawn into the net of a worldly, charismatic man. Weil's accent made Jake think of a steamer trunk plas-tered with stickers from everywhere in Europe: Warsaw, Budapest, Prague,

Berlin, Paris, London, Rome. There were dozens of stories about Weil, and no one knew for sure where he'd come from, only that he'd ended up in Berlin in the twenties, where he'd worked with Dorshka Albrecht and Stefan Ventura, and gone to Paris with them in 1933. He was a gambler, a womanizer, very possibly a crook, and an astonishingly successful producer of big, good movies.

Weil took the table adjacent to the Knights' and turned his full solar force on Jake. There was the offer of a large Monte Cristo, the ordering of another cognac. Talk flowed—of movies and movie deals, cities, bars, restaurants, hotels, gambling clubs, tailors, tobacconists, theaters, plays, writers, wars, cars, art, and horses. Weil put his arm around Jake and, with an innocent blink of his Tatar eyes, said, "Come now, Jake Lasker. Tell me the truth. Are you married to Irv Engel? Are you going to grow old and die at Marathon? Can you write only for America or for the rest of the world? I mean, can you write international funny? Don't tell me it's a medium only of words. You write physical comedy, so why don't you bring laughter to a billion people? Have breakfast with me tomorrow morning at the Ritz, and we'll talk about it."

Jake glanced around, looking for Veevi. He wanted to change their plans. He'd meet her later. He could move their date up a couple of hours. But she had disappeared. He caught Felicity's eyes and mouthed, "Where's Veevi?"

She shrugged.

"Tomorrow morning's kind of tough for me, Willie," Jake said. "Any time later?"

"I'm flying to London at noon. But we'll find each other—I just know it. I have a feeling about you. Do you feel it, too?" He smiled, a dazzling, flirtatious smile that promised everything. "I think we're going to fall in love and get married and make babies together."

Jake laughed. "Well, I'm crazy 'bout you too, but on my pictures I kind of like to be the guy in charge."

"Oh, we can take care of that," the older man said, letting the cigar smoke drift up to his half-closed blue eyes. Weil looked like a contented Siamese cat. "It's easy. I take care of all the details and let you alone to be the genius." He twinkled. "I'll be the prick and you'll be the pet." Jake could have kissed him. Weil was the ticket to a dreamed-of life. "Ask Hunt. He'll tell you what it's like to work for me. Tell him, Hunt."

"You want me to tell Jake what it's like to work for you, Willie? Felicity, should I tell him?"

"Yes, darling," said Felicity.

"Willie Weil is without doubt the most irritating, inconsiderate, selfish, tyrannical, insanity-producing human being I have ever known in my life. Take, for instance, what happened in the middle of *The August Wind*." Weil chuckled, and then Hunt launched into one anecdote after another, and soon everyone was telling stories, and Felicity's laugh rang out in peals of gaiety, and Jake was drinking more and more cognac and he was part of it, this delicious life, and nothing else existed.

He was drunk when he got back to the hotel and fell giddily onto his bed. Only by the most deliberate exertions did he manage to take off his shoes and trousers, but when he did, he crawled in under the crisp sheets and fell asleep at once in his T-shirt and boxer shorts. Yet even in Paris, his old insomnia woke him sometime after two. He had a raging thirst and a pounding headache. After drinking some bottled water and taking two Alka-Seltzers, he went to the window and looked out. The sight of street-walkers in high heels and tight dresses, with large handbags dangling from their shoulders, filled him with sadness. He was homesick for London. Paris smelled better, but he loved London's frumpish comforts. All those attractive young people tonight—what did he have in common with them? He staggered around the room in his shorts, trying to belch. I am a knock-kneed, balding, overweight Jewish comedy writer, he thought. What business do I have with these highfliers? They live as if they're never going to die; I feel a heart attack stalking me around every corner.

Felicity had said to him in London, "I have a life of unearned felicity, no pun intended. I know everybody worth knowing, and Hunt and I are each other's best friend, and every day I do something interesting and fun." How could he possibly live that way, when he woke up every morning thinking only of the difficulty of his craft and the limits of his talent?

He paced the large, elegant room, sat down on the brocade sofa, got up again, and opened the windows. For a moment he was tempted to go downstairs and negotiate with one of those girls—a skillful blow job would relax him and send him right back to sleep. But too many failed encounters years ago had taught him not to trust himself with hookers. Should he call Dinah? He missed her but somehow wasn't in the mood to call her, and that made him feel guilty and restless. He got up and drank more of the bottled water, which fizzed in his mouth, and then he went to the window and again looked out.

Down on the street there was a prostitute wrapped in a white coat. She was walking slowly up and down on high heels, and looked like a moving flashlight. She checked her watch, as if the night had been long and she hadn't yet made enough money to go home. Had she been standing out there all night or had she already serviced half a dozen men? he wondered. It had been years since he'd gone to a prostitute. The last time was at Queenie Boardman's place in Beverly Hills, which looked like a sorority house and where the girls wore tennis skirts and tennis shoes, for which reason he'd found it impossible to do anything with them. That was just before he met Dinah, when he was working so hard on the Crystaldent show that he hadn't taken anyone out in months.

To hell with it, he thought. I've proved I can say no. Now I can say yes. He slipped on his trousers and raincoat and took the elevator down to the street. He approached the girl he had watched from the window. Inside her white coat she looked small, and she had raccoon eyes from the black eyeliner she had drawn both across and under her lids. *"Combien?"* he asked. She rattled something off, and he shook his head. "No comprende," he said, aware that the words sounded Spanish—or something not quite French.

"Twenty dollars," she said in heavily accented English.

"Okay," he said, taking her elbow.

The hotel was empty, and the girl sniffled from the sudden warmth and took a handkerchief out of her coat pocket to wipe her nose. No one said anything, neither the concierge nor the bellboys. The elevator man, though, nodded as if he recognized the girl, and after an initial flutter of embarrassment Jake calmed down. This was France, he told himself. Men took women to their rooms, paid them, and had sex with them, and nobody gave a damn one way or the other. He remembered now a scene in Mike's first novel, *The Confession*—which Jake had competitively devoured after Mike and Veevi had gone back to Paris following their visit in 1946—some wartime interlude with a French prostitute who had been "affectionate and skillful." He'd wondered at the time if Mike had meant cocksucking, the one thing that Dinah didn't like and wasn't good at.

Jake's mind wandered back to Bonnie, in L.A. She was married now to some muscle-bound stuntman who probably kept her well supplied with healthy orgasms. He smiled at the girl in the elevator, and she smiled back shyly and said nothing. Had he really given Felicity a good time the other night? She was so aware of what she was doing, so smart, and had such good manners that he couldn't tell ("Oh, that was marvelous, darling") whether she had faked it or not. What was he doing now, taking this cold, sniffling girl with raccoon eyes to his room? And what about Dinah? If he were home right now he'd pace the house, raid the icebox, and then go back to their room. Instead of getting into his own bed, he'd get into hers and he'd put his arms around her still body and put his face against her warm neck and fall into a deep sleep. Who were these people he had eaten and drunk and danced with tonight? Who were they kidding? How did any of them manage to write anything with all that booze flowing down their throats?

Once they were inside the room, the girl stood waiting at the door, and he pulled the money out of his pants pocket. Then she disappeared into the bathroom and emerged wearing only panties. She beckoned to him with a crooked finger, whereupon she took a washcloth and soap, unbuckled his trousers, fished his cock out of his boxer shorts, and washed it; she wasn't especially affectionate, but she wasn't unfriendly, either—just businesslike.

He was dying to ask her all kinds of questions, but without French he felt paralyzed. He might have made jokes, or learned something about her, or at least charmed her enough to make her like him, but none of this was possible. How could he ask her for a blow job? He didn't know how to say it in French, and the thought of demonstrating with gestures struck him as unseemly. So he took her to the bed, and she reached over and turned down the light. She got on top of him. What followed was done with detachment and haste. There wasn't much pleasure, but he didn't fail, and was pleased with himself. *"Merci beaucoup, mademoiselle,"* he said afterward as she got up and went to the bathroom to dress. Perhaps it had worked because she was French? He wondered if he would tell Sandy Litvak about it, and then remembered that his analysis was finished. As the girl was leaving, he gave her some more money and she thanked him and slipped away.

It was about four in the morning. In a thousand years, he told himself, he could never find anything romantic or tender about this exchange, but it hadn't been sordid, either. And he hadn't failed, he repeated to himself. He'd got it up and kept it up, which was a far cry from what had happened at Queenie Boardman's so long ago.

He got back into bed and pulled the covers up to his nose. Was she out there walking the street again, in her white coat and high heels, with her bangs hanging limply over her eyebrows? He didn't have the energy to get up and look. It didn't take him long to admit to himself that he had had her because he was feeling competitive with Mike, Ben, and Hunt, all of whom had been in the war. Albrecht had killed Germans and fucked French prostitutes, whereas he, Jake Lasker, because of his deaf ear and flat feet and glasses, had missed out on the action and been declared 4-F. In any case, he'd been ordered by Irv Engel to write all-star comedy musicals for the boys overseas. He heard Sandy's voice saying to him, "Why do you need to compete with Michael Albrecht anyway? Or any of those guys?" Jake couldn't think of an answer, and he fell into a heavy sleep where there were no questions and no answers, and woke exactly at ten to eight.

Warily he lay in bed, afraid to raise his head, expecting the punishment of a hangover. But his head was miraculously clear. He even had a sense of well-being, as if he had been put through Miss Fanny's ironing machine and pressed and starched by its rollers.

Today he was going to see Paris and give Dinah's letter to Veevi, and in the evening he would fly back to London and send Dinah a telegram.

Veevi had told him to call her when he woke up, but it seemed too early. He showered and dressed and went down to the hotel lobby and bought a *Herald-Tribune,* then looked for a café where he could have breakfast. When he called Veevi's number about an hour later, Claire answered and said she was still sound asleep. Christ, he thought, that's irritating. I could have seen Willie Weil! He left a message with the girl, a teenager now, and included his hotel room number.

It was eleven-thirty when she finally rang. He thought it odd and rude that someone who had offered to show him around Paris would let the whole morning go by without calling, but he said nothing and at twelve-thirty she picked him up downstairs. There were other people in the car— Bill Nemeth, and a woman, Gerry Tuttle, whose husband, Veevi explained, was a foreign-car import czar in New York. They had a Park Avenue apartment and one here in the Sixteenth, which they visited about twice a month. The husband had gone to the Camargues for the weekend to meet Schuyler Gray and buy a horse, so she was here alone.

As soon as Jake managed to squeeze himself into the little car—no easy feat—he turned around to shake hands and make small talk with Nemeth. On the tip of his tongue he had a question about the photographer's new assignment in Indochina, but Nemeth and the stunning Mrs. Tuttle had instantly thrown themselves upon each other and, like two pythons, were intertwined in a ravenous embrace. He glanced uneasily at Veevi, who had started the engine but was lighting a cigarette. She had an unperturbed look on her face, implying that what was going on in the backseat didn't remotely engage her interest. She pulled into traffic and Jake put two and two together: Veevi was providing Nemeth and Mrs. Tuttle with a refuge and an alibi.

"Now for the grand tour," Veevi said with that brief intake of breath that always signaled a laugh. He met her sardonic look, which took him into her confidence and seemed to say, "Can you believe those two idiots in the backseat?"

The grand tour started at the bottom of the Étoile, from which they drove to the Madeleine and then to the place Vendôme, where Veevi pointed out the fancy stores. "Perhaps Monsieur Le Big Hollywood Producer wants to buy his wife some expensive French perfume?"

"With the filthy lucre I've made since she cleared me with HUAC?" he said in return, surprising himself with the remark.

"There are worse ways to thank her," was the cool reply. "Unless she's still wearing that god-awful Tabu."

He gave Veevi a sidelong glance of displeasure. Who needs this? he thought. The fact was, he kept Dinah well supplied with Femme and Joy. And he was bringing her a gold bracelet from London, made of antique jeweled necklace clasps strung together. "It's Sunday, isn't it?" he said.

"Right you are. Eiffel Tower, then?" she asked, and he knew she was still testing him, trying to find out if he was a cornball American tourist.

"Actually, Veevi, the only thing I'd really like to see is the Louvre," he answered. "And I'm happy to do it alone if it's a drag for you."

"Oh, Uncle J.," she said, startling him with this new nickname, "don't be an idiot." And she went back toward the rue de Rivoli, explaining that she was going to drive through the gates of the Louvre.

"Can you find a place to park?" he said under his breath, indicating to her with his eyes that more than heavy necking was now taking place in the backseat. "They're having it off," he mouthed. She shrugged. Jake, afraid he would burst out laughing, wondered what kind of a game Nemeth was playing. With all the fabled little hotels in Paris, why couldn't he simply rent a room for a couple of hours to bang Mrs. Tuttle? Why this adolescent clutching and gasping in the backseat of a dove-gray Aronde in the middle of Paris traffic? The car swayed and shook; he was tempted to turn around and yell, "Can you stop for a second till I get a life jacket!" But then he realized the scene was a gift and that the comedy he couldn't find last night was right here, right now, and that if he moved to Europe he'd find it elsewhere too, and be able to write it—and in his own language at that. In this car, the elements of pure farce were there for the taking. He'd use it all one day—if not in a movie, then in a play; if not in a play, then in a novel. It was a windfall, pure serendipity.

"We're here," Veevi said, stopping the car. Jake jumped out at once. Together they observed the car from a distance of about four feet. It rocked; it rolled; it shuddered. "What if a cop happens by?" he asked Veevi.

"They could stand bare-assed right here in the middle of the Jardin du Carrousel and nobody'd notice." She laughed, and her eyes lit up with hilarity.

"Well," he said, shaking his head and taking her arm, "I've never seen anything . . ."

"Really? Come. I'll introduce you to Mona Lisa."

They did the Louvre fast; Jake wasn't in a hurry, but he wanted to devour the whole place. He stopped quickly in front of everything, enjoying every moment too much to be dampened by Veevi's clipped remarks. She lived here, after all, and had probably been to the Louvre a thousand times. While drinking in the paintings, he plied her with questions about Nemeth's backseat antics. "Why doesn't he just take her to some jazzy little hotel?"

Veevi laughed. "It's obvious, isn't it? Bill Nemeth thinks everyone knows who he is and that he'd be recognized wherever they went. He's probably right. And the concierge could make a nice little bundle out of calling the sleazier press photographers."

"But it's the danger too, isn't it?" Jake added.

"Of course. Danger, passion—that sort of thing." She put her arm to her forehead, fluttered her eyelids, and tilted back her head in a mock swoon.

The dashing Nemeth, whom Jake had envied so last night, now seemed a buffoon of sexual vanity, but for Veevi, Jake thought, he he must be a reminder of Mike.

"Why are men such slobs?" he said. "These things," he added, knowing he was implicating himself and that Veevi was smart enough to get it, "can be done with a little more class, a little more discretion."

She laughed mirthlessly. "But then it becomes banal. Then it's not 'burning with a hard gemlike flame,' as Knight always says."

"Ben Knight didn't make that up, you know. I forget who did, but he's quoting somebody. That I know," Jake said. Unlike last night, he was willing to give Knight his due, but not more than that.

"These guys aren't like dentists in New Jersey," she said. "They don't play it safe."

"But you shouldn't be a horse's ass and put someone like Rue Melville at risk. She's one hell of a handsome dame. And nice, too."

"Yes, but Bill's home from some war. She wants to keep him in bed with her night and day until he flies out again," Veevi added. "He can't spend every minute with her. And, he likes variety."

They had come to a stop in front of Watteau's *Pilgrimage to Cythera,* and as Jake stood in front of it, giving it a quizzical look, Veevi turned to him and put her hand on his sleeve. " 'No' is not in Nemeth's vocabulary. They adore him," she said with another acid laugh. "I don't."

"What about Felicity Crandell? Does she adore him, too?"

"Oh, sure," said Veevi.

Jake winced. "Tell me something," he said, head cocked, scrutinizing the painting. "Are these people coming or going? It looks like they're leaving. They've had a lovely time and some of them are lingering, but the rest are going down to meet that ship that's in the distance. See it? Of course I don't know what *Cythera* means. Do you?"

"The island of Aphrodite—you know, Venus. A place for, quote, 'love.' " She smiled at him sadly, and her eyes lingered on his face. "Like it?"

"Crazy about it. Tell them to wrap it up. I'll take it now."

She smiled again. "I know you think Bill Nemeth's a bit of a shit," she said, pulling him away from the painting, "but it's his only way of dealing with fear. He's always in danger when he's working. He could get killed any day. So he comes here to find relief, and sometimes he has to get away from Rue. He loves her, she's his girl, but he's the kind of guy who has to get free of a girl even so. He'll go back to her apartment and do unto her what he did unto Gerry, and then he'll show up at Fouquet's again with Rue and keep his arm around her all night. By the way, want to take me? To Fouquet's?"

"Tonight?"

"Tonight."

"Geez, honey, I'm flying back to London tonight. Gotta be in Covent Garden at six tomorrow morning. Wynn has to knock over a couple of fruit-and-vegetable carts as he's being chased by two trench-coated heavies. It's going to be a long day."

"Oh," she said. Her face betrayed no disappointment, but it had a sharp brightness that hovered between warmth and mockery. "Well, come back and we'll try again."

"Love to." He took her arm and they moved ahead. Delighted, his chest swelled with the triumph of having passed a difficult test. He wished he could stay in Paris, but it was impossible. It occurred to him that maybe he was no more to her than a convenient escort. But it didn't matter. Now he had a Paris connection, and he was mindful of what she had done for him.

"Look, Veevi, you sure you want to be in that situation again?"

"What situation?"

"You know, running into Mike all the time. With the broad."

"Oh, that," she said. They came up to Géricault's *Madwoman,* looked at each other, and flinched. "Look," she said, "had enough art for a while? Let's go have lunch."

When they reached the car, the amorous couple was nowhere in sight, and Veevi took Jake to a brasserie on the Left Bank. The day was chilly. Sunbursts alternated with clouds, with swift changes from light to shadow. They ordered a roast chicken and a good white wine, and he began to feel the strong pull of friendship for Veevi, who ate and drank with robust appetite. He liked it that she didn't judge her friends. It was gutsy of her to insist on remaining part of her group, even if it meant seeing Mike and the blonde night after night. She was fun. She listened to what he said, she asked questions, she seemed to find much of what he said amusing and interesting. Over strong black coffee, he finally handed her Dinah's letter. When Veevi put it into her purse without opening it, he felt he had to say something.

"You can guess what this is about, Veevi. Look, she did it for me. She saved my ass. Without her, I wouldn't be making this picture. I couldn't be here, talking to you."

"It must have been a tough decision for both of you," she said, putting her hand over his. He saw that her fingernails were perfect: perfect ovals, perfect cuticles, perfect red enamel.

He hesitated for a moment, then put his own hand on hers. "And so, when we didn't hear from you . . ." he trailed off. She looked right into his eyes, and it seemed to him that they understood each other perfectly.

"Let's not talk about it, Uncle J. Let's just have fun. Look—both of you, I mean—stop worrying about me. I'm okay. Mike and Odile—well, that's something I have to sweat out right now. Tell Dinah for heaven's sake not to feel guilty. Tell her to enjoy her life. God knows I was a pain in the ass for her until you came along. She's earned everything she's got."

But suddenly, for the second time today, she had struck a note he didn't like. He picked up her lighter and leaned forward to light her cigarette but he was taken aback by the automatic presumption that her very existence put Dinah at a disadvantage. It irked him, as had her remark about Dinah's wearing Tabu (which she didn't and, as far as he could remember, never had).

"Well, honey, if you ever need anything—money, help of any kind—" he said nevertheless.

"Thanks, Uncle J., but no. If I don't write to Dinah, it's not because I'm angry. It's because I'd only whine and sound sorry for myself." She laughed. "Why bore everybody with my dreary little story?"

That tone—that sense of the dreary and the boring as the measuring stick of life—he had to admit that he found it spectacular. Veevi held up her glass for him, then took a lingering sip. She was one hell of a flirt, he thought, watching her face. That's where her acting had been, he remembered—not in her voice but in that face, which was never the same for more than an instant. You couldn't take your eyes off it, because if you did you might miss some nuance, some way of looking at the world you'd never thought of before. She had a gift, a vocation, really, for savoring the moment and bringing you into it, the way some people had a gift for the violin or acrobatics. He saw it and felt it, this need to relish every instant, every taste, every experience, until it yielded up its jewel of pleasure. Nothing could get in its way, even heartbreak. Hence her self-mockery, which he liked, the clipped, barbed rapid-fire speech that he had to bend closer to her to hear.

"So, Uncle J.," she said, blowing smoke and taking another sip of wine. "This is Paris. Still like it?"

"It'll do." And he said to himself in wonder, Who ever thought I'd end up sitting here as Veevi Milligan's brother-in-law? He saw the possibilities:

what he had with her was unique. No one could ever know her—observe her—in exactly this way.

Her irritating remarks about Dinah slipped from his mind as he refilled his glass and they looked admiringly at each other for a comfortable interval. It seemed to him that neither of them could possibly wish to be anywhere else and that there was a vast reservoir of things for them to talk about. After they finished their coffee, they walked back arm in arm, across the Pont du Carrousel, and then drove along the quai Voltaire and the quai d'Anatole France, finishing up at her apartment on the rue des Acacias so that he could visit with Claire and see the baby, Coco, before going back to the hotel in time to catch his plane.

In Sun Valley one movie and fifteen months later, Dinah lay on a soft blanket spread out over the grass reading *The Tunnel of Love,* by Peter de Vries, while Jake stood thigh deep in a stream casting for trout. Dinah breathed in the scent of pines and felt glad in her very bones. At the Challenger Inn, she dozed on a chaise longue by the pool or held an aluminum sun reflector under her chin while Jake swam laps. Her skin turned bronze, then walnut brown. He took 16mm movies as she figure-skated, long-legged and firm, on the opaline surface of the Sun Valley ice rink or rode a bike along wooded paths or sat in their rented car, counting the sheep in the flocks tended by Basque shepherds until she pretended to fall asleep. She and Jake took drives, danced in the evenings, and made love with the tenderness, abandon, and ardor that had accompanied their previous efforts to conceive a child, and conceiving a third child was what they had come here to do.

After dinner and dancing at the Challenger Inn, a silent signal would be exchanged, and they would go back to their room and throw off their clothes. They took their time and did everything every possible way, and when Dinah lay beneath Jake she felt their bodies dissolving into each other. The most accidental form of touch—even his toenail scraping across her leg—felt good to her, and full of meaning, full of proof of their oneness. She didn't think it was possible to be happier than they were. Here they were, in their forties, married for ten years, with two children, a new, successful movie out, and, despite big expenses and a consuming career, still they felt this bliss and connection with each other, this infinitely comfortable but undiminished passion.

Afterward, he did not fall into a heavy snoring sleep as he usually did at home, but lightly and playfully stroked her shoulders, her arms, her legs as she held them up against the wall for half an hour. They talked and told stories and made each other laugh. Then he would drift off, his head nestled on her breast, his arm around her midriff. She had bought this for them by testifying. Well, so what? she would say to herself. Wasn't it worth it? Isn't this exactly why I did it?

⁂

Two weeks after they got back from vacation, when she was late and felt her breasts swell and noted the arrival of that familiar languorous fatigue, along with small cramplike twinges, Dinah said to herself, *Jackpot.* She waited for a long month, not wanting to hurry the visit to Dr. Zuckerman. She savored, as she had with her first two pregnancies, the imagined division of every growing cell. But then when the month passed and she could feel a swelling hardness in her lower abdomen that seemed to be blossoming sooner than it had in the past, she wondered if she had miscalculated and made the appointment.

Dr. Zuckerman was six-five, and about her age—perhaps a few years older. As she sat across from him in his office after the examination, she had to lift her eyes a little because of his height. The results of the test, she knew, wouldn't be in for two days, but while examining her he had said, "After two kids together, I think you and I know your signals pretty well. If you say you're pregnant, why then, you're pregnant." Then he winked. "Get dressed, honey, and meet me in my office." She liked that wink, that "honey," and she remembered the feeling of being on a team with him when her babies were born. "Come on, Dinah, push that baby out!" he would holler at her, like a football coach.

He performed some rapid calculations on a sheet of paper in her chart. "May twenty-first," he said, more soberly than she would have expected, since he was usually generous with his rabbit-toothed smile when he figured due dates.

"W-W-W-Wonderful," she said. "A spring baby. Jake will be so happy."

"Now, Dinah," the doctor said, looking straight at her. "I think we have a problem." As she turned pale and began chewing the inside of her cheek, he explained that the hardness she had felt could mean they were way off and she was two months or more ahead of herself; but since she had been right on schedule up to her missed period, that seemed unlikely. So the hardness was probably a fibroid tumor, he said, judging from its location and the way it felt. Fibroids—she thought it one of the ugliest words she had ever heard—weren't dangerous in themselves but they often grew fast, especially when there was a lot of estrogen in the body, as there was during pregnancy. They tended to take up room the embryo needed. Dr. Zuckerman said all they could do was wait and hope that the pregnancy would continue in a normal way and that the tumor would shrink by itself. But he had to prepare her for the possibility that the tumor might—she saw that he wished he could spare her—crowd everything out and that the pregnancy would end spontaneously. If that happened, the only way to get rid of the tumor was with a hysterectomy.

"So it's all or nothing," she said. "If the baby doesn't make it, I'm done having kids."

"You need to prepare yourself," he said. He walked over to her and put his hand on her shoulder, and suddenly he looked like a helpless giant in his white coat. "I want you to take it easy. Rest every day. Put your feet up. Send your housekeeper to the store. Don't overdo and don't let things get to you. If Jake wants to give me a call, you tell him I'm always available. Is he here?"

"He's back in London doing publicity for the British release of the picture. I'll call him or send a telegram, I guess." She stood up and rested her head against Dr. Zuckerman's chest. "Oh, Shelley," she said. "This st-st-st-stinks."

He squeezed her shoulders. "I know, honey. You're in a tough spot. I'll do my damnedest to keep this baby for you. Okay?" And he kissed her on the forehead. She had always felt that Dr. Zuckerman liked delivering her babies because he liked the kind of woman she was. The most important moments of her life, she thought, the births of her children, she had experienced with him—not Jake. It was odd, really.

Later that morning, Gussie told her that Mrs. Albrecht had called.

"From Paris?" Dinah asked.

"No, Mrs. Lasker. Mrs. Albrecht senior, in Westwood. She left her number."

It was a long time since Dinah and Dorshka had last spoken—well over six months. Dinah was the one who usually phoned, so a call from Dorshka had to be important.

"I must speak with you, darling. Can you come today?" Dorshka said as soon as she heard Dinah's voice.

The only thing Dinah wanted to do was go upstairs and cry, but five minutes later she was headed west on Sunset toward Westwood.

Dorshka picked up an aerogram, the kind Veevi had sent to Dinah in the past. Despite Jake's visit with Veevi in Paris last year, Veevi had never written, and Dinah hadn't, either. Now she could see the black typewritten letters through the blue paper. She watched Dorshka as the older woman found a particular passage she had evidently read several times. Finally, Dorshka looked up from the letter and sighed. "He thinks she should come home."

"Who?" Dinah asked. Dorshka's vagueness annoyed her. "Who wants her to come home?"

"I'm sorry," Dorshka said, removing her reading glasses. Her large blue eyes looked directly at Dinah. "You must think I am a senile old woman." She waved the letter. "This is from Mike. Ordinarily, I don't read my personal letters to other people, but as this concerns you I will break my rule." And she read: " 'The situation can't go on this way. It's not healthy for me or V. I've told her there's no hope for the marriage, that I want a divorce and I'm going to marry Odile. She took it calmly enough, but that's what worries me. It's as if it hasn't really sunk in. I will do the right thing financially, but I have new pressures on me now and I think the Laskers, given what they've done, should share some of the responsibility for Veevi with me.' "

"Oh, does he now?" Dinah broke in.

"Shhh. Let me go on."

And Dorshka continued:

I have also told her that she should go back to the States and find something to do. In short, she should start a new life. It's increasingly uncomfortable for me, and I would think humiliating for her, that we know all the same people and that she always manages to turn up in the same places at the same times that Odile and I do. What I'm writing to ask is whether you would consider letting her and the girls move in with you. You've always said that you wish you could see more of Claire and Coco. Well, here's your chance. I would take care of their expenses, though I repeat that I see no reason why Jake and Dinah couldn't also help out. After all, as you know, V. has told the consulate here she won't name names. So she will be unemployable. Under the circumstances, I consider Jake just as morally obligated to her as I am—perhaps even more.

The biggest obstacle is getting V. to see the sense of going. She doesn't want to leave Paris, or Europe, although anyone can see there's nothing for her here. Frankly, I'd love it if someone came along and took her off my hands, and clearly that's one reason she keeps showing up night after night, hoping she'll find someone—preferably right in front of my nose. It's so obvious and so awful to see, Mom. Can't you try to convince her that her best chances of finding someone else are in the States? The men we know are all married or have girls, and she knows that. And you know what girls are like. They're not so crazy about having a single woman along. Of course Felicity Crandell is loyal to Veevi and thinks I'm a cad, and even says so to my face, but the Crandells are going on location to the South Pacific soon and won't be around to look after her. To put it bluntly, no one in our group is going to go near her, primarily because of me, and that's a fact. You'd be doing me a big favor if you would just write her and tell her to come. September is fast approaching, and she could be in Los Angeles in time for Claire to start school. Ma—help me out please, write to her, invite her to come and live with you.

She put the letter down and folded her arms across her bosom. Dressed in men's slacks and a man's sport shirt, her white hair tousled, she looked like an Amazon grandmother. Dinah waited for her to say something, but what could or should have been said failed to issue from her lips. A slight smile—what Dinah always thought of as Dorshka's "European" smile— sardonic, disabused, given not so much to suspending judgment as to disregarding it once it has been made—played across her mouth. Dinah took advantage of this withheld speech and plunged blindly off the edge with the question she had been wanting to ask her friend since 1938. "Dorshka—was Stefan Ventura Mike's f-f-f-father?"

Dorshka's blue eyes widened in speculation but evidently not in surprise. "You know, darling, all these years I've wondered about that myself. Frankly," she said without embarrassment, "it's entirely possible. And I have always wanted to believe it. But I don't know."

She sat back in her armchair, smiled, and crossed one leg over the other. "Let me tell you, I had a wonderful affair with Stefan. It is how we became the very best of friends. But Mike looks so much like me that I have never been able to make up my mind one way or the other. What do *you* think?"

The question startled Dinah. "What did Joachim Albr-br-brecht look like?"

"Not a bit like Stefan. He was not so tall, not so broad. Thin. Skinny. Very light brown hair—straight, not thick and wavy like Stefan's. And he didn't have Mike's enormous blue eyes."

"Has it ever occurred to you that Mike is Claire's father?"

"Mike? *Claire's* father? What on earth makes you say that, my dear? It's preposterous!"

Dinah broke out with a laugh. "My God, for once you're at a loss! I'm sorry to laugh, Dorshka, but I've never seen you so s-s-s-surprised by anything!"

"What makes you say that?" Dorshka asked again, her eyes blue fires of curiosity. "Is there something I should know?"

Dinah wished she had kept her mouth shut. "Well, Dorshka," she said, swallowing. "I s-s-s-saw something—on the beach one night. Before Stefan and Veevi left for France."

"Something? On the beach at night? Don't beat around the bushes."

"I saw Veevi and Mike on the beach, in the middle of the night. They didn't see me."

"They were making love?"

"Yes. But I shouldn't have told you."

"Oh, don't be silly. It's impossible to shock me."

But Dinah could tell that Dorshka *was* shocked. Very shocked.

"What does it matter now?" Dorshka went on rather too quickly. "Your sister was never in love with Stefan. She was fond of him, she admired him, and he was her ticket out of that horrible American nowhere you came from. And Mike wanted only to forget that he was European. All he wanted was to become an American. He still wants to be an American, only not here, and I can't say I blame him. So, really, it's not such a big surprise. On the other hand, I never suspected what you are telling me. That your sister slept with any man who desired her, as long as he had a name of some kind—this already I knew. I knew it from the beginning, I knew it without having to be told. Mostly, they were writers. She slept with all those American boys who came to the house with their one big screenplay or their one 'important' novel. All those comrades making two thousand a week at Metro and Marathon and Paramount and RKO."

"Are you sure, Dorshka? How did you know?" She was remembering all that heavy flirting between Veevi and Clifford Boatwright.

"My dear," Dorshka said. "I, too, was once young and desirable and every talented man I knew wanted me. There is a look and a way of acting when an ambitious and beautiful woman achieves power over the men who desire her, and it comes from granting oneself once, but never twice, to such men. When it's twice, they think they have a claim on you and become tedious. But once? Once and no more means they do nothing but beg. Especially if you belong to a man who is older and more important and it is in some mysterious way contact with him that the other man seeks through the woman. If she gives herself once, and no more, then he is her slave—forever. I saw your sister exercise this power over many men who came to Stefan's house, while he was suffering the agony of failure here. But those men failed to possess her, and they failed to weaken Stefan."

"Did he know?"

"I think so—" She looked reflective. "But I am not sure. Certainly he knew that the young men—the puppies, he called them—adored her. He seemed to find it amusing. He also knew that she was not in love with him. 'Give her time,' he used to say to me. He thought that if he was just patient enough she would truly fall in love with him. She wanted writers, but she had no idea how to live with a real artist. No idea!" Dorshka said with contempt. "No idea of what he was facing, really. Such a difficult time he was having. And we were both out of our minds with all that was happening in Europe." She shrugged, and with the rise and fall of her broad shoulders Dinah felt the full weight of Dorshka's tenderness for her old friend, whom she had known for so long and in so many ways. "It would have hurt him to know this . . . this abomination you tell me about now. I know he offered to return to Europe without her, and that she was the one who insisted on going with him. Perhaps Stefan asked her if she wanted to remain married to him, whether there was someone else. After all, Mike was still a child. A boy of sixteen! I had decided to send him to a good boarding school in the East. But she went with him. And eight months or so after they left, Claire was born. So perhaps what you say is true. Perhaps Mike is Claire's father."

She put her hand to her head. "He loved your sister, and then I think he saw that she wasn't . . ."

"A younger v-v-v-version of you?"

"Oh, not me," Dorshka said. "A younger version of all his hopes, I think."

"I've always w-w-w-wondered whether he knew," Dinah said, enjoying this retrospective probing.

"I miss Stefan every day of my life," Dorshka said.

"I remember, that night on the beach, hearing Mike say he thought Stefan was his father. That you had told him it might be true."

"It was stupid of me to tell him. If you think I am wise, it is because I have done every stupid thing a woman can do."

"Did he ever bring it up again?"

"Well, yes. When he went into the army, and knew he might die, he asked me again, and I said that I did not know but that I hoped it was true. I told him I wanted everything clear but that I had no way of knowing. He knew already that I had had love affairs. I suppose my example had a strong effect on him." She stretched her legs out and put a foot up on the coffee table. "He wants a working actress. As I was. To give up her career—this for Veevi is a very big mistake."

"You're blaming her? He told her he wanted her there all the time, in the same room with him, sitting on a sofa and reading while he wrote."

"No, darling, I don't blame anyone. I don't blame, period—especially in this matter of love. Even this ugly thing you tell me about, I don't blame. But Veevi should have put up a fight and resisted him and said she wanted to act again. She was lazy. She did not want to use her talent."

"But she never wanted to act!" Dinah cried. "*I* did. *I* wanted to. But I had this—this f-f-f-fucking stutter!" She laughed at the stutter, and squeezed her eyes shut for an instant, as if to force back tears.

"Yes," said Dorshka. "I understand. Still, your sister should not have given my son everything he wanted."

"You're blaming her, and that's unfair," Dinah said carefully. "I know he's your son, but a man does not c-c-c-c-customarily end a marriage when his wife is p-p-pregnant or has just given birth."

"Dinah darling, don't be naïve," Dorshka said. "There is never a good time to break up. If you fall in love, you fall in love."

So that's where he gets it, Dinah thought.

"Can you speak to Jake about her? Will the two of you help out? I will be glad to have her and the girls come and live with me," Dorshka went on.

These last utterances, so peremptory, brought Dinah up short, and all she could say was "Yes, of course." Wanting to leave, she gave Dorshka a quick hug. "We'll figure something out. I'll write to her myself. Tell him, tell her, we'll do everything we can."

She drove directly home, dying for her bed and the feel of the afternoon breeze blowing through the windows. When she arrived, however, there was a letter waiting for her in the breakfast room. She felt nauseated and asked Gussie to bring her a Coke and some saltines. Then she went upstairs, lay down, and tore open the letter.

Dear Dinah,

I can't stay here any longer. Mike wants a divorce and is going to marry Odile. So, I've lost him. It's over for good. I had hoped to live in Paris for the rest of my life, but it's time to bow out.

Can we stay with you until we get settled? I suppose some kind of job is the best thing, but I don't know what's possible. Everything's finished for me over here.

But I won't be coming home. I'll be going into exile.

xxxxxs V.

She put the letter down and stuck two pillows under her feet, then lay with her knees up and brooded. She wanted none of this now—not Veevi and her life and its complications. Alone in her spacious bed, Dinah felt crowded and jostled, and she put her hand on her belly and felt the too-hard, prematurely large roundness. All she wanted was to keep what she had intact and inviolate: her husband, her children, the life fighting to grow inside her. She wanted no changes and no invasions. Within her a voice snarled, *I don't give a fuck about Veevi, I don't want her here. I don't want her coming into my house and taking over, because that sure as hell is going to happen. She will come here and eat me alive.*

All this she said clearly to herself, lying with her hands on her belly, wondering whether the mass beneath her fingers was tumor or baby. As she felt the nubby white candlewick bedspread underneath her legs, she remembered the letter she had written to Veevi and thrown away the day after testifying. She wished now that she had kept it. It would have felt good to reread it and have its words look her in the face. No! she was shouting inside. I want no one and nothing coming into our life. But she felt herself being helplessly dragged toward the magnet of obligation and responsibility. A phrase from the past came to her: *We'll just have to get the hose and wash her down.* And then she saw, in her memory's eye, herself and her mother in all the backyards of all the little houses and bungalows in which the Milligans had lived. Alice would be standing there in an apron, her hands on her hips, her face a nest of worries, while Dinah, all business, took Veevi's clothes off and threw them in a pile and then picked up the garden hose and washed her sister down. Veevi, irrepressibly gay and nonchalant, was determined to squeeze every drop of pleasure out of the fun she'd had that afternoon with the other kids—the taste of the candy, the feel of the gooey cool mud between her toes, the splash and iridescence of the water in the balmy California afternoon.

6

*I*n his room at the Dorchester, Jake was restless and jumpy all right, but it wasn't because of what he had to do tomorrow. Tomorrow would be interesting but hardly difficult—a full day of newspaper, radio, and television interviews with Wynn Tooling and Glynis Carleton. He loved being back in London. No, it wasn't the picture; he expected rave reviews here. Ever since he had arrived in London two weeks ago, he had known that he simply did not want to go back to Los Angeles. He wanted to spend some time alone, in a lovely little flat, working on his new project. Only then would he be ready to go back to L.A., where he planned to sell the house and bring Dinah and the kids to Europe as soon as possible and make London his base of operations. It was time to get out of Hollywood, that goddamn company town.

It had to be London, though, not Paris. Paris was dangerous for him. It was too seductive, and he would allow himself to become something he couldn't afford to be—he felt this instinctively and with complete certainty, having flown back tonight from his second trip to Paris this weekend. It had been even more of a revelation than the first. That lunch yesterday with Gerry Tuttle and Veevi: the pleasure of it, the gaiety. Veevi had seemed a little sad, but it hadn't prevented her from having a good time. They'd been talking about Bill Nemeth, who had been shot to death by a sniper in Indochina last year. The two women toasted Bill, weeping a little and dabbing their eyes with white handkerchiefs. Veevi had laughed at some meshuga story of Gerry's that Bill had told her—about a dead American soldier found in a church cellar in France, nothing left of him but a skeleton and a dog tag, and how the office in charge of getting bodies back to the families had called every one of his relatives and none of them wanted him because he had been such a pain in the ass. Ben Knight had turned it into a short story for *The New Yorker* and everybody loved it. Seeing Gerry Tuttle again brought back that moment during his first trip when he had turned his head in Veevi's car and seen Gerry straddling Nemeth, her skirt drawn up to her thighs. He and Veevi had just looked at each other as if to say, "You and I aren't bothered by this. We know this kind of thing goes on all the time, and neither of us is a square or a bore about it." Now, once again, he was overwhelmed by a desire to live in this world. This time, too, he'd had a drink at the Ritz with Willie Weil, who had laid out for him every single advantage of making movies in Europe, with him as executive producer.

Saturday night in Paris had been clear and cool, and, Jake felt, alive with an exquisite understanding and acceptance of every human appetite. This was a city indifferent both to shame and self-control, and he felt all too comfortable there with Veevi and her friends as they migrated from Fouquet's to dinner to some after-hours jazz club where they knew all the musicians. This time Veevi called him, in front of the others, "Uncle J.," displaying for all the familial tie between them, with its hint of secrets and special understandings.

At two o'clock on Sunday morning, Jake and Veevi were back at her place, sitting on her worn brocade sofa and talking about the evening—and Veevi's plans.

"Has Dinah said anything to you?" she asked.

"About what?" He wouldn't have admitted it, but Dinah and his children were very far from his mind right now.

"About my coming home?"

"You can come whenever you like, honey. Just say when."

His spirits drooped a little. It was convenient to have a member of the family in Paris. He didn't have to be told what her situation was. Her friends cared for her, and wouldn't dream of excluding her or cutting her off. But in this set (as in all others, he thought), a woman had to have a man. Even Veevi, beautiful Veevi, was there because she had been, until now, Mike Albrecht's wife. It wasn't easy, and despite everyone's esprit de corps, her situation had become more and more awkward.

She took a sip of cognac and looked frankly at him. "One thing is sure," she said without emotion. "I'll never find another Michael Albrecht. Unless he comes back."

"Is that a real possibility? He wants a divorce. He's going to marry the girl."

"Oh, Uncle J. After so many years, I know him well. He loves me," she said. "He can't possibly love anyone else. But it's not going to happen overnight. I might as well go home to California."

"You mean, that way he'll know where to find you?"

"Well, yes," she said, and smiled ruefully. "I guess I've failed with Mike, but you know, really, I should have been a king's mistress."

He searched her face to see if she was being ironic. "What makes you think of yourself that way?" He was trying to get her to say more by adopting the neutral but encouraging tone his analyst used.

"Because I could have, that's all. I have the talent. The skills."

It was an odd thing for a rejected woman to say, Jake thought. "So it's power you want?" he said.

"God no. I don't want to be *bored*," she answered quickly. "I want to be amused. I want every day to be interesting and new. I hate monotony and routine and the bloody sameness of things."

But you and your friends live the same way every day, he thought.

"Crunched," she continued. "Christ, how crunched and squeezed we all were—Pop and Mom and Dinah and me in that little box of a house where you could hear every word any of us said."

"The petit bourgeoisie?"

"Lower! The fucking proletariat! God, just the thought of going back to L.A. makes me feel buried alive."

"Then why give Paris up? These people love you, I can tell. Stay here and keep out of Mike's way. You're still gorgeous, you'll find someone else. Why exile yourself from the world you love? Hollywood is just going to be hell for you if you love it here. Nothing in L.A. will ever be good enough for you—including us, I'm afraid."

She shook her head and her brown hair undulated in languid waves along the crest of her shoulders. "It's shit, you know, running into them everywhere. I don't want to be always trying to avoid him, always finding out whether it's my night or his night to have dinner with Hunt and Felicity or the Knights or Gerry and Walter Tuttle. And the worst of it is, I'm always getting paired with Rue now that Bill's dead. Rue and me, without men. Oh God, how dreary. She's got this wispy girlish little voice"—hers became soft and childlike in mimicry—"and she thinks the way to compete with me is to say nasty things about everyone. A real Malice in Wonderland."

He laughed. "If it's any consolation, you're going to do fine in Holly-wood if you come back."

"But wouldn't I be just as much of a sad old broad out there as I am here? Why would it be any different?" She'd been drinking all night, but she spoke clearly.

"You'd have us. We'd take you everywhere. Have everyone over to meet you."

She looked at him. "Uncle J.," she said with a tilt of her head. He got it: his idea of "everyone" wasn't hers.

"Has Mike suggested this to you? Does he want you to leave?"

"Yes," she said. "He says it kills him to see me in pain."

"And you believe him?"

She shrugged.

"Has it occurred to you that he's a first-class prick?"

"Even first-class pricks can feel guilty," she said with equanimity.

He kissed her on the cheek. "You're brave and wonderful," he said. "And I'd love it if we could just move here and live together in a big house somewhere."

"Oh, Uncle J., you're a panic," she said, using one of her pet phrases. It was slightly acidic, the way she said it, but the look on her face brought him into the exclusive society that they alone shared. It suggested that of all the people in the world, they were the only ones who understood every-thing, including his own extravagant fancies.

She walked Jake to the door, folding her arms and smiling sleepily. "Lis-ten, if you want to come home, do you think it would be soon?" he asked.

"Oh, I guess so. I've written to Dinah, so she knows. But talk it over with her. I can't possibly come unless it's all right with her. I was pretty mean to her, not answering when she wrote. And now you say she's having another baby. A real breeder, my sister."

"Dinah would do anything to help you," Jake said. "You know that, Veevi. Especially after—"

"Shh," Veevi said. "Good night."

⁂

If he had been sleeping, his good ear would have been pressed against the pillow and he wouldn't have heard the hotel telephone ringing its insistent,

British, double-trilled ring. But he was pacing the room in his shorts and pajama top, thinking—he enumerated his points to himself and jutted out a finger for each—that (1) it made no sense for Veevi to come to California, where her passport problem and her status in the industry would make it almost impossible for him to do anything for her, and (2) it was especially pointless now, just when he was thinking of getting out of California and moving to London, where (3) perhaps he really could find something for her to do and where (4), most important, she could, simply by remaining in Paris, be useful to him both socially and professionally. She could be—and he loved this idea immediately—his Paris office.

There was another thing on his mind. He couldn't get the image of Gerry Tuttle and Bill Nemeth in the backseat of the car out of his mind. If he lived in London, but flew often to Paris, there would be possibilities for him—interesting possibilities, without having to incur the guilt of being in the same city with Dinah. With Felicity, for instance! He could fly to Paris on a Saturday for a morning meeting with Willie Weil but spend the afternoon with Felicity. Where? Well, he'd have to invest in a pied-à-terre. It would be beautifully deductible, and maybe he and Weil could work things out so that it would in fact be Weil who paid for it. Dinah could fly from London to Paris whenever she wanted to see Veevi and do a little shopping.

It was at this point of inspiration, when every detail was effortlessly falling into place, that the phone rang. "There's a telegram for you, sir," a woman's voice said. "Would you like it to be delivered to your room now, sir, or in the morning?"

*T*hat was great, Mr. Perrin," Peter Lasker said, gently placing the separate parts of his clarinet in the red-velvet compartments of his clarinet case. Mr. Perrin smiled and put his own clarinet down. Peter's lesson had gone well, so he had rewarded the child by playing the clarinet solo to "Sing Sing Sing." "Ask your mother to get you the album for this," he said. "It's the 1938–39 Carnegie Hall concert. Listen to the Jess Stacy piano solo, too. It's thrilling." He smiled at Peter again, and his expression grew serious. "I guess one day you're going to have to decide whether you want to be a classical musician or a jazz player," he said. "Here," he added, writing something down on a slip of paper and handing it to Peter. "Tell your mother to get you the Rubank Intermediate book. We'll keep on playing the folk song duets, but it's time for you to move on to Mozart."

Mr. Perrin had given up jazz and big-band music in order to support his family. He was now a studio musician at Marathon, and Peter was well into his second year of taking lessons with him.

Peter forgot the rules and let the screen door slam behind him as he left Mr. Perrin's house, he was so excited. His mother's profile, with its straight nose and pretty mouth, her short brown hair caught on the side in a gold barrette that she always wore, seemed beautiful to him, as always, within the roomy seclusion of the station wagon. He climbed into the front seat beside her, putting his clarinet case on his lap. "Guess what, Mom! Mr. Perrin says I'm ready to start Mozart next time. I have to get this—" and he handed Dinah the slip of paper with the title of the music book on it. "Can we do it today?"

Dinah glanced at her watch. "Sure."

"And can we stop at the sword shop? Please, Mom, please?"

"We'll see," she said, which meant they would. "What's the M-M-M-Mozart piece?"

"A concerto, I think." He said the word carefully, liking the sound but not quite certain of its meaning. "Do you think Dad'll like it?"

"Of course." She hesitated. "Why wouldn't he?"

She knew perfectly well why he wouldn't. Jake was always nagging Peter with "Why don't you learn to play the piano?" or "I wish you'd play more baseball at school" or "If you like, I'll get tennis lessons for you at the club." Peter wanted to play the clarinet, not tennis or baseball. When he started fencing lessons his father said, "Tennis is a great social game. Later on, it's very useful for meeting people."

"He never likes anything I like," Peter answered.

She heard herself making excuses. "Dad just wants you kids to get out there and have fun with other kids."

The inaneness of this reply didn't escape Dinah, but she didn't know what else to say and she would never criticize Jake in front of Peter. It baffled and angered her that Jake was so critical of Peter. Lorna could do no wrong, but about Peter they always quarreled. "Why do you have to be so hard on him?" she would ask in their room at night after the children were in bed. "So what if he doesn't like baseball?" And Jake always had a ready answer, some wordy and superior explanation pulled out of a psychoanalytic hat. It invariably began not with Peter but with Jake himself and included references to his "unconscious" and his "inadequacies" and his "anxieties." Back in Chicago, in his Studs Lonigan youth, he'd been uncoordinated, knock-kneed, and Jewish, he explained, and he'd felt terrible about his inability to compete with other boys; and here was Peter, well formed and beautifully coordinated but indifferent to baseball and football and interested only in oddball and egghead things. Jake had therefore concluded that Peter must be having the same conflicts and anxieties and thus needed to learn, as he himself had been forced to learn, how to compete in a larger world, doing the things that normal boys do to learn how to be aggressive and strong.

Dinah always became furious when he talked that way. "How can you say these things about your son?" she would shout at him. Slunk back in the armchair, his silk paisley bathrobe spread open to reveal his T-shirt and blue boxer shorts and his skinny legs sprawling toward the floor, his hand held wearily to his forehead, Jake would say, "Honey, I'm trying to do my job as his father. I've got to prepare him for the struggle of life." And then she felt that she couldn't argue with him, even though she was sure he was wrong—not in principle, perhaps, but in the all-important particulars concerning Peter himself. But she couldn't put that into words. And so she would give up, resentful and angry. Increasingly, she noticed, Peter was reluctant to talk to his father or to play ball with him in De Neve Park, which was just a few blocks away, within walking distance of home and thus convenient for an impromptu game whenever Jake experienced a fit of paternal obligation or—what amounted to the same thing—the impulse to torture and needle his son.

It had been so calm at home since Jake had left for London—so peaceful, for instance, at the dinner table. Peter ate what he wanted to eat and she didn't sit there anxiously watching every mouthful he took. If he didn't want Brussels sprouts, she didn't make him eat them. Would Jake and Peter hate each other in the future? Jake was certainly doing everything he could to make sure his firstborn child would hate him later on. Yet now, driving into Beverly Hills with Peter, and feeling deeply that Jake was in the wrong, Dinah nevertheless missed her husband terribly.

At the music store, they bought the clarinet instruction book, and Peter browsed through new releases of clarinet performances. Then they walked up to the store on Little Santa Monica, where he gazed lovingly at a saber he planned to buy when he'd saved up enough money. Finally, they drove to the Wil Wright's just below Wilshire and Beverly and ordered hot-fudge sundaes.

They were wonderfully happy together, waiting for the sundaes. Dinah looked at her boy's solemn oval face and questioning eyes. She thought his musical talent came from her mother, who had played the piano in silent movie theaters, and she loved it in him. It was fine with her that he wanted to be a musician.

She asked him if he remembered his grandfather, Ed Milligan.

"Sure. I remember Papa Milligan," Peter said. "I remember the way his trailer smelled. It was kind of strong, but nice. Was it his pipe tobacco?"

"Yes. It had a very acrid smell."

"Mom? You know what?"

"What?"

"I never told you this, Mom, but once when Papa Milligan stayed overnight at our house—in his trailer, I mean—I went out there and he was brushing his teeth, only he was holding them in his hand."

"Those weren't his real teeth—they were false teeth."

"And, Mom, I looked at them and they were all black. He told me he chewed tobacco, and he gave me a piece of it and told me to chew. The taste was so horrible, I ran out of the trailer and threw up in the ivy."

"Golly, that must have been t-t-t-terrible," she said, making a ghastly face in sympathy. "In Little R-R-R-Rock, when he was a kid, all the boys chewed tobacco. They had cuspidors and would spit the wads of tobacco and tobacco juice into them." She made another face, and Peter laughed. "They made bets about who could spit the farthest. And he used to have a little saying. Imagine a little boy who lisps, and who says: 'I can thpit in a thraight line, I can thpit in a curved line, and I can thpit in a thircle. But when I thpit in my friendth eye, he'th both thurprithed and pleathed, but more thurprithed than pleathed.'"

Peter couldn't stop laughing, and asked Dinah to say it again. The ice cream sundaes were served, and they spooned up ice cream and fudge sauce in a familiar ritual of small, delicate bites. "Another thing I remember about Papa Milligan," Peter said, "was that he always sang the tobacco song: 'There was an old soldier, who had a wooden leg / He had no tobacco nor tobacco would he beg.'" Peter continued to the end.

"Gee, Petey," Dinah said, "it's great how you remember that. You can pass it on to your children—when you have them."

He looked up from his ice cream, finding it odd to hear his mother talk this way, and saw that her face, so lively and happy a moment ago, had suddenly turned a grayish white. "Mom? Are you okay?"

She got up slowly and reached for her purse. "I'm just going to go to the ladies' room for a minute," she whispered. She saw the worry on his face. "I'm okay, sweetheart. Just a tummy ache or something." But he turned to watch her as she walked away, and her walk, it seemed to him, was too careful, as if the stomachache was really bad or she really had to go to the bathroom. Uneasy but not alarmed exactly, he kept eating his sundae, scraping the sauce off the bottom of the silver dish and saving for last the little macaroon that always came in a waxed-paper envelope. He took his mother's from her saucer because he knew that she would have given it to him anyway. He kept waiting, but she didn't come back. He saw what was left of her sundae and wanted it, but he left it alone, feeling that it should be there for her when she came back. After fifteen minutes, it had begun to get soupy, so he finished it and ate both of the macaroons. Thirsty, now, he drank his glass of water and hers, and still she hadn't come back.

He was worried now. He supposed he should go to the ladies' room and knock on the door, but that would be really embarrassing. He was wondering if he should say something to the waitress, when he saw his mother walking slowly back to the table. She was still pale, and she had a strange look on her face. She didn't even sit down. "Have you finished, honey? Good, because we have to go home right away. I'm sorry, honey, but I don't feel well."

She looked terrible: her skin, usually coffee-and-cream-colored, was an eerie greenish gray.

"Mom?" he said, taking her hand and finding it cold and moist.

"It's okay," she said, and they both knew it wasn't.

"Mom? Are you sick? Mom?" he said.

Once they were back in the car, she lit a cigarette. "Don't be scared, sweetie. I just need to get home and lie down."

"Can you drive okay, Mom? I can drive. Dad taught me how in Palm Springs. It's an emergency. I can drive you home." He wanted desperately to drive the big station wagon. He wanted a policeman to stop them so that he could explain that his mother was sick and he happened to know how to drive and was driving her home because she couldn't drive. He wanted his father to know.

"Thank you, darling, but I'd better drive. I'd have to be dead first before I couldn't drive."

He fell silent, because she really did look very sick and her joke wasn't funny. He glanced over at her. She was still pale, and the expression on her face was sadder than anything he had ever seen in his life—sadder even than she had looked at Papa Milligan's funeral. He didn't want to make her talk, but he moved to the center of the seat and put his hand on her shoulder, and she glanced at him with love. He was a tender, sweet boy, she thought, and Jake was a son of a bitch for being so rough on him.

They took the long, winding way home, since there was late-afternoon traffic on Sunset. Even so, the blinding sun was bothering her, even with her dark glasses on, and she lowered the sun guard. He watched her drive, her mouth set, and still wished with all his heart that he could be the one behind the wheel. He was certain that something was very wrong.

"Does it hurt, Mom?"

"Yeah, honey. Yeah, it does."

"A lot, Mom?"

"Well, kind of. Yeah. A lot."

"Mom, are you still going to have a baby?"

"I don't know, sweetie. Maybe not."

Finally, his mother pulled the car into the driveway. "Now, Peter, when I stop the car, run into the house and get Gussie."

Peter ran, shouting, into the house, and Gussie, who had been peeling potatoes, flew out the back door. With a knot in his stomach, he saw her put her arm around his mother's back and help her up out of the car. His mother was bent over, but her head rested against Gussie's shoulder. Gussie, who was saying something too low for Peter to hear, guided her slowly into the house.

A few hours later, a doctor came. He was a huge man whom Peter had never seen before, and he went upstairs to his mother's room with Gussie, who closed the door. Then an ambulance came. Peter and Lorna stood at the top of the stairs with Gussie while the ambulance men brought their mother out of the bedroom and took her down the stairs, their feet making a muffled clomp-clomp on the carpet. "Careful," they said to each other. "Watch that turn there. Got it."

Peter and Lorna ran downstairs behind the stretcher. Dinah told them she was going to the hospital and that everything would be fine, but she looked sad.

"Oh, Gussie dear," she called out as the men lifted her into the ambulance. "Call Gladys at the studio and tell her to please wire London. And maybe you and the kids could go and pick up Jake's mother. She'll be happy to come and help out."

"Mrs. Lasker, honest, I don't need no help with the children. You know as well as I do Mrs. Lasker senior is just going to get in the way."

Dinah laughed and reached for Gussie's hand. "Oh, Gus, you're great. You're in charge now, so just do it your way. Kids, listen to Gussie. I'll call home very soon."

She awoke slowly. The incision hurt. It was early evening, and the fading light, with its orange streaks, filled her with desolation. Her eyes, only slightly open, took in Jake, sitting near the bed, his round head, with its receding hair, leaning against the back of his hand. He seemed to be staring at the dull linoleum floor. On his face was an expression of terrible weariness. She thought, with sudden anger, You'd think someone had just sentenced him to death. Why was he here? What had he come for? Was that expression on his face love? It couldn't be. No. It had to be obligation. She'd dragged him home from Europe.

They looked at each other. "How are ya, honey?" he said.

She didn't answer.

"The nurses tell me you've been crying."

"Well?" she said almost defiantly. Then her head drooped and she wept.

He sat on the bed and took her hand. "It's a big blow, honey. I feel it, too." He felt her hand limp in his own and squeezed it. Then he waited until the crying subsided.

She saw something on the windowsill—a bouquet of red, yellow, and pink roses. "Are those from home?"

"From the kreebnabbers," he said, using the private nonsense word that was his nickname for their children. "And Gussie. They're from your own flower beds. She cut them this afternoon."

"When did you get home?" she asked.

"Six this morning. I came as soon as I could."

He saw her head drop again, and he took her in his arms. She burrowed her head into his chest and wept again as he held her. She pulled back to look at his face and saw a thin line of tears. Then she reached her arms around him and they held each other, and she felt now that everything would be all right and wondered why she had been so angry. She looked up at him and smiled, and took his large round head in her hands, like a baby's, and kissed him where she loved to kiss her children, on the place just between his chin and his mouth.

"Oh, you're much better," he said.

"I want a cigarette."

He opened the bedside table and took out her cigarettes and lighter and gave them to her. She shook out a Camel and put it between her lips. "Do I have any lipstick here? Where's my purse? I want a hairbrush."

He explained that her purse was at home.

"Oh-shit-oh-dear," she said. "I must look like hell."

"You look fine. A little tired. But good, honey."

He flicked the lighter and held it while she lit her cigarette. She drew deeply on it and exhaled, and her expression became calm and peaceful.

"Honey?" he said.

"Yeah?"

"Now, do just as I say. Close your eyes."

He had gotten up and was standing expectantly at the foot of the bed.

"What do you have out there, a camera crew?" But she shut her eyes and smiled. "Wait," she said, putting the cigarette in the ashtray. Then she shut her eyes again, and put her hands over them for good measure.

"Just stay like that," he said. "Don't move."

Don't let me cry, she said to herself. Just don't let me cry when I see their faces. She remembered the stricken expressions—Peter's and Lorna's—when her father died and they saw her crying. Was Gussie with them? To gather them around her—the kids, Gussie, and Jake—and to hear their voices: that would make her stop crying for the lost baby, the lost womb.

In the darkness behind her scrunched-tight eyelids, Dinah listened. She heard steps, rustling, and movement, but not the rapid motion of children's feet.

"Honey—? Okay. You can look now."

Jake stood back against the dull, hospital-white wall and observed, with a director's interest, the scene that now took place: Veevi taking unhurried steps toward the bed, Dinah's eyes widening with what seemed like be-musement, as if she'd been expecting someone completely different and didn't recognize or know what to make of the figure that was moving toward her. Then the sisters did the same thing at the same time. They looked at each other and, pressing their lips together and widening their eyes until they resembled the eyes of baby dolls, each made at the other what Jake knew they had as children called a bubby face—the face of an infant, Dinah had once explained to him, squashed up against its mother's breast. Their mother had invented both the funny face and the name for it, or so they liked to think; nobody really knew where it came from. But here they were, making bubby faces at each other, neither of them saying a word. What fascinated Jake, however, was that Dinah's bubby face was different from Veevi's. Dinah's was worried and questioning, Veevi's beseeching and contrite.

Then Dinah held out her arms and Veevi sat carefully beside her. Dinah embraced Veevi, then quickly released her. The sisters did not cling to each other. Dinah's cigarette, Jake noticed, had burned down to a long, thin rod of ash, and now she gestured with her fingers for another smoke, all the while appraising Veevi's face as Veevi snapped open her purse and offered her a cigarette from a blue packet—a strong-smelling French cigarette.

Dinah shook her head and twisted around for her Camels. Then, with a sharp intake of breath, she said "Ouch!" and snapped at Jake, "For Christ's sake, honey, hand me a cigarette, will you? And don't make me l-l-l-laugh, because this incision hurts like hell."

Jake gave Dinah her cigarette and found a chair for Veevi. Then, with her husband on one side and her sister on the other, Dinah leaned back against her pillows. "This is a hell of a s-s-s-surprise!" she said, smoothing out the counterpane and folding her hands in front of her. "Jake didn't tell me you were coming."

"Well, how could I?" Jake answered.

He could have sent a telegram, but he figured she'd be too doped up to read it. Veevi and the girls—Claire and Colette, whom everyone called Coco—had flown to London and then on to L.A. with Jake, who had tried to get Burt Unwin to meet them at customs when Veevi's passport was confiscated. But Unwin, the lawyer who had coached Dinah in preparation for her testimony, had said there was nothing he could do. Peter and Lorna had been getting ready for school when the exhausted travelers trooped in from the airport, and had instantly fallen in love with Claire and Coco. Peter, Jake said, was already mad about Veevi.

"Natch," said Dinah, smiling. "He's male, isn't he?"

"My God," Veevi said, "what a swell kid. How did two such unattractive people as you produce such a beautiful kid?" Both Jake and Dinah laughed, as they knew they were supposed to, Dinah grimacing and clutching her bandaged belly.

There was a brief silence, and they saw that it was dark outside and the hills were dotted with lights.

"We won't be imposing on you too long," Veevi said. "I'm going to find an apartment in Westwood, maybe a house. With Dorshka. Dear God, she's going to live with us." Veevi rolled her eyes.

Dinah, again clutching her belly, laughed.

"A job, too," added Veevi. "Have to get a job. A bit of a challenge, that."

"I've been waiting for you to come home for a long time, Vee. Get settled first. Rest. We'll worry about the job l-l-later," Dinah said, just as an orderly came in carrying her dinner on a tray. Under the hot steel domes was a slab of dried-out roast beef, a mound of graying peas and discolored cubed carrots, and another mound of lumpy mashed potatoes with a puddle of mud-colored gravy at the center. Dinah took a forkful of mashed potatoes, made a face, and put the fork down. "Oh Christ, the f-f-f-food is god-awful. I'll be so glad to get home to Gussie's cooking. What's she making for dinner tonight? Wait—better not tell me, or I'll cry," she said, pushing the tray away in disgust.

"Actually, darling," Jake said, standing up, nimbly grabbing the slab of beef and devouring it as he spoke, "Reggie Pertwee just happened to call this afternoon, and since he remembers Veevi from the old days we started talking about her situation with the blacklist and the passport, et cetera, et cetera, and he said he'd think about it. I invited him out to Chasen's with us tonight so he can talk to her himself. In fact, we'd better push off any minute now, since we're meeting him at seven-thirty. He sends his dearest love to you, by the way. Said he didn't know about your being 'in hospital,' as he put it, and is going to send flowers immediately."

"You've already got oodles," Veevi said, nodding at the collection of vases with bouquets standing on the window ledge and on a nearby side table. "Of course, by the time you go home most of them will be dead."

Dinah hadn't noticed the flowers and looked at them with a puzzled expression. How had she managed not to see them?

"When can I go home?" She was feeling weak and tired again. Her belly was throbbing.

"I spoke to Shelley Zuckerman," Jake said, "and he said to give it five more days. He wants to talk to me about my deal on the picture—he thinks

Engel's trying to screw me, that we gave him too many deferrals. He's afraid the studio's accounting isn't kosher. So I thought, Well, let's get that worked out, and in the meanwhile Veevi can start lining things up right away—"

"Shelley Zuckerman? My OB thinks Irv Engel is trying to screw you?"

"No, darling, did I say that? I mean Reg Pertwee. Christ, I'm absent-minded. Must be the damned airplane."

He leaned over her plate again and helped himself to the mashed potatoes. "How can you eat that?" she said. "It's inedible."

Veevi, she noticed, was wearing a black wool crepe dinner suit with a white silk shirt. "Is that mine?" Dinah said.

"I hope you don't mind, Ina. Everything of mine is wrinkled. I didn't want to ask Gussie to press anything, she's so busy with the kids."

"It's fine. I'm glad you found them," Dinah said. "I'm taller than you, but it doesn't seem to matter. 'They're wearing them long this year,' " she said, and Veevi laughed, because years ago they had loved to make fun of fashion talk on the radio. She looked at Jake again and saw that he was wearing a dark blue jacket and tie. They certainly were going to Chasen's. "Jake, can you just see if the nurse is coming? I want my shot."

"Darling, I know it hurts terribly." He leaned forward and took her hand. "Do you want us to stay? I'll just cancel. In fact, Reggie told me to call if we wanted to change plans. He sends his love."

"You said that already. Listen, go—go and have fun. Just stop on your way out and ask them to send in some m-m-m-morphine, and a nurse to give it to me would be nice, too, okay?"

Jake and Veevi stood up. "Call me as soon as you wake up tomorrow. I'll be at the studio, and I'll come as fast as you can say 'Jack Robinson.' All right, darling?" He kissed her on the forehead, though she had lifted her face to meet his mouth with hers.

"I won't hug you," Veevi said. "I know how sore you are. Coco was a Caesarean."

"Fun, huh?"

"Lots," said Veevi. And the two of them made another bubby face, exactly the same one this time: a bubby-face-of-physical-suffering. That's the damnedest form of communication I've ever seen, Jake thought.

Then they were gone—out the door and out of sight and hearing. Dinah looked at her plate of hospital food, now cold and lumpy, pushed the tray away on its steel rollers, and pressed the button for the nurses' station.

It was forty-five minutes before a nurse came. "Mrs. Lasker? Remember me? I have your shot."

Dinah turned slightly, wincing from pain. The nurse gave her the shot in her backside, and Dinah turned around and looked her in the face. "It's me, Mrs. Lasker, Mary O'Donnell."

"Oh, Mary," Dinah said. "Sit down, dear."

The nurse, who was in her early thirties and had short, frizzy blond hair, promptly sat in the chair that Jake had occupied. She was Irish, and had taken care of Dinah during the births of both of her children. Dinah reached out her hand, and Mary took it immediately. "Why, Mrs. Lasker, dear, what's the matter?" Dinah's eyes were suddenly squeezed shut and pouring tears.

"Do you remember the last time, Mary, when my daughter was born? You took me out to the car, where my husband and my son and my housekeeper were all waiting for me. And, as you and my husband helped me into the car, you turned to me and said, 'Well, Mrs. Lasker, I suppose we'll see you next year,' and my husband looked at you and said, 'Uh-huh, we've found out what's causing them.' Do you remember that?"

Dinah, whose speech was becoming slurred from the morphine, nevertheless laughed with Mary O'Donnell, who was blushing. "You blushed then, too, dear. Well, Mary"—and the tears sprang anew—"it's finished. Everything's gone. I've lost my third, and all my pl-pl-pl-plumbing, too." Her head fell to her chest and she sobbed.

Mary O'Donnell never let go of her hand. "There, there, dear Mrs. Lasker." She waited while Dinah wept. Then, as the pain in Dinah's belly subsided and she began to grow drowsy, Mary spoke, knowing that Dinah wouldn't remember what she said but sensing that the sound of her voice would soothe her patient. "Your body's had a shock. It's the hormones, Mrs. Lasker. You know, going from before to after. Soon you'll be going home to your beautiful son and daughter. I remember those babies, Mrs. Lasker. I saw them come into the world. Beautiful, perfect children, Mrs. Lasker, and they'll be so happy to see you." She began to let go of Dinah's hand.

"Iz punishment?" Dinah murmured anxiously, squeezing Mary's hand.

"No, Mrs. Lasker. It's just nature up to her old tricks. Why would God want to punish a nice lady like you?" Dinah drifted off, and Mary felt her relaxing her grip. She waited and withdrew her hand to pull the covers up over Dinah's shoulder. Then she took her hand again. It was strange, what

Mrs. Lasker had said. Why would she think God would want to punish her? she wondered, recording the time at which she had given Dinah the shot.

Peter and Lorna had seen Dinah cry before, at Papa Milligan's funeral. Still, it was a shock for them when they went up to their parents' room after school five days later and she burst into tears. Both kids stopped dead in their tracks. Lorna's lips trembled, and Peter stared, speechless with horror at the sight of her sobbing, her face contorted in grief.

The two of them—Peter in a white T-shirt and jeans, Lorna in a plaid dress with a sash that tied behind in a bow, and barrettes and braids from which strands of thick blond hair were escaping—looked like statues.

"Lorna, darling, tie your shoe," Dinah finally said, reaching for a tissue to wipe her eyes. Relieved, Lorna looked down and saw that the laces on one of her scuffed blue-and-white saddle shoes had come undone.

"I'm sorry, kids," Dinah said. "I know, it's awful to see your m-m-mother cry."

Then she opened her arms and they approached, but in a gingerly fashion, afraid not so much of hurting her but of seeing her burst into tears again. But she didn't cry. She hugged and kissed them, and asked them about school and all the things that had happened to them while she was in the hospital, and was simply her mother again.

Still, now that she was home, she wept constantly. It happened when she was alone, often when she had gone back to bed after a session of going up and down the stairs with Veevi or Gussie helping her. Then she would slide under the cool sheets and sob. She mentioned it to Shelley Zuckerman when she went to have her stitches removed. "I c-c-c-can't stop crying," she said. He said it was normal and natural, and, like Mary O'Donnell, reminded her that she had been blessed with two beautiful children. She said nothing about feeling that she was being punished; how could she, she told herself, when she didn't even believe in God? She continued to cry, though, and Jake, at his wits' end, summoned Dr. Zuckerman. The doctor sat on the edge of Dinah's bed and talked to her as if he had read her mind and knew her deepest fears, and she found his words comforting: no, there would be no difference in their sex life; she and Jake could carry on just as before. His manner was warm, kind, candid. He suggested that she consider therapy if the crying persisted. Before leaving, he joked with Peter and Lorna about the way they hollered at him when they were born. His visit, Dinah felt, had done her a world of good. Time to stop all this, she commanded herself. After all, I've got a house to run. Shape up or ship out!

The evening after Dr. Zuckerman's visit, she came downstairs for dinner. The next morning she came down to breakfast, not in her bathrobe but dressed and in time to eat with the kids and to wait with them for the school bus. She smelled the fresh morning air and touched the flowers she had planted. She felt strong on her feet and full of energy. Back inside the house, she sat down in the kitchen with her Robinson Reminder open in front of her, and she and Gussie wrote out a grocery list.

Then she looked at her housekeeper across the gray Formica table, both of them smoking Camels. "Gussie, do you have too much to do?" she asked. "Do you need extra help?"

Gussie said that she'd spoken to Mr. Lasker while Dinah was in the hospital, and he'd said it was okay to give Miss Fanny an extra day so they could keep up with all the laundry.

Dinah, who hadn't known about this change, said it was fine. Was there anything else? she wanted to know.

"I hate to complain, Mrs. Lasker," Gussie said, "but Mrs. Albrecht junior wants me to bring her up a tray, just like I was doing for you. If you want me to, I'll do it, but far as I can see she ain't had no hysterectomy, and I got my vacuuming and all my housework to do, and it do cut into my morning." Whenever Gussie switched from "proper" English to her own way of speaking, Dinah knew the conversation was confidential, and she resolved to do something about the problem before it went too far.

Privately, she thought, We were Communists, for Christ's sake, and here we are running this Negro woman ragged going upstairs and downstairs bringing us breakfast in bed.

Was there anything else? Gussie gave her a peculiar look. "Mrs. Lasker," she said in a low voice, "you best be checking your gin supplies. I found an empty bottle in the trash out back, and I sure ain't the one done put it there."

"My sister?"

Gussie nodded. "There's a bottle under the bed," she added. "There's one in there right now. But what worries me the most, Mrs. Lasker, is that she smokes in the bed. Now, I'm safe and sound out there in my room over the garage, but all of you is here in the house and I'm afraid she gonna set fire to the place. Just the other day, I found some burn holes in the sheets."

Dinah drew in her breath sharply. "Oh, boy. This is bad. What're we gonna do?"

Gussie shook her head. She didn't like Genevieve Albrecht, who asked her what she thought about *Brown v. Board of Education* and headlines in the newspapers, and then, while Dinah (which is what Gussie privately called her employer) was in the hospital, told her what to make for dinner that night. It was a relief to have weekends off and to go home to her house in the Crenshaw District. The Lasker house was getting a little too crowded.

Dinah went out that morning to do some errands, but when she came home she was so tired that she could barely get upstairs to take a nap. She slept deeply, however, until she sensed someone in the room. Opening her eyes, she found Veevi turning to leave. "It's okay, I'm awake, Vee," she said.

Veevi, who slept until after one o'clock every day, was still in her pajamas. She sat down on one of the upholstered armchairs in front of the fireplace opposite Dinah's and Jake's beds. The pajamas were pink cotton, and they peeped through her navy blue bathrobe, revealing bare feet, very white, with red toenails, and ankles that looked almost blue below the hem of her pajamas.

"Want to go downstairs for c-c-c-coffee?" Dinah asked her.

"Just had it. I told Gussie to wake me up at one, and she brought it up to me."

"With orange juice and toast?"

"Mmm." She smiled.

"Well, Vee, I'm glad you enjoyed it but, you know, Gus has an awful lot of work to do, now that we've got eight people living here. Maybe you ought to come downstairs from now on."

"Did she say something?" Veevi looked perturbed.

"No, of course not."

"It's such a small thing."

"No, dear, it isn't a small thing. You should see her nights when we go out and come back—she's absolutely conked out in the den. Gussie works hard—and I mean hard."

"Fine," said Veevi. "But she didn't seem to mind."

"There's a lot of laundry now, and—"

"Don't you have Fanny, or Miss Fanny, or whatever you call her?"

"There's a lot for both of them. Veevi—"

"Hmm?" Veevi had nestled into the armchair, her knees pulled up against her chest. She had just lit a cigarette. "I guess I'm a big burden," she said, removing shreds of tobacco from her lips.

"You're not a b-b-b-burden at all. There's extra work, that's all. Let's make it easy on her. Listen, Vee," Dinah said, sitting up and slipping on her loafers. "Gussie did say she's finding empties in the trash out in back and cigarette b-b-b-burns in your sheets."

Veevi looked away, then back at Dinah, and smiled, at once dismissive and abashed. "Well," she said. "Really. Imagine being spied on like that. It's simple. I can't sleep. It's, you know, this change from Paris to Los Angeles. People tell me it can take weeks. I'm all discombobulated and upside down. If I have a little drink before I turn off the lights, it relaxes me. I threw the bottle out myself because I didn't want anyone to know. Honestly. There's no need for her to spy on me."

"Veevi, she's not sp-sp-spying. She found the bottles. The burn holes," Dinah said hurriedly, not wanting to prolong the conversation. "But, Vee, you can't smoke in bed. Otherwise I'll be the one who can't sleep. I mean, the kids . . ."

"Fine," said Veevi reasonably. "I won't smoke in bed."

"Look, get dressed and come downstairs. I'm dying to get back to my garden. There are a million things I want to do out there, and old Joe said he'd help me. Wanna come, too?"

"Look at you," said Veevi, "with a gardener and a maid and a laundress. *La châtelaine.*"

"Yes," Dinah said, "and I l-l-l-love it." She looked directly at her sister and remembered that out in Malibu, Veevi had proclaimed that she didn't believe in household help. Then one of the refugee women asked for a job doing the laundry and she gave it to her, as a favor, she said, and Dorshka did all the cooking. That left Veevi free to read all she wanted to when she wasn't working.

"Help me downstairs, Vee. I'm still a little woozy going down."

Veevi stood on Dinah's left, bracing her as she held the banister with her right hand and went, step by step, down the pale green carpeted stairs. Dinah had to admit that her sister's breath was sour with old alcohol. But, she reminded herself, that's why she came home. She's sad and exhausted, and drinking to get to sleep. She'll get settled and find a job, and then she'll be too busy to drink. But the thought of the drinking oppressed her, and she felt her knees sag as she turned a sharp corner on the stairs. "Oops," she said to Veevi. "Maybe I overdid it this morning."

"Want to go back to bed?" Veevi asked brightly.

"No," Dinah said. "I want to put in a full day. Staying in bed is depressing. I want to get out there and get d-d-d-dirt on my hands. If I can bend over," she added, laughing.

"The Duchess of Delfern," Veevi said with a mirthless laugh. "I guess you've come a long way from Claggett Oil."

"You're goddamn right I have," Dinah said as they went into the breakfast room.

*U*ntil lately, Dinah had loved the enormous spaces of her house and its many silent and secret places. But now it swarmed with people. The kids had friends over to swim after school or to play inside when it was too cold to swim, and Claire, a tenth-grader, brought friends home from the private girls' school she attended. Dinah learned from Jake that at first, while she was in the hospital, Veevi's old friends had stopped by late in the day for a drink, and sometimes, at her invitation, for dinner. Sometimes Jake was there, but usually he wasn't because he was visiting Dinah. At those times, the Lasker kids and Coco ate in the kitchen, while Claire and her mother and their friends ate in the dining room. Poor Gussie then had two meals to prepare, the second one often improvised at an hour's notice. But the friends had stopped coming, now that she was home, Jake told Dinah.

"So what else is new?" she said.

She was too glad to be home, and at the same time too sad, to worry about people's reactions to her testifying, especially when they were eating at her table. Jake said it didn't matter anyway, because they weren't people who counted in the industry anymore—they'd all been blacklisted. Then he changed the subject and said it was time for them to start entertaining again. There were a lot of people they owed, and he'd been too busy with the Tooling picture to do much entertaining. If they started giving parties, he added, Veevi might meet somebody, and that would solve everything.

As far as a job was concerned, Jake and Veevi had worked out an arrangement: she would be his private story editor, which involved reading manuscripts and writing synopses, and he would pay her a weekly salary. Meanwhile, through Jake and Reggie Pertwee, she would try to find work as an actress, though this, they all admitted, was a long shot. Movies were out, for the time being, but television was a nut that might be easier to crack. Dinah told Jake that it was taking a while for her to get back on her feet, but she promised to give a party within a month.

Late one evening in November, when Dinah was almost herself again, she, Jake, and Veevi were sitting in the den, as they often did on fall nights. Jake had made a fire, and each of them had a brandy snifter. They were going through Veevi's books—not the books she'd left behind in Paris, but the ones from her years with Stefan. Their furniture had been in storage for fifteen years now. Though Veevi wouldn't claim her belongings until she found a house of her own, she and Dinah had agreed that she shouldn't have to live without her books. A Bekins truck with roughly fifty boxes had pulled up several days ago, and two hairy-armed moving men had carried them into the house and stacked them in the entryway. Since then, at around ten every night, Jake had followed "the girls," as he called them, into the den for a nightcap and an unpacking of books, which the three of them would scrutinize not only as candidates for temporary inclusion in the Laskers' library but as potential movie properties that Veevi could summarize for Jake.

Jake was energetically slitting open boxes with a Swiss Army knife, pulling out books, and handing them to Dinah, who stacked them in piles in front of the sofa.

"What's this? I never heard of it," Jake said, handing a heavy volume to Dinah.

"Oh my God!" Dinah exclaimed. "Vee, look. Remember this? *Sunset Song*? And"—she took two more books from Jake—"look at this! *Cloud Howe* and *Grey Gr-Gr-Granite*! God, how we loved these."

"We were so sure they'd be classics," Veevi said, taking the books from Dinah. "Now, who on earth has ever heard of poor old Lewis Grassic Gibbon?"

"Just tell me one thing," said Jake. "Is there a movie in it?"

Dinah and Veevi looked at each other and pondered this great question. "I don't know," said Veevi. "It's a little on the *Grapes of Wrath* side—noble peasants in the Scottish moors and all that."

"Yeah," said Dinah. "The people endure forever."

"We ate it up, though, didn't we, Ina?" Veevi patted the books affectionately as they lay in a stack beside her, and Dinah was happy to see her sister taking such pleasure in having them back.

"Well, read 'em again," said Jake to Veevi. "That's an order."

Veevi actually looked pleased.

Jake pulled out a large tome in an engraved apple-green leather binding. It turned out to be the *Histories* of Herodotus. "Jesus, this weighs a ton," he said, handing it to Veevi.

"Look," she said. "Stefan inscribed it to me: 'To my most beautiful and beloved wife, Genevieve—here is the world I promised you.' " There was a pause, and she added, " '*Je t'aime.*' "

They fell silent. The fire crackled, and they sipped their brandy, and the sisters lit cigarettes. "He wanted to educate me," Veevi said matter-of-factly. "So he said I had to begin at the beginning."

"Forgive my ignorance," said Jake, "but why was this fellow the beginning?" She began to explain, but he wasn't listening so much as just enjoying that feeling of consummate well-being he'd experienced in London and Paris. To be in this room with his wife, whom he loved, and Veevi, whose company he enjoyed and whose life fascinated and impressed him, to have conversations like this with these two attractive women, to breathe the air of all their reciprocal references and allusions, and to listen to their memories, gave him a feeling of intense pleasure he would easily have called happiness. His den, his house, his wife, and Veevi now seemed to him part of the larger world—the literary world, the world of talk and stories, and, of course, of Europe and the war, which he had missed, and the whole tumultuous century to which he felt he absolutely belonged. These hours with his wife and sister-in-law, he believed, despite Veevi's sad situation and Dinah's recent grief, could do nothing but good for his work. He, too, was sad about the lost child, but it was a relief—and he could never confess this to Dinah—that he would have to pay for only two, not three (or more!), college educations.

The taste of brandy suddenly gave him an intense desire to smoke a cigar, so he went into the bar, found one, and lit it, listening closely to what Dinah and Veevi were saying. It seemed to him that they spent the days in endless talk, and he wished he could hear all of it, because he was convinced that Veevi had stories he might be able to use one day.

For this reason, he was in no hurry to have Veevi move into a place of

her own. The convivial time they spent together in the evenings, the anecdotes they told each other: it was all "material."

"You know," said Dinah, "I think about Stefan all the time." She searched
for words. "He was such a mensch, and I was so fond of him." (She felt
quite certain that he had never told Veevi about that afternoon on the
beach.)

"He was crazy about you, too," Veevi said.

Dinah knew that "crazy about" in Veevi's sense had nothing in common
with the "crazy about" she herself had felt for Stefan. "Was he?" she said.
All she remembered was Veevi's telling her so many years ago: "He thinks
you have a long way to go. Educationally, that is."

Now she said, "I sure as hell felt d-d-d-dumb around him."

"If I think to myself, If only we hadn't gone to France, I sort of start to
feel insane," Veevi added matter-of-factly.

Dinah couldn't help thinking, Uh-huh, you were already monkeying
around with Mike when Stefan decided to leave.

"How did he ever become a director, coming out of Bulgaria?" Jake
asked. "I didn't know they had movies in Bulgaria. I mean, where is Bulgaria?"

"In the Balkans," said Veevi. "You *do* know where they are, don't you?
Speaking of which, where's *Black Lamb and Grey Falcon*? Let me know the
minute you find it."

"Is there a movie in it?" asked Jake.

"*No*," she said with a laugh. "Unless you're interested in old bridges in
Yugoslavia. Now, listen, of course they had movies in Bulgaria. Stefan saw
them and knew he wanted to make them, and he went to Berlin in 1917 to
work for a director named Robert Wiene—remember *The Cabinet of Dr.
Caligari*? Well, that's how he got his start. After that he went to Moscow,
came back to Berlin, and then in 1933 dear old Willie Weil—a friend from
Berlin who also wanted to leave—got him a job in Paris, so he left—with
Weil and Dorshka, because, of course, they were all Jews. Everyone in the
film world in Paris knew who he was, which is one reason it made sense to
go back when we did."

"But what about Moscow?" Jake asked. "What was in Moscow?"

"Think, Jake." She smiled at him.

"What? Who?" he said with an edge, irritated at the way she always had
to seize the advantage.

"Eisenstein, to begin with."

Dinah couldn't help thinking that Veevi was trying to make Jake feel like an American bumpkin. She reached for a pile of books Jake had absently placed on the table. "Plays," she announced. "These are almost all plays. From the thirties. You want to keep them out or put 'em b-b-b-back?"

Veevi took the books and began scrutinizing them. "Remember how we were always reading these, stuck in godforsaken Southern California and wishing we could be in New York? Look at this. *Winterset.* Maxwell Anderson. I don't even remember whether I ever read it. *The Women.* Oh God, that awful Clare Booth Luce." Then, before Dinah or Jake could answer, she said in a rush, "Christ, look at this! Odets! Jesus."

"Which one?" Jake said, holding out his hand for the book. He looked transfigured, as if someone were holding a bright candle flame up to his face. "I'll never forget the night I saw *Awake and Sing!* I was still living in Chicago. Gee, I think it must have been '35 or '36. In my whole life, I've never had a night like that in the theater. I'd been so discouraged—selling advertising for the *Jewish Sentinel,* trying to work on a play, my folks yammering at me all the time and telling me how I could work for my uncles in the wholesale meat business. I'd try to write at night, and then I'd read it over in the morning and hate it. Then I saw that play, and I knew I had to keep writing."

His eyes were glistening, and he opened the book to the play and tenderly turned its pages.

"Oh, Uncle J.," Veevi said. "You're a panic. Crying over that thirties crap. You don't really think it's any good, do you?"

Dinah had never seen Jake humiliated—until now. He turned red, and his eyes widened with surprise at the ridicule and contempt in Veevi's voice. He's been struck dumb, Dinah thought, and she remembered those Saturdays, so many years ago, at the Venturas' house in Malibu, when Veevi, with her stunning face and her perfect figure, reclined in the sun in a two-piece bathing suit, and, listening to the young Communist writers trying to outdo one another in clever literary and political talk, kept them all at heel with her barbed remarks. The young men would flush and shut up, nonplussed by this beautiful, sharp-tongued woman in her twenties, who hadn't gone beyond the ninth grade, and who often, when she cut them, did so in slow and languid tones, her flawless face held up to the burning sun as if to a handmaiden.

"You can think what you like about it, Veevi," Jake answered in a tone of injured dignity Dinah had never heard from him before. "But the evening I saw that play was and always will be one of the most important nights of my life. I reread it recently and it's magnificent. I only hope one day I can put the life and passion into my work that Odets put into his."

Not once, Dinah thought, had any of those men—men with novels and screenplays to their credit—not once had any of them answered Veevi as Jake just had. And she was glad, with a swift and deep satisfaction, that Jake had stood up to her sister.

"You can't be serious," Veevi said with a sneering laugh. "It was so corny! What the English call 'too much of a muchness.' Well, perhaps I should reread it," she said with a shrug, taking the book and putting it on top of one of the piles. "I heard," she said, quietly, "that he squealed."

"Yes," Dinah said. "We heard it, t-t-t-too. But I don't remember whether it was before or after I did."

She reached over and put out her cigarette and sat back on the sofa, folding her arms in front of her. There was silence as Jake quickly slashed through another cardboard box, but his expression had become grim and preoccupied, and he put the letter opener on the table. "Gonna hit the sack," he said, getting up and leaving the sisters to themselves.

If Veevi noticed that the mood had changed, she didn't comment. She was going through the small stacks of books in the den, making a new, special pile that consisted, she said, of books Stefan had made her read and that she now wanted to reread. She lovingly stroked the covers. "Look, Ina," she said, reading the names of the authors: "Mann, Joyce, Kafka, Dostoyevsky, Tolstoy, Proust, Aeschylus, Sophocles, Euripides." She picked up another apple-green leather-bound volume. "Oh, look," she said. "Thucydides."

"Who?" said Dinah.

"Another Greek. Historian, that is. He gave me this one after we had an argument about the Party, which he said I took too seriously."

"I didn't know you argued with him."

"Well, it wasn't a real argument." Veevi picked up the book and thumbed through it. "He told me I had to read it because it showed how everything always falls apart. He thought Hitler was going to destroy everybody, and he was right. 'We Communists can't stop this,'" he said.

"But that means"—Dinah struggled to put her thoughts into words—"that he must have felt that going back to Fr-Fr-France wouldn't help."

"Well, there was nothing for him to do here," said Veevi. "Not after he blew it with old man Engel."

" 'Blew it'?" Dinah said.

"Oh, come on, he blew it."

"How can you say that? How did he blow it?"

"His kind of integrity always had something suicidal about it," Veevi said.

"And yours?"

"Mine?"

"Yes. About HUAC."

"Oh, that's nothing," Veevi said dismissively. "Stefan knew if he went back to Europe he could get killed. I can't get work, but nobody's pointing a gun at me. I don't think my integrity's so great, and I don't think your snitching's so terrible."

"You don't?" Dinah said. "What about that letter from Mike?"

"That letter," Veevi said bitterly, "was written by a man who was feeling guilty as hell about having an affair with a younger woman. 'The Knight of the Burning Pestle'—that's who wrote that letter. It wasn't principle. It was his prick—his goddamn guilty prick."

"Jesus Christ, Vee," Dinah said, a look of horror on her face. She thought of the letter she'd found in her father's trailer, the days she waited to hear from Veevi, the feeling, when Mike's letter had come, of being socked in the gut. But she mentioned none of this.

"He didn't give a shit about me or anything else at the time except Odile Boisvert," Veevi said. "And that's still true. By God, she's got some kind of hold on him, that's for sure."

The two sisters sat looking at each other in silence, but it wasn't an uncomfortable silence. Well, she's really back now, Dinah thought. Now I can do something for her.

"Tell me," Dinah said. "Why did you go with him? Stefan, I mean. Why did you go to Europe with him? Nobody in their right mind would have gone to Europe at that point. Talk about s-s-s-suicidal."

Veevi shifted her weight and pulled her right leg up onto the sofa. "I don't know, Ina," she answered. "Did I really understand how dangerous it was? He kept saying we'd be safe, there were people, he would always look after me. Listen, Ina, I wanted to get out of L.A. I wanted to go to Europe."

And, Dinah thought, you were pregnant with Claire, and you wanted to make sure that Stefan thought it was his child.

"Anyway," Veevi added, slipping the Thucydides back in the storage box, "Stefan had friends there."

"Friends?" Dinah said. "You mean the Party, don't you."

"Mmm," Veevi murmured. "I do mean the Party. Remember those people in Mexico who came up to hear Malraux?"

Dinah nodded.

"They had connections in France. They had people meet us when we got off the boat. There was an apartment for us. Stefan got back into the swing of things there, started working on a movie. Everything was more or less normal for a while. We felt safe. Still, all the time we were getting ready. He kept wanting me to go to London, but I didn't want to leave France. Then, in the summer of '41, it got dicey." She yawned.

A little later, when the two sisters were upstairs, Veevi made what Dinah would have called "an apologetic bubby face." "Do you think I hurt Uncle J.'s feelings? I mean, about that silly Odets business?"

"Yes," Dinah said. "You did. You know, Vee," she said, "it would be great if Jake woke up tomorrow morning and suddenly discovered he was Marcel Proust. But he isn't. He's Jake Lasker, he writes comedy, and he has three dependents to support, and a mortgage. So if reading Odets helps him be Jake Lasker, then it's kind of, you know, unfair to make him feel he should be somebody else."

She had never spoken to her sister in that way.

"Sorry," Veevi said.

Dinah shrugged and leaned forward to kiss Veevi on the cheek, but Veevi stepped backward toward her room, so that Dinah was left with her head thrust forward, like a great awkward bird bobbing its beak in the air.

"Sleep well, Vee," she said. "Don't set the house on f-f-f-fire, okay?"

※

Dinah found Jake in bed with his half of the night-table lamp turned off. She thought he was asleep, but as soon as she returned from her dressing room he said, in a muffled voice, "Scratch my back?" She climbed into his bed, though her belly was still sore, and she found it uncomfortable to lie on her side and ply her nails underneath his cotton pajama top and across the familiar fuzzy mesa that was her husband's back. She felt him relax and expected to hear snores, but he turned suddenly and pushed up the black eyeshade he was wearing. "In case you haven't guessed," he said, "that sister of yours can be a real coozeburger."

"Yeah," Dinah answered. "She can. But please, honey, don't hate her."

"Who said anything about hating her? I thought she was nice. At least in Paris. I thought she was fun. I even thought she was bright and interesting. And, craziest of all, I thought we were friends. She talked to me very frankly about her life when I was in Paris. But who's she kidding? That's all I want to know. What gives her—she has no right to say what she did about Odets." He reached for a stick of Doublemint gum from the pack he kept in the night table. "She just sits there waiting for you to say you like something," he continued, angrily chomping on the gum, "and then she says something that's supposed to make you drop dead or feel like an ass. To hell with that. In Paris she told me she hates monotony, can't stand to be bored, but she has zero curiosity about anything, and no desire to find anything out. God forbid she should ever be at a loss for something barbed and stinging to say! Everything has to be ironic—snide and ironic. Since when has she ever tried to write a play or a screenplay? Since when has she read everything that's ever been written? What the hell does she know about dramatic construction?"

To see him seething with hurt was a revelation to Dinah, who had never considered Jake thin-skinned. "Honey," she said, "forget it." And she reminded him that Veevi had been back from Europe for only a month or so, and that as soon as they got their lawyer to work out the details with Mike's lawyer, she would be able to find a place of her own.

"I don't like a person who has to belittle others," he said. "Why doesn't she ever say anything nice about anybody?"

"Turn around again," Dinah said. "I'll scratch your back some more."

She pulled the little metal cord on the lamp and the room went dark. She wanted to calm him down. It would be a nightmare if they were all living in the same house and at one another's throats. As she massaged his shoulders, it occurred to her that maybe there was another reason for Jake's anger at her sister. They hadn't made love since before she went into the hospital, and Dr. Zuckerman had told her that it would be another two or three weeks before they could, as he put it, "resume relations." Neither she nor Jake had said anything to each other; she assumed that he understood the necessity for delay and was waiting for a signal from her. But what surprised her—and hurt her a little—was that he hadn't said anything about even wanting to. To her, the absence of sex was beginning to feel like an interrupted conversation—a conversation that had been going on since 1941, but had now come to a stop—and neither of them knew how to pick up again from where they'd left off.

So, bravely yet shyly, she reached down to the soft parts faintly tickling her thigh and clasped them in a warm squeeze. She found his instant tumescence reassuring.

"Is it really okay?" he asked.

"Well, this—not the other, yet."

"But is that fair?"

"Fair?" she replied.

"I mean, what about you?" he said.

"Oh, me. It's for you."

"Oh, sweetie, I can wait. Let's wait," he said, putting his hand over hers.

But instead of thinking he was being considerate, Dinah felt rejected. In all the years they'd been together, he had never wanted to wait. Even right after the births of their children, he had required some sort of improvised ministrations. "Is there something wrong?" she asked, her lower lip quivering.

He raised his head and looked at her in the dark. "God *no*," he said. "But I don't want to be selfish, after what you've been through."

"Why not?" she answered. "You always were before, and it was always kinda fun." Her voice broke, and she started crying.

Jake turned on the light and took the gum out of his mouth. It was late, he said, and they were both tired. Only a selfish bastard would insist on his own pleasure at a time like this, and he knew she would tell him when everything was okay again. Of course he wanted her, he always wanted her, and he didn't need a hand job to tide him over. In fact, as soon as the doctor gave her the green light they'd go to Palm Springs for the weekend, away from the kids and Veevi and Dorshka and the whole teeming swarm of people in the house, and he'd reserve a suite at Deep Well and bring his golf clubs and she could walk with him around the golf course and they'd go at it just the way they used to.

"Here, give us a kiss," he said, and they kissed. He turned out the light and they settled in together—first on their backs, with his arm around her, then nestled together on their sides, since she couldn't sleep on her stomach. Soon he began to snore and she pushed him away gently and lay beside him with her arm over his belly.

Before long, his snores grew so loud and ragged that she knew she would have to take a Seconal to get any sleep at all. She slipped out of bed and went into her bathroom and swallowed a red-and-orange capsule and returned to her own bed. While she waited for the drug to sink her body with its leaden weights, she cried, silently. Instead of reassuring her, his words seemed to mark the beginning of a change between them—the loss of the one thing of which she had always been sure. Fortunately the sleeping pill soon did its work; otherwise, as his snores sawed the air, she would have wept through the night.

It would have shocked Jake to learn that Dinah believed he no longer felt desire for her. Of course he still wanted her. But so soon? When he felt her hand closing around him, instantly warm, familiar, knowing, he had thought her generous to a fault and told himself that to allow things to take their course would be tantamount to taking advantage of her. He had also been using the time since she came home from the hospital to adjust to the idea—where he had gotten it, he couldn't have said—that his and Dinah's sex life would invariably undergo a change. Any woman, he believed, who had lost her capacity to bear children would naturally have a reduced interest in sex—especially the wanton sex he and Dinah had always had. The simplest, least disruptive, and most convenient way for him to obtain basic satisfaction would be to just go and get it elsewhere.

He had, in fact, been splendidly laid that afternoon on his way home from the studio. Hortense Leavitt, a shapely costume designer at the studio, had invited him over for a drink after work and had capped the occasion with a lively, sporting fuck, and no questions asked. He hadn't showered at Horty's place, thinking he'd jump into the pool when he got home, but at home there had been no time, what with telephone calls from Irv Engel that had to be returned, Lorna's asking him for help with long division, and, after dinner, that irritating exchange with Veevi. By the time he went to bed, he still hadn't had a chance to shower. One of his cardinal rules was never to have sex with Dinah if he still had traces of another woman on him, and that was another reason he had avoided Dinah's overtures.

Soon, he was sure, he and Dinah would be back to their regular routine. He was saddened by the thought that they would never again have a child together; there truly was a special excitement in their coupling whenever he had tried to make her pregnant. But that part of their life was now over, and it seemed perfectly reasonable not to expect her to welcome his embraces with her former enthusiasm. Still, hadn't they always had a great time together? That didn't have to change.

One morning Dinah looked up from the newspaper she was reading as Veevi came into the breakfast room. "Look at this, Vee," she said. "V-V-V-V—oh shit, I can't say it—Vishinsky's dead."

Veevi, still in her bathrobe, looked at her with a sleepy blankness. "Who? Vishinsky? Dead? God, I haven't thought about him in years. Now he's dead, Stalin's dead. They're all dead, those fellows."

She poured herself a cup of coffee.

"We hung on his every word," Dinah said. "Vishinsky's, I mean. Norman Metzger made me pick up a copy of the *New York Times* every day after work and cut out articles about the tr-tr-trials so he could study them. That was one of my official assignments."

"Hmm," said Veevi. "What's happened to Metzger?"

"Moved to England. He was one of the guys I named. Of course, he'd been named by God knows who else by the time the Committee got to me."

"Ah," said Veevi, getting up. "Do you think Gussie could make me some toast?"

Before Dinah could tell her to make it herself, Veevi disappeared behind the swinging door for a moment and came back. "Gussie wants to know if you want anything." Dinah shook her head and looked at her sister. There were sleep creases on her face, but she no longer reeked of booze.

"So you're not still in, Vee?"

"The Party?" She looked out the window. It was a gray, cold morning, and she pulled her bathrobe tightly around her.

"Yeah. The P-P-P-Party. In Paris."

"Are you kidding? Not on your life. And you?"

"What do you think?"

"Well, obviously not."

"Obviously."

"When did you leave, Ina? Did you have a"— she smiled ironically— " 'formal break,' as they say?"

"Well, not exactly. It was early '44, just before we got married. Jake said get out or else no dice with the marriage. Actually, I was sort of out anyway by then, since I was spending all my t-t-t-time with him and wasn't going to meetings anymore."

Veevi nodded but didn't ask more questions. The sisters stared out at the pool, and seemed hypnotized by the steamy mist rising from its surface. Gussie came in looking preoccupied, set down a plate with buttered toast for Veevi, and disappeared through the swinging door.

"When," Dinah began carefully, "did you leave?"

Veevi bit into the toast as she gazed out the window. "It wasn't a question of leaving or staying. I'm alive because Communists hid me, that's for sure. Everyone we knew there was a Communist, I think. But when I went back to Paris after the war and heard about Stefan, I didn't look up anyone he'd known. A lot of them had been killed, anyway. Everything had changed. Then Mike found me, and nothing else mattered."

A picture of Mike and Veevi embracing somewhere in Paris flashed through Dinah's mind—the happy ending to a war movie. Apparently, for Veevi, time had stopped at that moment. Or, rather, everything that had happened up to then was unimportant. Then Dinah remembered what her soggy nightgown had felt like that night on the beach in Malibu.

"You know," she said, "I used to ask Stefan about the trials. They didn't make sense to me, and they still don't. You and Tola Klein and Norman Metzger, and everybody used to say the bourgeois press was slandering St-St-St-Stalin, and that he was heroic to stand up to the saboteurs and counter-r-r-r-revolutionaries. But I used to ask Stefan, 'How can this be? Weren't these old men Stalin's friends?' And Stefan said to me, 'Stalin's a monster, but history needs him.' Christ," she said, shaking her head, "I've thought about that for years, and I can't figure it out. It means one thing if you wake up on a Tuesday morning and it's f-f-f-foggy outside and you slept badly, and another if it's Saturday and the sun is shining."

"He said that? To you?"

Veevi spooned strawberry jam onto her plate, spread the jam on a piece of toast, and took a big bite.

"I guess you don't remember, Vee, but Stefan and I used to talk quite a lot."

"Poor Stefan," Veevi said, putting down her toast. "Poor dear old man." She took a handkerchief from her bathrobe pocket and daubed her eyes.

Poor dear old man my ass, Dinah said to herself, adding, Whose son you were fucking just when L.J. was letting Stefan know he was through out here. Then she felt ashamed, and her face turned hot as the wave of anger spent itself.

"Yes, it's awfully sad," Dinah said. She glanced at her sister and turned away. Veevi's hair looked dry and dull. Her skin, so blooming once, was rough, coarse. She wasn't fat, but her muscles were flabby. And the grief Dinah saw in her eyes, day after day, often gave her normally shrewd expression an oddly hapless cast. "How did I end up like this?" her eyes seemed to be asking, and in truth Dinah wondered, too. For Veevi to have come to this seemed eerie, as if some fundamental law of nature had been broken. How had it happened, anyway? Every time Jake came home at night and kissed Dinah on the mouth, Dinah felt Veevi watching and wondering how she, who had been so beautiful and brilliant, could have ended up desolate and forlorn while Dinah, for whom no one had predicted anything beyond a dull and ordinary life with a dull and ordinary man, had triumphed over the odds. It embarrassed Dinah and gave her the oddest, most uncomfortable sensation to be kissed by Jake in front of Veevi. If another adult had been watching too, Dinah was certain, Veevi would have caught his eye with an expression of mockery and disbelief.

Dinah thought Veevi lingered over the toast and jam as if it were her only pleasure now. She knew that Veevi would go upstairs ostensibly to read scripts and books for Jake, but that she would actually spend most of the day in bed crying. Then at three she would get up, shower, dress, and come downstairs to the den, where Dinah and her two kids and Claire and Coco usually congregated before dinner. She would make herself a martini, with either a green olive or a pearl onion. Then another. She would come in to dinner and eat with such gusto that Jake remarked one night, as he and Dinah were lying in bed together, it was "as if Hitler were in Beverly Hills."

They would talk after dinner, the three of them—Jake, Dinah, and Veevi—or Jake would go upstairs to work, leaving Dinah and Veevi together with the children. For a time, the den was a hive of family happiness. Lorna played with Coco. From the living room, Dinah could hear the sound of Peter practicing his clarinet. Veevi would have a brandy and read *The New Yorker* and the *Saturday Review*. Claire would sit at the inlaid wooden chess table and write out the answers to her algebra problems. Then, one by one, the den emptied. Gussie would come in to take Coco upstairs for a bath and bed. Claire would traipse off to her room behind the kitchen. Peter disappeared into his to listen to Benny Goodman records. Once her brother had left, Lorna would pointedly ask Dinah if it was time for her bath. Before Veevi came, Lorna had insisted that she could bathe herself. Now she wanted her mother to scrub her back and shampoo her hair. So Dinah would put her knitting away and go upstairs with her daughter. Left behind in the den, Veevi watched television. And drank. That was her day.

Sometimes Dinah did hear typing, which meant that Veevi was writing a synopsis. Jake had hoped to have two or three of these a week; Veevi took a week and a half, on the average, to do one. He complained to Dinah that Veevi wasn't very productive; after all, he was paying her a salary. Dinah told him to go easy on her, and on sunny afternoons when Dinah didn't have to do errands or pick up the kids for after-school lessons, she sometimes managed to persuade Veevi not to go back upstairs to her room but to put on something comfortable and join her out by the pool, where the two of them read together or Dinah knitted while Veevi read. Dinah thought the fresh air and sunshine would be good for Veevi and liked being with her.

One day Dinah turned the book she was reading—*Nine Stories,* by J. D. Salinger—upside down on her lap and said so, adding, "It reminds me of that summer we lived on McCadden Place when we lay all day in that big hammock Pop tied from one tree to the other and read library books and ate c-c-c-celery."

"What summer was that?" Veevi asked.

"You don't remember?"

"No," said Veevi. "I try to remember as little as possible about our childhood."

"Really?" Dinah said, astonished.

"I couldn't wait for it to be over. But the hammock. When did you say that was?"

"You were ten and I was almost thirteen: 1925."

"Hmm," Veevi said, as if she were hearing a mildly interesting detail about someone else.

Dinah was stunned. They had been inseparable during that hot California summer. They had scarcely communicated in complete sentences and had been so telepathically linked that a couple of words murmured by one would be instantly understood by the other. Dinah remembered the sound their mouths had made as they munched celery, and the nice, musty smell of the library books and the yellowing paper that sometimes crumbled onto their laps when they turned the pages. How could Veevi not remember it? she wondered.

Suddenly Veevi looked up from her book. "When did you start reading?" she asked Dinah. "I never knew you read."

Dinah thought she must be sitting with a creature from Mars who had somehow invaded her sister's body. "Veevi, are you nuts? I've always been a reader. How can you p-p-p-possibly not remember me reading?"

"I was the reader and you were the dancer. I was the introvert and you were the extrovert. You were the homebody and I wanted to get the hell out. Fast."

"You danced, too. I taught you. And I was always reading—when we were kids, in high school. And when you were with Stefan I was always asking the two of you which books I should read. What about all those books we read at the same time? You know, Steinbeck and Malraux and Poe and Mann and Proust and God only knows who else? Not to mention Marx and Engels and all their ilk."

At the sound of this word both sisters laughed, as they had many years ago, and Dinah felt as if she had broken through Veevi's bizarre amnesia, for *ilk* was a word they had always found funny. At least some part of their old world of secret jokes was intact, or almost intact, even if Veevi pretended it had never existed.

They were beginning to talk more. Late in the afternoons, perched on either end of a long upholstered love seat in the den under the windows that looked out onto the pool, Dinah got Veevi to talk. They watched the evening news together, and found themselves riveted by footage of Hurricanes Carol, Edna, and Hazel, discovering in their mutual pleasure at the names and the spectacle of natural disasters a topic over which neither had to exercise discretion. They also watched the Army-McCarthy hearings, and in early December, when Welch finally let McCarthy have it, Dinah looked at the television and said, "I hope that's the end of *you,* you evil s-s-s-son of a bitch!"

Veevi, looking at her, threw her head back and laughed. "You sound just like Pop," she said with a sad smile.

Then Veevi got up, took her drink, and went into the living room to visit Peter while he practiced. She often did this, settling herself on one of the sofas with one leg tucked under her. She blew her cigarette smoke away from him because she knew it bothered him. He found her visits disconcerting at first, but he got used to them. For one thing, his aunt was very pretty, and she always said nice things to him whether he played well or not. And when she was there he did play well, because he thought of her as an audience at a recital. He always apologized if he happened to be learning a new piece, as if preparing her for the mistakes he was sure to make. She said she didn't mind at all, that it was a pleasure to watch a working musician. He loved that phrase: "a working musician." She would wait for him to finish, and when they went back into the den together she would tell Dinah how gifted he was. But this made him uncomfortable, because he had noticed that Veevi was mean to Lorna.

Dinah was aware of it, too. She couldn't help observing that Veevi's first martini was quickly followed by a second and a third, which seemed to liberate a sharp tongue that was always aimed at Lorna. Yet Dinah was always too startled to say anything about it. She couldn't believe that her sister would treat her own niece, who was now eight, with such overt nastiness— and right in front of Dinah, too. "Stop eating peanuts," Veevi said once to Lorna after the child had taken a handful from a ceramic dish on the coffee table. "They'll make you even fatter than you are!" Lorna's face turned red and she ran out of the room. Another time, Lorna, who adored her cousin Claire, brought her reading homework over to the chess table where Claire was doing Latin exercises and spread her book out on her side of the table. "Don't sit there, Lorna," Veevi snapped at her. "Can't you see you're getting in Claire's way?" Claire was concentrating so hard that she wasn't even aware of what her mother was saying, but Lorna burst into tears and ran from the room.

Lorna, who had expected to love her aunt, now hated her and told her mother so one night when Dinah gave her her bath. "Why didn't you say something when Veevi was mean to me?" Lorna asked. "It's our house, Mom, and she should be polite." Dinah explained that Veevi's harshness was just her way of being different, like her preference for being called

"Veevi" and not "Aunt Veevi." She pointed out to Lorna that Veevi wasn't particularly warm even with her own children—it wasn't her style. Hadn't she noticed that Veevi never kissed Claire or cuddled with Coco? She said that Lorna shouldn't take offense at Veevi's tone of voice because Veevi was a member of the family and people in families sometimes talked to children this way.

But Lorna wasn't having any of it and keenly felt the injustice of her aunt's barbs and her mother's cowardice. She could feel that in spite of the nightly bathtimes with her mother, she was not uppermost in Dinah's thoughts. And she was right. What was more important right now to Dinah were the brief but powerful bursts of euphoria she felt during those late afternoons, when their enlarged family seemed to come together in—she used the word pointedly to herself, making a private joke—"relative" harmony. Jake would come in, tired and hungry, grabbing handfuls of peanuts, and his face would light up at the sight of them—Dinah and Veevi and the children, gathered together in the cozy, plush-carpeted, book-lined room, a fire glowing in the fireplace.

Once Dinah got past the embarrassment of being kissed in front of Veevi, she was proud that it was in her house that they were all together, and that Jake, unlike her own father, was providing handsomely for them all. His ebullience was infectious. He often remarked now that this was how families used to live, with aunts and cousins often under one roof. He said his new project was about an immigrant family living together and working together, and it was good for the work that he should come home and find them like this; in fact, he told Veevi that she should drop whatever she was reading and start doing some research on immigrant families in Chicago at the turn of the century.

"Research?" she said. "Where?"

"It's simple," Dinah said. "You go to UCLA and get a library card and start looking up whatever you want to know."

"I know that, dear," said Veevi acidly. "The point is, I'll need a car."

"We'll get you a car," Jake answered. "But I need the material fast. Can you do it?"

Dinah looked up at him: "Go easy on her," she seemed to say. He grabbed another handful of peanuts and Lorna came over to him, took a handful of her own, and climbed onto her father's lap, looking at her aunt with a hatred Dinah pretended not to see.

After dinner, the Lasker children loved to go into the living room to dance and sing and engage in a little horseplay. It was a family tradition. Dinah played the piano, Jake played show tunes on the new hi-fi system he'd brought from the studio, and Lorna and Peter invented silly dances, getting their little cousin, Coco, whom they loved and petted, to join in. Jake got out his cameras and took pictures or made home movies, ordering Dinah to place the living-room lights just so, and calling out "Action" and "Cut" and making them do several takes. They called in Gussie to join the fun and she danced with the family, picking up Coco and snapping her fingers and singing "Toot, Toot, Tootsie, Goodbye" and Nat "King" Cole's "Keemo-Kymo," which she'd sung to the Lasker kids when they were babies. Dinah would get up from the piano and do the time step and a soft shoe and the Charleston while Jake captured it all on film. Veevi and Claire sat on the couch and acted as the audience for these impromptu show-biz antics. They smiled at the children, but Dinah caught their sidelong glances of shared superiority and disdain. It was at such moments that Dinah was certain that Veevi disliked her and looked down on her life, and was staying with them only because she had nowhere else to go. And that, Dinah told herself, was her fault. It was her testifying that had brought this all about.

Night after night, the light stayed on in Veevi's room. When Jake and Dinah turned off their own light and closed the door connecting Jake's office with the dressing corridor that led to their bedroom, Veevi's light was always on, and at two or three in the morning, on the way downstairs for his insomniac's snack, Jake often saw the flicker of the television Veevi had asked them to get for her when they bought her a car. If he knocked on her door, he told Dinah, and asked why she couldn't sleep, or invited her downstairs for a snack of vanilla ice cream, Hershey's chocolate syrup, and kosher pickles, she always said no thanks, complaining of pain in her shoulder, her neck, her arm. She had pain pills, she said, but she didn't want to take more than she had to. She always added that she hated to take medicine of any kind, even an aspirin for a headache. There was still a bottle of gin under the bed, but Gussie had reported to Dinah that it was going down only a little every few days. All the same, Jake sometimes saw her quickly shove it under the covers when he knocked. At the same time, Veevi never seemed really drunk. At least not to him.

It was the smoking that terrified them both. Jake found her smoking in bed, watching television, and begged her to put out the cigarette. Veevi's room was right next to Lorna's; what if Veevi fell asleep or passed out with a lit cigarette in her hand? The thought was horrifying enough to wake Dinah out of her own sleep. Once Dinah crept down Jake's dressing corridor toward Veevi's room and, seeing a streak of light under the door, gently turned the doorknob. She found her sister sitting cross-legged in bed, her head bent forward and her once lustrous dark hair hanging by the sides of her face in great unbrushed clumps. With one hand holding a cigarette and the other clasping the bottle of gin, she sobbed and sobbed as the television flickered with a movie called *Little Boy Lost*.

"It's Bing Crosby, in Paris," Veevi said. "Trying to find a lost kid after the war."

Dinah sat down beside her. Veevi didn't look up. Dinah put her arms around her sister and held her, as she had often held a sobbing Lorna, or Peter. Veevi felt small and shrunken in her arms. Ugly sounds hemorrhaged from Veevi's chest—horrible squeals and coughs, hoarse moans, and hiccups. Dinah felt pity and revulsion at Veevi's late-night staleness—the smell of booze and smoke and sweat that steamed damply upward from her nightgown. "There, there," she said, pressing her sister's body to her own. "It's all right. Just cry, honey. Just cry as much as you want. We're going to fix you up, lovey." She stroked Veevi's hair and pushed it back from her damp forehead. "It's going to get better."

Neither of the sisters saw Jake standing behind the open door of the corridor. He had just come upstairs from the kitchen, where he had eaten half a salami and drunk a Cel-Ray Tonic. As he watched Dinah and Veevi, his eyes filled with tears and he said to himself, I've got to use this one day. My God, what a scene. He turned and crept back to his own bed, happy as a child who has just found a quarter in the crack of a sidewalk.

11

wo days later, the two sisters drove into Beverly Hills, past the Indian fountain, which spouted clear water by day and brilliant rainbow colors by night, and under the Santa Claus and reindeer that were suspended above traffic at the intersection of Wilshire and Santa Monica. Soon, they were strolling arm in arm down Rodeo Drive. The day was balmy and clear, and it pulled Dinah, as such days always did, back into the past and the Milligan family's first years in California.

"Do you remember the way Mom used to say, 'Smell the air, girls! Just smell the air'?" she said to Veevi.

They had stopped in front of Juel Park to admire a pink satin nightgown with hand-stitched lace trim.

"Mmm," Veevi answered absently. "I *think* so. You know, your memory is incredible. I don't remember half the things you do. You have total recall. I sure as hell don't, though I do remember when I used to buy things here."

"Well, that wasn't so long ago. Jesus, the stuff you got. No Communist ever had fancier lingerie. What happened to all of them?"

"Oh, they lasted a long time. Very well made. I gave them to Madame Rochedieu and her daughters. God, it was so cold in the farmhouse that we had to wear them as layering under heavy wool sweaters."

Dinah remembered that Veevi had spent hundreds of dollars on these gowns and that she herself had, on seeing them spread out on Veevi's bed at the Malibu house, felt pure, naked envy, followed by self-disgust, because she despised envy—anyone's, including her own. Once she had married Jake and could spend whatever she liked, and was even commanded by Jake to dress well, she still couldn't bring herself to buy handmade nightgowns as expensive as these.

"If I say to myself, 'I was a Communist,' " Veevi remarked, laughing, "the words sound so *peculiar*. It just doesn't seem like anything someone could *be* anymore. Yet I know I *was* one," Veevi said. "Wasn't I?"

She turned and looked at Dinah with an expression of mock puzzlement. "I still believe in the ideas. Who wouldn't? But if I were to use all the old phrases, like 'working class' or 'proletariat,' I'd feel s-s-s-silly. Wouldn't you?"

"We felt pretty silly using them even then. Remember how we used to laugh at the word 'toilers'?"

Veevi squeezed her eyes shut and nodded her head, as she did whenever she found something particularly amusing.

"B-B-B-But I agree with you about the old ideas," Dinah continued. "About haves and have-nots. Only now I'm a have and I never thought I would be."

She realized that she had just said something tactless.

"Well, I never thought you would be, either," said Veevi, taking Dinah's arm. "But it's nice that you are." Dinah felt warmed to the core by Veevi's gesture. She remembered how much she loved her sister, who, she had felt ever since she'd come home from the hospital, secretly despised her. "Mmm, that's nice, isn't it?" Veevi added, looking admiringly at the beige lace trim on the neckline of a pale green silk nightgown.

"Oh God, this is wicked, Vee," Dinah began. "But remember June Palmer? Well, you know, she has a big hit television series now, and last year *Life* magazine sent a journalist and a photographer out to do a piece on her, and she and Reynaldo—"

"Who?"

"Reynaldo Perez. Bandleader? Cuban? Gosh, maybe you were in Europe when—"

"Anyway . . ." Veevi said expectantly.

"Well, anyway, June and Reynaldo are sitting in her 'boudoir' and she's wearing a nightgown and robe, very elegant, and the interviewer, who's a young woman—some Vassar girl or something—says how gorgeous the nightgown is, and Reynaldo says, 'Yeah, but you don't have to see the shit stains on it!' "

For the next two minutes, the sisters clung to each other, laughing until they cried. Then they stood in front of the window, admiring the nightgowns and peignoirs, and laughing some more. Dinah felt all the old feelings come back—the old days of their childhood, when they were always together, played after school together, slept in the same bed together, thought the same thoughts at the same time, and found everything funny.

Dinah took Veevi's hand, clasping the soft roll of flesh at the top of her palm as she had done when Veevi was six and she nine and in charge of walking the two of them home from school. They strolled down the street like this without embarrassment. A bleached blonde in her forties, wearing a yellow V-necked sweater set with elaborate sequin and bead flowers, passed them. The skin of her cleavage was freckled and wrinkled from the sun. Her breasts, well fortified with falsies, pointed outward like guided missiles. She had poured herself into skintight turquoise toreador pants. Her shoes were high wedgies in white-and-gold leather, and she was accompanied by a white toy poodle on a rhinestone leash attached to a rhinestone collar. The two sisters exchanged silent looks but waited until they reached the end of the block to burst once again into laughter.

"God, I had forgotten about those types!" said Veevi. "Jesus, the hair! The tits! Those colors! What a ridiculous place this is!"

Dinah felt herself draw back a little, and she let go of Veevi's arm. "Well, it's true," Dinah said. "There *are* a lot of ridiculous-looking characters out here. But I like it. I like Beverly Hills on a w-w-w-weekday morning. It's peaceful, and empty. It probably won't stay this way forever. But right now it's fine. I come here and go to the hardware store, the stationery store, get a ham sandwich and a Coke for lunch, then pick up whatever Gussie needs from the grocery store. Then I drive back and I'm ready for the kids to come home and t-t-tear into each other and for Jake and his worries. Otherwise," she said with a laugh, "he's too tough to live with. God, especially when he's writing. I come here, and it's kind of a refuge. I like the guys at the hardware store. I like saying hello to them and asking them how they are. Sure, there are silly-looking people, like that woman, but so what?"

"It's just that . . ."

"Oh, Veevi, I know. This isn't Paris. Or anyplace *you* would rather be. Come on," Dinah said, pulling her ahead. "Let's get you something to wear."

In the dressing room at Jax, Dinah sat on a small settee and watched as Veevi, stripped to her underpants and bra, tried on slacks and shirts. Hoping to work her way back to that momentary idyll of unity with her sister,

Dinah reproached herself for getting miffed at Veevi's comment. Of course, Veevi was right. Beverly Hills was a ridiculous place—where else in the world did women go around wearing outlandish outfits accompanied by poodles in rhinestones?

She and Veevi were doing what sisters were supposed to do—shopping, buying clothes—but neither of them was a particularly enthusiastic shopper or especially fond of spending money for its own sake. So, quite uncharacteristically, Dinah coaxed and urged.

"That one's good," she said now, nodding toward a pair of white toreador pants. "Let's get two. They look great, and you can always use the other one."

"Do you think so? But look," Veevi said, taking off a pink shirt with a high neck and crossing her arms over her chest. "My tits are terrible."

"Your t-t-t-tits are fine—you just need new brassieres," Dinah said, eyeing the way Veevi's small but high and once firm breasts now sagged inside the lace bra she was wearing. It, too, was from Paris and had once been a beautiful thing, Dinah saw, but it was dingy and worn. She looked at her sister's body. Veevi's abdomen had thickened. In the dull light of the dressing room, her nostrils seemed too wide, her mouth too large, though the white teeth, like Dinah's, remained straight and perfect. But it was a thing of the past now, that beauty that had singled Veevi out for a remarkable destiny—at least as a phenomenon of nature, absolute and incontrovertible in itself—and Dinah, glancing briefly over at herself in the mirror, realized that for the first time in their lives her own looks were not unequal to Veevi's. The discovery seemed not only sad, though, but somehow wrong. This wasn't supposed to happen.

"I'll tell you something very strange," Veevi said, standing with her hands on her hips as she, too, took inventory of her body. "Do you know how I survived in France, during the war?"

"You mean at Madame Rochedieu's? When you were doing R-R-R-Resistance things?"

"I mean, do you know how I managed not to be afraid? Not to be too afraid, that is?"

"How? All I know is how Mom and Pop and I were worried sick about you."

"Ina, I thought I was so beautiful nothing could ever happen to me."

Dinah nodded, understanding at once what she meant.

"I thought to myself, If the Nazis catch me, one of them—an officer perhaps—will see that I'm beautiful. He won't kill me; he won't torture me." She let her hands drop to her sides. Standing there in her panties and bra, she let her head fall to the side and continued looking at herself in the mirror, which also reflected Dinah, dressed in slacks and sandals, sitting cross-legged on the settee, holding clothes in her lap for Veevi to try on. "It had gotten me everything before. Everything. I never had to work at anything. It was my gift, you see, and I was smart enough to use it."

"True," said Dinah, remembering that point, after Veevi had started dancing at Marathon, when life had opened up for her and lifted her up and out, and she had left Dinah and their parents without even meaning to.

"I thought that the beauty"—Dinah noticed how she said "the beauty," not "my beauty," as if she were talking to a doctor, the way Jake's mother did when she said "the limb," "the womb," "the foot"—"the beauty gave me so much power over people that I assumed that nothing could ever hurt me. Dumb, wasn't it?" She turned and looked down at Dinah. "I mean, breathtakingly idiotic, don't you think?"

"Well, no, Vee, not really," Dinah said. "On the c-c-c-contrary. It kept you brave. Maybe you saved a lot of l-l-l-lives because of it."

Veevi seemed not to have heard her. "I've got to do something about my hair," she said, holding up one lifeless brown clump. "Jesus, look at me. Where the hell did it all go?"

Dinah said that Ken, her own hair guy, would take care of Veevi. Veevi could go with her to her next appointment. They could go to the Griffith Park Observatory afterward, have lunch somewhere. But Veevi didn't respond. She kept trying on and taking off new outfits and looking at herself in the mirror, and rambling, "My skin is terrible . . . I'm too fat . . . I look lumpy . . . I'm too short. Why couldn't I have gotten your legs? . . . I'd trade my face for your figure . . . I look like hell in this. Christ, no wonder Mike found himself some little French number."

Dinah had an answer for every lament: "The light in here is terrible. Your skin is fine. But if you like, we'll go to Elizabeth Arden for facials. You've never been too fat. Your legs are great. You have a waistline; I don't. I'm built like a boy; you're not. You have a really feminine figure. P-P-P-Perfect pr-pr-pr-proportions. I'm too short-waisted. Everything about you is just right. Mike's a shitheel, and the sooner you realize that the better. You're still beautiful; you'll always be beautiful. Your face is sensational, Vee. There's no one in the world as beautiful as you," she chanted.

She heard herself conjuring up in fashion-show mumbo jumbo—the kind they had always laughed at in the old days—a wonderful life in which every item of clothing would have infinite uses.

"Now, try those bl-bl-bl-black pants on with the white shirt. You can wear it for company or just hanging around the house, and you can wear it out, too—to a c-c-c-cocktail party, or to Chasen's." She began exaggerating the fashion-show voice, turning it into parody: "And try on that black jacket, too. You can coordinate these 'separates' "—she snickered at the word—"elegant for evening but still sporty. 'Cause, you know, we're so fucking sporty out here you can put one outfit on in the morning, shop for groceries, pick up the kids, take a swim, have a drink, meet your husband at Ciro's, and never have to change."

Veevi was laughing now. "You think?" she said. She was wearing the black pants and the white shirt and black jacket. Finally, she looked good, very good, and smiled at herself in the mirror.

"Well, why not? It's not Paris, but it's not the asshole of the universe either, you know. You might actually meet some people you'd like out here. Including some fellas."

"Who the hell is going to invite *me* anywhere?" She was getting back into her old blue slacks and a white silk shirt whose seams, Dinah noticed, were frayed. In Dinah's lap, however, was a sizable haul of new outfits. She picked up each piece and looked at it and folded it on her lap, patting the accumulating pile with satisfaction.

"A lot of people. Everyone we know, to b-b-b-begin with. And then you'll meet people on your own. Before you know it, you'll be surrounded by worshipers and adorers, just as you've always been."

"I'm not twenty, Ina, I'm not beautiful, and I'm not married to somebody famous or important," Veevi said with bitterness.

"Veevi, you *are* beautiful. Look at yourself. You look great in that outfit. To hell with age—just forget it. What you've got left over is more than most girls start out with. And I promise you in two years at most you'll be married again—to somebody terrific. Don't forget who you are, Vee. You're a class act, a prize. You always were and you always will be, and I could kick that son of a b-b-b-bitch Mike for making you forget it."

Veevi made a bubby face full of doubt and fear.

After Dinah had paid for the new clothes and given instructions for the delivery of the packages, the sisters left the store and were just setting out into the late-morning Los Angeles haze to have lunch when they ran

smack-dab into Belle Pomerantz. "My God," she screamed, nearly dropping her Dick Carroll box on the pavement. "I don't believe it! Veevi Albrecht! Dinah Lasker! Both at the same time! How lucky can I get?"

Belle was the wife of Clement Pomerantz, one of the great songwriters
of the century. After several heart attacks, he was now a semi-invalid, but
they still lived in stupendous luxury on his ASCAP millions, in a fifty-room
palazzo high above Sunset. Belle entertained lavishly and frequently, often
for the Democratic Party, to which they were famously generous donors.
The Pomerantzes had come to Hollywood in the early thirties, almost as
soon as talkies appeared, after innumerable successes on Broadway, and
had instantly become Hollywood aristocracy. They had great respect for
the refugees, and had courted Stefan and Veevi until Stefan told Veevi how
much he disliked going to their overcrowded, amorphous affairs, which
were ostensibly given for good left-wing causes but served the more general purpose of feeding Belle's insatiable appetite for social domination.
She was now a stout, expensively and tastefully dressed woman in her late
fifties, with a large mouth, a firm jaw, and a cap of silver hair. Dinah saw
how she instantly registered the changes in Veevi and her glance shuttled
inquiringly from one sister to the other. She had obviously got wind of the
Albrecht breakup, and no doubt read about Dinah's testimony, too.

"Well, honey, what brings you home?" she asked Veevi. The sisters
weren't deceived by her motherly warmth, which, they understood, con-
cealed a raving nosiness.

"Europe began to bore me," said Veevi, smiling. "And I began to crave
the food served in my sister's house—corn bread, lima beans, and anything
that goes with ketchup. You know our grandfather was from Little Rock,
don't you, and served in the Confederacy? Seems we're always on the
wrong side, our family." She smiled at Belle, squeezing Dinah's arm in an
uncharacteristic gesture of protective and pre-emptive complicity.

"Dinah Lasker," said Belle, who was given to calling people by both
their first and last names. "I simply have to tell you—Clem and I ran
Cousin Jonnycake the other night, and when I say we loved it, I mean we
loved it. Merv and Ethel Kramer were over, you know, and he said, 'That
Jake Lasker's a major talent.' And Clem said, 'You can say that again,' and
you know what? He said it again: 'Jake Lasker's one hell of a major talent.' "
Merv Kramer, Dinah later explained to Veevi, was the head of Coronado
Pictures, one of Marathon's major rivals and, like the Engels, part of Holly-
wood's old guard.

"Oh, how nice of you to tell me," Dinah said, beaming, though not so brightly as to let Belle think that her compliment was all that out of the ordinary. "I'll p-p-p-pass it along to my husband."

"You know," Belle offered, her throat husky from cigarettes and depleted estrogen. "Looking at you beautiful girls"—she bent her head forward confidentially and fixed them with a momentous stare—"I can't help thinking: you two could be a power in this town."

"Oh, that's your job, dear," Veevi said quickly, giving Belle one of the most winning, flattering, and completely phony smiles Dinah had ever seen.

"I mean it, you know," said Belle, clearly pleased at Veevi's rejoinder. "You two could have this town at your feet." She kissed Veevi on the cheek, which she stroked with her hand. "All it takes is one party—one perfect party. I know the best caterers, too, let me tell you. And I'd give you my guest list." She twinkled.

Then she said pointedly to Veevi, "Come see me someday. We'll have lunch and you'll tell me all about it. And who knows—maybe I know a fellow or two you might want to meet. Though who could be good enough for you, huh? Well, not everybody out here's a schlepper, right?" Her expression became shrewd with matchmaking possibilities. "And Clem would love to see you. It would do him good. God, how he used to talk about you. 'Prettiest girl who ever lived,' he'd say. 'And so smart. Who ever thought a beautiful gentile could be so smart?'"

"Do send him my love," Veevi said girlishly. Dinah realized that Clem Pomerantz was no doubt one of the enchanted suckers on whom Veevi had bestowed her favors once, and only once. Belle probably suspected it and might even have used it to get something she wanted—a great piece of jewelry, for instance, or a trip to Washington to have dinner with the Roosevelts.

The Pomerantzes had never invited the Laskers over for an intimate evening. Jake and Dinah had gone to their big parties, the ones that were held in their acres of backyard with two or three hundred people and for which they'd first had to make a sizable donation to the Democrats, but that was all.

"Well, girls, I'm off with some new shirts for Clem," Belle announced. "I buy him two dozen every month—can you believe it? He grew up on Rivington Street and now he's got a thousand shirts."

"Is he still writing?" Veevi asked.

Now that, Dinah thought, shows how long my sister's been away from Hollywood. She would have to remind her: you never ask people what they're doing; they either have something good to tell you or they don't. But you *never* ask.

"Nah," Belle said, waving her hand dismissively. "We're too rich. He talks to the stockbroker four, five times a day and the business manager another half dozen. He says somebody's got to know where everything is. God knows I don't. We get him up and dressed, the chauffeur takes him to Hillcrest; he has lunch with Groucho and the boys, comes home, takes a nap, we have dinner, somebody comes for bridge or a movie, we see our grandchildren—it's a nice life. Every weekend, we drive to the Springs and the nurse takes him into the pool, and when they think I'm not looking she plays with his weenie."

Both sisters laughed with Belle, who shrugged "Whaddya gonna do?" She had a long string of marble-size pearls around her neck, which Dinah figured must have cost somewhere between seventy-five and a hundred thousand dollars, and a square-cut sapphire nestled against her wedding band. Her red lipstick, rouge, and powder didn't conceal the many tiny wrinkles all over her face, but there was still something soft about her full cheeks, and she was handsome in her sky-blue wool suit.

This is how she dresses when she comes into Beverly Hills, Dinah observed—as if she were walking down Fifth Avenue. Belle had the look of a woman who spent whatever she liked on herself and had stopped worrying about the results. After all, she could wake up every day and go to sleep every night secure in the knowledge that she was entirely safe and limitlessly comfortable within a world that she thoroughly understood and to which she completely belonged. Her husband was beyond the possibility of failure. He would never surprise her again with an achievement; perhaps, Dinah mused, she missed being around the ferment of work—his work. But that was a wisp of romantic regret, hardly important compared with the infinite protections of her life, or so it seemed to Dinah.

Again, Belle looked at Veevi and Dinah and shook her head. "My God, you girls could run this town. I'm serious. With your looks"—a nod to Veevi— "and your personality"—another to Dinah—"you could *enslave* this whole stinkin' place." She sighed at the opportunities she could feel them passing up, blew kisses, clutched her package, and, with a brief wave, marched over to a waiting Rolls and chauffeur.

The sisters went in the opposite direction, toward Wilshire, and when they reached the stoplight and were certain that Belle Pomerantz was out of sight, they turned to each other and burst out at the same time: " '*A power in this town!' 'A power in this town!'* Ha! Ha!" They laughed long and hard—Dinah with her machine-gun laugh, Veevi's breathier, almost choking.

❧

"So, look, you've been here over two months, Veevi. Are you ever going to tell me what happened?" Dinah said some twenty minutes later, putting down her BLT and looking fixedly at Veevi.

"Oh, all right," said Veevi, lighting a cigarette. She leaned forward and began to talk in her whirring hummingbird way. "Mike loves Paris as long as it's cool. Fall is good for him. He's disciplined then. Writes for hours at a stretch. When it gets cold, though, he wants to ski, and when it's warm, in the summer, he needs tennis. So, when was it—three years ago? Two? I was pregnant with Coco. So it was whenever that was. The Crandells and the Knights took a place together on Cap Ferrat—Hunt and Ben were working on a screenplay and they invited us down. I wanted to go, but I'd been bleeding a little and the doctor at the American Hospital told me to stay in town. Also, Claire was in school. Mike said he'd stay, but I could see he was dying to go and get that last taste of summer before the cold set in. He'd been so standoffish when we first met the Knights, a couple of years after the war. Such a snob, really. *Hacks. Pretentious hacks,* he'd say. But by now he and Ben and Hunt were inseparable. He knew, too, that Ben was as good as they come. And Ben and Hunt got Mike to do all the things they loved to do."

"Such as?"

"Nightclubs, races at Deauville, skiing in Klosters, fishing in St-Jean-de-Luz, bullfights in Pamplona. And, of course, they had the war between them. They'd all had an interesting war and never ran out of stories. Pretty soon we started doing everything with them. I liked their wives, Felicity—who's great, as you know—and Sylvia, who's a little middle-class about things, but nice. It got so that Mike, or I guess I should say we, couldn't live without them and they couldn't live without us. When we were all in Paris at the same time, which was pretty often, we saw one another every night. Until then, writing had been Mike's whole life. He'd work, and we'd be together all day, and he didn't need a reward. But once we hooked up with them, being with them became a way of life. He lived only to be with them at night and would go to bed full of brotherly love."

"And brotherly rivalry that would get him up in the morning and over to the t-t-t-typewriter?"

"Exactly."

"And there was, of course, the added spur of his b-b-b-belief in the superiority of his own talent, alternating with the fear that maybe he *wasn't* as good as Knight and had to beat him."

"Of course he's better than Ben, but he didn't always know it. It's one of the reasons he depended so much on me."

"Mike has more talent than Ben Knight?"

"You bet."

"No, Vee, he doesn't," Dinah said. "He had promise. But it hasn't gone anywhere. He doesn't have Knight's power. Or warmth."

"Since when are you a literary critic?"

Dinah let that pass.

"Listen, Vee, Mike's only modest when someone t-t-t-tells him he's a genius. He's been rotten to you."

"Anyway," Veevi went on, "I told him to go and he went."

"To Cap Ferrat?"

"Yeah, Cap Ferrat. There's a great hotel there, right on the sea. You go down from the pool to these rocks and dive right into the bluest water in the world."

"I thought you two were inseparable," Dinah said, thinking in particular of one letter, written around Christmas of '47 or '48, in reply to one of her own, in which she had asked whether Veevi would consider a visit to California soon, to see Pop. *"I can't leave now,"* Veevi had written. *"Mike wants me with him all the time. In the same room, all day. I sit and read, and then I go out for the lunch things and come back and make lunch. After lunch, he reads me the morning's work and asks me what I think, and we take a nap for an hour and then he goes back to work. He can't write without me. And, of course, Claire's in school and has a regular routine. Please find some way to explain this to Pop."*

Veevi sighed. "Well, we were, for a long time. And then he found the Crandells and the Knights, and somehow the routine sort of fell apart. I did love it all those years, listening to him hunt and punch on the typewriter. Idiot that I was, I thought I was indispensable." She paused, took a sip of coffee, and went on: "That was my first big mistake. Giving up that little ritual. I should have stood my ground and not given in so easily to the"—she paused, searching for a word, and laughed a little—" 'collective' life. Except that it was so much fun."

She continued with her story. She and Mike agreed that he would go for two or three weeks and come back immediately if she needed him. So he went, and he sent her a postcard every day showing the hotel and the outdoor bistros in Beaulieu. He wrote to her all the time, telling her how much he missed her and how concerned he was about the pregnancy. He kept asking if she wanted him to come home, so of course she said she was fine and that he should stay. Then out of the blue he wrote and said that the only thing Hunt and Ben talked about was show business and that he was bored to death by it and was going to spend a week with Gastang if that was all right with her. She said of course it was. She knew Gastang and thought it would be fine.

From Veevi's letters, Dinah knew that Gastang was a famous French sculptor—a Basque, actually—who lived just outside St-Jean-de-Luz. He had been a friend of Stefan's, a member of the Ossau network in the war, and had hidden Stefan a couple of times in the mountains. That's what Mike learned when he started investigating what had happened to Stefan. Mike had gone to visit him and they'd become friends, or, more precisely, Gastang had become a kind of father figure for Mike—*"with a lot of guzzling of red wine from goatskin flasks and throwing their arms around each other's necks,"* Veevi had once written.

Now Veevi leaned forward on her elbows, and her eyes narrowed. "Whenever Ben Knight publishes a new story in *The New Yorker,* Mike worries that Ben's getting ahead of him and goes off and visits Gastang," she said. "Gastang tells Mike, 'You aire ze real ting, you aire ze real artiste,' and they go fishing, and Mike comes back as if he's been blessed by the goddamn pope."

If she hadn't exiled herself from these people, she wouldn't be saying these things, Dinah thought. She's trying to find things to ridicule about them, because she can't bear not having them anymore.

"K-K-K-Keep talking," Dinah said.

Mike had said that he would stay at Gastang's for about a week, no more. During that time, Veevi had another bleeding episode and was weighing whether to call him and tell him to come home, when he called her from St-Jean-de-Luz to say that he'd decided to write a book about the sculptor and needed to spend another week observing him in his studio. Of course, watching Gastang had very little to do with seeing him make sculpture and everything to do with having fun: fishing in the choppy Atlantic off St-Jean-de-Luz, drinking with Gastang's Basque smuggler pals in the mountains. The extra week became two, then three. Then he wrote to say that the Crandells and the Knights had driven up from Cap Ferrat. In another letter, he casually mentioned that there was a girl with them— a French girl named Odile Boisvert. She was an actress of about nineteen or twenty and the girlfriend of Jock de Maistre, the Paris chief of *Newsfront*. He had left her in Cap Ferrat with the Crandells when he went back to Paris to cover the American presidential campaigns.

"You know the kind of girl she is," Veevi went on. "The kind that always makes friends with the wives first. Felicity told me that the girl zoomed in on her. Tried to turn her into her best friend—seeking motherly advice and all that rot. Felicity was contrite when she told me, but she bit at once. The girl had been in operation since she was fifteen and had already had a fair number of rather conspicuous boyfriends—a French duke who was also a racing car driver, an Iranian prince—and Felicity can't resist the gossip that a girl like that brings with her—it's like party favors. Felicity said Odile kept going on about how much in love she was with Jock, who had apparently delivered her from the unwanted attentions of Willie Weil, who had persuaded Hunt to put her in his last picture. So Felicity took her under her wing, supposedly. You know," Veevi said, "Felicity eats at home with her own kids twice a year and decides she has to play mama with Odile."

"What happened next?" Dinah asked, taking Veevi's hand in anticipation of difficulty. Veevi withdrew it and lit a fresh cigarette.

"Well, the Crandells showed up at Gastang's with Odile in tow. Gastang went nuts. He wants every woman he sees. He's *priapic*."

"You mean he's got a p-p-p-permanent hard-on?"

"Beyond permanent. *Eternal*. And he's sixty-seven years old, for Christ's sake."

"Okay, so he's after her."

"He wouldn't leave the girl alone. But she wasn't interested. I guess after you've had a French duke, an Iranian prince, and who knows how many counts and earls, a horny old artist who reeks of wine and tobacco that smells like horse manure isn't all that exciting. Mike wrote and told me all about it, as if he were taking notes for a novel—a Ben Knight novel, by the way, not a Mike Albrecht novel."

"He *wrote* to you about it?"

"Uh-huh. I heard all the details. The old man kept bothering her, kept grabbing her knee under the table, putting his hand on her ass. He asked her to sit for him in the studio, and then tried to tear her clothes off. It went completely bonkers when Mercedes got involved."

"Mercedes?"

"Madame Gastang. Oh boy, is she ever *formidable*," Veevi said, pronouncing the word in French. "She was getting sick and tired of Gastang's foolishness with the girl. But when Mike told Gastang to lay off Odile, Mercedes blamed her, not Gastang, and ordered her and Mike to leave. That was fine with the girl, but the Crandells and the Knights had gone back to Cap Ferrat, so Odile asked Mike to drive her back to Paris because she had found the experience too nerve-racking to take the train alone."

"Poor little thing," said Dinah, who knew what was coming.

"The first phone call: 'The car's broken down—have to stay in this little town for two days. Bored out of my mind. Miss you terribly, darling.' Next call: the car part from Paris still hasn't arrived, and it's raining. But he has the typewriter—he can work. About three days later—and he calls every day—I call Felicity to see if she's back, 'Come over,' I say, 'I'm stuck. Can't go anywhere—doctor's orders.' An hour later, she waltzes in and says, 'How do you like the Arpège?' 'What Arpège? I can't stand Arpège.' Well, the look on her face, I tell you. She asked me if I had a birthday coming up. No. Not a chance. She's not the kind to tattle, and I know she must have been kicking herself mentally, but I'd caught her in something, and told her she *had* to tell me, whatever it was. Well, she'd run into Mike that morning at Lanvin. She'd just assumed the perfume was for me. So I told her she was crazy, it couldn't possibly be Mike, because he wasn't even in Paris. But she just shook her head and said, 'I'm so sorry, baby. That fucking girl.' Then I called Gastang's and put Felicity on, since my French is so terrible, and the maid told her Monsieur Albrecht and Mademoiselle Boisvert had left together five days ago. Later, I found out they'd gone right back to Paris that day and were shacking up at her apartment, which wasn't even ten blocks from me."

"What'ja do when he came home? Hit him over the head with a f-f-f-frying pan?"

"Oh, come on. One has to have a *little* class."

"For Christ's sake, Vee, I didn't mean it literally," said Dinah testily. For a moment, she thought that her sister was both an idiot and a snob. "Anyway, what happened then?" she said, chewing the inside of her cheek.

"I sweated it out. He had to come home at some point. Two days later, to be precise. It was a Saturday morning. I'd decided not to say anything. He'd come and gone before, and I'd learned the hard way that you don't ask questions. Felicity had taught me that. She told me you have to have perfect manners about these things if you don't want to blow the marriage."

"That's her c-c-c-contribution to the fund of human wisdom?"

"Believe me, she's right. But in this case it didn't matter. He came home that morning, unshaved. He had tired, contented eyes and he smelled like someone—I can't put it any other way—who'd been fucking his brains out all week. You know, sort of gamy. Fetid. Satiated." She made a face. "He started to speak. 'Take a shower first,' I told him. That was hard, waiting for the shower to end. Finally, he comes in and sits down, pulls up a chair, and says, 'This is going to be hard for you.' I said, 'Is it really necessary to tell me?' I wanted to use my brave, civilized silence. 'Yes,' he said. And then he told me what I already knew, and he added, 'I'm completely in love with her. I can't live without her.' There were several repetitions of 'I can't tell you how sorry I am.' But not too many, of course, because that would mark the difference between *regret,* which he was feeling, and *apology,* which is a no-no as far as he's concerned—not then, not before, not at any time."

This was a distinction Dinah had never thought about, and as she listened to her sister she puzzled over it, as if she were trying to follow an algebra formula she couldn't understand while the teacher has moved on to a new one. Her sister's eyes glinted. Three-quarters of her sandwich lay uneaten on the plate. She was speaking so rapidly that Dinah had to lean in to follow her. "He told me he was more than willing to stay and get me through the birth. 'I know it's bad timing,' he said. 'With the baby coming.' As if the whole thing were a muck-up in the timetable of the gods."

"What horseshit," Dinah said. She would have liked to add, "But that's the way you guys live. I know. I've read Ben Knight's novels. I know your world."

"At any rate," Veevi said, lighting a Lucky Strike, "that's when I found out how much he loves himself. I hadn't realized it before then. God, I'd been stupid. I'd always believed the main thing in his life was his work and me. I thought he'd love me forever. I was sure of it. He always had. Did you know he had a crush on me when we were living in Malibu?"

Was this the time? Dinah wondered. Swiftly, she had to make a decision.

"Yeah," she said. "I did. Actually, Vee, I heard you two, you know—on the b-b-b-beach. One night."

"You did?" Veevi made a mock-guilty "Oops!" kind of face and nodded, smiling dreamily. "It was strong between us right from the beginning."

My God, Dinah thought. "And Stefan?"

"Dear Stefan."

Dear Stefan? That's all she could say? *Dear Stefan?*

Then Dinah saw that Veevi was looking at her with her mouth closed, except for a slow puff on her cigarette, and she knew that her face must have betrayed her feelings of shock and bafflement and that Veevi wouldn't say another word if she was going to start being "dreary." Just listen, Dinah commanded herself. That's what you're here for. Forget everything else.

"You were saying about Mike—"

"Mike fell for me the day he arrived from Paris. One look, and that was it. He was fifteen years old. He wrote me a letter." She laughed lightly. "Put it between the covers of a book. Very sweet. But I was crazy about him, too. It was overpowering. But it was—"

"In two words, as Sam Goldwyn used to say, *im-possible.*"

Veevi nodded. "Of course, that's the main reason I went to Europe with Stefan. I tried to fight it."

"And you were pregnant?"

"Yes. I thought I'd never see Mike again. Or Mom and Pop and you, for that matter."

Not that you gave a good goddamn, Dinah thought.

"When the war ended, he looked for me in Paris. He was wild when he found me. I was sure we'd be together forever." She blew smoke and stubbed out the cigarette. "So much for romantic wartime stories."

She took a bite of her sandwich, a sip of Coke, and lit another cigarette. "Where was I?"

"After the war? In Paris? Undying love?"

Veevi laughed. "No, I mean with the girl."

"Well, he's in the shower and then he comes out and tells you everything."

"Oh, yes. True Confessions. Yes. He'd been wild about me? Well, now he was wild about her. But now I saw something different. You see, he was so kind. So fucking kind. And I saw that he approved of himself for being kind. He loved himself for being that way. 'Can I get you a cup of tea?' he said. He'd never ever gotten me a cup of tea! He'd never needed to! I thought about it later and figured it out. He felt sorry for *me* for losing *him*. He was putting himself in *my* place, imagining what it was like for some-one to lose *him*. Trying to soften the blow. He was in love with himself the way he thought I was in love with him."

Dinah shook her head in enormous sympathy.

"He held me while I cried. He was so *understanding*. His manners were perfect. If I could reproach him for the large things, he wanted to make sure I couldn't do it for the small things. So he *thanked* me for our years to-gether. Imagine being *thanked,* for Christ's sake. Imagine receiving his gratitude, when for the last fifteen years you'd had endless love—or thought you did."

"That's a t-t-t-tough one."

"What he said was," Veevi continued, " 'It's better for us to break up while we still care for each other than wait and tear each other apart.' 'Care'! Can you imagine? *'Care'!* This way, we would always be 'friends,' al-ways be 'on each other's side.' And then a few days later, when he came back to pack up his things, he said, 'Be strong, baby. Who knows, maybe this'll pass. Think of it as 'a spell of rough weather.' ' "

"Isn't that the title of a Ben Knight story?"

Veevi nodded.

"I could kill him," Dinah said. "The phrase-making, lying son of a bitch. He was t-t-t-torturing you."

"But, you see, he wasn't really sure what he wanted. He still isn't. He loves me. I just know it. Remember that letter he sent, after you testified? Well, he wrote that after I had the baby—after he left. He made a carbon copy and sent it to me."

"And you think that means he loves you? That the letter is some kind of pr-pr-pr-proof?"

"Why else would he have written it?"

"Are you kidding? There he is, guilty as all hell, and suddenly he has a chance to make himself smell good again, in your eyes and his own. Jesus Christ, Veevi. Can't you see that?"

"He's suffering, Dinah."

"Veevi, I think this guy knows exactly what he wants: a divorce."

"Well," Veevi said, "that's what he said. But I think it'll just run its course, and it's better if I'm here and he's there until it does."

Dinah's heart sank.

"And your passport?"

"This HUAC craziness can't last forever, can it?"

Dinah got it now. She understood that, far from being reconciled to a divorce from Mike, Veevi was determined to wait it out. Even if there was an actual divorce, she wasn't going to let go of Mike. Over the uneaten ham-and-cheese sandwich on her plate, Veevi's face was sad and resigned—but not to final loss, only to a limbo of waiting.

"You love talking about him, don't you?" Dinah said.

Tears welled in Veevi's eyes. "Is it boring?" she asked.

"No," Dinah answered, instinctively opening her purse and handing her a tissue. "Not at all. You can talk about him all you want. You just have to put up with my editorials. Because I'll be goddamned if I'm going to think of him as anything other than a lousy two-bit r-r-r-road-show imitation of some jerk in one of his novels. Or, rather, one of Hemingway's or even Ben Knight's, of which Mike's are but p-p-p-pale imitations."

Veevi frowned. "That's not fair," she said. "And it isn't true."

"Okay, fine, what do I know about literature? But let me tell you something, Veevi. You married a man and not his talent, and so far the man has turned out to be a louse. What are you holding on to, anyway? What's this crap about having 'perfect manners'? Is that your idea of how to act when someone leaves you when you're sick and pregnant? I couldn't do it. I'd tear his eyes out."

Veevi rested her chin in her hand and didn't answer. Then Dinah asked practical questions: Well, what about the divorce? How much alimony could she get? Child support? Did it include Claire? Then she slipped in: was Claire Mike's child?

"I don't know," Veevi said. "She looks like him. But, well, she might be Stefan's."

"And Mike might be Stefan's as well. What are you guys, the Hatfields and the McCoys? Jesus Christ, Veevi!"

Suddenly, in a flash of memory, Dinah saw Stefan and Mike wrestling on the beach, Stefan lifting Mike and throwing him on the ground, Mike grunting as he lifted all 185 pounds of Stefan and did the same to him, both of them gasping, concentrating, shouting. A big grin on Stefan's face, his solid grown man's body clasping the boy's with its tight new muscles, its washboard rib cage and hairless chest. A fierce burst of love for Stefan exploded within her.

"If Dorshka could do it, why couldn't I?" Veevi said.

Dinah suddenly got it: Dorshka was the model; Dorshka was the influence—and the rival. But she went on, not wanting to appear shocked and naïve. She returned to the question of alimony. It seemed to Dinah that Veevi was entitled to a great deal, and she said so, her voice full of cheerleading spirit.

But Veevi took a deep breath and glanced away. "Well, I'm not ready for that yet." She pressed her lips together, as if hesitating about something. She had decided that it was beneath her to ask for alimony, then, Dinah surmised. It was unstated, but nevertheless clear: she and Jake would have to support Veevi for the rest of her life. Dinah saw that her sister wasn't going to finish her sandwich, and she called for the check.

At night, after long days of listening to Veevi telling stories, Dinah would get into bed next to Jake and rub his back and share the day's catch, telling the same stories, word for word, although her own recounting of them was even more animated than her sister's. Despite her essentially unsophisticated distaste for the erotic shenanigans that ruled Veevi's world, she wanted to appear, both to herself and to Jake, capable of taking the measure of that world, and to seem unperturbed by its terms and assumptions. It was one way of fighting back against the feeling she got, whenever she contemplated Veevi's Paris life, that she herself was a "real square," as she put it. Moreover, it helped to stanch her old envy that, like a leakage of black blood, rose up in her whenever she talked with Veevi or discussed her with Jake—reminding her of all that her sister had once been, and all that she herself was not. She throbbed with sudden desire for evenings in cafés and bistros—wherever you got to dance with handsome strangers who had had "good" wars, written books you'd liked, lived for the moment, and said charming, sexy things to you in French. Why, Veevi knew enough French to speak it badly! Dinah's high school French was like a storefront dummy—frozen and stiff, unable to move a single limb on its own.

But these surges of wanting whatever it was she thought she was supposed to want passed quickly. Rubbing her warm feet against Jake's, pressing her torso against his back and shoulders, she wanted no life other than the one she had. Were routine and habit, a comfortable house, eating dinner with your kids, enjoying your husband's triumphs and helping him with his worries, something to be sneered at?

Nevertheless, it seemed to Dinah that Veevi's stories of a life of restless

joys, with its changes of place and partners, its rhythm of arrivals and de-
partures, were meant to diminish her own. And Veevi's contempt for Hollywood was so grating. Whenever Veevi spoke of friends who had put aside
their difficult novels to make a fast buck "tossing off" screenplays, Dinah's
jaw stiffened. As if screenplays could be "tossed off"! As if the long, grind-
ing months Jake put into his own made him a hack.

"Well, Jake is a joke writer," Veevi said once, explaining why Mike
would never return to Hollywood. "He belongs here, this is his element.
But Mike is an artist."

The remark had riled Jake, too, when Dinah reported it to him. "About
screenwriting, she doesn't know her ass from a hole in the ground," he'd
snorted. "You know, I like your sister. I really do, honey. She's kind of an interesting broad. But Jesus, she's got that coozeburger side, and I do think
for everybody's sake she ought to get a job and find a place of her own, and
soon."

But every time Jake said this or made some damning remark about her
sister, Dinah simply could not forget the realities of Veevi's life. Where
could she go? Dinah was all the family she had. So, as she kneaded her
husband's muscles and felt them slacken into sleep, she would say, not so
much to him as to the air and the night, "Don't be hard on her. Give her a
chance, that's all."

Jake came home from the studio early one afternoon. Finding Dinah and
Veevi sitting in the den together with the kids, he patted his chest, coughed
slightly, announced that he had "a little throat" coming on, and asked
Dinah to go with him upstairs and take his temperature.

Once they were inside their room, he closed the door and told her to sit
down. "What about your throat? Do you want me to get the thermometer?"

"No." She felt a sudden dread. Was there bad news? He had a glittery
look in his eyes; it came from exhilaration—the exhilaration with which he
always confronted crisis or disaster, as if there were, for him, a keen pleasure in coming up against adversity.

"We've got a problem," he said. "A very definite problem."

"Well?"

"I decided to call Reggie Pertwee and see if I couldn't 'utz' him a little
about Veevi. I don't mind being the 'employer of last resort' if that's what I

have to be, but what if there's some way she could get back into acting? And what he said was, and these are his exact words, 'I've been calling all over town to find something for her, but the fact is, your sister-in-law's unemployable. It seems that half of Hollywood named her during the investigations.' "

"Oh, Christ," said Dinah. "My G-G-G-God, what did I do to her?"

"*Darling*, that's just the point," Jake barked at her, and now he really did sound hoarse. "*You* didn't do anything that lots of other people hadn't already done. She was a lodestar, for Christ's sake. The fucking queen of the Stalinist Left out here. Everyone knew her and knew who she was. All that trouble with her passport would have happened even if you hadn't named her. Even if nobody had ever subpoenaed you, she would have been blacklisted. This whole situation she's in is all her choice and isn't your fault. You and I both know goddamn well that she could call up that son of a bitch Marlow today and clear herself and find a job. And that's where you can help. Tell her to go and testify and get it over with, for Christ's sake. It would just be a formality. She wouldn't be naming anybody who hasn't been named a thousand times already. Whoever she would hurt has already been hurt. And it would get her off our backs. I don't know if you can admit it, but you have to be blind not to see she that hasn't the slightest intention of moving out of here and getting on her own. Didn't you have to tell her to stop asking Gussie to bring her orange juice on a tray in the mornings? Some fucking Communist!"

Dinah sat forward in her chair, her whole body stiffening. "Now, just a minute, Jake. I have never for one moment told myself that going down there and t-t-talking to those two cr-cr-creeps was anything other than degr-gr-gr-grading and humiliating. But I did it for you, and for us, and I would do it again for you and for us. But don't ever tell me to tell Veevi to do it, and don't tell me to throw her out of this house. I don't care how many other people named her. Maybe my testimony was the one they nailed her with, and maybe it wasn't. *It doesn't make any difference.* I named her. She's my sister. I love her. She's lost her husband and her passport and now Reg Pertwee says she's been blacklisted, as if that's some b-b-b-big s-s-s-s-surprise. She's up shit creek, honey. She can't work in pictures, she has no future, no prospects, she's damn near forty years old, and her beauty's fading fast. As far as I'm concerned, *I* named her, and that means that *I'm* going to take care of her."

"You've got a neurotic, compulsive, dare I say sick, sense of responsibility toward—"

"DON'T PULL THAT FR-FR-FR-FR-FREUDIAN SHIT ON ME!" she exploded at him.

"Darling," he said, regretfully putting away his psychoanalytic formulations, which he liked to trot out like a magician pulling a stream of fancy-colored scarves out of his hat. "It'll never end. We'll never be just us again. Veevi's taking over everything in our lives. Why can't I come home and just have dinner with you and the kreebnabbers anymore? Why does every family dinner we have turn into some kind of contest between 'dreary' Hollywood and 'fun' Paris?"

"She's just trying to bring a little civilized conversation into the house."

"What's so fucking civilized about it? She laughs that velvety laugh and sticks it to you. If I say the sun is shining, she says it's raining. If I say I like Tennessee Williams, she says, 'Oh, but you haven't read Ionesco.' I like Sinatra; she says 'Listen to Piaf.' I make Hollywood comedies; she brings up Jean Renoir."

"Well, what's so wrong with that? That's, you know, what people do when they talk about c-c-c—shit, I can't say it, 'cause I hate the word! C-C-C-Culture!"

"I hate it, too! Well, okay, it's fine hearing you two talk books, but Jesus H. Christ"—he brought his hand to his forehead, as if testing himself for a fever—"I hate the way she does it. Those light laughs that are, when you think about it, little sneers. Little barbs. I'm sick and tired of it. As if we have to live up to some standard of taste that never is clear in and of itself but always turns out to be *not* whatever it is we happen to like."

"You're exaggerating. You're being unfair. You sound like Peter c-c-c-complaining about Lorna."

"This isn't about sibling rivalry between your sister and me for your attention!"

"Did I say it was?"

"Well, you implied it."

She stuck a thermometer into his mouth, and they sat in silence as they waited for the result. She saw that he was shivering. Unbuttoning his shirt and unbuckling his belt, she helped him into his pajamas and his silk paisley bathrobe, in which he looked, she thought, like the fastidiously dressed aristocratic elephants in the *Babar* books she read to the children.

"Darling, the point is, none of us ever gets enough of you anymore," he said, taking out the thermometer. "We miss you."

At that, she melted. This wasn't the sort of thing he said easily, though sickness—his own, not anyone else's—made him tender; she had seen that before. She sat down and pulled him to her, and he buried his head between her breasts while she waited another minute. The thermometer read 100.6. "Herm the Germ is here," she said, using the phrase she had made up for her kids whenever they got sick. "You've got a real bug. Better get into bed."

He rolled under the covers, which she pulled up to his chin. His eyes glittered with fever. "I'm taking a big risk with the new project," he said, his voice cracking. "But now, instead of having four mouths to feed, I have seven."

"Honey," she said. "Just give it a little more t-t-t-time. She'll get settled in her own place. Meanwhile, we've got to find someone who'll take her off our hands. Though I hate like hell to p-p-p-put it like that."

"Not to mention that she's costing me something like two hundred a week. What does she do all day in the office? Stay in bed and play with herself?"

"Jake." She made a wry face.

"She should be doing two or three synopses a week, and I'm lucky if I get one twice a month."

"Jake, isn't it obvious that she's had some kind of collapse? All this stuff she says, about books and things. Don't take it so seriously, all right? She m-m-m-misses her friends. She's trying to talk to us the way she'd be talking with them."

"I didn't notice any highfalutin *Partisan Review*–type talk in Paris," he croaked. "You know what I saw in Paris? A lot of sidelong glances, a lot of close dancing and necking, not to mention two people having it royally off in the backseat of your sister's car. A lot of Ben Knight, Mike Albrecht, Hunt Crandell, and Bill Nemeth kissing each other on the cheek and calling each other '*mon vieux*' while engaged in literary pissing contests. I didn't hear anything especially brilliant."

"But you told me you had such a good time."

"I did, darling. It was interesting and new. I wish to hell you'd been there." His eyes opened wide, and he reached for her hand and squeezed it. His, she noticed, was hot and dry. "Oh boy, you really lay it on when you're sick," she said, and kissed him on the mouth. "Honey, I'm going to get you some tea."

"And crackers? I want crackers."

"Graham or saltines?"

"Both—I want both. And I want you to bring them to me and stay with me all evening."

"Veevi will have to eat with the kids in the kitchen if I do that. Can't I bring her up here with us?"

"Oh shit," he moaned, turning on his side. "Can't it be just us?"

"Jake, come on."

"Do what you want," he said, sounding sleepy. "That's what always happens anyway."

They actually had a pleasant and early evening together. Veevi and Dinah brought pot roast and mashed potatoes on trays, and Veevi volunteered to go downstairs again to get Jake some ginger ale. They watched Milton Berle, whom Jake had written for years ago, and Steve Allen, taking time out to put their kids to bed. When they came back and found Jake snoring, they kept the television on and watched until Veevi finally said she was going to bed.

When Dinah turned out the light and got into bed beside Jake, he squeezed her tightly, kissing her cheeks and her neck. Then he stuck his leg between hers and began to move up against her, and she lay back in his arms, surprised and happy that he wanted, fever and all, to make love.

13

*K*nowing there was to be a party that night, Lorna wandered into her mother's dressing room after supper. For Lorna, watching her mother bathe and dress for a party was a sacred ritual. She liked to examine her mother's body, which she adored, and was always transfixed as Dinah scrubbed her long tanned legs and arms and sloshed the washcloth along her neck and shoulders. Every detail seemed necessary, from the silly pink shower cap fitted like a swollen bubble over her mother's newly done hair to her mother's reciting the same old saying she had heard a thousand times: "Wash up as far as possible, then down as far as possible, and then"—as Dinah rose to her knees and washed between her legs—"wash possible." Dinah had learned the saying from her own mother and had passed it along to Lorna. Then there was the exciting talk about the people who were coming over—the stars, the stunning actresses. Lorna wanted to hear everything her mother would tell her about these endlessly fascinating creatures. All the while, Dinah smoothed cream on her legs and daubed perfume on her neck and wrists, dressed, applied makeup and jewelry, and magically transformed herself into what Lorna thought was the incarnation of absolute loveliness.

This evening, however, a soft February twilight, Lorna was startled to discover not just one but two naked women bustling in and out of the many-mirrored dressing room and the adjacent bathroom, with its dark pink tiles: her mother, of course, but also her aunt Veevi, who followed Dinah to the dressing table.

"Well, he called back and said he was c-c-c-coming," Dinah said. "So I guess his desire to see you has won out over his political conscience. A m-m-m-mighty battle, no doubt. Oh, by the way, I picked up your Amelia Gray sheath and it's hanging in my closet."

Lorna, who hadn't the faintest idea what Dinah was talking about, observed that Veevi was much whiter and somewhat shorter than Dinah but had the same high round breasts, though, like everything on Veevi, they sagged more than her mother's.

Lorna was aware that Veevi knew she was there, but her aunt said nothing, not even greeting her with her eyes. She hates me and I hate her, Lorna said to herself. She thought crossly that Veevi had her own bathroom; why didn't she use it? Then she remembered that Veevi's bathroom was really her father's, and that he was taking a shower in there and getting ready himself.

"Mom—?" Lorna began, as she heard the double roar of the bathtub filling and the shower gushing.

"Hi, darling!" Dinah turned and smiled at her.

Lorna went up to her mother and possessively grabbed the flesh of Dinah's stomach in a roll and kneaded it between her fingers. "Ooooh, squishy Mommy tummy," she said, using an intimate and familiar phrase.

Dinah gently pulled her hand away and got up, and Lorna followed her into the bathroom, where she sat down cross-legged in her usual position on the shaggy bath mat. Dinah turned off the faucets and dipped her toe in to test the water. "P-P-P-Perfect," she said. Reaching out to steady herself against the wall, she stepped into the tub and lowered herself by her haunches down into the hot water. The bathroom smelled deliciously of fragrant steam, perfumed soap, and freshly laundered towels.

"Dear," said a voice.

Both Lorna and Dinah turned to see Veevi standing by the shower, holding the steamy door open.

"Why don't you go downstairs, dear, and let Mommy and me have the bathroom to ourselves?"

Lorna, who did not at first realize that Veevi was speaking to her, blushed and looked up questioningly at Dinah. There was a pause, during which Dinah averted her eyes from both her sister and her daughter. Dinah finally looked at Lorna. "Better go downstairs, honey," she said. "Just this once."

Lorna hung her head. She looked up again at her mother, eyes imploring.

"Oh, don't be tedious, dear," Veevi said. "Just go."

Dinah motioned with her head and eyes: yes, you'd better go. Lorna saw that her mother wasn't going to tell her to stay. Furious at Veevi, and stunned by her mother's failure once again to stand up for her, she got up from the bath mat and fled, her cheeks flaming. She left the bathroom door open just as Veevi went into the shower, so that Dinah, to avoid a draft, had to get up and, with goose pimples and dripping skin, step out of the bathtub to close it.

14

*S*o that's the famous Genevieve Al-
brecht, thought Nelly Steiner, noting the entrance into the Laskers' den of
a well-proportioned woman close to forty, with a lovely, intelligent face. She
was wearing, Nelly noted, an elegant black crepe sheath, with a piece of
transparent short-sleeved black chiffon that covered her from the neck to the
curved edge of her small high bosom. She wore simple pearl earrings and no
other jewelry. Nelly recognized in the total picture something understated,
chic, and French. She noticed, too, that Veevi, except for a clear red lipstick
and mascara, wore no makeup. What struck her foremost about Veevi,
who, she knew, had once been an actress, was her disciplined and elected
resistance to any form of willed display. A queen had certain responsibilities to fulfill, but that didn't mean that she had chosen her lot in life.

Well, on second thought, Nelly reflected, perhaps she did take some
pleasure in it. After all, Dinah's sister had delayed her entrance just long
enough to guarantee the attention of a small audience, all of whose members would know something about her. Everyone looked up; the room,
without becoming dramatically quiet, seemed to take a large collective
breath and hold it for the moment. At last Nelly understood why it was that
Dinah, whose face she loved, had so little confidence in her own looks.
Anyone could see that at one time Veevi had completely obliterated Dinah
and any other woman in her sphere. Even now, through her majestic presence, she erased the little English actress who was sitting with Wynn Tooling, next to Groucho Marx, and who, Nelly recalled from the trades, was in
the States to make a new picture. Suddenly there wasn't a woman in the
Laskers' den whose beauty, of whatever degree, wasn't extinguished by
Veevi's.

Watching Dinah take her sister by the elbow and firmly lead her around, Nelly saw Dinah's welcoming smile and lambent vitality fade into inconsequence as Veevi locked eyes with every person, male or female, to whom Dinah introduced her. A conqueror, a predator, Nelly remarked to herself, suddenly prey to an unexpected sadness. She observed how one man, whom she didn't know, after embracing Veevi and kissing her on the cheek, stayed close to her and drew her over to the place he had occupied on the sofa. He watched with intense satisfaction as other men got up from their Windsor chairs and clustered around her, drinks in hand, to pay their respects. If I had had a sister like that, Nelly said to herself, I would have moved to the South Pole.

Of course Dinah had much to do, and the old, aching invisibility that had stolen over her the moment Veevi came into the den was partly absorbed by the obligation to greet her guests and set them up with drinks and introductions. Some of the Laskers' friends had already met Veevi at various parties, and some remembered her from her pictures and others from her politics. Even the comedy writers from Jake's radio writing days on the George Joy show, who had always preferred the track and poker games to Party meetings and left-wing fund-raisers and who, like him, had moved successfully into screenwriting, producing, and directing, knew that she was, as one of them secretly remarked to himself, a "high-class broad," with an impeccable marital pedigree (Ventura, Albrecht) that remained unblemished by the breakup with Mike. Milty Ostrow, who had attended Party meetings but had never joined, had signed a loyalty oath at Marathon and was now a much sought-after composer and arranger of movie scores, went right over to Veevi, got down on one of his knees, lifted his watery blue eyes to hers, and shrilled loudly, "You're here? You're actually here? This is unbelievable. Veevi Milligan's back in town, and I can die happy now."

Veevi, slightly embarrassed at first, was laughing now, her eyes half closing with pleasure. Saul Landau, the man who had kept a place for her on the sofa, moved closer to her, as if acknowledging that even if he could never play the fool as Ostrow just had, he would nevertheless be the first to concede that adulation to the point of hyperbole was nothing less than Genevieve's due.

Saul, Dinah estimated, had been in love with Veevi since approximately 1935, when he had been a shy young Communist radio producer who showed up at meetings and was a weekend regular at the Venturas' house.

He had left radio to produce movies and was blacklisted in 1948 for refusing to testify. Nowadays, he made a modest living running a charter-fishing-boat business in Trancas and a jazz club in Venice. With Dinah's encouragement, Veevi, who had gone out to dinner with him a couple of times, had invited him to the Laskers' tonight. He had greeted Dinah and Jake with the curtest of nods, thus indemnifying himself against the risk of moral contamination by treating them, in their own house, as if they were bellboys or elevator operators.

Dinah didn't care what he thought of her or Jake. What mattered was that at last a man had appeared who was romantically interested in Veevi. Saul Landau was a real "candidate," as she said to Veevi—not especially rich or talented, and hardly well-known for his achievements, but someone from the old days who adored her in the old ways; that is to say, he would gladly cut his heart out for her were she only to ask.

Other men approached. Mel Gordon, one half of the writing-producing-directing team of Gordon and Morocco, came up to welcome Veevi home and to say that he would remember her all his days as Liza, the young ward of Alice Brady in Stefan Ventura's *Queen of Spades*. Dick Telford, the very East Coast WASP producer, came over with his chic wife, Louise, each clasping one of Veevi's hands: they had last seen her two years ago in Paris, with Michael, and heard what had happened. Dinah saw the half-aghast, half-hilarious "what on earth are we doing here with these bumpkins in Hollywood?" look Veevi gave them—the look that managed to lift them in conspiratorial fellowship above the present moment and spirit them away to the worldly expatriate crowd that was their real milieu at the red-hot center of the earth. But Dinah recognized that trick from long ago: it was the very old and familiar arrangement of Veevi's holding court, surrounded by admiring men and women, with Dinah herself standing invisibly by on the sidelines. The only difference was that it was now taking place in Dinah's own house.

But that was just the way she wanted it, Dinah reminded herself. This was Veevi's coming-out party, her debut. "We're gonna launch you like a r-r-r-rocket to the m-m-m-moon," she'd said in her dressing room that evening, as the two sisters had sipped Scotch on the rocks and curled their eyelashes.

Where was Jake? She wanted to find out if they were both noticing the same things. She scanned the room and discovered him seated on an ottoman, talking to Groucho and Wynn Tooling and the "winsome" and "gamine" Maureen Tolliver, from whose puzzled expression Dinah realized she had mistaken Groucho's gripes for insults. Tooling and Tolliver had joined again to make a new movie together and this time won Gordon and Morocco, who were probably making what Jake had referred to as a little "pre-production whoopee" while they waited for the principal photography to begin.

On the pretext of seeing whether either of the two stars needed a new drink, Dinah approached them in time to catch Jake telling a story she loved—about the time his celebrity-loving mother had come over on a Sunday and asked if he and Dinah had met anyone famous at the party they'd attended the night before. "Well, actually, Ma, I did," Jake told her. "The playwright Lillian Hellman." "And what was she like, darling?" Rose Lasker inquired. "When I first laid eyes on her, she was the ugliest dame I'd ever seen. But the minute she opened her mouth this really grotesque-looking little woman took on a strange fascination. She was not only magnetic, intelligent, and witty; she was intensely seductive and sexual, and before I knew it she had turned into one of the most attractive women I've ever seen in my life." At this point Rose Lasker had paused, and pondered, and then remarked, "Just like Mrs. Diamond in Chicago." Dinah watched and waited for the expected laughter, which came exactly as she knew it would.

As she moved about the warm and richly paneled room, Dinah caught snatches of conversation. Almost everyone there was a screenwriter. Norma Levine, who had been subpoenaed in 1948 and had testified and now didn't even cast a glance at Veevi, was leading two other couples, the Copelands (he was a Bob Hope writer) and the Sussmans (producer and head writer on a comedy series about the principal of a midwestern high school), through a methodical and detailed report of changes she and her writing-partner husband, Lenny Korman, were making to the screenplay they were adapting from their last Broadway play, *Beyond the Beyond*. She saw Evelyn Morocco talking with Saul Landau, who wouldn't take his eyes off Veevi. For her part, Veevi had come over and sat down beside Groucho, and was listening to him as he held a cigar between his fingers and whispered something that made her laugh so hard she had to wipe her eyes. Jake had insisted on inviting the Moroccos, and Evelyn had been cordial at the front door, as if the incident four years ago between her and Dinah at Mort Berman's had never taken place. Izzie Morocco and Manny Steiner traded Harry Cohn stories with Milty Ostrow: "It's 'schmucks with

Underwoods,' for Christ's sake," cried Ostrow in his high voice, referring to the legendary studio head's definition of screenwriters. "Not 'schmucks with typewriters'!" Gerry Sellers—the former Geraldine Stanhope—who had stopped acting in the mid-thirties when she married the journalist-and-Algonquin-regular-turned-screenwriter Norman Sellers, was discussing the fine points of bonsai cultivation with Anne Gordon, Mel Gordon's wife. Audrey Sears, Jack Sears's wife, was having an earnest discussion about Aldous Huxley's work with Dorshka, whom Dinah had insisted upon inviting to the party, and who had known Huxley for many years.

Finally, just when Dinah was thinking she ought to tell the caterers to serve dinner, the Engels arrived.

"The goddamn phone," Irv apologized, kissing Dinah on the cheek. "I spend my life on it. And it's always New York, always. What a curse that three-hour difference is."

"Where's that beautiful sister of yours?" Anya said, offering neither her hand nor her twisted cheek in greeting.

"Come on—I'll take you to her," Dinah replied.

Anya spotted Veevi snugly ensconced in her corner of the sofa, her shoes on the carpet, her legs tucked up demurely beside her. "Oh, isn't she still the eighth wonder of the world!" Anya murmured to no one in particular.

Enough of this, Dinah thought. At the same time, her fluttering heart told her how nervous she was about introducing, or, rather, reintroducing, Veevi and Irv. Don't let this go wrong, she prayed. Taking the plunge, she said, "Vee, you remember Irv Engel—"

"I certainly hope so. I'd be crushed if you didn't, Miss Milligan," Irv said. He bent slightly and took Veevi's hand. "I was a great admirer of yours when you were the youngest star on the Marathon lot, and I remain a worshiper of Stefan Ventura's work."

Dick Telford promptly left Veevi's side and gallantly gestured for Irv to take his seat. Dinah, feeling her heart would simply stop, looked at Veevi, who saw her but gave no indication of her intentions. "I've often felt that my father did not treat him with the respect and encouragement he deserved," said Irv, arranging himself next to Veevi. "I hope you realize that I always stood up for him and believed in him."

She reached out her hand and smiled, enigmatically, brilliantly. "But, Irv, you know perfectly well that if Stefan were alive today you wouldn't allow him to work at your studio."

Dinah froze. Oh dear God, she's going to blow it, she thought; she's going to fuck it up right here, right now, before dinner is even served.

But Irv only put another large, fleshy hand on top of Veevi's. "I'm afraid you're probably right, my dear," he said soothingly. "These are tragic times for America. And I don't think there's a man alive who deplores it more sincerely than I do. But tell me, how do you find us, now that you're back?"

It was an agonizing moment. Dinah didn't know what Veevi was going to say. Then she saw Veevi making room for Anya on the sofa, and thought she would faint with relief. Saul lit his pipe, staying proprietarily close to Veevi. Dinah wished she could get rid of him—drown him, do anything just to get him out of the way. By God, she thought, he's useless and socially inept, with his principles and his resentments. Desperate for ammunition should things go terribly wrong, Dinah remembered how cruel Veevi had been to him; well, not to him directly, but about him. He had come out to Los Angeles from New York with a fellow named Lester Weissman (now a moderately successful director), who had also fallen for Veevi and told her in spiteful rivalry that on the train out to California, Saul had masturbated so vigorously all night, every night, that the berth above his had shaken so much that he would wake up out of a deep sleep thinking the train had derailed. One Sunday afternoon at the Malibu house, lounging by the pool and surrounded as always by admirers, Veevi had glimpsed Saul, dressed only in his bathing trunks, and said, "Oh God, here comes Landau, that mover and shaker!" Then she revealed what Lester Weissman had told her to her circle of worshipers, each of whom believed himself to be exempt from similar remarks because he, unlike the others, had a secret bond with her.

Dinah doubted that Landau had ever found out about this remark. Looking like everybody's cliché of a college professor in his tweed jacket and leather elbow patches, corduroy trousers and sober tie, he did have a boringly kind demeanor, and from his quiet, weathered face, she knew that he would never hurt Veevi. But she also knew that Veevi didn't think he was sexy, and that if she didn't want sex with him she would never accept anything else he had to offer. Was he still a Communist? Well, maybe, but who cared? As long as he was there to court her sister, and behaved himself, and didn't have a seizure of righteous indignation, he was welcome in her house. He had a drink and a pipe to puff on, but he made no attempt to talk to anyone and seemed not just content but in a state of pure bliss to be breathing the same air as Veevi.

What Veevi said in response to Irv's question, Dinah didn't know. Veevi had motioned to him, and then to Anya, to draw in close—excluding Saul—and was whispering something to the two of them like a child telling a naughty secret to her parents. Then both of them, Irv and Anya, threw their heads back and laughed. Dinah couldn't help feeling that Veevi was in some way making fun of her, or her house, or the other guests.

Dinah checked her watch. It was nearly nine. The hum of steady talk had filled the den. Everyone had arrived. She motioned to the bartender and told him to let the catering crew know that dinner could be served.

"Two Jews meet on a road," Jake began an hour and a half later. Dinner was over, and everyone had moved into the living room for coffee. "One is from Minsk and one is from Pinsk, and they compare rabbis. The one from Minsk says"—Jake spoke in an understated Yiddish accent—" 'You should see our rabbi. Such a learned man! Studies Torah night and day—never stops even to eat. And he's wise, fair, and just.' The man from Pinsk replies, 'That's nothing, for not only is our rabbi wise, fair, and just, but he is now ninety-two years old, and every night for the past seventy years he has had sexual intercourse with his wife.' 'Every night?' says the man from Minsk. 'Yes, every night,' says the man from Pinsk. 'When the clock strikes midnight, twelve angels come and pick the rabbi up out of his bed and put him on his wife, and at one o'clock in the morning one angel comes and takes him off his wife and puts him back in his bed.' The man from Minsk asks, 'Why does it take twelve angels to put the rabbi on his wife and only one angel to take him off?' 'Ah,' the other answered. 'The rabbi fights!' "

Laughter poured through the room, and through Dinah, filling her with love for her husband. At such moments—when everyone had eaten well, and people were telling stories, and the children were asleep, and her large, beautiful house was alive with all its uses—Dinah's happiness was a bright speechless buoyancy. It seemed that life was everything it could be, and that she and Jake together were harvesting their share of all that it should be.

Manny Steiner, his brown egg of a bald head shining, launched into a story of his own without preliminaries: "Some men are praying in Jerusalem, at the Wailing Wall. They're davening back and forth"—and Manny started to daven—"and one guy says, 'How do you know when you're praying to God and when you're praying to a wall?' Another fellow answers, 'When you ask for the sun to shine or for your wife to make a good dinner, you're praying to God. But when you ask for twenty-five thousand dollars, then you're praying to a wall.' " Again, the room, like a large lung, expanded with laughter.

Then Irv Engel tried his hand with an interminable story, stuffed with "he said"s and "she said"s, and endless dialogue, and, unforgivably, Irv's own anticipatory giggles. Irv hadn't been raised on the streets of Chicago or New York but in a sixty-room mansion on a twenty-acre estate above Sunset in Beverly Hills. Shiksa that I am, said Dinah to herself, I know a good Jewish accent when I hear one and his is always phony and terrible. His timing was off, he added unnecessary details, and he meandered. But he was Irv Engel, president and head of production at Marathon Pictures, and he got his laughs. Gratified, he ran his hands over his thick hair, which was brushed back from his forehead.

"Tell us about your next play, Irv," the normally sedate Dick Telford burst out. He may have been hoping to deflect Irv from launching into another endless story.

It was about Andrew Jackson, Irv said, and it was the third in a series of plays about critical moments in the lives of great American presidents. The first two were on Jefferson and John Adams, and they'd been quite successful. Everyone nodded and listened as, for several minutes, Irv expatiated on this subject.

The room went quiet, and somebody coughed. Norma Levine got up to go to the powder room. Shrewd and affable mogul that he was, Dinah wondered, didn't Irv know that before dinner people talked deals, shooting schedules, Guild strikes, and Eisenhower, but that after dinner they wanted stories, music, and laughs? Dinah and Jake caught each other's eyes; his face said, "Do something."

The moment Engel finished his discussion, she made her move. "Milty! How 'bout it?" she called out.

Immensely tall and gawky, with blue eyes that quivered in pale pink sockets, the composer got up from the sofa, where he had been talking with Izzie Morocco. Stopping on his way to the piano, he extended a hand and pulled up a short, stout woman wearing a diamond as big, Dinah might have said, as her ass. This was Elaine Marcus, the songwriter Buzz Marcus's wife; as Elaine Adams she'd been an understudy in *Finian's Rainbow* and had left the stage to marry Marcus and raise a family. She had put on weight since her marriage, but she was a belter, a girl with a huge voice, and when she and Milty started with "Old Devil Moon," men loosened their ties, women let their high heels drop to the carpet, and everyone sank back with a happy sigh into the Laskers' silk sofas.

In Hollywood, a good party becomes a great one when people who entertain the public for a living sing and play just for one another's pleasure. During those moments, there is nothing beyond the singing and playing itself. Those making the music do so to a knowing and appreciative audience. Receiving as a gift what the rest of the world must pay for, those in the audience feel themselves exempted from the entanglements and rivalries they are forced to confront every working day in "the industry." Out across the capacious living room soars the live voice, undubbed, without microphones, so close that you can see the vibrations in the singer's throat. The awkward, modest, but supremely talented Brooklyn expatriate, forever shy with women, becomes a witty and generous accompanist, singing harmony with perfect pitch, gliding effortlessly with the singer from show tunes and standards to blues and jazz. The singer, having renounced her profession for the joys of domesticity, easily reclaims her birthright. Song follows song, and the room fills with bliss.

Then someone called out for Jake to get up and sing the parody lyrics for which he was renowned. He went over to the piano, murmured something to Milty, leaned back with both elbows, and sang in a gravelly, respectably on-key, and faintly Bing Crosby–ish voice:

> *Though my doctor has toyed*
> *With both Adler and Freud*
> *He is Jung at heart.*
> *And he has a dislike*
> *For both Horney and Reich*
> *'Cause he's Jung at heart.*
> *He's convinced, don't you see*
> *That what's troubling me*
> *Is the very same thing*
> *That is bothering he—*
> *And every time that I lie down upon his couch,*
> *I find him right beside me and that boy's no slouch—*

Before he had finished the song there were cheers, laughter, and applause. Norma Levine called out for Milty to play "Black Bottom," so that Dinah and Groucho could do the Charleston together. Elaine Marcus got up again and sang Rodgers and Hart, Gershwin, Johnny Mercer, and Burke and Van Heusen songs, while people lolled on the sofas and the carpet, shoes off, legs stretched out.

It was well past twelve when Milty finally lowered the keyboard cover and, one by one, the couples reluctantly rose to go. Dinah felt the warmth of Jake's hand on the back of her neck, stroking it a little, and she knew he was pleased and that everything had gone well. At the front door, there were good-night kisses and thank-yous, the distant sound of cars on Sunset, cold air drifting in through the heavy oak door. In the living room, couples still lingered on the sofas—the Steiners, Wynn Tooling and Maureen Tolliver, snuggled up against each other, the Telfords, Veevi and Saul, the Engels with their shoes off. Jake headed toward the den for a bottle of brandy, and Dinah went to the kitchen.

She was just coming back, carrying a tray with a pot of hot coffee, a pitcher of cream, and a new box of chocolate mints, when she noticed that something was different. There were loud voices—she wasn't sure at first whose. Then she saw Anya Engel clinging tightly to Irv's arm, both of them with their shoes back on, her brows furrowed and the twisted porthole of her mouth tightly closed.

Waving his pipe, Saul Landau was saying, "What do you mean, it's 'blowing over'? When, Irv, when? Are you rehiring all the people you fired? How many is it now, Irv? Forty, fifty, a hundred people? All out on their asses? When did you ever stand up to the Committee and the American Legion?"

"We've all suffered, Saul. Believe me, both of you," said Irv, looking earnestly at Veevi. "A man in my position has to make difficult decisions—sometimes excruciating decisions, let me assure you." His eyes flashed with anger, and his face, with its fleshy, overdefined features, contracted into a scowl. "And I am"—his voice rose higher and higher, until it was almost a falsetto—"ready to be responsible for them. I will say only this: I did whatever I had to do to save the studio. It's true that I urged some people to testify, to give in to the bastards. I hated doing it. In my heart I knew it was not something that in ordinary circumstances any of them would do. I knew that none of them—almost none of them—did it with an ounce of sincerity in their hearts. It was—you know—*acting*. You should have as much compassion for them as you do for your holy and unsullied self. I know, too, that some of the martyrs, the great moral heroes we all admire for refusing to talk—and I, for one, will not name them—live as strictly under Party discipline today as they did fifteen years ago. They scream and yell bloody murder about the violation of their constitutional rights, when they themselves have nothing but the most cynical and contemptuous opinion of democracy and have actually held trials for fellow writers whose work deviated from the Party line. . . ."

"Prove it," sneered Saul. "Prove it."

"Prove it? Happily. I suggest that you call up Clifford Boatwright tomorrow morning and ask him what happened when he published *If You Want to Know the Time*. Ask him if, by God, they didn't put him on trial. Ask him if anyone demanded that he write a letter to the *New Masses* acknowledging the error of his ways. Ask him if Anatole Klein and Norman Metzger and Guy Bergman threatened him with expulsion from the Party. Go ahead and ask him."

"It's not so easy to call him," Veevi said coolly. "He's been living in Ireland since he got out of jail, writing for English TV."

Dinah looked sharply at Veevi. Did she remember that sinister exchange beside the pool, when Metzger and Klein ganged up on Boatwright?

"No, Veevi, he's back in New York, living at his mother's," Irv said. "I've been in touch with him. And that's all I'm going to say about it at this point."

Veevi looked startled at this piece of information. Saul glanced at her face, saw her eyes brightening, and bit down on his pipe.

"But what about Franklin Shaw?" Veevi said. "Come on, Irv. Franklin Shaw offered to talk. He wasn't subpoenaed. Who does that, for Christ's sake? Have you ever heard of anybody actually calling the Committee up and volunteering?"

"He's bitter, Veevi. He's another one they put on trial."

"Nonsense," said Saul. "Another malcontent."

That word, Dinah thought. *Malcontent*. He's still using that word. She looked at Veevi, and Veevi looked at her. She got it, Dinah thought. She heard it, too.

"He had better things to do with his talent than weave baskets in

Mexico," said Irv. "And he honestly thought it over and decided he wanted to get back to work. You may not agree with him, Saul—that's your privilege. But just because it isn't your position doesn't make it unprincipled."

"Snitching isn't unprincipled? Snitching on your friends?"

"Well, you know what they say," Irv fired back. " 'With friends like that, who needs enemies?' "

No one laughed.

"He was called to account, as he damn well should have been," Saul broke in. "But a trial? Nonsense. Franklin Shaw wasn't put on trial."

"Yes, he was, Saul," Veevi said. "I know, I was there. It took place in my living room."

"I was there, too. It was a lousy book, a reactionary book, and they had every right to tell him so. "

"It was a trial, Saul," said Veevi calmly. "A trial, a public humiliation, and idiotic. We were all idiots then."

A muscle under Saul's right eye twitched almost imperceptibly.

"Look, you guys," Irv continued. "If I can hold on to the studio, then I'll have a place for everybody to come back to when this whole fucking thing blows over. Hell, I'll even hire you back, Saul."

"And he doesn't even like you," Anya snuffled, squeezing her husband's arm. "You're a bore—a smug, self-righteous bore. And your music's dull, too."

For the first time, Dinah understood that until then she had had only the shallowest view of the Engels' marriage, and that Anya was a fiercely loyal wife. "I'll rehire everyone I fired—the talented ones, anyway," Irv said, smiling cruelly at Saul. "So Anya's right—that rules you out. And then, through art, we'll tell the truth about this time."

Oh shit, thought Dinah. Talk about bores. He always hits that note.

"That's a very nice plan for the future, Irv," said Veevi. "But nevertheless you caved in and Saul didn't. No matter what you say, doesn't that make you rather a public martyr and a private shitheel?"

Dinah cringed. The entire evening crumbled like a stale cracker.

"No, Miss Milligan, it does not. Stand in my shoes and tell me what you would have done."

"What you've done is made it as easy on yourself as possible," said Saul. "You've got an excuse for every concession you've made. If they want you to fire people, you fire them and then you tell the press you deplore the blacklist. Why don't you quit your job if you feel such anguish? Oh, I know: it's because you're planning to pull the nails out of the hands of all the people you've crucified."

"Get off the cross, Saul," said Irv.

There was silence. Dinah's heart was pounding. She looked at the carpet and then at Jake, who was standing, as if paralyzed, with the Telfords, their faces blank with genteel neutrality. Dinah tenderly put her hand on Anya's elbow. "Come on, honey." She led Anya to the coat closet, and just as she was gently wrapping Anya's mink around her, she saw Veevi and Saul moving through the screen door and out to the pool.

"Well," said Irv at the front door, engulfing Dinah's hand in his two paws. "I certainly admire a woman of principle. I'm surprised she was able to tolerate being in the same room with me all evening."

Anya, scowling, took his arm. "Come on, darling. It's time to go home," she said softly. Then, looking up at Dinah, she said, "You know, you're much more beautiful than your sister."

"Oh, Anya," Dinah said, leaning forward to kiss Anya's cheek. "Thank you. But I'm not."

"You know," Irv continued, speaking to both Jake and Dinah. "When my poor brother Tal first saw Genevieve Milligan on the Marathon lot, he came home and told me that he'd found his destiny."

He shook his head, and Dinah saw tears in his eyes and remembered the rumor that L. J. Engel had never gotten over his grief of Tal's broken engagement to Veevi, when she eloped with Ventura. And then Tal had died a few years later up in Vermont, where he'd gone to get out of Hollywood and to write another novel. It was unfinished at the time of his death, and it was rumored to be about Veevi.

"She's still a pretty girl," Anya said, again taking her husband's elbow. "But nothing like before. You gave your sister a lovely party, Dinah. It was a generous gesture on your part. But I don't see a future for her in this town. Good night, Dinah. Good night, Jake."

And that was it. They were out the door.

And soon so was everyone else.

———※———

Jake and Dinah embraced, but as they did Dinah felt her body sag with fatigue. "So much for Veevi's coming-out party," she said with a sigh.

"I don't want that horse's ass in this house again," Jake said.

She knew that he meant Saul Landau. "Don't worry. He didn't want to be here. Though what he said was right."

"What do you mean, 'right'?"

Jake was locking the front door, which had been imported from some ancestral English house when the house was built in the thirties. He unlocked the door to make sure the lock worked correctly, then locked it again.

"I mean, he was right about Irv. But Irv was right about what happened to Franklin Shaw. I was there for the two nights of the trial. Veevi told me to stay out of the living room, but I listened from the kitchen. Stefan came in and sat down and told me what was going on. He was depressed. Things weren't going well for him at Marathon. And he said, 'These robots. They have one idea, and they think this writer should obey this one idea. How is this different from Moscow, right now? Tell me, Dinah, should I stay here? Should I go? Where do I go if I don't stay here?' "

She had never told this story to anyone, and she did not add the following: Stefan had taken her in his arms and said, "I make two mistakes: I come to America and I marry the wrong sister." She believed the first but not the second, and broke free of his embrace, but she had never stopped wishing, with all her heart, that he had meant it.

She and Jake went into the kitchen, and while he stuffed himself with several pieces of strawberry meringue covered in strawberry syrup and drooping whipped cream, Dinah slipped into the darkened breakfast room and looked out the window. "They're out there, by the pool," she said, coming back into the kitchen. "He's got his arms around her and they're kissing. How could she possibly find him attractive? He looks," she added, using an expression of her mother's, "like Skygak from Mars."

"She sure as hell blew it tonight," Jake said.

"I know. It was a gamble, darling, wasn't it?"

"You mean, for us?"

"No, for her. She's not stupid. None of that was about principle. It was a test. In the past, she could say anything, and she was so beautiful she would be forgiven. She could have said, '*Heil,* Hitler!' and it wouldn't have made any difference. She was testing that old law of the universe, and it didn't work. Her b-b-b-beauty isn't a cosmic force anymore."

"You can say that again."

"And that's why she's out there necking with Saul Landau."

"Well, he's not the only single guy in the world. What about Mort Berman?"

"Christ no, honey."

Jake turned next to the refrigerator, from which he withdrew a casserole with cold leftover beef Stroganoff and noodles, and asked Dinah for a bottle of beer. He belched happily and loosened his buckle. "What's wrong with him?"

"Everything."

"*Oy!* I suppose that rules out the guys I play golf with."

"It does."

"Then I suggest she marry that tweedy loser who at this very moment has probably got his hand up her dress." He went back to the refrigerator, searching for more leftovers. "The problem with a guy like Saul is that he's got nothing but principle, which is very useful if you don't have any talent. But it's of no use in the industry. You can be as principled as you want, but finally you might have to make a movie with Hitler's grandmother. Then where does it get you? By the way, one thing was settled tonight. Your sister sure as hell isn't going to get a nice inconspicuous little part in my picture or anybody else's. Irv's hardly going to look the other way after that contretemps."

A sudden ecstasy flooded Jake's entire being: he had always wanted to use the word *contretemps*. He took a forkful of cottage cheese and horseradish and bit into a stalk of celery. And he had discovered a jar of kosher pickles and a can of Hershey's syrup with two triangle-shaped indentations in the top, and he knew exactly where in the deep freeze he could find a pint of Wil Wright's Chocolate Burnt Almond ice cream.

But Dinah grabbed the pickle jar and the syrup and put them back into the refrigerator. "Stop eating, darling! You're going to k-k-k-kill yourself, for Christ's sake. Come on, let's go to bed."

On their way through the house toward the stairs, they heard an engine starting up, followed by the sound of a car taking off. They paused, waiting for Veevi to come through the breakfast-room door from the pool yard, or into the kitchen from the back door. But she didn't.

"I better lock the other doors," said Jake. "She's not coming back tonight."

"I'll come with you, sweetheart," Dinah said, accompanying him as he made the rounds of all the doors in the house, starting with the front door once again. Thus together they locked out danger, cold, and darkness—at least for tonight.

15

*O*ne afternoon some weeks after the party, Dinah sat at the antique secretary in the corner of the bedroom signing checks and putting them into an envelope addressed to the business manager. The breeze drove the scent of eucalyptus through the windows, stirring the long panels of heavy silk drapes. The house was empty, and Dinah found the solitude delicious.

She took a sip of coffee and listened to the traffic on Sunset. In the years since she and Jake had moved into the house, the sound of speeding cars, even the shrieks of skidding tires on the snaking curves, had receded from her awareness. Unless she made an effort, she almost never noticed it anymore, and even now, when she tried to listen, it was distant and un-troubling. Under her hand, she felt the bulky weight of the checkbook—not the kind that you put in your purse, but a large album with leather covers. In the thirties, at Sprague Paper and Claggett Oil, when she had owned two dresses and gone to work nine-to-five five days a week for eleven years, she hadn't known about albums of checks or business managers. She hadn't known how to dress, or dream up a menu for a party, or hire and fire household help, or cheat on receipts saved for itemized deductions. But the biggest shock had been that it wasn't hard to sign checks, buy good clothes, and have a housekeeper, laundress, gardener, and pool man. It wasn't painful to be a person who had a successful husband and a fine house and beautiful children. It wasn't hard to have things.

Yet she had never forgotten what it was like to be poor. Every day, she saw the Negro maids on Sunset waiting in their street clothes for the bus (she couldn't stand for Gussie to have to wait like that, and she and Jake had given her his old red Mercury convertible when they bought the green Caddy) and felt a sharp sadness and resentment at the meanness and unfairness of things. That the world had remained a place of toil and futility for most people most of the time, she had no doubt. And in this darker mood, which often came upon her in even her most tranquil moments, she would remember her father, with his hard blue eyes and grim mouth, and she would shiver with the knowledge of his sour resentment and hard disapproval, his bigotry and selfishness, and feel how much he had never loved her but also what a lousy life he'd had, selling steel, drinking away his chances, and finally giving up and going to live in a trailer.

Then, in the very center of peace and solitude, she would be overcome by uneasiness—a sense that bad things were going to happen and that there was something fundamentally wrong with her life. A panic would seize her: Why did she and Jake have to have so much? Why did they need such a big house? Sell it, sell it, a voice would say. It's too big, and Jake will kill himself working to keep it up. They were not Hollywood aristocrats; they were not, despite Jake's success, free of worry. Why, then, did he need to live like a baron? Yet it was only by refusing to give in to this panic that she could escape from that picture of her father she carried with her—the harsh and lonely man in the garden chair in her backyard, smoking his pipe, taking the sun amid surroundings he hated. To hell with him, she would say to herself at the memory of his mirthless silence. The house stays. We stay. This is my life, and I'll be damned if I'll give it up.

A sound disturbed her reveries. Was it a car door being slammed shut, Jake's perhaps, or Saul Landau letting Veevi out of his car and escorting her to the back door? She hoped not; she wanted her solitude to last a little longer. For a moment, she listened for Jake's heavy tread on the stairs but heard nothing. She signed a few more checks and then put her pen down. Time for a ham-and-cheese sandwich and a Coke—and then she would read for the rest of the day, until the kids came home. It was Gussie's weekend off and she would cook tonight, or they might all go down to Olvera Street for tacos and enchiladas.

She would get the book first and read while she ate. It was in the den, where she had left it the day before in her knitting bag. Her steps were noiseless on the soft peridot-colored carpet. Absorbed in her small happy purpose, Dinah did not register that the heavy wooden doors of the den were wide open.

Then she saw something. The brown sofa, always the first thing anyone saw upon entering the den, was occupied. Stretched out full length on it was Veevi, her head resting on one of the big cushions. On the floor, Dinah observed, stopping dead in her tracks, knelt a man. His solid upper body was bending over Veevi's, and his head was slowly descending toward hers in what would, inevitably, become a long kiss. It was Jake, and his face was a mask of concentrated, solemn tenderness such as Dinah had never seen in him before.

She turned around and tiptoed out of view, before either of them could see her, and lunged on tiptoe, with the stealthy rigidity of a silent-movie comedian, into the powder room, just to the left of the front door. Here she sat down in a blue velvet armchair, her heart pounding violently.

Two thoughts flamed up simultaneously: that this was, of course (how could she have failed to predict it?), fated to happen, and that she was going to stop it. *I'll be goddamned if she's going to get her hands on him.* But it's happening right now. My God, he's kissing her right now. They're gonna do it right now.

My ass, she said to herself, looking for all the world exactly like the grim and hardened father whose image she had banished from her thoughts only moments ago. As he would have done, she slapped her knees with both hands. Then she stood up, took a deep breath, and slowly walked toward the den, singing out, "Yoo-hoo, anybody home? Yoo-hoo!" She gave them enough time to execute what she vividly imagined were the contorted disentanglings required to present a convincing picture of virtuous conversation.

It must have been Jake's car she'd heard in the garage, while Saul had probably dropped Veevi off sometime earlier and very quietly. Or perhaps it was vice versa. She steadied herself with these musings and forged ahead. At the door of the den, she exclaimed in mock surprise, "Why, look who's here . . ." to Veevi, and to Jake, "Honey! . . . I didn't hear a sound."

Jake was sitting in one corner of the sofa, the one where Veevi's head had been, and Veevi was sitting in the other. Her legs were crossed, her arms folded, and she was lighting a cigarette with a heavy silver lighter. There was a slight flush in her cheeks, a feverish brightness to her eyes, but her demeanor, which included the slightly cocked head and the mouth now eagerly dragging on the cigarette, was composed.

"Well, hello, hello," she said in a mock-British accent.

Jake, completely at ease, didn't look particularly disheveled in his golf slacks. "Where've you been, honey?" he asked, and smiled at her, as if delighted to see her. "Come and give us a kiss."

But Dinah could see only what might have happened if she hadn't wandered in: Veevi's legs wrapped around his back, Jake pumping away, white behind in the air.

"I've been upstairs writing checks," she said smoothly.

She ignored his request for a kiss and settled down in one of the armchairs.

"Did the kids get off to their various rendezvous?"

"Mmm. How was your g-g-g-game?"

"The goddamn gout started up a little while ago, and it hurt like hell to walk across the golf course. Otherwise, it was fine. A beautiful day." He delicately pointed to his knee and grimaced, and she refrained from saying, "If it hurt so goddamn much, how come you were able to rest your substantially overweight self on it while swooning over my sister?"

"Did you take your Benemid?" Dinah asked.

He shook his head and again squeezed his eyes and his lips shut in pain. "Honey, would you mind getting it for me? It's in the top drawer of the dresser."

She flew out of the den and upstairs. Were they even now falling back into an embrace? Was he bending over her again, grotesquely lowering himself for a kiss—or more? Was his knee really acting up? Had he sent her upstairs just to be alone with Veevi? She couldn't get out of her mind the look she had seen on his face, the completely unfamiliar look of a man playing a part in which he would never ordinarily have been cast: the solemn, unsmiling lover, bending over as if into a baptismal font, to bestow a kiss that would inaugurate—what? A slow-motion pornographic movie so harrowing it took her breath away: his body and hers entwined, doing, in a tumult of images, everything—everything a man and a woman can do together.

Perhaps she hadn't seen anything. Perhaps she had made it all up. Suddenly, she wasn't sure.

She opened the dresser drawer and stared into the clutter. There was no time to sift through it all and find an incriminating note. In a flurry of disappointed suspicion, she shook a pill from a little brown vial, slammed the drawer shut, and raced back downstairs to the den, where she found her husband and her sister once again in changed positions. To Dinah's relief, Veevi was completely vertical, standing at the bar getting Jake a root beer, though Dinah felt like snatching the bottle out of her sister's hand. This time, he was the one stretched out on the sofa, with a cushion under his raised knee. His eyes were squeezed shut, his jaw clenched in pain. Good, Dinah thought, I hope it hurts like hell.

"Here's your p-p-p-pill," she said, too quickly, as she walked into the den. Dinah took the full mug of root beer from Veevi and gave it to Jake, who grimaced in pain as he swallowed the white tablet.

"Tell Gussie not to cook any red meat for a couple of weeks," he said. "Chicken's okay. Veal, too. Christ, how'm I ever going to go to New York in a month with my knee this way?"

"Best stay off it," Veevi said. Dinah thought, You perfect bitch, having a private joke with him thinking I don't get it.

"Have you been *on* it recently, d-d-d-dear?" said Dinah.

"You mean, like getting down to measure the angle on a putting green? I did do that today. Big mistake," said Jake.

Nice alibi, Dinah thought. She looked at her sister, and then at her husband, and then at her sister, and at her husband again. She told herself point-blank that it was impossible that she should have seen what she surely had. Slowly, she began to feel safe again. If she saw what she thought she had seen, there would have to be a reasonable explanation. Since she didn't want to ask, the best conclusion was that she hadn't seen anything at all.

At dinnertime, Jake's knee began to throb again, so he went upstairs to lie in bed and watch TV. Only the two of them were in the house, Veevi having gone out with some old friends Dinah remembered from the Malibu days—people whom she went outside to wait for in the driveway, since, Dinah assumed, they had refused to set foot inside the house of a stool pigeon. Jake's knee made it impossible for him to come down to dinner, so on a tray she brought up what she called one of her "white trash" meals; that is, the kind of food her father loved—corn bread, macaroni and cheese, pineapple slices with cottage cheese, and lima beans with plenty of salt and pepper and butter. He winced as he sat up in bed, but ate, as he always did, with gusto, his eyes glued to the baseball game.

Dinah sat on the edge of his bed with her arms folded, chewing the inside of her cheek. For a while, she watched the game with him, and then she went over to her own bed. She thumbed through the *Saturday Review,* irritated by the gray roar of the baseball crowd, which sometimes surged and sometimes diminished but never changed pitch. It accompanied every athletic event on television, and Jake watched them all.

Eventually, she lit a cigarette. "Jake, I have to talk to you about something," she said. And she got up and turned off the television.

"Honey!" he objected.

"You didn't hear me. I have to t-t-t-talk to you." She sat down on the nubby candlewick bedspread, facing him.

"What about?" His eyes drifted back yearningly to the television.

"Your knee."

"My knee?"

"I'm not surprised it's hurting you so much, though I wonder why the other one isn't just as sore."

He looked at her, mystified. "What's eating you?"

"Just when I was coming into the den this afternoon, I looked in and saw you on your g-g-g-gouty old knees, leaning over my sister, like you were just about to kiss her. Or crawl on top of her or G-G-G-God knows what. So I turned around and hollered out to you and came back and made a completely f-f-fake entrance."

Jake took a sizable square of buttered corn bread and slowly bit into it. "Well, you should have walked right in the first time," he said with his mouth full. "You could have gotten me out of a real jam."

"Oh? How's that?" She folded her arms across her chest.

"When I came home from golf, I found Veevi in the kitchen. She was crying, and I think she was hungover—she smelled kind of boozy. It seems that Saul proposed to her last night—said he wants to marry her as soon as she gets the divorce from Mike. And I said, 'So what's the problem?' 'I don't want to marry him,' she said. 'Then don't,' I said. 'No one's holding a gun to your head.' She said, 'I'm such a burden to all of you.' And then I said, 'Come into the den, we'll talk about it.' I felt sorry for her, but I thought this was a good time to discuss her plans. So we went into the den, and then, Jesus, we sat there, and she said she had a terrible headache, so she stretched out and put a pillow under her head. Meanwhile, my knee is killing me and I'm wondering where you are. But she keeps talking. Says it's all her fault that she and Mike split up. That he'd had affairs from the beginning but expected her not to, and she was jealous because he fooled around and she didn't, so she had an affair with that artist Gas Bag, or whatever his name is—"

"Just c-c-c-c-cut to the bending-over part. You haven't explained that yet."

"That's true. I won't lie about it. She asked me if I found her attractive, and asked me to kiss her. Just that once. As a favor."

"I see. What if she had asked you to put your th-th-th-thing in her mouth? As a favor."

Dinah kept furiously chewing the inside of her cheek, while smoke from her cigarette drifted upward into her hair.

"Oh, honey, please," he said, showing a sudden prudish distaste for the vulgarity he normally loved in her. He had consumed the hot buttered corn bread and pushed the tray to the side, and now, his hand on his knee, his face again grimaced with pain.

"Well, do you find her attractive? Are you in l-l-l-love with her?"

"Hon-ey! For Christ's sake, *no*."

"You said, in her kitchen in 1938—or was it '37—that she was the most gorgeous creature you had ever laid eyes on."

"I didn't know you then." He smiled.

"Okay, but you were talking to me! I never forget a face. It was you all night. Goddamn drooling over her."

"I will make a sworn statement and have it notarized: I am not personally attracted to your sister. Moreover, I didn't want to kiss her, and if I had actually gone ahead and done it I would've told you."

"She's after you. Just like she was after you the night you guys got back from Paris. You took her out to Chasen's! You didn't even stay and have dinner with me in the hospital!"

He put his hand on his sore knee and winced. "Sweetheart, I can't tell you how wrong you are. If I'd known you didn't want me to go to Chasen's that night, I would have stayed with you. Honest. And your sister isn't after me—not by a long shot. It's a grotesque thought, by the way. She wants what she had, and there's nobody out here who's going to give her that. Anyway, how could I possibly want anyone but you? Huh? She was just testing the waters and wanted to find out—she just wanted me to tell her, or show her, that she doesn't have to be stuck with a rebarbative bore like Saul Landau. She's never had to face the future without a man, and she's scared. It was pitiful, actually. That Veevi Milligan Ventura Albrecht should have to ask a guy to kiss her is just pathetic."

Dinah sat back, chewed her thumb, and stared at him.

"I feel sorry for her," he said. "I know she was a legend all those years ago, and had every writer in Hollywood at her feet, but Jesus, those days are over and that stunning young woman is gone. She knows it, too. She's drowning in self-pity, and I'm dying for her to get out of this house and into a place of her own. If giving her some kind of kiss is going to jump-start her on a new life, it's a small price to pay. Problem is even then it won't do any good. If you're not part of that Paris world she's fled, then you don't exist for her. And don't think I haven't noticed the way she treats you, either—like a slave. You love her, I can see it, and maybe she loves you, too, if she still has the capacity to love anyone, but it's not a very kind or thoughtful sort of love. It's, you know, family love—the kind you take for granted, the kind everybody takes for granted."

"So now you're a philosopher of love. Well, 'home is where you hang,' as my father used to say."

"Exactly. I've put that in my notes, too."

"Do you put everything in your notes, like 'Today I humiliated my w-w-w-wife'?"

"Come here, baby," Jake said, beckoning to her with his arm. "I'm sorry you had to play that undignified little charade this afternoon."

He patted a place beside him on the bed, and she went over to him, lifted the tray onto the floor, and sat down. She felt limp, and ashamed. He put his arm around her and she melted against him. "You didn't make it up," he said huskily. "I was leaning over her, and I was going to kiss her. But only because she asked me to. I would've given anything not to do it. It wouldn't have been for real."

He kissed her, softly at first, then harder. "Like this," he said.

But Dinah drew back. "You never tell me I'm b-b-b-beautiful."

He laughed a little. "I don't?"

"No. Never once."

"Well, the word I would use is *handsome*."

Again, she pulled away and made a face. "What's wrong with *beautiful*? What would it cost you, huh?"

"Oh, honey, you're my wife. I love you. But you know the kind of guy I am. It's hard for me to say things like that. I love the way you look. You're better than beautiful. *Beautiful* is a fucking cliché. There are thousands of girls out here who are beautiful. I see them every day at the studio, and let me tell you, honey, they're boring as hell—boring to look at, boring to talk to. I can't remember one face from the other. But handsome? Classy? Elegant? Interesting? Intriguing? Sexy? That's you." Pulling her toward him, he squeezed her and nuzzled her neck. His hands felt warm on her skin. "We're one person, you and I. When I'm not with you, I'm only half alive. You're my wife. It's you I want. Always."

She swallowed. There was a sudden heat in her throat and eyes, a sprouting of tears. He pressed his large warm hand around her cheek again. "There's nobody in the world for me but you." She groaned a little, and the tears rolled and splashed. She knew that he had now seen her naked need for love, and her fear of losing it. She pressed her face into his T-shirt with shame. And as she clung to him, allowing herself to be held, a different heat stole over her—the heat of safety, of completeness, of belonging, and desire.

She tore off her clothes and, naked, lay on her side, straining to fit her body to his. "Will you do something for me?" he asked suddenly. "Something I've never asked you to do?"

"What? Stand on my head? Do s-s-s-somersaults? What?"

His eyes were bright, as if he were taken with his own ingenuity.

"Go into your dressing room and put on something sexy."

"Like what?"

"I don't know. Stockings, maybe. One of those things you put on, you know, to hold up the stockings."

"A garter belt?"

"Yeah. And put some makeup on—you know, eye stuff, lip rouge."

"What for?" He had never asked her to do anything like this before, and she was bewildered.

"Because I'd like it. Because it's sexy."

"You just told me how s-s-s-sexy I am."

"Of course you are, baby. This is just to do something a little different."

"Well, I don't *have* a garter belt—I only have girdles. And if you think they're sexy, you're in real tr-tr-tr-trouble."

"Don't you have something black? What's that kind of a lacy thing that pushes your knockers up?"

"A merry widow?"

"Yeah. Don't you have one of those?"

Her own desire was rapidly fading and his erection was shrinking, but, feeling she was to blame, she got out of bed and disappeared into her dressing room. Trying not to think too hard about why he wanted her to put on this weird getup, and why she didn't, she opened a drawer and began sorting through her underthings. She found a black lace merry widow with a tiny red satin bow. She sucked in her belly and, one by one, methodically worked from waist to breast the long row of hooks and eyes, although what she really wanted to do was tear off the tight, scratchy "garment," as, she suddenly remembered, her mother-in-law would have called it. She found a pair of stockings, the kind with seams, pulled them on, and hitched them to the garters. Then she slipped into a pair of black suede high heels.

Sitting at her dressing table, she could feel the upholstered raw silk of the stool against her bare behind, and she felt ridiculous. Nevertheless, she applied red lipstick to her mouth, and green eye shadow to her eyes, adding black mascara, which she dried with the eyelash curler. Everything was taking so long that she wondered whether Jake had fallen asleep. What if she walked into the bedroom in this getup and he was no longer interested? She would feel like an idiot, she told herself. She daubed some perfume on her neck and in her artificially pushed-together cleavage and her pubic hair, which exposed the scar from her hysterectomy and struck her as grotesquely ugly under the edges of the merry widow. Feeling unfamiliar to herself, and hurt by Jake's sudden whim, she went out to him as if he were a stranger.

He lay dozing on top of the sheets. His pajama top was unbuttoned; his penis small and limp. She lay down beside him and fondled it again, and he blinked but didn't open his eyes. He began to grow hard again in little leaps and stretches. Resenting him, she thought, I've gone and done myself up like he asked and now it's going to be one of those half-dead ones where he never opens his eyes. "Jake," she said. He opened one eye.

"Let me look at you," he said drowsily, as if chronic somnolence were his natural state and the bursts of energy required for daily life only a brief respite from permanent exhaustion. "Stand up," he murmured.

She got up from the bed and stood in front of him. His eyes swept over her.

"You look great. Come here. Dance a little."

She approached him the way she thought he wanted her to, with a bump-and-grind—something that she, with her dancer's body, knew how to do. She had done it long ago, before they were married, and since then, too—in her nightgown or her underwear or with a towel around her or naked. And it had been she herself who did the sexy, slinky dance, and not some gotten-up imitation of a five-dollar whore.

He smiled at her with half-closed eyes, reaching out to grab her. For a moment, she stood over him and he kneaded her ass. Then, not wanting him to sense what she felt, and knowing what he loved, she leaned over and put her mouth around him. "Oh, boy," he said.

Oh, boy, she thought. That's what he says when he's about to eat a hot dog at a baseball game.

After a few moments, he stopped her and motioned to her with both hands. "Climb aboard," he said. "And watch my knee!"

It wasn't what she wanted, and she couldn't let go. So often, in the past, her love for Jake and her faith in the rightness of their marriage had been wordlessly renewed when they made love, and every little familiar routine—his hands sliding underneath her buttocks when he lay on top of her, her rooting in his chest hair and his neck—had spoken of their knowledge of each other's body, of their soldered selves. She yearned now for the old connection, but it wasn't there. And again she blamed herself and did what she had never done before: she moaned and groaned and clutched and bucked, faking it all. He came quickly—too quickly—but powerfully, explosively, with a hoarse cry and a sudden shrinkage within her. Lengthening herself on top of him, carefully avoiding his knee, she brought her head to his chest. His heartbeat was subsiding, and she reached up and felt the sweat on his forehead.

She felt sure that it wasn't she who had caused that explosion of lust, but whatever character she had become for him in this "costume drama," as she silently called it. Perhaps it was a memory of themselves, when they weren't yet married, hadn't had children, and were still in the throes of their stormy on-again, off-again three-year affair, with its quarrels and passionate reconciliations? She did not know and could not ask. There were certain things they had always been able to say to each other. Organs could be named, dirty words used, jokes made. But some kinds of talking were beyond her, because she was shy and proud and embarrassed, and, glib as he was, with his ready store of answers to everything, there were things—

tender, loving things—he could not bring himself to say, although she yearned to hear them.

She rolled off him and sat up. "Sorry, but this thing is driving me n-n-n-nuts," she said. She unhooked the stockings and rolled them down, letting them fall to the carpet; then she unhooked the merry widow and tossed it to the floor. Naked, she was herself again, and even felt the return of desire. She snuggled up against Jake, placing his hand inside her spread legs.

"Didn't you come?" he said, his voice muzzy. "It sounded like you'd landed on the moon."

"Well, of course I did," she said. "But I want more. 'Cause you were so great."

"Uh-huh," he said drowsily. He dispassionately began to play with her, using a series of practiced moves that had been worked out between them many years ago.

A couple of times, she put her hand on his to make him pause, because his fingers were working stolidly, mechanically. Oh God, he's on the assembly line tonight, she thought; this was the expression she used when she felt that his heart just wasn't in it. It was obvious that he wanted more than anything else to drift off to sleep.

But now, as if to erase what she had just recognized, she felt that she had to come, had to find pleasure, had to obliterate the vision of herself in the merry widow and high heels. She wanted everything to be the way it used to be. Oh, give up, she said to herself—just let him go to sleep. But she continued to labor away in the solitary confinement of unfulfilled desire, while sensing acutely her husband's satiation and indifference. She told him to touch her nipples, to suck them. Why, after all this time, do I have to ask? she wondered. Why doesn't he just *do* these things? Doesn't he *know* by now? I know what *he* likes, I do what *he* wants without having to be asked; why doesn't it work the other way?

She could tell that he wanted to sleep—that the automatic moves learned long ago were, for him, a chore. So she got him to stop and start, fighting her own resistance to pleasure with small escapes from it that she used to force-feed desire. I am being *serviced,* she told herself. Finally, she realized that the climbing and the retreating were futile. Her body gave up, and she said to herself, indignant at her own recalcitrance and nearly exploding with anger at herself and at him, *I want this*. Through slightly opened eyes she guided his hand, instructing him to put two or three fingers inside her and then to press hard with his thumb on the outside. In

this way, with these precise movements and unromantically detailed instructions, the pleasure mounted, like a donkey climbing a mountain in
Peru, and she came, but in a searing explosion of loneliness and despair,
without joy or connection.

It seemed to Dinah that she should say something to Veevi. But what? And
how? She brooded, and waited for the right moment, and had imaginary
confrontations in her head. "Now, listen," she said, her speech clear as
January in California, "I don't care how down and out and pathetic you are;
keep your goddamn hands off my husband." Every time she rehearsed this
scene she felt exhilarated, and she decided, about a week later, that she
would actually speak her piece. It was a hot Sunday afternoon. Jake was
away playing golf, and the Lasker kids, along with Veevi's little Coco, were
splashing and shrieking in the pool. Claire was stretched out on a towel
along the hot terra-cotta tiles, roasting herself through a glaze of coconut
oil. Any moment now, Dinah expected Veevi to come out to the pool after
a long lunch date with Saul. She decided that she would say what she had
to say quietly and firmly, though she shuddered at the prospect. After all,
she couldn't remember when she had ever spoken with true harshness to
her sister.

She took a drag on her cigarette and continued knitting, determined
not to cave in.

Veevi did at last appear, wearing a two-piece bathing suit and a terry-
cloth jacket, and carrying a large paper bag in which, Dinah assumed, she
had some crocheting, books, cigarettes, and the Sunday papers. Dinah was
counting stitches herself and barely glanced up as her sister settled in a
comfortable pool chair. Both women wore straw hats and sunglasses. Veevi
smiled at Dinah and began to apply suntan lotion to her arms, shoulders,
and midriff. Dinah immediately began to relent. Then her resolve doubled.
"Vee . . ." she began.

"Mmm," Veevi murmured, not looking up.

"There's something I have to say to you."

"Mmm?"

"Vee. Look at me."

Veevi looked up, blank-faced. Dinah couldn't see her eyes behind the
dark glasses.

"I saw you and J-J-J-Jake. Last week. In the den."

"Oh, my God," Veevi said, speaking rapidly. "So embarrassing . . . entirely my fault. Made an absolute ass of myself. Christ, I'm sorry."

"F-F-F-Forget it," Dinah said. "It never happened."

She looked up. Veevi was making a "Can-you-forgive-me?" bubby face, to which Dinah nodded and made her own: "Of course I forgive you."

Desperate to change the subject, she took a closer look at the large paper bag Veevi had brought with her. "What're all those clothes in there?" she asked.

Veevi explained that they were clothes Saul had collected for old friends and their families who had been blacklisted and were now living in Mexico; he was terribly busy with work and had asked her as a favor to pack them up and send them for him. Some of them were very nice, actually—donated by people like Evelyn Morocco, who made annual trips to Bergdorf's and believed fervently in cashmere. Saul had said that Veevi was to let Claire take a look and pick some of them out for herself before she sent them off.

As she spoke, she pulled one item of clothing after another out of the bag, and soon there was a large pile at her feet, out of which she selected individual pieces to show Dinah. Calling softly to Claire, she told her to go through them, and the girl, who had her mother's good proportions, held up one piece after another, deciding which ones to take. It was at this point that Lorna, who adored her older cousin and was fascinated by everything she did, came out of the pool to see what was going on. She stood with water dripping down her legs and a large towel around her shoulders, listening as Veevi repeated to Claire that the clothes were being sent to poor friends in Mexico but that Saul had distinctly told her that Claire was to have as many of them as she liked.

"Oh, can I have some, too?" said Lorna.

"Why, no, dear," Veevi answered at once. "Claire's thin, and you're fat, and Claire's poor, and you're rich."

Stung to the quick by these words, Lorna looked from Veevi to her mother, her face reddening and her eyes filling with tears.

Dinah did not lift her eyes from her knitting, and said nothing.

"I hate you, Veevi," said Lorna. "I hope you die. I hate you too, Mommy." She turned away and walked toward the house, pulling the wet towel tightly around her. Dinah saw Lorna through Veevi's eyes, saw her fat behind, and knew without a doubt that she had failed her child once again—failed to protect her and stand up for her, failed to rebuke Veevi for the delicate cruelty of those words.

When Dinah finally glanced in Veevi's direction, she still couldn't see behind the dark glasses. But Veevi kept giving clothes to Claire, and telling her how marvelous she was going to look in them and what a good figure she had and how much the poor children of the blacklisted writers in Mexico were going to appreciate the rest. Since Claire didn't ask what *blacklisted* meant, Dinah assumed that she knew, and that Veevi had told her why Jake was not blacklisted and why Veevi herself was.

Dinah brooded all afternoon about that incident. She went upstairs to Lorna's room and found her sitting on the cork floor next to the dollhouse she had gotten for Christmas. Dinah had bought it for her because it looked so much like the Laskers' house—a large Tudor mansion with an upstairs and a downstairs and a great many rooms. If Lorna made her bed, kept her room neat, and helped Gussie out after dinner, she was allowed to buy one piece of doll furniture and one piece of doll clothing a week; the house was becoming quite amply furnished with tiny sofas and tables, lamps and bathtubs and numerous beds and cribs for the Doll family's many children.

In fact, the nursery already boasted four baby dolls. The Doll mommy liked having babies, and, according to Lorna, her goal was ten. When Dinah looked inside the house today, she found Mommy and Daddy Doll and the three larger Doll children at the dinner table. There was a Negro maid doll wearing a white uniform and an apron. She was standing in the dining room holding a tray with tiny bowls in which Lorna had placed minuscule carrots and cauliflower and steaks. Her name was Gussie. There was also a white-haired grandmother doll. Dinah asked Lorna what the Doll family were talking about at dinner and what kind of day they had all had, but Lorna didn't answer. Usually Lorna had a long story to tell about the dolls, with elaborate details about the babies—who was walking, who was talking—and which older Doll kids had gone to a birthday party, nursed a sick baby through a cold, or tried to fly. But today she sat with her lips tight, not looking at her mother.

"Maybe tonight, when it's bath time, you can tell me what happened with the D-D-D-Dolls today," Dinah said, standing up and lightly touching her daughter's blond braids, but Lorna jerked her head away.

"Why can't you talk right?" she spat out. "What's wrong with you, any-way?"

Dinah paused, but the child refused to meet her eyes.

Next door, in the bathroom next to Jake's office, Veevi was taking a shower. Dinah went in and sat on the unmade bed to wait. She was going to say something. Folding her arms, she leaned back against the wall and allowed her eyes to travel around the room. Veevi's clothes were stacked haphazardly on the armchairs. She used the closet in Coco's room for her dresses and slacks because there was really nowhere to hang anything in the office.

Lying next to the pillow was a book—the new John O'Hara, *Ten North Frederick*. She picked it up and opened it and a letter fell out. Carefully, she unfolded it. The shower stopped. Breathing fast, she skimmed the let-ter. Phrases leaped out at her: "heavily camouflaged trip . . . absolute cir-cumspection . . . figure out a place to meet . . . never stopped loving you all these years. Cliff." She folded the letter and put it back in the book just as the door opened and Veevi came out, looking scrubbed and fresh.

Cliff Boatwright and Veevi? Now, this was interesting. Was he married? Divorced? What was his situation? What did he mean by "heavily camou-flaged"? All Dinah's resolve to say something to Veevi about Lorna disap-peared as she watched her sister remove her bathrobe and slip into one of her new pairs of Jax slacks and a light blue cotton shirt and fasten her hair back with a tortoiseshell barrette. There was no doubt about it: Veevi looked better. When had the letter come?

"Shall we?" Veevi said.

"Shall we what?"

"It's five, Sister Ina," Veevi said. "Time for a drink."

She went to pick up her book.

"Any good?" Dinah said as they headed toward the stairs.

"Well, it's not—"

"Ben Knight or Mike Albrecht. But would it make a picture?"

"For Jake? Haven't read very far. But I don't think so. Not his sort of thing. Here," she said, taking the letter out of the book and handing it to Dinah as they reached the foot of the stairs. "You read it while I was in the shower, didn't you?" She was smiling.

"Sk-Sk-Skimmed it, actually."

They reached the den. The kids were watching television and didn't look up. "Read it," Veevi said, going into the bar. "Chivas on the rocks?" Dinah nodded and settled on the love seat, and this time she read Clifford Boatwright's letter to Veevi with great care.

While Jake was in the middle of his new project, Izzie Morocco and Mel Gordon called and begged him to take over their picture, whose director had dropped dead of a heart attack right on the set. It meant a lot of good fast money, a nice credit, and a chance to work again with Wynn Tooling and Maureen Tolliver. The minute Jake said yes, the household went on what he called "military alert." Dinah took charge: everything and everyone had to follow a strict schedule, for nothing was allowed to disturb Jake or interfere with his requirements for food, rest, sleep, and order. No fugitive crayons were to be left in the den, waiting to bruise an unsuspecting adult's tender barefoot instep. No wet bathing suits dripping on the stairs. The large house, with its great white-painted brick façade; Gussie at the vacuum cleaner; the gardener working in the flower beds; the pool man's quiet strokes as he plied his net across the surface of the water, scooping up dead bugs and sodden leaves; the children eating early in the kitchen and sent to bed before their father came home—all were ruled by Jake's one great purpose: to finish shooting the picture in five weeks, obtain first-rate performances from the actors, win undying love from cast and crew, and remain in or under budget.

So Veevi's affair with Clifford Boatwright couldn't have come at a better time. He was on the Coast for a month, talking secretly with Irv Engel, and working on a play for a new and very ambitious television project, *Electro's American Scenes.* It was the brainchild of Ira Zeigler, who would be producing for NBC hour-and-a-half-long original plays once a month on Tuesday nights, sponsored by the Electro Corporation, a huge home appliances company. He wanted only top writing, acting, and directing talent, and he'd gone straight to Clifford for the first play.

"But Clifford's blacklisted," Dinah said to Veevi. "How's he gonna do it? A fr-fr-fr-front?"

"Exactly. He's out here writing the play, consulting with Zeigler, but when he's done Ira will fly to New York and meet with him and the front—who's—who's a relative of Eve, Cliff's wife"—Dinah locked eyes with Veevi at this information, but Veevi just continued—"and after Ira and Cliff coach him—the kid's a graduate student in classics somewhere—Ira's going to take him to meetings with the NBC execs. Oh, Jesus, they're going to put one over on those guys." She threw her head back and laughed as she headed out the door toward her new MG, a bag of books in her hand. Every day she drove to the Château Marmont and worked for Jake in Boatwright's suite, he typing in the bedroom, she reading in the living room. More often than not, she stayed overnight and came home to the Laskers' only to type up a report for Jake, shower, change, and see Coco and Claire in the afternoons.

She was transformed, Dinah thought, no doubt about it. Her skin was clear, her eyes shone, she walked and moved with the old majesty and assurance. She and Boatwright were crazy about each other, Dinah explained to Nelly Steiner one day as they ate lunch together under the awning of Nelly's pool house. Boatwright had been insanely in love with Veevi forever—since he'd first come out to Hollywood. But they'd lost touch during the war. He'd written her once in Paris, after he'd read about her marriage to Mike, and she'd written him back. He'd written again, but she hadn't answered. "But you know about his wife, don't you?" Nelly said, pouring Dinah a cup of tea.

"Eve Leyburn? I know she's a damn good actress. And that it's her cousin who's the front for Cliff."

"Don't you know about her and Clifford's brother?"

"Wait a second," Dinah said. "I think I heard something. They were engaged?"

"They were engaged, and he was sent to the Pacific. And killed on an aircraft carrier that was kamikaze'd. She was pregnant at the time. Had the baby. Cliff came back from the war—I think he flew bombing missions—and married her, and now they have five kids, plus the first one."

"The brother's?"

"Six altogether. Eve works, but the blacklist has made it tough for her, though it's not as tough for people in the theater, in New York, as it is out here. They live with his mother, according to my friend Shirley Dunlop, who's an old friend of Eve's from summer stock. The mother has money."

"In other w-w-w-words, he's never going to get a divorce," said Dinah.

"Never. Does your sister know that?"

"I don't see her anymore!" Dinah said. "She's spending her time with Cliff, and it's fine this way. Delicious, really. I've got my thoroughly exhausted husband to myself again at night."

When Jake was directing, Dinah was more indispensable to him than ever, and she went about her days in a state of ascetic rapture. The short hours between his homecoming late at night and his headfirst dive into oblivious sleep were hers. And then, of course, there was the prestige, the glory of it all. There were mentions in the trades. The telephone rang; invitations poured in. Joyously, she turned down almost all of them: "Can't do it—Jake's shooting right now." The pleasure of saying those words was immense. She didn't have to entertain, or go out. When friends called to ask "How's the picture going?" she gave them the vague "Oh, great, great." As Jake had instructed, she admitted no problems or impediments, even if the night before he had come home cursing Irv, Izzie, and Mel, who had criticized the rushes and had pointed out to him that Maureen Tolliver was obviously stuffing her bra with Kleenex, since her boobs changed size from one scene to another.

Had Veevi been there, Dinah would have had to share him, and these times when he needed care and attention were too special for Dinah to want her sister there. Veevi, in turn, wasn't about to bring Boatwright over to the house. Of course, he wouldn't have come anyway; he had notoriously defied the Committee and spent a year in jail.

he picture was difficult. Mel and Izzy had written a sharp, gag-filled satire on the advertising business, and everything had to be fast—the one-liners, the physical comedy, the tempo of the scenes. Lothar Selz, the director who'd died—both Dinah and Veevi remembered him from the old days in Malibu, after Dorshka managed to get him out of Germany—and whom Jake greatly respected, had nevertheless his own rhythm, which was terrific for physical comedy but too fast for the jokes. Jake spent a lot of time in the cutting room at night going over the scenes that had already been shot and making sure his own tempo didn't clash with Selz's, while at the same time keeping the emphasis on the words. By the third week, he was irritable and anxious and couldn't wait for the picture to be over. So, for Easter vacation the Laskers rented a house in Palm Springs, sight un-seen, right on the edge of the desert. Veevi was back on Delfern Drive again. Boatwright had gone home to New York to finish his play, and there were no plans for him to return to L.A. for the time being.

Dinah and Veevi drove down alone with the Lasker kids and Coco. Gussie had taken the week off to visit relatives in Marlin, Texas, and Claire had gone skiing in Mammoth with friends from school. Dinah did all the cooking and watched over the children, while Veevi parked herself on the patio, supposedly reading scripts and novels and writing synopses for Jake. Dinah noticed that she had become very quiet. Opening the sliding doors to invite Veevi in for lunch, she waited for her sister. As Veevi stepped into the house, Dinah said, "He's not going to leave his w-w-w-wife, is he?"

"No," Veevi answered, coming into the kitchen and sitting inside the breakfast nook. "But I never thought he would."

Liar, thought Dinah.

"You'll meet someone else, Vee. But he's been great for you. You look wonderful. Got those roses in your cheeks again."

Veevi laughed. "He's not that great in the sack, if that's what you mean."

"But he loves you, doll. I knew it eighteen years ago."

"A lot of good that does me." She took a sip of iced tea. "Oh, stupid men and their dreary wives."

Dinah was looking forward to Good Friday, when Jake was finally driving down for the weekend. After two or three days in the small, unprepossessing house, she regretted the decision to rent it and wondered why she had let Jake have his way with the fantasy of "camping out" in what to her was a thoroughly dull and unattractive place. She wished they had gone to Deep Well, where they usually stayed. But he had been anxious about money recently, despite the windfall of the directing assignment, and he was adamant: the children were growing up amid too much luxury, and they were beginning to take it for granted. She knew the real reason for his skittishness: he was about to dive into something he'd never done before, and when the movie was over, he'd go back to this new project, something exciting and scary—a Broadway show, which he was doing on spec. And it was crucial for them to economize, now that he had Veevi on the payroll and was supplementing the paltry sums Mike sent for Claire and Coco. With her own doubts about luxury, Dinah was glad when they weren't spending money, or planning to spend money. But this house was a mistake—a charmless, cramped assemblage of concrete, plate glass, and synthetic-wood paneling in a development that had been thrown up now that the building shortages of the Korean War were over. The dull ocher sofas, bought, she imagined, from some department store in nearby Indio, depressed her. And there was only one bathroom—not nearly enough, she thought, to accommodate three adults and three kids.

The house was, moreover, in a small, anonymous neighborhood where year-round residents, needing relief from the heat and relentless sunshine that L.A. weekenders craved, lived in the long purple shadows cast by the nearby mountains. So the day's swimming ended early. Lorna and Coco slept on cots in the dining alcove; Peter had agreed to share his room, which had twin beds, with Veevi. He was very fond of his aunt, and had no intention of sleeping with the girls. On Saturday, Jake and Dinah drove off to Tamarisk Country Club, where he played golf and Dinah had a lesson; Jake wanted her to learn the game so that the two of them could eventually play together. At first, Dinah told him she couldn't go, since there was no one to take the kids to the neighborhood pool, but Veevi had uncharacteristically volunteered to watch over them, adding quietly that anyone could see that Jake had had a hard week and obviously needed to have some time alone with her.

That afternoon, while Jake and Dinah were on the golf course, Veevi lay stretched out by the side of the small neighborhood pool, which was filled with kids. She read *The New Yorker* while they swam, occasionally clasping it to her chest to save it from cannonball splashes, or gazing up at the mountains as she smoked. Peter found her interest in his dives gratifying and asked her repeatedly to watch him when he did a swan dive or a jackknife, and she did watch, praising him and appearing to be altogether more interested in his diving than his mother usually was.

The sun shone clear and hot until three o'clock. Then the shadows tumbled down from the mountains in a violet avalanche. By three-thirty, it was no longer hot enough to swim and Veevi and the kids started the short trek home. There were very few cars in sight, but they walked along the desert side of the road, against traffic, just in case. Chilled by their clinging wet bathing suits, the kids, with towels slung around their shoulders, walked in their bare feet, feeling the sharp edges of pebbles in the newly laid asphalt road. The desert breeze raised goose bumps on their skin, which smelled of chlorine. Lorna and Coco were absorbed in comparing water wrinkles on the tips of their fingers. Peter walked slowly beside his aunt, his head down and his eyes riveted to the selvage of sand between roadway and desert.

"Pete, I've been meaning to ask you all week," said Veevi, "why you always keep your eyes on the road. Are you looking for rocks or something?"

"Well," Peter said, giving her a quizzical look, as if he were debating whether to answer her. "I hate to say this, but I'm really scared of lizards and snakes. Especially rattlers."

"Are you? I didn't know."

She reached over and took his hand. He didn't like her taking it, although he liked her, and he let it lie limply in hers, as if it belonged to somebody else.

"They come out when it's hot and lie on the road," he said. "And there's probably lots of them just a little ways from here. Out there." He nodded toward the desert, which stretched out to his left the way beach turned suddenly into ocean.

"But have you ever actually seen one?"

"Yep. One time Mom took us to the Agua Caliente reservation and there was this huge yellow-and-black diamondback rattler curled up by the side of the road, ready to strike."

He let go of her hand to form the size and shape of the snake's head with his own. His face, too, became the snake's face, his teeth the bared fangs. Then his frightened eyes returned to the black asphalt road, which was still warm underfoot.

"I don't think you've got anything to worry about," Veevi told him. "There are too many people here."

"I saw two this week: one on the back porch and one just off the road."

"Snakes, or lizards?"

"One snake, one lizard. The snake was a rattler. I mean, I'm pretty sure it was a rattler. It was in the sand—gliding really fast. The lizard was on the porch."

"Well, rattlers *are* scary. But they're scared of you, too. And lizards aren't dangerous. Snakes can be dangerous, but not lizards. Why are you so afraid of them?"

"I don't know," he said, as if he, too, were puzzled by this. "There's just something about them."

"I used to see lots of desert creatures—lizards, snakes, Gila monsters—in Death Valley, when I went camping with Grandpa Milligan. Do you remember him?"

Peter nodded. "He had these false teeth, Veevi, and they were stained all black from chewing tobacco."

"Pop was a real old-timey kind of guy," Veevi said. "He loved the outdoors."

Peter paused, because he could tell that he was supposed to say he loved it, too. "Actually, I don't like the outdoors that much."

"Oh, I know, you like music. You're an artist. But you can like the outdoors, too. You don't have to like just one and not the other."

"Well, I like fencing. I brought my foil down with my clarinet. Did you see me practicing foil out on the patio?"

"Oh, I did, my love. Now, that's an elegant sport. I like that very much about you, you know, that you're a fencer."

It made him feel funny when she called him "my love" or when she came into the living room to watch him practice the clarinet. She hadn't done that for a while; lately, she hadn't been there when he got home from school. But now, here she was again, part of the family, and he found it pleasant, despite her endearments, to walk beside her while she listened so intently. "There was this kid at school," he said. "He stepped on a lizard one day. It was on a brick patio right outside the classroom, and when the kid stepped on the lizard's head its eyes popped out. They were all red. It was *disgusting*. My dad wants me to go to a psychiatrist because I'm afraid of lizards, and because I like fencing but not baseball, and also because I don't like vegetables and having short hair. My mom says I don't have to if I don't want to, but he says I'm an oddball."

He waited to hear whose side she would take.

"No," she said, "you're not an oddball. You're special. You're going to be a great musician one day. I can tell."

"My father thinks the clarinet's a weirdo instrument. He thinks I should play the piano. Or the sax. He says if I learn sax I can play in a band in high school and meet girls at dances."

"Your father, if I may say so," said Veevi, "is full of shit."

He laughed out loud, free, for the moment, from his rattlesnake watch. But when Veevi reached for his hand again, he stuck it into the pocket of his wet bathing trunks before she could grab hold of it.

When they reached the house, they saw Jake's moss-green Caddy in the garage, next to Dinah's big Pontiac woody. Lorna dashed ahead to find Dinah, leaving Coco dawdling behind. But the bedroom door was closed, which meant, everyone knew, that Jake and Dinah were taking a nap, a situation that always made Peter feel uneasy, though he didn't know why. Disappointed, the Lasker children each went their separate ways—Lorna into the shower and Peter to his bedroom to get out of his wet trunks and into something dry. Since his parents were sleeping, he couldn't practice the clarinet. He stretched out on his bed and opened his Freddy the Pig book. Later, he'd go out and practice with his foil. Veevi was in the kitchen, getting Coco graham crackers and milk.

After her shower, Lorna bounded into the living room, her hair in a dripping ponytail, and plopped down on the rug with several members of the Doll family and a box of clothes for them. Ignoring Veevi, she handed a baby doll to Coco. Veevi sat on the sofa with her legs tucked up underneath her, reading *The New Yorker*. Then she yawned, gazed blankly out the plate glass window, and got up and went into the room she shared with Peter.

She let her pool slippers drop to the rug and lay back on her bed on the other side of the room with her arms folded under her chest. "You don't mind if I have a li'l nap, dear, do you?" she said.

"No, it's okay," he said, getting up and putting his sneakers on.

"You don't have to leave, dear."

"That's okay," he said. He didn't mind it when she slept in his room at night, but there was something about being awake in a room with a sleeping grown-up that made him feel strange, and he took his book and his long, gleaming foil and slipped out as quickly as possible.

No sooner had he settled himself on the sofa than Veevi padded back into the living room. "Can't sleep," she said almost apologetically. He was lying full length, the book propped up against his knees, but he sat up to make room for her.

"Oh, don't get up, Peter," she said.

"That's okay." He liked her, but he wished she wouldn't always pay so much attention to him.

"When are Mom and Dad gonna wake up?" he said to no one in particular.

"They're resting for a party tonight," said Lorna importantly. "At George Joy's."

Lorna raised her eyebrows dramatically, as she did whenever she spoke of the famous people her parents knew.

"He has a house down here, too, huh?" Peter asked, not especially interested.

"Of course," said Lorna. "Don't you read the movie magazines?"

"No, birdbrain, I don't. But you do. They're written for birdbrains like you."

Lorna replied with dignity, "Don't call me a birdbrain. I hardly ever read movie magazines."

"You do, too. You give your allowance to Gussie and you get her to buy them for you."

"I do not."

"Liar. You do, too."

"I dislike you intensely," she said, turning away from Peter to concentrate on pulling a formal white tulle ball gown, a pair of tiny white satin high heels, and a little white fluffy fur stole out of her box of doll clothes.

"I dislike you intensely," Peter retorted.

Although she didn't want to talk to Veevi, Lorna needed to check the plans. "Who's coming to baby-sit for us tonight?" she asked, all business.

"No one."

"Aren't you going to the party, too?"

"Heavens, no. I can't stand big parties. I'm staying home. So I guess I'm the babysitter."

"Why?" said Peter. "We don't need a baby-sitter. I'm the oldest and I can do it."

"I can do it, too," said Lorna.

"We'll have lots of fun!" said his aunt. "We're going to dye Easter eggs. Your mother got me all the equipment. We'll do it tonight!"

"Why can't you stand them?" Lorna probed.

"Why can't I stand what?" Veevi said.

"Big parties."

"Because I can't, that's why."

Lorna persisted. "Didn't you like them when you were a big star, in the olden days?"

"No. I never went to that many even then. I've always loathed them."

Lorna eyed her aunt skeptically, disbelieving every word. Moreover, the thought of having to dye Easter eggs under her aunt's supervision didn't thrill her.

"What does 'loathe' mean?" Peter shouted out excitedly. "You and Mom always use that word. 'Oh, I loathe him,' " he mimicked.

"It means hate," Lorna said. "Anybody knows that, birdbrain."

"Fuck you," Peter said.

"Fuck you, too," Lorna said.

"I dislike you intensely," Peter said.

"I dislike you intensely, too," said Lorna.

"You think you know everything, but you don't, moron," said Peter.

"Actually, Peter, Lorna's right," said Veevi. She was smiling at him, as if to say, "Lorna *is* a birdbrain. You and I both know that, of course. But sometimes even a birdbrain knows something we don't."

Lorna caught it all—the looks between them and everything they implied. She began taking off the ball gown in which she'd dressed one of the dolls. "She's changed her mind," she said. "She doesn't want to go to the big, fancy party. She's going to go to *college*. 'Cause she's so smart."

Peter put his book down, took up his foil, and headed for the sliding screen doors. He thought he might as well go out to the patio and practice lunges. Veevi got up and followed, leaning against the glass door, with a drink in one hand and a cigarette in the other, watching as he stood sideways, in profile. Holding up his left arm in a stiff curl, he lunged forward until his left calf nearly touched the ground and the foil in his extended right arm tipped forward into the empty air.

"En garde!" Veevi cried out, to his embarrassment.

He advanced and advanced, lunging and thrusting, then retreating, his left arm still held up in a half-moon curve above his head.

"God, you're getting so good at this," said Veevi. "It's so great for your muscles. I wish Mike could see this. He'd go crazy for it."

He knew that Mike was her husband, or used to be her husband, and that they were getting divorced. But he had no memory of a face to match with the name.

Suddenly he saw his mother sliding the screen door open. She came up to Veevi and stood beside her, wearing her soft blue wool bathrobe, with the belt tied around her waist and one satin-edged lapel folded over the other to keep out the early-evening chill. She rubbed her tanned forearms and yawned.

"Who're you slicing up out there, darling? Anyone I know?" she called out to Peter.

"You know, Dinah, he's really very good," Veevi said.

"Yes, I *do* know, actually. Even in Los Angeles we hicks are able to recognize gr-gr-gr-grace and agility." She was surprised at her sarcasm. The words had just slid out, and she wished they hadn't. She was irritated that Veevi had refused to come to the party tonight. How was she ever going to meet someone single and available if she didn't make an effort? Why did she insist, Dinah wondered, on isolating and removing herself from any chance of a new start, especially since the Boatwright affair was clearly a fizzle?

"Come on, give your muddoo a hug," she said to Peter, using his old baby word for mother. Peter came over to her, placing the foil tip backward under his arm, and threw his arm around her, kissing her and letting her tousle his hair. He didn't often let her do this anymore; he usually shrank from kisses and caresses. But at the moment the nearness of his mother's body pleased him. She was deeply tanned after a week in the desert. She smelled like warm toast, and her voice sounded like the notes of a piano.

About twenty minutes later, Dinah called everyone to the round Formica table in the eat-in kitchen. Supper consisted of Dinah's tried-and-true macaroni and cheese, heated baked beans from a can, saltines, cottage cheese, and pineapple cubes. Lorna pestered her with one question after another about the party: What time was it going to start? Which famous people were going to be there?

Jake strode into the kitchen, pulled open the refrigerator door, pulled off a leg from a broiled chicken wrapped in foil, and tore into it.

"Here's old Dads," Dinah said, "curing himself of malnutrition." She shook her head but smiled up at him, an especially intimate smile. "Honey," she said, "Lorna wants to know who's going to be at George's tonight."

"You mean name-type folk?" His mouth was full. "I'm not sure. He knows a lot of non-movie people. Magnates, industrialists, big Republican goniffs of various stripes. He owns almost half of California himself."

"Dad! Tell me about the movie stars. Not boring people—movie stars."

"Darling," he said to Lorna, knowing Veevi was listening, "actually there probably won't be that many movie stars. George likes songwriters and comedy writers. And rich reactionaries. But if I see any movie stars I'll be sure to tell them about my beautiful daughter."

He smiled at her and finished the chicken leg, and then he returned to the refrigerator for a breast. "Why don't you come, Vee," he said. "We can still get a sitter."

She shook her head and smiled. "I want a nice, quiet evening with the kids. And a book."

Dinah, not listening, watched as Jake now stripped hunks of white meat from the breast of the chicken. "Stop eating!" she burst out. "For Christ's sake—you eat in the middle of the night, you eat before we go out to dinner, you eat on the set, in the commissary, before parties, after parties. You're going to weigh five thousand pounds."

"Well, what's the difference?" he said mildly, searching the vegetable crisper for something else. He grabbed some celery stalks, which he shoved into his mouth. Loud crunching sounds filled the kitchen.

"Jesus," said Dinah, "you sound like an army of t-t-t-termites."

"You know, a lot of people you think you can't stand might actually turn out to be nice, and very interested in *you*," he said to Veevi.

"It's not the people, honestly. I just want to stay home tonight. In fact,

I can't tell you how glad I am to be going absolutely nowhere." She put her arm around Coco and stroked her hair.

"I'm going to get dressed," Dinah announced. "You kids clear the table and wash the dishes." Ignoring this command, Lorna followed Dinah out of the kitchen to watch her and talk to her while she dressed for the party. If Veevi wasn't going out, she wouldn't be getting dressed up and Lorna could have her mother and their beloved ritual to herself again.

Satisfied that he had left nothing untasted, Jake closed the refrigerator door. "Why don't you and Veevi go out for a walk right now?" he said to Peter. "This is a great time of day to explore the desert. The air smells great and it's not too cold, and you can still see where you're going."

"Want to?" Veevi said, smiling at Peter.

"*Dad!*" He felt his face flushing.

"Oh, for Christ's sake," Jake exploded. "Don't tell me you won't go out there because you're afraid you might see a lizard."

"There *could* be one, Dad."

"Come on, Pete. You've got to get over this thing. You're nine and a half. You've been to sleepaway camp. How can you still be afraid of lizards?"

"I just am," he said simply. He didn't care whether Veevi witnessed his humiliation. It was too frightening even to consider—going out in the desert at twilight. He ran out of the kitchen, hating his father, and threw himself down on his bed. He wished he were at home, in his own bed, with his Benny Goodman records; he couldn't stand this poky house where you could see and hear what everyone was doing and where you couldn't get away from them. If this was how regular people lived, he hated it.

Soon he heard his father go into the bathroom; the shower roared up, and then, after a while, he could hear his father singing a song and snapping his fingers and clapping. That was his father, all right: exploding in anger one minute, honking out some dumb song the next. Peter turned on his back and lay very still. Something about his father often made his mind go blank.

Veevi came into the room and sat down on the edge of his bed. "I'm going to take that walk now," she said. "Why don't you come? The desert's just across the street, and we'll walk along the edge. We can come home any time you like."

She reached out and clamped her hand on his calf; it was something his mother might do, and in just the same way, yet he liked it when his mother did it but not when Veevi did. "You know, when I was little and went out to the desert with Papa Milligan, he would tell me marvelous things. How the desert used to be the bottom of the ocean. How you can go out there and find seashells that are millions and millions of years old and rocks with fossil fishes in them."

Did she want him to go looking for rocks with fossil fishes in them now? he wondered. Right now? In the growing darkness?

"You saw lizards and snakes and Gila monsters out there?" he asked.

"Sometimes. But never at night. Come on, it's beautiful out."

She jumped up and held her hand out to him. She was smiling; he saw her perfect white teeth, her red mouth, her shoulder-length brown hair, the warm hazel eyes with black stuff on the lashes. "Sorry, Veevi," he said miserably. "I just don't want to go out there."

He picked up one of his Freddy the Pig books off the floor and opened it.

She waited, briefly, and watched him becoming absorbed in the book. "Well . . . all right then," she said quietly, and she went back to the living-room sofa and her *New Yorker*.

During the next hour, the light in the desert darkened to a deep blue, and the thin air, which had been hot and dry in the daytime, became sharp with cold. Peter could feel it coming through the screen door, which he got up to close. He was absently aware of Coco's and Veevi's voices, of the bright light just beyond the bedroom door illuminating the small passageway that connected the room he shared with Veevi to his parents' bedroom. Then his mother came out, and in her wake Lorna, with all the self-importance of a lady-in-waiting. "Where's Pete?" he heard his mother say, and he got up and went into the living room.

Dinah was wearing a tangerine-colored strapless chiffon evening gown with crystal bugle beads sewn on the breast and the bodice. When she moved, the dress rustled and wafted the smell of perfume throughout the whole house.

"You look really pretty, Mom," he said. He saw Veevi's head jerk sharply as she looked up to appraise his mother. But she said nothing.

"She's not pretty. She's beautiful," Lorna corrected him.

His sister was right, he thought, but it was embarrassing to tell your mother she was beautiful. "Pretty" would have to do.

Jake came out. His head seemed very large and round to Peter, who couldn't imagine a time, ever, when he would be big enough to look the way his father did tonight in the dark blue suit. Jake cleared his throat conspicuously and held his white handkerchief to his mouth, sickening Peter, who hated the way his father was always coughing up gobs of phlegm in front of everybody. If his father sniffled, he wanted to throw up; anything physical his father did—cough, sneeze, belch, fart—revolted him. Yet, as he watched his father help his mother wrap around her shoulders a long shawl made of the same tangerine-colored stuff as her dress, he felt that Veevi was looking at him, and he glanced at her. There was a strange expression on her face, and it was directed at him—something mean, a faint smirk that, he felt, was supposed to be a secret between them. Her eyes darted back and forth between him and his mother and father, as if she were inviting him to make fun of them in a private understanding of something about which he hadn't the faintest clue; he knew only that it had something to do with his parents, and the way they were dressed up tonight, as if she wanted him to make fun of them with her.

"Doesn't Mom look great?" Jake said.

"Uh-huh," he said.

"Can't you do better than that?"

"He already told me he thinks so, honey," Dinah interjected.

"It's time for him to learn how to give his mother a compliment," Jake said.

"I think Peter is very gallant," Veevi said. "At least with me."

"C-C-Cut it out, both of you," Dinah said. "He's nine years old, for heaven's sake."

"But he's very smart, and sensitive," Veevi continued, undeterred. "And he sure knows how to be nice to girls. Don't you, Pete?"

He smiled bashfully at her and went back to his book.

After kissing Lorna and Coco, Dinah came over to where he lay on the carpet and bent over to kiss the top of his head again. Peter could smell the perfume in the gauzy folds of her dress. Jake bellowed that they would be late, and she hurried to join him, her high heels skittering across the kitchen floor. A door slammed shut, and the Cadillac coughed and started up. He had gone back to his book when suddenly there was a flash of orange before his eyes, and a manicured hand thrusting a slip of paper toward Veevi: "George Joy's number, just in case. Don't lose it. He's unl-l-l-listed."

Veevi took the scrap of paper, stuck it in her shirt pocket, and returned to her magazine. He heard the car pull out of the driveway and take off down the street. Then he felt the desolation that always came over him when his parents went out for the evening—the feeling of filled space suddenly emptied out, leaving a vacuum in the heart.

Lorna must have felt it, too. She called out to him, a plea in her voice: "Watch TV with us?" She and Coco were lying on their stomachs, their faces in their hands and their legs hinged upward and waving from the knee. On the television screen, there was a choir of women in white robes singing at the top of their lungs. Lorna sang along, imitating their high, operatic range.

Peter and Coco giggled. Peter got up from the sofa and crouched on his knees, reaching over to the television set to change channels.

"There's nothing else on. There's only about three stations, and they all have Easter junk," Lorna declared.

"There's got to be something better," said Veevi. "Go ahead, Peter. If anyone can find something, it's you."

He flipped the channels, passing another program with a preacher, until an old western flickered on the screen.

"There, that one!" Lorna cried.

The movie had nobody they recognized, just the familiar sights and sounds—thunderous hooves, gunfire, a stagecoach teetering on the dusty plain. The children happily settled in to watch, and Veevi watched too, her magazine set aside. Outside, it was completely dark. At some point, she was supposed to tell them to come into the kitchen and dye Easter eggs. She had to get up and boil the eggs first. But she would do it later.

A good guy rode into town, tied up his horse, and walked down the middle of the street with his hands poised just above his two holstered guns. Suddenly the children heard a choking laugh and turned toward Veevi. "My God, look!" she said. "That's the western set at Marathon. It's been there forever. It was there when I worked on the lot a thousand years ago. Look! Do you recognize that saloon? Your father's office is right across the street from it."

The children scrambled up closer to the set. Lorna claimed to recognize the western street; Peter wasn't so sure. "It might be the western town they have out at that ranch in Santa Barbara."

"Well, I can't prove it right now, because they've just switched to an interior, but if they go back to an exterior, check and see if it says 'Hicks's Dry

Goods' next to the saloon. If it does, then it's the Marathon set. Meanwhile, I'm going to make popcorn."

She went out to the kitchen, and soon the children could hear the bursts of popcorn popping on the stove, but after it finished she stayed in there for a long time. Peter vaguely remembered his mother's telling him earlier in the day to help his aunt with the Easter eggs that night, but Veevi hadn't asked him yet and he didn't want to get up. When she came back, holding a big steaming bowl of buttered and salted popcorn, her face was flushed and the children grabbed fistfuls even as she was setting it down on the floor for them. "Heavens!" she exclaimed. "I forgot the Cokes. You guys want Cokes? You can't have popcorn without Cokes!"

Her heartiness struck Peter as odd; he had never heard her take that tone before, but he was beginning to have fun and to forget his shame at being too scared to go for a walk in the desert with her. He was getting caught up in the movie, caught up in waiting to see if the western set really and truly was Marathon's, as she had claimed. Once again, she was gone for a long time, but when she came back she was carrying a tray with a plate of chocolate chip cookies and four ice-filled glasses of Coca-Cola.

"We saw 'Hicks's,' " he said, grabbing a cookie. "You were right. It's the western set at Marathon."

"Process shot!" Lorna called out as a gang of villains raced alongside a speeding train.

Veevi laughed. "You Hollywood brats don't miss a thing, do you? Every other kid in the world thinks it's real cowboys and a real train. Not you guys. Nobody can fool you," Veevi said. Peter found her speech different and odd. It sounded lazy. And he wasn't used to her making cracks; that wasn't like her, though it was something his mother always did.

Veevi resumed her place on the sofa, watching the movie with them, smoking cigarettes, and reaching over now and then for a handful of popcorn. When the bowl was empty, she took it back to the kitchen and again stayed a long time and brought back another full bowl; but this time the kids had had their fill and barely touched it.

After the movie ended, *Have Gun, Will Travel* came on, followed by *Gunsmoke,* both of which were favorites with the Lasker kids. At ten o'clock, Lorna simply picked up Coco, who was nearly comatose after swimming all day, and put her to bed in the alcove off the living room.

When she returned, she and Peter and Veevi watched television together for another hour or so, until *The Fabulous* 52 came on. That week's movie opened with a murder in which a man was thrown screaming off a building, and Lorna, who was frightened of violent deaths in movies, decided she didn't want to see any more and asked Peter to change channels.

"But, dear, *we're* not frightened and we want to see it," Veevi said.

"Yeah," said Peter. "It's two against one."

Lorna stood up, put her dolls away, and went to her cot in the alcove next to Coco's.

Peter and Veevi watched a little more of the movie alone, with the sound turned down low. But Peter felt himself growing sleepy, and he went into the bathroom to change into his pj's. When he turned out the bathroom light and came back into the living room, he saw that the television was off and that Veevi had disappeared into the kitchen. He heard running water, and he thought, Oh, she's going to dye the Easter eggs. He knew he was supposed to help, but he was tired. He, too, had had a long day of swimming, and he went into his room and got into bed.

Outside it was quiet, much quieter than it was at home, where from his room every night Peter could hear cars whooshing by on Sunset Boulevard, sirens screaming through the canyons, dogs howling from their chained posts outside kitchen doors. Sometimes the sounds of outdoor parties drifted by, with vibrant waves of band music, the splashing of pool water, and laughter. Here in Palm Springs, though, the house was a half mile from the new freeway, much too far for the sounds of cars to reach his ears. Just across the street lay the desert, where small animals huddled under dry shrubs at night. Where, he wondered, did the lizards go? Surely, being cold-blooded creatures, they had to find someplace warm. Maybe they came into people's houses. The desert temperatures could drop to almost freezing, couldn't they? Then where did the snakes and lizards go? Wouldn't they want to come in and warm themselves?

He knew this didn't happen, but it didn't matter. With the thought that lizards and snakes might be crawling across the street and into the house, his breathing, which until that moment had been peaceful, came hard. In his mind's eye, he saw hordes of fierce scaly lizards, their eyes red and their claws extended, scrambling across the cold night sand and finding their way through cracks in the walls into the small, unprotected house, where an army of them would march over his feet and under his blanket.

He bolted upright, sweaty and gasping, the way he sometimes did when he thought about death. His heart pounded in his chest; the back of his throat was dry. He needed a drink of water, but was too scared to get up: what if he stepped on a lizard? This is *stupid,* he said to himself. This is *dumb*. He got out of bed and walked toward the bathroom. On the way, he glanced at the living room and saw Veevi sitting back on the sofa, staring dreamily out the sliding glass doors at nothing at all, a cigarette dangling from her fingers. Her book lay facedown on the rug at a funny angle, as if it had slipped from her hand. He hoped she wouldn't hear or see him, but she did.

"Are you all right, dear?" she said. Her voice sounded high, childlike—strange.

"I'm just getting a glass of water."

"Go back to bed, darling. I'll get it for you."

"That's okay. You don't have to."

He didn't want her to see him hot and trembling with fear, so he quickly went into the bathroom, drank the water, and went back to bed without looking in her direction. But in a minute she was leaning over him, whispering, "Here, dear. Here's a glass of water."

"Thanks." He took a sip and handed the glass back to her.

She took it, but her hand was wobbly and a little of the water spilled onto his blanket. "Oops," she whispered, with her other hand rubbing the wetness into the blanket. "All right, dear, try to sleep now," she said.

Her speech was strange. The words were all slurred together, and her breath stank. As she leaned over and with her free hand fumbled with the blanket and sheets, trying to pull them up over his shoulder, her breath hit him again square in the face. Suddenly he understood what was wrong with her. She was drunk! The terrible smell was liquor. He had seen the bottle on the kitchen counter. Every night, before dinner, his mother poured herself a drink from it—one for herself and one for Veevi. The stuff that came out had an orange-brown color that became lighter when it was splashed over ice cubes.

But he hadn't seen her drinking; how, then, had she gotten drunk? Then he remembered that each time she'd gone into the kitchen, she'd stayed for a long time. His deduction impressed him. He had never seen a drunk person before, although Lorna had told him that one night when she and Coco were brushing their teeth, Veevi had crawled into the bathroom on all fours. He had already gone to bed and was listening to Benny Goodman when Lorna rushed in and described in great detail the way Veevi had swayed on her hands and knees and spoken in a weird high voice. Lorna had run downstairs for Gussie, who had picked Veevi up off the bathroom floor and carried her back to bed.

Go away! Go away! Peter said to himself. He shut his eyes tight and pretended to be suddenly and deeply asleep, which any sober person would know was impossible, since he had just thanked her for the water. But Veevi was too drunk, he saw, to tell. To his relief, she finally left and he heard her grunting and lurching her way back to the living room.

He had to do something, he thought. She was dangerous. She might set the house on fire with her cigarettes! She might try to hurt someone. He turned over on his side, his eyes wide open. What was she doing in the living room, anyway? He didn't want her to come back into their room, but she was too close to Lorna and Coco, and he had to figure out what to do. The passageway between his and Veevi's room and his parents' room was almost completely dark, and Veevi had turned off the living-room light and the television. If he could just call his parents! If he could just become invisible and go into his parents' room and call them! But the number, he remembered, was in Veevi's shirt pocket. He had seen that quick orange flash when his mother had rushed back into the house to leave it.

His heart tightened and he held his breath. The grunting got louder. She was coming again, coming to their room. What would happen now? Was he going to have to listen to her falling asleep in the bed across from him? He squeezed his eyelids until they were almost shut, then, through a sliver of light, saw her steady herself in the door frame, then stretch out her hands, like a blind person, in the darkness.

Frozen under the covers he heard her soft, uncertain footfalls on the carpet. She was in the room now, but she wasn't going to her bed; she was coming toward his! She was leaning over, groping along the edge of his bed. He could smell her sour, fumy breath and feel her hands tugging at the covers, patting his back. "There, now. Cover 'oo. Lovely boy. Not idiot. Nice boy. Veevi make 'oo warm." She giggled. He felt her patting him, tucking him in, or trying to, and he stiffened. If only he could disappear! She had leaned over so far that he thought she was going to collapse on top of him. Then what would he do? She would smother him! He lay petrified while she tried to pull the covers back. "Move over, baby. Veevi keep 'oo nice 'n warm."

She was getting into bed with him! No! He remained rigid, but as she slid a leg in beside him she pushed and shoved him, and he felt himself being squeezed against the wall.

He felt her entangling him like an octopus. Her feet, two cold fishes, rubbed up against his. Somewhere in the region of his ankles he felt her ankles, and the nylon of her pajamas. With horror, he felt her face pressing against his neck and the back of his head. Her lips made strange noises: kissing noises. "Veevi love 'oo. Give Veevi kissies," she said, kissing the back of his neck. One hand was wrapped around his head; the other lay along the length of his back and hips. He felt her breasts through her pajamas, soft against his back. Then, suddenly, her whole body collapsed, with one leg under the bedclothes pushed up against his, and the other like a fallen log on top. He was pinned under the covers—he couldn't move. Her head was a dead weight on his shoulder. Whisky fumes swirled around him.

She had passed out.

He waited, unable to move. The minutes passed slowly, and he had no idea when his parents were coming home. He had to get out from under the dead weight of his aunt's drunken body, but he was afraid that if he moved she would wake up.

Sharply alert himself, he could not have felt more fear and revulsion at the body lying next to him if it had been a corpse. A maddening restlessness surged through his legs. If he could wait a little longer, he told himself, and not panic, he could start to disentangle himself and get out from under her. So he kept as still as he could, and waited. He wanted more than anything just to change the position of his legs, but he was afraid any movement at all would disturb her and give her a chance to start making those terrible kissing sounds again.

All of a sudden, she gave out a great sigh. A warm wetness began to seep into his pajama bottoms. It was pee! Warm pee! Veevi's pee! She was peeing the bed, peeing all over him! The wetness grew and spread, soaking the sheets and himself—and he could smell it, too, acrid and inescapable.

In desperation, not caring whether he woke Veevi or not, he pulled himself back from under the sheets and managed to hoist himself up over his aunt. His pajama bottoms dripped pee onto the blanket, and he retched. She didn't stir or make a sound. Moving quickly, he grabbed the jeans and the T-shirt he had been wearing earlier in the day and went into the bathroom.

Quickly, he scrambled out of his pajama bottoms and left them on the floor. He wet a washcloth and wiped his skin where the pee had touched him, and dried himself, and then put on his jeans. Then he went into his parents' room and closed the door. They would come home, eventually, and find him. Meanwhile, he would lie in their bed with his eyes open, waiting for them; he was the baby-sitter now.

Time passed, and he was drifting off when he heard sounds in the passageway, faint groans. "Jeez Chrize, pee my panzs." She was up again! She was going into the bathroom. She would see his pj bottoms on the floor and come looking for him.

He sat up suddenly, waiting to hear what she was doing. The toilet flushed. Water poured out of a faucet. Then there was a terrible thud.

He ran across the living room and into the kitchen, grabbing his foil. The bottle of liquor was still on the counter, and he read the label: Chivas Regal. The bottle was empty, and for an instant he felt triumphant. He was right; she *had* gotten drunk, and he had recognized it.

But now he had to do something. Lorna and Coco were asleep in the alcove; he couldn't leave them alone. He had to find a way to telephone his mother and father. But how? The telephone was here in the kitchen, but he couldn't go into the bathroom and get the phone number out of Veevi's shirt pocket. He was too afraid—afraid that if he tried to call his parents Veevi would hear him and come out of the bathroom and—he wasn't sure what—do something to him. He didn't want to go in there, because he was also afraid that she might be lying on the floor—dead—with maybe a lot of blood all over the place. Without thinking further, he opened the kitchen door and stepped barefoot onto the cold garage floor.

Then he ran, foil under his arm, the blade sticking out behind him, fly-ing past the three palm trees on the small patch of clipped front lawn, and onto the coarse new road. Sharp-edged particles of asphalt and sand bit into the soles of his feet as he raced down the middle of the pavement. On his left, he could just make out the silhouettes of houses and palm trees; on his right, the desert was a forbidding expanse of darkness and cold. Snakes and lizards! Lizards and snakes! They were out there in the sand, he thought, and perhaps even closer. What if he stepped on one? Well, it didn't matter now. He had his foil. He could fight them if he had to. All he knew was that he had to do something to save his sister and his cousin. Running, his chest heaving and aching, he looked for a house whose lights were on.

It was past the neighborhood swimming pool and in front of a house that was dark except for the dim gray flickers of a television set that he finally stopped. He was gasping, and his mouth felt so dry that he was afraid the words would stick in his throat. He ran up the flagstone path and pressed the doorbell. Two chimes followed, one high, the other low; he was bothered by the absence of a third, which would have made a full chord.

The door opened, and Peter found himself looking at the wary face of a heavy-set woman in a housedress, a scarf over a full set of curlers. Words heaved out of him; he was afraid she would slam the door on him. "Please, ma'am, I'm staying down the street, in this house, and my aunt's there. She was baby-sitting for us, but she got drunk and fell down in the bathroom. My mom and dad are at a party—can I please call them from your phone?"

The woman, who was in her early forties, saw a thin pale boy of about ten, with a sweet oval face, dark eyes and dark hair, a heaving chest, panting and hugging himself. He was barefoot. And in his left hand he was holding a thin, gleaming foil.

"You've got a sword?"

"It's a foil, ma'am. I'm a fencer. I brought it to kill lizards and snakes."

"All right, Errol, come on in," she said with a faint western twang. "But give me that sword, son. There's no reptiles in my house, that's for sure."

Peter handed her the foil and stepped inside. The woman's husband was standing next to a television lounger, looking at him curiously.

"Errol Flynn here needs to phone his parents," she explained. "His aunt's the baby-sitter and she got drunk and fell down." She held up the foil. "He's a fencer."

"Is this a game?" the man asked, but not harshly. "Are you playing pirates?"

"No, sir. My aunt got drunk and fell down. I want to call my mom and dad."

"Where is she now, son?" the man asked. "Your aunt." He, too, had a western accent, and he was wearing, Peter noted, a plaid cowboy shirt with pearl buttons and a string tie.

"She fell down in the bathroom," Peter said.

"Passed out?"

"I *think* so," Peter said.

"Is she hurt?"

"I don't know. I need to call my mom and dad."

"Well, the phone's here, hon," the woman said, motioning to the coffee table. "Do you have the number?"

"My parents are at George Joy's house," Peter explained. The woman's eyes opened wide. "I don't know the number. It's on a piece of paper my mom gave my aunt, but it's in her pocket. My mom said it's 'unlisted.' I don't know what that means. Do you have a phone book?"

The woman disappeared for a moment and came back with a phone book that Peter could see was about a quarter of the size of the Los Angeles phone book at home. "You can look in here," she said, opening the book. "But if it's an unlisted number you won't find it. Did you say George Joy? *The* George Joy?"

"Yeah," said Peter.

"Your folks know him?"

"Uh-huh."

Peter explained that his father made movies and that George Joy had been in a lot of them. She asked him to name some of the movies his father had made with George Joy, and when he finished she said, "Son of a gun. I've seen them all. What's your father's name, Errol? And what's yours?" He told her. "Son of a gun," she said again.

"Try Information for him, Velma," the man said. He had a deep, slow kind of voice. His belly hung over his underslung pants, and Peter noticed that his belt had been loosened and the button at the top of his trousers was undone.

"I'm just doing that now, Garnett," said the woman. "Here, hon, you just set down." She pointed toward the sofa, and Peter obeyed. The woman dialed Information and asked for the number of a Mr. George Joy in Palm Springs. She waited and then scowled slightly. "Thank you," she said, and hung up. "She says the number's unlisted and can't be given out." She dialed Information again. "Operator, this is an emergency. There's a child here with a drunken baby-sitter who might be injured. He says his parents are at Mr. George Joy's. Can't you give us the number?" She listened and put the phone down again. "She says to give her our number and she'll call the George Joy residence and then your parents can call you here. Unless you want me to call the police."

Peter shook his head. He wanted his parents to come.

The woman gave the operator Peter's name, and then her name—Mrs. Garnett Holman—and the number. Then she and Peter sat on the sofa while her husband sat in his recliner, and they waited for Jake and Dinah to call back.

꧁

His parents had left the party, Mrs. Holman explained to Peter after the operator had called back. They were already on their way home. Mr. Holman said he would go and wait for them at the house; that way, he could see whether the boy's aunt was injured and call an ambulance if necessary. Peter explained to him that their house was the one down the street with the three palm trees in the front yard. He saw Mr. Holman button his pants and take a pair of high cowboy boots from the coat closet near the door. The man sat down on the sofa and pulled on the boots. He did this slowly and methodically. Then he took out a leather fringed jacket and a ten-gallon hat. Peter wondered whether he had a holster and a gun.

"All right, son. Now, don't worry," Mr. Holman said. "I'll be back here in no time with your folks. Velma, put him to bed in Glendora's room. All right, I'm going," he shouted.

"All right, Garnett," Velma called back. "Be careful, now."

Within minutes, Peter was settled under the tight sheets of the couple's daughter's bed.

The daughter was sixteen and was at a slumber party, Mrs. Holman said. "You try to get some sleep, hon," she said to him. "I'll let you know when your mom and dad get here."

He felt deliciously happy to be in the strange house and the strange bed. Velma. Garnett. Glendora. The man and woman teasing him, calling him Errol. His getting the joke and not minding it. Then their calling him "son." He liked the names. He liked the man with the string tie and the cowboy boots, who was going to meet his parents. He was proud of himself for going for help, proud for running along the scary street in the middle of the night, proud of himself for noticing what was different and nice about these people. No one could say he was afraid of lizards and snakes now. Even if there had been a thousand of them out there, he told himself, he would still have run for help. That means I'm brave, he said to himself. I'm not a sissy. He wanted his father to know—to know and to stop picking on him all the time about his fear and his fencing, and everything else.

he voice, the rustle of chiffon, the perfume, pulled him from the dark burrow where he was no longer conscious, yet at the same time not quite deeply asleep. Opening his eyes, he saw his mother sitting on the bed and felt her taking his hands. When he sat up, she took off the orange chiffon shawl and wrapped it tightly around him. It felt warm and smelled like her. "C'mon, honey, I have the c-c-c-car running outside."

"Where's Dad?"

"I'll tell you in the car, honey. C'mon, sweetie."

"My foil, Mom."

"Mrs. Holman's got it. She'll give it to you on the way out."

In the car, she told him that there was an ambulance at the house that was going to take Veevi to the hospital. She had fallen and hit her head; there was some blood on the bathroom floor and she just wanted him to know and not to get upset. He saw the ambulance and its flashing red light in the driveway of the house. He wanted to look inside its open back door, but Dinah steered him through the kitchen, across the living room, and past the bathroom, where, leaning against the doorway, were his father and Mr. Holman. They were watching something that was going on inside the bathroom. He thought he could see two men in uniforms kneeling over something that he couldn't see but that he knew had to be Veevi.

"Don't l-l-l-look," said Dinah, putting her left hand like a visor over his eyes and pushing him gently toward her room. On the way, she took his foil and leaned it against the wall in the living room.

Peter sat on his parents' rumpled bed. He took off the chiffon shawl and sat with his arms crossed and his legs dangling over the edge. His mother had gone for a glass of water. The door was closed, but he could hear the sound of men treading back and forth across the living room to the ambulance outside and back to the bathroom again. He felt stranger than he ever had before. Nothing like this would ever have happened at their Delfern house, he reflected. It was all because this house was so small. If Veevi had been baby-sitting at home and had gotten drunk and fallen downstairs in the den, he would never have known it. She could have died or shouted for help, and he would have been too far away in his own room to know it.

He got under the covers and listened, tensely. Then his mother came back. "I had to get some clothes for Veevi."

"Yeah," he said. "She peed herself. And she got into bed and peed all over me."

"She got into b-b-b-bed with you?"

"Yeah. She got in and started making kissing sounds, Mom"—he made a face—"and then she peed the bed."

"That must have been awful. Here," she said, "take this." She took a little bottle of pills out of her vanity case, opened it, and let a capsule roll into her palm; then she took the needle of a safety pin and pricked the capsule's brilliant orange-and-red skin, so that some of the white powder fell into the ashtray on the bedside table. "I'm giving you half of this," she said. Then she told him to swallow the pill.

"What is it?" he asked.

"You'll get sleepy real s-s-s-soon. But tell me what happened."

He did, lingering on the peeing and kissing part, and on the terrifying thud. "Oh, poor you. Poor Veevi," his mother said. When he was finished, she said that since the sheets on his bed were probably wet he would have to sleep in Veevi's bed.

"I don't want to sleep in her bed," he said. He didn't want to be close to anything that smelled of her in any way.

"She won't be there, honey. You've got to go to sleep."

She took him by the hand and led him, again shielding his eyes, into the bedroom, where he got into Veevi's bed as his mother sat beside him and tucked him in.

"Mom?"

"Yes, honey."

"Do you think I'm brave?"

"I think you're very br-br-br-brave. It took a lot of guts to go and get help."

"Mom, I *was* brave. Before, I was so scared of lizards and snakes. But I went anyway. I thought they were out there, and I went anyway. And it didn't bother me. Do you think that was brave?"

"It's the bravest thing you've ever done."

"Mom? I'm not scared of them anymore."

"That's really something, honey."

"Scratch my back?"

She made a circular roll-over gesture with her fingers, and he flopped happily onto his stomach. Then he felt her long hard nails lightly tracking his shoulder blades, the top of his neck, the length of his spine.

"Scratch to the left. Up a little. Down. More down. Right *there*."

His mother knew exactly where he meant. Lulled, soothed, he drooled a little onto the pillow. Then the pill hit him and everything went black.

It was almost noon when he woke up. His mother was sitting beside him on the edge of the bed. He had never slept so deeply in his life, and the sensation of thick, headachy grogginess was new and unpleasant. His mother put her hand behind his neck and helped him sit up. She handed him a glass of orange juice, which he drank slowly, as if he had forgotten how.

"Honey," Dinah said. "Come into the living room. Your f-f-f-father wants to talk to you."

"Is Veevi here?"

He dreaded having to see her.

"She's still in the hospital, but she's okay. She had to have a couple of stitches where she cut her head. Daddy's driving her home this evening. I'm taking you guys home this afternoon. That way, she can have some time to take it easy and you guys can swim today. She told me to tell you she's sorry about what happened. I think she's pretty embarrassed."

"Are we going to have an Easter egg hunt?"

"Not today. We'll do it next Sunday, at home."

"After Easter? Why?"

"The eggs didn't get dyed last night."

Dinah waited for him to get out of bed; then she followed him into the living room. Lorna had been instructed to take Coco out to play in the front yard, by the palm trees. Jake was sitting in a corner of the sofa. Peter sat down in the other corner, across from his father, and Dinah perched herself on the arm of the sofa, next to Peter.

After asking his son whether he'd slept well, Jake asked him to give a full account of what had happened the night before. This Peter did. His father listened, pursing his lips. And then he spoke. "What I don't understand is why you didn't call us. From here."

Peter tried to explain: when he heard the thud, and realized that Veevi must have fallen down in the bathroom, he knew that the piece of paper with George Joy's phone number was in her shirt pocket, but he'd been too scared to go in and get it.

"What were you scared of?"

He was scared, he said, that she might be badly hurt and he wouldn't know what to do. And he was just scared—scared she might do something to him.

"What kind of thing? What would a woman who has passed out and fallen and perhaps given herself a brain injury have done to you?" Jake asked.

He didn't know what. Just something. Also, he remembered that there was something funny about the number—it was "unlisted" and he wasn't sure what that meant, and he thought the best thing to do was go for help.

"But why didn't you first go into the bathroom to see what had happened?" Jake pressed him. "She could have been badly injured—she could have been bleeding to death."

His father's words stunned him. Expecting praise, so certain that he had done something good and right, he couldn't fathom his father's harshness. He looked at his mother, trying to find an answer there. But all he saw was that she was chewing the inside of her cheek and had folded her arms tightly across her chest, her worried eyes glancing rapidly back and forth between him and his father. Again, he explained: "I was scared, Dad. I wanted to call you. I knew she might be hurt. But I didn't think I could take care of her by myself. Dad! She *peed* all over me."

"So she peed on you! So what! It's pathetic, and embarrassing for her, but it's no reason to be *afraid* of her."

"Let up, Jake," Dinah said sharply. "He did what he thought best, and I'm pr-pr-proud as hell of him."

"Hold it right there, darling," Jake said, his voice loud and sharp. "I don't see anything to be proud of. In fact, I don't mind saying that I'm very disturbed by what he did."

Peter went perfectly still, sitting there on the sofa. "Peter," his father continued, his legs crossed comfortably. "What I still don't understand— what I absolutely *do not understand* is, number one"—he held up his little finger, bending the others—"how you could leave your little sister and your baby cousin *all alone* in this house with your aunt while she was drunk and possibly smoking cigarettes, and, number two"—and he held up the fourth finger on his hand—"how you could leave the house at all with Veevi lying in the bathroom, where she might well have been bleeding to death. She could have died; she could have set the house on fire and your sister and cousin could all have been *killed*. Burned to death!"

"Jake! Enough!" Dinah shouted.

Tears fell one by one from Peter's eyes, though he sat erect. He tried to wipe them away with the back of his hand. He wanted to speak, but instead he blinked and clenched the muscles of his mouth, because he knew that if he tried to explain further he would begin to sob. The tears kept coming.

"If you were that frightened, why didn't you simply go to the phone in the kitchen and call the police? They could have found George's number in a second. Why this production number with strangers down the street? What if *they* had turned out to be drunk themselves, or criminals, or God knows what? What the hell possessed you to *leave this house?*" His father's voice had risen to an enraged roar. "You're almost ten years old!" he bellowed. "You left your family! You ran away! You failed them! And us! And yourself! And, frankly, I'm *very* concerned. Very concerned about what this means for your future. What this says about your *character*. You're a goddamn coward."

"How *dare* you speak to him that way!" Dinah shouted. "How *dare* you call our son a c-c-c-coward. He did the b-b-b-best he could, Jake! He used his judgment. He thought about what to do. He went to get other adults."

"Horseshit! He jumped ship. Thought only of himself."

The tears flowed steadily down Peter's face. He sat on the edge of the sofa, his long, thin arms limply by his sides. Dinah sat beside him and put her arm around him, and the boy turned his face to his mother's breast and sobbed.

"Now, you listen to me, you s-s-s-sadistic pr-pr-pr-prick," she said, her eyes flashing. "He wasn't responsible for her. *We* were. We knew she's a drunk. We went out and left our kids with a drunk. And she was responsible for him, not the other way around."

"Sweetheart, you're overreacting."

"I'm overreacting? That's a scream."

"People sometimes get drunk when they're sad and lonely, as we all know Veevi is, and Pete is old enough to cope with that. When I was ten, my parents left Evelyn and me alone in the apartment when they went out and we knew what to do in emergencies."

"Well, b-b-b-bully for you, b-b-b-buster. Sitting in judgment on your k-k-kid and calling him a c-c-c-coward and throwing around your fancy Fr-Fr-Fr-Freudian words."

Dinah released Peter, who sat, watchful and listening. "Now wait a minute, darling," Jake countered sternly (Peter hated the way his father called everyone "darling" and "sweetheart" and "honey" when he was yelling at them). "Pete left your *sister,* a member of this *family,* who in a moment of frailty, or God knows what, slipped up, as all human beings do on one occasion or another, left her injured in this house, which she could easily have set on fire, when his sister and cousin were sound asleep and helpless, when all he had to do was go into the bathroom, reach down and pull the number out of Veevi's pocket, and walk calmly into the kitchen and call us. Peter had a clear responsibility, and he didn't meet it. And I mean it when I say I'm very concerned. He's been running away from reality all his life, and this is just the most severe example of it."

All the strength in Peter's body suddenly drained away. He felt not simply small and weak but insubstantial, as if he had been changed by a powerful magician into something that wasn't even human anymore, just smoke or air. Staring out the open screen door at the concrete patio and the empty blue sky, he no longer felt that he was himself, and his parents might as well have been two complete strangers. He hates me, he said to himself. He doesn't care that I ran out for help and wasn't afraid of snakes or lizards. He hates me. I hate him, too.

Meanwhile, his parents had begun to shout at each other.

"Does he have to think of *everything* an adult would?" his mother yelled. "Why aren't you reserving one word of censure for Veevi? God help me, she's my s-s-s-sister, but she's the one who put all these kids in danger. Not Peter!"

"I'm not concerned about Veevi. I don't even like her!" Jake said. "She takes up all the oxygen in this family. I'm suffocating with her in our lives. We all are! It's my son I'm worried about. Why can't he follow the rules? And, for that matter, why do you always protect him from the demands of normal life? You refuse to make him compete with other kids in normal sports; you let him fence instead of taking him to Little League. You don't force him to go to birthday parties. Did you ever hear of a kid who doesn't like birthday parties?"

Peter looked at his father and thought, What a jerk.

"He ran away from his responsibility last night the way he runs away from team sports."

"How can you say that? How can you call a kid who practices his in-strum-m-m-ment two hours a day irresponsible? And how can you put this whole thing on him?"

"He won't play baseball! Doesn't that say something to you? He wants to fence—a violent, snobbish sport, for European aristocrats, not normal American boys! He won't compete like a normal kid. He's so afraid of his own competitive aggression that he runs away from it and seeks gratification in places where he won't find any competition."

"Speak English, Jake, not Freudish!"

"You don't see it!" he shouted. "You're blind where Peter's concerned. It's a moral question, too—a matter of principle. He should have known what to do."

"Pr-Pr-Pr-Pr-Pr . . ." She absolutely could not get the word out, and her eyes opened so wide they looked like two round brown nuts. Finally, she took a deep breath that filled the sails of her lungs and blew out, " 'PRIN-CIPLE'?"

Her face registered bitter incredulity. But she could see that the silent connections she was making in her mind between his indictment of Peter and his desire for her to testify were nowhere near each other in his. She wouldn't make them for him, because Peter was there. But she was boiling now, steaming, lathering, erupting, and she leaped up from the couch and went for Peter's foil, grabbed it, and in a single movement strode across the living room and banged its handle over and over on Jake's round balding head and shoulders. "You *prick*!" Her voice was at once hoarse and shrill. "You absolute *prick*! Pete's our child! Do you want to d-d-d-destroy him?"

Peter sprang away from the sofa and stared as his mother hit his father over and over with the gleaming handle. She seemed possessed, a creature none of them had ever seen before—not her son, her husband, or herself. His father shrank a little, protectively hunching his shoulders and ducking the blows, but then, laughing loudly, he reached up and seized the lower end of the blade, its tip swathed in thin white soiled bandage tape for Peter's lessons, and wrestled the foil away from her. Dinah, with redoubled fury, began pounding Jake with her fists. He did little to fend off the blows, only shielding his face slightly and laughing again, as if Dinah's fists were Ping-Pong balls. "I'm taking these kids back to L.A. now, and I don't give a good goddamn if I ever see you or that pain-in-the-ass sister of mine again," she said. "As far as I'm concerned, you two deserve each other, and I've fucking had it with both of you! She's never going to p-p-pee on our son or be cruel to Lorna again!"

"If you could hear yourself, you'd see how funny this is," Jake said. "But suit yourself. No one can reason with you, Dinah. You always do just what you want to do." He shrugged and folded his arms.

She collapsed at the other end of the sofa and glared, while Jake leaned back and looked at her in his imperturbable way. There was a long silence. And then, to Peter, it seemed as if Jake was about to break into a smile, as if he had been studying the whole scene and enjoying it very much. He rubbed his large hand over his balding head and looked at his fingers. "No blood," he said. Then he laughed.

An airplane droned overhead. Outside, Peter could see that it was going to be a clear, hot day. "Pick up your foil, Peter," Jake said. He got up and went to the sliding glass door, opened it, and took a deep breath. "Christ, it's gorgeous outside. I hate like hell having to lose that eighteen holes with George. This is nuts, really. Why don't you take Peter to see Vee in the hospital and let them have a little talk together, and I'll go play golf and you'll have the Easter egg hunt, and then we'll all go back at the same time later today like we'd planned and stop in Redlands at the nineteen-cent hamburger place."

He yawned like a great happy hippopotamus, and waited, without apparent concern, for her answer.

"Pete, honey," she said finally. "Go get dressed and tell Lorna and Coco to come in and pack up. We're going home. Right now."

"You can do what you want, darling," Jake said to Dinah. "But you're making a big mistake. The whole thing should just blow over. We should just have a normal day here. All of us together."

"C'mon, Pete," Dinah said, ignoring her husband.

Peter picked up his foil and went into his room. Under his bed was a duffel bag, and he reached for it and took out a clean white T-shirt. Then he sat on the edge of the bed. He would get dressed to leave in a minute, he told himself, but for now he just wanted to sit and do nothing.

PART

Three

1

*A*bove the garage, in her small, neat room, Mrs. Augusta Crittenden, known to her friends, family, and employers as Gussie, stirs in bed, awakened in the June night by the sound of the Cadillac starting up. She turns on the bedside light and picks up the clock: a little past two. Where he off to again? she wonders, but her body, needing sleep, pulls her back down into the warm sheets.

Dinah also stirs, looks across the bedroom, and sees that Jake's bed is empty. He's restless again, she thinks.

Anxious about the final cut of the picture—worried that it's too long. He doesn't like the score Mel and Izzie have commissioned, wishes they'd bring Milty Ostrow in to fix it, but they don't want to spend the extra money; they won't listen to him. But they're the producers, he's reminded her. He's only being paid to direct it. Most of all, he's wild to get it over with, wild to go back to the other project—the book for the Broadway musical he's dreamed of doing for years.

For the past few weeks, ever since he began cutting the picture, every night, after about two hours of deep sleep, he starts awake with what he calls the restless heebie-jeebies—sizzling electric currents of intolerable restlessness running up and down his legs, making it unbearable for him to stay in bed. Until he began taking these night drives, his tossing and turning and gum cracking, not to mention his mooselike snoring when he did sleep, had been driving Dinah crazy. She would wake up in the middle of the night to find him sitting up in bed, noisily munching saltines and celery and swigging from a bottle of ice-cold root beer. Nothing seemed to work.

"Take a hot bath," she would say to him. "Go for a swim, warm up a cup of milk, read a book. Or take a Seconal."

"You know I can't read unless I'm looking for material," he would reply. "Either that or I get so caught up in the words, it takes me two hours to get through the first paragraph. If I take a Seconal, it doesn't kick in until the middle of the next afternoon, and then it knocks me out."

"Why don't you stop at Finlandia on the way home from the studio?" she'd suggested. "What about taking night swims? We built the pool and now you don't use it."

Then one night he got up and dressed and went for a long drive and didn't come back until it was almost light out. But the drive had soothed him, he told Dinah, and he had taken another drive, and another. Now it's part of his routine. He likes to drive down to the beach or all the way out to Zuma, he tells her. There's a twenty-four-hour Jewish deli in Santa Monica. The greatest pastrami sandwiches ever. He takes a drive and gets a sandwich, then he's able to sleep for a while. But she can't stop worrying about him. The fact is, he's always tired.

As Dinah falls asleep again, she wonders whether what took place in Palm Springs has anything to do with Jake's insomnia. That incident, however, remains for her the worst thing that has ever happened between them. It passed, of course. For three days they hardly spoke, and then life just went back to normal. She's happy to see him when he comes home at night from the studio, but she can't forgive his harshness toward Peter. She's still appalled by his cruelty and imperturbability. But then he wakes up and she hears him putting on his slippers. "Darling, is that you? Can't sleep again?" she asks, and the anger melts away.

The day after the Palm Springs fight, as she calls it to herself, Veevi had come down to breakfast early. There was a bandage on her temple that didn't quite cover the ugly cut at her hairline. Dinah looked up: Veevi was making a contrite bubby face. Dinah shook her head. "Oh, Vee," she said.

Her sister sat down at the table and began to cry. "I'm so sorry," she said through sobs.

It was a familiar scene, for Dinah and Veevi alike, and an ancient one. They both recognized that this was exactly what their father had done whenever he'd come home from a bender.

Dinah poured coffee for Veevi. Then, as she handed it to her, she looked at her sister and bit her lip. "Veevi," she said. "I think it's time—"

"I know," Veevi said.

They went out together that afternoon and the next, taking Dorshka with them, and a few days later they had found a house for Veevi in the Pacific Palisades. Dorshka agreed to move in with Veevi and Coco. Letters, telegrams, and phone calls were exchanged between Veevi's attorney in L.A. and Mike's attorney in Paris. Then everything was settled. In early May— a little more than a month after the Palm Springs fight—Dorshka, Veevi, and Coco moved into the new house. Claire remained at the Laskers' because she would be closer to her school.

Jake drives west on Sunset Boulevard, going as fast as he can while keeping an eye out for the squad cars that sometimes lurk on the margins of the road. The window is rolled down, and he breathes in the heavy sweetness of night-blooming jasmine. Past Bel-Air, past Brentwood, out toward the Palisades, he notices that the big houses along the road are all dark, though now and then a fugitive light casts a pale glow on gardens and shrubs, warning thieves against trying their luck.

He thinks about Gussie and their conversation that morning at breakfast.

"Hey, Gus, didja catch the doubleheader yesterday?"

"Sure did, Mr. Lasker."

"My Cubs finally beat Newcombe," he said, putting aside the sports page as she poured his coffee.

"It done took 'em long enough. Ten in a row. But you'll see. This is our year."

"Naw, Gus. This is the beginning of the end."

"Oh no it ain't, Mr. Lasker." She laughed and gave him a look, and then stood holding the coffeepot with her other hand on her hip. "Tell me something, Mr. Lasker," she said. "Am I crazy or do I keep hearing someone starting up the Cadillac in the middle of the night?"

"I'm sorry if it's waking you up, Gus. I can't sleep, and I find that it soothes me to go out for a drive."

"Well, the only thing about the driving is, you're liable to fall asleep behind the wheel. And, Mr. Lasker, you got to stay away from that refrigerator."

"Do you think you could put a lock on it for me?"

She and Jake were always trying to figure out ways for him to lose weight. "You got to put a lock on your stomach, Mr. Lasker."

"You said it, Gus. But the driving doesn't have any calories."

"How old are you now, Mr. Lasker?"

"Forty-three, Gus."

"That's the age when gentlemen need to get some relaxation."

She leaned over the lazy Susan in the breakfast room, the coffeepot still in her hand. Tall, with carefully coiffed straightened hair, crisp white uniform, maroon lipstick, and clear rimless glasses, Gussie was an imposing figure. Like Dinah, he adored her, and liked having her company all to himself early in the morning, before the kids came downstairs.

As she goes back and forth between the swinging doors, bringing him toast, half of a grapefruit, and a soft-boiled egg, he wonders whether she's figured it out by herself. Because she's a Negro and was once, as a young woman, the head housekeeper in a Texas whorehouse—she's told him enough stories to fill a book, and he's written them down for future use— he likes to imagine that she has an all-encompassing wisdom about the sexual follies of men, and with it the tolerance and forbearance he believes such follies deserve. There are times when he wishes he could go to her and unbosom himself of his own. But he is her employer, and she his employee. More important, he knows that although she's fond of him, it's Dinah and the kids to whom she's really devoted.

So he keeps his secrets to himself. Only now, taking the long, leisurely curves on Sunset, does he think about where he's going and what will happen when he arrives. Finally, when he can smell the ocean, he makes a turn to the right just beyond Pacific Palisades village and parks on a street across from a two-story brown shingled house with green shutters. He is careful to mute the shutting of the car door, and when he crosses the street and walks up a brick path to the kitchen door, he clutches his keys in his pocket to keep them from jingling.

He turns the door handle and walks in, and she's standing there, waiting for him, luminous in a white satin bathrobe. He follows her into the bedroom, which is situated on the first floor. She gives him a glass of root beer and ice and perches on the foot of the bed while he sits in an armchair across from her.

"Hello, Uncle J.," she says.

That's all he needs to hear: he rises and goes over to her. He leans down and kisses her, and she puts her arms on his shoulders and pulls him down. Next to her bed there is an intercom; its faint red light glows in the dark. If Coco wakes in the night, Veevi will hear it, but it will be Dorshka who goes to her, for she occupies the room across from the child's on the second floor. Since Jake's visits began, the child has awakened only once. Like most children in Southern California, she plays outdoors all afternoon and therefore her sleep is long, deep, and undisturbed.

He unties the satin belt to the white robe. Their movements are quick and fierce—not so much with passion as with marksmanship, as if they were taking aim at each other. She pursues her own pleasure with a sharp, incandescent greed. Always, at the beginning, he can't help being aware that she's the same flesh and blood as Dinah. But desire heightens the differences, and the comparisons turn into contrasts. Dinah has more muscle, more suppleness, longer limbs. She is generous, warm, vocal. Veevi is compact and quick, but not as athletic as her sister, not as free with her movements, and she never makes a sound, never laughs with intimacy or lust. Dinah, who doesn't use perfume on these hot, clear spring days when she works in the garden, and is often too tired to shower at night, smells of healthy sweat and sun. Veevi smells of soap; her body is exquisitely clean. He can't help asking himself, every time, as he goes inside her, whether she feels different there from Dinah—is it just his imagination that Dinah seems roomier than her sister? He's certain that Veevi is tighter.

Early on, she'd asked him point-blank what he did to Dinah to make her come. When he told her and agreed to demonstrate, she laughed and said triumphantly, "Nobody should have to work that hard! Not necessary with me." She comes, she claims, while he's inside her—and always before he does, silently, except for her quickened breathing. "Do you know what Dorshka told Mike, when he was sixteen years old and had started fucking?" she said once. " 'Never come first, and always remember the working class.' "

So he had always given her enough time, and she'd learned how to get what she wanted. Mortified, calling himself a schlepper and an amateur, he realized that he was in general not as scrupulously and fastidiously attentive to Dinah as Mike had been to Veevi. "Well," he said, "unlike Mike, I never got instructions from my mother." But he tried to do what he thought Mike had done, and when she hit her target fairly quickly, or so she said, that made him feel that he was up there in the major Parisian expatriate-novelist-educated-lover leagues.

He and Dinah do make love perhaps once a week now. It's understood that because of his insomnia and his anxieties about the picture and the new project, this is a slow time for them. He likes to fall asleep in her bed, with her arm around him and his head on her shoulder. A moment comes when she gently unfastens her arm and rolls over into her own cave of sleep, and then he moves back to his own bed. When they do make love, they fall into their regular routine, so that every move is comfortable and predictable, but this is not a time of passion.

Veevi asks coolly about what she calls "beddy-bye" between him and Dinah. It irritates him, but he responds vaguely, thinking it just as well for her to believe that he and Dinah have an indifferent time in bed. Nor does he tell Veevi that when he makes love to Dinah he feels intensely that she is a good human being, whom he trusts and relies on—that he loves her, that she's been a good wife. No longer able to make babies with her, he feels, nevertheless, that entering Dinah is like walking into a sanctuary at night after a long day at the studio. He cannot renew himself in her, because she's too familiar, but there is refuge and warmth. When he makes love to Veevi, he can feel, despite the way she tears her pleasure out of him like a shark biting into a human limb, that there is no union between them. But that excites him. He tells her often that he loves her, that he's in love with her, and he believes it.

He dozes for a while as they unclench and lie side by side in her bed. When he wakes, and rises, knowing he must go, he sees her sleeping on her back, with her hands resting one over the other. It is an unsettling sight, for she looks like a woman in a coffin, or like one of those stone effigies in a medieval tomb. At the same time, the effect is not so much of eerie remoteness as of a cold, imperious perfection that exudes censoriousness and the unspoken demand that he measure up to something which she has yet to name. He leans over and kisses her and tells her that he's crazy about her. "That's nice, Uncle J.," she murmurs, turning on her side, and again he's unsettled, for she has curled up the way Dinah does at night.

The moment he hits Sunset, he's ravenous. The craving overwhelms him, so he turns right on Allenford and drives down to Olympic and over to Itzik's. The owner, who has numbers tattooed on his left forearm, wipes his hands on his apron and makes Jake a pastrami sandwich on rye. He takes the sandwich, wrapped in aluminum foil and dripping mustard, and a Cel-Ray Tonic, and sits in his car, watching the sky change from deepest indigo to a pearlescent gray, delirious with joy at the spice and tang of the food, and the fizzing scrape of the soda against the back of his throat. He has to go home, shower, and get to the studio. He has to fight with Izzie and Mel today, and he isn't looking forward to it; he has to beg them one more time to bring in Milty Ostrow to fix the music, then he's going to wash his hands of it. Previews are starting soon; then he'll go back into the cutting room, fix the timing on jokes that don't work, do whatever dubbing and voice-overs might be necessary, and that'll be it. He'll be able to work on the show, which he's doping out in his head, during the long drives to and from Veevi's.

He gets out of the car, throws the crumpled-up aluminum foil into a trash can, and waves good-bye to Itzik, who looks out the window and waves back. Jake has a talent for getting people to talk about themselves. He does it on airplanes and in doctors' waiting rooms; he can get a hat-check girl's life story in the time it takes her to give him his coat and help him on with it. But he has never been able to do this with Itzik. Often, he feels himself on the point of saying, "When did you come here? What year did you arrive?" But he can't do it. He wants to say, "Auschwitz?" But he's shy, afraid of causing Itzik pain. Instead, he brings him jokes—new jokes he's heard at the studio or on the golf course—and he tells them, and since he's usually the only person in the deli at three in the morning they have a good laugh together. When Itzik sees Jake's eyes filling with tears, he thinks it's from laughter. But Jake once sat in the car and stuffed his mouth with a pastrami sandwich and a kosher pickle and cried at the sight of Itzik standing in his rolled-up shirtsleeves and apron, churning a vat of coleslaw.

The long curves of Sunset Boulevard are bleak and tedious as he drives home. The night air is chilly, the ocean mist raw. He is so tired now that he could fall asleep on the road, and he yawns, over and over, and belches, and thinks, What the hell am I doing in this? I'll see her a few more times, and then it's got to end.

After the fight in Palm Springs, Dinah and the kids left within an hour. Jake gave Veevi a good long day to rest, then he picked her up at the hospital at about eight o'clock. It was Veevi who drove, however, despite the bandaged cut on her head, insisting that nothing would relax or steady her nerves like being behind the wheel of a car. Jake hesitated at first but let her have her way. He was glad to be free of his family, and as he sat back in the passenger seat and let Veevi drive—something she did extremely well—he forgot Dinah's rage and the sight of his son sitting on the sofa nestled against Dinah's arm, expecting to be praised for a decision that filled Jake with such contempt that he'd had to fight the impulse to slap the boy across the face. He had never really liked Veevi before, but now, reminded of the day in Paris when they had visited the Louvre, he lost himself in the feeling that he and she were two self-sufficient, sane adults who understood each other perfectly and knew that families could be a bore. He was wishing he had never gotten married and had children, and he blamed Dinah for trapping him in a situation he'd known from the beginning he was never cut out for.

Veevi had tied a silk scarf under her chin, and the wind coming through the open windows whipped up wisps of thick brown hair that escaped from the scarf's edges. Except for the bandage at her temple, no one would have known that she had drunk herself into a state of oblivion the night before, peed on a young boy, passed out in the bathroom, and hit her head. For a long time, they said nothing. She smoked, and struck him as completely in command of the car and the driving. Then they began to chat, and, discovering that it was difficult for them to hear each other because of the air whooshing by, they rolled up the windows. Veevi untied her scarf, so that her hair fell in waves along her shoulders.

"Poor Peter," she said. "It must have been ghastly for him."

"Oh, he'll survive," Jake replied. "Unless his mother turns him into a faggot, which I'm afraid she may well do."

Veevi agreed. "Dinah's afraid of strong men," she said. "She's going to break him if you don't watch out. He's much too sensitive for his own good."

Jake had evidently never been around to hear Veevi telling Peter, as she often did, how wonderful it was that he was so sensitive.

"You know," he said, enjoying her dig at Dinah, "she just doesn't get anything."

"She's hopeless, I'm afraid. And, Jake, her taste! You've got to do something about it—her clothes, the things in your house!"

He heard how far she was trying to go, and he didn't tell her that he approved every item of clothing Dinah bought and made her take back anything he didn't like, and that it was he who had supervised the furnishing of the house, the consultations with the interior decorator—everything. So he ignored this last remark and, instead, asked her if she remembered the times when Ed Milligan had gotten drunk when she and Dinah were kids. She did, she said. She remembered her mother holding her, and Dinah always being the one to put him in the bathtub and clean him up. Jake asked whether it was true that Pop had loved her more than Dinah, and Veevi answered that it was, but that Alice had loved Dinah more than her, so it all come out even. "They were allies, Mom and Dinah. The responsible ones. The ones who always had to clean up after me or Pop. The virtuous, long-suffering ones. Domestic, dreary martyrs."

There was a not-very-subtle web of implication that he was gladly allowing her to spin around him. The world was divided into those who lived interesting lives, broke the rules, and didn't give a good goddamn about the consequences, and those who, because of inherent cowardice, self-pity, and lack of imagination, always chose safety over risk and then lorded it over the scapegrace others with their noble sufferings. It needn't be said which group the two of them belonged to.

When they got back to the house in Los Angeles, the lights were out. Dinah, he guessed, had put the kids to bed and then probably taken a sleeping pill, which she did often to get through a night of his snoring. She was unlikely to wake up and surprise them, but his conscience was bothering him, as if he'd been drawn into a conspiracy. He thought he ought to go upstairs and check. When he came down to say that Dinah and the kids were sound asleep, he discovered that Veevi had made grilled ham-and-cheese sandwiches—so like Dinah, he couldn't help thinking!—and brought out a couple of bottles of ice-cold beer from the bar in the den, just for the two of them. As they ate and drank, Jake plied her with questions about her life in Europe; he couldn't seem to get enough. When they had finished eating, she got up to put the dishes in the sink. Jake glanced up from the Sunday funnies he'd been skimming, saw that she was looking at him. A smirk played on her lips. Her eyes, which were the color of dark vinegar, danced with mischief.

"Uncle J.," she said with an ironic laugh. She laughed again, and he understood what it meant: what, after all, could be funnier! He saw this recognition between them in the lambent mobility of her mouth, the sardonic quickness of her laugh, and he stood up and went over to her, and she put his hands on her shoulders.

"What are you up to? Hmm?" he said.

"Uncle J.," she said again.

They did it on the brown tweed sofa in the den. Jake kept his pants down around his ankles, and his socks on, which Veevi found hilarious.

*H*e became familiar with the things in her house, even though he saw them mostly in the dark: the bookshelves filled with books she had collected during the Malibu days with Ventura; the long antique refectory table and benches in the dining room; the French landscapes; the pair of African masks with thin ridged geometric noses and mouths protruding like corks; the small framed photographs of her and Mike with everybody famous and literary in postwar Paris.

They had a ritual before they went to bed. He would talk, and she would listen and smoke. Always, it was the same thing: what did he want? To stay in Hollywood and keep making well-constructed romantic comedies at Marathon or to uproot Dinah and the kids and move to Europe? Of course, the answers were complicated by the new project, which he was dying to get to and which, he believed, offered the greatest possibilities of anything he had ever done. If everything worked out with the show, he would be spending a lot of time in New York, and that would be exciting.

As he paced the carpet in her bedroom, they played the game of "Ifs" so common to people in the movie business: if the show was a hit, they would all move to New York—Veevi and the girls, too. Or maybe he'd just have an apartment in Manhattan and she could fly there and spend a week or two at a time with him. If the show died, maybe they'd move to Europe—all of them.

"What about my passport?" she asked him.

"This situation won't last forever," he told her. "Look at your friend Boatwright. It's just a matter of time until he's working again under his own name. The whole stupid blacklist will collapse. Just hang on. I'm putting at least two years into this show, and a lot can happen in that time; maybe it'll all be over by then."

But he had to get out of Hollywood, and she agreed. He couldn't stand being attached to a studio anymore. It made him feel like a horse in a stable. He wanted to go independent, in Europe.

"Where, in Europe?" she asked him. "Paris?"

Paris was great, he said, but he had to go where he could make pictures. He didn't think he could do that in France. "Sure you can," she told him. "The French love American-type comedies."

"I don't know—I write jokes, I need the English language," he said uncertainly.

"Talk to Willie Weil. He'll tell you—you can make any kind of picture you want in France. Ask Hunt Crandell, too."

They went over every point again and again. There was something about Paris that made him nervous, he said. "Look at Ben Knight—look at Mike. Paris is great for weekends, but I don't want café life."

"Why not?" she said. "They work during the day. Why shouldn't they have fun at night?"

"It isn't me," he answered.

"Of course it's you. Look how much fun you had there."

"Veevi," he said, "I get up every day and I go to work. I don't need that much fun. If I wake up and just find my glasses in the morning, that's enough fun for one day."

There were endless variations on these themes. For instance, there was his novel. He wanted to take out the novel he'd written in college—the one about his uncles in the meat business in Chicago—and rewrite it.

"A Jewish *Studs Lonigan*?" she asked.

"Kind of," he said, admiring her sharpness but uncomfortable at the ease with which she'd pigeonholed the project.

"After your show," she said, "you'll write your novel. In Paris. We'll get a flat there. And a country place, small and cheap—a farmhouse in Brittany, maybe. Or an Irish fishing village. A chalet in the Swiss Alps. A villa with a vineyard in Italy."

"With the size of this family, I'll need a goddamn château."

"By then," she said, "perhaps you won't be so encumbered."

She caught his eye with a bright glance of conscious wickedness. He could take it any way he liked. He wasn't ready to say out loud what they were both thinking. Meanwhile, he was grateful to her, because she listened so well, and knew people he wanted to know, and had lived the life he sometimes wanted, and sometimes didn't. In any case, he believed she could teach him how to live, one way or the other. It was good for him that he was having this affair, he decided. It forced him to think things over, take stock, get ready for the next move.

One night he asked Veevi, "What happened with Boatwright?" He felt sure that what happened in Palm Springs had something to do with that affair.

"Things were going swimmingly," she said. "He said he'd waited all these years for me, hoping I'd come back from Europe, and he wasn't going to lose me now. Wanted me to move East. Said he'd get out from the stranglehold of wife, mother, the barbarian horde of kids."

But she wasn't so sure she wanted that, she said. Cliff was fun, bright, witty, and he adored her. But if he made his move, it was going to be messy and drawn-out. Then one night his wife walked in. They were in bed at the Château Marmont when Veevi heard the key in the door. She jabbed him with her elbow. " 'Cliff, Cliff,' I said. 'Stop, for God's sake, somebody's here.' And by God somebody *was* there. It was Eve, just off the plane from New York. Marches right up to me," Veevi said, "pulls off her white gloves, and slaps me across the face. Then she picks up my clothes, throws them at me, and starts taking off hers. Suddenly I'm dressed and she's starkers. She gets into bed with him, glaring at me, and says, 'You know what I'm gonna do right now, you home wrecker! I'm gonna fuck him to death.' " Veevi squeezes her eyes shut and laughs. " 'You're too late, dear,' I say. 'I just called the undertaker.' Cliff peeks out from under the covers, sits up, and bursts out laughing. 'What's so funny, hotshot?' the wife says. God, was I ever out of there fast!"

"Jesus Christ," said Jake, stroking her leg. Dinah had told him that Veevi was devastated by what had happened and had really believed Boatwright would leave his wife for her. That's why she'd gotten drunk in Palm Springs. "Just p-p-p-pure despair," Dinah had said a few weeks later, when she'd had time to think it over. Pure despair over the feeling that she'd never find anyone again. But Jake thought Dinah'd got it all wrong. Veevi never wanted Boatwright. She'd set her sights on *himself*.

"Well, you've been awfully sporting about it," he said, adopting a phrase she often used.

"Haven't I?" she said, laughing again, beautiful in her pajamas, her eyes lively with promise.

He looked at her. "Tell me, Genevieve, what do *you* want?"

She shrugged. "Let's put it this way. My sister wants *things*. I *want* things."

He nods. She's being unfair to Dinah, but he gets it now—that quality in her that attracted all those men in the past, that sense that nothing mattered so much as living up to what she wanted you to be and what she made you think you had it in you to be. If you met that standard, if you could get her to love you, it meant you were someone, someone she would choose over all the others. How could Mike Albrecht give that up? How would Boatwright survive without it? He himself, Jake thinks, has to have it forever.

Thus two or three nights a week, for the past few months, he's been the man he believes she wants him to be. She sits back against the headboard with her legs stretched out on the bed, sometimes tucking her pedicured feet underneath her and running her fingers through the rich brown waves of her hair. Night after night, she says the same thing, and he can't get enough of it: "Jake, darling, don't you see? All these doubts and worries you have? They're ridiculous. You're too damn good for this town. You've got to think of yourself in an entirely new way. You don't belong here anymore."

He's complained to her about his deal at Marathon. Irv loves him as long as he keeps to the same old formula: bumbling schlemiel outsmarts the city slickers and turns out to be an American hero. He wants to make pictures that have some sex in them, some truth. He wants to write, for instance, about infidelity, but to do it as comedy. He's told her about how he's had girls on the side ever since Dinah was pregnant with Lorna, and that he wants to write about that, too. He wants to do a picture about Stefan Ventura in Hollywood.

"Don't get your hopes up," she said. "Nobody here is going to touch it. You need France for that—somebody like Willie Weil to produce it. He likes you, you know."

Despite the time they spend in conversation, it amazes him how little has to be said. There always comes a point in the talking when she murmurs, almost inaudibly, "Uncle J.," and gives him that look. Then he reaches for her as she turns off the light.

It's afterward that he finds her puzzling. The way she immediately moves away from him and lights a cigarette seems strange and unfeminine.

Don't all women want to be held after sex? Why doesn't she? He wonders what Stefan had thought of it, and Mike, and Boatwright. He knows there have been others, but they don't count—only those other three, and himself, of course, in what he likes to think of as an ascending order of talent. Well, take that back, he says to himself. Let Ventura be first. After all, he's dead.

As soon as Jake delivered the picture to Izzie Morocco and Mel Gordon, his work was essentially done, and he moved swiftly to his Broadway project, *My Grandfather's Saloon*. Now that Veevi had moved to a house of her own, he had his upstairs office at home again. Gladys, his secretary, came early every morning, had coffee with Gussie, pinched the kids' cheeks while they waited for the bus to take them to summer day camp, and then went upstairs where, chewing endless sticks of Juicy Fruit and smoking Kools, she typed up last night's pages while Jake sat in bed until noon and wrote in his nearly illegible longhand on yellow legal pads.

Lunch was now a big production at the house. Jake, Dinah, Gladys, and the songwriters Johnny O'Rourke and Sammy Hart came to the table in the breakfast room every day at twelve-thirty. After a leisurely hour the men disappeared into the living room, where they worked all afternoon on the music and lyrics for the show. O'Rourke, when he wasn't supplying his friends with his own ex-girlfriends, was a hard-drinking piano player from Georgia who'd started working in speakeasies at the age of fourteen and was renowned for both the words and the music to dozens of American standards. Hart had gone to Carnegie Tech to study engineering, but the lyrics he wrote for fraternity reviews were so good that he'd quit school and gone back to New York, where he immediately began playing in nightclubs and peddling his songs to top performers. Both men had come to Hollywood in the thirties. Later, they teamed up to write songs for Jake's George Joy movies, so Jake had known them for a long time and had set his heart on hiring them for the project.

With O'Rourke at the piano, and Hart and Jake stretched out on the sofas, there issued, on these afternoons, what anyone who listened in (and both Gladys and Dinah frequently did) might have called a ceaseless stream of musical babbling: the sound of the piano resonating with chords and phrases, single and blended male voices echoing through the house. Both O'Rourke and Hart were marvelous singers—O'Rourke's voice a thin, reedy warble with a honky-tonk intonation, Hart's robust and smooth—and as experienced collaborators each knew how to build on what was best in the other. Jake's was the only voice occasionally off-key, but he brought appetite and invention to the work. These afternoons induced in him such a state of concentrated bliss that he forgot everything else: Veevi, Dinah, the kids, the house, moving to Europe, and the obsession that afflicted him and everyone else in the movie business: what was going to happen next. He jotted down phrases, strung rhymes together, listened, interrupted, shouted, got up, sang out loud, and danced. Watching him, Dinah adored him; he seemed like a dolphin leaping into the sky—alive, on fire, ecstatic.

As Dinah and Gladys hovered at the entrance to the living room, Jake often waved them in and asked them what they thought. What about this, for instance, for the opening number, which had to introduce the audience to the world of the show: "All the Harolds / all the Sidneys / Max and Jack with ailing kidneys / South Shore Temple, Temple Sholem / Contraceptives when we stole 'em"? " 'Contraceptives'! You can't use that," Gladys said. "You'll lose the Catholic audience on the out-of-town tryouts."

"She's right, Jake," Dinah said. "You can just forget the c-c-c-contraceptives."

Jake's face fell. Hart and O'Rourke were laughing: we told you so.

"How about 'Grandma's kreplach / When we stole 'em'?" Gladys said. Jake looked at Hart and O'Rourke, who nodded "Okay." Dinah smiled at Gladys, radiant, and formed her fingers into an "okay" sign.

It was Dinah, however, and not Gladys, who asked hard questions late at night, as she and Jake talked in their room. Jake would think for a while, and pace, and hit golf balls with his electric putter, and try to answer out loud the problems she brought up, and she would feel appreciated and indispensable and a very serious part of his work. And he would say to himself, Am fucking I crazy? What would I do without her? And then he would think, as he watched the clock, and knew that he would be getting up in the night before long: But we'd always be friends. I could come to her for help any time I wanted to. You don't have to be married to your wife to get her advice on a project.

Three or four times a week, Veevi would show up at about four o'clock, bringing Dorshka and Coco over for a swim and dinner. While Coco ran into the kitchen to get a cookie from Gussie, Veevi and Dorshka would go into the living room and listen as the three men brought the day's work to a close. Jake was always scrupulously careful about avoiding anything—a look, a tone of voice, a gesture—that would betray the connection between him and Veevi. Even so, having her there in the room, watching him work, made the hairs on the back of his neck bristle. He always had the feeling that she and Dorshka were exchanging private glances, and this unnerved him. Dorshka was effusive in her praises, though, and this elicited a tight, approving smile from Veevi.

Once, out at her house in the middle of the night, Jake called this her "you'll-never-be-better smile."

" 'You'll-never-be-better smile'?" she asked.

"Yeah," he explained. "You know, when you go backstage and you say to an actor whose performance stank, only you don't want to say so, so you say, 'You'll never be better.' "

"Oh, don't be silly, Uncle J."

But he pressed her.

"All right, then, since you keep asking," she said, joining him in the shower. "Broadway musicals are all very well. Lots of fun, big stories, people who 'belt out' songs that audiences go home and sing in the shower. But for God's sake, get it out of your system and move on. What about that novel you want to write?"

"Right now, I love what I'm doing."

"So love it. And move on."

"What would I do without you?" said Jake, soaping her all over.

"Have to shower by yourself."

They stood together, under the hot spray, arms locked around each other.

"I love you," he said. "I'm crazy about you. I've never loved anyone in my life the way I love you. I've never talked to anyone this way in my life. Do you love me?"

"What a question."

"Come on. Do you?"

"Oh, Jake, don't be such a boor!"

Dorshka Albrecht, too, wakes in the night. She craves something delicious to eat—some black bread with a slab of cheese schmeared with plum preserves. Across from her room lies her granddaughter Coco, asleep with one leg jutting out from under the covers. She walks over to the child and gently adjusts the bedclothes. Her legs are a little stiff and her hips ache, so she clutches the banister as she begins a gingerly descent down the carpeted stairs. She is amused by the jiggling of her pendulous old breasts, which hang down nearly to her waist, like collapsed hot-water bottles. The lacy nightgown—a Christmas present from the Laskers (she remembers with disdain that they had given one very much like it to Jake's mother, Rose)—is so long that she must be careful not to trip on it. Taking each step slowly and cautiously, she listens to her own breathing, appalled at the effort it takes her merely to go down a flight of stairs. So many lives she's had! And now here she is, an old woman with creaky joints hobbling downstairs for a stolen treat.

Suddenly she pauses: she sees fields of rye in back of her father's house, Malka the kitchen maid plucking feathers from a goose, Wojcek the peasant boy who had kissed her under a linden tree, the theater in Warsaw where Papa took her to see Sarah Bernhardt's Phèdre. If Mama and Papa had not died before the war, they, too, would have been ashes in the Auschwitz mud, like her cousins and her aunts and uncles. And Ziggy, her brother the violinist, who had stayed in Berlin after she left for Paris, and had then, in 1939, gone with his wife to St-Jean-Cap-Ferrat—to safety, they said—only to be put on a bus and then a train back to Poland. Better not to think of that. Better not think of him and Stefan. . . .

Not a day passes that she does not think of them.

Reaching the bottom of the stairs, she takes slow steps, her bare feet sinking into the luxurious plush of the carpet (all these American houses have carpets from one end of the room to the next—never a beautiful rug), turns right into a narrow hallway that leads past the dining room to the kitchen, and stops. She hears something. It is coming from Genevieve's bedroom. She concentrates. These sounds cannot be mistaken for anything else. She shrugs, almost involuntarily: so, she tells herself, there is someone who comes to Genevieve's bed in the middle of the night. What else is new? Genevieve is still a young woman—why shouldn't she have a man in her bed?

But who, she wonders, making her way undaunted to the kitchen.

Who? Who would come in the night? Is it that dullard Saul Landau? Probably not. He hasn't been around for a while. Dorshka knows that the affair with Clifford Boatwright—whom she is fond of and respects—is kaput. She quickly reviews the men who have come to the house. There's Mort Berman, that writer fellow the Laskers introduced Veevi to, who takes her out to dinner from time to time. Veevi isn't interested in him. "He's just a gag man, a joke writer," she says of him. There is Irwin Shoemaker, that blacklisted fellow who writes TV scripts behind a pseudonym and likes to call up old friends who held out for only so long but who have finally testified and are now working again under their own names, invite them to breakfast at Nate 'n Al's on the pretext of reconciling, and then screams at them loudly and walks out, leaving them with the check. He takes Veevi to the movies once in a while. "A tiny talent," she says of him. "Very tiny," she adds, winking. But there has been no one interesting, no one exceptional. No one remotely able to compete with Mike.

Usually the snack does what it is supposed to do and lulls Dorshka with a pleasant fullness in her belly, but she's awake and astir, wildly curious about whoever it is who is now so energetically providing her daughter-in-law with the pleasure she herself has not had in years and remembers almost as an abstraction. Her steps on the climb upstairs are labored; she is afraid of making noise. Back in her room, she goes quietly to her bed, where she props herself on her elbows and gazes out the window. Whoever it is must leave before dawn, she reasons.

So she waits and waits. The moon pours cold light down on the trees, and she can even see, with the help of the street lamp, the skeins of black asphalt baked into the pavement. Her eye discerns a large humpbacked car parked on the opposite curb. It must belong to the lover, for in this neighborhood all the cars are parked overnight in garages. The car looks vaguely familiar, but since she pays no attention to the make and model of American cars she can't identify it properly.

Eventually, her ear catches the sound of a screen door quietly shutting. Next, she hears steps, and then, incongruously, a low whistle. A man emerges into view, walking with an awkward, lumbering gait toward the street and reaching into his right trouser pocket for what seem to be car keys. She follows him with her eyes and sees that she was right about the car parked across the street: it does indeed belong to him. She has heard the toneless whistle before, too, and suddenly recognizes the walk and the large, broad body and the round, well-formed head. And she wonders, too, why she waited up, because as he gets into the car she realizes that she has known all along whose car it was and could have had a couple of hours of much needed sleep. She just hadn't wanted to believe it.

It is only the next day, between sessions with acting students in the downstairs study, that she contemplates what she now knows, sighing with disapproval and foreboding. And, to be truthful, she feels envy, too. But she is not envious of the man, whom she would never have chosen for herself, or of the woman, whom she loves but about whose character she has no illusions. It is herself she envies, her long-lost self; or rather, her long-past self, since she has never stopped being the person she is. There have been times when she's been relieved that it's all over for her—desire, intrigue, passion, lust, danger. All the same, she tells herself as she lights a cigarette or drinks the good coffee that she makes herself when she eats a big piece of cake at four in the afternoon, she always treated love as an art that had to be respected. She was skillful and clever at it, and, despite any number of thrilling escapades (the assignation made onstage with the wink of an eye, with no one in the audience being any the wiser), she never compromised the peace and safety of those she truly loved. These Americans—so naïve, so unpracticed, so ignorant, so unsatisfied with their lives—how could they possibly carry this off without disaster? Even her own son: how stupidly he has handled this business with Genevieve, causing such needless pain. Amateurs, she says to herself. Absolute amateurs.

Shortly before Jake started working at home on the show, Gladys told him Irv Engel had called and wanted him to come in.

"When?" Jake said, as he glanced at some memos Gladys had placed on his desk.

"Pronto," said Gladys.

"Do you have everything ready to bring out to the house?" he asked her.

"Everything. My brother's coming on Friday with his car, and with mine and his we'll shlepp it all out and be set up and ready to go by Monday morning. You want me to sharpen the pencils while you're with Irv or can I go to lunch?"

He nodded and headed toward the door. "If I'm not back in fifteen minutes, go ahead. I don't think this'll take very long," he said. "Probably just one of his little checkups."

A few minutes later, he was shown into Irv's office and took his familiar place across from the studio head's desk. He was eager to get back to work. The sooner the Gordon-Morocco job was done, the sooner he could get back to his own project. "What's up, Irv?"

"Oh, you know, I like to have these little chats once in a while. See how everything's going. We're very happy with the numbers on this last picture, by the way."

But Jake knew this, and said so. "What am I here for, Irv? Something must be up."

"Well," Irv said calmly. "I don't think there's anything to get really upset about, but there's been some talk."

"About?"

"Veevi—that she's working for you."

"Oh? Since when is that common knowledge?"

"Well, someone—I don't know who—managed to spill the beans to V. Z. Aldrich, who called me, and wants you to let her go. I know, you're paying her out of your own pocket, but we're paying you out of ours, and as my father would put it, it don't look so good, if you know what I mean. It's just a matter of time before somebody calls Louella, Hedda, Winchell, the trades, you name it, and gets the studio's name plastered all over the goddamn gossip columns. The whole thing will cost us at the box office. So better just nip it in the bud and let her go."

"How can I do that, Irv? The divorce is being held up because Mike's claiming he has to pay too much alimony since she can't work, and she can't work because Dinah named her."

"She can't work because she won't clear herself," Irv said. "She could turn this around in a minute if she'd just call up Burt Unwin and have him arrange a nice little private session with the boys."

"We're not talking Dinah here, Irv. We're talking about Veevi. Veevi's different."

Irv looked up at Jake and seemed about to say something but changed his mind.

"Irv," Jake said, "roughly speaking, how much money have I made for this studio in, say, the last five years?"

"I know, my boy, I know. It's idiotic. But I'm just telling you the situation."

Jake stood up. "Listen, Irv. I haven't got time for this shit anymore. I threw my wife to your fucking lions and I'm not throwing Veevi. If you can't stand up to those bastards, I can. I'm onto something hot right now. I've got one hell of a property cooking, and when I'm ready to show it to you it's gonna knock your socks off. But it has to go to Broadway first—"

"Broadway? Since when are you writing for Broadway and not us?"

"I *am* writing for you. But it'll go to Broadway first."

"Then come back to us? Okay, okay, we'll talk about it. But you gotta solve this other thing first."

"No, Irv, I'm not solving anything. You solve it. And, by the way, I'm packing up my office here and moving it home. I've had it here, Irv. From now on, I write at home. I'm working with Hart and O'Rourke and we need a piano. I can't bring Veevi on the lot. I can't even put her on my payroll without some anonymous red-baiting loser calling the New York office. I've proved what a valuable asset I am, and I'm gonna work the way I want to work and hire the people I want to hire, blacklist or no blacklist. If you don't like it, that's your problem."

"Are you threatening me, Jake? You gonna break your contract?"

"I owe you one more picture. And you'll get it after I go to Broadway. That's it."

"You keep Veevi on your payroll and we'll go right back to the loyalty oath."

"Do it, Irv. Go ahead, call my lawyer, call my agent, and then fucking do it." He stood up, put his hands in his pockets, and turned to leave.

"Well, Jake, I see you're a man of mettle, after all. Tell me," he said, as Jake headed toward the door. "What's she got that Dinah hasn't?"

Jake drew himself up stiffly. "I'm not going to dignify that disgusting remark with an answer."

"My poor brother used to say that she didn't even like sex that much. Sex is, you know, messy, and she's too fastidious. But power? That's another story."

"You're licking the garbage can, Irv. Tell your secretary to get the Lysol and wash your mouth out with it."

He slammed the door behind him and hurried back to his own office, where he announced to Gladys that they were moving right then and there, and that she should call home and tell Dinah to send Gussie down in the Pontiac to help with the boxes.

At two the next morning, he and Veevi were sitting across from each other in her bedroom, and he was telling her what had happened. He expected praise.

"You shouldn't have moved out of the studio," she said. "So what if it comes out that I'm working for you? That should be open and public. The whole world should know. Now they've won."

"They've won?" said Jake. "Naw. I'm just going to do things my way, that's all. I haven't broken any deals. They'll still get another picture from me."

"But you could simply have told them to make whatever fuss they were going to make and stayed put and let the waves crash over you. You need," she said, "to exercise more sovereignty."

"More what? Jesus, Veevi, what do you want from me?"

"I'll tell you exactly what I want," she said promptly. "I want you. And I want us to have our own life. I want what I deserve. You know, darling, that it's just a question now of when, not if."

He sat back and looked at her. She had just said the unsayable.

"Veevi, darling . . ." he said weakly. "What are you saying?"

"I just told you."

"What you want is impossible."

"Nonsense. You're poised for the next step. New York. London. Paris. Where's Dinah going to do her gardening? Where's she going to prune her damned roses? What's she going to do with herself? Who's she going to talk to? She simply can't keep up with the really interesting people you and I need to be around. Make the break now, darling, because then she'll have a chance to meet someone out here—some nice fellow, some television director or something—and she can grow vegetables and drive a station wagon, which is all she wants out of life anyway."

"My wife," he said solemnly, "is a wonderful woman."

"Yes. A Wonderful Woman. That's what a man always calls a wife he's fallen out of love with. The world is full of Wonderful Women, whom you're terrified you might have to sit next to at a dinner party. And my sister is one of them. So virtuous! Paints her own rooms! Installs the redwood rounds herself for the garden path! Picks up the kids at school and schlepps them to music lessons! And wouldn't know how to talk to Ben Knight if her life depended on it!"

He sat paralyzed in the armchair and touched the tips of his fingers together. He had to admit that what Veevi was saying made a lot of sense.

Who, after all, knew Dinah better than her sister? Dinah just didn't have the dimensions that he and Veevi had. Of course, at first it would go hard for her. Dinah did, after all, truly love him. In fact, he had realized long ago that she loved him far more than he wanted to be loved; her love was a burden. She could love him considerably less and he would still have all the love he needed, he decided. Well, who knew him better? Dinah or he himself? And he hated that way she had of being lovey-dovey with him. It was the kind of thing you always saw in nightclubs—broads with their hands all over a guy—and it made him feel as if he were trapped in an elevator with the oxygen running out. He didn't like it when she said she loved him. It made his throat close up, as if he had strep. Years ago, he had taken Dinah's arms with his hands when she had put them around his shoulders and said to her gently, "Let me be the one to do that." Stung, she had said, "Wh-Wh-Wh-Whatever you want."

Night after night, when he made the long drive out to the Palisades and found Veevi waiting for him, he heard what he needed to hear. "I've got to get you to Villie Vile," she said. "Engel's strictly road show compared to him. Imagine being free to do exactly what you want to do—write and direct. Without any of the hassles you have to put up with in the studio system. Villie's an independent's independent. I know, because that's what Hunt Crandell says about him. Hunt loves him. 'I'll be the prick and you'll be the pet,' he told Hunt."

Jake didn't tell her that Weil had said the same thing to him.

"I thought," he said one night, "you were going to wait until Mike has had it with Odile. What if Mike wants to come back and I'm in the middle of divorcing Dinah. What then?"

"Jake, we're not negotiating a treaty. Why should I wait for him when I have you?"

She looked at him, her eyes soft with promise, and touched his arm, and he said to himself, *I am equal to this. I want this.*

"A divorce won't be easy, you know," he went on with a light laugh. "We'd have to wait a long time before we got married. Leaving one woman to marry her sister? Guys have been boiled in oil for less."

"Married? Who said anything about getting married? We'll have two apartments, and then nobody can say anything. My friends won't care, and most people, anyway, are too involved in their own affairs to pay attention for long. Once we're back in Europe, it won't be a problem."

She had an answer for every question. So there it was, he thought: she who had had Ventura and Albrecht wanted him—the little knock-kneed, flat-footed, high-waisted, not-athletically-gifted Jewish comedy writer from Hyde Park—Hyde Park, Chicago, that is. Now what did that say about his talent and his future?

4

*B*ut once he left Veevi's bed and began the drive toward Itzik's, he couldn't stand the thought of losing Dinah. Didn't it make more sense, he reasoned as he pulled into the parking lot next to the deli, to just have them both?

When he finished his sandwich and Cel-Ray Tonic and went north again along Sunset Boulevard, he knew that within minutes he would be getting into his own bed, across from Dinah's, where he would find her curled-up, still, unsuspecting body, with its warm scent of sun-baked skin, and he did not know how he could ever leave her. It was inevitable, he knew, but how could he actually do it? How would he tell her, for instance? What words would he use? And where? Where would he tell her?

He also told himself that, at any rate, this wasn't something he had to do right now.

Dinah and Dorshka joked about ladies' lunches, but they were happy to be in each other's company once again at the little open-air Brentwood Mart on San Vicente and Twenty-sixth Street. They ordered chicken enchiladas and sat as they had the last time at a large wooden table whose wide canvas umbrella shielded them from the sun and the wind. It was Dorshka who had invited Dinah, ostensibly to compare notes about Veevi, and they had quickly agreed that, despite the alarm they had each felt after the Palm Springs episode, Veevi had rallied and was looking well. She seemed to enjoy her job as Jake's reader, and she appeared to have stopped grieving over Mike. Dorshka, who cleaned the house, had found no empty gin bottles under the bed. Veevi, she said, was seeing old friends too, going out for dinner now and again, and to occasional parties as well.

This review of Veevi's situation concluded, Dorshka displayed far greater interest in Dinah, who was startled and flattered by the attention. Dorshka had known the girls' parents, and she asked Dinah many questions about their childhood. Dinah found it easy to talk. Dorshka was a good listener, with her mobile, intelligent face and ironic smile.

"You know we are both exiles, in a way," reflected Dorshka. "Each of us started out somewhere else."

"True. But, Dorshka—everybody comes to California because something didn't work out somewhere else. They want a life they never had. You're the opposite. How can life here ever be what it once was for you? Think of the things you've done! The adv-v-v-ventures you've had!"

"Well, you can have them, too, darling." Dorshka leaned forward a little and smiled at Dinah in a way that she found puzzling.

"Me?"

"Yes, you. Now listen carefully."

Dinah leaned forward.

"You are too involved with your children. You should spend more time with Jake. Go out more in the evenings. Have more—more romance with your husband."

"Oh heavens, Dorshka," she said. "Is that what you wanted to tell me? I'd love to, but Jake's so involved with the show right now he doesn't have time for fun. He never wants to go out when he's writing like this. As it is, he has terrible insomnia and takes these long night drives and then comes home absolutely exhausted. We barely go out even to Chasen's anymore."

Dorshka slammed her fist down on the wooden table. "Don't give in to it! Be the one he turns to for—for 'refreshment'!" she said. "Make yourself alluring. Be, you know, an enchantress."

"An en-ch-ch-chantress? Oh, Dorshka," Dinah said, laughing. "I'm about as enchanting as a bowl of cornflakes."

"It is very dangerous to think that way, darling. Very dangerous. You must seduce him! Away from his worries and his work." Dorshka gripped her by the wrist and looked at her with a ferocious expression. "Down there. You must exercise those muscles. *Sqveeze* them! Fifty times a day! Otherwise, he will complain that it is like a football stadium! And this, my dear"—she wagged her finger at Dinah—"you do not want! You must put cold cream in there. You must stay young! Juicy!" (She pronounced it *joozy*.)

Dinah laughed out loud. "Dorshka!" The older woman smiled tolerantly. "Tell me," said Dinah, "where'd you learn all these female 'secrets of the deep'?"

"Ah," she said, her eyes lighting up. "In Vienna, when I was very young, I had a friend—she was an actress, and she was of 'a certain age.' She had learned them from Sarah Bernhardt herself, who had learned them from her mother—a great courtesan, you recall. There was a time when I thought I needed an education in these matters. Or, rather, my friend saw that I needed this education. I didn't know I needed it, but I had taken a lover, and my friend knew that I knew nothing. And let me tell you, it works! It makes you like a girl of sixteen."

"So have you got any special lore to imp-p-p-part?"

Dorshka smiled her mocking, good-natured smile. "Yes. As a matter of fact, I do."

"And?"

"At your age a woman should have a lover. That, too, keeps you young. And it is very good for the circulation, the skin, and, most of all, the mind! With a lover you talk about many things, and you become more interesting to your husband. A woman like you, so bright and"—she searched for the word—"so full of zest! Yes, zest! . . . should have a lover."

"Got anybody in mind?" Dinah said with a broad laugh. "I had a fling with poor old darling Art Squires in the old days before I married Jake, during one of those times when he'd tell me he loved me and then get so scared at the sound of those words that he'd take a powder the next day and I wouldn't hear from him for months. Poor Art." She had learned recently that Art had died suddenly of a heart attack. Refusing to name names had cost him his career.

"Well, perhaps I know someone for you."

"*Who?*"

"There are some very attractive young men who come to me for acting lessons. I could arrange for you to come for tea someday when one of them is there."

There was a pause, during which Dinah drank from her paper cup of Coke and lit a cigarette.

"What would a young actor want with a married woman with two children?"

"This young man—why, a thousand things he could want! You are attractive, Dinah, and witty, and you are now a woman with experience; you have much to tell him about the way things work in Hollywood. You could, you know, provide him with a 'sentimental education'!"

They looked at each other and burst out laughing.

"Dorshka, don't you know by now that I'm hopeless?"

"Indeed you are, Dinah. You are one of those impossible creatures who are actually in love with their husbands. What am I going to do with you?"

A serious, even sad expression came over Dinah's face. "You know, Dorshka, ever since I've been with Jake I don't think I've found anyone else attractive. I can't imagine anyone out there who would interest me. I have everything I w-w-want with him."

Dorshka sighed. "I must tell you something, Dinah. It is too much, this love you have for your husband. No one should love anyone that much, my dear."

But she did not press Dinah. Their conversation moved on to other things—Veevi's daughters, Dinah's kids, what would happen if Jake got the backing he wanted from Marathon for the show. Dinah, Dorshka knew, would never have an affair, but it was also true that she would never figure out, on her own, about Jake and Veevi. Really, she thought in exasperation, there was nothing one could do with these abominably chaste, virtuous wives.

That night, unaware that she and Dorshka had met, Jake made love to Dinah, as he sometimes did on nights when he didn't visit Veevi. When it was over, he kissed his wife on the cheek. "Do you still love me?" he asked her.

"Of course I love you," she said. "I adore you. You know that, don't you?" She tightened her arms around him. "Are we still one person? Are you still only half alive if we're not together?" she asked.

"Of course, darling," he said. "You don't ever have to ask."

As usual, Jake believed every word he said, at least at the moment he said it.

On Sunday afternoon, as on all Sunday afternoons over the summer, after golf or after writing, when Jake woke up from a nap, he went out on the balcony outside the bedroom, held the camera up, and, in a shot that included the whole backyard, captured his entire family: Dinah, Peter, and Lorna; his mother, Rose; Veevi, Claire, Coco, and Dorshka; his sister, Elsinore, her husband, Dave, and their daughter and son, Phyllis and Jerry. Later, there would be friends with their kids, more swimming, a barbecue by the pool, with hot dogs and hamburgers. After it got dark, he would pull down the screen in the living room and run a picture he had brought home from the studio.

The moment he went downstairs and out to the pool, however, he saw Elsinore emerging from the wood-slatted dressing room, her large bulk so much like his in shape but made ungainly by feminine swellings and bulges exposed by her bathing suit. She was followed by Phyllis, who had also gone in to change for a swim. At thirteen, Phyllis was tall like her mother, but though no beauty, she had so far been spared Elsinore's inheritance of fat and awkwardness. Dave was lying on a pool chaise, his eyes closed, soaking up the sun. He had large patches of scarred skin on his thighs and forearms, grafts from burns he'd gotten in the Pacific; he held a big unlit cigar in his hand while he dozed in the sunshine. Jake was glad to see him relaxed and tranquil. The man spent his entire life—Monday through Saturday—on his feet, selling shoes. At that, he barely made a living.

"Jacob," Elsinore said. "May I have a word with you?" He nodded and got up, and they went over to a couple of chairs under a bay tree, where there was shade and some privacy. "I need to ask you for a favor, Jacob," Elsinore said.

"You're on my deaf ear."

She got up and dragged her pool chair over to Jake's right side. When she sat down again, he made a point of not looking at her Jell-O thighs. He remembered the time he and Bobby Nathan had spied on her taking a pee in the bathroom on Calumet.

"Can you hear me okay?"

"Yeah. Shoot." Whatever she was going to ask him for was going to cost money.

His sister took a deep breath and tears filled her eyes. She smiled, and Jake became uncomfortably aware of her extensive bridgework. His sister was, to him, a patchwork of physical imperfections and charmless mannerisms. He saw her nearly every Sunday, when she and Dave brought the kids over to swim. They stayed for dinner, and he was generally affable and kind, but he avoided long conversations with her.

"You know, Phyllis could be a very pretty girl," she began. "Not like me." She gave a brief, bitter laugh. "Now that a lot of her friends are becoming teenagers, they're getting nose jobs."

"Say no more. She's got it."

She reached out to touch his hand. "Please," he said, wincing. "Don't do that."

"You'll really do it?"

"You've got it, Elsie. I just said so."

"Don't you want to know how much?"

He withdrew his hand to the safety of his lap. "Okay. How much? Never mind. Don't tell me. Just set it up and tell them to send me the bill."

"A good one is about three thousand dollars."

"*Oy vey.* Consider it done."

"Jake, they're all getting them, the girls in the ninth grade. You should see them. They come over with their eyes all bloodshot and their faces black and blue, like they've been in a prizefight. It looks terrible. Then, a month later, you can't believe your eyes. Gorgeous. They're absolutely gorgeous. I want her to have this chance, Jacob."

"Elsie, stop already. I told you: she's got it."

How we Jews hate ourselves, Jake thought, though he admitted to himself how glad he was that both of his kids had inherited the straight, well-proportioned, and very gentile Milligan nose.

"It's just, you know, that you do so much for Dinah's family."

She never knew when to stop. She did it every time, whether it was the loan for the down payment on their house or extra money so they could take Grandma Rose on vacation with them to Murietta Hot Springs.

"What do you mean, Elsie?"

"Well, you know—putting Claire through private school, supporting Veevi and Dorshka. You treat them better than you treat us."

"Elsie, don't blow it. We don't support Dorshka. Mike takes care of her."

He knew that she knew he'd send her the money anyway, no matter how she needled him.

"Thank you, Jacob," she said. "You know, my kids go to public school."

"Guess what, Elsie? So do mine."

"Yes, but for how long?"

He got up. "Elsinore, go take Mother into the goddamn pool and make her exercise her knee. Would you do that for me?"

"I did it already, Jacob," she said triumphantly. That was their unspoken deal: she took their mother to the doctor and the chiropodist; he paid the bills. And when the time came she would be the one to take her mother in, or change her diapers, and Jake would be the one to pay for it.

"Well, go for a swim," he said. "Phyllis'll have her nose done."

If Phyllis had a nose job, she'd have a crack at marrying a guy who could make a buck. That's what this was all about, and both of them knew it. He'd had a nap only a little while ago, but conversations with his sister always exhausted him. Yawning, he caught Veevi looking at him with a secret smile that said, "We're going to leave this one day. Just say the word."

With sudden irritation, he went up to Dinah and leaned over her. Startled, she put down her knitting and looked up at him. "Will you please pay some attention to my sister and my mother? It's not too much to ask, is it, considering all I do for Veevi."

She looked at him, her mouth open, flabbergasted. "You're out of your fucking m-m-m-mind," she said. "Who do you think looks after them while you're upstairs working or playing golf? Or napping all afternoon?" She was stunned by his outburst.

Suddenly he knew he couldn't keep his eyes open. "I don't know what's the matter with me," he said. "I gotta go lie down again. Be nice to them, okay?"

She looked at him and scratched her head. "I don't know what's gotten into you, b-b-b-bud. That sure as hell came out of nowhere."

But he was already on his way into the house. Passing through the kitchen, he told Gussie to wake him up in an hour, when it was time to light the coals for the barbecue.

"Mr. Lasker, you're too tired," she said. "It's all that night driving. You got to relax, but that ain't the way. What if you get so relaxed you was to fall asleep at the wheel?"

"Oh, Gus. I've got a lot on my mind," he said. "You have no idea how much."

He went to the ice box and opened the door.

"Mr. Lasker," Gussie said, glaring at him. "Are you fixing to eat something?"

He had told her not to let him raid the ice box. "I'm so tired I'm not even hungry," he said, peering inside, then closing the door.

About an hour later, he woke up to find Dinah sitting beside him, holding his forearm. "Jake? Are you all right? Gussie says it's time to come down."

He looked up into her brown eyes and smelled the suntan lotion on her skin. What a nice smell that was—hot skin smooth with suntan lotion. "I must have fallen asleep," he said.

She leaned over and kissed him. "You're so tired all the time, honey. I've never seen you so tired. Look, darling, if this show is doing this to you, it just isn't worth it."

"Actually," he said, abruptly sitting up, "I feel marvelous now."

He had been thinking of Veevi lying in bed with her nipples hard, but now, looking at Dinah, smiling at him so lovingly, he thought, I've got to get out of this. He pulled on his pants, and together they went out to the balcony. With his arm around her shoulder, he cupped his free hand to his mouth and shouted, "Everyone out of the pool! Everyone out of the pool!" The sun was going down, and Gussie was lighting coals in the barbecue. It was time for him to go down and flip hamburgers.

Not every night was what he called a Veevi night. But even when he stayed home, desperate to catch up on sleep, he still woke up at two, as he had tonight, and went downstairs to the kitchen. He had dunked five Oreos, one after the other, in a glass of milk, swallowed each soggy one practically whole, and then moved into the den.

He was there now, pulling a book down from the shelf. It was one of Mike's novels, and he read the final paragraph:

Darling, he said. Darling, darling. It's dawn.

She stirred next to him in bed, and he could feel her body through her satin gown.

No, she said in French. It can't be. No, darling, not yet.

It's time, he said.

When will we . . . ? she began to ask. He put his finger to his lips and silently shook his head. They knew, each of them, that there could be no answers, and therefore no questions.

The sound of the military transport roaring through the village drowned out the thud of his boots as he made his way downstairs and out into the pale light of day.

Jake felt both moved and embarrassed, but he only said to himself, What crap. That was Mike and Veevi's way of living: you fell in love and seized the moment and you did it in wartime or in impossible situations and you took what you could in the face of fate. It certainly wasn't life on Delfern Drive, where you just lived with your wife and your kids, you got up and worked all day, and you functioned almost automatically but you never questioned that you were together and would stay together forever. But which guy was he? A good Jewish husband and provider who raided the ice-box at night and worried desperately about bringing his pictures in under budget and the grosses in Cincinnati, or a Mike Albrecht, one of those seize-the-moment guys for whom life without passionate sexual love wasn't worth living?

*P*acing back and forth in Veevi's bedroom eight months later at two in the morning, he watched her face.

"So it's done, finally?" she asked.

"Went off to New York today. Which means," he said, "that I can finally tell you the story."

"Yes, I know. You've been very good. So far, all I know is what I've picked up from the songs. So go ahead. I can see you're dying to tell me."

"Don't you want to hear it?"

"By all means! Deliver yourself. You're bursting!" She turned on her side, propping her head against her hand, and looked at him brightly, eyebrows raised in anticipation.

He paced again for a moment, then stopped and opened his arms, suddenly a master of ceremonies in blue boxer shorts, a white T-shirt, and black socks.

"Okay. It's Chicago, 1918. The war has just ended. David and Dolly's Budapest Café—my grandfather's saloon. Dolly makes the goulash that's killed more Jews than Hitler—"

Veevi let out a laugh.

"And David conducts his Royal Hungarian Orchestra on Friday and Saturday nights. Got the picture?"

She nodded and listened as he resumed pacing, and poured out the story of the Jewish immigrant family with its four sons, among them Munish, the baby, whom the other three are putting through medical school, and who falls in love with a Polish waitress. Prohibition hits, and the whole family, including the Polish waitress, make "sacramental wine" in the cellar and turn the saloon into a speakeasy. But the cops find out and shut the place down. Whenever there was a musical number, Jake paused and sang the first eight bars, softly, so as not to disturb Coco and Dorshka, then went on with the story. When he reached the part where Munish dies of pneumonia, and with him the family's American Dream, he sniffed and went over to the ottoman to retrieve a handkerchief from his jacket pocket. "Second Act curtain," he said, wiping his eyes. Soon, as he brought together all the strands of the plot, which included Prohibition, gangsters, cops, and mayhem, tears began to stream down his face, and he made no effort to stop them. "Suddenly," he said hoarsely, moving into the finale, "we're at the big wedding scene, with David leading the Royal Hungarian Orchestra, the whole ensemble dancing and singing—and the stage goes dark except for a spot on Buddy, the grandson. He's standing in front of the saloon. Only now it's 1955, and it isn't there anymore. And that's the final number—his farewell to the family and his memories and that time in American life."

He coughed and wiped his eyes. "I can't help it," he said. "I love it so much."

He looked at her. "So?" he said. "What do you think?"

She paused and cocked her head a little to the side and smiled. "It's fine, dear. Fine."

"*Fine?* As in, 'How are you today?' 'I'm fine'?"

"Jake. It is what it is."

" 'It is what it is'? What the hell is that supposed to mean?"

"It means exactly that. It is what it is. Obviously it's something you have to get out of your system before you can go on."

"You don't love it?"

"No, I don't love it. Do I have to?"

"No, you don't *have* to! But if you love me, as you've been telling me you do all year—"

"I have?"

"Yes, you have, though you seem to have developed a sudden and devastating case of amnesia. But if you love me, then you can't fail to love this show. This show *is* me. This show is about everything I've come from. And you don't love this show."

"Jake, really. What can I tell you? It's *corny*. It's 'too much of a muchness,' as the English say. It's—it's *Broadway*. Not my sort of thing."

"What *is* your sort of thing?" he said with fury. "Tell me that! Half-assed

Hemingway imitators like Ben Knight and Michael Albrecht? International literary snobs with very tiny talents and very large bar bills? Where's the heart in their work? Where's the laughter and the human struggle, huh? Who the hell are you to be snide and disdainful of something I've been pouring my absolute guts into? Huh?"

"I've told you all along: do your little show and then get to the real stuff you've got it in you to do."

" 'Your little show'? Don't you know what this means to me? Haven't you seen me killing myself this last year? I'm staking everything I've got on this!"

"Jake, don't be ridiculous. I said it's fine."

" 'Fine' is the operative word you use when the proctologist asks you if he's gone in too deep! And when Veevi Milligan Ventura Albrecht says it's 'fine,' it means it stinks. It means she thinks it's a piece of shit."

"Oh, really—"

"You think I don't know every tone of your voice by now? To think I stood here crying my eyes out, spilling my guts, while you sat there coolly laughing at the whole thing!"

"I wasn't laughing."

"You were laughing. You're always laughing. You have that light little laugh that covers up the venom running in your veins. Jesus Christ, Veevi. What kind of person are you, anyway?"

"Until this moment, someone you've been ready to change your life for. Someone you've been ready to get out of your pathetic charade of a marriage for. Someone you've dreamed of sharing a life with. All I've said is that I don't like your show. Suddenly that makes me Medusa—a monster with snakes in her hair!"

"Very apt, believe me! It was stupid of me to think you'd ever like anything I do!"

"That's not true. I believe absolutely in you. More even than you do."

"Bullshit! You believe in something you want to turn me into! Something I'll never be in a million years. Meanwhile, this project, which I adore, which is more me than anything I've ever done, you dismiss with one word: 'Fine.' Tell me something, Veevi, what do you know about putting yourself on the line? Have you ever written one goddamn word? No! Oh, I know, every writer in Hollywood has been in love with you, and considered it a privilege for you to bite his balls off with a snotty remark and a snide look, but those guys are horses' asses, and don't I know it now!

You've got a stinger, baby, and you're always trying to use it. You're a god-damn Johnny one-note. You're never *for* anyone or anything. You nourish yourself—excuse me, gorge yourself—on ridiculing others. At least Dinah knows what happens when you sweat out a project like this. She remembers what it's like to sit down in front of the goddamn typewriter and try to think of ways to make people laugh and cry and feel something except the numbness of their lives. She's my wife, goddamnit, and she was a damn good radio writer, and I can't believe I've come *this* close to fucking up her whole life to hear your snotty snap judgments about the best thing I've ever done!"

"Then," said Veevi, stubbing out her cigarette and turning out the light, "I suggest you go home to her and finish out your little tantrum there. Nighty-night."

He made no rejoinder.

The room went completely silent. He knew what she was doing: lying there curled up in a ball. Did she think he was going to come to the bed and get in beside her? Did she think he was going to fit his body to hers and tell her she was right?

In the dark, he fumbled for his trousers and shoes and shirt and jacket, which lay in a heap on the ottoman. The keys jangled as they fell out of his pants pocket onto the carpet, and as he groped for them, he sensed the small body under the covers becoming so defiantly still that it seemed to have stopped breathing.

Upstairs, Dorshka sat up in bed. His angry voice had risen through the ceiling. Is it over? she thought. She listened at the window and detected the back door closing, steps crunching across the gravel in the driveway, the engine turning over, and the car driving off.

"You nincompoop, you horse's ass, you all-time schmuck," Jake fumed at himself. He was driving all over Brentwood, then down into Santa Monica, not sure where he was going, not noticing streets, not caring, just berating himself, cursing himself, exploding at her, shouting, repeating the same things over and over. The window was down, and the night air filled the car, and he began to feel cold. But just as he told himself he had better get home, he realized that he had driven across Santa Monica to Itzik's deli-catessen.

Soon he was sitting behind the wheel of his parked green Cadillac, ecstatically stuffing himself with a pastrami sandwich on rye, slathered with mustard, and guzzling Cel-Ray Tonic, feeling deliriously alive and rapturously free of Veevi—free of guilt, free of complications, practically reborn. *I'm out of it,* he said again. *It's over!* I'll do whatever Dinah wants, I'll support that cunt of a sister of hers until the day she dies, but I'm out of it now.

He got out of the car and threw the mustard-streaked waxed paper and the empty soda bottle and the sliver that was left of the kosher pickle into a metal garbage can, and emitted a tremendous belch. He couldn't wait to get home to Dinah, to get into bed beside her and snuggle up against her. To think he had planned to leave her! To think of the hours he and Veevi had spent describing to each other the apartment they would have in Paris! "You perfidious lout!" he fumed at himself. To his relief, no one else was around; the street was deserted, and there was no one to accuse him. He waved good-bye to Itzik, who, looking up, wiping his hand on his apron, and waving back from behind the counter, evoked in Jake an overwhelming tenderness for his fellow Jew. That's the kind of love I feel, he said to himself, not that romantic crap Veevi wants. And the show—he felt tears rising again—that show would mean something to Itzik if he got a chance to see it; Jake made a note that if it ever came to L.A. he would arrange free tickets for Itzik and his wife. Who had ever put the Jewish immigrant struggle on Broadway before? With singing and dancing and joy and tragedy and heartache—the way he was going to do it? What did Veevi know of that? Dinah—now she understood it! No one had to explain it to her. Have I been crazy? he asked himself. To think of how close he had come to giving her up!

He leaned against the car for a moment; he thought he could hear the roar of the ocean six or seven blocks away. The blue Pacific, he said to himself. When I die, I want them to scatter my ashes there. I want them to be spread across the whole world. I want to be a part of everything, not rolled up into a tight little ball of cruel passion with Veevi. The very thought of her filled him with disgust.

He started the car and turned the radio on. June Christy's husky voice flowed out: "I could cry salty tears / Where have I been all these years?" Oh Jesus, he thought. He had sung it so many times with Dinah, on car trips; held her close while dancing to it; crooned it in the shower. Driving slowly, carefully across Santa Monica, looking for Twenty-sixth Street, which he would take, as usual, to Sunset and home, he savored his warm belly, his mouth glowing with a spicy aftertaste, and the way the song reminded him how much he loved his wife. He checked his watch: four. He had a meeting with Jimmy and Sammy at nine that he couldn't cancel. That was okay. He wanted to work. He would get in three hours of sleep, and then take a nap in the afternoon. The night drives were over. He could get some rest now. The next time he saw Veevi, he would be friendly and businesslike, and make it very clear that she could keep her job. There would be no discussions; she would realize, just from his demeanor, that it was finished between them, but that family life would go on as before. Thank God, he repeated to himself, he hadn't yet made a move. Dinah and the kids were still his; nothing at home was changed. Treat the whole thing, he said to himself, like a bad investment. Just put it behind you. Write it off.

He yawned, and stared ahead, and switched stations. He recognized piano music by Debussy and let it enfold him in its surges and vibrations. Then an elephant stepped on his chest, and he fell into a chasm of crushing pain, nausea, and blackness.

Gussie wakes again at about four-thirty, as she so often does, anticipating the sound of the Cadillac slowly easing itself into the garage downstairs.

Why ain't he back yet? she wonders. Usually he's back by now.

She decides to check. Putting on her bathrobe and her slippers, she quietly eases her way down the back stairs. It is still deep darkness, and she can see stars. She opens the creaking wooden gate that separates the front of the house from the back and moves into the driveway.

The garage door is open. No sign of the Caddy.

Now, where is he? she wonders again.

It isn't like him not to be back by now, and she can't go back to sleep. So, wrapping the bathrobe tightly around her fifty-six-year-old frame, she goes out to the mailbox and leans down to pick up the *Los Angeles Times*, wrapped in wet plastic. Then she goes back to the house. She might as well wait up for him.

The water is on the boil, the kettle just beginning to whistle. She's turning toward the sports section and is about to light the first Camel of the day when the phone rings.

Oh, these movie people, she says to herself as she reaches for the receiver. Sooner or later, they always gets into trouble.

*E*verything was in turmoil at the Laskers'.

Jake, home from the hospital the day before, was propped up in bed against a backrest and joyously ordering everyone around. Gussie and Dinah kept running up and down the stairs, nearly colliding with each other as they outdid themselves carrying a steady load of trays to the patient, who was permitted only toast and weak tea or boiled chicken and wedges of iceberg lettuce or sliced melon and melba toast—and nothing else. Every few minutes, either the phone rang or the doorbell chimed, with the children doing their share of escorting the never-ending parade of visitors, as well as huge bouquets, telegrams, and baskets of fruit, upstairs to their parents' bedroom.

Not only had Jake had a heart attack but he'd broken two ribs and was in great pain, for which he was taking a strong painkiller that made him giddy with euphoria. Peter, Lorna, and Coco brought friends, who asked him to pull up his pajama top and display the truly magnificent purple and green bruise that, even after two weeks, was still the size of an eighteen-inch pizza. It was dramatic evidence that his big belly, into which the steering wheel had slammed when the Cadillac crashed into an old juniper tree on the edge of the Palisades polo grounds, had saved his life. Grown-up visitors sat across from Jake on Dinah's bed and listened in wonder to the tale of his miraculous brush with death. They, too, were shown the bruise, and regaled with his quest in the night for the perfect pastrami sandwich, the ecstatic fulfillment of that goal, the blissful start for home, and then the plunge into pain and oblivion. He had awakened, he said, in an oxygen tent at Cedars, with the terrible feeling that he was still alive, that the car had been wrecked beyond salvation, and that he would have to go on with his show.

At five-thirty, after the visitors had left, Jake's cardiologist, Justin Brody, showed up to check on his patient's progress. Dinah told Gussie, Dorshka, and Veevi, who were present, to stay while the doctor, who had become very fond of his new patient, listened to his heart, and they paid close attention as he repeated what he'd said in the hospital, namely, that Jake had almost died, that the scarring at the back of his left ventricle, though minor at this point, would be permanent, that he had been abusing his health with the cumulative effects of overwork, lack of sleep, and suicidal eating habits, that if his broken ribs had pierced his lungs or oxygen-deprived heart he would have bled to death within seconds.

"Well, Uncle J.," Veevi purred. "No more midnight snacks for you!"

"I done told you, Mr. Lasker, that you was liable to get yourself killed," said Gussie.

"You damn f-f-f-fool! You're lucky to be alive!" Dinah said, handing the doctor a cup of coffee and a large slice of the chocolate cake Dorshka had brought over and that Jake now longingly followed with his eyes. "You know, dear," Dinah said, grinning broadly, "I kept thinking night after night, when you went out on those drives, that you must be having an affair. Little did I know you were going down on a pastrami sandwich!"

The doctor threw his head back and laughed so hard that he began choking on his cake. While Dorshka pounded his back, Dinah ran to the bathroom for a glass of water. "Justy, dear, are you all right?" she said.

The doctor loosened his tie. "You guys better take out laugh insurance in case someone dies in your house," he answered, daubing his eyes with his handkerchief. "Wait till I tell my nurses what you said."

"Tell me, Justy. When can I have sex again?" Jake asked, looking mischievously at Dinah and pointedly ignoring Veevi. "And, more important, will it kill me?"

Everyone laughed, including Veevi, who, Jake noted, was smiling at the tall, dapper physician in her loveliest, most beguiling way.

"Actually," he began, "the research that's been done on this very topic shows that one act of sexual intercourse with a familiar partner in a longstanding relationship—your wife, for instance—is the equivalent of running around a city block and is not only *not* harmful but very good for the heart."

"Oh, great," said Dinah. "The old d-d-d-donkey ride."

"But," he added, giggling in a most unscientific way, "with anyone new, or if you engage in any unusual practices—you know, like 'going down on a pastrami sandwich' "—he was laughing uncontrollably again—"you'd better call me first."

"What're you going to say?" quipped Jake. " 'Okay, but hold the mustard'?"

Justin Brody winked at him. "I'm a very discreet guy, Jake. And I want you alive for the opening of that show. Do me a favor. Stay away from Jewish food for a while—say, six months. Sex—well, give that a couple of weeks, and then do whatever comes naturally. Then come into the office. I'll check you out, and if everything's fine and you've lost weight and you're exercising regularly, then once in a while you can go to the deli."

"But I'm going to New York!" said Jake. "That's like sentencing me to death row. The theater's five minutes from the Stage Delicatessen!"

Dorshka, glad of the change in subject, asked why he was going to New York, and Jake and Dinah excitedly took turns explaining that *My Grandfather's Saloon* was going full steam ahead—rehearsals were scheduled for the summer, out-of-town tryouts in the early fall, and then the opening, in November, at the Breckinridge Theater. The minute Justy Brody gave the word, Jake would fly East, where Dinah and the kids were going to join him for the summer.

"Well, bravo and well done, and all that," Veevi said. "You must be pleased." Only Jake could hear the edge in her words.

"If you behave yourself," said the doctor, accepting a second piece of cake, "and start taking walks and stop eating like a kamikaze pilot, you can leave in six weeks. Until then, no work at all, strict bed rest, and no aggravation."

"Did you hear that?" said Dinah sharply.

"Hear it?" Jake said. "I've been dying for a little heart attack for the last ten years. First real rest I've had in ages."

"Joking aside, Jake," said Dr. Brody, coming up to the bedside and clasping Jake's hand and shoulder. "You're forty-three, and you've had your first heart attack. Make it your last. There are easier ways to go on vacation."

"When you're in love, the whole world's Jewish," Jake sang out in a codeine-induced non sequitur, followed by a loving grin at the doctor.

"You got yourself a real handful here, Dinah," the doctor said, leaning over and kissing Jake on the forehead.

Dr. Brody turned, noticed Veevi looking at him with interest, brushed cake crumbs from his shirtfront, and went downstairs, followed by Dorshka, Dinah, and Gussie. Dinah consulted with him about the days ahead; Gussie was given strict orders to wrap up all the pies and cakes people had brought over and take them home with her for her church socials; Dorshka went to round up the children for dinner.

Upstairs, Jake and Veevi found themselves alone. His face radiant with benevolence, his hand on his chest by his ribs, he looked at her in silence as the warm spring air blew in through the windows.

"Well, Uncle J.," she said, amused, scornful, her voice full of the memories and assumptions of recent months. "I know I've had a certain effect on various characters, but I've never killed anyone before!"

"Seems I'm still alive, actually. So I wouldn't give yourself too much credit yet." He frowned. "How are you, Vee?"

"Fine."

He winced, remembering their last exchange.

"Did Dinah tell you about New York? I mean, about our going there for the summer?"

"No. She's been too busy playing Florence Nightingale."

"Don't, Vee. She's been an angel. Look—"

"Don't say it. Not necessary."

"Anyway, the deal's set."

"That's hardly surprising. You always get what you want, don't you? Isn't that 'the iron law' around here?"

"I'm a comedy guy, Vee. Always will be."

"And a pastrami-sandwich guy, too."

"Look," he said. "Nothing's going to change. You still have your job, if you want it. You're still part of this family. That's forever."

"Oh, shut up, Jake," she said with a light laugh. "You always think everything has to be spelled out. It doesn't. There's nothing drearier than an explanation."

He took a deep breath and made a face. The codeine was wearing off. She looked so bitterly intelligent, so determined not to be a bore, that he didn't want it to be over. But the ribs on his left side were throbbing, and he couldn't get comfortable, and all he wanted was to be free of pain.

"Listen, honey, could you just get me a glass of water so I can take an Empirin and codeine?"

"Natch." She got up, moved to the bedside with her usual quick grace, and poured him a glass of water. He could smell her perfume and remembered her body. But he did not feel desire, and this both surprised and disconcerted him.

As he swallowed the pill, she stood there, her arms folded, looking down at him. For a moment, he half considered reaching out and touching her arm. "I'm sorry, baby," he said. "It was killing me."

"Evidently."

He drew the covers up to his nose, aware that he looked silly but wanting Veevi to see him completely as himself. He wanted her to find him lovable and endearing, but not to be in love with him (if indeed she ever had been, which he now doubted). "You're brave, kiddo," he said.

"I am? What makes you say that?"

"No explanations, remember?"

"Agreed."

As she stood looking at him, he closed his eyes and half dozed, waiting for the lifting tide of relief, musing on how she had peed on Peter, how Peter, Dinah had told him, had felt suffocated under her body in that bed. Damn it, he did love her, he told himself. Loved her for just that—for betraying all that gargantuan hunger she otherwise pretended not to have. She was reckless and even vicious, but, like a rattler curled up along the desert road, she struck only when she had to, and she fought, in her own way, for herself. Like him, she wanted everything from life, and she hated losing what she'd had. Opening his eyes, he held out his hand and she took it. "You're one helluva dame," he said.

"I think you're looped on this stuff," she said, holding up the vial of pills.

Again, he dozed. Nothing need be said. They were in-laws again, no more and no less.

She watched him for a while and then went back to her armchair, where she settled herself and began thumbing through *Holiday* magazine.

Dinah returned fifteen minutes later and whispered to her sister, "Is he asleep?"

Veevi nodded.

"Let's go downstairs," Dinah suggested, "and have a drink."

"Don't go!" Jake cried out. "Stay here! I love falling asleep with you girls around me. Go ahead and talk. I love it. I love falling asleep to the sound of your voices."

"Shh. Go to sleep," Dinah said. "We'll st-st-st-stay."

He drifted off to the sound of their whispers and the rustling of pages. He couldn't know that Veevi was passing the *Holiday* over to Dinah, and pointing out to her an article about writers who regularly went to Klosters to ski during the winter. There was a photograph of Michael Albrecht; his fiancée, the young actress Odile Boisvert; the producer Willie Weil with Lady Fiona Berkeley; the director Hunt Crandell and his wife, Felicity; the author Ben Knight with his wife, Sylvia; and assorted other chic and attractive people Veevi knew. They were all gathered around a pot of fondue, at a big wooden trestle table, eating and talking.

As Jake's chest rose and fell, and he lapsed into mighty snores, Veevi whispered stories about each one, and Dinah, who had come upstairs intending to tell her sister how helpful she had been and how she couldn't have gotten through the past few weeks without her, understood that her words would have meant nothing, and that for Veevi, being here in Dinah's house, living in Los Angeles, and helping out weren't really life at all.

By early June, Dinah's whole life had become consumed with details and arrangements. Jake, fully recovered, was already in New York, living in an apartment in the East Sixties and spending eighteen-hour days in a rehearsal hall on West Forty-sixth Street, where he held auditions with Hart, O'Rourke, and the director-choreographer, Buzz Keegan. Dinah, the kids, and Gussie were due to leave as soon as school was out. She was on the phone several times a day with Elsinore, explaining where everything was, giving her phone numbers for the plumber, electrician, exterminator, gardener, pool man, and laundress; Elsinore and her family and Jake's mother would be living in the Delfern house while the Laskers spent the summer on Long Island in a house Jake had rented in Springs. He would do as New York families did: work in the city during the week and go out to the country on weekends. For the Lasker kids, who had never been out of California, this custom, and everything connected with New York, was as exotic as going to the moon. The previous fall Jake had ordered the upcoming salmon-pink '56 Chrysler station wagon, and Dinah had come up with the very ambitious idea of driving the kids and Gussie across the country. Let them see America, she proposed to Jake, who was all for it, especially since the house in Springs wouldn't be available until the first of July.

About three weeks before school let out for the summer, Dinah went to the AAA office in Beverly Hills, where a grandmotherly woman cheerfully mapped out a cross-country route for her with a green felt pen and gave her a stack of booklets with the names of motels and hotels in various states along a generally northern route from Nevada to New York. Jake was going to meet them in Chicago, where they would stay with his cousin's family in

Highland Park. He had an interview on the Kupcinet show, and then he would drive Dinah and the kids to the South Side and point out all the places where he had lived as a kid and some of the places he was putting in the show. When they got to Pennsylvania, Dinah, in turn, would show them where the Milligans had lived in Beaver Falls, Pittsburgh, and Phila-delphia.

Her errand completed, she was thinking about how many hours a day she would realistically be able to drive with a car full of kids when she pulled up to a red light a couple of blocks west of the intersection of Santa Monica and Beverly Glen. She was in the right lane, squinting a little against the sullen orange-gray glare that was determined to burn its way through the June cloud cover, when her eyes lit on a two-story motel on her right. A man and a woman were exiting a room at street level, moving briskly toward a black Chevy convertible parked in front of their door. The couple looked absorbed and silent: "postcoital," thought Dinah. They couldn't possibly see her, which was awfully lucky for everyone concerned, because the man was Michael Albrecht and the woman was Jill Trevor. The actress was still blond and beautiful despite her stalled career—the result, Dinah had heard, of a nasty divorce several years ago from Willie Weil, who, Dinah remembered, had so charmed Jake in Paris.

The couple quickly got into the convertible, and Dinah could see the back of the man's head as he leaned forward to start the engine. She felt a panicky urge to escape, and pressed the accelerator the instant the light changed, moving swiftly ahead into what was still fairly light morning traf-fic. That it was Mike Albrecht she had seen, she had no doubt. He had the same head of thick curly hair that she remembered; the same broad shoul-ders; the same round face and high cheekbones (now that he was older, she could see that they were unmistakably Stefan Ventura's); the same stiff-backed yet forward-tilting walk so exactly like Dorshka's that she would have recognized it anywhere.

The next time she looked in the rearview mirror, the Chevy was gone. She had planned to go into Westwood to buy a new bathing suit for the East Hampton beach, but she made a sharp right turn. Some ten minutes later, she was climbing up a steep lane off Stone Canyon Road. She stopped in the circular driveway of a white colonial house that looked out over a vast hilly sweep to the sapphire Pacific. As she parked, she saw a wiry brown man running around the circumference of the driveway. He was wearing blue bathing trunks and white tennis shoes, and his bald head glistened with suntan oil. A blob of white cream shone on the end of his nose. Around his waist was a belt to which he had attached a small transistor radio; he was enjoying the baseball game at full volume. He waved and blew her a kiss but didn't stop to talk, motioning, instead, to the back of the house with a jerk of his thumb. She knew where to go, and, walking down a series of brick steps, she saw her friend Nelly Steiner doing her daily hundred laps in the pool. Planting herself in a chair in the sun, Dinah sat for another ten minutes or so before Nelly noticed her. Her friend held up her hand and squeezed her fist open and shut twice, meaning that she had ten laps to go.

Finally Nelly came out of the pool and wrapped herself in a white terry-cloth bathrobe.

"I'm sorry I didn't c-c-c-call first," Dinah said. "But I've got to talk to you."

"Uh-oh," Nelly said, putting coconut-scented oil on her tanned legs and arms. "Should I brace myself?"

"Yes, br-br-brace yourself."

Dinah then told her what she'd seen.

"Well?" said Nelly. "And what of it?"

"Well, the thing is, shouldn't I do something or say something, Nelly? To my sister?"

"You're sure it was Michael?"

"P-P-P-Positive."

"So where's the French girlfriend?"

"How the hell should I know?" Dinah said. "Probably pining for him in Paris. Probably getting l-l-l-lovesick telegrams from him saying how much he misses her."

"Well, maybe he does. Maybe he's just, you know, having one of these meaningless little flings."

Dinah shrugged. "Well, sure—maybe that's all it is. But, Nelly, I'm at the end of my rope with Veevi. She's still in love with Mike. She doesn't know he's a c-c-c-cad. She doesn't know they're through."

"Now listen, Dinah," Nelly said with her slight lisp and precise German accent. "The fact is, you don't know anything about them. You don't know whether Mike is still with the French girl. You don't know if the thing with Jill Trevor is just a big nothing. You don't know why he's here, how long he's staying, or even if he's in contact with your sister. True? These things always look like one thing to outsiders and another thing to the people concerned."

"True. But I know he's not coming back to her."

"How do you know it?"

"I can't say, but I know it. Just like I know our husbands aren't like that."

Nelly laughed. "Well, that's what *we* think. Tell me, has Veevi said anything to you about his being in town?"

"Nothing."

"So most likely she doesn't know. Well, what you're going to do is very clear: nothing. Do you hear?"

"Yes, *mon c-c-c-commandant.*"

"You didn't see it, you know nothing about it, it didn't happen."

"But, Nelly," Dinah protested. "She's bound to find out. If it's for a short visit, she'll be let down as all hell if he doesn't see her, and if he does, she's in for a miserable time. She ought to just get away for the summer—Jake really ought to change his mind and invite her to Spr-Spr-Springs with us."

"He doesn't want her to come? Why on earth not?"

The sun ducked behind a swirl of clouds and the wind blew ripples across the pool, giving Nelly goose bumps. She beckoned to Dinah to come up into the house. Over tuna salad sandwiches, Dinah explained that Veevi, after a pretty good year in which she seemed to be on an even keel, had been having a difficult time again. She'd been a big help while Jake was in the hospital, but as soon as he'd come home she'd started seeing that awful Saul Landau again. He was still in the Party, apparently, and Veevi had gone to a couple of meetings with him somewhere in the Hollywood Hills.

"You wouldn't believe how depressing it was," she'd told Dinah. "There were four or five people I recognized from the old days. It was like visiting a cemetery. The thinking hadn't changed at all. You know, Khrushchev's Stalin speech was a pack of lies and just a way of furthering his bourgeois counterrevolutionary compromise with the West. Stalin couldn't have killed all those people, and if he did, then he knew what he was doing—he was protecting the revolution. All the old clichés came out. You know—'to make an omelet you have to break eggs.' It was unbelievable. I couldn't breathe in there. It was like time had come to a complete standstill. But it was terribly sad, too."

Of the four or five old-timers Veevi knew, all had refused to testify and had been cited for contempt. One, an art director at Paramount, had served time in jail and was selling men's clothes at Desmond's; another, a cutter, was selling radio advertising over the phone. Landau wanted her to come back to the Party, and they'd quarreled about it and she'd stopped seeing him. There didn't seem to be any likely prospects in sight. Besides, she'd told Dinah, she couldn't stand him in the sack.

"I don't know what to do with her, Nelly," Dinah said, putting down her glass of iced tea in exasperation. "She still reads, supposedly, for Jake but produces maybe one synopsis every other week. She has no training for any other kind of job. She can't even type. Because of the blacklist, she can't get work in TV or the movies. I can't think of a single single guy to introduce her to."

"So where does New York fit in?"

"Two big reasons, Nelly. Blacklisted actors have been doing more or less all right in the theater—at least some are s-s-s-surviving. And there's the social life. Jesus, everyone in the theater goes to East Hampton in the summer—writers, directors, producers, actors. Everyone. If she comes with us, she's bound to meet someone. Her best hope is a new fella, and Jake knows that."

"So why he is so against it?"

Because, she answered, he didn't trust Veevi to take advantage of the situation. She wasn't making an effort in L.A. Why would she do it in New York? And if she didn't make an effort, she'd start drinking again, and stay in her room all day, and be critical and superior about everything, Broadway in particular. He just wasn't in the mood for it, he'd explained to her, not when he was devoting himself a thousand percent to the show.

"He doesn't really like her that much," Dinah said. "I mean, he likes her, but she p-p-p-pisses him off."

"But what about acting? Doesn't she want to get back to that."

"Not really. She never liked it even in the thirties," Dinah explained. "She doesn't really believe in herself as an actress. She says things like 'Actors are children,' and 'I hate all forms of public display.'" Jake had said he could just see it: he'd set up auditions for her, and she wouldn't show up. She'd have an excuse for everything, just as she does for the synopses that are always late.

"Perhaps she just needs a push. To get her self-confidence back."

"Well, that's why she should come East with us," Dinah said. Then she explained, a little shyly, that since his heart attack Jake had been very, well, sort of sweet with her. He'd insisted on having his family all to himself.

"I just want the four of us, plus Gus, which makes five," he'd said. "We cannot devote our entire lives to your sister's emotional and social rescue. We've done everything we can, and she's having none of it. She doesn't like our friends, she can't stand Hollywood, she has nothing but contempt for the show and my career. You've got to face the fact," he'd told Dinah, "that your sister doesn't like you or us or our family. We're all she's got right now, but that doesn't mean she loves us. For some reason, she needed to exile herself from her own crowd in Paris, but every time she thinks of them she wants to punish us for not being them."

"How do you know all this?" Dinah had asked him, suspecting that he was right but wanting to stand up for Veevi, too.

"Because I've talked to her about my project. I've asked her to do research on it. She thinks it's a big pile of schmaltz—a big load of cornball commercial horseshit. And if we're in East Hampton and having people over or going to somebody's house"—and he'd exploded—"I'll be god-damned if I'm going to sit by while she gives those nasty little looks and those contempt-filled little smiles whenever the subject of my show comes up. To hell with that. I've just had a heart attack, and Justy Brody says I've got to take it easy and avoid aggravation. Honestly, honey, if you bring her East with us I might just as well drop dead. I've been supporting her un-complainingly all this time. I have a right to a vacation from Her-Royal-Pain-in-the-Heinie."

"So you see," Dinah said to Nelly, "maybe I should tell him about Mike. Maybe that would soften him a little. I'm worried about her, Nelly. The last thing she needs right now is a brush with that shitheel husband of hers."

"You don't have to tell me about Veevi's little 'everybody-in-this-room-is-an-idiot-except-you-and-me' smiles," Nelly said, shaking her head so that her egg-beaten curls fluttered as she spoke. "But you know," she said, with her mild lisp, "somewhere in a Tolstoy novel—I think it's *Anna Karenina*—a character says, 'Things will shape themselves.' And I tell you, Dinah, for your own good and for the good of your sister, this thing you saw today you did not see. Do not say a word. Let things shape themselves."

Manny Steiner suddenly came through the kitchen door, brown and glistening. He ran up to the table, grabbed his wife's face and kissed her on the mouth, ran to Dinah's side of the table and kissed her on the mouth, and ran out the back door and down the steps toward the pool.

The two friends smiled at each other, and then Dinah's face became serious again. "You're right, Nelly. You always are. I'll just forget the whole thing."

⁂

In Jake's upstairs office that afternoon, Dinah sat restlessly behind his desk. He wasn't at the apartment; his secretary said he'd just left for the rehearsal studio. She wouldn't get a chance to talk to him until that night, because he couldn't be disturbed during auditions. Was there someone else she could call? Dorshka, perhaps? But if Dorshka didn't know that her own son was in town, Dinah reflected, *she* wasn't going to be the one to tell her. And if Dorshka *did* know but hadn't said anything, she must have had a good reason for keeping it to herself.

Resigned to a long wait, and feeling guilty for going against Nelly's advice, Dinah put the phone down and went into her dressing room, where she changed into her gardening shorts and halter. This would be her last day of gardening until she came back in September.

Soon, squatting on her haunches, she was contentedly troweling holes for the blocks of pansies that would border the pool patio. Seeing Manny Steiner had reminded her to bring out her own little transistor, and she listened to old swing tunes as she lost herself in the dirt and the flowers and felt the sun beating down on her back. She loved her house and making things grow outdoors in the California sun, and she wondered what it was going to be like to live in the East again for the first time since 1922. She was remembering the bugs and the humidity in Pittsburgh when she heard Veevi's customary "Hello, hello!" so mock-British, as she approached from the house.

"I don't know why I'm doing this," Dinah explained a few minutes later. "I'm not even gonna see these darling little creatures this s-s-s-summer." Veevi had emerged from the dressing room wearing a two-piece bathing suit.

"You like putting your hands in the dirt—you do it for the fun of it," she said. "You like gardening; I like books."

" 'How true,' " Dinah answered, lapsing into the sisterly banter they had shared for aeons, in which every word was a self-consciously deployed cliché, a deliberately arch or archaic turn of phrase. It was as if everything they said to each other had to have implicit quotation marks around it, lest they be caught talking to each other in just a simple, ordinary way. Had

Dinah wanted to play it straight, she could have added that she also happened to like books, but Veevi always had to accent their differences: I like this, but you like that. Though she never said so, Dinah found this tallying of differences tedious.

She waited for Veevi to stretch out, as she usually did, on a pool chaise, but instead Veevi turned the chaise away from the sun and toward Dinah, sat down, crossed her legs, and leaned slightly forward. Dinah made a half turn so that she could work the soil and talk to her sister at the same time.

"Tell me, Sister Ina," Veevi began, lighting a Lucky Strike. "What was it like when you testified? What did you say? What did they ask you?"

Dinah sprang up and stood with her legs apart and her gloved hands on her hips. "What was it like when I t-t-t-testified? That's what you want to know?"

Veevi nodded.

"I thought you'd never ask," she said with a sardonic mock aside.

"Tell me."

"It was cold, imp-p-p-personal, matter-of-f-f-f-fact," Dinah replied without hesitation. "And awful. Simply awful."

"How so?"

Dinah pulled off her gardening gloves and sat down on the edge of the chaise opposite Veevi's. Then she told Veevi everything that had happened from the moment the man in the gray hat had shoved the subpoena into her hand to the instant she had seen poor Artie Squires in the hotel corridor. She described the Honorable Curtis P. Kingman (who had died recently, she'd read) and Horace Marlow, and repeated every question they had asked her—all of which she remembered with photographic precision and a sense of horror that even now she could feel running up and down her spine.

She spoke evenly, directly, and without hesitation, even though she had to endure the usual lockup in the jailhouse of her throat. But, ultimately, the stutter didn't get in the way. It was as if she had saved up her story until this very moment, and as it poured out of her she felt the release of finally getting it out. Yet she wasn't offering a confession or an apology. Her comely face and clear voice did not ask for absolution. Neither did she attempt antic facial expressions, ironic asides, or put anything, so to speak, in quotation marks. She did not measure her words to fit her sister's expression, which she nevertheless watched closely. For once, Veevi listened without raising her eyebrows, pursing her lips, glancing aside at invisible interlocutors, or assuming any of the repertoire of a thousand expressions with which she conveyed disdain, belittlement, mockery, or skepticism.

"And that's it," Dinah concluded. "I came home and wrote you the next morning. And never heard from you, although Mike certainly gave us a piece of his mind."

Veevi glanced away ever so slightly. "Mmm," she said abstractedly. "Yes, I know. But, Ina?"

Dinah looked at her again. Was it coming now? The "How could you?" Dinah had been expecting since the summer of 1951. She was ready for it, and braced herself by looking away from her sister's face momentarily and simply waiting for the bullet. It was three-thirty. The light had begun to change and the shadows to lengthen; the afternoon heat was letting up, and the fragrant air she loved so much chased the smog away with a thousand scents.

"Ina?" Veevi said in a strangled voice. "Would you take a look at this?"

Veevi reached into her purse and pulled out a letter, one of those tissue-thin blue airmail letters that immediately signified "Europe" for Dinah.

"Is it from Mike?" Dinah asked.

Veevi nodded. "Here, read it."

The moment she saw the salutation, *"Dearest V.,"* Dinah's heart sank. *"As you know, we're making progress with the divorce, which I've tried to make as easy on you as possible. I'm doing everything I can to make sure you get the alimony you need. But I need hardly remind you that divorce is a pretty expensive proposition. I have finally bent to necessity and decided to let them make a movie of* The Confession." Dinah quickly read on, making an effort not to react, and learned the following: that Willie Weil had bought the property and had scheduled meetings in Los Angeles to pitch the story to Seymour Mandlin, the head of Palomar. Willie had gotten commitments from Brando and Kurt Jurgens—even without a script. If Mandlin went for it, Weil was reasonably certain he could get Mike twelve weeks' work in L.A. to write the screenplay. A whole summer in L.A. was just what Mike wanted, he said, because he needed to catch up with Coco, Claire, and his mother. And, of course, Veevi herself, if she felt they could be friends. He didn't mind telling her that he would be coming alone; Odile was going to be in Italy and Austria on location with the Crandells for Hunt's new picture. The whole plan, however, had come up against a gigantic snag. *"Mandlin won't do the deal,"* Dinah read, *"unless you clear me with the Committee."*

"Oh shit," Dinah said. "Oh g-g-g-goddamn it to hell."

"Keep reading, Ina."

Being separated and even almost divorced from her didn't make a bit of difference, Mike explained: Seymour P. Mandlin, according to Willie Weil, wanted the deal but was adamant about keeping his studio absolutely pinko-free. *"It's evil and insane,"* Dinah read out loud, *"but that's how it is. Anybody who thinks this lousy business is dying down is out of his mind. I know it's been rough on you these past couple of years. Believe me, I think about you all the time. But the only way I can meet my responsibilities to you is by getting this job, and I can't get the job if I don't have the clearance. I never thought I'd have to ask you for something like this—I know how abhorrent it is to both of us. But I wouldn't be asking you even to think it over if I felt we had a real choice in the matter."*

He'd be arriving sometime in early June and would call her when he got in. He wanted to take her out to dinner, so she had plenty of time to think it over.

But he's here already, Dinah almost blurted out. Veevi must have sent him a telegram at once saying she'd do it, since he would never have risked coming to the States with the question still up in the air. "When did you g-g-g-get this?" she asked instead.

"Couple of weeks ago."

"And you've agreed to do it?"

"Well, I've been thinking about it."

Oh, you liar, Dinah didn't say. "You're not going to do it, are you?"

"Mmm. I am. That's why I asked you about, you know, your session. I need the name of that lawyer you used."

"Veevi—" Dinah said. "You don't have to do this, you know."

"Oh," said Veevi, sighing. "But I do. The Khrushchev speech."

"The Kh-Kh-Kh-Khrushchev speech? What about it?"

"It's changed everything, hasn't it? It doesn't mean the same thing anymore, standing up to the Committee."

"Is that what you're t-t-telling yourself?"

"Oh, really, Ina. We were all such fucking idiots."

"But, Vee, that's b-b-b-beside the p-p-point."

"You're telling me not to do it? Why?"

Dinah took a deep breath and let it out. "Simple. It's wrong. And I wish I hadn't done it, that's all."

"But all this—" Veevi gestured grandly, mockingly, toward the pool and the house. "You'd have lost it."

"So?" Dinah said.

"It's easy for you to say now."

"True. I'm not k-k-k-killing myself over it, Vee. But, on b-b-balance, I wish I hadn't."

Dinah put her gardening gloves back on, sat down on her haunches, and resumed digging. Veevi lit a cigarette. Dinah worked, and Veevi smoked in silence for a while.

"You know, Ina," said Veevi, "it was the Communists who killed Stefan."

Dinah dropped her trowel and turned around. "What are you *talking* about?"

"Somebody in the Party sold him out to the Gestapo."

Dinah stared at Veevi, speechless.

"You see," Veevi continued, "they were planning ahead, those clever French Communists. Of course, they had their instructions from Moscow, and they were *very* worried about having a bunch of Jewish Resistance heroes in postwar France. Wouldn't look good in elections, when they'd have to compete with the Nationalists."

"Who told you this?"

"A friend of Bill Nemeth's, a journalist. Another dashing Hungarian— is there any other kind?—and an ex-Communist, or so he said, who'd done sabotage with Stefan. I don't know where he got it, but he was a reliable type."

"You never told me this. Are you sure?"

"Absolutely one-hundred-percent foolproof sure? No. How can I be? But that's what he told me."

Dinah got up and sat down across from her sister. "Look, Vee, even if it's true—don't kid yourself. You're not thinking about who nailed Stefan or what Khrushchev said in that sp-sp-speech. Come on, Vee. You're just cooking up reasons to testify."

"If I clear Mike, I'll get my passport back," Veevi said with a dreamy smile. "We'll go back to Paris together and be just as we were. We'll bring Dorshka home with us and the girls. She doesn't exactly want to die in 'the land of the free and the home of the brave.' Or is it 'the home of the free and the land of the brave'? Hard to keep it straight."

She gave a light laugh. Her eyes were sparkling. There was a touch of gaiety about her, and a look of anticipated joy suffused her face.

Dinah gave her back the letter, which Veevi carefully folded and tucked inside her cigarette case. "Can you get me that lawyer's number? I need to call him today. Mike should be getting here sometime this week."

"You don't want to think it over some more, discuss it with him when he gets here?"

"I want the lawyer's number."

She looked up at Dinah and made a triumphant bubby face that Dinah understood at once to mean: I always knew he'd come back. Everything will be wonderful again.

"Ah, you want it now. This minute. Okay," Dinah said, rising. "It's your life, dearie Vee. But listen to me, please. If you're really going to go ahead with this, make sure you name me. Name Renna Schlossberg, Cliff B-B-B-Boatwright—"

"Oh, not Cliff! I could never name him!"

"Why not?" Dinah turned to face Veevi and stood with her hands on her hips.

"Well, he'd think—"

"He'd know goddamn well why you were doing it and he'd understand completely. He's been in love with you his whole life, and he'll love you till the day he d-d-d-dies. You know what, Vee? When I testified, there were people who stopped talking to me. I knew they would and I didn't give a royal f-f-f-fuck, and I still don't. But that's not going to happen to you. You're the exception, Vee. You could be an ax murderer and no one would blame you for it. So listen to me. I'll say it again: name the fewest people you can, and make sure the ones you do name are p-p-p-people they al-ready know about and can't screw twice, like Cliff."

"Mmm," Veevi said. Dinah saw that she wasn't listening. "Just think, Ina. He'll be here. The whole summer!"

"Vee—"

"Without the French Open."

The sisters laughed. "Okay, I'll get the number. Be right back."

It took only a few minutes for Dinah to go upstairs to Jake's office and find Burt Unwin's number, but during that time she realized that she would be lying to herself if she didn't admit that the thought of Veevi's going back to Paris didn't fill her with a certain satisfaction. It was exactly what every-one needed—for Veevi to be back with the man she adored, in the city she loved—and it would certainly make her own life once again peaceful and calm, or as peaceful and calm as life with Jake Lasker could ever be. But so what? she reproached herself. It was so simple and obvious, she thought, as she headed for the stairs. For Veevi to testify would be a disaster. Mike wasn't going to come through in the end. And when that happened, Veevi would be left alone, abandoned, with the knowledge that she had testified; it would shatter her. She might not think she had principles, Dinah reflected, but she did, and it would matter to her greatly what Cliff Boatwright, for example, thought of her. Aware, though, that Veevi had made up her mind, Dinah wondered what more she could do.

Midway down the stairs, she collided with Lorna, who was stampeding toward her room. Tears streamed down her face, and a half-eaten Eskimo Pie dribbled down the front of her bathing suit.

"My God, what is it, honey?" Dinah asked, catching the child in her arms and sitting down with her on the carpeted steps.

"Veevi told me," the little girl sobbed, "not to eat ice cream in front of her. She said I'm so fat it's *disgusting* to watch me."

The child's wails rang through the house, bringing an alarmed Gussie from the kitchen. Together, Dinah and Gussie led Lorna upstairs, where Gussie wiped her face and tried to soothe her down. Dinah went down to talk to Veevi.

She hadn't heard the kids come home, and as she returned toward the backyard she saw Peter already in the pool, wearing a mask and a snorkel, and pointedly ignoring Veevi, who was calling out to him to show her his best swan dive. Dinah hesitated. Ever since the Palm Springs incident Peter had stayed as far away from Veevi as possible, and it filled her with a wavering pity for her sister.

Nevertheless, Dinah pulled up a pool chair and sat down directly across from Veevi. "Goddamnit, Vee, how dare you speak to Lorna like that!" she said quietly and fiercely. "You've done it over and over, and I'm sick of it. If you ever d-d-d-do it again, you will not be welcome in this house. Do you understand?"

Dinah had never spoken to Veevi this way.

"Oh," Veevi said, shaking her head and smiling, as if the topic were too ridiculous to be discussed. "Really. If she can't take a little kidding—"

"Veevi," Dinah said, now shaking with rage and yanking Veevi up by the hand. "Get the f-f-f-fuck out of here. Now. We need a v-v-v-vacation from each other. A big one. You've said one s-s-s-savage, vicious, cruel thing to Lorna after another, and God knows why, but I've let you get away with it every time. But you're never going to do it again." She pulled the scrap of paper from her pocket and placed it in Veevi's hand. "Here. Go testify, for all I care. Live your life, and stay the hell out of mine!"

Veevi made a bubby face.

"Put it away, Vee. I've had it with you."

She picked up Veevi's cigarette case and her lighter and put them in Veevi's purse and snapped it shut. "Here," she said, putting the purse over Veevi's arm and leading her through the wooden gate that separated the yard from the driveway.

Veevi, unresisting, looked at Dinah as if she had lost her mind.

"You're going home, right now," Dinah said, opening the door to Veevi's MG. "And if you ever hurt Lorna's feelings again, I will fucking k-k-k-kill you."

Dinah turned her back and walked toward the pool, not waiting for a reply.

Later that night, Jake called Dinah from New York and she poured out the whole story. When he put the phone down, he whooped out loud for joy. This calls for a celebration, he said to himself, pulling off his sleep mask and hurrying to the refrigerator in his Sixty-third Street apartment. Free of Veevi! he rejoiced, as he pulled out two pieces of rye bread and some smoked turkey. Free of that pain-in-the-ass snobbish, disdainful cooze! Thank God for Mike Albrecht! Thank God for Willie Weil and Seymour Mandlin and the Marlon Brando Committee! he said to himself as he twisted open the jar of mustard, slathered some on the bread, and un-capped a bottle of root beer.

Clearly, there was a god of timing, he thought to himself as he sat at the kitchen counter. Mike couldn't have come back into Veevi's life at a better time, as far as Jake was concerned, because, from the moment he'd set foot in the rehearsal studio and started auditioning actors and dancers for the show, he'd been in a state of utter bliss. Finally, after all these years of churning out one bitch of a movie after another, he was doing theater, he was doing it in New York with people who were brilliant talents, and he had the greatest faith that the show would be a hit. Even if it failed—if it died, if it stank—he would still have had a crack at doing what he now believed he'd been born to do. Furthermore, while he and Dinah were talking tonight, he realized that this state of utter bliss and absorption in the show was the perfect antidote to the bilious nausea that overcame him whenever he thought about his affair with Veevi. His memories of himself in bed with her brought him nothing but cold-sweat shame toward himself and revulsion toward her. He wanted nothing to do with her, except the longest, most formal distance he could imagine between them. What an idiotic mistake the whole thing had been! And now, after Dinah's call tonight, he felt like getting down on his knees and kissing Albrecht's feet! Take her, she's all yours! Just get her out of our hair!

Once Veevi testified, Mike could take them all back to Europe. Dorshka, too, with that phony European bonhomie of hers, that semi-superior *Gemütlichkeit* that let you know, as she handed you a piece of five-thousand-calorie cake with a lethal dose of schlag, that *any* novelist is better than the best screenwriter. The only thing that worried him was Dinah's bawling Veevi out today. She should have handled that better—put it more diplomatically or just let it pass the way she always had. After all, Lorna did have a weight problem. Like him and his mother, she'd never met a calorie she didn't like. But if Veevi were to get mad back at Dinah and tell her everything . . . The thought was too horrible to finish. Well, he'd deny it. There was no proof, no receipts—nothing on paper. He wasn't a fucking amateur.

But, oh boy, had he ever learned his lesson. As for now, he wouldn't rock the boat. He'd pretend nothing had happened, keep Veevi on the payroll until she'd had her session with the Committee, have her send the synopses to Gladys, who would send them to him to gather dust on his desk. As far as extracurricular fun went, from now on he was going to stick to tootsies. He figured he needed a little setup, a nice little arrangement like the one he'd had with Bonnie. That Bonnie. Now, that was a sweet kid. "Come and lay down," she used to say. That's what he wanted. A nice, sweet girl with lousy grammar and a great body. A girl who wouldn't be a pain in the ass when it was over. Maybe somebody he could put in the show.

He took his plate over to the sink and washed it with a little sponge, feeling happy and virtuous to be washing his own dish, though he left the root beer bottle in the sink for the maid to throw away the next morning. As he turned off the kitchen light, he had a thought: What about the dancer he and the boys had auditioned yesterday afternoon? She was a friend of Jimmy O'Rourke's, said she'd met Jake about a month ago when he'd flown to Vegas to talk to Victor Lewis about the part of David in the show. The girl—a redhead from England, with a cockney accent—had been in Vic's dressing room at the Flamingo. God, who was that guy she was with, the crime writer—Burgoyne, Duff Burgoyne? The guy mentioned something about sending him a treatment, but had been talking to Jake's deaf ear, and Jake hadn't caught all the man had said.

At first, he'd gotten the idea that she was Burgoyne's girl. Then she'd said he was like an uncle to her, a friend to her brother and father, croupiers who'd come over to Vegas from London. Jake didn't remember telling her to come to New York to audition, but apparently he had. She'd also called Jake's friend Jimmy, and he'd told her to come, too. If she was a friend of Jimmy's, that meant she knew the score—knew how to behave around a certain kind of guy. And Buzz Keegan liked her. The choreography in the show was going to be very athletic, robust, and sexy, and Buzz wanted well-trained dancers with energy to spare. Keegan had said after her routine that her tits were really too big for a dancer's, but Jake had liked the way she looked onstage—the big smile, the good legs. He'd said to Keegan, "Take a chance. She looks kind of zaftig, like the immigrant broads I grew up with," and had taken her number, impressed, too, that she'd come all the way to New York and staked everything on getting into the show. She looked like fun—like she knew how to handle herself. He'd be nice to her, and that part of life would be all squared away.

And if she wasn't available, he'd find somebody else. He was seeing more gorgeous girls every morning than he'd seen in years on the Marathon lot. Dancers, with sensational bodies. He wasn't worried.

He opened the window in the living room and looked out toward the river. Late-night city sounds flew up in a roar that he loved. He had had this feeling in London and Paris. If things worked out for him, he'd have a place in New York and a place in London. He'd go from picture to play to novel to picture to play to novel. The image of a sign saying We Never Close came into his head and made him laugh. His productivity would be staggering. He wanted to buy that house in Springs that he'd rented. Oh boy, was Dinah going to love it—and the kids, too. Not like that crappy little house in Palm Springs. What a mistake that had been. This one was small but not cramped, a charming, Dutch farmhouse next to a potato field. And this summer it would be just the four of them, and Gus; and if the show was a hit he'd buy the place in a minute. And see what he could do about buying a place here, too. He'd have to come back every two weeks or more, maybe even move the family to New York for the run of the show if—and he used that "if" a thousand times a day—if it was a hit. And he would be doing this all on his own, without Irv Engel and Marathon, and without Veevi or some big romance that would be a complete drag on his time and energy.

Here it was two in the morning, and below him the cars were rushing by, thousands of them, on the FDR. What were they doing, all those cars? Where were people going? It was so different from L.A., where at night all you could hear was dogs barking and raccoons scurrying on your roof; if you couldn't sleep and went out on the porch, you could hear the coyotes barking back at the dogs. He thought of Peter's fear of snakes. The La Brea tar pits: now, that was the real L.A., he thought. Land of the saber-toothed tiger, snakes, earthquakes, and floods. A fucking inhuman place. He didn't want nature and animals; he didn't know one tree from the next, and flowers bored him. He wanted people, cities, human voices, people trying to accomplish things and succeeding or failing. How could you be a writer unless you could eavesdrop and snoop and overhear and look out windows? L.A. was nowheresville. All those big mansions with their secrets and their landscaping and no way to listen to any of it. He wanted to live on a river and stare out across the night into other people's apartments and watch them while they scratched their asses or picked their toes. He wanted—well, he admitted to himself, he just wanted. And wanted.

9

All journeys begin in exhilaration, and Dinah's cross-country adventure was no exception. She and Peter rode up front; Gussie and Lorna commandeered the backseat, along with a cooler filled with ice, sodas, milk, and four huge grocery bags stuffed with potato chips, Fritos, pretzels, Ritz crackers, cheese, bananas, grapes, peanut butter, and Oreos. The kids sang, shouted good-bye to L.A., listened to the radio, talked about the sights they were going to see, and opened the windows to let the wind flap against their faces and whip their hair.

The four of them felt almost as if they were flying as Dinah skimmed along on the new freeway into the desert toward Nevada. It was so hot that the air in front of the car seemed to melt in shimmering waves above the road, empty except for trucks, which she passed at speeds well over eighty. Driving with her legs apart and her skirt hitched up over her thighs, Dinah smoked Camels, drank Coca-Cola, and pointed things out to the kids: crumbling, sand-abraded corrugated steel and wood shacks lone prospectors had once built for themselves and abandoned, tumbleweed rolling in the wind, giant green cacti rising up like cowboy hats, the rusting corpses of cars left to freeze at night and burn in the day. But these sights abruptly reminded her of her father and how lonely he had been when her mother finally left him, and then she thought of him coming over in the trailer and getting all dressed up in his pin-striped wool suit just to read Veevi's letters, and she couldn't stand it—she had to get him and Veevi out of her mind. She told Peter to read to her from the AAA guide to Nevada, which he did, as she tried to listen.

Late in the afternoon they reached Las Vegas, their first stop, right on schedule. The kids wanted to swim, Dinah wanted to take a shower, and Gussie wanted to stretch her legs. Dinah had called ahead earlier in the week and made a reservation at an AAA-endorsed motel at the far end of the Strip. She parked the car in front of the motel office and went in to register. At the front desk, she rang the bell and a young woman came out from behind a multicolored beaded curtain. She smiled, confirmed the reservation, and gave Dinah a clipboard with a registration form and a ballpoint pen. As Dinah was filling out the form, the woman said, "Is that a colored woman out there in your car?"

Dinah raised her eyes. "Why, yes, it is. Why?"

"Is she with you?"

"Yes. Why do you ask?"

"She can't stay here."

Dinah's face was gray when she got into the car. In silence, she started the engine, and the children and Gussie asked her what was the matter. But she didn't answer them, not until she'd stopped at a gas station. When she told them, Lorna burst into tears; Peter looked at Gussie and reached out to touch her shoulder.

"Oh, Mrs. Lasker—"

"I'm just so sore!" Dinah interrupted her. "Of all the l-l-l-lousy places in the world. Las V-V-V-Vegas! Wait till I tell Jake about this! Gussie, I'm so sorry. . . ."

"Don't be sorry, Mrs. Lasker," said Gussie. "It isn't your fault, and I should have thought of it myself. Let's not pay it no nevermind. Let's find out where the colored motel is. You can put me there."

But the kids burst out, "*No!*"

"We'll sleep in the car!" Peter shouted.

"I wouldn't dream of l-l-l-letting you sleep away from us," Dinah said. "But we're not going to sleep in the car."

"Why can't we all sleep at the colored motel?" Lorna asked.

"Well?" said Dinah to Gussie.

"No, Mrs. Lasker. I don't recommend it."

"No?" Dinah looked at Gussie.

"Not with the children," she added.

Peter looked at her, puzzled and curious, aware, since Palm Springs, that things often went on in the adult world that kids knew nothing about.

"You sure, Gus?" said Dinah.

"Mrs. Lasker, I don't want to take these babies to one of those places.

It ain't that it's colored. But, you know—this is *Vegas*." She looked at Dinah significantly.

Dinah nodded, grabbed her purse and the AAA booklet, and went to a phone booth. She dialed a number from the book and said, very distinctly, "I am traveling by car with my three children and my N-N-N-NEGRO housekeeper. Can we get two rooms for the night?"

"No," said the voice on the line. "We don't take colored."

"Well, thank you very much, you h-h-h-horse's ass."

She tried another number from the AAA book. This time the voice said, "We don't allow niggers here."

"F-F-F-Fuck you," she said, and hung up.

She tried two more places: "We don't allow coloreds." "We don't take Negroes."

She stood in the phone booth biting her thumbnail. Where was she going to find a place to stay? Maybe this whole trip was a mistake and she should drive back to L.A. and put everyone on a plane the next day. Then she thought of the Flamingo, got the number from information, and dialed. To the hotel management, she explained that she was the wife of producer-writer-director Jake Lasker, who had recently stayed there, and happened to be a very good friend of Victor Lewis's, and that she needed two rooms. Did she want single or double beds? "Double. By the way, my housekeeper is traveling with us and she is a N-N-N-Negro. Is that going to be a problem?"

"Certainly not, Mrs. Lasker. We're all great admirers of your husband's work." This could only mean, she told herself, that they appreciated Jake's great achievement in losing five thousand bucks at blackjack the last time he'd stayed there.

Indeed, they gave her—free of charge—an air-conditioned suite with a bathtub the size of a small swimming pool. The kids, tired and hungry by now, just wanted dinner, so she took them and Gussie—who at first was reluctant to accompany them—downstairs to the main restaurant for dinner. Then Gussie took Lorna upstairs for a bath and bed, while Dinah allowed Peter to stay with her and watch the floor show.

To Peter's astonishment, the show included several numbers with lines of nearly bare-breasted dancers dressed in skimpy costumes bedecked with flashing beads and feathered headdresses. Mesmerized, Peter kept looking back and forth between his mother and the chorus girls, saying to her, "Wait till I tell Joelly," his best friend, and giggling.

During one of the numbers, she felt a hand on her shoulder and looked up. "I'm Duff Burgoyne," he said, shaking Dinah's hand, then Peter's. "The fellas tell me you're staying here tonight. I'm a big fan of your husband's work, Mrs. Lasker. Ran into him in Vic Lewis's dressing room last time he was here. Vic says he's having a ball rehearsing your husband's show in New York. I see you've got a very open mind about your son's education. I admire that in a woman." He gazed into her eyes, and his friendliness and charm vanished for her immediately. She was looking at a stocky, muscular man in his late thirties with closely cropped prematurely salt-and-pepper hair. His rust-colored tie was loosened from an open collar around his thick neck. His leathery skin was tanned to a swarthy burnish. An old scar over his left eyebrow and another on his chin, a nose that had more than once been smashed and reconstructed, a Boston accent and a mouth full of re-arranged teeth spoke of an embattled and streetwise past and gave him a studied and decorative tough-guy look about which, Dinah could tell, he was extremely vain. His voice—a smooth, controlled bellow—was saturated with sexual innuendo and educated violence.

"I also don't mind telling you how much I admire you for having the courage to testify," he said.

"Mr. Burgoyne," she said quietly, leaning over behind Peter's back. "As you can see, I'm here with my son?" Her voice went up slightly, as if she were making a request. "It's nice of you to stop by. I'll tell my husband we met."

"Please do, Mrs. Lasker," he said, raking her with his eyes. "Your husband's a very talented man. I wish he had liked a treatment of mine a bit better, though. I admire someone who can make comedy out of crime."

"Good night, Mr. Burgoyne," she said, having no idea what he was talking about, but smiling her phoniest, broadest, most white-toothed smile. "You know, my husband's quite a fan of yours, too." It was a lie, of course.

"Glad to hear it!" he said, squeezing her hand again and slapping Peter on the back so sharply that the boy turned around and glared at him.

Back in the room she shared with Peter, Dinah tried calling Jake after Peter had fallen asleep, but he didn't answer. She tried to imagine what he was doing, worried that he might be at a deli somewhere, stuffing himself with deadly "Jew-food," as he liked to call it. She fell asleep wondering what it would have been like at the colored motel, and what it was about Burgoyne that gave her the creeps.

In the car the next morning, the kids asked Gussie questions, and she told them what it was like to grow up in Texas—Marlin, Texas. Peter wanted to know if there had been separate entrances and Colored Only benches and drinking fountains.

"Yes, we had the Jim Crow laws," Gussie said. But she added that most of her childhood had been spent on her grandfather's farm, which was so big that it had its own church and its own store, and that she'd never spent any time around white people until she turned fourteen, when she went to work.

By the middle of the afternoon, Dinah began to worry about the coming night's lodging and whether Gussie would be turned away.

But at Bryce Canyon and at Salt Lake City, nobody said anything about Gussie, and they spent the nights in comfortable, air-conditioned motels. There was one, though, that had no air-conditioning, and during the night Dinah woke up sweating and overwhelmed with remorse at having rebuked Veevi for the way she'd treated Lorna. Then, remembering Lorna's tears, she got sore at Veevi all over again, and even more at herself for having said nothing so many times. No, the words had been said, and they were going to stay said. But she remained apprehensive, nonetheless, and knew it was because of Veevi and Mike and the subpoena.

After two full days in Yellowstone, they left on the third morning. The Lasker kids were subdued. They had seen enough sights for a while. It was Peter's turn to sit in back, where he read "Little Lulu" and "Archie" and "Donald Duck" comics, while Lorna, beside her mother in the front seat, looked dreamily ahead and stuck her arm out the window so that she could let the air play across her skin. Gussie hummed "He's got his eye on the sparrow" to herself, and Dinah hummed along.

Sometimes Lorna and Peter quarreled over who was going to sit where, told each other to shut up, and shouted "I hate you intensely" at each other. At those moments, Dinah felt the trip had been a mistake and just wanted to get it over with.

※

I've got to get there before Jake does, Dinah kept repeating to herself as she drove the next day. I've got to get to Chicago before Jake does. He was scheduled to arrive that night from New York. She no longer pointed out every farmhouse and cornfield but kept her eyes fixed on the road and only half heard the kids' by now ritualized talk about dead-bug splats on the windshield, their games of Twenty Questions, their songs. It was close to five when she pulled into the driveway of a three-story house in Highland Park. Hubie and Betty Lasker, Jake's cousin and his wife, ran out to greet the travelers, their two daughters, Karen and Paula, behind them.

Just as the Lasker family stepped out of the car, they heard a whirring, buzzing hum in the air, which was thick with brown vibrations. To their horror, they heard and felt their shoes crunching down on layers and layers of brown-ridged capsules. Betty Lasker, a brisk and energetic woman with thick arched eyebrows, shouted, "Seventeen-year locusts! They won't hurt you."

Nevertheless, Gussie and Dinah and the Lasker kids hurried into the house as fast as they could, shrieking as they crunched more insects underfoot.

"What is this?" Dinah asked. "Some kind of b-b-b-biblical pl-pl-pl-plague?"

"They drive us nuts for a couple of weeks and then disappear. Seventeen years later, out they come, and the whole thing happens all over again." Betty laughed, and Dinah liked her warmth and her rich, fruity Chicago accent.

Dinah shivered. "Have you heard from Jake?"

"I'm just leaving now to pick him up at the airport," answered Hubie. "Wanna come?"

"You take the kids and I'll take a shower and a nap," Dinah said. "Actually, I wonder if I could use the phone?"

Betty took her to a guest room, which had twin beds. The air-conditioning blocked out the sound of the locusts, though myriad dead ones were heaped up like stale chocolates on the ledge of the closed windowsill. Minutes later, with the door locked, instead of taking her clothes off to get into the shower, Dinah placed a long-distance call.

Please be there, she said to herself. Please pick up the phone. Right now. Pick up the goddamn phone right now.

Finally, there was a click, and a voice on the other end.

"Vee? It's me. Listen, Veevi, don't do it. Don't t-t-t-testify."

Her voice was calm and firm, urgent but not agitated.

"Why not? You did it for Jake. Why shouldn't I do it for Mike?"

"Veevi! L-L-L-Listen to me. D-D-D-DON'T DO IT." She was stuttering badly. "It's WR-WR-WRONG. There are NO good reasons to do it."

"Oh, come on," she said, with her old, familiar disdain. " 'Birds do it,' " she began to sing. " 'Bees do it . . .' " She was off-key and slurring.

"Veevi, stop. Listen to me. We could have made it, Jake and I. I know that now. We could have survived it—jail, M-M-Mexico, the works—whatever happened. And you can, too. Look, Vee—this is a t-t-t-terrible c-c-c-country." Her stutter was maddening; it was impossible to get the words out. " Am-m-m-merica is all wr-wr-wr-wrong. Do you hear me? AM-M-MERICA IS ALL WR-WR-WR-WRONG."

" 'Movie people on their knees do it . . .' "

"V-V-V-Vee! SH-SH-SHUT UP. I'm tr-tr-tr-tr—oh, SHIT!—I'm tr-tr-tr-trying to tell you something. D-D-D-DON'T give in to it. If I could go back and choose again, I'd g-g-g-g-go to—Jesus Ch-Ch-Ch-Christ!" she exploded in frustration. "JAIL."

" 'Show me the way to go home,' " Veevi sang. It was a song the girls' father had sung to them a thousand times. Their mother had sung harmony with him, in the Model T, on Sunday afternoon excursions along the Pacific Coast Highway, until Dinah and Veevi had been old enough to sing harmony with them, and then all four of their voices had harmonized. " 'I'm tired an' I wanna go to bed.' "

"Stop singing, Veevi," Dinah said. She heard a voice in the background—muffled, irritable, and male. There was a thick intake of breath, and the sound of ice clinking in a glass. Then laughter. "Is he there now?" Dinah asked.

"Mmm."

"Oh shit, you're f-f-f-fucking him again."

"So? We're having a lovely time together. Everything's wonderful. Isn't it, darling?" Veevi's voice seemed faraway as she spoke to someone in the room.

"Christ, Veevi. Don't d-d-d-do this to yourself!"

"Can't talk about it now," Veevi said, her voice gay and thick.

"Oh, fuck it, Veevi. Ask him what he was doing with Jill Trevor at the G-G-G-Golden Horn Motel on Santa Monica Boulevard on the morning of June 3rd. Because I saw him come out of a room with her and get into a car. Just ask him."

"Jus' a minute!" Veevi said. Dinah heard her slur out the question, laughingly, and cringed—*Not now, idiot! Not now, not this minute, while I'm on the phone and you're shit-faced.*

"What is this, Dinah?" a male voice suddenly asked.

She spoke firmly, though her legs wobbled beneath her.

"Veevi's all set to go and s-s-s-sing for your supper, Michael. But I saw you, b-b-b-buster. I saw you with Jill Trevor at the motel near the Mormon Temple on Santa M-M-M-Monica Boulevard a whole week or two before you were supposed to get here. I know what you're up to."

"Stay out of it, Dinah. You're way over your stupid little provincial head. Whatever you think you saw has nothing to do with Veevi and me. Stay out of our lives. You of all people, the stool pigeon of Holmby Hills, have no right to interfere. Leave Veevi alone. I'm taking care of her from now on."

"The hell you are. If you l-l-l-loved her you wouldn't l-l-l-let her do this, Mike."

She heard a click. For a moment she sat motionless, blinking. Then, glancing at her watch, she reached for the phone again, dialed the operator, asked for a number in New York, and waited to be connected, poising her finger so that if she had to, she could cut off the call in a second.

Sitting up, her back so rigid that it ached, she waited as the phone rang. "Hello?" said a voice finally.

"Cl-Cl-Cl-Cl—"

"Dinah? Dinah Lasker?"

"How'd you guess?" she said with a deep laugh, relieved that his wife hadn't answered the phone. "Can you talk?"

"More or less. If I start telling you I've already sent a check to the relief fund, you'll know who's entered the room."

"Got it. Listen, Cliff, Vee's in big trouble."

She filled him in, including the exchange she had just had with Mike.

"When's it supposed to happen, Dinah?"

"Soon. Middle of July."

"But what can I do?"

"Call her, Cliff. Talk her out of it. Not now. She's loaded, and he's there. He may even be there when you call, but if you try tomorrow, late morning, she'll be up by then. Maybe she'll be sober, and maybe she'll listen to you. You count, for her."

"Not like Mike counts. I never did."

"Not true, Cliff. She respects you more than anybody. She knows, somewhere, you l-l-l-love her."

"Well, you know, I'm under surveillance here."

"I know. I've heard. But doesn't she ever go out of the house? Can't you go somewhere?"

"I'll do what I can."

"Thanks, Cliff."

"Don't get your hopes up, Dinah."

"Try, Cl-Cl—shit, you know your name."

"Listen, if you don't mind my asking, how come you've switched sides all of a sudden? I didn't think you were in the business of saving souls, including your own."

Dinah took a deep breath and laughed softly. "Well, as my sister always says, 'Don't be an idiot.' "

"Ah," he said. "Dumb question."

"Yeah. V-V-V-Very."

She put the phone down and dialed another number. "Dorshka?" she said. "It's me, Dinah. In Chicago, at Jake's cousin's. Do you know what's going on with Vee and Mike?"

"Do I know?" Dorshka said. "Dinah, you cannot imagine. A real glass of worms, this is."

"Can of worms," Dinah said.

"Okay, okay. Worms, snakes. Nest of snakes is better." She was in agony. "Listen, Dinah. It's like this. Truly, I can't *stand* it here anymore. I don't want to die in this awful country, and if I can't go back to Europe I *will* die. *I will!* But still, if she does this for me and for him, how can I live with myself? How? That lawyer you gave her, Unwin, says it's a package deal. Two for one. If she clears Mike, and maybe gives them some names they don't already have, she gets her passport back again, and I, too, get mine. Back to Paris we all can go. Mazel tov all around. All of us—me, the girls, the two of them. Dinah, listen to me. I lost everybody, Dinah. They killed my mother and father, my brother. Mike and the girls—they are all I have left. I cannot live without my family anymore. But God help me, I don't want her to do it. I tell her not to do it and I mean it, but if she doesn't do it I will die here. Dinah, did I tell her the right thing? I don't know what is this right thing anymore."

"You've got *me*," Dinah almost said. But she knew it was no consolation.

"You said the right thing, Dorshka," she murmured without satisfaction in either herself or Dorshka. After she said good-bye, she took a hot shower, changed her clothes, and waited for Jake to arrive.

∗

She wanted to tell him right away about her phone call to Veevi, but she couldn't find a way to do it. The second Hubie and Jake and the Lasker kids marched through the front door, Betty announced dinner. This was a long, cheerful affair, with Hubie and Jake telling stories about the old days: how they'd giggled hysterically at their Hungarian grandfather's funeral and been picked up by the backs of their jackets and thrown out on the street; about Sunday dinners at this same grandfather's, when their grandmother would speak only Hungarian to her sons and completely ignore their wives; and then how the sons—Jake's father, Eli, and his brother, Sidney—would do comedy routines that had everyone peeing with laughter.

Although Jake considered Hubie one of the purest comedy talents he had ever known, Hubie had not gone out to Hollywood with him, despite Jake's invitation, in the winter of 1937. He owned a very successful advertising agency, had a summer house in Michigan, and played golf every weekend with Betty, who, Dinah noted, did her own housework and cooking. Hubie and Jake looked like brothers. Their voices were alike, gravelly and warm, and their laughter and their facial expressions and ways of talking were not just similar but identical. They laughed at each other's jokes with an instinctiveness funded by years of growing up together, though Hubie's father had become rich in the furniture business and Jake's father had stayed poor. Whenever Jake's father managed to make a decent living, it was because he was working for Hubie's father. Whenever he went into business on his own, he failed. Hubie was sent to private school, and his father dressed elegantly and belonged to good clubs. Jake's father gambled and fooled around with women. And, Jake used to say, "If you just boiled his ties, you'd have a hell of a soup."

In the living room, after dinner, Hubie played the piano and Jake sang, the two of them keeping up an endless patter. Dinah saw that Hubie could, just by looking at him in a certain cockeyed way and clearing his throat, cause Jake to dissolve into an eye-streaming, quivering lump of helpless laughing protoplasm. In the past, when the two families had gotten together for weeklong vacations in Palm Springs, or Hubie had come over for dinner while on a business trip to L.A., Dinah had loved watching the cousins in action. Yet she was having difficulty concentrating on the moment. She laughed where she was supposed to, but she chain-smoked and she couldn't find a comfortable position on the sofa. The fun continued until just past midnight, when Jake and Dinah finally went up to their room. It had twin beds, which Jake said a guy his size couldn't possibly sleep in.

Wide awake, talking his head off about the show, Jake was happier than she had ever seen him. "If this thing goes," he said as he took off his shoes and unbuckled his belt, "I'm never gonna make another picture. We'll move to New York, get a great apartment, put the kids in private school, get a house in East Hampton, and I'll do theater, nothing but theater, from here on in. I've never loved anything so much in my life." On and on he went about rehearsals, auditions, actors, dancers, fights with the director, problems with the budget—all of which were dramatic without being catastrophic, all interesting and amusing. He was excited about everything, chucked her under the chin, and talked nonstop about showing the kids all the places where he'd lived as a kid. At the same time, he couldn't wait to get back to New York and take her to rehearsals, which had now started in earnest.

Hearing *that,* of course, delighted her so much that she decided to wait until the next day to bring up her phone call to Veevi. It wouldn't register with him, she argued with herself; he wouldn't be able to take it in right now. That she must tell him, somehow, she felt sure; she didn't exactly know why she had to, she reflected, only that she felt uncomfortable with his not knowing. But to do it now, as he stretched out on the bed to her right, wearing only his familiar boxer shorts and pajama top, seemed pointless. It was as if nothing existed for Jake except the magnificent present. That they had a house in Los Angeles, that the show could fail, even that he had a movie that was about to be released in time for the Fourth of July—and that her sister was scheduled to testify in closed session at Palomar Pictures in two weeks—never came up.

They had been separated for nearly a month. "Come here," he said, lying back on the bed, displaying a ready, ripe erection.

"How's your heart?" she said.

"We can run around the block and find out."

"But that's for a guy who's been m-m-m-married for a hundred years. Don't I qualify as new and exciting?"

"Just come here."

Within moments she was astride him, trying to control the laughter that accompanied their attempts not to make noise. But that only heightened their pleasure, so that everything was over very fast—but happily, for both, and for each.

Soon he began to snore, and she went to her own bed, leaned against the headboard, and smoked a cigarette. She couldn't sleep, not yet; she was too happy to go to sleep. She felt he loved her deeply, she was sure of it now, and nothing else mattered. His face had lit up when he saw her downstairs and he had been so hungry for her, just like the way it used to be. And his energy, his excitement about his work, and New York, and the future! She believed him, felt herself caught up in the fire of invincibility that burned so brightly within him now. She looked over at him, and drank in his physical nearness, his big shoulders and chest, the broad forehead: these were her protection and her safety.

She went into the bathroom to brush her teeth. All right then, she said, looking at herself in the mirror, if Veevi wants to testify that's her business. Mike's going to fail her, and it will go hard for her when that happens, but we'll just keep taking care of her and life will go on. But when she got back to her own bed, in the room that wasn't their bedroom at home, somehow she couldn't get under the covers but sat down on the edge of the mattress, with her hands clasped on her thighs. She couldn't just let it go—what was happening in Los Angeles. She couldn't give up so easily. Jake had to know. He was the one who should call her up and tell her not to do it. It wasn't right for her to keep him from knowing, not when Veevi listened to him and trusted him as her brother-in-law. I have to get him to see it my way, she thought.

She went over to his bed and, gently shaking him by the shoulder, woke him up out of his sleep and told him about her telephone call, earlier that day, to her sister.

The next day Jake took Dinah and the kids on a tour of Rogers Park, where his grandparents had eventually moved after becoming prosperous. She drove while he issued directions. The children had never known their great-grandparents and were not greatly interested in them, but he was full of memories of himself as a child, and they listened to those.

He pointed to a storefront with a large sign in plain red letters: ACME BARGAIN CENTER. "I'm sure of it. That's the saloon. I mean, that's where it used to be." The children dutifully looked at the storefront, straining to see what he was trying to conjure with words. Their faces, however, showed nothing but blankness. "You'd go in that door, and there'd be tables by the window, little candles on the tables, and fancy white tablecloths that Grandma Lasker had ironed herself. And there was a cousin—her name was Manya, I remember, and she worked the cash register, and her boobies were so big they interfered with the keys. . . ."

He stopped in front of other buildings, telling stories out loud that delighted him but were lost on his children. It was hot and they wanted to go back to Highland Park, where they had been promised an afternoon of swimming in Lake Michigan. Nevertheless, Jake was determined to complete the tour. Dinah could feel his delight in the generosity of the day, giving him back the world of his childhood at just the point when he could make use of it. Oddly, for her the one detail that stuck had to do with a Dutch door he described to her in a building he had lived in at the age of four: "One day a man came to the door and was talking to my mother, and I remember being so frustrated because I wasn't tall enough to see through the window, too." The thought of him as a little boy wanting to be bigger moved her. She tried to imagine him at that age, with skinny little legs, standing on tiptoe.

"Strange, isn't it," he said, "how you remember things. I thought I'd remembered everything in my analysis, but I don't think I even mentioned that one."

At the university, he pointed out his old fraternity house, and then the apartment in Blackstone Mansions that he had shared with Izzie Morocco before Izzie went out to Hollywood. Izzie summoned Jake some ten months later, after the up-and-coming radio comedian George Joy had accepted the batch of two dozen jokes plus a guest spot for Groucho Marx that Izzie, who worked for Joy, had gotten Jake to write and had then submitted for him.

Jake instructed Dinah to drive further, and then he stuck his arm out the window and said in a tour guide's voice, "And right over there, ladies and gentlemen, is where they first split the atom—right here at the University of Chicago. The most important scientific development of the modern world happened right over there."

"Did you see it?" Peter asked.

"No," he answered. "I didn't even know it was happening. That was one of the worst times in my life. I could barely make it through my accounting class. It was the middle of the Depression, and every week in class I was putting together and dissolving multimillion-dollar corporations when I didn't know if I was going to have enough money to pay for school. That was the only class I ever took that I passed by cheating. Now, don't ever go and do this," he said sternly, "but I had some of the answers written down on my wrist and palm. I swear I would never have gotten through that course without it."

"A useful lesson to pass on to the kids," said Dinah drily. Then under her breath she said, "Where's the apartment where your friends helped to c-c-c-carry you after your first—"

"We passed it. Two slums back," he answered, knowing exactly what she was referring to. He had told her, long ago, that his high school friends believed the loss of body fluids through ejaculation drained one of physical strength. So after Benny Kravitz arranged for him to lose his virginity to his cousin Irene Moskowitz, Jake made sure Benny and two other friends, Ed Cole and Phil Weinberger, were waiting outside on the stoop to carry him home.

"Ah," said Dinah. "Too bad there isn't a historical plaque to commemorate the event."

He noticed something hard and biting in her tone, and looked at her, surprised and a little hurt, and at a loss for a quick retort.

⁂

"Let's go over this again," he said later that day when they were supposedly taking a nap in their room before going to a dinner dance at Hubie and Betty's country club. "You told her *not* to testify?"

"What I said was that I wished *I* hadn't done it and that *she* shouldn't do it."

I thought this might happen, he said to himself. Humor her. Don't oppose her.

"Jake," she said. "I shouldn't have done it. It's wrong."

"Well, of course it's 'wrong,' darling. I thought we went over that. We never told each other it was 'right.' We never kidded each other about that. It was a dreadful thing, to be asked to do what you did. And God knows, darling, I didn't want you to do it. You made the choice, darling—and I'll always be grateful. Always. My God, you made the ultimate sacri—"

"I wish I hadn't, Jake."

She had said it, finally.

"Okay," he said slowly. "You're entitled to think that."

They looked at each other in silence for a while.

"But we're not talking about me," she said. "This is about Veevi. She's doing it because she thinks Mike will come back to her. I did it for you and us and the kids, and I have you and us and the kids. But she thinks Mike will see how much she loves him and come back for good, and he's just not going to do that. He's sleeping with her, lying to her, deceiving her, just leading her on."

"How do you know he doesn't mean it?"

"I just *do*," she said. "He's just taking advantage of her—anyone can see that. Help me, Jake. Call her and tell her not to do it. You've got to. I will be like a gh-gh-gh-ghost walking the earth for the rest of my life if you don't do this."

He had never seen such a look of anguish on her face. It made her skin waxen and yellowish. She smoked fiercely, sucking down and pulling hard on her cigarette, while she chewed the inside of her cheek and stared at the carpeted floor with her haunted brown eyes.

"And what if it works out for her and Mike? Suppose that happens? You want to stand in the way of that?"

"It's not going to happen. He's going to leave her again. I just know it. He's playing with her, Jake. I can feel it. And when it's over, and she realizes she testified for him and it didn't make any difference, she's going to fall apart and it's going to be bad. I know her, darling. Believe it or not she's got a conscience, and she won't forgive herself for giving in to the Committee."

"Wrong, baby. You're the one with the conscience. You've got so much conscience you could bottle it and sell it. Here's her chance to start over with Mike, and you want to fuck it up with conscience. What right have you got to stand in the way of her happiness? Anyway, you wait and see. If she testifies, she and Mike and all their friends will tell themselves it was different. It won't be like yours. They're always the exception. And they'll sneer at people like you and me and never think they've given in."

"That's not true of Veevi. She's not like that."

Oh, if only you knew, Jake wished he could say. "Look, darling, I understand what you're feeling. But this is her chance to start over, with or without him."

"I'm so sure of it," she went on, "that I told her . . . about . . . about seeing him with Jill Trevor. I know you told me not to, but she's in d-d-d-danger, Jake."

"You didn't! Ah, honey. You shouldn't have."

"I had to, Jake. I had to make her see she's kidding herself. It didn't make any difference. She thinks she's going home with him to Paris and it's all going to be just like it used to be."

"Listen, darling," he said, leaning forward and grabbing her wrists so hard that it hurt. "Don't ever, ever do that again. Do you understand? So he was with a broad. So what? It has nothing to do with anything. If he's coming back he's coming back, and whether he sees a broad or not means nothing."

"How can you say that?" she said, pulling away from him. "And let go of me. You're hurting me!"

They argued back and forth, going over and over what it meant for Mike to have been with another woman, for Dinah to have seen it, and for her to have told Veevi about it. Jake kept scolding her, and she was so angry she wanted to find a hairbrush or a magazine and thwack him with it to make him stop browbeating her. "Besides," he said, "what makes you think I have any influence with her? She knows I was glad you testified. You know, I think the safest thing to do with a small talent is to find a cause that makes you the helpless victim of people who won't let you use it. As far as I'm concerned, that's the story with ninety-nine percent of those martyrs."

"I'm only interested in Veevi's case, nobody else's. I don't give a good goddamn about the others—the heroes or the finks. Including me."

"What you're forgetting is that your sister isn't going to listen to you, because she doesn't like you."

"I don't c-c-c-care. Just call her for me. Just tell her she doesn't have to do it. Help me out, Jake."

"Did it ever occur to you that you're so jealous of your sister—of her beauty and the life she's led—that you're unconsciously trying to hurt her? That you're doing everything you can to undermine her chance of happiness?"

"That's a l-l-l-l-lousy, mean, stupid thing for you to say." She felt herself ready to explode, the way she had in Palm Springs. But they were guests in someone else's house, and they had to go to a fancy party with a lot of "civilians"—doctors, lawyers, businesspeople, manufacturers, Hubie's advertising friends—and she was paralyzed.

"But think about it. Lots of couples go through rough times and break up and think it's over forever and then find their way back to each other. It's happening with Mike and Veevi. It's a damn good thing. Let them alone."

"I trust my instincts, honey, and my instincts tell me that Mike Albrecht doesn't give a good goddamn anymore whether Veevi lives or dies as long as he, that great, pure, incorruptible artist, gets paid to make his masterpiece of postwar fiction into a Hollywood movie produced by Willie Weil, who, according to Veevi, likes to have girls pee on him, and worse. Just go and call her. Tell her she doesn't have to do it. You don't have to say 'right' or 'wrong.' You don't have to lecture her. Just tell her she doesn't have to do it."

"What makes you think she gives a good goddamn what we think? You and I don't count. She calls us 'idiots' to other people."

"How do you know that?"

"She calls everybody else an idiot. What makes you think she spares us?"

"That doesn't matter. Just tell her she doesn't have to do it. I told her; now you tell her. She likes you, and she listens to you. You're her brother-in-law."

He said nothing, but let her continue. He was hoping she'd run out of steam.

"Jake, it's not just that I feel certain he's going to leave her faster than you can say Jack Robinson. There's something else. I don't want her waking up the next day telling herself she didn't have to do it, that she could have made it, that you survive these things and you don't give in."

"Is that how you feel?"

"S-S-S-Sometimes." She looked at him. "Yes."

She put her cigarette out and leaned back against the wall and put her arms around her drawn-up knees. "We could have made it, that's all. We would have been okay."

He waited for a while. "Maybe you're right," he said.

She dropped her head onto her knees. "I don't want to argue with you, Jake. I don't care about j-j-j-j-justifying what I did or comp-p-p-paring it with what she's going to do. I just don't want Veevi to fall apart. I don't want her to die. Please. Go downstairs and call her."

"Okay," he said. "I'll do it. But first I'm gonna take a shower and get something to eat. I'm starving!"

At about six o'clock, while Dinah was sitting in the kitchen with Gussie and Betty and both sets of Lasker kids, Jake took his cousin aside and asked him if he could use the phone in his study.

"Sure, sure," Hubie said.

He looked at Jake, who winked at him.

"Ah," said Hubie. "Lucky you. Some doll in New York?"

"L.A., actually. I'm kind of winding things down."

"Nicely, nicely now. Good pickings in New York, huh?"

"Sensational. You know, dancers. You wouldn't believe the muscles they've got. And the places they've got them."

Hubie had taken Jake by the elbow and was leading him into his study, which had a piano loaded with music composition paper, a coffee cup filled with pencils, and a mantelpiece covered with golf trophies and advertising awards. Jake immediately felt at home in it. He was proud of his cousin's career, though he would never have wished it for himself, and toward which, in addition, he felt a certain superiority—the kind he felt toward television writers as well.

"You know, Betty and I have been married—let's see now—nineteen years, and in all that time I've never once been unfaithful to her." He waited for a moment. "In the same city."

He laughed at his own line—a rapid, infectious laugh, in which Jake easily joined him, storing the line away for future use.

"Tell me something," he said as he sat down behind Hubie's desk and pulled the phone toward him. "Do you and Betty still do it?"

Hubie looked at him with a straight face.

"We sure do," he replied as he headed toward the door. "Every single year."

Twenty minutes later, Jake returned to the guest room, pulled out the book of his musical, and began going over one of the pages with a sharp pencil he had brought up from downstairs. He informed Dinah, who was putting on eye shadow and mascara for the evening ahead, that he had told Veevi exactly what she had wanted him to tell her.

He had, of course, done nothing of the kind. What he had told his wife's sister was that he would always love her, and wanted her to be happy, and that nothing in the world should stand in the way of her finding happiness again with Mike. He said that if testifying would make it possible for the two of them to have a new life together, then she should go ahead and do it. "And God bless," he added, using a phrase that Dinah loathed and considered the height of Hollywood phoniness.

11

*D*inah pulled the thermometer out of Jake's burning mouth: 102.4. He was shivering under the heap of extra blankets and looked like a balding child with glittering eyes. It was two-thirty in the morning, and outside a hard November wind pushed against the windows. He drew out a hot hand from under the covers and gestured for her to give him the newspaper again.

"No," she said. "You've already read it a dozen times. Forget it. It doesn't matter." Then she relented and handed him a much-creased *New York Times.*

In a dry, cracking voice, Jake read: "Lasker's tasteless one-liners will not go over well with those seeking a night of wholesome entertainment. While the raucous and lively streets of Chicago receive their due in O'Rourke's lyrics and Hart's tunes, the book's endless family intrigues are unremittingly noisy and off-color. Buzz Keegan's choreography, though exuberant and energetic, crosses the line from suggestive to salacious."

"I don't want to hear it again," said Dinah, grabbing the newspaper out of his hand and throwing it on the floor. "You're torturing yourself. This is just one guy's opinion."

"Two whole fucking years of my life," he croaked. "What does that son of a bitch Quincy Bradford know about musical comedy?"

"GO TO SL-SL-SL-SLEEP."

She was waiting for the Seconal she had given him twenty minutes earlier to take effect, but now, putting her hand on his forehead, she wondered whether the fever wasn't giving him abnormal energy that would keep him ranting and raving for the rest of the night. "The audience loved it," she said. "Think of all those curtains calls. P-P-P-People were standing, and shouting. This is just one guy."

"Doesn't mean a thing if the critics hate it. And he's the top critic in this town. I wish I were dead."

"Shh."

"We'll have three more performances, and then we'll close. I'll be home next week. For good. Then what'll I do? I don't have a picture in me or on me right now. We've got a mortgage, a housekeeper, a laundress, a pool man, and two kids eating me alive. Not to mention—"

"Would you be quiet and go to sleep, please? Here. Your chest is tight, I can hear it." She dipped her index and third fingers into a purple jar of Vicks VapoRub and spread the mentholated goo all over his chest. His eyes looked at her pleadingly, as if he wished she could change everything with a word.

"Do me a favor and go out at five for the papers, will you, honey?"

"Sure. Now, turn over and I'll rub your back."

Reaching under the covers, she glided her hand over his flat, almost shapeless behind, up along the broad shoulder blades, and began to press firmly against his flesh in broad, soothing circles. He turned to her suddenly. "Suck my dickie?"

She laughed and pushed his head back down on the pillow. "Forget it, Charlie. You're b-b-b-burning up! Go to sleep."

"Yeah," he said, his voice murmurous and drooling. "What kind of a meshugana thinks he can bring a musical about a bunch of Hungarian Jews in Chicago to New York? You know what? This town is square. Deeply square. They think they invented life. They think they're the standard for everything. I've never liked it here. Let's pack and go back to Hollywood, right now. I wanna go home and see the kreebnabbers and get back on the golf course. Let's go home tomorrow."

"Shh." She kept massaging his shoulders, his neck, waiting for the sleeping pill to work. The smell of VapoRub rose up to her own nostrils, clearing her head. He was hot, but she knew his fevers and felt certain that he would have a good sweat in the night and that the fever would break by morning.

The phone rang, and she picked it up, annoyed that anyone would call at this time of night. "Hello?"

There was no answer. "Hello? Hello?"

No response on the other end. She put the phone down. "Wrong n-n-n-number," she said, and saw that in the seconds between the ringing of the phone and her putting it back on the receiver, Jake had fallen asleep. She turned off the light and sat on the edge of the bed for a while, just listening to him breathe, as she often did with her children.

※

Had he noticed, she wondered, when she eventually got into bed beside him, what happened when Thelma Ostrow, Milty's ex-wife, and her new husband came up to them, pushing their way through the crowds of people in the foyer of the theater? There they all were, she and Jake, and Buzz Keegan and his wife, Lou, and Jimmy O'Rourke and a girl, and Sammy and Lois Hart, receiving congratulations ("It's a hit, an absolute hit," "It's gonna run forever," "Absolutely sensational," she had heard over and over), when up come Thelma and this new husband of hers, Eugene Strong, a good, working New York actor, and still, she'd heard, a dedicated Party guy. Thelma seizes Jake's hands and pulls him down and kisses him on both cheeks. "It's sensational!" she says. "The best thing since *Guys and Dolls*—a classic, an absolute classic American musical." And then she introduces the new husband, and he shakes hands with Jake and offers praise and congratulations, and then they cut Dinah dead, both of them. They turn their backs on her, after darting glances of icy hatred at her, and they move past her to Buzz Keegan, with whom they once again do the grabbing and kissing routine.

Two pure and incorruptible saints, Dinah said to herself, stretching herself out in the small cool space left unoccupied by her husband's snoring hulk. Where did Thelma Ostrow suppose that Jake had gotten the wherewithal to keep working and do the show? Couldn't she figure it out?

It wasn't that Dinah minded being cut. Clearly, this was going to happen for the rest of her life, and she knew it could happen anytime, anywhere. But the way they left Jake out of the equation: now, that was funny. Kissing his ass because she thought he had a hit and might, just might, give her husband a job.

She laughed out loud and then turned on her side, facing Jake. She could feel the heat from his body and stretched her hand out to touch his arm and his upturned hand lying on the pillow. She closed her eyes, then opened them again. The wind was making a whining sound, but the night-time glow of the lit-up city flamed in through the windows. The bedroom was dry and stuffy from central heating, but Jake was a fervent believer in the pneumonia-causing properties of fresh air, especially in the East. And it was cold outside, colder than it ever got in L.A., cold with the menace of coming winter.

Once again, she was in the East. Last June, after Chicago, they had driven through Indiana and Ohio to Pennsylvania, back to Beaver Falls, and Pittsburgh, and then to Philadelphia, where she had taken out the AAA map and found a street, and told Jake to park the car in front of a house with a set of high front steps. Looking at it for a long time, she had said, finally, "Grandpa Milligan built that," and pointed to a garage. "He took me down to the Baltimore docks and got the materials, just the two of us in his Model T, and built it himself, so that the garage would be toasty warm in the mornings and he could start up the car to get to work on time. God, it was cold in the mornings. We always had coughs and sniffles. The snot would freeze under our n-n-noses, and they'd be raw and sore."

Gussie and the kids and Jake urged her to ring the doorbell. Maybe whoever lived there would let her in and show her the house. Her heart froze. "Should I?" All together they cried, "Yes! Yes!" And then maybe if the owner let her in, Dinah would be able to show them around, too.

So she walked up the steps where she had once tried to fly and broken her arm, next to the patch of grass where Veevi had sat in the sandbox holding out a little bag of brown sugar she had stolen from the kitchen— holding it out so that all of Dinah's friends stopped watching the roller-skating race between Dinah and her rival, George Schmidt, and stood around Veevi in the sandbox, getting their faces and fingers sticky from licking the sugar.

She pressed the doorbell. The door opened and revealed a thin young woman in a housedress holding a baby in her arms. She wore no makeup, and a scarf was tied around her hair and knotted in the front. She looked at Dinah with caution. That could have been Mom forty-two years ago, opening the door with Veevi in her arms, Dinah thought, explaining why she was there. The woman said it was okay with her but her husband had told her never to let anyone in. She said she was sorry. Dinah asked her if the boiler was still in the garage, and the woman shook her head and said there was a boiler there but she honestly didn't know whether it was old or new; she guessed it was new. As they spoke, Dinah looked beyond the woman and into the parlor, with its sofa and armchairs from Sears, and the television in its "console," and the open-topped cube of the baby's playpen set on the vomit-green carpet. "Was there wallpaper here when you moved in?" The woman said there had been wallpaper, but it was old and faded, with big brown stains from leaks in the roof. "Do you remember the pattern?" Dinah asked. "Was it roses? Little bunches of roses? In f-f-f-festoons?"

"Honestly, ma'am, I don't remember. I think so. But we had it all scraped off before we moved in. My husband said for the price we were paying the other owners should have scraped those walls themselves."

It would have been so easy to say the next thing, to continue the conversation, to ask about the kitchen, the yard, the bedrooms, and the bathroom upstairs, where Dinah had undressed and washed her father so many decades ago when he came home staggering and reeking after yet another three-week binge. But she stopped herself cold. "Thank you, dear," she said, the "dear" mixing warmth and gratitude with the condescension of a woman who now belonged to the upper middle class, and who would never stand in a doorway, as her mother had, in a shapeless housedress and a knotted kerchief, with the upright vacuum plugged in and waiting in the parlor.

12

It is deep in the mid-November night, and in West Los Angeles a relentless Santa Ana wind strips the eucalyptus trees of their dry and brittle leaves and flakes the bark peeling back from their swaying trunks. Below the star-encrusted sky, yucca, juniper, sage-brush, and thyme pour scent upon scent through the open window screens, while family dogs, chained outdoors for the night, smell coyotes in the canyons and howl in cascading echoes. Yet Veevi neither hears nor sees and, under the sheets thrown back from her shoulders, lies perfectly still, her knees tucked up almost to her breasts and her two hands placed vir-ginally together underneath her cheek.

She has been yearning for this state of ecstatic oblivion. How hard she has worked to get there, fighting her way downward to the blackest dark-ness. She could not do it alone, but needed help from big gulps out of the bottle hidden underneath the bed, and from the red-and-orange jewels in the vial on the night table.

Each by itself could not do the job. With gin alone, she could still feel the body of the man lying beside her, feel its grossness and wrongness. She does not want to see and know this fat and hairy belly, these fleshy eyelids, these sensualist's hands that lie only inches from her own. With gin alone, he cannot turn into the one she wants, the one with the beautiful boy's face as it had been in 1938, his young beard dark and still rough after shaving, and his chest hot and sweating above hers on the beach in the middle of the night. With gin alone, she cannot go down into the velvet darkness with the boy lying full length above her. For that, she needs the red-and-orange jewels. When she washes them down with a big swig of gin, soon there is a curling wave that lifts and cups her as she falls again into the darkness, and not a moment too soon, for it wraps its black cloak around her just as she sees the pornographic scene in all its perfect detail: the young French actress with her short blond hair and her long legs spread and Mike taking aim—one, two, three, he's in! And oh, are they ever at it, hour after hour!

So she sinks to the dark place where dreams turn to nothing, and nothing turns to dreams. It's so droll, really, that she wishes she could tell Dinah about it. She is floating in delicious oblivion but having the dream all the same, the way kids talk at night after the lights are out. But she's honored, too, because inside this dream, which she's laughing at while she's having it, Sleeping Beauty is walking down the street—our Sleeping Beauty—side by side with the president.

Yes, the president of the United States of America! President Dwight D. Eisenhower. Ramrod straight, with the bluest blue eyes you've ever seen. He is looking at her, with a sidelong glance of adoration and desire and eyes so blue they are the exact shade of the deep skies at Madame Rochedieu's, in the late fall afternoons—the only time that it is safe to walk in the woods and look for firewood. They are the blue of Pop's eyes, too, when he takes her out to the desert, just the two of them, to teach her to shoot. Propping up the .22 on her shoulder, he stands back, and when she fires, and the bullet hits the tin can set up on a rock, his blue eyes flash with pleasure. "Atta girl!" he says. They get into the Model T, and he strokes her hair, shyly, and they say delicious mean things about Mom and Dinah. "Don't they ever shut up?" "Everything they like to do is boring, and everything we like to do is fun." "They're just stick-in-the-muds." "You're my favorite and you're always gonna be my favorite."

And now, in her sleep, she smiles, her lips twitch and blink with pleasure, for in her dream (sunk now so far below the murk of barbiturate and booze), President Dwight D. Eisenhower walks beside her but does not touch her. A parade is going by. They are part of the parade, and it's—for him! People are throwing ticker tape into the air! Some of it falls on them like confetti, and he looks at her again, and she feels safer than she has ever felt with anyone in her life (though she is still laughing at herself having the dream, it is really too ridiculous that she's with Dwight D. Eisenhower, and she laughs and tells him, "I never voted for you! I never would! I'm a Communist!"). But he finds it charming, and he lets her know with his eyes that there is no one in the world who is so beautiful, so wonderful. But he doesn't touch her; his arms remain straight against his sides. His uniform fits him perfectly, and his medals glint in the sun. No one says it out loud, but everyone in the parade knows that he cherishes her and loves her *more than anything on earth,* and that he has *chosen* her out of all the women in the world to be his, forever. That's why he looks at her the way he does. The most important man in the world, the man who is the president of the United States of America and the world and the universe, loves her more than anyone he has ever loved, and more than any man has ever loved any woman. Everybody sees it; everybody knows it. And now, in front of the whole world, he puts his hands on her face and kisses her, and she feels happier than happiness itself. As the people in the parade roar by him, he leans over and whispers in her ear, "Oh, you darling Communist!" and smiles at her, his face blazing with adoration. And she says to him, with a smile that promises the most spectacular time in bed he will ever have in his life, "We think Stalin's the cat's meow, don't we?" And she throws her head back, laughing, and he laughs, too; it's their private joke, and in the whole world only the two of them have that special understanding. After all, everything is fine now. She is supposed to be with a great and important man. She is fulfilling her destiny, and she turns to him and says, "I should have been a king's mistress, but I'm yours instead," knowing that he will find this as funny as she does.

But suddenly he's gone. It's dark, and the parade has ended. The street is deserted. Everyone has gone home. Sleeping Beauty isn't in a city anymore but lying in her actual, mussed-up bed, whose fetid sheets haven't been changed in weeks. She turns on her stomach, and as she does so, a long thick groan escapes from her, because despite the flow of hot air streaming through the windows, she is cold and has goose bumps on her arms where the short sleeves of her nylon nightgown stop. The covers lie bunched around her feet. Dwight D. Eisenhower is nowhere in sight. Neither is the street. Sleeping Beauty is standing on a cold, deserted beach. Water widens toward infinity in a gray mist. Cold waves lap her feet and make her want to pee. Oh God, she has to pee; it's such a bore, and she's being dragged up out of sleep, dragged by the hand, by her sister, away from a chocolate soda, and all the good tastes of life, dragged away from the sprinkler she's running through stark naked and that she wants to stand over with her legs spread so she can just pee, dragged up through the darkness and blackness and left stranded in her bed, on her stomach, with her eyes opening in the darkness and a heavy, keen pressure in her pelvis, because the one thing she won't do (and her eyes open slowly in the dark room), the one thing she won't do ever again, is pee the bed. No, she won't do that. She did that with Peter Lasker, and she is determined, no matter how bad things are, never to pee another bed. You crawled, sobbing, on all fours up to his knees when Mike said he was going back to Paris and Odile, she tells herself, but you will not pee that damn bed.

And so, in the darkness, where a man she despises lies insensate beside her, stinking of gin, Sleeping Beauty, awakened by her bladder, puts one bare foot and then the other on the carpet. She pushes the right foot under the bed and finds a bottle, because she badly needs something warm going down her throat. She bends down, slowly, unsteadily, almost keeling over, and reaches out for it. After a nice, warm slug, she puts it back under the bed. It helps right away; she feels much better, and she gropes for her cigarettes and matches. Oh, but she will want to go right back to sleep, to dreaming in the velvet darkness, when she gets back. It will be too, too dreary if she can't go back to sleep, so although she is stuporous, she is nevertheless deft as she opens the amber vial and picks out two of the red-and-orange jewels, and takes another swallow from the bottle she again retrieves, laboriously, from under the bed and again laboriously puts back. Then she thrusts her hand out and pushes herself up from the bed, feeling for the hardness of the wall. The crinkle of the cellophane around the pack of Lucky Strikes in her left hand reassures her; she will have more pleasure soon. She gropes, walking with exaggerated care, leaning against the wall. Her eyes adjust to the darkness, she's unsteady, her head lolls onto her shoulder, but there's nothing surprising about this. She's been drinking all day, and with the two she has just taken, that makes a total of eight lovely red-and-orange Seconals since nine o'clock tonight.

At last she moves into the bathroom, and there is enough moonlight coming through the window for her not to have to turn on the light. That is very good, because anything brighter would hurt her eyes. These days, she can't stand bright light and always wants her room to be dark, with cool shadows. These days, she hardly ever leaves her room. With a long sigh of relief and happiness, she lowers her unsteady behind onto the toilet seat, pulling her nightgown up so that the hem rests along her thighs. With one hand pressed against the wall, she relieves herself and sighs again, and feels, in her lap the pack of cigarettes and decides that she's going to sit there and have a smoke. She places the pack of cigarettes on the counter by the sink, wipes herself, and reaches back to flush, hating it when people pee in the night and don't flush. She gagged when the man now lying in her bed first spent the night and the next morning, when she came into the bathroom and found the seat up, saw his dark yellow urine in the bowl. Then she reaches for the pack of cigarettes and holds it so that just one cigarette slides out. She places it artfully between her index and third fingers and holds it to her lips. With one hand, she bends a match over and strikes it, and it is at just this moment, this very instant, when she is lifting the flame to the tip of her cigarette, that a fresh gust of hot wind pours through the window. Perhaps it's the gin and the pills alone roiling upward in a huge volcanic crescendo, or maybe it's that bump on the head in Palm Springs, or all of them stomping on her together, an enraged mob—it's anyone's guess. But suddenly, in the bathroom, the tiles that gleamed only seconds earlier with moonlight now light up with a terrible red glow and the small figure on the toilet seat slumps to the floor as the flames eat her up like a sweetmeat.

Dinah didn't need to set the alarm. She woke up at five to five, slipped on a pair of slacks and a sweater and her coat, and went down to the lobby, where the doorman directed her to a newsstand outside in the cold blue morning. The city was already alive with traffic; she liked being part of the hum and the roar. There was an open coffee shop on Lexington, and she went in, holding the papers under her arm, and ordered a coffee with cream to go. She was very tired, having slept so little, and wanted to brace herself for when Jake woke up, as he soon would, to see if the morning reviews were as bad as that first one last night. When she let herself into the apartment, she was surprised to find him already up. The light on the night table was on, and he was sitting on the edge of the bed, in his pajama top only, with the phone on his knees. What he was saying confused her. First he said, "It's Dorshka," and then he said, "It's Veevi," and she thought, Dorshka's dead. Then he rasped through his sore throat, "Bad news," as he handed her the phone, and she thought, Veevi's dead.

Some thirteen hours later, Dinah put out her cigarette and fastened her seat belt as the DC-7 descended through an invisible stairway to the L.A. basin. The plane rocked, and she gripped the armrests with both hands. It must be the Santa Anas that Dorshka had told her about. Her palms were sweating; her heart was not so much pounding as flittering, skittering—an animal in panic, but not from the turbulence. She did not know how she was going to do what she would have to do once the plane landed.

The first thing would be to conceal her loathing of Byron Cole. She detested him. When she described him to Jake over the phone, after Veevi brought him over to the house to swim one Sunday, she called him a "heavy, because he looks like the bad guys in movies—you know, a kind of sexual thug," aware of something not quite right about her own response that only made her hate him more. Upon meeting him in September, when she and the kids had flown back from New York to L.A., she had figured him out and hated him at once. She knew exactly what he was up to with her sister, and impotently watched as he took over every aspect of Veevi's life. But now he was picking Dinah up at the airport and taking her immediately to Cedars, and she would have to behave politely, although she blamed him for what had happened, blamed him almost as much as she blamed herself.

He had moved in on Veevi like a coyote, at the end of the summer, plying her with booze whenever she asked for it, drinking with her. But he had a hollow leg, while she got smashed on the first drink, her blood already soggy with the sleeping pills he procured for her from who knows how many Beverly Hills doctors. He was a "serious actor," no less, who came to Veevi's house for lessons with Dorshka twice a week. When he couldn't pay, he did favors for her and Veevi, yard work, handyman stuff, in tight jeans and a sweaty T-shirt.

Veevi wouldn't have looked at him twice, but in the miserable days after Mike left, in August, when she was literally unable to get out of bed, he made himself indispensable to her. When she woke up, he got her orange juice laced with gin. A transplanted New Yorker, he claimed to be a photographer as well as an actor, said he had been a painter in the late forties, dropped every name in the book, and, immediately after he started sleeping with her, began referring to himself as the latest in the line of Veevi's consorts: Stefan, Mike, and Me. Dinah hated his lewd blue eyes, hated the way he would lean over the sofa at the Laskers' and, in a coarse display of ownership, tweak Veevi in the crotch, hated the sweat that broke out on his upper lip when he drank beer, hated the tight bathing suits he wore around the pool, hated the way he talked about the "art" of acting, and hated the way he played in to Veevi's disdain for everything that wasn't New York or European. Above all, she hated him for taking possession of Veevi.

Thinking about him, Dinah remembered the argument she and Jake had had over the phone before she left L.A. in early November for the last out-of-town tryouts and the opening. She had wanted to stay, worried about Cole's grip on Veevi, but Jake had put his foot down: "I'm sick of your putting her first. This is the biggest risk of my career, and I want you with me." Ordinarily, she would have been thrilled, but his words now left her with a sickening uneasiness. Veevi was drunk so often when she called on the phone that Dinah simply held the phone to her ear, listened to Veevi's sodden slurring and weeping, and could only murmur in response, over and over: "Yes, Vee . . . sure, Vee . . . I know, Vee."

Now, flying into L.A., knowing only that whatever she had to face in the coming hours would be worse than anything she had ever experienced in her life, she cursed herself. If only I hadn't left. If only I hadn't accepted Dorshka's version of things last summer—that Veevi was fine, that she had accepted it completely when Mike went back to Paris, that they had parted as friends, with an understanding about everything, that Byron Cole was a dear, kind man and a stabilizing and calming influence on Veevi. Wrong. All of it wrong. It appalled her, the whole situation. She was mad at Dorshka, whom she had always thought so wise, because she had accepted Byron Cole into the house as if he were one of her beloved refugees and refused to see what he was doing to Veevi. Of course, having him there made things easier for her; Dinah understood that. It meant that she didn't have to bur-den herself with Veevi and could devote herself to Coco, who had no one except Dorshka. She did have her passport back, thanks to Veevi, but Mike hadn't insisted that she move to Paris. In fact, he had told her that it was best for her to stay with Veevi and the girls (though Claire, fortunately, spent most of her time with her boyfriend and was hardly ever at home). Because he seemed so eager for her to have Coco, she had refused to ac-knowledge his cruelty to Veevi.

Dinah had bought more newspapers at Idyllwild, intending to reread the morning reviews on the plane. Jake had tried to read them out loud to her as she packed, and later in the limousine, hoping to distract her—and capture some small particle of her attention for himself—but she couldn't concentrate on listening to him. Still, she knew that she had been right. The reviews were great, and despite the Quincy Bradford review last night, the show was a hit—a big one, in fact—and would be running for a long time to come. But it didn't matter to her now; it meant nothing at all, and she had shoved the newspapers unopened under the seat in front of her and forgotten them. She had been silent, unresponsive, tense, as she packed, listening to him as he lay on the bed taking calls of congratulations from people whose excited voices she could hear through the phone even though she was on the other side of the room.

⁂

Byron was waiting for her, his swarthy face unshaven, a roll of tanned hairy belly visible under his T-shirt. She barely nodded hello, and ducked away from his attempt to embrace her; she nearly outpaced him in her rush to get to the car. Arrangements had been made in New York to have her baggage delivered to the house, so there was no need to claim it. She fired questions at him: Was Veevi conscious? What about the pain? Was she getting morphine?

That, more than anything, was what she couldn't bear—the thought of Veevi's pain from the burns. When she reached the left side of the green MG, Veevi's car, which she and Jake had bought for her with its British right-hand drive, she saw that the top was down and the front seat soaking wet. Dinah didn't want to sit down in a puddle of water, and she looked around for something to wipe the seat with.

Byron was already starting the ignition and seemed not to notice that she was still standing.

"I'm not driving to C-C-C-Cedars in the rain, with the top down," she said, trying to steady her voice. "I need something to wipe the seat with."

He gave her a doleful look with his hooded eyes, as if he'd been startled by emotions too deep for her to fathom. "She's in agony, Dinah."

You prick, she thought. You fed her booze and pills day after day, and then you drive her MG here in the rain with the fucking top down and get the seat soaking wet because you're so overcome with grief. Dinah turned swiftly and began to walk in the other direction. "Fine. I'll get a t-t-t-taxi," she said furiously.

"Hold on, hold on." He jumped out of the car and grabbed some rags in the back to wipe off the seat. As they raced downtown on the Hollywood Freeway, Dinah asked questions. What were Veevi's chances? The next six weeks would be crucial, he said. How badly was she burned? (She knew the answer to this, but had to ask again.) Third-degree burns, over fifty percent of her body. How did it happen? She was feeling bad that day, he said. A letter had arrived from Mike saying that he couldn't live without Odile, after all, and that it was best if they went ahead with the divorce after all. He had left L.A. promising to think everything over. He'd always love her, he said, but the marriage was no go anymore.

"I took her out for a drive, down to the beach," Byron said.

Yeah, you got her good and crocked first, Dinah said to herself.

"She seemed to accept it all. I asked her to marry me when the divorce was final. You know how much I love her," he said with a sob.

Dinah turned away and looked out the window. Everything was freeways now, looping in and around one another, the palm trees hanging over them breathing in the exhaust. He kept talking. They had had dinner that night with Dorshka and Coco, then a couple of drinks, and gone to bed. A couple of drinks my ass, Dinah said to herself. They must have gotten tanked. It was just a freak thing, he said. He was asleep when it happened. It was Dorshka who woke him up, because she'd smelled the smoke rising, and the other smell—the hideous smell of Veevi burning, Dinah knew. Then they went into the bathroom and found her on the floor, moaning.

"Prepare yourself," he said to her. "It's bad."

Indeed, it was worse than anything she could have anticipated. It was the worst thing she had ever seen. When she was finally allowed into the room, swathed in a sterile cap and gown and mask, and the smell hit her nostrils, she gagged and gagged again, and her mouth watered, and she had to swallow quickly, to keep her spit from running into the mask. Then, oddly, she was standing so close to Veevi's bedside and watching her so intently that the smell ceased to matter and all she was aware of was Veevi herself.

Everywhere that the fire had bitten deep into Veevi's flesh, including the two patches on her cheeks, there were thick white dressings. From her neck down to her knees, Veevi was encased in layers of white gauze through which Dinah could see seeping yellowish fluids. Her lips, unburned but dry, were covered with petroleum jelly. The hair that had been burned had been cut, and what was left lay thick and luxuriant against the pillow. There were tubes everywhere that flesh remained—in her ankles, up her nose, in her hands, her back. A nurse, covered head to toe in white, stood on the other side of the bed, checking the tall poles with bags of fluid suspended from them, a clipboard in her hand, writing down numbers.

The nylon nightgown that Veevi had been wearing ended just above her knees, and had melted on her and burned her wherever it touched her. Third-degree, Dorshka had said on the phone, and Byron again in the car, and again she had heard the phrase from the nurse in the burn unit who had given her the green gown and the cap and the mask. *Third degree.* The *third degree. Give him the third degree,* ran through her mind as she draped herself in the regulation coverings.

"Vee?" Dinah spoke through the mask. What she saw amazed her: Veevi, her eyes closed and only semiconscious, raised her right arm, brought her fingers to her mouth as if she were holding a cigarette, pressed her lips together, as if taking drag after drag, and smiled with pleasure—the pleasure of smoking, of putting something good into her mouth.

That first day, Dinah was instructed not to stay long, because the risk of infection was too great. But she said everything to Veevi she could think of: I'm right here, I'll be back tomorrow, I love you, you're going to be fine, Uncle J. sends his love, we all love you. Over and over, the same plain words. Over and over: I love you. Veevi smiled, it seemed to Dinah, then again made the smoking gesture.

"What about her lungs?" Dinah asked the nurse outside in the hall. "Did she breathe in the smoke?"

"Yes. There's tissue damage there, and diminished pulmonary capacity," the nurse answered. Dinah could see only her eyes above the mask, but they were intelligent and thoughtful. She was young, Dinah thought, but she knew how to take care of the worst kind of injury that exists. Her name was Kirsten Fisk, and burns were her specialty. It comforted Dinah to see how calmly she tended to the poles and tubes while never seeming to take her eyes off Veevi.

Dinah had asked Byron to let her have some time alone with her sister, but after only ten minutes or so he came in, gowned as Dinah was, and stood by the bed. "Oh, baby, baby," he said, crying. Beside herself with anger, Dinah left the room and waited in the corridor, listening to the soft padding of the nurses' white oxfords on the linoleum floor.

She drove back and forth between the hospital and her house twice a day, day after day. She gave blood, and called friends, and they gave blood. She drove Claire to the hospital and back, and listened to her as she wept quietly, and was hurt when, at home, or at the hospital, the girl went stiff when Dinah tried to hug her. Soon Claire began driving to the hospital with her boyfriend—an older man of thirty-two named Vernon Ashby. He was an ex–vice squad cop whom she had met out at Saul Landau's dock at Trancas, where he was the captain of one of Landau's three charter-fishing boats. Dinah was put off by him at first, and she couldn't help thinking there was something wrong with a man of that age going out with a girl of seventeen. There wasn't a doubt in her mind that Claire was sleeping with him, and she had a feeling that her niece would marry him when she graduated from high school the following June.

But gradually she began to like him. He came to the hospital day after day with Claire, and he comforted her when she cried; and Dinah found out that he had been tireless about getting his cop buddies and fisherman friends and their wives to give blood. When he told her that he couldn't stand Byron Cole and had told him to move out of Dorshka's house and back to his own place, an apartment somewhere in West Hollywood, she thanked him and realized that she trusted him and was grateful he was there. He was an odd-looking fellow—tall and sinewy, with deep-set gray eyes that were a little too close together, and sharp-angled cheekbones. He told her his parents were Okies who'd come to California in the thirties and now had a pig farm near Fresno. When Vernon saw Byron at the hospital, his look became mean and hard—just like Pop, Dinah thought approvingly.

But nothing helped her with the horror of what had happened to Veevi. Dinah couldn't get used to visiting her. Fear swept over her every time she turned in to the hospital parking lot. Veevi remained heavily sedated, but she was still in indescribable pain. Every time her dressings were changed, she had to have general anesthesia, and when that wore off she needed morphine. It was this presence of unceasing agony, and the knowledge that it wasn't going to stop anytime soon, that ate into Dinah. She felt Veevi's flesh as her own. For a long time now, she had wondered whether she truly loved her sister. There had been times when she wasn't sure. But the question no longer even existed. She did not know where she ended and her sister began; she and Veevi were the same body; Veevi was her child, her sister, herself.

"It's unb-b-b-bearable," she said to Kirsten when Veevi moaned in pain.

"Yes, I know," the nurse answered, hooking up a fresh bag of morphine to one of the IV tubes. "How can it not be? She's your own flesh and blood. But if you don't mind my saying so, Mrs. Lasker, try to remove yourself just a little. It will make it easier for you, and if it's easier for you it will be better for her."

Every day when she drove the long hours in traffic along the Hollywood Freeway, passing all those streets where the Milligans had lived in stucco bungalows and cramped one-story houses, she said to herself, Thank God Mom and Pop don't have to see her this way. Thank God they're not here for this.

Yet it seemed to Dinah that if she had truly loved her sister none of this would have happened. It seemed to her that if she had loved her sister she would have walked out of that room at the Hollywood-Griffith. I sacrificed her for Jake, she told herself. It is not possible to do that to someone you love. I named Veevi because . . . (Go on, she said to herself behind the wheel, driving away from the hospital and into the western glare, Go on, *say* it) she had never, not even once, been unloved. She had never, ever, been hurt. She had never been passed over. She had never been rejected. And she was never going to be rejected. It was unthinkable. Unimaginable. It was a law of the universe that she would always be adored. For Veevi to be hurt was as impossible as the ocean's running dry. All she had ever had, Dinah admitted to herself, was Jake and the kids. Before that, there had been nothing and nobody. I did whatever was necessary to keep what I had, and look where it's brought us now, she said to herself.

13

She stood beside the bed, and reached out to touch Veevi's hand. The skin was hot with fever. Veevi moved her head back and forth, moaning. Small croaking sounds came from her throat; her breathing was labored.

"She's in agony, Kirsten," said Dinah. "C-C-C-Can't you t-t-turn her? I think she can't stand lying on her back all the time without moving."

"Can't do it, Mrs. Lasker. Mustn't lose fluids."

Dinah longed to touch Veevi, to soothe her, and she rubbed her sister's feet and legs, which were splotched with bruise marks from the endless IV needles. When she touched her sister's body, she remembered Pop's words: "It's food and drink to see you." It was food and drink to touch her sister's legs and feet. When she gave blood, it upset her that only a pint could be taken. She wished she had quarts and quarts to give; why couldn't she give all of her blood to her sister? Her appetite had fled with the phone call in New York, but she forced herself to eat red meat, which she hated, so that she could manufacture new red blood cells—billions of them, all for Veevi.

Dr. Hershel Epstein, the burn doctor at Cedars of Lebanon who was in charge of Veevi's case, showed Dinah a photograph in a textbook about four inches thick. "We will slice off a piece about this size." He made a small square with his hands, and held up an instrument. "I call it my cheese slicer. See? We'll just peel off a thin layer of skin." He spoke with a soft precision. She nodded. She had driven to his office in Beverly Hills on her way downtown to the hospital. "We'll take the first piece from your thigh." He opened the medical gown she was wearing and, holding his pen just above her right thigh, drew on her skin. "And then we'll take another piece the same size from the left thigh—about here." He was tanned, and had one of those chronically peeling noses she associated with tennis players. She could imagine him dressed in white shorts and a striped V-necked tennis sweater, with one of those jaunty khaki hats on his head. "We can take more, when we need to, from your buttocks, your belly, and your back," he added. He picked up her two arms and held them out and scrutinized them. "You've got nice, healthy skin, so we can harvest a good deal of tissue."

"I'm darker than my sister," Dinah said. "She was always so fair."

"Doesn't matter. The important thing is that she won't reject your skin. At least, that's what we're banking on."

"Okay," she said. "That's fine. I'm glad I can d-d-d-do it."

He scrutinized her body again, and she felt, suddenly, a sexual flutter that surprised and embarrassed her.

"Now, Dinah, you have to be aware that it will be, you know, somewhat disfiguring." He let go of her arms and showed her another page in the book. "It'll look like this—kind of bumpy, like oatmeal. I can send you to a guy I know who can smooth it down, but you will have some scarring."

"I don't care. It's not important, compared to the scarring *she'll* have. You can't imagine how b-b-b-beautiful she was."

"Oh yes I can. I remember her movies. Her face isn't that bad, Dinah. There are the two patches on her cheeks. That's where we'll put your skin, to start."

How odd, she thought, with a quiver. Her skin on Veevi's face. She had wondered all her life why she hadn't been given that face, or a face just like it. And now her own skin would be Veevi's—on Veevi's cheeks, saving what was left of that commanding loveliness.

Dr. Epstein clicked and unclicked his ballpoint pen with his exquisitely clean hands and manicured nails.

"When can we start?" she said. "I'm ready now. Today."

He explained that if Veevi could hold on for another three weeks or so, until January, they could begin. Until then, they had to keep fighting infection, build her strength, get her to the point where she could accept the grafts. He would harvest skin from the older daughter, too.

"Claire?"

He nodded.

"Oh, no. Don't take hers. She's so young and pretty. As for me, you can flay me alive for all I care."

He smiled at her with a look of playful wisdom. "Now, you wouldn't be of any use to anybody without your skin. So I'd advise you to keep it."

The situation was kind of unusual, Kirsten explained to Dinah out in the hallway, while Dorshka stood on one side of the bed, crooning a Yiddish lullaby to Veevi, and Anya Engel stood on the other, holding Veevi's bluish fingers. The two women were covered head to toe in green hospital gowns; both of them wore masks. Anya had come to the hospital to give blood and bring flowers, but she hadn't been allowed to carry the flowers into the room and had left them at the nurses' station; the environment in Mrs. Albrecht's room, Kirsten had explained, had to be kept sterile. Dinah found it difficult to leave Veevi for even a minute, but with the two women keeping watch over Veevi like fluffy hens, she was free to step outside.

"We've discovered why the morphine isn't as effective with your sister, Mrs. Lasker," Kirsten said. "You see, her body has become so accustomed to alcohol and barbiturates that the morphine just can't do that much. The relief isn't as deep, and it wears off faster. If we give her more, we're taking too big a risk."

But it was also because the morphine wasn't getting that much mileage that Veevi was beginning to have lucid moments. Dinah went in and stood at the foot of the bed. Veevi lay very still; her eyes were half open. All three women bent over to listen, because she was trying to say something and her voice was faint: ". . . such a funny dream, you know, a parade! And there was . . . a character, Eisenhower! With the bluest eyes, and he loves me! Have you ever!" Dinah rejoiced at that *have you ever!* It meant that Veevi was still there. Dinah, Dorshka, Anya—all three of them laughed, wanting Veevi to know they were listening. A smile hovered around Veevi's mouth. "Gone now," she said to Anya with a hoarse laugh. "Beauty all gone! Oh God, such a burden, dear. Oh, you have no idea! All gone now."

Dinah couldn't see Anya's face, only her eyes, above the mask, and her forehead, which contracted, as if she wanted to protest something. It seemed to Dinah that Veevi was apologizing to Anya for having been beautiful, as if she were accepting punishment.

"Not true, sweetie," Anya said. "You still have your marvelous face."

Veevi opened her eyes wide and looked at Anya. "No," she said. "All gone. Mirror. I wanna mirror."

"There's no need for a mirror, darling. It's not all gone, and you will still be the envy of us all," Dorshka said definitively before she and Anya slipped away, leaving the two sisters alone. Veevi and Dinah began to talk, and Kirsten, who day after day had kept Veevi from dying, heard between them a patter that was indistinguishable from the sound of hummingbirds' wings—low rapid murmurings, flutterings, whirrings, always interspersed with laughter. It was a good sign.

That Mrs. Lasker, Kirsten thought, even with that awful stutter, had bent over her sister every day, talking through the mask, getting Mrs. Albrecht to laugh or smile or talk a little. She overheard Mrs. Lasker telling stories, and often they were about their father and their childhood. " 'This is no time for jollification!' " she heard Mrs. Lasker say, and that seemed to trigger a memory for Mrs. Albrecht and made her laugh. " 'You could be a power in this town!' " Mrs. Lasker said to Mrs. Albrecht another time, after the visit of an important-looking older woman, and again there came laughter.

One day she heard them making plans. That was good. They were talking about the future: that was very good. She saw Mrs. Lasker pull up her skirt and show her sister where the grafts would come from. Mrs. Lasker apologized for not being allowed to give her sister a cigarette; Mrs. Albrecht constantly made that smoking motion, bringing her hand to her mouth as if she were holding a cigarette and taking a puff on it, especially whenever she came out of the anesthesia for the dressing changes. They talked about Mr. Lasker's show in New York and what a big hit it was, and how Mr. Lasker was coming home for Christmas and on Christmas Eve they were going to drive all the children into Beverly Hills to see the the colors spouting from the Indian fountain and the Santa Claus and his reindeer installed above the intersection of Santa Monica and Wilshire.

Mrs. Lasker sounded so happy when Mrs. Albrecht said she was going to start her own literary agency, and that way she could do what she had always loved to do: read books and talk to authors. And she would have an office right in her own house, so no one would ever have to see her, she said.

"N-N-N-Nonsense," said Mrs. Lasker. "You won't have to hide from anybody."

Mrs. Albrecht said, "You're too nice, Dinah. You're lying about my face. I know about my face. Hideous! Give me a mirror. Let me see my face."

"No, it's not hideous," Mrs. Lasker said. "But it's too soon for you to see it."

"But who's going to want me now?" Mrs. Albrecht said.

"Plenty of people," Mrs. Lasker answered. "Everybody loves you." And then she reeled off the names of all the people who had given blood and who had come to visit Mrs. Albrecht in the hospital when she was too doped up to know it. "Saul Landau comes all the time," she said. "And I don't think you were conscious yet, but Cliff Boatwright came, too, Vee. He flew out here just to see you, and he stood here and talked to you and told you he would love you forever. Said it right here in front of me. Cried, too, and came every day for three days. Both the Steiners have given blood. Everyone we know has given blood. Gussie's given blood, and gotten her friends from church to give blood. Hell, the blood of half of Hollywood is flowing in your veins."

"Even Republicans?" asked Veevi.

"Even R-R-R-Republicans," said Dinah, with a laugh.

"Where's Uncle J.?" Mrs. Albrecht asked.

"He's coming soon," Mrs. Lasker said. "He sent his love. He's going to give blood, too."

Then Kirsten heard Mrs. Albrecht say, "I'm so sorry, Dinah."

"About what, dear?"

"Ohhhhh . . ." What came out was something between a sigh and a moan. "Everything."

"There's nothing to be sorry for, sweetie."

Kirsten was busy checking fluid levels, but she was also listening.

"Ina?" Mrs. Albrecht's voice was small and weak, like a child's.

"I'm here, Vee. What is it, dear?"

"You ended up me, and I ended up you."

"We haven't 'ended up,' lovey. There's lots ahead, for both of us."

Mrs. Albrecht seemed to do better when Mrs. Lasker was there, Kirsten observed. Talking about the skin grafts and the future and what she was going to do seemed to wake her up. She had more fight in her then. Her vitals improved. Mrs. Lasker held a cup up to her with a straw in it and got her to drink juice, and that was good, getting those fluids into her.

But there was always late afternoon, when Mrs. Lasker drove home to her family, and sometimes she didn't come back. It was a long, tiring drive home to West Los Angeles, and Mrs. Lasker needed to see her kids. It was usually around seven, when Mrs. Lasker wasn't there, that Kirsten found a heavyset figure bending over Mrs. Albrecht. Mr. Cole was his name. He always came then, she supposed, because that was when Mrs. Lasker wouldn't be there. He had said that he was Mrs. Albrecht's fiancé and had told her to report any change in her condition to him, and had scolded her for not informing him of decisions about her care. "I'm not authorized to do that, sir," she had replied. He always had a five o'clock shadow, and he smelled like liquor. "Our understanding is that Mrs. Lasker is Mrs. Albrecht's next of kin." He had scowled darkly and threatened to go to her superior, and she had invited him to do so. Of course, he hadn't done it.

But something else had happened that Kirsten had reported to Mrs. Lasker right away. One evening she came in with fresh supplies of antibiotics and found him leaning over Mrs. Albrecht, holding up a pocket mirror so she could see her face. Another time Kirsten heard him saying, "Where's the money, Veevi? Where's the money?" He had grabbed her wrist very near the place where there was an IV line going in, and Kirsten had spoken to him sharply. Mrs. Albrecht had smiled at him, almost a baby smile, as if she didn't understand what he was asking her. Kirsten decided she would tell Mrs. Lasker about it, and she did. "She can never be alone with him, Kirsten," Dinah said. "What are we going to do? Should I hire a private nurse so that someone will be there whenever I'm not?" Kirsten had promised her that she would always be there when Mr. Cole came, and that she would tell Dinah if she heard him saying anything to Veevi about money again.

Day after day, Dinah tried to pull Veevi up out of the ash pit. Nothing else was real to her, and nothing else mattered. Somehow, she drove home in the evenings and put her children to bed. Somehow, she did her chores every morning—went to the grocery store, wrote checks, talked with the business manager, reported Veevi's condition to friends, comforted Dorshka and Claire. She did everything that needed to be done. She bought a Christmas tree at Wilshire and Beverly Glen, and trimmed it with the kids.

And she wrote a cordial and heartfelt response to Michael Albrecht's equally cordial and heartfelt letter of a week before, announcing his shock and grief at what had happened to Veevi. He also congratulated Jake on the success of his Broadway show, news of which had traveled across the Atlantic via the Paris edition of the *New York Herald-Tribune,* and asked if Jake and Dinah would pay half of Veevi's medical bills. He would be hearing from Veevi's lawyer, Burt Unwin, Dinah pointed out in her reply. Surely, she said, he must remember the name, since it was the very same fellow who had accompanied Veevi to Seymour Mandlin's office at Palomar last summer. Thanks to Veevi, he could now make the picture with Willie Weil, Dinah reminded Mike, and, under the circumstances, she and Jake frankly considered Veevi's medical bills to be entirely his responsibility.

She bought Christmas presents for Jake and the kids, and for Gussie and Grandma Rose, Dorshka and Claire and Coco and Claire's boyfriend, Vernon. Jake came home from New York, and that night, before they went to bed, he gave her a small box, inside of which she found a ring from Buccellati. It was made of brushed gold, with a raised mound of ivory at the center of which lay a large emerald. She loved it, put it on at once, and felt that it gave her strength when she went to the hospital.

Christmas came and went, and Jake flew back to New York. Every day, Veevi was a little more lucid. The dressing changes remained agony for her, but when she came out of the anesthesia she talked about the future. The idea of starting her own literary agency became stronger. She wanted to edit books as well. She wanted to work with writers. That would make her happy. She was going to start a new life. "In *your* skin," she said to Dinah.

14

*S*aul Landau showed up one afternoon at the hospital. Veevi had been relatively clear that day, expressing pleasure in the red and yellow roses Dinah had brought with her from the garden, and shock at the things Dinah reported to her about the situation in Hungary. Whenever Saul encountered Dinah at the hospital, he said as little as possible. And just as he always perched himself on the arm of the sofa at her house, and never fully sat down, he stood on the opposite side of Veevi's bed. His eyes above his hospital mask avoided Dinah's above her mask. He was as determined as always, she knew, to preserve the moral distinction between them: he had refused to testify; she had not.

But, she had to admit to herself as she watched him stroking Veevi's hand, he was certainly devoted to her sister; she had to give him credit for that.

"You know, Saul, with this disaster in Hungary you might as well look my sister in the eye," Veevi said to him, her voice thick with sedation but still barbed. "Guess you've got nothing on her now, you old idiot."

"How do you know about Hungary?" he asked her.

"Spies," she said.

Dinah looked over at him and saw his eyes darting nervously between her and Veevi. "Genevieve," he said, "I stand by every position I've ever taken."

"God, Saul. It's not 1935 anymore! Don't you ever think?!" She laughed, and it was her familiar, choking laugh, full of gay contempt. But she hissed with pain. And then her eyes caught Dinah's and drew her into the lovely, irresistible cruelty of two conspiring against one. "Why do you always have to be such a bore?" Veevi groaned at him.

"At least I never betrayed my friends," Saul said with dignity.

"You're such a goody-goody," Veevi countered. "We're bad guys, aren't we, Sister Ina?"

"Yes," said Dinah. "We're bad guys. We're f-f-f-finks and stoolies and songbirds, Saul. I don't think you want to spend too much time around us."

"I wouldn't ever put your sister on the same level as you," he said.

Inspired by her children, Dinah said, "I d-d-d-dislike you intensely." Then she laughed and shook her head.

"Look," he said, "I didn't drive all the way down here to talk politics or to be ridiculed. Would you let me have some time alone with her?"

Dinah saw that he couldn't quite look her in the eye.

"Sure." She began to get up.

"No, Dinah, you stay. Go away, Saul," said Veevi. "I'm tired of you. Go away and don't come back. I hurt. I want a shot. Dinah, ring Kirsten, please. And stay with me. Tell me stories." She closed her eyes, shutting out Landau and his injured adoration.

Dinah pressed the buzzer.

"I've got nothing to apologize to anyone for. Let me know if you need me," he said to Veevi, as Kirsten came in carrying a tray with a long syringe and a needle.

"Oh, bless you," Veevi said.

Landau lingered, waiting for Veevi to say something more to him. When she didn't, he finally left.

Kirsten gave Veevi the shot in her foot, where there were areas of unburned skin, and Dinah, holding Veevi's fingers, waited for her to relax.

"Was it Uncle J. who made you leave?"

"The Party? Mmm," said Dinah. "You know that, dearie."

"The real reason Stefan and I left Hollywood," whispered Veevi, who was getting drowsy, "was that the French wanted him. PCF. French Party." Her speech was becoming slurred now. " 'Future,' " she mumbled. "Wha' funny word. Fu-shhhure. WherezuncleJ? WhycannahavncleJ?"

"Shh," said Dinah. "Go to sleep. He sends his love. Shh."

"Mirror. Wanna mirror. Face all gone. All over now."

"Hush," Dinah said softly. "You are beautiful. Now and always."

Her sister drifted away from pain, and the hospital room went still.

Dinah, forgetting husband and children and house and roses, sat beside the bed of the sleeping, suffering woman and gazed out the window. Through her mask, she breathed calmly and fully. She no longer felt the need to protect herself against the smell of her sister's burned flesh. Streaks of orange flamed in the darkening blue over the Pacific. She held her sister's limp hand, and felt, without naming or questioning it, love.

15

eter Lasker reached over and plugged down the button of his alarm clock. It was five-forty-five on a dark February morning. He woke early on Fridays. That was because he was always picked up at six-thirty, a whole hour earlier than usual, by Joelly Rosen and his father, Dr. Rosen, for orchestra practice. It was fun. Dr. Rosen took them to a drive-in for breakfast and then dropped them off at school at seven-thirty. Joelly and Peter would each bring their issues of *Mad,* and go over the parts they loved, making jokes about Alfred E. Neuman and Smilin' Melvin and all the other characters.

He put on jeans and a plaid flannel shirt, socks and black high-top sneakers. He opened a window and looked out at the pool. February mornings were dark and cold, but the air was fresh, without the smog that gave him a catch in his chest and made him cough when he practiced the clarinet. He waited and watched the sky, and loved it that as he stood there he could see the deep blue becoming lighter by the moment. He closed the window, carefully picked up his clarinet case and a manila envelope filled with music, and headed for the stairs. On the landing next to his parents' room, he paused and listened. It was nice when his father was away in New York and there were no disgusting snoring sounds coming through the walls. It would be nice if his father stayed in New York indefinitely.

Halfway down the stairs, he stopped and his nostrils flared with the good smell of fresh coffee. Then he remembered something. Something was supposed to happen today. But what was it? Oh, he knew now: Mom was going to have something done to her. She was going to go to the hospital and give skin for Veevi. He shuddered. It had been horrible, these past weeks, hearing about Veevi's burns.

The coffee smell had to mean that someone was up, though, and he hurried down the stairs toward the breakfast room. At the doorway he stopped cold, for there, in the shadows, with the blue light fading to a grayish pink outside, he saw his mother leaning over the marble lazy Susan. She was holding her hand to her forehead, and she was perfectly still, like a statue. A cigarette in the ashtray sent up a ribbon of smoke. The telephone, black and heavy, stood on the table beside her left hand.

She hadn't heard him, and she didn't look up.

"Mom?"

He went over to her and leaned against the edge of the table. "Mom?"

Her head turned slightly, and she looked at him. "Veevi d-d-d-died a little while ago."

"Died?" He was aware that he had never used the word *died* before in reference to anyone he had ever known, and it felt strange to say it. Then he thought, Mom'll be home today when school's over.

He reached out and, awkwardly, softly, put his hand on his mother's shoulder, and at his touch she gave a deep sigh. He braced himself, expecting her to cry, but she didn't. "Dr. Epstein called a little while ago," she said. "And I called Daddy in New York. He's coming home later today."

"I thought she was going to be okay. I thought you were going to do that skin thing today so you could give it to her."

"I was, honey. But now I can't. You know what's strange?"

"What?" He moved backward and sat down at the place where his father usually sat. "She didn't die of the burns. It was a blood clot—an embolism. From lying so still for so long. It formed, maybe in her legs, and traveled through her blood and finally it hit her heart or her lungs. Anyway, she was gone like *that*." She snapped her fingers.

He felt immensely privileged and awed; except for his father, he was the first one to know. "She was asleep," Dinah continued. "Never knew what hit her."

"Is that good?"

"Yes. I think so."

"I'll stay here with you, Mom," he said, and he reached for the phone. "I'll tell Joelly not to come."

"No," she said. "Go to practice and school." Then she thought for a moment. "But go upstairs and knock on Gussie's door and tell her, honey. Tell her I need her to come down a little early."

Many years later, he remembered how grateful he was that morning that she had given him something to do.

16

*S*he came over at about eleven-thirty, her red hair pulled back in a ponytail. As usual, he was struck by the look of softness and sweetness about her. Another thing he couldn't get over was her accent.

"You really are a cockney?" he often asked her.

She laughed. "I'm as cockney as you can be and still be Jewish." Although she was only twenty-two, she had been working since she was fifteen, starting out in the chorus line of imported American musicals in London and living at home in Poplar. Then, after her father found jobs at the tables in Vegas for both himself and her brother, she'd gone out there with her mother to join them, and gotten hired right away in the line at the Flamingo. Duff, yeah, well he was like a second father to her. He'd even given her the money to come to New York when Jimmy O'Rourke said she should audition for the show.

Jake liked to listen to her tell stories about her family. He had no doubt whatsoever that her father and brother were well-connected criminals; he had a hunch that there was a picture in it somewhere, if he could just get her to talk about them. He couldn't get enough of the Jewish-cockney angle. She told him that the family name in Poland had been Sidlowski. It fascinated him, too, that a cockney should be named Rivka Sidlowski, although she had changed it to Grace Siddons.

Why "Grace"? he asked her.

"Mum and I, we put hours into it. We went through Ginger, for Ginger Rogers, but with my ginger hair, it didn't sound right, and besides, she's a has-been now. Then I thought of Rhonda, after Rhonda Fleming. There was the hair connection, but on the other hand, you know, it's kind of an unusual name, so everybody would know I'd pinched it. We tried out Vivien, for Vivien Leigh, but you know, everybody wants to be like her; Joan and Bette—well, they're finished, aren't they? I thought of Cyd, after Cyd Charisse, 'cause I'm a dancer, too. But then my name would have been Cyd Siddons."

"Sounds like a dentist I know at my country club."

"Then Mum said, 'I've got it, Shayna'—she always called me Shayna, for *shayna punim*—'you're Grace. For Grace Kelly. That's it.' And I said, Righto. I'm Grace. Even though I look like Kim Novak. She's Polish too, by the way. Did you know that? But Grace it was. Before we left for Vegas, my dad got our name changed. Legally. Sidlowski to Siddons. I said, 'Right you are, no more bloody Rivka Sidlowski for me. I'm Grace. Grace Siddons. But you're the only one who knows I'm Jewish, guy. Keep it to yourself, okay?"

"Who'm I gonna tell?"

She snuggled up to him. "Oh," she said with a light laugh, "you never know. There are anti-Semites everywhere."

"You can say that again," he said, drawing her closer to himself. With her high cheekbones and broad face, she *did* look like Kim Novak. Suddenly, thay had a lot to talk about. His family, her family. Jokes. Food. Itzik's Deli in Santa Monica. He had always avoided Jewish girls, hearing, in the back of his mind, his parents yammering at him, "It's just as easy to marry a rich girl as a poor girl." And maybe Sandy Litvak had been right. Maybe he'd always been afraid of waking up one day and finding himself in the sack with his mother. But this doll, he found himself explaining in an imaginary conversation with his former analyst, didn't look anything like his mother!

The day after she auditioned, it had been so simple, really, so natural to give her a call and invite her over to his apartment. He had said to her on the phone, with an almost British gentility to his voice, "Would you mind terribly if I met you at the door in my slippers and robe?" and she'd said, "Oh, Mr. Lasker, of course not. Just be as comfortable as you like." From the beginning, everything had been very comfortable between them, just as it used to be with Bonnie. She was, in fact, about as close to Bonnie, he believed, as he would ever find again, and he felt very lucky. She was useful to him, telling him all the backstage gossip, including the things people said about the director and the stars of the show, so he was always up on the latest scandals and sleeping arrangements.

She was, he had to admit it, a wonderful companion. Naturally, he had become aware of how much he needed to have someone that terrible day after the show opened, when he'd been left all alone. God, what a day that had been, he explained early on to Grace. He would remember it for the rest of his life: going to bed with a high fever, afraid he was developing pneumonia, absolutely certain, because of the review in the *Times,* that the show was a disaster. Then the next morning the phone ringing with the horrible news of his sister-in-law's accident (which he described to Grace in detail), and Dinah having to leave, and the indescribable irony of putting his wife in the car to Idyllwild, then going back to the hotel room and reading one great review after another.

Jake established ground rules with Grace: he loved his wife and would never leave her. There was to be no talking to anyone about him—no one in the show, no one she knew. Nor was he going to ask the director to fix her up with a speaking role. The show had certain casting requirements, and a role for someone with a cockney accent wasn't one of them. But later, when the show closed—and he didn't know when that would be, since the projections were for an indefinite run—or if she decided to leave the show and look for something else, he would do what he could for her. And that was a promise—a cross-my-heart-hope-to-die-stick-a-needle-in-my-eye promise (backed up, not long afterward, by a real contract he had Harvey Lefkowitz, his lawyer in L.A., draw up for her—in absolute secrecy, by the way, but putting her on his payroll, as he had done for Veevi).

Jake told himself that while he would have preferred to have Dinah with him, even without Veevi's horrible situation, he was sure that she would have been unwilling to leave the children for more than two or three weeks at a time, and it was impractical to uproot them in the middle of the school year and move everyone to New York. But most of all, the Veevi situation left her no time or energy for anything else, and he, of course, understood that. So by taking care of his needs in New York, he reasoned, he was in effect protecting Dinah, leaving her free to devote every available ounce of energy to her sister.

When he went home in December for five days, he made no attempts to make love to Dinah, and it seemed to him that she neither noticed nor cared, exhausted as she was by her daily vigils at the hospital. From his perspective, he was behaving with exemplary thoughtfulness, even nobility. After all, here he was having the most exciting, most successful time of his professional life, and he would have loved to have Dinah in on it at all times, but he understood that right now she couldn't think of anything except Veevi.

He was relieved to have Grace Siddons around. She took such an interest in everything that concerned him, and was fun to talk to, and a remarkably mature listener, and damn good in the sack. Everything about her body was trim and fit, for she had a trained dancer's lean muscles, and the combination of hard muscle, soft curves, and buttery bosoms delighted him. Though he flew home to Los Angeles every couple of weeks for three or four days, when he was back in town he managed to see her two or three times a week, and when he was in Los Angeles he called her often from his office at home. There really was no danger, because Dinah was always at the hospital, so she was unlikely to pick up the phone in mid-conversation.

When he told her about visiting his wife's sister in the hospital, she sucked in her breath and screwed up her eyes. "Oooh, painful, idn'it, being all burnt up like that." Then she said, "Must've been bloody difficult for you to go and see her." And he said, "More difficult than you can imagine," although he stopped short of telling her why. But she did have the nicest way of taking an interest in him, and he could listen endlessly to her stories. Her father was born in a village in Poland and had gone to London when he was only sixteen. He had learned English and been a street gambler until Georgie Higginbotham, the criminal from Liverpool, who co-owned a club in London called the Snow Leopard, discovered his talents. Her mother was Jewish too, but her family had come to England from Latvia at about the turn of the century. Her grandfather on her mum's side had been a tailor who made bespoke clothes for people in the West End. She used the word *fantastic* a lot. She would say, "Aren't you fantastic, a man your age having it off with a young girl like me three times a night!" And that would make him laugh.

That first night, when he greeted her at the door in his pajamas and bathrobe, she had delighted him with her soft girlish face and her matter-of-fact brazenness. As if sensing that he was tired, too tired for romantic ceremony, she had leaned across the sofa, untied his bathrobe and pajamas, and buried her head in his crotch. Sometimes, he told himself, as he gave in to the pleasure, you just had to follow your hunches about people.

On this February morning, however, they were both still asleep, after a very busy and gratifying night together. It was she, stark naked, who shook his shoulder and called out to him: "Jake, the phone! The phone! Wake up!" He sat up, pushed his black sleeping mask up on his forehead, and glanced rapidly at the clock as he reached for the receiver. It was a little past eight. Grace lay on her side and watched his face. "This is he," she heard him say in a sleepy voice. He was wearing his pajama top only, but it was unbuttoned. Immediately alert, he scratched his chest.

"Honey?" Ah, then it was his wife calling. She had heard him talk on the phone to her before. He always called her Honey or Darling or Sweetheart and almost never by her Christian name. But it was so early out there! Why was she calling?

He frowned and his head dropped, and so did his voice. "When?" His voice was so low that Grace could barely hear him, and she moved closer and put her head on the sheet covering his thigh. She wanted him to stroke her hair, and she picked up his hand and put it on her hair, but it lay there, inert. "I'm so sorry, darling," he said.

Grace didn't have to be told. The burnt-up sister must have croaked. It had to be for the best, really, when you thought about it. Who'd want to go through life being all scarred and all? Specially if you'd once been a beauty, like Jake had said about her.

Only when he put the phone down did he begin to stroke her hair. "Your wife's sister?"

He nodded.

"Is she dead?"

"This morning."

"Your face dropped right down. Like this." She imitated him.

He smiled. "You're some little actress, aren't you? Listen, honey, I'm afraid I have to fly out to the Coast today."

"Yeah, well of course you do."

He sighed. "It's a tragedy, her story. A real one. It would make a hell of a novel. I'll tell you all about it when I get back."

He made an airline reservation and ordered a car for later that morning. It was too early to call his secretary, however, and he didn't need to pack, since he kept a complete supply of clothes in both New York and L.A. There was nothing he had to do except be ready to leave in an hour and a half, and this left plenty of time to explore the possibilities, which struck him as delightful, of a shower with Grace.

※

Five days later, Dinah, Jake, Dorshka, Claire, Clifford Boatwright, Vernon Ashby, Byron Cole, Saul Landau, Felicity Crandell—who had flown in from Paris—Nelly and Manny Steiner and Irv and Anya Engel stood gathered around a rectangular plot of rosebushes in a cemetery in Westwood Village, California. Dressed in a dark gray suit, the cemetery official pulled open the drawstring on a blue velvet bag and matter-of-factly drew out a small polished wooden box with a shiny brass clasp. He opened the box and took out a plastic bag, tightly closed by another drawstring, which he unloosened. Holding out the bag, he invited each of the mourners to approach and receive a handful of ashes and scatter them inside the shallow hole that had been dug in the black earth, speckled with flecks of white, around a sturdy, thickly blooming rosebush that Dinah and Claire had chosen together.

Dinah held out both of her hands to receive her portion. A wave of nausea rose up and receded, as she felt what seemed to be dry gravel and grit against the skin of her palms. Like the born gardener that she was, however, she opened her fingers slowly, letting the stuff fall gently and then she crouched and reached in to knead it into the soil, while a cloud of minuscule particles rose like powder into the air.

When she finished, she saw how Claire's eyes had opened in horror at the realization that the ashes weren't really ashes but coarse pieces of bone—human bone—imperfectly pulverized as yellowish-gray grains and chips and pea-size pebbles, with traces of black where they had been seared by the crematorium flame. So it was neither dust-to-dust, Dinah reflected, nor ashes-to-ashes. It was wet, gooey sperm-and-egg turned flesh-and-blood-and-bone that burned in fire until it cooled as scorched gravel that you could pave a driveway with, scooped up into a plastic bag. You didn't go back to your beginnings, and nothing could be reversed.

About two hours later, a smaller collection of people sat together in the den of the Laskers' house. Boatwright hadn't stayed but had taken a waiting taxi to the airport after a cordial and warm farewell; the Steiners had come over for coffee but had retreated, and so had the Engels, who had hugged Dinah at the door. So it was basically just the nearest and dearest, as it were, who were there. Vernon Ashby, with his lean Appalachian features, had his arm around Claire, who wept; Dorshka, at the opposite end of the sofa, was eyeing Claire watchfully, tears slowly running from her eyes. Jake occupied one of the deep-red armchairs, and Dinah sat in front of him on its ottoman—near him but not touching. It was just as well, because he couldn't take his eyes off Felicity Crandell, dressed in a chic black suit and sitting very straight-backed in a Windsor chair, well-bred as usual, companionable, and unembarrassed by the silence. God, he was fond of her. She could go anywhere, and she would know what to do and say on any occasion. Not for one moment had she said or implied anything about their time together in London. She was, in fact, serious and sober. She had been sent to Los Angeles by Mike to pack up Coco and Dorshka and bring them back to Paris to begin a new life with him and Odile, and she behaved with perfect tact. As always, though, she was her irrepressible self, and Jake saw her catch Dinah's eye, indicating that she, too, was aware of the man who sat on the love seat, sobbing—a particularly histrionic kind of sobbing, with his jaw hanging open and his grotesque pink tongue visible.

At the cemetery, when it was his turn to toss his handful of burnt bone into the ground, he had wailed, "Oh God, Veevi, how I loved you!" And now he gasped, "She was everything to me. To you she was only a sister"—he nodded in Dinah's direction—"and to you a mother"—this nod was for Claire—"and to you a—" He glanced at Jake and then turned away with a wrenching sob. It was then that Jake felt a kind of electric twitch in his legs. How much did Byron know? Had Veevi told him?

"I assure you," said Saul, "that she meant a great deal to everyone in this room, and that—"

But Dinah's hatred of Byron exploded before Landau could finish. "How d-d-d-dare you put yourself at the head of the line. How d-d-d-dare you!" she broke in. "You slept with her for what? Three months? And you sit here telling her daughter and her friends that she means more to you than she does to them? What kind of a h-h-h-horse's ass are you?"

He cast an injured look at her. "I didn't mean . . . Oh God, I'm sorry," he said, pulling a soggy handkerchief out of his pocket.

"Honey, not now," Jake said.

"Yes, N-N-NOW, " retorted Dinah. She stood up in her dark blue dress and went over to him. "Listen to me. I'm not going to say this again," she began. "I want you to take your freeloading and unsavory self back to Veevi's and get your things and leave. I will drive Dorshka and Coco and Felicity home by eight. If you haven't cleared out by then, I will call Vernon, who is sitting across from you, and knows I mean b-b-business, and tell him to get some of his pals from the LAPD to personally esc-c-c-cort you from that house. And no monkey business, mister; don't take anything that doesn't belong to you. You preyed on my sister and pandered to her misery, and dragged her down, and I never want to s-s-s-s-set eyes on you again."

Byron's heavy, dark eyes dropped, and he shrugged, "Okay." She saw Jake scowling at her but ignored him and stood tall, with her arms folded. Byron looked at Claire, who had buried her face in Vernon's shoulder, and then at Dorshka, who gave him one of her worldly smiles, with the corner of her mouth turned downward, but then she, too, looked away.

And then, as if asking "How about you, Jake?" Byron turned to him, and again Jake thought he saw an intelligent, mocking look come into the bulging blue eyes. "Do what the lady says," Jake said softly.

Byron made no effort to get up, and again fixed Jake with a look that he could have sworn was a smirk. Jake jerked his head toward the door. Byron smiled at him again, an obscene, leering smile, and Jake knew for sure that he had something on him.

At the door that evening, Dinah told Saul that he had loved Veevi more faithfully than any man in her sister's life, and had helped keep her alive, and that she was very grateful to him; he was always welcome in her house. Then she held out her arms to give him a hug. But without a word he cut her, turning himself, his tweed jacket, his pipe, his brown loafers, and his inviolable principles briskly away. Like the process server five years earlier, he disappeared down the brick path along the rose garden and toward his parked car in the driveway.

On his first night back in New York, as they talked in bed at his flat, Jake told Grace about the funeral and lavishly praised his wife. "She's one hell of a dame," he said, and explained how she had ordered Veevi's boyfriend out of the house. "I was a little worried about it," he confessed.

Why? Grace wanted to know. What was there to worry about?

"Look," he said, "I've got to be able to trust you with this."

"Oh, come on, love, you keep my secrets and I'll keep yours. Mum's the word."

Well, he said, there had been a kind of an—an interlude, he would have to say. Of course, he had learned so much from it—it was invaluable, price-less, really, from a creative standpoint. He knew now that he could write a story about his wife's sister—a novel, a screenplay, he wasn't sure which.

"An interlude? What do you mean?" said Grace, her big eyes open wide.

It was snowing outside. As thick flakes piled up against the windows, throwing pale light into the dark bedroom where Jake lay with his young mistress snuggled up beside him, he began to tell her the story of his affair with Veevi, but also the story of Veevi's life, in which, he modestly explained, he had actually played a very small role. And as he spoke he realized that what was coming out was really a first draft, and that telling this story one day would be the greatest challenge of his career—telling it right, finding the right form. So he listened to himself and answered Grace's questions, and instructed her to remember his answers, and wondered how, and when, he would get around to actually doing it. He knew only that one day he would, when he was good and ready. In the meantime, he was awfully glad that Grace was there, to get him started. She was such a good listener.

PART

Four

hico Burke, the assistant director, held up his megaphone and boomed, "Places, people!" throughout the hangarlike soundstage. The dancers filed quickly and obediently into the Maxwell Street set, an exact replica of the stage version in New York. Jake took a deep breath, willing in himself the patience he did not and could not feel, reminding himself that he must fight against the urge to rush through the final shots of the picture. Take your time, he told himself. God forbid you should have to go back and do something over because you were sloppy. But he felt like a kid on the last day of school before summer vacation. Ahead lay freedom from what had been a very tough directing job, and four years of the same project, if you counted both the stage and the movie versions. It was the last day of ensemble work, the last day he would need the dancers. After that, two days for covering shots—reactions, close-ups— and that was it. Time was very tight, but he thought he could get a rough cut of the picture ready in six weeks; that is, if he spent sixteen hours a day at the studio, which would make him ready by the end of July to hand over the picture for scoring. It was killing but doable.

He searched the faces as the dancers converged in front of the camera in their 1919 costumes. "Chico, where the hell is Grace?"

"That guy Cole's off taking her picture. Jeez, boss, I swore I'd keep my mouth shut, but I wish you'da used my cousin Diego for the stills. This guy you got wanders around all the time, you can never find him when you need him, he gets in the way of the grips, and he's always moving in on the girls."

"Guess he'd better not ask *you* for a reference. Get everything set up while I find her myself."

"Okay, boss," said Chico, letting his eyes linger understandingly on

Jake's annoyed face. He was a stocky, mustached, superbly competent man from New Mexico who had been the assistant director on every picture Jake had made at Marathon. Jake loved him and was going to miss him very much. Yet, like everyone on the set, Chico knew too much, which was one reason Jake wanted the picture over and done with.

"Goddamnit," said Jake under his breath as he went off to look for Grace and Byron. As far as the latter was concerned, Jake considered his mitzvah quotient more than met. For a long time after Veevi's death, nobody had heard from him. But once it was announced in the trades that Jake was directing the film version of *My Grandfather's Saloon,* Byron had come to him at Marathon to ask for a job. Jake didn't like him any more than Dinah did, but he felt a vague obligation, coupled with an equally vague intuition of menace. With Byron, dignity would never be an issue; he had none and pretended to none, though he had presumptions of importance. Jake would never forget his "Stefan, Michael, and Me," his promotion of himself to the position of primus inter pares among Veevi's musketeers—a delusion that Jake himself, he cringed to remember, had once entertained.

He glanced at his watch as he searched everywhere. He was losing time. Then he saw them on the dancers' rehearsal floor: Grace with one long leg in high-heeled dancing shoes raised on the piano bench, the voluminous long hot-pink net petticoats of her costume fluffed out and her fishnet stockings revealing her calves and thighs. A long red false ponytail, also part of her costume, hung down her back. She was smiling, eyes huge with makeup and false lashes, into the lens of Byron's Nikon. A spasm of pain constricted Jake's chest, and he felt his pocket for the vial of nitroglycerin tablets he always carried with him and wondered whether the girl was going to kill him.

"Gracie, didn't you hear the call? Chico's waiting for you. I need a run-through, and we've been looking for you all over."

"Sorry, guv," she said. "I just wanted some stills, you know, for when the picture's over. Got to fink of me future, you know." She was flaunting her accent, the exaggerated one she used to caricature herself. Usually it made him laugh. But not now. She knows, he said to himself. She knows it's coming.

"When the picture's over, you can do anything you want. But you've just blown ten minutes of time, at roughly a thousand bucks a minute."

"I said 'Sorry,'" she snapped, hanging back familiarly nonetheless, as heavy-lidded Byron smiled at him the way he always did—with an enigmatic seediness. Jake had been about to bawl him out, too, to remind him that he was the stills photographer for this picture and that he was not to have private clients on the set. But he thought better of it. Getting Grace set up for the future was precisely what had to be done.

"Send her a set of the ones you just shot," said Jake. "And charge them to me."

"Sure, guv," Byron said. "Anyway, we're finished," he said, smiling intimately at Grace and pointedly moved away, as if to leave Jake and Grace alone.

Jake, not wanting to be observed lingering with her, moved decisively toward the set. Grace kept pace with him, brushing up against his arm and irritating him even more. They had been involved for more than three and a half years now, and she was provokingly careless, always finding ways of sidling up against him in front of others.

He paused for a moment, as if taken by a sudden thought, and she paused, too. "By the way," he said, lowering his voice, "be home at seven." She nodded. "Are you and the missus still having that cast party Saturday night?" she asked.

"If you don't stop me from finishing the picture today."

"I was just wondering if I could bring a date," she said.

"Got someone in mind?" His half smile was ironic and edgy.

"As a matter of fact, I do."

Chico was at his side. "Okay, boss, we're ready. Grace, On the double."

Watching her as she scampered over to the line, Chico scratched the back of his neck. So she had nice knockers. So what? Personally, he couldn't understand why a classy guy like Jake would go and get himself mixed up with a pain-in-the-ass broad like that.

※

"Honey?" Jake said later into the cutting-room phone.

"How does it look?"

"Not bad. But this dance sequence is an absolute ballbreaker. Cutting in tempo is no picnic. I'm gonna be late again with Bill"—his cutter—"just to make sure I don't have to reshoot anything. I'm sorry, darling. You'd better eat with the kids again. I don't think I'll be home till ten—maybe later."

"It can't be helped, honey. Did you have that m-m-m-meeting with Irv?"

"Yeah. Lunchtime."

"And?"

"He said he hated to see me joining 'the bandwagon of runaway production,' but that I'd fulfilled my deal with them and if he couldn't persuade me to stay I could leave with his blessing. Marathon is still available to me for distribution deals."

"Golly, I remember him so well when he was home from college for the summer and smitten with Veevi. He used to tell her about the books he was reading. Like he wanted her approval. Sometimes we went to dinner at his parents' house. It was a Renaissance palace above S-S-S-Sunset, with an indoor marble pool. His father was jealous of Hearst and wanted the place to look like San—"

"Gotta go, sweetie." He knew that if he didn't cut her off, she would go on like this forever.

Jake was worried about Dinah. Veevi had been dead for more than three years already, but Dinah went every day to the rosebush where they'd scattered her ashes. He had the feeling that she nipped a little. He had had to leave her alone a great deal while he was in New York, and when he came home for visits it seemed to him that whenever she came back from the cemetery he could smell booze on her breath. She eagerly looked forward to a drink before dinner. She never drank after dinner, but until Veevi's death she had been strictly a one-drink-before-dinner girl. What bothered him most was the way she talked all the time now about the past. Anything would set her off—a remark about the weather, a phone call, hearing the mention of somebody from the old days. Again and again, she turned whatever they were talking about into something connected with her sister and their parents, life before they came to California, life after they came to California, days at Marathon and Malibu. Sometimes he felt that Dinah no longer lived in the present and that he and the kids were phantoms, and that she felt alive only when she was talking about the old days. Since coming home from New York and starting the picture, he'd been exhausted at night from shooting and simply fallen asleep when she started in, so she had turned the kids into a captive audience. Lorna had asked him why Mom told the same stories over and over. "Does she?" he'd asked. "Yeah, only about a million times." And Lorna said that if she or Peter said anything about it their mother started crying.

He left the studio promptly at six and drove to Sunset and then up Crescent Heights over to Franklin, parking his '57 Chevy Bel-Air convertible in front of an olive-green stucco apartment building, a stack of bald cantilevered rectangles overlooking a cluster of palm trees. The neighborhood both aroused and depressed him. You either lived here when you first came to L.A. or you ended up here if you failed. Loveless desire hung in the pale blue of the summer dusk, and memories of blinding pleasure, of heat and sweat. He had allowed it to go on far too long; it was time to end it. And it was dangerous here, with traffic coming down off the Ventura Freeway and the Cahuenga Pass. Had anyone he knew ever seen him getting out of the car?

He went up a flight of concrete steps to the second floor, then, clearly knowing the way, followed the path of a naked wraparound concrete porch, stopping in front of a rust-colored door with a peephole and a buzzer on the doorframe. Over the railing lay a mean little swimming pool, in which he had actually swum a number of times. He hadn't found it satisfying, though—unheated, too shady, the drain clogged with leaves, the surface stippled with drowned insects, the bottom streaked with dirt. Once he retrieved what looked like the corpse of someone's old red turned-inside-out bathing trunks and wondered who had worn them and why they had been taken off.

In recent months he had become afraid of having a heart attack in the pool, as well as in Grace's bed, where, so often now, he would lie with his chest tightening with guilt and the urge just to get up and leave. Three times he had had to take nitroglycerin. It just proved that the whole business of setting her up out here in L.A. had been a mistake, and a bad one. She wasn't like Bonnie, whom he often thought of with nostalgia. That had been an arrangement, convenient and easy; but Grace had become an addiction, a requirement, an obligation, and thus a yoke around his neck. Yet he couldn't end it, though he had resolved to time and time again. When he needed her, he needed her. It was like a physical pain that couldn't be relieved until he had plunged into the hot springs of her body. He paid for this in the hard cash that he gave her to cover everything from rent to clothes to food to television repairs to contraceptive jelly to car insurance.

He pushed the buzzer. Then he heard the dull ching of the brass chain being slid through its notch and saw, behind the opening door, the soft pale round face, studio makeup and false eyelashes removed, her own thick red hair falling to her narrow shoulders, the by now completely familiar body hidden inside the also completely familiar green silk robe. She said nothing, but held the door open for him, giving him the look that told him she knew where to go and what to do. "Wait, honey," he said, as she headed toward the bedroom. She stopped and raised her eyebrows. He motioned toward the ugly sleeper sofa that had come with the other cheap-looking pieces in the furnished apartment. Stacks of mysteries were piled on the coffee table, the end tables, and in the corners of the sofa lay a heaped-up assortment of dolls Grace had collected. She liked dolls that represented different countries and costumes, and in New York she once took Jake to a shop at the United Nations, where he had bought her a dozen dolls— Japanese, Dutch, Polish, each in a separate national costume. Bringing them out to L.A. with her made the apartment feel like home, she said.

They walked across the wall-to-wall synthetic ocher carpet and sat down. Then the phone rang and she ran into her room to answer it. "Yeah. Yeah. Right. Ta, love, talk to you later," he heard her say. "That's just Ninky," she said, mentioning a friend who had been in the show and had also come out to California to be in the movie. Ordinarily Jake, always curious about everything, would have asked her why the friend had called. Not today, however.

"Listen, honey," he began. "I've come to a decision."

"Have you? Well, I know what you're going to say."

"You do?" Was it possible she was going to make it easy for him?

"You're ending it. I've guessed it now for a while. And I knew it would be today."

"You did? How's that?"

"I just knew, that's all."

"I wish I didn't have to."

Her face reddened and her eyes filled with tears.

"Honey," he went on, "we've sold the house and we're moving."

"*Moving?* Where?"

"To Europe."

"Where in Europe?"

"We're not sure yet. Paris or London."

"London!"

"Well, maybe."

"No. You can't be. When?"

"Well, soon. Next week. August 1st. We're all going—me, Dinah, the kids." He didn't add that he would be back, after he got them settled, to finish cutting and scoring the picture, previewing it, and so on. The less she knew of his whereabouts, the better.

"You're going to hate it. It's a filthy, depressing, wet, cold, hateful place."

"Honey, let me explain something to you."

He made a speech: he had been thinking this over for a long time now, but had decided after a great deal of wrestling with himself that he had to go independent, be on his own, leave the studio system, and work as a writer-producer-director with the freedom to shop his stuff around himself and head his own production company. He'd go to studios for financing, marketing, and distribution, but he wanted to be in charge of his own material—what to make and how to make it. He was tired of making the same kind of picture; he wanted to try different things, make serious stuff. European countries subsidized their film industries; Americans making movies abroad got great tax breaks from the U.S. government. It was just too good to pass up, and he owed it to himself, his talent, and his family to take that next step and get out of Hollywood.

"Right, then. Take me with you. I guess I could stand being back over there if we had each other."

This was the hard part. He swallowed. He now pretended to search for the lines he had prepared and rehearsed so often.

"Gracie, darling. You know, this situation we have—this arrangement— well, this is something a lot of guys like me get themselves into. And it always comes to this point. A friend of mine was once in this predicament. I said to him, 'Do you love your wife?' 'Sure I love my wife.' 'Do you love the girl?' 'Of course I love the girl.' Then I said, 'Do you love the girl enough to give her up?' You know, give her a chance to find the right guy to settle down with and have a family? And I've had to ask myself those same questions. They're tough questions, baby, because I do love you. You know I love you. But my wife has had a tough time, what with the death of her sister and my being away so much. Frankly, I'm very concerned about her. We're going to start fresh in Europe. I can't give you what you want, and it isn't fair to pretend I can when I've got responsibilities to her and the kids."

He waited. He didn't want to have to listen to her; he just wanted it to be over with.

"You waited till the last day of shooting to tell me."

"Well, I didn't want us to have to work together, see each other every day. It would be too painful for both of us. We've been together—what is it, three, almost four years now. And then, you know this business. I wasn't absolutely sure I could get things going over there. I couldn't talk about it until I was sure I had a project lined up. But I've got one now."

"Oh, what is it?"

"Better not go into that now. You know, don't want to hex it." He winked, trying to make her feel that if she could share its superstitions, she belonged to show business as much as he did.

He had expected tears. But she only looked thoughtful. "But the apartment. My acting lessons. My—expenses. What am I—?"

"I've thought it all out, baby. Don't you worry." He took out an envelope. "You're still on salary at the studio, though that ends next week—I'm aware of that. Here's enough dough for three months. Should cover everything. I had a meeting with Irv Engel today, and I told him all about you. I reminded him that he met you when he visited the set, and I told him you're going to call him for an appointment to talk about your future. And I have a referral here from my agent, Reg Pertwee, who gave me the number of someone named . . ."

He reached into his jacket pocket.

"Why did Pertwee give you a referral? I want *him* for my agent."

"Be realistic, honey. He doesn't handle unknowns."

"If you'd given me a speaking part in the picture, I bloody well wouldn't *be* unknown!"

She glared at him and he stayed calm, though his left foot was jiggling in its loafer. "We talked about that at the time. Your American accent needs work. You've been doing that work, and you've made progress. I know how much time you've put into those lessons. But you still have a way to go."

"I thought you were going to call up all your producer and director mates for me when we reached this point. Don't think I didn't know it was coming. I bloody well did know. I'm not a fool, you know."

He got up while she was speaking and went into the kitchen and came back with a handful of Ritz crackers and a bottle of root beer. A sound came through the open window—a colliding, scraping sound, as of an aluminum pool chair being dragged along a concrete deck. "Shit!" he heard a man say in annoyance.

"You know, honey," he said, munching the crackers, ignoring what she had just said, "I think you're going to do awfully well out here. People will notice you in the picture. I've given you a number of close-ups."

"But I'm dancing. The camera's on me for all of a second and a half."

"Not true," he said. "I let it linger long enough to really show your face. You make a real impression. I'm not worried about you at all."

She crossed her arms over her chest and her lower lip trembled. "Look, Jake, I think I'm being one hell of a good sport about this."

"I think you are too, sweetie." He sat down and brushed the crumbs off his shirt front, took a swig of root beer, and puffed out his cheeks in a controlled belch. "In fact, one helluva good sport."

"We've had some nice times together, eh, guv?"

"The nicest." His voice was husky, and his eyes glistened. "You've been a real friend, Grace. You've seen me through some very tough times."

"Can I still come to the cast party?"

"Of course! But, sweetie, don't make this too hard on yourself." In other words, they both knew he was saying that his wife would be there.

He leaned back, scooping up a handful of dolls, whose tiny legs and feet were poking him in the back, and placed them gently in a pile on the floor. Having said all he had intended to say, he was ready to leave, but he didn't want to seem callous. He covertly glanced at his watch and comfortably gazed at her, reaching across for her hand.

"Oh, Jake, I'm going to miss you, you randy old bugger."

He had resolved not to touch her. But she snuggled up against him, opening her kimono, placing his hand on her breast and her own on his fly. End-of-affair sex, he reminded himself, could be awfully good—intense and deliberate. And he wanted her to feel appreciated.

An hour later, she told him to let himself out while she stayed in bed and dozed off. "Are you okay?" he asked her.

"I'll be fine," she said. "But I'm not going to see you out. That might be a bit sticky for me."

"Me too," he said, huskily.

"Just go. Now." God, he thought, she's being so great about this. "Okay," he said. "Thanks, honey. For everything. You've been terrific."

Inside his car he felt that he and Grace had experienced moments of real love over the past three years, and that she had been altogether good for him, and he for her. He wanted to keep his nose clean for a while, but once he was settled in London he'd look for someone just like her and find a way to duplicate the situation. In the meantime, he would try to do what he could for her while he was still here, though of course he hoped she understood that he couldn't perform miracles—out of bed, that is.

A Saturday night in late June, and the Laskers' pool shimmers a bright turquoise. All afternoon and into the evening, the water has been churning and splashing as a storm of young, athletic dancers clad in bikinis and close-fitting trunks jump and dive into the water, toss volleyballs and one another up into the air, and abandon themselves to every possible aquatic combination with which they can entangle their perfect bodies. On the pool deck and patio, more dancers and other guests eat, drink, and dance to rock 'n' roll music and Broadway songs played by a studio band. The night is warm and balmy, the heavens clear and pricked with stars.

The picture is finished; this is the final cast party for the movie of *My Grandfather's Saloon,* and, as Jake has just put it at the end of the barbecue dinner, making a speech to the assembled group, a night that brings to a close nearly four wonderful years together—the two years during the run of the show on Broadway and the time it has taken to shoot the picture in L.A. They have been a family and he's going to miss them very much, he says, but he knows that great things lie ahead for each and every one of them—the most singularly talented bunch of people it has been his privilege and delight to work with. Buzz Keegan, the former ballet dancer who is the show's original director and choreographer, has made a speech too, thanking Jake for preserving so much of the original stage version on film and wishing him the greatest luck and success at his new headquarters in London. Jake, speaking again, toasts his relationship of nearly fifteen years with Marathon Pictures and its brilliant, generous, visionary head of production, Irv Engel. He lifts his glass to Irv and his wonderful wife, Anya, and thanks them from the bottom of his heart for their friendship and support.

It's about nine now, the speeches are over, and it's time for more fun. Peter Lasker and his sister, Lorna, who are now fourteen and thirteen, respectively, mesmerized by the sight of the young beautiful flesh before them, and uneasily aware of the other's embarrassed and aroused fascination with it, sit on the patio steps, modestly dressed, each preferring to die rather than put on a bathing suit and take part in the swimming-pool follies.

They roll their eyes at each other, and exchange glances that are comments on comments. Peter knows that Lorna has a crush on a "gypsy" dancer in the show named Tony Romeo, whom she had noticed onstage when she was taken to see the show in New York. Her cheeks had burned to a bright cherry when, during a visit to the set in Los Angeles, her father had introduced her to him by saying loudly, "Hey, Tony, she has a big crush on you. Can you give her a kiss?" She could have killed her father, on the spot. Romeo is a short man in his early twenties, with rippling muscles in his back and arms—the most athletic and absolutely the sexiest male dancer in the show. In New York, Jake had to triple his salary to keep him from being stolen by *West Side Story* and *Li'l Abner*. He is wearing a tight elastic brieflike bathing suit, with a bulge so prominent that Peter jabs his elbow in his sister's arm and whispers to her in his best Hollywood-brat fashion, "Well, look at that: there's a garden at the bottom of our fairy." He's certain that she won't know the source, and he's right; she doesn't, because the only other kid he knows who reads Shakespeare is his friend Joelly Rosen. But she gets a little bit of his meaning, nonetheless, and says, "Like hell he's a fairy, and you know it, too. You just wish . . ." Before they can banter themselves into either a fit of giggles or a loud quarrel, they are struck by a singular commotion.

Over by the Ping-Pong table, a man and a woman have entered the vast backyard of the Lasker demesne. The man is stocky, five-nine or so, with broad shoulders and a swagger. Dressed in a dark suit, he has graying hair that, Peter sees at once, he wears in a military crew cut. Moving up to get a closer look, they observe that he has a square-shaped face ("He's lantern-jawed," whispers Peter to Lorna. "You could keep a pet cricket inside his head") and tanned, weathered skin. "Wow, a real tough guy," says Peter under his breath, noting the man's cocky stance and his big-knuckled hands, as well as the protective and proprietary arm wrapped around the shoulders of a voluptuous redhead; she's wearing an electric blue strapless sheath with sequins all over the place, and matching electric blue three-and-a-half-inch spike heels. The red hair is pulled back in a French twist, and the girl's lipstick is a hot thick red. Her cleavage is visible, her large breasts squeezed upward, hinting at full nested globes lying cupped within the warm receptacles fastened inside the dress. Accompanying them is that all-around Lasker unfavorite, one Byron Cole, at the sight of whom Lorna turns to Peter, sticks her finger into the back of her mouth, and makes an exaggerated gagging sound.

"Stop that," Peter says. "Concentrate: who's the babe?"

Lorna stares. She knows the name of every one of the dancers. "It's Grace Siddons," she says.

"And you know what?" says Peter. "That guy was in Las Vegas."

"What guy?"

"That guy with her. You were asleep, with Gussie. But he stopped at our table at the Flamingo and said something to Mom. Mom said he's a jerk."

All of a sudden, before either of them can add a further comment, a human cannonball, all tight muscles and wet black hair, shoots through the air and lands in a horizontal explosion mid-gut on the man in the suit, socking and pounding the guy wherever he can, landing blows on his ribs and shoulders, to which he clings like an enraged squid. The stocky guy opens his mouth and laughs, and, peeling the little dancer off limb by limb, lifts him up under the shoulders, strides over to the wall opposite the Ping-Pong table, and slowly and sadistically rakes the dancer's naked back along the white stucco wall. He then repeats the motion, the dancer howling and kicking, then drops him in a heap on the terra-cotta tiles.

As Jake and Dinah tear over to the fight, and other dancers pick up the injured man, Peter and Lorna see the girl, Grace, smile mysteriously at their father and at Byron Cole. She moves in closer to the stocky man, who is still laughing with his head thrown back, so that the edges of his crew cut are silhouetted like shark's teeth against the light. The two Lasker kids hear their father calling their names. "You guys come with me, on the double. I'm taking Tony upstairs," and they have no choice but to follow, though they are now horrified by the sight of the dancer's back—a mess of bloody streaks where the skin has been torn to shreds against the coarse sharp wavelets of white stucco.

"Lorna, get Band-Aids. Pete, get the iodine, on the double," Jake barks in his upstairs bathroom, and they rush into the kids' bathroom and back again, in time to hear what the dancer is saying. He's punchy, gasping, and he dances lightly side to side like a prizefighter in the ring, while Jake instructs Lorna to daub his wounds with iodine-soaked cotton balls. Though her face is one large scarlet moon, and she feels almost sick from the waves in her belly that she doesn't yet recognize as sexual desire, Lorna does as she's told and the dancer hisses each time the antiseptic touches his flesh. Meanwhile, he talks nonstop.

"I knew it, Jake. I swear, I knew that cunt was two-timing me. I knew she had some big motherfucking bigshot on the side. She gives me the brush-off in New York even before we get out here, see. Then somebody tells me the bigshot's out here, too, but I'm such a dumb fuck I don't believe it, see. Then out here she calls me. She says, 'I'm lonely, Tony, come over and love me up, baby,' in this crazy accent of hers, and I'm such a sucker for her. You know I've always been crazy about her, Jake. So I go and keep her warm at night, and I says, 'Come on, move in with me,' but she says she can't, she's got stuff going on with her career. Then here she comes tonight with this big fucking guy, and I'm in the pool and I says, 'Who's that?' And Bobby Collins—you know Bobby? Right? He says, 'Don't you know who that is? That's Duff Burgoyne, the writer—you know, plays his own character, Axel Duke the detective, in all the movies they make outta his books?' Well, I says, 'I'm gonna kill that son of a bitch,' and I'm gonna do it, too, Jake. I'm gonna go downstairs right now and kill that motherfucker just as soon as you fix me up. And then I'm gonna strangle that cunt, I swear."

"Hold still," Lorna shouts. "You're bleeding!" As he speaks, his breath permeates the confined space of the bathroom with the smell of booze. Lorna can't stop blushing; she's so crazy about this dancer.

Tony looks at her and grins. "Thank you, darlin'," he says, still moving from one leg to the other. "You're a doll, you know that? Hey, Jake, you don't mind if I tell your daughter she's a beautiful girl, do ya? You're a nice girl, too, ain't cha, not like that fucking cunt downstairs. Excuse me, sweetheart, for using them kind of words."

Jake looks at Lorna as if to say, "You're doing fine, you're taking it in stride."

But she's so embarrassed that she's afraid she's going to cry as Peter leers at her. Oh, he's going to tease her later; she'll never hear the end of it.

Jake murmurs, "No kidding," and "What do you know?" to everything the dancer says, but when the boy says yet again that he wants to go and kill the guy, Jake tells Peter and Lorna to keep fixing him up while he runs downstairs.

He returns ten minutes later to say that Burgoyne has been a real gentleman, and agreed that it would be best for him and the young lady to leave.

"Byron, too?" says Lorna. "That ick."

And Jake says Byron, too.

"Ah, she ain't nothin but a whore," Tony sobs, bringing his hands up to his face. Then he grins at Jake and the kids and hisses again, suddenly feeling the pain of his red, shredded back and noticing the cotton balls piling up in the sink, bloodied and stained with orange iodine. "Ooooh," he hisses again. "That fuckin' bastard." He grins at Lorna. "Listen, beautiful, don't go kissin' nobody till youse is sixteen. Then call your friend Tony. 'Cause I'm gonna thank you then for bein' so sweet to me tonight, darlin'. And hey," he says to Jake. "Leave off with the Band-Aids on me. I'm goin' back in the pool. Fuck *her*," he adds. "I'm gonna have some more fun." Then he turns away and calls out, "Thanks, Jake. Thanks, youse guys." He runs out of the bathroom and downstairs.

Jake and his two kids are left standing at the sink with a dozen opened Band-Aids stuck to the porcelain edge, waiting to be applied, and a spreading pink puddle on the floor, where the dancer had dripped blood and water. Jake sees the pink flush on his daughter's face and chucks her under the chin.

"Stay away from guys like that," he says.

She blushes again. "Dad!"

Out by the pool, Jake finds Dinah talking to Tony, to whom she has given a cup of strong coffee. "Well, she's very pretty," he hears her say. "And very pretty girls can be very cr-cr-cr-cruel sometimes."

"Ah, she ain't worth it," Tony says sadly.

She tells him what a good dancer he is and that she once danced in pictures.

"Oh, yeah? What pictures?" he says, and she describes a routine she did when she was just sixteen, in 1928, in *Bewitching Brunettes*. "Let's see it," he says.

So right there, Dinah does a tap routine, a cramp roll, a buck-and-wing, and an assortment of time steps. She is wearing a white sleeveless dress, and her arms are very brown and she looks good.

"Hey, Jake," Tony says. "Your wife here's a real hoofer. You shoulda fired that bitch and put your wife in the picture instead."

"You can say that again," says Jake. Then Tony gets up and begins dancing with Dinah, improvising with her to the music on the speakers. The guests gather around, shouting and clapping, while Peter and Lorna look at each other in mute disgust at their mother's movements, which are gracefully but unmistakably sexual and therefore appalling to them, although they enchant everyone else.

"Did I tell you I met that Burgoyne fellow in Vegas? I didn't like him one bit. Did Veevi reject a story of his or s-s-something? He said something about you not liking a treatment of his. What's going on between him and the redhead?" Dinah asked later, after the party finally ended—at 4 A.M.— and they had retreated, exhausted, to their bedroom.

"Oh, he's got Vegas connections," Jake answered vaguely. "I think he's like an uncle to her or something. She must have known Tony would be here and wanted protection," he added. "Anyway, it's none of our business, and I don't want to think too hard about the lives and loves of the Very Nebbish."

But with her question he had himself become one of the Very Nervous.

She had slipped into her nightgown and was sitting cross-legged in bed. "Who? That girl? She doesn't look so nebbish to me. Tell me about her. Isn't she that dancer Grace something or other? The one Peter has such a crush on?"

"I didn't know he had a crush on her," said Jake. "What makes you think that?"

"Lorna told me. It's not something he's going to tell *you*, you know." She shook her head. "I don't like that B-B-B-Burgoyne. You know he's a famous red-baiter, don't you?"

"Is he?" Jake said. "I've never read a word the man has written."

"Oh, yeah. He makes all these pronouncements all the time. In the junk magazines I read at the beauty parlor."

Jake yawned. "I didn't know that."

"How come they showed up with Byron Cole?"

"Well, he's the stills photographer on the picture, and I saw him taking pictures of her the other day. So I guess they know each other or something. Who cares?"

He went over to her and led her to his bed, and they talked together about the party and the big changes that were about to take place in their lives. He'd been so proud of her, he said, when she danced with Tony—she still looked great and danced great. There was so much they were going to do together when they moved to London—take the kids skiing in Switzerland, go to museums, expose the kids to art and music. He'd been so worried about her, he said. She'd seemed so sad since Veevi died, and he wanted her to know how much he loved her and how completely the two of them were one and how much he wanted to spend the rest of his life with her. Holding her, nuzzling her, making her laugh, he talked on and on, as the gray and pink California dawn spread its gradual light through the bedroom.

3

*K*nowing that she would soon be leaving Los Angeles, Dinah continued to visit the cemetery in Westwood every day to stand alone for a few minutes, and cry. She kept a small bottle of Scotch in the glove compartment of her station wagon, and she always poured out two capfuls—never more—after she'd been to Veevi's rosebush, and went on with the day. But Veevi was never out of her mind. Driving Jake's mother back to her apartment on a Monday morning, she noticed the railroad tracks in Beverly Hills, long abandoned, and they reminded her of the big red streetcars she and Veevi had taken to school or the Santa Monica beach or downtown to the Hill Street Theater, with their mother, for eight acts of vaudeville and two movies plus a newsreel. You couldn't grow up with your sister and then leave her where her ashes lay and move to an unknown city, could you? You couldn't sleep in the same bed with her for years, pee while she took a bath, stretch out with your legs parallel on the old sofa reading library books, practice dance steps together on the sidewalks, wash the dishes together, and then leave her ashes behind just like that.

Then quickly clearing away the dry leaves from the rosebush, Dinah said to herself, No. This is not a reason to stay. I go where my husband goes. I belong with him.

She spent most of her days now packing Bekins cartons, wrapping plates and cups and saucers in newspaper, stacking pictures, lovingly filling boxes with books. The house had been sold in May. She was leaving her flowers, the children's bedrooms she had painted, and the den where she had spent so many hours talking to her sister and hearing the sound of Peter's clarinet as it drifted in from the living room. Jake spent every available minute in the cutting room, even Saturdays, desperate to get the picture ready by the end of the month.

Gussie worked with Dinah, who had gradually given up trying to persuade her to move to London with them. Leaving Gussie behind was turning out to be the hardest part of all, but she had her sisters and her daughter and son-in-law in Los Angeles, her church and her friends, and she had decided to retire.

"The llama," she announced, "is going out to pasture. I done toted all the laundry I'm ever going to tote."

Jake had arranged a pension for her, and Dinah knew that her life would be comfortable. Nevertheless, it would be a hard parting.

"Jake's going to miss talking to you about sports," Dinah said. "And I'm going to miss talking to you about politics. You'll be here when the convention starts. Will you write me all about it? You know, everyone we know is fighting with everyone else about who's going to give the biggest party for this guy Kennedy."

"My cousin Mamie," who worked, as Dinah knew, for the movie star Robert Tipton and his wife, Jeanie, "says they're going to give him a party with three hundred people. She even wants me to come and help out. She's got to be kidding. 'I'm retired as of August the first,' I told her, 'and I ain't gonna hand round no trays of rumaki to nobody, even if he's going to be the president of the United States.'"

Later that afternoon, at about three o'clock, Dinah was in the pantry, wrapping platters and serving dishes, when she heard the front doorbell ring. "Gus, can you get that?" she called out.

Gussie shouted back, "No, I can't, Dinah, I'm peeling potatoes right now."

So Dinah shouted back absently, "Never mind, Gus, I'll get it myself."

She decided it must be a real estate agent who was unaware that the house had been sold, but then she thought, How is that possible? There's a sticker saying Sold on the For Sale sign stuck in the ivy beds near the street. She remembered, too, the day the doorbell had rung and the man in the gray suit had shoved the pink subpoena at her. Wondering if she was about to get hit with some new political catastrophe, Dinah went uneasily to the front door. Then she thought, This is nonsense. It has to be the moving company with extra cardboard cartons.

Opening the door, she saw a young woman, with great swirls of red hair, wearing a pink sundress with ruffles at the shoulders, high-heeled pink sandals, and a large white straw hat. The girl took off her sunglasses, and Dinah scanned her face, trying to remember where she had seen her. "Mrs. Lasker?"

Dinah suddenly remembered. "The party! Of course. You were at the p-p-p-party. Did you forget your bathing suit?"

The big red mouth opened, and Dinah thought, The outfit and makeup are all wrong for this girl. God, what these girls do to themselves when they come out here. She smiled and waited for the girl to speak.

"May I come in?"

The girl had an accent, an English accent of some kind. Dinah suddenly recognized it: cockney. The girl had a cockney accent.

"Yes, of course. I can take you out to the pool house to look for it if you like."

"Actually, Mrs. Lasker, I didn't lose my bathing costume." The girl's mouth trembled. "May I talk to you, Mrs. Lasker?"

"Follow me."

Dinah's first thought was: She needs an abortion. Of course, she would help her out. Of course.

She took her past the open cartons and half-filled boxes that littered the entrance hall and the den. Motioning to the love seat, she gestured for the girl to sit down directly opposite her, by the leaded windows that looked out over the pool, whose still water, Dinah thought, looked as if it had already forgotten the Laskers and was anticipating the new people who were moving in and the splashing and cavorting of their children.

"What can I do for you, d-d-d-dear?" Dinah said.

The girl clasped her hands and held them primly in her lap. "Mrs. Lasker, what I've come here to tell you is that I've been having an affair with your husband for the past three and a half years."

"No k-k-k-kidding," said Dinah, without missing a beat. She reached into the pocket of her dusty toreadors and, pulling out a pack of Camels, lit one, blew out the smoke, and observed that the girl was wearing thick clotted black mascara, black eyeliner, green eye shadow, rouge, heavy powder, and gloss. The face was a mask, taut and caked with artifice.

"And, well, the reason I'm here is because he always said if we ever broke up he wouldn't leave me stranded, he'd get me a good agent, introduce me to the right people, but he hasn't done a single thing he promised. I tried to see Mr. Engel, but Mr. Engel's secretary said he's booked and can't see me. The agent he told me to call hasn't called me back. And he's only given me three month's, you know, support."

"He was supporting you?"

"Yes, of course, Mrs. Lasker. He was paying for everything, and, well, my new boyfriend, Duff Burgoyne—the writer? I'm sure you've heard of him?"

Dinah nodded. "He's your new b-b-b-boyfriend?"

"Yeah, well, new and old, anyway, he told me to come see you for a heart-to-heart and tell you that if Jake doesn't behave like the gentleman we all know he is, and take care of me for at least the next two years"—she took a deep breath here—"he's going to call Louella Parsons and Hedda Hopper and his friends at the trades and Walter Winchell, who happens to be a very good friend of his, and tell them about how your husband hired a known Communist and had her work at Marathon studios right under the nose of Irv Engel, who was probably in on it all the time, anyway."

"How does Duff Burgoyne happen to have that piece of information, may I ask?"

The girl smiled very sweetly. "From me."

"From you? How so?"

"Well, you see, your husband and I were really quite good friends, Mrs. Lasker. Bosom buddies. And I do mean 'bosom.' He confided in me quite a bit. Know what I mean? Like, you know, what they call 'pillow talk.' He told me about you being a Communist and your sister being a Communist. And you naming names and naming her, but she didn't name anybody until she had to because she decided to do it for her husband, too. And how much of a wreck she was when she got out here, and how sorry he felt for her, which was why he had an affair with her."

"An affair with her?"

"Oh, yeah. A big one. It lasted, like, for a year, or more. They were absolutely crazy about each other. He was really in love with her. I mean, madly in love. He'd never been in love like that before, and he was just going crazy about it, and they were making all kinds of plans for him to leave you and the kids, too. But then she didn't like his show, and he got mad at her and just dropped her, like that; and then her husband acted like he wanted to come back and got her to testify. And then your husband wanted to go back with her. He was still madly in love with her, but she didn't want anything to do with him. And, believe me, it broke his heart. So much that he needed all the comfort he could find. That's where I come into the picture."

"How very interesting," said Dinah. "And you have such a c-c-c-colorful, fr-fr-fresh way of putting things, dear. Tell me, what is your name?"

The girl smiled at her with murderous sweetness. "Grace Siddons." She leaned forward and touched Dinah's emerald ring. "Nice ring. Oh, before I forget, this is for you."

Suddenly Dinah noticed a heavy manila envelope whose clasp, with its two flaps, the girl was bending upward. As Dinah watched, she took out a book and handed it to her. Dinah read the cover: it was a collection of plays by Clifford Odets. Opening the cover, she read an inscription:

Darling,

I don't care what you say—this man's a genius. And I wouldn't trade you for two pitchers and an outfielder.

I love you, baby,

Jake

"Hmm," said Dinah, coolly shrugging. "Where'd you get this?"

"From the same person who took these."

Then she handed the manila envelope to Dinah and watched, her hands once again folded primly in her lap, as Dinah pulled out a dozen large black-and-white glossy photographs of Grace and Jake in various postures of sexual congress.

Dinah turned them over and saw an inscription, stamped in black ink, which she read out loud: "Byron Cole, Ph-Ph-Ph-Photographer. I see," Dinah continued, "that we have a mutual acquaintance. Well, young l-l-lady, any other surprises for me?" She smiled at the girl—a rich, warm, patronizing smile.

"He owes me, Mrs. Lasker. I mean, there's a lot of men I didn't meet during the past three years. Men who could've done lots more for me than he did."

"Then I'd say that that was v-v-v-very stupid of you. I think you'd better go. What you're telling me really doesn't interest me."

She got up and folded her arms.

"Mrs. Lasker, if I don't have twenty thousand dollars in cash by August first, those photos—and I have copies, you can count on that—are going to Duff's friends at the newspapers, and so is a letter about your Communist sister working for Jake. I'm going to do whatever I have to do to take care of myself. I'm not going to end up like your sister or some of these girls out here—dead in their beds with a bottle of empty sleeping pills next to them and all choked on their own vomit."

"Well, I can certainly see you're not. You're obviously a girl who knows how to g-g-g-get what she wants."

The girl stood up and touched the brim of her hat, leaving the manila envelope on the love seat. "I've got clothes of his—socks, underwear, ties— all kinds of stuff. You ought to come by sometime and pick them up."

"Just give them to G-G-Goodwill," Dinah said. "Or any charity of your choice. I'm sure you'll think of something, a resourceful girl like you."

The girl took a slip of paper out of her handbag and gave it to Dinah. "Here's my address. I want cash."

Dinah took the slip of paper and pushed it into the pocket of her slacks. "Shall we?" she said, leading the way out over the noiseless peridot carpet.

When Dinah finally opened the door, Grace turned and said, "I hope I haven't hurt you."

"Well, shouldn't you have thought of that before you came over?" Dinah smiled brightly and slammed the door in the girl's face.

Nausea overwhelmed her; she had to vomit. In the small bathroom off the entrance hall, she heaved and heaved, throwing up her lunch in a couple of strong convulsions. She felt as if she'd been socked in the solar plexus, and gasped for air. Her legs buckled, and collapsed beneath her. On her knees, she grabbed the rim of the toilet bowl and spat into it, trying to clear the vile taste from her mouth.

At three o'clock that afternoon, just when Grace Siddons was ringing the Laskers' doorbell, Jake Lasker was at Marathon, hard at work in the cutting room with his editor, Bill Wilkinson. They were counting out loud the beats for the number "What Can You Do in Minsk (That You Can't Do in Chicago)?," so that he and Bill would know exactly where to splice the film and insert close-ups, when the telephone rang. "Shit," said Jake. He hated to be interrupted. "Hold it there, Bill, while I get this."

"Lasker?" said a gruff but surprisingly high voice.

"Yeah?"

"Burgoyne here."

"And?" Jake said. He spoke neutrally, not wanting Bill to suspect anything. But he instinctively felt fear. There could be no good reason for this call.

"I was just wondering if you know where Grace Siddons is right now."

"Haven't a clue."

"Told me she was going to drop in on your wife for a little girl talk."

"That so?"

"You're a cheap bastard, you know that, Lasker? You owe her, baby. Twenty thousand bucks, in cash, now—before you take off for London. You know what I'm saying? Between her father and her brother and me, we know everyone between L.A. and Vegas who could break your skinny Jew legs if you don't do right by her, you hear me?"

"I'm well aware of that."

Bill looked at Jake and saw sweat breaking out on his forehead. He mouthed, "Everything okay?" Jake held up his hand and nodded.

"You pay up or you're gonna see your name plastered all over the trades, all over the L.A. *Times,* the *New York Times,* and every TV station in the land."

"Only those ones, huh?"

"Very funny. A joke writer. A very funny guy. And we're gonna tell 'em how you hired your wife's sister, a known Commie, and had her work right under Irv Engel's big Jewish nose. But that's not all we're gonna tell 'em. We're gonna tell 'em how you shtupped her—isn't that the Jew word?— shtupped your own wife's sister, and then took advantage of a sweet little girl in the chorus line of your show. Oh, and you know what? Gracie's been brought up right, so she's bringing your wife a little thank-you gift for the lovely time she's had with you. You know—a nice little black-and-white thank-you gift." There was a loud laugh.

"I'm a busy man, Burgoyne, so if you're finished I'd suggest we—"

"Not so fast, Lasker. Meet me at Joe Brogan's Monday night at seven. With the money—twenty thousand. To keep her in the style to which you've made her accustomed. Only better than that cheap place you set her up in. Wouldn't give her a speaking part. Haven't made good on your promises. Letting a sweet little thing down like that. She thought you had class, Lasker."

"I think the delusion was perhaps mutual."

"Don't try to be clever, Lasker, and don't try anything funny. To begin with, there isn't a cop in L.A. who wouldn't lay down his life for me. Get it?"

"Got it."

"So don't try any funny stuff. 'Cause I also got my eye on that faggot kid of yours. The one who plays the clarinet."

This time Jake gestured quickly to Bill and held up the phone so that they could both hear the voice bellowing on the other end.

"He'd have a hard time playing that faggot music he likes with two broken arms. Just like you couldn't hit a golf ball too good with two broken legs."

"You know, I'm deaf in one ear," said Jake. "Would you mind repeating what you just said?"

"Don't get funny with me. You heard me. I promised her people I wouldn't let you get away with it. Brogan's, seven sharp, Monday night. And remember, no monkey business if you ever want to walk again."

There was a click. Jake's face had turned ashen, and he clutched his chest.

"Boss?" said Bill. "What the hell was that?"

"Reach in my pocket," Jake gasped, his face contorted with pain. "And get me my nitroglycerin."

"Sure, boss. What's going on?"

Jake couldn't speak until the tablet had dissolved the searing pain. Then all he said was "Duff Burgoyne. Bad news. Keep it to yourself for now, please. Take Monday off. I won't be coming in on Monday."

"You serious, boss?"

"Wish I weren't. Help me to my car, will ya, Bill?"

If Burgoyne was on the level, then Grace was at the house right now, and he had to get home right away.

"Can you drive, boss?"

He nodded, and gestured to Bill to hand him his jacket, which was hanging on a coat hook by the editing-room door. Then he reached into the pocket in the lining, withdrew a small black memo book, and placed a call to Trancas. After that, he dialed home. Peter answered the phone. "Let me talk to Mom, Pete," said Jake.

"She went to bed, Dad. She's sick or something. Are we still going to leave next week if she's sick?"

"I don't know. Did you just get home?"

"Yeah. Byron Cole and that girl—you know, the one that dancer guy socked the big guy over at the party?—they were just driving off when I came up the driveway. Why were they here?"

"I don't know. Maybe they left something at the party. You think Mom's asleep?"

"I guess so. I'm riding my bike over to Joelly's."

"No, honey, don't," he said, using an endearment he had never used before with his son. "Stay home. Don't go out. In case Mom needs you. Wait till I get back."

"But, Dad, Gussie's here. And this may be the last time I get to hang out at Joelly's."

"Just do as I say, Pete. I want you at home with Mom."

"But, Dad—"

"Remember Palm Springs? Don't run out on Mom now. She's not feeling well, and we may need you."

"All right." His son's voice was sullen. That his son hated him, and mystified him and disappointed and irritated him, made absolutely no difference to Jake in his desire, overwhelming and fierce, to protect him.

In the car, he took another nitroglycerin and pressed his foot down on the accelerator, alternately driving faster than the speed limit, and then slowing and looking anxiously out the rearview mirror and the side windows. On the one hand, he was hoping that a cop would stop him, so that he could confess everything and get help. But then he broke into a cold sweat, in case what Burgoyne had said was true and every cop in L.A. was already on his tail.

Gussie looked up when he came into the kitchen through the back door. She was smoking, and reading the sports section of the *Examiner*. "Where's Mrs. Lasker, Gus?"

"Dinah's upstairs, Mr. Lasker," she said pointedly, using Dinah's first name. "She ain't feeling too good."

She gave him a long, unsmiling look. He nodded. "I'm expecting someone here in about an hour, Gus. Let me know when he comes, will you? Where's Peter?"

"He's upstairs in his room, packing up his stuff."

"You see anybody around here today—any cars sitting out in the street that maybe shouldn't be here? Anything or anyone that bothered you?"

"You mean anyone besides that dog-ass Cole and that red-haired woman? He done sat in the car the whole time the girl was here, and then he drove off with her."

"But you didn't see anybody else, did you?"

"Like who, Mr. Lasker?"

"Gussie, you just keep a lookout for me, will you? Just let me know if you see anybody you don't like the looks of."

"Well, I'm lookin' at one right now." She fixed him with a steady gaze.

"Gus, please. You can think whatever you like of me later, but right now I need your help. Pete might be in danger."

She stood up and went over to the kitchen window and looked out. "No," she said. "There ain't nobody out there. So you just go on upstairs, Mr. Lasker. Ain't nobody gonna touch that boy or anybody else in this house long as I'm here."

His eye filled with tears. "Thanks, Gus."

"You better go upstairs, Mr. Lasker. You is in the doghouse now. You better grease your chops, too, 'cause you got some explainin' to do."

"Gus, can you keep on with the packing? I've got a plan, and we've got to get the packing done as soon as possible."

"Well, you want me to do the packing or the looking? I can't do both at the same time."

"Packing." He started to go toward the stairs. "But then, every fifteen minutes or so, just take a look out the windows, too. Okay?"

4

*H*oney?" he said, standing by Dinah's bed. She was lying on her side with her knees drawn up and her hands between them.

The manila envelope lay on the floor. He picked it up and pulled out the book and the photographs. He looked and saw the open kimono, the sofa with the dolls. The open bottle of root beer. The bedroom. His fat belly and flat ass and skinny ankles arched over her body.

They had all been taken on the evening of the day he'd finished shooting. He remembered a phone call—from her friend Ninky, he thought. The pictures had all been taken through a window, with a zoom lens, in the early summer evening, when it was still light enough to get an image. The sound, that night, of somebody tripping on something, or scraping a metal thing along the ground, and muttering "Shit!" That had been, he realized now, Byron Cole.

He moved over to the bed but dared not sit down. "Listen, honey, I know this is hard for you. But listen to me, please. Burgoyne called me today. Just when . . ." He couldn't bring himself to say her name. "When, you know, what's-her-name was here. And he's made some threats. Some serious threats."

She sat up suddenly and blinked at him, and rubbed her arms, as if she were cold. Her voice was low, and dead. He smelled booze on her breath. "What k-k-k-kind of threats?"

"Against Peter. And me."

"What do you mean?" She lit a cigarette and stared at him. Her eyes were swollen, her lips puffy and dry.

He explained what Burgoyne had said.

"You I don't care about," she said. "I hope you d-d-d-die. But what about Peter?"

He had a plan, he said. He had already called Gladys at the studio, and she was making all the arrangements. "You and the kids are leaving tomorrow. Not for London. For Paris. The George V. You'll see Felicity. You'll see Dorshka and Coco. And then I'll join you, and we'll go back to London together and move into the flat there. On Green Street, just as we planned, only you're going a little bit earlier."

She blinked at him. "I'm not going anywhere with you, Jake. I'm not leaving, and the kids aren't leaving. I'm taking them, tomorrow morning, to the Beverly Hills Hotel, and then I'm going to find a house in Brentwood, and a divorce lawyer, and you are n-n-n-never going to see them or me again."

"Wait till this is over, and then you can do whatever you like. I know this is hard on you."

"Not as hard as it's going to be on you. You've blown it, b-b-b-buster. I'm through with you."

"Honey, promise me you won't do anything, judge anything, say anything, until we clear up this mess with Burgoyne. Then we'll talk it through. None of it meant anything."

"None of it *meant* anything? What kind of human being are you, anyway? A girl you fuck for three years doesn't mean anything? Veevi didn't mean anything?"

"What I mean is, none of it changes one bit the feelings I have for you—and have always had, and always will."

"Which is no doubt how you felt when you were f-f-f-fucking my sister."

"Please, honey, it wasn't what you think. Listen to me, darling. Let me explain."

"Explain? What is there to explain? You're a *prick,* Jake! A *pr-pr-pr-prick!*"

She burst into sobs. He sat down on the edge of his own bed, his arms folded across his chest, and looked at her while she sat there, shaking, the ugly, squealing sounds of rage and grief racking her body.

He felt far away, and patient. This is all very normal, he told himself. She'll get over it in time. They always do. That's what George Joy had told him—and the other guys, dozens of them, over golf, at Finlandia, at the commissary. If you get caught, stay cool: keep her busy, treat her well. A vacation in Cap Ferrat, a new place to fuss over in London, getting the kids settled in schools over there, some sweet talk, trips to Paris, jewelry. For every broad, she gets a brooch. In the meantime, he'd just have to stand it, like serving a short jail sentence. Of course she was angry and hurt. They're always like that. The Burgoyne thing had to be cleared up first, though. Then he could go to work on her.

The telephone rang. "I'll get it," she said, glaring at him.

"Dinah Lasker?" bellowed a voice on the other end.

"What do you want, Mr. B-B-B-Burgoyne?"

"I know about your Commie past, and I'm calling to tell you how proud I am of you for coming clean about it."

"You said that in Vegas. What do you w-w-w-want?"

"Girls like you should get the Congressional Medal of Honor, doing your country a service like that. Too bad you spilled your guts for a horse's ass like your husband. I know you must be feeling pretty rum tonight, but believe me, Mrs. Lasker, my sweet little Jewess friend Gracie here did you a favor. Didn't you, kitten?" he said, his voice suddenly becoming distant, as if his face had been turned away from the phone.

"You evil b-b-b-bastard." Jake ran quickly down the corridor and picked up the phone in his office. "You love your son and I love my kitten. Don't I, baby?" Again, the voice faded out and returned. "So your husband should act like a gentleman and take care of Gracie like he said he would. He shouldn't get any ideas about leaving town in a hurry. I hear your son's a faggot, anyway, and could use a little toughening up." Dinah heard a mirthless laugh. "Grace's old man and I have very good friends in London. Good friends here, too. Right, doll? I've seen the pictures. Your husband's got skinny Jew legs. We can break 'em like matchsticks. Same with your son. We can do whatever we want until he makes good on that contract."

"What contract?"

Another rolling laugh. "You ask him about that. Like I told him, and like Grace told you, if she doesn't get the money by Monday night, come Tuesday morning I'm calling Hedda and Louella before I even take a morning crap. I got a copy of that contract your husband gave Grace, and I can tell my good friend Winchell about the apartment he paid for and the job he gave your Commie sister while he was banging her."

"If you touch my son, I will kill you, B-B-B-Burgoyne," said Dinah.

"Oooh, I like your cute little stammer."

Dinah slammed the phone down. She started toward the attic.

"Where are you going?" he said.

"I'm getting Pop's .22. It's still in there."

"Oh no, you're not." He was aware that she was absolutely capable of using it—that she wouldn't hesitate to get into the car, find Burgoyne, and blow his head off if it meant protecting Peter. He grabbed her by the shoulders and forced her down onto the bed. She drew up her knees and kicked him, knocking him backward toward the antique chest of drawers where he kept his chewing gum, cuff links, and socks. She sat up, breathless, and he held his hand to his chest.

"Angina," he whispered, panting. "Acute angina."

"I'll say you've got ang-g-gina!" she sneered. "And I'm sure hers was very cute! You're up to your ears in ang-g-gina, you schmuck."

He reached into his pocket for the nitroglycerin.

"Gee, you could have died screwing her. Then what would have happened?"

"Then I'd have been dead and you'd have gotten a million bucks in insurance."

She stared at him. In the past, they would have laughed at this together.

"Now, what's this about a contract?" she said.

His voice, usually so rich and gravelly, so that it seemed he sometimes spoke like a radio announcer, was tight and thin. "Well, I did have kind of an arrangement with her."

He moved in gingerly fashion over to the armchair, careful to sideswipe the foot of the bed in case she tried to clobber him again.

"You better tell me everything, Jake."

She sat cross-legged on his bed, listening and crying softly, while he started at the beginning—the night he drove back into L.A. with Veevi, after the fight in Palm Springs. When he finished, she wasn't thinking about the contract. "Jesus Christ, Jake," she said. "My sister."

"Dinah," he said. "Please, listen to me. You're not getting the important part. Which is that I ended it. I ended it with Veevi. I ended it with Grace. I didn't want them. I only want you."

"The girl said you were so much in love with Veevi you were going to leave us for her."

"Not true. I never, ever, had that thought."

"I don't b-b-b-believe you."

"I swear, Dinah. It wasn't like that. Ever. Well, look, for a while I didn't know what to do. I thought maybe it would have been the decent thing.

Not for me, but for you. That I didn't deserve you. That's the only reason I even contemplated it. But I got over that quickly. I couldn't stand the thought of losing you."

Dinah shook her head. "What kind of an idiot do you think I am?"

"Dinah, darling—"

"You're a fucking liar. And this girl, Grace. You didn't do anything for her."

"That's a load of crap. I did all I could. A girl like that, whatever you do is never enough. She's not rare, honey. She's not Monroe. She's not even Jayne Mansfield. She's got an accent problem. She's not very talented."

"Except at bl-bl-bl-blow jobs. She's a genius there."

"Stop, Dinah. Look, I gave her enough dough for the next few months. The contract was just a convenience, and she knows that. She never took it seriously. Burgoyne's another story. He's dangerous. I want you and the kids to get out of here, now, till this blows over. Go to Paris. Go to Cap Ferrat. The Crandells are there. After that, you can do whatever you want."

"By God, Jake, I feel sorry for you. I've never seen a fuckup like this one. You're gonna lose the whole thing, Jake. I'm not leaving the country. I'll take the kids to East Hampton, but I'm not going to France."

"No, Dinah, you've got to get out of the country. This is a bad guy— a real one."

She looked at him and shook her head. "You don't get it, do you?"

"What's to get?" he said wearily. "Look, Dinah. I love you. I want to stay together, I want the family. I can't say any more than that."

There was a knock at the door. It opened a little, and Gussie stuck her head in. "Mr. Lasker, Vernon Ashby's downstairs. He said you asked him to come over."

"Tell him I'll be right down, Gus, thank you."

"I'm coming too," said Dinah.

"Let me have fifteen minutes with him alone, then come down. Okay?"

"No," Dinah said. "I'm coming down now. If Pete's in danger, I'm not leaving anything to you."

This time it was Jake who started in the direction of the attic. She watched as he disappeared into her large walk-in closet, and reemerged a minute or two later, holding a long object encased in a canvas bag. "This," he said, "I'm giving to Vernon. I don't want you anywhere near it. You've got too much Milligan in you not to use it. On me."

"Very funny," she said. "Very funny."

inah and Jake hadn't seen Vernon and Claire (whom he had married a week after her high school graduation) since Veevi's death. Neither had they spoken to them. Jake had always been fond of Claire, and he was fascinated by Vernon and his stories about his years as a vice-squad cop. But there had been an unfortunate incident, or moment, rather, only a few days after Veevi's death. Dinah, Dorshka, Felicity, and Claire were all out at Veevi's house going through her things when Dinah came across an album she and Veevi had put together from the years in Malibu. There were pictures of everyone from those days: Dorshka and a young teenage Mike barely able to speak English; Stefan in his American bathing trunks, with his arms around Dinah and Veevi; groups of people on the beach, mugging for the camera; then, clusters of refugees in straw hats and sandals, talking together under striped umbrellas. Dinah had actually taken most of the pictures herself, with her own Kodak, and remembered pasting them in the album with Stefan. Looking at them again, she became desolate. Grief overwhelmed her. It seemed impossible that she was alive and that Veevi was dead, impossible and incomprehensible. "I'm sorry," she'd said. "I have to go." Dorshka and Claire looked at each other, somewhat put out, since there were a great many things to do, and only two days left before Felicity was to take Dorshka and Coco back with her to Paris. Dinah caught their look on her way out, as well as Felicity's far more forbearing expression. But she simply couldn't help herself; she had to get away. She ran, blind with tears, to her station wagon and sat behind the wheel, thinking she would drive home. But putting her head down and clutching the wheel with both hands, she sobbed and sobbed, holding nothing back, allowing the sadness to have its way with her completely.

In a while, it subsided. She blew her nose and smoked a cigarette, and then, instead of starting the car and driving home, she felt she really ought to get back to work. So she returned to the house, and entered through the kitchen door, quietly, so quietly in fact that as she approached the living room she heard a voice, a very clear young voice, saying: "Why wasn't it Dinah who died? Why did the good one have to die?"

"Shame on you, Claire," Felicity said. "What an awful thing to say. I was friends with your mother and Dinah, for years, and loved them both. How could you say such a dreadful thing?" Then she caught sight of Dinah in the doorway.

"I came back to help you f-f-f-finish the job," she said to all of them. Then she looked directly at Claire. "You know, Claire, there were many t-t-t-times, in the hospital, when I wished it had been me, too."

She and Claire hadn't spoken since that day. Dinah longed to see her, to give her things, to help her set up her household. But she could not, would not, call her.

ernon Ashby was so tall, lean, and lanky that he looked like a caricature of someone tall, lean, and lanky. Whenever Dinah saw him, she thought of Ichabod Crane and his feet "like shovels." But somehow it all made for a strange kind of handsomeness.

He had quit the vice squad, after a fight with a pimp in which he'd gotten his jaw broken. Through a fisherman friend he'd met Saul Landau, who'd made him a partner in the business; he loved taking out the charter boats. Jake had gone out with him one Sunday with some country club pals, though he hadn't been able to do it again because of the show in New York. But he thoroughly liked and respected the younger man.

Vernon listened as Jake told him about the jam he was in. When Jake came to the part about his affair with Veevi, Vernon interrupted him. "Is this something you want Claire to know about?"

"Not if we can help it," Dinah answered for him.

"Okay," said Vernon. Then he listened some more, rubbing the side of his clean-shaven face from time to time.

"How long were you in the LAPD?" asked Jake.

"Oh, close to ten years."

"Did you ever hear of him? Burgoyne, I mean?"

"No. Never did. But that doesn't mean he's lying. Still, it sounds kinda funny to me. If you hang on, I can find out for you."

"Can you call someone right now?" said Dinah. "He's threatened Pete."

"Not to mention me," added Jake, making an attempt at levity.

"Well, I need some time alone with a phone," he said.

Jake took him upstairs to his office, while he and Dinah, treating each other with deliberate and artificial courtesy that was not lost on Peter and

Lorna, had dinner in the breakfast room, on paper plates with plastic knives and spoons. Their real plates and silverware had been packed up in preparation for the move to England.

Vernon came downstairs just as Gussie was serving coffee, in paper cups. He had dinner, too, and then he and Jake and Dinah went into the den. What he reported was this: He had checked out Burgoyne with the guys downtown. The connection to the LAPD was real enough, though it wasn't quite what Burgoyne had made it out to be. They knew him pretty well; some of the boys drank with him, gave him tips. He liked to be in on the action when there were busts and such. He was like a kid—got a kick out of hanging out at cop bars and riding around in cop cars, liked using the radio equipment, enjoyed hearing the lingo. He was friends with the chief, so the boys humored him. He had his loves and hates: worshiped J. Edgar, hated reds. "He's pulled this before; he likes intimidation stunts. He gets his books made into movies—starring himself—but he thinks he's been slighted by respectable Hollywood folk and likes to get the dirt on them," Vernon added. "Remember that Swedish actress Astrid Bengston? Came out here, had an affair with an actor—oh, what's his name, you know, Kent Tempest? Well, Burgoyne started snooping, got the American Legion involved, and Tempest—"

"I remember it well. Bengston was deported, Tempest blacklisted, because he wouldn't talk," said Jake. "Remember him, honey? Nice fellow."

She nodded but kept her eyes fixed on Vernon.

"But the truth is, most of the guys laugh at him behind his back. Give him their old toys—handcuffs, radios, bulletproof vests—just to keep him happy. Still," he said, looking back and forth between a stricken Dinah and a rapt Jake, "it doesn't mean he can't do some damage. He does have pals, on and off the force, who'll do favors for him. A guy like Burgoyne's got himself confused with the guy in his stories—what's his name, I can't think of it right now. Likes to use his fists. And maybe other things, too. So the threats are real. Burgoyne should be arrested for them, though you'll have a scandal on your hands if you do; there's no two ways about it."

"I want Dinah and the kids to leave the country."

Vernon nodded. "Good idea."

Jake looked at Dinah. "Do you hear, honey?"

She said nothing. She was thinking about something.

"Meanwhile, you and I have a little date on Monday night at Joe Brogan's, right?"

Vernon laughed. Dinah scowled at them. "You're both crazy."

"Let's go upstairs," said Jake to Vernon, "and punch out some dialogue together."

A huge grin widened on Vernon's face. "You know, just living out here, you can't escape the movies."

"Darling," he said to Dinah. "You and the kids finish packing. You guys are leaving on the 7 A.M. flight to Paris tomorrow morning."

"What do I tell the kids?" Dinah said.

"Anything you want," he said. "Except the truth."

*S*he was in her own bed, her last night in her own bed, and he was in his, flat on his back. She wanted him to fall asleep, but she couldn't let him—not yet.

"I knew it," she said. "I knew it that time I saw you b-b-bending over her in the den. You had that look all the boys used to have, like you wanted to disappear into her."

"It was nothing like that."

"You know, if I'd just followed my g-g-g-guts, I could have figured it all out. One week you can't stand her, the next week you're dying to hear all her Ben Knight stories. And I knew Veevi. She couldn't get up in the morning without thinking about whom she was gonna conquer that day. She was a born pr-pr-pr-predator, with the conscience of a cat. I didn't put a little flirtation past her. A little seduction. I mean, that was her nature. And yours, too. She charms you; you charm her, you have a crush on her, maybe you neck a couple of times. Okay, it killed me, but so what? But the two of you ending up in the s-s-s-sack? My sister and my husband?"

There was a long pause between them in the dark. Then Dinah glanced at her watch. It was eleven-thirty. "This is the last night I will ever sleep in the same room with you."

"Let's just get through this part together. Then you can do whatever you want to, darling."

" 'Darling.' 'Honey.' 'Sweetheart,' " she said, stuttering on them all. "Horseshit. All horseshit." She turned on her side and pretended to go to sleep.

An hour later, as Jake snored within the cavern of Nembutal-induced slumber, she eased herself out of bed, dressed quickly, tiptoed through Peter's room, covered him up, kissed his pale oval face, and let herself out, crossing the painted planks that connected the house with the apartment above the garage. She knocked lightly three times on Gussie's door until it opened and Gussie slipped out.

The night was warm and clear, as July nights in Southern California can be, and the two women, each wearing slacks and a short-sleeved shirt, stepped lightly down the back stairs.

"Did you park the car in the street, Gus?" Dinah whispered.

"Right on over by the mailbox," Gussie replied. "You got the address, Dinah?"

"Yes, Gus. Got it right here." And she pressed her hand to her breast pocket.

Together they drove, with Dinah behind the wheel of her station wagon, down Sunset Boulevard, past the mansions in Beverly Hills, the two of them smoking Camels in tense but companionable silence. When Dinah turned left onto Crescent Heights, and then made a sharp right onto Franklin, Gussie said, "Ain't this where you grew up, Dinah?"

"Sure did, Gus. On Selma Avenue and Gardner Street. Right after we came out to California. I used to roller-skate around here. I'd roller-skate up and down Hollywood Boulevard. Once I saw Charlie Chaplin. He was looking at us from a restaurant window. I wanted him to discover me and make me a child star, and I started doing all my fancy dance steps—on roller skates. He smiled at me, and then he took one look at my sister and stuck a rose in his mouth."

Gussie laughed—a roll of chesty guffaws, one right after another. But she had heard this story a hundred times and had noticed the way Dinah talked all the time now about the past.

Dinah stopped the car across from the eight-unit stucco apartment house and then checked the number against the slip of paper in her shirt pocket.

Blue lights from the patch of landscaped shrubbery illuminated the address. "Okay," Dinah said. "We're here." She opened the glove compartment, took out the bottle of Chivas, and offered it to Gussie, who shook her head no. Dinah took a swig and put it back.

"Okay, if I'm not back here in twenty minutes, come in and get me in apartment 3B."

But Gussie opened the door on her side of the car. "Uh-huh, Dinah. You ain't going in there by yourself, and I sure ain't going to sit alone here in the middle of the night. You know about the police out here and how they treats the Negroes."

"Sorry, Gus. I should have remembered. Come on."

When they reached the apartment, Dinah could see light through the curtains at the window. She knocked firmly and then pressed the buzzer. The door opened with the chain still in place.

"I came for his l-l-l-laundry," said Dinah.

The girl opened the door farther. "I am with my housekeeper, Mrs. Crittenden," Dinah added.

Grace was wearing her kimono. Her red hair had been rolled into big metal curlers that moved backward in orderly rows off her freckled face. A movie was playing softly on the television, and there were magazines strewn about the sofa and the floor, a bottle of red nail polish, emery boards, white cotton balls, and two bottles of Coke on the coffee table.

"Turn the television off, dear," said Dinah.

"You can sit down if you like," said the girl. There was no bravado in her cockney accent this time. She seemed tired, and shy.

"Thank you," said Dinah, sitting down on the edge of the sofa after pushing a copy of *Confidential* out of the way. Noticing all the dolls piled in the corner, she motioned for Gussie to sit as well, but Gussie shook her head and remained standing near the door.

"Please, sit down too, G-G-G-Grace," said Dinah. She nodded toward the opposite end of the sofa, and waited for the girl to arrange herself.

"This is for you," she said, pulling off her emerald ring. In the shadows, Dinah heard a groan escape from Gussie. "Oh, Dinah, don't . . ."

"It's all you're going to get, but I think it will get you through the year that's left on your contract."

The girl took the ring, warm with the heat of Dinah's skin, and looked at it. "How do I know it's real?" she said.

"You pathetic creature. You really don't know sh-sh-shit from Sh-Sh-Sh—"

"Shinola," echoed Gussie.

The girl put it on her finger and then, keeping it there, looked at Dinah.

"Now, I'd like you to get on the phone and call Mr. Burgoyne and tell him there's no need to meet my husband at Joe Brogan's tomorrow night—

the matter's settled and he's not to lay a hand on my husband or my son. Please do it now, while I'm here."

"That's impossible," said the girl.

"No, do it now, dear."

Gussie took a step closer to Dinah and crossed her arms.

"Well, what I mean is," the girl said with a giggle, "he's here. Asleep in the bedroom. Go on and see for yourself if you don't believe me."

The girl nodded her head in the direction of the bedroom. Gussie disappeared for a moment and came back. "He's in the bed, all right."

"Tell me, dear. Were you involved with Burgoyne while you were seeing my husband?"

"Of course. But," the girl leaned forward. "He doesn't know I'm Jewish. I suppose Jake told you I'm Jewish?"

"No, dear," said Dinah, "he hasn't told me."

The girl covered her eyes with her hands, in relief.

Dinah shook her head in pity, but continued. "Listen, honey. Tell Burgoyne that if he persists in his desire to torment us and wants to make a sc-sc-sc-scandal, tell him to save his breath. To b-b-begin with, I couldn't care less who knows whether or not I testified; it's public knowledge. I also don't care who knows that my husband slept with my sister. Or gave her a job while she was blacklisted. Or had anything to do with the l-l-l-likes of you. It's of no importance to me one way or the other. I'm through with this town, and this industry. And him."

A hulking figure in a white terry-cloth bathrobe now appeared at the back entrance to the living room. "Mrs. Lasker," he roared. "What a pleasure."

"Well, maybe for you, but not for me," said Dinah, standing up. "This is my housekeeper, Mrs. Crittenden."

Gussie looked at him and snorted contemptuously.

"We're just leaving," said Dinah. "I've given Miss Siddons something she can depend on for a while—not the money you and she tried to blackmail out of us but enough for her to get her away from earning her living on her back." She looked at Grace. "You ought to go to school, dear. You're still young, and if you're clever enough to get involved with a blackmail scheme, then maybe you're clever enough to get a c-c-c-college degree. Perhaps you can avoid the mistakes I've made."

Grace Siddons was looking at her now, her expression abject and deferential.

"And I was just telling her to inform you," she said to Burgoyne, "that the d-d-d-date is off tomorrow night at Joe Brogan's. You can say anything you like about us; it doesn't matter. Of course, if you continue to bother us, or threaten my husband or my son, you will pay d-d-d-dearly for it."

Then Dinah turned toward the girl. She tightened her hands into two fists and stood taking deep breaths, while the girl drew back, alarmed. "Dinah," Gussie said, coming up to her and putting her hands on her shoulders. "Come on, sugar, let's go home."

"You. Are. A. Vicious. Stupid. Pathetic. Malevolent. Ignorant. Little. C-C-C-C- . . ."

"Dinah," Gussie said again, firmly now. "Come on, honey. Don't waste your breath on this trash."

"The whole thing was Duff's idea," the girl burst out. "He made me do it. It was just his idea of a joke. Honestly, Mrs. Lasker, I'm sorry!"

Trembling, the girl put her thumb to her quivering lips. "Here, I'll just get Jake's things for you."

"Oh, for Christ's sake, dear, burn them. I don't want them!" She turned to go. Gussie's arm was around her waist.

"Ah, you guys're no fun. I'm going back to bed. Turn the lights out, kitten," said Burgoyne. "So long, Mrs. Lasker." He began to lumber back toward the darkness from which he'd emerged. Then he paused again. "Why didn't your sister like my treatment?"

"She read a treatment of yours? Ah—the one you mentioned in Vegas."

"Yeah. I thought it would make a good Jake Lasker picture. She thought otherwise. I made sure V. Z. Aldrich found out about her."

"Oh, you're the one who tried to make trouble," Dinah said.

Burgoyne laughed. "I wonder why she didn't like my story."

"Perhaps," said Dinah, "it was because she could smell a hack a hundred miles away. She was attracted only to real t-t-t-talent."

"Oh, who needs this shit? Kitten, make sure you turn off the lights when you come to bed!" He shuffled off, looking oddly, to Dinah, like Jake at night when he wandered through the house in his bathrobe, racked with insomnia.

"Did Byron Cole know about my s-s-s-sister and Jake?" Dinah's arms hung slackly at her sides.

"Yeah," Grace said. "She told him about it. She told him she wanted to live your life. Thought she'd do a better job of it than you had. Said you were too simple to be the wife of a, you know, a guy like Jake."

"Did my husband want to leave me for her?"

"Yes. But only for a little while. I lied when I told you he wanted to go back with her. He didn't. He was glad it was over. He really loves you, Mrs. Lasker. Honest. In New York, when he was away from home so much, and your sister was falling apart and then had that frightful accident, why, that's when he found me! I was just supposed to take his mind off his worries about you. He never liked having it off with her, either. Said she was too . . . what was his word? De-something. Detached. Said she was too detached. He said the fucking was much better with you. And me. That between us we took great care of him."

Dinah felt the girl trying to make it right somehow, trying to tell the truth.

Grace took the emerald ring off and held it out to Dinah.

"No, dear. You keep it. You've earned it. Now, look after yourself."

The girl took a sharp inward breath. " 'Cor," she said. "I don't know what to say."

"Come on, Dinah," said Gussie, who looked at the girl. "You heard all you got to hear."

Dinah felt Gussie's arm around her, steering her out the door and around the patio and down the concrete flight of steps to the street, where the car sat parked under a palm tree that was dipping its fronds in the night wind like oars in a stream.

PART
Five

*E*arly one Sunday in November, some three months later, Dinah saw Peter putting on his peacoat and Westminster School muffler. She asked him where he was going. Just up to Hampstead, to meet his new friend Gideon. It was really weird, he said. Of all the kids he'd met at Westminster, the one he'd made friends with was American. He had an English accent and all, because he'd lived here so long, but he was an American and he'd even been born in L.A. His father had been a film writer—Peter said "film" now, not "movie"—out there. They were going to a YCND meeting.

A what meeting?

"Youth Campaign for Nuclear Disarmament. They're going on the Aldermaston march, and I'm going to a planning meeting. I told you about it two weeks ago. Don't you remember?"

"Oh, I'll drive you," she said.

"No," he said irritably. "I don't want you to drive me. I'm taking the tube: Central Line to Oxford Circus, change to the Bakerloo, get off at Hampstead." He liked reciting the tube stops. From the day the Laskers had arrived in London, Peter had been going everywhere alone by tube. He knew the entire system by heart.

"No, I'll take you."

"Mom, please don't. I want to go alone."

"No. I'm taking you, and that's that."

He scowled at this encroachment on his independence. "Why? I'm not a baby!"

"I know you're not a baby. But it's dr-dr-dr-dreary indoors, and I want to go out for a while."

Jake had gone to Paris for the weekend, as he often did now, staying at the Crandells' flat, and meeting with Willie Weil, who was the executive producer on the new picture he was due to begin shooting in Paris in the spring. She had refused to go with him, saying that sometime soon she was going to fly to Paris alone, during the week, when she could stay with Dorshka and watch Coco from a safe distance in the Bois. Michael had forbidden her ever to see Coco again.

She called the garage and asked for the Vauxhall, and then she and Peter walked together down Green Street, where they'd been living in a maisonette since September, to the garage on Audley Street, past the rubble of a pub that had been bombed during the war. Peter looked glum and embarrassed to be seen, even by the garage attendants, with his mother.

"You know, Mom, I want to go alone," he said.

"End-d-d-dure it."

Dinah had mastered the art of driving on the left, a feat her son admired. He now became absorbed in watching her shift, stop, and start in the Sunday traffic on Baker Street. "You're still in second, Mom. Go into third."

"I know what I'm doing, dear. Tell me, where does this kid live?" she asked.

Peter took the *London A–Z* from the glove compartment and looked up the street. "Hampstead," he said. "Frognal. That's a funny word, isn't it?"

"Yeah," she said. "Tell me about this YCND stuff. What is it, again?"

He explained to her that the Hampstead group was important and well-known; one of the kids was the son of a big Labour M.P. There was going to be another demonstration soon, next week, in Trafalgar Square. Bertrand Russell was going to be there. People might get arrested. "I'm joining this group, Mom, and I'm going to the demonstration."

"Oh no you're not," she said. "We're not citizens here. We're v-v-v-visitors. If you get arrested you could jeopardize our residence permits, and for Christ's sake," she added, "don't sign anything. Not now or ever."

"I won't get arrested," Peter said, looking out the window with a put-upon expression. "But I'll sign anything I damn well want. Mom, why don't you just let me out here. We're in St. John's Wood. I'll walk the rest of the way."

"No, I'm driving you there, and that's that. Now tell me again about this kid. Did you say he was born in California?"

"Yeah. It's the weirdest thing. I was talking to him at school, and he had this YCND button on his jacket. I asked him about it, and when I said I was American and from L.A., he said he was born there, too, and that his dad had been some kind of screenwriter. But he doesn't remember it. He was only four or something when they moved here."

"What's his name again—your friend, I mean?"

"Gideon Metzger."

"Oh," she said. She was sure now.

"And," Peter said, "he has this really pretty sister. . . ."

"Oh?" said Dinah. She smiled at him knowingly, but all the same abruptly edged the car over to the side of the road and brought it to a complete stop.

"What's the big idea, Mom! What're you doing?"

Since the Laskers had left Los Angeles, Peter's voice had changed. It cracked often, and was deepening unmistakably. He was shooting up, too, getting taller and thinner by the minute, and had started wearing glasses. When he wasn't in his school uniform, he usually wore a big navy-blue pullover from Marks & Spencer and his school muffler wrapped around his neck. It was as if every day, except for his accent, he was losing the traces of his California childhood and becoming instead a thin, delicate-featured, serious-looking young man, completely at home in this new city he loved, consumed by a secret, independent life that he pursued ecstatically on the London tube, free of the humiliation of having to be driven everywhere, as he had been in Los Angeles.

"Listen to me, Peter," she began. "There is something I have to tell you."

"What?" He looked bewildered, annoyed, and impatient. "Do you have to tell me now? I don't want to miss the meeting."

"You won't miss the meeting. But there's something you have to know." She lit a cigarette with the car lighter, and then turned and looked directly at her son. "I used to know Gideon Metzger's parents. Their names are Norman and Helen. You're right: he was a screenwriter, and a pretty good one, too. But he was blacklisted; that's why they're living over here. Do you know what the blacklist is?"

"No."

"Well, I'm going to tell you."

And she did. "If your friend's parents have figured out that you're my son," she said, when she had finished, "the same way I've figured out that Gideon is theirs, you might walk in there today only to be thrown out. Because I named Norman Metzger when I t-t-t-testified." She had placed her arms on the steering wheel and was looking right at him, searching his face. "They probably won't want him to associate with you. A lot of people hate me and consider me a traitor, a fink, and a stool pigeon. And among those who do, the Metzgers probably have me right at the top of their shit list." She pulled the lighter from the dashboard and lit another cigarette. "And that's why you aren't walking into that house alone."

His eyes opened very wide. "You were a *Communist?* A *real* one?" There was surprise and something close to delight, or pleased amazement, in his expression. But then, as if the rest of what she said had just sunk in, he added, "You named people? You *ratted?* You *told* on people? How could you *do* that? That's *terrible.*"

She started the car and pulled out into traffic. "I did it to protect D-D-D-Dad."

"To protect *Dad?* God, Mom," he said, his voice cracking. "I can't believe it! My mom a *fink!* And for whom? For Jake Lasker. All-time asshole. Don't think I don't know about Veevi and that girl. I know all about it. We listened to you fighting with Dad—Lorna and me. We heard you yelling at him. We heard you crying and stuff. But Jesus, Mom, you named people's names. For him! Shit, Mom, why'd you have to do it?"

She opened her mouth to say something, then thought better of it and simply sighed. "I remember Norman and Helen out at Veevi and Stefan's," she said quietly. "I didn't like him, and someday I'll tell you why. But she was nice—very nice. I remember one night we all went grunion hunting. Everybody was running into the waves, trying to catch these millions of slithery little f-f-f-fish. We were very young, and they'd just come back from Russia and were telling everybody that night how great it was over there. The grunion were flopping up onto the beach, and we all had baskets to catch them. God, I remember it like it was y-y-y-yesterday."

"Mom, let's go. I'm going to be late."

As she drove, and found her way with the help of his *London A–Z,* which he laughingly pronounced "zed," she saw his fists repeatedly clenching and unclenching. "It's down there," he said. "There. There's the number. Stop, Mom," he said. "Let me out."

She pulled over and began to open the door, then felt his hand clamp down on her left shoulder. "You are *not* going in with me."

"Hush up," she said sharply. "I'm taking you to meet them whether you like it or not."

"*No,* Mom." His hand was firm and dug into her flesh, pushing her away. "I can take care of myself. I don't want to be protected."

"I'm not letting you go in there without facing those people myself. I have to protect you. I'm your mother. That's my job."

"Oh, Mom, cut it out. I'm fifteen, for Christ's sake." He let go of her shoulder but took her chin in his hand and then stroked her cheek. "You don't have to protect anyone anymore," he said. "You protected Dad and you tried to protect Veevi, and look what happened."

"What if they say something to you? What if they throw you out of the house?"

"Then they'll throw me out of the house. Big deal. Look, Mom. I wish you hadn't, you know, done this thing with the names. I really, really wish you hadn't done it. But I don't care what his parents think. That's their tough luck. This time, I'm protecting *you.* And I'm going in there alone."

He got out of the car and came around to her side, where she looked up at him through the open window. "I'm not coming home for dinner," he said.

Then he pushed down the lock on her side.

"When will you be home? You have school tomorrow."

"So what? Don't wait up. I might see if I can find a concert tonight, after the meeting, over at the Albert Hall."

He grinned at her and shook his head at the same time. "Jesus, Mom. You were a real dope. What was the matter with you, anyway?"

She shrugged. Love, she said to him silently. Love. Love. Love.

"Am-scray," he said. "Go to the Heath, Mom. Take a walk. Feed the ducks. Okay? See ya later, alligator."

She watched him, hands in his peacoat, casually wait for a car to pass, and then cross the street and walk up a stone path to the front door of a brick house. He knocked and the door opened, but she couldn't see who had opened it. Then he disappeared inside.

❧

She drove to the Heath, got out, and began walking.

The afternoon was cloudy, with a tumultuous vaulted sky whose pale blue and gray haze softened and misted the yellowing leaves, what few were left, on the oaks and planes and beeches that trembled in the cold. Oddly enough, the weather now often seemed familiar. London made her think of Pittsburgh—the grayness and the grime, the smoke and the smell of coal dust in the air, the children on the streets with their pink cheeks and grimy raincoats, who could have been herself and Veevi so long ago. Every day she was no sooner out in the streets, doing her errands with her string bag on her wrist, than the bleak weather knocked her backward into the past—the streets of Pittsburgh and Philadelphia, where she was always, always, guarding her little sister.

She came to a spot high on Parliament Hill, tightened the belt of her trenchcoat, and sat down on the grass to smoke a cigarette. As far as she could see, all London lay before her—sprawling, teeming, a place where she still knew practically no one. The city stretched out as far as she could see. How many, she wondered, of those millions I do not know, and who don't know me, are deluded and deceived, as I was, are fools, as I have been?

I haven't left Jake, she reminded herself. I still haven't made my move. It seemed impossible that she wouldn't, someday, but she hadn't the least idea how. She had lived with him for so long, and she had never stopped loving him. She couldn't imagine not loving him. But continue to live with him? She couldn't, and yet she was, still.

What she did was walk—all day, every day, when she was doing her daily chores and when she wasn't. She walked and looked around her and thought and didn't think. She walked down to Blackfriars Bridge and sat in the garden of Gray's Inn and thought about Stefan and Veevi, Mike and Veevi, her parents and Veevi, Jake and Veevi, herself and Veevi. She walked in Regent's Park and asked herself, How did things end up the way they did? What am I going to do? It wasn't that she lacked answers. There were dozens of them, hundreds of them—answers, reasons, explanations, plans—and she was a target for every single one of them, for none arrived without its accusing voice. What do you have to show for your life? asked one persistent voice. If she could bedeck herself with all she had done, and all she had failed to do—to see, to know—she would look, she thought, like someone in a *National Geographic* photo, covered head to toe with beads, shells, and feathers, each one an error, a folly, a sin, and a crime.

Yet, no matter how hard she looked at her life, it seemed to her that everything would have turned out the same. Veevi and Mike would have broken up, Veevi would have come home, Veevi would have tried to take Jake, and Jake would have taken whatever he could get. "I'm sorry," Veevi had said in the hospital. Now Dinah knew why. But there was nothing to forgive. Veevi couldn't help being who she was. "You ended up me, and I ended up you," she had said. Meaning: you weren't supposed to be the one who made it. You weren't supposed to have lived.

There had been one choice she could have made. But she hadn't. It was useless wondering if things would have been different if she had walked out of that room and gone to jail. And now, here she was, on Hampstead Heath. To her amazement she wasn't dead. Her heart was beating, and the cold air smelled bitter with autumn smoke and she liked it. She felt again the tenderness of Peter's hand on her face, and for the first time in months she wondered what his life was going to be like, his and Lorna's. They were thriving here in London. They didn't miss California. They were getting an education, and they felt they were in the world, finally. Lorna looked out her window at night and watched the people walking up and down the street and listened to the sounds of a great city. The Irish maid, Olive, came in at six every morning and woke her for school with a cup of hot tea and two pieces of toast. To dress for school, she wore an orange-and-white-striped necktie and a pair of crimson knickers under her tunic, and a black hat that looked to Dinah like some kind of homburg. And she loved it. She loved playing hockey and learning Latin. And Peter? He was making great strides on the clarinet, but he had also started to compose. At dinner one night, he had announced to her and Jake, "I'm going to be a composer."

If she left now, if she took the kids back to Los Angeles, it would be a disaster for them. But if she stayed with Jake, she would die.

Again she felt Peter's hand on her cheek. The firm way he had pushed her shoulder and locked the door on her side of the car.

One recent Saturday, she had picked out a small silver flask from an antiques dealer on Portobello Road, taken it home, and filled it with Scotch. Now she reached into her pocket, took it out, opened it, poured out the whisky on the ground, and got up to find someplace to throw the flask away.

She was trying. She went to the market and shopped for groceries; she went to the theater with Jake and dinner at R. Parks with friends from Hollywood when they came to town. For laughs, she took them to the Tower and to Westminster Abbey, but told them that if they really wanted to see England they had to go with her to the lamp department at Harrods. People took the stories of her London adventures home with them to Hollywood, New York, and Paris, and in four months she had become a legend—someone you had to see when you went to London—and so at five o'clock there were usually people at the Laskers' flat on Green Street, with its view of a formal garden, where she sometimes sat on an iron bench and read *The New Statesman* and smoked her Camels and wondered why she was alive. She went out to parties with Jake and took excursions with him on Sundays to new English friends of his who had grand houses in Marlow, High Wycombe, and Gerrards Crossing. He wanted to get a dog and buy a house. She told him she didn't care what he did, and slept by herself in the maid's room downstairs, in a small single bed. In the early-morning hours, she could hear the horse-drawn milk carts clop-clopping in the street.

A windy drizzle had begun to fall. She arranged her silk scarf on her head, with the knot just under her chin. A young solicitor, out for the after-noon by himself to take a break from a case concerning the sale of a hotel in Penzance, noticed her springy walk, her shapely ankles, and her slender figure. That's an American walk, he thought to himself. He got up and hur-riedly approached her, and when he asked her for a light she smiled. "Sure," she said. He was right: American.

She held up her lighter and flicked it, and in the wind he cupped his hand around hers to protect the flame. Her hand was steady. He decided to take a chance. She was older than he, he saw that at once, but she had a marvelous smile.

"I say, care to go round to the pub for a drink?" he said.

She threw her head back and let out a mighty laugh.

"What's the date today?" she said, speaking to him as if she had known him all her life.

"The date? Sunday, November 12, 1960. Why?"

"Young m-m-m-man," she said, and he noticed at once that she had a stammer. "I'll tell you what. I'll gladly go and have a drink with you. In four years. Four years from today, to be exact. November 12, 1964. Maybe by that time I'll have figured it all out. Maybe by that time I'll have left my phi-landering husband, sent my kids off to college, and decided what to do with the rest of my life. Maybe by that time I'll have the courage to go and have a drink with a nice young guy I meet on Hampstead Heath. But till then, if you want a drink, here"—she handed him the flask—"it's yours."

"Are you sure?" he said, taking the silver flask and grinning at her in wonder as she turned to go.

She didn't answer, but only waved and smiled—the warmest, kindest smile he had ever seen. She wasn't a beauty, he saw, but comely, with something sweet and lively and disabused about her eyes. For an instant, he had thought her a bit mad. But he saw now, wanting to follow her and catch up with her, hoping that she would turn around, that she had meant it when she said no, that she had told him the truth. He watched through the gathering downpour as her step quickened, and he saw that she moved gracefully, like a dancer. My bloody luck, he thought. I meet someone smashing and she's a heartbroken married American.

Once inside her car, she started up the engine and drove off along Spaniard's Road. It was cold, and she turned on the heater. There was no rush to get home. Peter would be out until late. Lorna was spending the night with a school friend in Hammersmith. She could go anywhere she pleased. It might be nice, she thought, to drive down to the Embankment and have a cup of tea by the Thames. Or just stay in the car and drive around by herself. There was nowhere she had to be, and she had plenty of time.

ABOUT THE AUTHOR

ELIZABETH FRANK won the 1986 Pulitzer Prize for her biography *Louise Bogan: A Portrait.* She is also the author of *Jackson Pollock* and *Esteban Vicente.* She has written many articles and book reviews on art and literature for *The New York Times Book Review, The New York Times Magazine,* and *Art in America,* among others. She is the Joseph E. Harry Professor of Modern Languages and Literature at Bard College.

ABOUT THE TYPE

This book was set in Fairfield Light, the first typeface
from the hand of the distinguished American artist and
engraver Rudolph Ruzicka (1883–1978). Ruzicka was
born in Bohemia and came to America in 1894. He set
up his own shop, devoted to wood engraving and printing, in New York in 1913 after a varied career working as
a wood engraver, in photoengraving and banknote printing plants, and as an art director and freelance artist. He
designed and illustrated many books, and was the cre-
ator of a considerable list of individual prints—wood engravings, line engravings on copper, and aquatints.